Also by Peter S. Prescott

NEVER IN DOUBT
Critical Essays on American Books, 1972–1985

THE CHILD SAVERS
Juvenile Justice Observed

A DARKENING GREEN
Notes from the Silent Generation

SOUNDINGS
Encounters with Contemporary Books

A WORLD OF OUR OWN
Notes on Life and Learning in a Boys' Preparatory School

The Norton Book of American Short Stories

The Norton Book of American Short Stories

Edited by Peter S. Prescott

W · W · Norton & Company · New York · London

Published simultaneously in Canada by Penguin Books Canada Ltd.,
2801 John Street,
Markham, Ontario L3R 1B4.
Printed in the United States of America.

The text of this book is composed in Avanta, with display type set in Bernhard Modern. Composition and manufacturing by The Haddon Craftsmen, Inc.
Book design by Antonina Krass.

First Edition

Library of Congress Cataloging-in-Publication Data
The Norton book of American short stories / edited by Peter S. Prescott.
p. cm.
1. Short stories, American. I. Prescott, Peter S.
PS648.S5N69 1988
813'.01'08—dc19 88–14181

ISBN 0-393-02619-1

W. W. Norton & Company, Inc., 500 Fifth Avenue, New York, N. Y. 10110
W. W. Norton & Company Ltd., 37 Great Russell Street, London WC1B 3NU
1 2 3 4 5 6 7 8 9 0

For my parents,
who got me started on it all

CONTENTS

INTRODUCTION

The short story in its modern form is much younger than most of us realize. The lives of just two American short story writers span its entire history. Mark Twain was born in 1835, just at the time that Edgar Allan Poe began publishing stories which were in a significant way different from what readers had come to expect. Mark Twain was still alive in 1909, when Eudora Welty was born—and she is writing now.

Poe was responsible for perhaps half of the change that brought about what we think of today as the modern (if not the contemporary) short story. His stories did not, as stories had formerly done, convey a sequence of incidents; they dealt with, and above all elaborated upon, a single effect. The other half of that change, which involves a psychological approach to the events related, was invented at about the same time by Nathaniel Hawthorne. In recent years a third and equally important change has occurred: a writer's use of language and his deliberately skewed perspective are now often more important to his story than either plot or psychology. We may thank Donald Barthelme for this event, to which I'll return in a moment.

The point I think worth considering is that alone among literary forms, the short story is the one at whose creation Americans were present. Because we weren't around when foreigners invented epic and lyric verse, drama, history, the novel, the essay, even journalism, we came to these concerns at an unavoidable disadvantage. To be sure, foreigners tried to invent the short story and may even have thought they had; they did manage to skirt all around the territory by giving us sketches, fables, tales, and anecdotes. But the short story is not merely a story told short; it is a particular kind of literary construction. The thing itself is ours, invented by us a century and a half ago and dominated by Americans ever since.

That point, too, may be worth consideration. A handful of the most adept short story writers have not been Americans—Kipling, Conrad,

Joyce, Maugham, V. S. Pritchett, and Frank O'Connor—and a few more have not even felt obliged to write their stories in English: Chekhov, Babel, Kafka, Borges.* But after these, and perhaps a few others, the field is ours, all the way. It is ours in part for a typically American reason: the weight of numbers. In the past 150 years, Americans have published many times the number of short stories produced everywhere else in the world.

Numbers are unimportant. What's interesting about American short stories is their distinctive character. More frequently than short stories from other countries, American stories tend to be conveyed by a tone of voice that is not omniscient, that cannot be identified as its author's own in the sense that it continues from story to story; instead, this voice has been invented for the particular story at hand. It's an ad hoc means of narration that may take the form of the third person—as in Langston Hughes's "Slave on the Block"—but more frequently shows itself in first-person narration. We find it in Poe, we find it Barthelme. These stories won't work unless we can hear the narrator's voice in our ear; both the point and the character of the story emerge through the manner of its telling.

Such first-person narrations remind us of the oral tradition that lies behind all stories, long and short. The first stories were *told* by someone to an audience; many of the best stories today—like Richard Brautigan's "Revenge of the Lawn"—rejoice in their debt to that tradition. We can see the importance of the teller's voice here in early stories by Benjamin Franklin and Joel Chandler Harris—*spoken* tales that show the modern form of the short story being born. We see it in its rough, grab-you-by-the-lapels form in James M. Cain's story, which begins: "Of course there was plenty pieces in the paper about what happened out at the place last summer, but they got it all mixed up, so I will now put down how it really was. . . ." We see it again at its perfected peak in Eudora Welty's "Why I Live at the P.O.," a very funny story told in an unmistakably Southern tone of voice. It's a story that wouldn't work if the voice weren't Southern; it wouldn't work if we couldn't *hear* someone tell it.

Perhaps the short story's principal appeal is its throwaway effect: a few dabs with a brush, then wash your hands and throw away your materials; you won't be using *them* again. The short story will always be with us

*Indeed, one of the Americans in this collection chooses not to write in English, though he has lived in this country for over fifty years: Isaac Bashevis Singer's "Gimpel the Fool," written in Yiddish, is most widely known through Saul Bellow's translation, reprinted here.

because it's so useful; it's the only means of conveyance for certain themes, situations, and, yes, tones of voice that would prove unendurable if we had to live with them much longer. Think of Mary, who narrates "The Yellow Wallpaper," or Push, the schoolboy who's related to the Satan of Milton and Job, in Stanley Elkin's "A Poetics for Bullies." I wouldn't want to miss a word of what they said, but I'd ease my way out of the room if either began talking again. (On the other hand, you might think that Lorelei Lee, who narrates Anita Loos's *Gentlemen Prefer Blondes,* would, like Kleenex, prove to be a use-once-and-throw-away device. Not so. She hung around for quite a while, returning here in the little-known "Liquor Makes You Smart," just as pert and deadly as before.)

It's partly for this reason—the quickly approaching limit to our tolerance of a theme or a condition—that so many short stories are concerned with loneliness and her stepchildren, desperation and madness. The situation that Conrad Aiken develops in "Silent Snow, Secret Snow" could not very well have been further drawn out. It is the same with Jerome Weidman's "My Father Sits in the Dark": this memorable story works only because we learn nothing about the son who narrates it and virtually nothing about the father of whom he speaks.

By reason of its brevity, the short story can develop an intensity of style, as well as of vision, that would be difficult to sustain for the length of a novel. I like several things about Toni Cade Bambara's "Gorilla, My Love" and Jean Stafford's "In the Zoo," but I like especially the energy of language both writers achieve in what are basically realistic stories. Yet in the 1950s a number of writers who cared particularly for energetic language—writers like Donald Barthelme, Robert Coover, and William Gass—turned their backs on realism and began to do with short fiction what the Cubists had achieved in painting half a century earlier. That is to say, they rejected the traditional aspects of a story's design and contents, relying instead on perspective and style to create their often satirical effects.

Two of the stories in this anthology—Barthelme's and Gass's—seem to me as fine as anything this school of writing has produced. Barthelme's alertness to the tremors of our culture has never seemed more prescient than in "Robert Kennedy Saved from Drowning"; it's important to bear in mind that he wrote this story *before* Kennedy was killed. Gass's story about small-town life in Indiana reminds us that even the most revolutionary artists are constantly waving their acknowledgments to their predecessors. In "In the Heart of the Heart of the Country" Gass gives what turns out to be a postmodernist twist to Zora Neale

Hurston's "The Eatonville Anthology"—which he may then not have read—and to Sherwood Anderson's *Winesburg, Ohio,* which he surely had.

What these writers are trying to accomplish becomes a little clearer if we contrast the method of, say, Joyce Carol Oates with that of Robert Coover. Oates's vision of urban American life has its roots in naturalism; she transforms the banalities of its physical and psychological violence into melodrama and then takes one step further: she transforms her melodrama into a tightly controlled, even visionary narrative. Had she stuck at the first stage, she would be writing journalism; at the second, she would be writing readable, if not admirable fiction. It's her ability to take that last step that makes her traditional stories worth serious attention. Coover's method is quite the reverse. If Dr. Seuss had sat down to write *To Think That I Saw It on Mulberry Street* and had come up with an R-rated story for adults instead, the result might have been Coover's "The Babysitter." With Coover, you get the visionary element on the surface; the reader who cares to may scratch for the naturalistic body of the story. This Coover has dismembered and distributed throughout his pages. Here, for the perplexed, is what actually happens: A babysitter arrives, fusses a bit with three children, cleans up the kitchen, and does her homework while watching TV until the parents return. How can anyone make a workable story from such static banality? Coover does it by jettisoning the author's traditional problem with choices: if I make my character do *this,* then I can't have my story do *that.* Have it all, is this story's unwritten epigraph. What can happen to this girl? Well, everything, including the erotic fantasies of a male author who sets himself to think about babysitters.

Having suppressed an early fantasy of my own—that I would write brief comments about all of these seventy stories, each indispensable, that I've chosen for this anthology—I'll write a few words instead about why I chose the stories I did, and then a few more about some notable absentees. From the start of this enterprise, I decided to resist the temptation to define to any strict degree what a short story is. To define is to exclude, and there's something in the American character that resists exclusion; for a collection of American stories I needed a vulgar comprehensiveness. The art story, of course, but also the story with no other ambition than to tell a good tale. Had I drawn my wagons into too tight a circle, I'd have had to leave out the stories by Benjamin Franklin (a surprise there, surely: Franklin also wrote short stories? Yes, he did, and this brief satire is as amusing as it is little known), Mark

Twain, Joel Chandler Harris, and James Thurber—and my book would have been the poorer for their loss.

I wanted to include most, but not all, of the most famous American writers of short stories—but not necessarily their most famous work. Some of the classics have been overpublished. I admire "Rip Van Winkle" as much as the next sixth grader, but I'm quite sure I'll never read it again: enough is enough. The same goes for Mark Twain's jumping frog. Many readers never get past Irving's and Mark Twain's two or three most famous stories, yet there's every reason to do so. "The Devil and Tom Walker" is a fine story with many nice touches: the Devil, for instance, is no gentleman here, but a swarthy woodsman, and the anti-wife humor is even sharper than that in "Rip Van Winkle." Mark Twain's story about "crime in Connecticut" is known to only a few of its author's enthusiasts, but it's good fun: Mark Twain enjoying himself as he stands conventional morality on its head once again.

The fact is, an honest anthologist must feel uneasy as he pokes around in the short fiction of the American 19th century. With the exception of Hawthorne, James, and Ambrose Bierce, the celebrated writers he most expects to sustain him will let him down. Melville, for example, wrote few short stories, none of them very good; he *did* write a handful of impressive novellas. Because anthologists are more conscience-ridden than normal human folk, they feel obliged to stuff Melville into their collections. Inevitably they fall upon *Bartleby, the Scrivener,* the shortest of Melville's novellas. Readers who expect to find *Bartleby* in their anthologies of American short stories are hereby urged to consider Melville's *Benito Cereno,* a longer and better novella, a ghostly presence hovering within these pages. Mark Twain wrote a lot of short fictions that have been collected as short stories, but it can be argued that he was not a short story writer at all; even in his novels he seems most at home as a purveyor of anecdotes. As for Poe, who delighted us all when we were twelve, his stories seem to many adults almost unreadable. To make this book, I stumbled through a great many of them, including all that had thrilled me once, looking for one that would do—and settled upon one that offers a blessedly brief, if familiar, example of Poe's Grand Guignol, with less than his usual fustian. I had trouble, too, with Bret Harte. Until the First World War, sentimentality was the prevailing fashion among male American writers not quite of the first rank. Of "The Outcasts of Poker Flat" I can say that it's not as sentimental as his equally famous "The Luck of Roaring Camp"—it's a story with a plot we can't quite admire told in a style we can.

The women writers of the 19th century, those whom we have only recently begun to read seriously, seem much more satisfactory. Feminist critics like to insist that "The Yellow Wallpaper" was neglected until recently, but that's simply not so. The story has always been read, if not for the right reasons. At the age of twelve, I read it all unwittingly aloud to my mother, thinking it what my book said it was: "a tale of horror and madness." To reread it as an adult is to reassess it: Farewell the horror story; welcome to the symbolical tale of a woman trying to break free from her cage. For some reason this story is always published in corrupt versions: words are changed, phrases dropped, the parts rearranged. In a recent important anthology, the meaning of a sentence that the author wrote—"John laughs at me, of course, but one expects that in marriage"—is warped by the omission of the final two words. The text used here is that which originally appeared in the January 1892 edition of *The New England Magazine.* Its author's name is Charlotte Perkins Stetson; years were to pass before she married a cousin named Gilman.

Sarah Orne Jewett's "A White Heron" is another early feminist story, an unmistakably great one. What makes it so is partly that it's a version for girls of an abiding American theme reserved for boys: the boy who escapes from civilization, goes into the woods, down the river, off to the territory, or wherever, thereby discovering himself and truths about the world. This girl comes of age by *rejecting* her man—one in the eye for D. H. Lawrence, who later proposed that a woman becomes herself only by accepting the male. The symbolism in this story is heavily sexual; had it been read in its time as we must understand it now, it could not have been published.

Once past the 19th century, the going gets easier. O. Henry poses a problem: when he took himself seriously, as he did in famous stories like "The Gift of the Magi," sentimentality overcame him. But he could write with cheerful cynicism, as he does in "Mammon and the Archer." I like its emphasis on the pleasures of money (a rare theme in fiction anywhere) and I like its candor: this is certainly *not* a story about love. Edith Wharton posed a different kind of problem. I think her "Roman Fever" one of the best of all American short stories, yet I wanted a good ghost story in my collection. Wharton's "Pomegranate Seed" is one of the greatest of all ghost stories; it also seems to me just what a ghost story should be: the ghost proper is never seen, only its traces, yet the power the ghost exercises over the living is nonetheless awful for that. I made my reluctant choice: "Roman Fever" is widely anthologized; "Pomegranate Seed," a masterpiece, is little known.

It may be that every anthology has a shadow anthology flickering in its nimbus—stories that the editor knew should be included but which for one reason or another could not be. If that is so, put "Roman Fever" in this book's shadow anthology, along with *Benito Cereno.* Include in it, too, J. D. Salinger's "For Esmé—with Love and Squalor," omitted only because its eccentric author will not release his stories to anthologies. Add three more that I dropped most reluctantly because of their length: Saul Bellow's "A Silver Dish," Philip Roth's "Eli, the Fanatic," and, most particularly because it is so American, yet written specifically for a British audience, Raymond Chandler's "The Pencil."

Otherwise, I wanted . . . well, everything. Stories about a woman in league with nature (Jewett) and men up against it (Crane, London, Anderson). Stories by forgotten writers worth another look (Slesinger, Steele). Stories about religious revelation (O'Connor, Ozick). Allegories (Cheever, Jackson); a war story (Bierce); a fantasy (Le Guin). Stories about being a parent (Apple, Paley, and Olsen—hers is the most moving account I know of how a mother feels about a daughter). Stories emphasizing what is just now, temporarily of course, an unfashionable interest in plot (Cain, Flanagan). Robert Flanagan's "Teller's Ticket" is the kind of story that Roald Dahl wrote 30 years ago; *The Saturday Evening Post* would have published it, had the *Post* survived, and had the *Post* ever published stories with sex as the motivating element. Finally, stories by writers whom you may not have encountered yet (Gilchrist, Martone, Wiggins), but surely will.

And, as the barker says, more, much more.

The thing to remember is that we live, right now, in the Golden Age of the short story. The magazines that once paid highly for short stories have almost entirely disappeared, but, perversely, the short story flourishes. Until recently, book publishers—even the best of them—routinely snubbed collections of stories, but now these collections appear, albeit infrequently, on the best-seller lists. More good short stories are being written, right now, than ever before. More than in the 1920s and 1930s, when Hemingway and Fitzgerald, Faulkner, and O'Hara were writing theirs. It's hard to believe, but it's true.

My sincerest thanks to friends who helped me with suggestions for this volume, among them Joe and Kit Reed, John Seelye, Marguerite Barzun, and especially Anne Lake Prescott. I am particularly indebted to Alfred Bendixen of Barnard College, who advised me in the areas of my ignorance and provided me with authoritative texts.

P.S.P.

The Norton Book of American Short Stories

BENJAMIN FRANKLIN

The Speech of Polly Baker

The Speech of Miss Polly Baker before a Court of Judicature, at Connecticut near Boston in New England; where she was prosecuted the fifth time, for having a Bastard Child: Which influenced the Court to dispense with her Punishment, and which induced one of her Judges to marry her the next Day—by whom she had fifteen Children.

"May it please the honourable bench to indulge me in a few words: I am a poor, unhappy woman, who have no money to fee lawyers to plead for me, being hard put to it to get a living. I shall not trouble your honours with long speeches; for I have not the presumption to expect that you may, by any means, be prevailed on to deviate in your Sentence from the law, in my favour. All I humbly hope is, that your honours would charitably move the governor's goodness on my behalf, that my fine may be remitted. This is the fifth time, gentlemen, that I have been dragg'd before your court on the same account; twice I have paid heavy fines, and twice have been brought to publick punishment, for want of money to pay those fines. This may have been agreeable to the laws, and I don't dispute it; but since laws are sometimes unreasonable in themselves, and therefore repealed; and others bear too hard on the subject in particular circumstances, and therefore there is left a power somewhere to dispense with the execution of them; I take the liberty to say, that I think this law, by which I am punished, both unreasonable in itself, and particularly severe with regard to me, who have always lived an inoffensive life in the neighbourhood where I was born, and defy my enemies (if I have any) to say I ever wrong'd any man, woman, or child. Abstracted from the law, I cannot conceive (may it please your honours) what the nature of my offense is. I have brought five fine children into the world, at the risque of my life; I have maintain'd them well by my own industry, without burthening the township, and would have done it better, if it had not been for the heavy charges and fines I have paid. Can it be a crime (in the nature of things, I mean) to add to the king's subjects, in a new country, that really wants people? I own it, I should think it rather a praiseworthy than a punishable action. I have debauched no other woman's husband, nor enticed any other youth; these things I never was charg'd with; nor has any one the least cause of complaint against me, unless, perhaps, the ministers of justice, because I have had children without being married, by which they have missed a wedding fee. But can this be a fault of mine? I appeal to your honours. You are pleased to allow I don't want sense; but I must be stupefied to the last degree, not to prefer the honourable state of wedlock to the condition I have lived in. I always was, and still am willing to enter into it; and doubt not my behaving well in it, having all the industry, frugality, fertility, and skill in economy appertaining to a good wife's character. I defy any one to say I ever refused an offer of that sort: on the contrary, I readily consented to the only proposal of marriage that ever was made me, which was when I was a virgin, but too easily confiding in the person's sincerity that made it, I unhappily lost my honour by trusting to his; for he got me with child, and then forsook me.

"That very person you all know, he is now become a magistrate of this country; and I had hopes he would have appeared this day on the bench, and have endeavoured to moderate the Court in my favour; then I should have scorn'd to have mentioned it; but I must now complain of it, as unjust and unequal, that my betrayer and undoer, the first cause of all my faults and miscarriages (if they must be deemed such), should be advanced to honour and power in this government that punishes my misfortunes with stripes and infamy. I should be told, 'tis like, that were there no act of Assembly in the case, the precepts of religion are violated by my transgressions. If mine is a religious offense, leave it to religious punishments. You have already excluded me from the comforts of your church communion. Is not that sufficient? You believe I have offended heaven, and must suffer eternal fire: Will not that be sufficient? What need is there then of your additional fines and whipping? I own I do not think as you do, for, if I thought what you call a sin was really such, I could not presumptuously commit it. But, how can it be believed that heaven is angry at my having children, when to the little done by me towards it, God has been pleased to add his divine skill and admirable workmanship in the formation of their bodies, and crowned the whole by furnishing them with rational and immortal souls?

"Forgive me, gentlemen, if I talk a little extravagantly on these matters; I am no divine, but if you, gentlemen, must be making laws, do not turn natural and useful actions into crimes by your prohibitions. But take into your wise consideration the great and growing number of batchelors in the country, many of whom, from the mean fear of the expences of a family, have never sincerely and honourably courted a woman in their lives; and by their manner of living leave unproduced (which is little better than murder) hundreds of their posterity to the thousandth generation. Is not this a greater offense against the publick good than mine? Compel them, then, by law, either to marriage, or to pay double the fine of fornication every year. What must poor young women do, whom customs and nature forbid to solicit the men, and who cannot force themselves upon husbands, when the laws take no care to provide them any, and yet severely punish them if they do their duty without them; the duty of the first and great command of nature and nature's God, *encrease and multiply;* a duty, from the steady performance of which nothing has been able to deter me, but for its sake I have hazarded the loss of the publick esteem, and have frequently endured publick disgrace and punishment; and therefore ought, in my humble opinion, instead of a whipping, to have a statue erected to my memory."

WASHINGTON IRVING

The Devil and Tom Walker

A few miles from Boston in Massachusetts, there is a deep inlet, winding several miles into the interior of the country from Charles Bay, and terminating in a thickly-wooded swamp or morass. On one side of this inlet is a beautiful dark grove; on the opposite side the land rises abruptly from the water's edge into a high ridge, on which grow a few scattered oaks of great age and immense size. Under one of these gigantic trees, according to old stories, there was a great amount of treasure buried by Kidd the pirate. The inlet allowed a facility to bring the money in a boat secretly and at night to the very foot of the hill; the elevation of the place permitted a good lookout to be kept that no one was at hand; while the remarkable trees formed good landmarks by which the place might easily be found again. The old stories add, moreover, that the devil presided at the hiding of the money, and took it under his guardianship; but this, it is well known, he always does with buried treasure, particularly when it has been ill-gotten. Be that as it may, Kidd never returned to recover his wealth; being shortly after seized at Boston, sent out to England, and there hanged for a pirate.

About the year 1727, just at the time that earthquakes were prevalent in New England, and shook many tall sinners down upon their knees, there lived near this place a meagre, miserly fellow, of the name of Tom Walker. He had a wife as miserly as himself: they were so miserly that they even conspired to cheat each other. Whatever the woman could lay hands on, she hid away; a hen could not cackle but she was on the alert to secure the new-laid egg. Her husband was continually prying about to detect her secret hoards, and many and fierce were the conflicts that took place about what ought to have been common property. They lived in a forlorn-looking house that stood alone, and had an air of starvation. A few straggling savin-trees, emblems of sterility, grew near it; no smoke ever curled from its chimney; no traveller stopped at its door. A miserable horse, whose ribs were as articulate as the bars of a gridiron, stalked about a field, where a thin carpet of moss, scarcely covering the ragged beds of pudding-stone, tantalized and balked his hunger; and sometimes he would lean his head over the fence, look piteously at the passer-by, and seem to petition deliverance from this land of famine.

The house and its inmates had altogether a bad name. Tom's wife was a tall termagant, fierce of temper, loud of tongue, and strong of arm. Her voice was often heard in wordy warfare with her husband; and his face sometimes showed signs that their conflicts were not confined to words. No one ventured, however, to interfere between them. The lonely wayfarer shrunk within himself at the horrid clamor and clapper-clawing; eyed the den of discord askance; and hurried on his way, rejoicing, if a bachelor, in his celibacy.

One day that Tom Walker had been to a distant part of the neighborhood, he took what he considered a short cut homeward, through the swamp. Like most short cuts, it was an ill-chosen route. The swamp was thickly grown with great gloomy pines and hemlocks, some of them ninety feet high, which made it dark at noonday, and a retreat for all the owls of the neighborhood. It was full of pits and quagmires, partly covered with weeds and mosses, where the green surface often betrayed the traveller into a gulf of black, smothering mud: there were also dark and stagnant pools, the abodes of the tadpole, the bull-frog, and the water-snake; where the trunks of pines and hemlocks lay half drowned, half rotting, looking like alligators sleeping in the mire.

Tom had long been picking his way cautiously through this treacherous forest; stepping from tuft to tuft of rushes and roots, which afforded precarious footholds among deep sloughs; or pacing carefully, like a cat, along the prostrate trunks of trees; startled now and then by the sudden screaming of the bittern, or the quacking of wild duck rising on the wing from some solitary pool. At length he arrived at a firm piece of ground, which ran out like a peninsula into the deep bosom of the swamp. It had been one of the strongholds of the Indians during their wars with the first colonists. Here they had thrown up a kind of fort, which they had looked upon as almost impregnable, and had used as a place of refuge for their squaws and children. Nothing remained of the old Indian fort but a few embankments, gradually sinking to the level of the surrounding earth, and already overgrown in part by oaks and other forest trees, the foliage of which formed a contrast to the dark pines and hemlocks of the swamp.

It was late in the dusk of evening when Tom Walker reached the old fort, and he paused there awhile to rest himself. Any one but he would have felt unwilling to linger in this lonely, melancholy place, for the common people had a bad opinion of it, from the stories handed down from the time of the Indian wars; when it was asserted that the savages held incantations here, and made sacrifices to the evil spirit.

Tom Walker, however, was not a man to be troubled with any fears of the kind. He reposed himself for some time on the trunk of a fallen hemlock, listening to the boding cry of the tree-toad, and delving with his walking-staff into a mound of black mould at his feet. As he turned up the soil unconsciously, his staff struck against something hard. He raked it out of the vegetable mould, and lo! a cloven skull, with an Indian tomahawk buried deep in it, lay before him. The rust on the weapon showed the time that had elapsed since this death-blow had been given. It was a dreary memento of the fierce struggle that had taken place in this last foothold of the Indian warriors.

"Humph!" said Tom Walker, as he gave it a kick to shake the dirt from it.

"Let that skull alone!" said a gruff voice. Tom lifted up his eyes, and beheld a great black man seated directly opposite him, on the stump of a tree. He was exceedingly surprised, having neither heard nor seen any one approach; and he was still more perplexed on observing, as well as the gathering gloom would permit, that the stranger was neither negro nor Indian. It is true he was dressed in a rude half Indian garb, and had a red belt or sash swathed round his body; but his face was neither black nor copper-color, but swarthy and dingy, and begrimed with soot, as if he had been accustomed to toil among fires and forges. He had a shock of coarse black hair, that stood out from his head in all directions, and bore an axe on his shoulder.

He scowled for a moment at Tom with a pair of great red eyes.

"What are you doing on my grounds?" said the black man, with a hoarse, growling voice.

"Your grounds!" said Tom, with a sneer, "no more your grounds than mine; they belong to Deacon Peabody."

"Deacon Peabody be d——d," said the stranger, "as I flatter myself he will be, if he does not look more to his own sins and less to those of his neighbors. Look yonder, and see how Deacon Peabody is faring."

Tom looked in the direction that the stranger pointed, and beheld one of the great trees, fair and flourishing without, but rotten at the core, and saw that it had been nearly hewn through, so that the first high wind was likely to blow it down. On the bark of the tree was scored the name of Deacon Peabody, an eminent man, who had waxed wealthy by driving shrewd bargains with the Indians. He now looked around, and found most of the tall trees marked with the name of some great man of the colony, and all more or less scored by the axe. The one on which he had been seated, and which had evidently just been hewn down, bore the name of Crowninshield; and he recollected a mighty rich man of that name, who made a vulgar display of wealth, which it was whispered he had acquired by buccaneering.

"He's just ready for burning!" said the black man, with a growl of triumph. "You see I am likely to have a good stock of firewood for winter."

"But what right have you," said Tom, "to cut down Deacon Peabody's timber?"

"The right of a prior claim," said the other. "This woodland belonged to me long before one of your white-faced race put foot upon the soil."

"And pray, who are you, if I may be so bold?" said Tom.

"Oh, I go by various names. I am the wild huntsman in some countries; the black miner in others. In this neighborhood I am known by the name of the black woodsman. I am he to whom the red men consecrated this spot, and in honor of whom they now and then roasted a white man, by way of sweet-smelling sacrifice. Since the red men have been exterminated by you white savages, I amuse myself by presiding at the persecutions of Quakers and Anabaptists; I am the great patron and prompter of slave-dealers, and the grand-master of the Salem witches."

"The upshot of all which is, that, if I mistake not," said Tom, sturdily, "you are he commonly called Old Scratch."

"The same, at your service!" replied the black man, with a half civil nod.

Such was the opening of this interview, according to the old story, though it has almost too familiar an air to be credited. One would think that to meet with such a singular personage, in this wild, lonely place, would have shaken any man's nerves; but Tom was a hard-minded fellow, not easily daunted, and he had lived so long with a termagant wife, that he did not even fear the devil.

It is said that after this commencement they had a long and earnest conversation together, as Tom returned homeward. The black man told him of great sums of money buried by Kidd the pirate, under the oak trees on the high ridge, not far from the morass. All these were under his command, and protected by his power, so that none could find them but such as propitiated his favor. These he offered to place within Tom Walker's reach, having conceived an especial kindness for him, but they were to be had only on certain conditions. What these conditions were may be easily surmised, though Tom never disclosed them publicly. They must have been very hard, for he required time to think of them, and he was not a man to stick at trifles when money was in view. When they had reached the edge of the swamp, the stranger paused. "What proof have I that all you have been telling me is true?" said Tom. "There's my signature," said the black man, pressing his finger on Tom's forehead. So saying, he turned off among the thickest of the swamp, and seemed, as Tom said, to go down, down, down, into the earth, until nothing but his head and shoulders could be seen, and so on, until he totally disappeared.

When Tom reached home, he found the black print of a finger burnt, as it were, into his forehead, which nothing could obliterate.

The first news his wife had to tell him was the sudden death of Absalom Crowninshield, the rich buccaneer. It was announced in the papers with the usual flourish, that "A great man had fallen in Israel."

Tom recollected the tree which his black friend had just hewn down, and which was ready for burning. "Let the freebooter roast," said Tom; "who cares!" He now felt convinced that all he had heard and seen was no illusion.

He was not prone to let his wife into his confidence; but as this was an uneasy secret, he willingly shared it with her. All her avarice was awakened at the mention of hidden gold, and she urged her husband to comply with the black man's terms, and secure what would make them wealthy for life. However Tom might have felt disposed to sell himself to the devil, he was determined not to do so to oblige his wife; so he flatly refused, out of the mere spirit of contradiction. Many and bitter were the quarrels they had on the subject; but the more she talked, the more resolute was Tom not to be damned to please her.

At length she determined to drive the bargain on her own account, and if she succeeded, to keep all the gain to herself. Being of the same fearless temper as her husband, she set off for the old Indian fort towards the close of a summer's day. She was many hours absent. When she came back, she was reserved and sullen in her replies. She spoke something of a black man, whom she met about twilight hewing at the root of a tall tree. He was sulky, however, and would not come to terms: she was to go again with a propitiatory offering, but what it was she forbore to say.

The next evening she set off again for the swamp, with her apron heavily laden. Tom waited and waited for her, but in vain; midnight came, but she did not make her appearance: morning, noon, night returned, but still she did not come. Tom now grew uneasy for her safety, especially as he found she had carried off in her apron the silver tea-pot and spoons, and every portable article of value. Another night elapsed, another morning came; but no wife. In a word, she was never heard of more.

What was her real fate nobody knows, in consequence of so many pretending to know. It is one of those facts which have become confounded by a variety of historians. Some asserted that she lost her way among the tangled mazes of the swamp, and sank into some pit or slough; others, more uncharitable, hinted that she had eloped with the household booty, and made off to some other province; while others surmised that the tempter had decoyed her into a dismal quagmire, on the top of which her hat was found lying. In confirmation of this, it was said a great black man, with an axe on his shoulder, was seen late that very evening coming out of the swamp, carrying a bundle tied in a check apron, with an air of surly triumph.

The most current and probable story, however, observes, that Tom Walker grew so anxious about the fate of his wife and his property, that he set out at length to seek them both at the Indian fort. During a long summer's afternoon he searched about the gloomy place, but no wife was to be seen. He called her name repeatedly, but she was nowhere to be heard. The bittern alone responded to his voice, as he flew screaming by; or the bull-frog croaked dolefully from a neighboring pool. At length, it is said, just in the brown hour of twilight, when the owls began to hoot, and the bats to flit about, his attention was attracted by the clamor of carrion crows hovering about a cypress-tree. He looked up, and beheld a bundle tied in a check apron, and hanging in the branches of the tree, with a great vulture perched hard by, as if keeping watch upon it. He leaped with joy; for he recognized his wife's apron, and supposed it to contain the household valuables.

"Let us get hold of the property," said he, consolingly to himself, "and we will endeavor to do without the woman."

As he scrambled up the tree, the vulture spread its wide wings, and sailed off screaming, into the deep shadows of the forest. Tom seized the checked apron, but, woful sight! found nothing but a heart and liver tied up in it!

Such, according to this most authentic old story, was all that was to be found of Tom's wife. She had probably attempted to deal with the black man as she had been accustomed to deal with her husband; but though a female scold is generally considered a match for the devil, yet in this instance she appears to have had the worst of it. She must have died game, however; for it is said Tom noticed many prints of cloven feet deeply stamped upon the tree, and found handfuls of hair, that looked as if they had been plucked from the coarse black shock of the woodman. Tom knew his wife's prowess by experience. He shrugged his shoulders, as he looked at the signs of a fierce clapper-clawing. "Egad," said he to himself, "Old Scratch must have had a tough time of it!"

Tom consoled himself for the loss of his property, with the loss of his wife, for he was a man of fortitude. He even felt something like gratitude towards the black woodman, who, he considered, had done him a kindness. He sought, therefore, to cultivate a further acquaintance with him, but for some time without success; the old black-legs played shy, for whatever people may think, he is not always to be had for calling for: he knows how to play his cards when pretty sure of his game.

At length, it is said, when delay had whetted Tom's eagerness to the quick, and prepared him to agree to anything rather than not gain the promised treasure, he met the black man one evening in his usual woodman's dress, with his axe on his shoulder, sauntering along the swamp, and humming a tune. He affected to receive Tom's advances with great indifference, made brief replies, and went on humming his tune.

By degrees, however, Tom brought him to business, and they began to haggle about the terms on which the former was to have the pirate's treasure. There was one condition which need not be mentioned, being generally understood in all cases where the devil grants favors; but there were others about which, though of less importance, he was inflexibly obstinate. He insisted that the money found through his means should be employed in his service. He proposed, therefore, that Tom should employ it in the black traffic; that is to say, that he should fit out a slave-ship. This, however, Tom resolutely refused: he was bad enough in all conscience; but the devil himself could not tempt him to turn slave-trader.

Finding Tom so squeamish on this point, he did not insist upon it, but proposed, instead, that he should turn usurer; the devil being extremely anxious for the increase of usurers, looking upon them as his peculiar people.

To this no objections were made, for it was just to Tom's taste.

"You shall open a broker's shop in Boston next month," said the black man.

"I'll do it to-morrow, if you wish," said Tom Walker.

"You shall lend money at two per cent a month."

"Egad, I'll charge four!" replied Tom Walker.

"You shall extort bonds, foreclose mortgages, drive the merchants to bankruptcy"—

"I'll drive them to the d——l," cried Tom Walker.

"You are the usurer for my money!" said black-legs with delight. "When will you want the rhino?"

"This very night."

"Done!" said the devil.

"Done!" said Tom Walker.—So they shook hands and struck a bargain.

A few days' time saw Tom Walker seated behind his desk in a counting-house in Boston.

His reputation for a ready-moneyed man, who would lend money out for a good consideration, soon spread abroad. Everybody remembers the time of Governor Belcher, when money was particularly scarce. It was a time of paper credit. The country had been deluged with government bills, the famous Land Bank had been established; there had been a rage for speculating; the people had run mad with schemes for new settlements; for building cities in the wilderness; land-jobbers went about with maps of grants, and townships, and Eldorados, lying nobody knew where, but which everybody was ready to purchase. In a word, the great speculating fever which breaks out every now and then in the country, had raged to an alarming degree, and every body was dreaming of making sudden fortunes from nothing. As usual the fever had subsided; the dream had gone off, and the imaginary fortunes with it; the patients were left in doleful plight, and the whole country resounded with the consequent cry of "hard times."

At this propitious time of public distress did Tom Walker set up as usurer in Boston. His door was soon thronged by customers. The needy and adventurous; the gambling speculator; the dreaming land-jobber; the thriftless tradesman; the merchant with cracked credit; in short, every one driven to raise money by desperate means and desperate sacrifices, hurried to Tom Walker.

Thus Tom was the universal friend of the needy, and acted like a "friend in need"; that is to say, he always exacted good pay and good security. In proportion to the distress of the applicant was the hardness of his terms. He accumulated bonds and mortgages; gradually squeezed his customers closer and closer: and sent them at length, dry as a sponge, from his door.

In this way he made money hand over hand; became a rich and mighty man, and exalted his cocked hat upon 'Change. He built himself, as usual, a vast house, out of ostentation; but left the greater part of it unfinished and unfurnished, out of parsimony. He even set up a carriage in the fulness of his vainglory, though he nearly starved the horses which drew it; and as the ungreased wheels groaned and screeched on the axle-trees, you would have thought you heard the souls of the poor debtors he was squeezing.

As Tom waxed old, however, he grew thoughtful. Having secured the good things of this world, he began to feel anxious about those of the next. He thought with regret on the bargain he had made with his black friend, and set his wits to work to cheat him out of the conditions. He became, therefore, all of a sudden, a violent church-goer. He prayed loudly and strenuously, as if heaven were to be taken by force of lungs. Indeed, one might always tell when he had sinned most during the week, by the clamor of his Sunday devotion. The quiet Christians who had been modestly and steadfastly travelling Zionward, were struck with self-reproach at seeing themselves so suddenly outstripped in their career by this new-made convert. Tom was as rigid in religious as in money matters; he was a stern supervisor and censurer of his neighbors, and seemed to think every sin entered up to their account became a credit on his own side of the page. He even talked of the expediency of reviving the persecution of Quakers and Anabaptists. In a word, Tom's zeal became as notorious as his riches.

Still, in spite of all this strenuous attention to forms, Tom had a lurking dread that the devil, after all, would have his due. That he might not be taken unawares, therefore, it is said he always carried a small Bible in his coat-pocket. He had also a great folio Bible on his counting-house desk, and would frequently be found reading it when people called on business; on such occasions he would lay his green spectacles in the book, to mark the place, while he turned round to drive some usurious bargain.

Some say that Tom grew a little crack-brained in his old days, and that, fancying his end approaching, he had his horse new shod, saddled and bridled, and buried with his feet uppermost; because he supposed that at the last day the world would be turned upside-down; in which case he should find his horse standing ready for mounting, and he was determined at the worst to give his old friend a run for it. This, however, is probably a mere old wives' fable. If he really did take such a precaution, it was totally superfluous; at least so says the authentic old legend, which closes his story in the following manner:

One hot summer afternoon in the dog-days, just as a terrible black thunder gust was coming up, Tom sat in his counting-house, in his white cap and India silk morning-gown. He was on the point of foreclosing a mortgage, by which he would complete the ruin of an unlucky land-speculator for whom he had professed the greatest friendship. The poor land-jobber begged him to grant a few months' indulgence. Tom had grown testy and irritated, and refused another day.

"My family will be ruined and brought upon the parish," said the land-jobber. "Charity begins at home," replied Tom; "I must take care of myself in these hard times."

"You have made so much money out of me," said the speculator.

Tom lost his patience and his piety. "The devil take me," said he, "if I have made a farthing!"

Just then there were three loud knocks at the street door. He stepped out to see who was there. A black man was holding a black horse, which neighed and stamped with impatience.

"Tom, you're come for," said the black fellow, gruffly. Tom shrank back, but too late. He had left his little Bible at the bottom of his coat-pocket, and his big Bible on the desk buried under the mortgage he was about to foreclose: never was sinner taken more unawares. The black man whisked him like a child into the saddle, gave the horse the lash, and away he galloped, with Tom on his back, in the midst of the thunder-storm. The clerks stuck their pens behind their ears, and stared after him from the windows. Away went Tom Walker, dashing down the streets; his white cap bobbing up and down; his morning-gown fluttering in the wind, and his steed striking fire out of the pavement at every bound. When the clerks turned to look for the black man, he had disappeared.

Tom Walker never returned to foreclose the mortgage. A countryman, who lived on the border of the swamp, reported that in the height of the thunder-gust he had heard a great clattering of hoofs and a howling along the road, and running to the window caught sight of a figure, such as I have described, on a horse that galloped like mad across the fields, over the hills, and down into the black hemlock swamp towards the old Indian fort; and that shortly after a thunder-bolt falling in that direction seemed to set the whole forest in a blaze.

The good people of Boston shook their heads and shrugged their shoulders, but had been so much accustomed to witches and goblins, and tricks of the devil, in all kinds of shapes, from the first settlement of the colony, that they were not so much horror-struck as might have been expected. Trustees were appointed to take charge of Tom's effects. There was nothing, however, to administer upon. On searching his coffers, all his bonds and mortgages were found reduced to cinders. In place of gold and silver, his iron chest was filled with chips and shavings; two skeletons lay in his stable instead of his half-starved horses, and the very next day his great house took fire and burnt to the ground.

Such was the end of Tom Walker and his ill-gotten wealth. Let all griping money-brokers lay this story to heart. The truth of it is not to be doubted. The very hole under the oak-trees whence he dug Kidd's money is to be seen to this day; and the neighboring swamp and old Indian fort are often haunted in stormy nights by a figure on horseback, in morning-gown and white cap, which is doubtless the troubled spirit of the usurer. In fact the story has resolved itself into a proverb, and is the origin of that popular saying, so prevalent throughout New England, of "The Devil and Tom Walker."

NATHANIEL HAWTHORNE

Young Goodman Brown

Young Goodman Brown came forth at sunset into the street of Salem village; but put his head back, after crossing the threshold, to exchange a parting kiss with his young wife. And Faith, as the wife was aptly named, thrust her own pretty head into the street, letting the wind play with the pink ribbons of her cap while she called to Goodman Brown.

"Dearest heart," whispered she, softly and rather sadly, when her lips were close to his ear, "prithee put off your journey until sunrise and sleep in your own bed to-night. A lone woman is troubled with dreams and such thoughts that she's afeared of herself sometimes. Pray tarry with me this night, dear husband, of all nights in the year."

"My love and my Faith," replied young Goodman Brown, "of all nights in the year, this one night must I tarry away from thee. My journey, as thou callest it, forth and back again, must needs be done 'twixt now and sunrise. What, my sweet, pretty wife, dost thou doubt me already, and we but three months married?"

"Then God bless you!" said Faith, with the pink ribbons; "and may you find all well when you come back."

"Amen!" cried Goodman Brown. "Say thy prayers, dear Faith, and go to bed at dusk, and no harm will come to thee."

So they parted; and the young man pursued his way until, being about to turn the corner by the meeting-house, he looked back and saw the head of Faith still peeping after him with a melancholy air, in spite of her pink ribbons.

"Poor little Faith!" thought he, for his heart smote him. "What a wretch am I to leave her on such an errand! She talks of dreams, too. Methought as she spoke there was trouble in her face, as if a dream had warned her what work is to be done tonight. But no, no; 't would kill her to think it. Well, she's a blessed angel on earth; and after this one night I'll cling to her skirts and follow her to heaven."

With this excellent resolve for the future, Goodman Brown felt himself justified in making more haste on his present evil purpose. He had taken a dreary road, darkened by all the gloomiest trees of the forest, which barely stood aside to let the narrow path creep through, and closed immediately behind. It was all as lonely as could be; and there is this peculiarity in such a solitude, that the traveller knows not who may be concealed by the innumerable trunks and the thick boughs overhead; so that with lonely footsteps he may yet be passing through an unseen multitude.

"There may be a devilish Indian behind every tree," said Goodman Brown to himself; and he glanced fearfully behind him as he added, "What if the devil himself should be at my very elbow!"

His head turned back, he passed a crook of the road, and, looking forward again, beheld the figure of a man, in grave and decent attire, seated at the foot of an old tree. He arose at Goodman Brown's approach and walked onward side by side with him.

"You are late, Goodman Brown," said he. "The clock of the Old South was striking as I came through Boston, and that is full fifteen minutes agone."

"Faith kept me back a while," replied the young man, with a tremor in his voice, caused by the sudden appearance of his companion, though not wholly unexpected.

It was now deep dusk in the forest, and deepest in that part of it where these two were journeying. As nearly as could be discerned, the second traveller was about fifty years old, apparently in the same rank of life as Goodman Brown, and bearing a considerable resemblance to him, though perhaps more in expression than features. Still they might have been taken for father and son. And yet, though the elder person was as simply clad as the younger, and as simple in manner too, he had an indescribable air of one who knew the world, and who would not have felt abashed at the governor's dinner table or in King William's court, were it possible that his affairs should call him thither. But the only thing about him that could be fixed upon as remarkable was his staff, which bore the likeness of a great black snake, so curiously wrought that it might almost be seen to twist and wriggle itself like a living serpent. This, of course, must have been an ocular deception, assisted by the uncertain light.

"Come, Goodman Brown," cried his fellow-traveller, "this is a dull pace for the beginning of a journey. Take my staff, if you are so soon weary."

"Friend," said the other, exchanging his slow pace for a full stop, "having kept covenant by meeting thee here, it is my purpose now to return whence I came. I have scruples touching the matter thou wot'st of."

"Sayest thou so?" replied he of the serpent, smiling apart. "Let us walk on, nevertheless, reasoning as we go; and if I convince thee not thou shalt turn back. We are but a little way in the forest yet."

"Too far! too far!" exclaimed the goodman, unconsciously resuming his walk. "My father never went into the woods on such an errand, nor his father before him. We have been a race of honest men and good Christians since the days of the martyrs; and shall I be the first of the name of Brown that ever took this path and kept—"

"Such company, thou wouldst say," observed the elder person, interpreting his pause. "Well said, Goodman Brown! I have been as well acquainted with your family as with ever a one among the Puritans; and that's no trifle to say. I helped your grandfather, the constable, when he lashed the Quaker woman so smartly through the streets of Salem; and it was I that brought your father a pitch-pine knot, kindled at my own hearth, to set fire to an Indian village, in King Philip's war. They were my good friends, both; and many a pleasant walk have we had along this path, returned merrily after midnight. I would fain be friends with you for their sake."

"If it be as thou sayest," replied Goodman Brown, "I marvel they never spoke of these matters; or, verily, I marvel not, seeing that the least rumor of the sort would have driven them from New England. We are a people of prayer, and good works to boot, and abide no such wickedness."

"Wickedness or not," said the traveller with the twisted staff, "I have a very general acquaintance here in New England. The deacons of many a church have drunk the communion wine with me; the selectmen of divers towns make me their chairman; and a majority of the Great and General Court are firm supporters of my interest. The governor and I, too—But these are state secrets."

"Can this be so?" cried Goodman Brown, with a stare of amazement at his undisturbed companion. "Howbeit, I have nothing to do with the governor and council; they have their own ways, and are no rule for a simple husbandman like me. But, were I to go on with thee, how should I meet the eye of that good old man, our minister, at Salem village? Oh, his voice would make me tremble both Sabbath day and lecture day."

Thus far the elder traveller had listened with due gravity; but now burst into a fit of irrepressible mirth, shaking himself so violently that his snake-like staff actually seemed to wriggle in sympathy.

"Ha! ha! ha!" shouted he again and again; then composing himself, "Well, go on, Goodman Brown, go on; but, prithee, don't kill me with laughing."

"Well, then, to end the matter at once," said Goodman Brown, considerably nettled, "there is my wife, Faith. It would break her dear little heart; and I'd rather break my own."

"Nay, if that be the case," answered the other, "e'en go thy ways, Goodman Brown. I would not for twenty old women like the one hobbling before us that Faith should come to any harm."

As he spoke he pointed his staff at a female figure on the path, in whom Goodman Brown recognized a very pious and exemplary dame, who had taught him his catechism in youth, and was still his moral and spiritual adviser, jointly with the minister and Deacon Gookin.

"A marvel, truly, that Goody Cloyse should be so far in the wilderness at nightfall," said he. "But with your leave, friend, I shall take a cut through the woods until we have left this Christian woman behind. Being a stranger to you, she might ask whom I was consorting with and whither I was going."

"Be it so," said his fellow-traveller. "Betake you to the woods, and let me keep the path."

Accordingly the young man turned aside, but took care to watch his companion, who advanced softly along the road until he had come within a staff's length of the old dame. She, meanwhile, was making the best of her way, with singular speed for so aged a woman, and mumbling some indistinct words—a prayer, doubtless—as she went. The traveller put forth his staff and touched her withered neck with what seemed the serpent's tail.

"The devil!" screamed the pious old lady.

"Then Goody Cloyse knows her old friend?" observed the traveller, confronting her and leaning on his writhing stick.

"Ah, forsooth, and is it your worship indeed?" cried the good dame. "Yea, truly is it, and in the very image of my old gossip, Goodman Brown, the grandfather of the silly fellow that now is. But—would your worship believe it?—my broomstick hath strangely disappeared, stolen, as I suspect, by that unhanged witch, Goody Gory, and that, too, when I was all anointed with the juice of smallage, and cinque-foil, and wolf's bane—"

"Mingled with fine wheat and the fat of a new-born babe," said the shape of old Goodman Brown.

"Ah, your worship knows the recipe," cried the old lady, cackling aloud. "So, as I was saying, being all ready for the meeting, and no horse to ride on, I made up my mind to foot it; for they tell me there is a nice young man to be taken into communion to-night. But now your good worship will lend me your arm, and we shall be there in a twinkling."

"That can hardly be," answered her friend. "I may not spare you my arm, Goody Cloyse; but here is my staff, if you will."

So saying, he threw it down at her feet, where, perhaps, it assumed life, being one of the rods which its owner had formerly lent to the Egyptian magi. Of this fact, however, Goodman Brown could not take cognizance. He had cast up his eyes in astonishment, and, looking down again, beheld neither Goody Cloyse nor the serpentine staff, but his fellow-traveller alone, who waited for him as calmly as if nothing had happened.

"That old woman taught me my catechism," said the young man; and there was a world of meaning in this simple comment.

They continued to walk onward, while the elder traveller exhorted his companion to make good speed and persevere in the path, discoursing so aptly that his arguments seemed rather to spring up in the bosom of his auditor than to be suggested by himself. As they went, he plucked a branch of maple to serve for a walking stick, and began to strip it of the twigs and little boughs, which were wet with evening dew. The moment his fingers touched them they became strangely withered and dried up as with a week's sunshine. Thus the pair proceeded, at a good free pace, until suddenly, in a gloomy hollow of the road, Goodman Brown sat himself down on the stump of a tree and refused to go any farther.

"Friend," said he, stubbornly, "my mind is made up. Not another step will I budge on this errand. What if a wretched old woman do choose to go to the devil when I thought she was going to heaven: is that any reason why I should quit my dear Faith and go after her?"

"You will think better of this by and by," said his acquaintance, composedly. "Sit here and rest yourself a while; and when you feel like moving again, there is my staff to help you along."

Without more words, he threw his companion the maple stick, and was as speedily out of sight as if he had vanished into the deepening gloom. The young man sat a few moments by the roadside, applauding himself greatly, and thinking with how clear a conscience he should meet the minister in his morning walk, nor shrink from the eye of good old Deacon Gookin. And what calm sleep would be his that very night, which was to have been spent so wickedly, but so purely and sweetly now, in the arms of Faith! Amidst these pleasant and praiseworthy meditations, Goodman Brown heard the tramp of horses along the road, and deemed it advisable to conceal himself within the verge of the forest, conscious of the guilty purpose that had brought him thither, though now so happily turned from it.

On came the hoof tramps and the voices of the riders, two grave old voices, conversing soberly as they drew near. These mingled sounds appeared to pass along the road, within a few yards of the young man's hiding-place; but, owing doubtless to the depth of the gloom at that particular spot, neither the travellers nor their steeds were visible. Though their figures brushed the small boughs by the wayside, it could not be seen that they intercepted, even for a moment, the faint gleam from the strip of bright sky athwart which they must have passed. Goodman Brown alternately crouched and stood on tiptoe, pulling aside the branches and thrusting forth his head as far as he durst without discerning so much as a shadow. It vexed him the more, because he could have sworn, were such a thing possible, that he recognized the voices of the minister and Deacon Gookin, jogging along quietly, as they were wont to do, when bound to some ordination or ecclesiastical council. While yet within hearing, one of the riders stopped to pluck a switch.

"Of the two, reverend sir," said the voice like the deacon's, "I had rather miss an ordination dinner than to-night's meeting. They tell me that some of our community are to be here from Falmouth and beyond, and others from Connecticut and Rhode Island, besides several of the Indian powwows, who, after their fashion, know almost as much deviltry as the best of us. Moreover, there is a goodly young woman to be taken into communion."

"Mighty well, Deacon Gookin!" replied the solemn old tones of the minister. "Spur up, or we shall be late. Nothing can be done, you know, until I get on the ground."

The hoofs clattered again; and the voices, talking so strangely in the empty air, passed on through the forest, where no church had ever been gathered or solitary Christian prayed. Whither, then, could these holy men be journeying so deep into the heathen wilderness? Young Goodman Brown caught hold of a tree for support, being ready to sink down on the ground, faint and overburdened with the heavy sickness of his heart. He looked up to the sky, doubting whether there really was a heaven above him. Yet there was the blue arch, and the stars brightening in it.

"With heaven above and Faith below, I will yet stand firm against the devil!" cried Goodman Brown.

While he still gazed upward into the deep arch of the firmament and had lifted his hands to pray, a cloud, though no wind was stirring, hurried across the zenith and hid the brightening stars. The blue sky was still visible, except directly overhead, where this black mass of cloud was sweeping swiftly northward. Aloft in the air, as if from the depths of the cloud, came a confused and doubtful sound of voices. Once the listener fancied that he could distinguish the accents of towns-people of his own, men and women, both pious and ungodly, many of whom he had met at the communion table, and had seen others rioting at the tavern. The next moment, so indistinct were the sounds, he doubted whether he had heard aught but the murmur of the old forest, whispering without a wind. Then came a stronger swell of those familiar tones, heard daily in the sunshine at Salem village, but never until now from a cloud of night. There was one voice of a young woman, uttering lamentations, yet with an uncertain sorrow, and entreating for some favor, which, perhaps, it would grieve her to obtain; and all the unseen multitude, both saints and sinners, seemed to encourage her onward.

"Faith!" shouted Goodman Brown, in a voice of agony and desperation; and the echoes of the forest mocked him, crying, "Faith! Faith!" as if bewildered wretches were seeking her all through the wilderness.

The cry of grief, rage, and terror was yet piercing the night, when the unhappy husband held his breath for a response. There was a scream, drowned immediately in a louder murmur of voices, fading into far-off laughter, as the dark cloud swept away, leaving the clear and silent sky above Goodman Brown. But something fluttered lightly down through the air and caught on the branch of a tree. The young man seized it, and beheld a pink ribbon.

"My Faith is gone!" cried he, after one stupefied moment. "There is no good on earth; and sin is but a name. Come, devil; for to thee is this world given."

And, maddened with despair, so that he laughed loud and long, did Goodman Brown grasp his staff and set forth again, at such a rate that he seemed to fly along the forest path rather than to walk or run. The road grew wilder and drearier and more faintly traced, and vanished at length, leaving him in the heart of the dark wilderness, still rushing onward with the instinct that guides mortal men to evil. The whole forest was peopled with frightful sounds—the creaking of the trees, the howling of wild beasts, and the yell of Indians; while sometimes the wind tolled like a distant church bell, and sometimes gave a broad roar around the traveller, as if all Nature were laughing him to scorn. But he was himself the chief horror of the scene, and shrank not from its other horrors.

"Ha! ha! ha!" roared Goodman Brown when the wind laughed at him. "Let us hear which will laugh loudest. Think not to frighten me with your deviltry. Come witch, come wizard, come Indian powwow, come devil himself, and here comes Goodman Brown. You may as well fear him as he fear you."

In truth, all through the haunted forest there could be nothing more frightful than the figure of Goodman Brown. On he flew among the black pines, brandishing his staff with frenzied gestures, now giving vent to an inspiration of horrid blasphemy, and now shouting forth such laughter as set all the echoes of the forest laughing like demons around him. The fiend in his own shape is less hideous than when he rages in the breast of man. Thus sped the demoniac on his course, until, quivering among the trees, he saw a red light before him, as when the felled trunks and branches of a clearing have been set on fire, and throw up their lurid blaze against the sky, at the hour of midnight. He paused, in a lull of the tempest that had driven him onward, and heard the swell of what seemed a hymn, rolling solemnly from a distance with the weight of many voices. He knew the tune; it was a familiar one in the choir of the village meeting-house. The verse died heavily away, and was lengthened by a chorus, not of human voices, but of all the sounds of the benighted wilderness pealing in awful harmony together. Goodman Brown cried out, and his cry was lost to his own ear by its unison with the cry of the desert.

In the interval of silence he stole forward until the light glared full upon his eyes. At one extremity of an open space, hemmed in by the dark wall of the forest, arose a rock, bearing some rude, natural resemblance either to an altar or a pulpit, and surrounded by four blazing pines, their tops aflame, their stems untouched, like candles at an evening meeting. The mass of foliage that had overgrown the summit of the rock was all on fire, blazing high into the night and fitfully illuminating the whole field. Each pendent twig and leafy festoon was in a blaze. As the red light arose and fell, a numerous congregation alternately shone forth, then disappeared in shadow, and again grew, as it were, out of the darkness, peopling the heart of the solitary woods at once.

"A grave and dark-clad company," quoth Goodman Brown.

In truth they were such. Among them, quivering to and fro between gloom and splendor, appeared faces that would be seen next day at the council board of the province, and others which, Sabbath after Sabbath, looked devoutly heavenward, and benignantly over the crowded pew, from the holiest pulpits in the land. Some affirm that the lady of the governor was there. At least there were high dames well known to her, and wives of honored husbands, and widows, a great multitude, and ancient maidens, all of excellent repute, and fair young girls, who trembled lest their mothers should espy them. Either the sudden gleams of light flashing over the obscure field bedazzled Goodman Brown, or he recognized a score of the church members of Salem village famous for their especial sanctity. Good old Deacon Gookin had arrived, and waited at the skirts of that venerable saint, his revered pastor. But, irreverently consorting with these grave, reputable, and pious people, these elders of the church, these chaste dames and dewy virgins, there were men of dissolute lives and women of spotted fame, wretches given over to all mean and filthy vice, and suspected even of horrid crimes. It was strange to see that the good shrank not from the wicked, nor were the sinners abashed by the saints. Scattered also among their pale-faced enemies were the Indian priests, or powwows, who had often scared their native forest with more hideous incantations than any known to English witchcraft.

"But where is Faith?" thought Goodman Brown; and, as hope came into his heart, he trembled.

Another verse of the hymn arose, a slow and mournful strain, such as the pious love, but joined to words which expressed all that our nature can conceive of sin, and darkly hinted at far more. Unfathomable to mere mortals is the lore of fiends. Verse after verse was sung; and still the chorus of the desert swelled between like the deepest tone of a mighty organ; and with the final peal of that dreadful anthem there came a sound, as if the roaring wind, the rushing streams, the howling beasts, and every other voice of the unconcerted wilderness were mingling and according with the voice of guilty man in homage to the prince of all. The four blazing pines threw up a loftier flame, and obscurely discovered shapes and visages of horror on the smoke wreaths above the impious assembly. At the same moment the fire on the rock shot redly forth and formed a glowing arch above its base, where now appeared a figure. With reverence be it spoken, the figure bore no slight similitude, both in garb and manner, to some grave divine of the New England churches.

"Bring forth the converts!" cried a voice that echoed through the field and rolled into the forest.

At the word, Goodman Brown stepped forth from the shadow of the trees and approached the congregation, with whom he felt a loathful brotherhood by the sympathy of all that was wicked in his heart. He could have well-nigh sworn that the shape of his own dead father beckoned him to advance, looking downward from a smoke wreath, while a woman, with dim features of despair, threw out her hand to warn him back. Was it his mother? But he had no power to retreat one step, nor to resist, even in thought, when the minister and good old Deacon Gookin seized his arms and led him to the blazing rock. Thither came also the slender form of a veiled female, led between Goody Cloyse, that pious teacher of the catechism, and Martha Carrier, who had received the devil's promise to be queen of hell. A rampant hag was she. And there stood the proselytes beneath the canopy of fire.

"Welcome, my children," said the dark figure, "to the communion of your race. Ye have found thus young your nature and your destiny. My children, look behind you!"

They turned; and flashing forth, as it were, in a sheet of flame, the fiend worshippers were seen; the smile of welcome gleamed darkly on every visage.

"There," resumed the sable form, "are all whom ye have reverenced from youth. Ye deemed them holier than yourselves, and shrank from your own sin, contrasting it with their lives of righteousness and prayerful aspirations heavenward. Yet here are they all in my worshipping assembly. This night it shall be granted you to know their secret deeds; how hoary-bearded elders of the church have whispered wanton words to the young maids of their households; how many a woman, eager for widows' weeds, has given her husband a drink at bedtime and let him sleep his last sleep in her bosom; how beardless youths have made haste to inherit their fathers' wealth; and how fair damsels—blush not, sweet ones—have dug little graves in the garden, and bidden me, the sole guest, to an infant's funeral. By the sympathy of your human hearts for sin ye shall scent out all the places—whether in church, bedchamber, street, field, or forest—where crime has been committed, and shall exult to behold the whole earth one stain of guilt, one mighty blood spot. Far more than this. It shall be yours to penetrate, in every bosom, the deep mystery of sin, the fountain of all wicked arts, and which inexhaustibly supplies more evil impulses than human power—than my power at its utmost—can make manifest in deeds. And now, my children, look upon each other."

They did so; and, by the blaze of the hell-kindled torches, the wretched man beheld his Faith, and the wife her husband, trembling before that unhallowed altar.

"Lo, there ye stand, my children," said the figure, in a deep and solemn tone, almost sad with its despairing awfulness, as if his once angelic nature could yet mourn for our miserable race. "Depending upon one another's hearts, ye had still hoped that virtue were not all a dream. Now are ye undeceived. Evil is the nature of mankind. Evil must be your only happiness. Welcome again, my children, to the communion of your race."

"Welcome," repeated the fiend worshippers, in one cry of despair and triumph.

And there they stood, the only pair, as it seemed, who were yet hesitating on the verge of wickedness in this dark world. A basin was hollowed, naturally, in the rock. Did it contain water, reddened by the lurid light? or was it blood? or, perchance, a liquid flame? Herein did the shape of evil dip his hand and prepare to lay the mark of baptism upon their foreheads, that they might be partakers of the mystery of sin, more conscious of the secret guilt of others, both in deed and thought, than they could now be of their own. The husband cast one look at his pale wife, and Faith at him. What polluted wretches would the next glance show them to each other, shuddering alike at what they disclosed and what they saw!

"Faith! Faith!" cried the husband, "look up to heaven, and resist the wicked one."

Whether Faith obeyed he knew not. Hardly had he spoken when he found himself amid calm night and solitude, listening to a roar of the wind which died heavily away through the forest. He staggered against the rock, and felt it chill and damp; while a hanging twig, that had been all on fire, besprinkled his cheek with the coldest dew.

The next morning young Goodman Brown came slowly into the street of Salem village, staring around him like a bewildered man. The good old minister was taking a walk along the graveyard to get an appetite for breakfast and meditate his sermon, and bestowed a blessing, as he passed, on Goodman Brown. He shrank from the venerable saint as if to avoid an anathema. Old Deacon Gookin was at domestic worship, and the holy words of his prayer were heard through the open window. "What God doth the wizard pray to?" quoth Goodman Brown. Goody Cloyse, that excellent old Christian, stood in the early sunshine at her own lattice, catechizing a little girl who had brought her a pint of morning's milk. Goodman Brown snatched away the child as from the grasp of the fiend himself. Turning the corner by the meeting-house, he spied the head of Faith, with the pink ribbons, gazing anxiously forth, and bursting into such joy at sight of him that she skipped along the street and almost kissed her husband before the whole village. But Goodman Brown looked sternly and sadly into her face, and passed on without a greeting.

Had Goodman Brown fallen asleep in the forest and only dreamed a wild dream of a witch-meeting?

Be it so if you will; but, alas! it was a dream of evil omen for young Goodman Brown. A stern, a sad, a darkly meditative, a distrustful, if not a desperate man did he become from the night of that fearful dream. On the Sabbath day, when the congregation were singing a holy psalm, he could not listen because an anthem of sin rushed loudly upon his ear and drowned all the blessed strain. When the minister spoke from the pulpit with power and fervid eloquence, and, with his hand on the open Bible, of the sacred truths of our religion, and of saint-like lives and triumphant deaths, and of future bliss or misery unutterable, then did Goodman Brown turn pale, dreading lest the roof should thunder down upon the gray blasphemer and his hearers. Often, waking suddenly at midnight, he shrank from the bosom of Faith; and at morning or eventide, when the family knelt down at prayer, he scowled and muttered to himself, and gazed sternly at his wife, and turned away. And when he had lived long, and was borne to his grave a hoary corpse, followed by Faith, an aged woman, and children and grandchildren, a goodly procession, besides neighbors not a few, they carved no hopeful verse upon his tombstone, for his dying hour was gloom.

EDGAR ALLAN POE

The Tell-Tale Heart

TRUE!—nervous—very, very dreadfully nervous I had been and am; but why *will* you say that I am mad? The disease had sharpened my senses—not destroyed—not dulled them. Above all was the sense of hearing acute. I heard all things in the heaven and in the earth. I heard many things in hell. How, then, am I mad? Hearken! and observe how healthily—how calmly I can tell you the whole story.

It is impossible to say how first the idea entered my brain; but once conceived, it haunted me day and night. Object there was none. Passion there was none. I loved the old man. He had never wronged me. He had never given me insult. For his gold I had no desire. I think it was his eye! yes, it was this! One of his eyes resembled that of a vulture—a pale blue eye, with a film over it. Whenever it fell upon me, my blood ran cold; and so by degrees—very gradually—I made up my mind to take the life of the old man, and thus rid myself of the eye for ever.

Now this is the point. You fancy me mad. Madmen know nothing. But you should have seen *me*. You should have seen how wisely I proceeded—with what caution—with what foresight—with what dissimulation I went to work! I was never kinder to the old man than during the whole week before I killed him. And every night, about midnight, I turned the latch of his door and opened it—oh, so gently! And then, when I had made an opening sufficient for my head, I put in a dark lantern, all closed, closed, so that no light shone out, and then I thrust in my head. Oh, you would have laughed to see how cunningly I thrust it in! I moved it slowly—very, very slowly, so that I might not disturb the old man's sleep. It took me an hour to place my whole head within the opening so far that I could see him as he lay upon his bed. Ha!—would a madman have been so wise as this? And then, when my head was well in the room, I undid the lantern cautiously—oh, so cautiously—cautiously (for the hinges creaked)—I undid it just so much that a single thin ray fell upon the vulture eye. And this I did for seven long nights—every night just at midnight—but I found the eye always closed; and so it was impossible to do the work; for it was not the old man who vexed me, but his Evil Eye. And every morning, when the day broke, I went boldly into the chamber, and spoke courageously to him, calling him by name in a hearty tone, and inquiring how he had passed the night. So you see he would have been a very profound old man, indeed, to suspect that every night, just at twelve, I looked in upon him while he slept.

Upon the eighth night I was more than usually cautious in opening the door. A watch's minute hand moves more quickly than did mine. Never before that night had I *felt* the extent of my own powers—of my sagacity. I could scarcely contain my feelings of triumph. To think that there I was, opening the door, little by little, and he not even to dream of my secret deeds or thoughts. I fairly chuckled at the idea; and perhaps he heard me; for he moved on the bed suddenly, as if startled. Now you may think that I drew back—but no. His room was as black as pitch with the thick darkness (for the shutters were close fastened, through fear of robbers), and so I knew that he could not see the opening of the door, and I kept pushing it on steadily, steadily.

I had my head in, and was about to open the lantern, when my thumb slipped upon the tin fastening, and the old man sprang up in the bed, crying out—"Who's there?"

I kept quite still and said nothing. For a whole hour I did not move a muscle, and in the meantime I did not hear him lie down. He was still sitting up in the bed listening;—just as I have done, night after night, hearkening to the death watches in the wall.

Presently I heard a slight groan, and I knew it was the groan of mortal terror. It was not a groan of pain or of grief—oh, no!—it was the low stifled sound that arises from the bottom of the soul when overcharged with awe. I knew the sound well. Many a night, just at midnight, when all the world slept, it has welled up from my own bosom, deepening, with its dreadful echo, the terrors that distracted me. I say I knew it well. I knew what the old man felt, and pitied him, although I chuckled at heart. I knew that he had been lying awake ever since the first slight noise, when he had turned in the bed. His fears had been ever since growing upon him. He had been trying to fancy them causeless, but could not. He had been saying to himself—"It is nothing but the wind in the chimney—it is only a mouse crossing the floor," or "it is merely a cricket which has made a single chirp." Yes, he has been trying to comfort himself with these suppositions; but he had found all in vain. *All in vain;* because Death, in approaching him, had stalked with his black shadow before him, and enveloped the victim. And it was the mournful influence of the unperceived shadow that caused him to feel—

although he neither saw nor heard—to *feel* the presence of my head within the room.

When I had waited a long time, very patiently, without hearing him lie down, I resolved to open a little—a very, very little crevice in the lantern. So I opened it—you cannot imagine how stealthily, stealthily—until, at length, a single dim ray, like the thread of a spider, shot from out the crevice and full upon the vulture eye.

It was open—wide, wide open—and I grew furious as I gazed upon it. I saw it with perfect distinctness—all a dull blue, with a hideous veil over it that chilled the very marrow in my bones; but I could see nothing else of the old man's face or person: for I had directed the ray as if by instinct, precisely upon the damned spot.

And now have I not told you that what you mistake for madness is but over-acuteness of the senses?—now, I say, there came to my ears a low, dull, quick sound, such as a watch makes when enveloped in cotton. I knew *that* sound well too. It was the beating of the old man's heart. It increased my fury, as the beating of a drum stimulates the soldier into courage.

But even yet I refrained and kept still. I scarcely breathed. I held the lantern motionless. I tried how steadily I could maintain the ray upon the eye. Meantime the hellish tattoo of the heart increased. It grew quicker and quicker, and louder and louder every instant. The old man's terror *must* have been extreme! It grew louder, I say, louder every moment!—do you mark me well? I have told you that I am nervous: so I am. And now at the dead hour of the night, amid the dreadful silence of that old house, so strange a noise as this excited me to uncontrollable terror. Yet, for some minutes longer I refrained and stood still. But the beating grew louder, louder! I thought the heart must burst. And now a new anxiety seized me—the sound would be heard by a neighbor! The old man's hour had come! With a loud yell, I threw open the lantern and leaped into the room. He shrieked once—once only. In an instant I dragged him to the floor, and pulled the heavy bed over him. I then smiled gaily, to find the deed so far done. But, for many minutes, the heart beat on with a muffled sound. This, however, did not vex me; it would not be heard through the wall. At length it ceased. The old man was dead. I removed the bed and examined the corpse. Yes, he was stone, stone dead. I placed my hand upon the heart and held it there many minutes. There was no pulsation. He was stone dead. His eye would trouble me no more.

If still you think me mad, you will think so no longer when I describe the wise precautions I took for the concealment of the body. The night waned, and I worked hastily, but in silence. First of all I dismembered the corpse. I cut off the head and the arms and the legs.

I then took up three planks from the flooring of the chamber, and deposited all between the scantlings. I then replaced the boards so cleverly, so cunningly, that no human eye—not even *his*—could have detected any thing wrong. There was nothing to wash out—no stain of any kind—no blood-spot whatever. I had been too wary for that. A tub had caught all—ha! ha!

When I had made an end of these labors, it was four o'clock—still dark as midnight. As the bell sounded the hour, there came a knocking at the street door. I went down to open it with a light heart,—for what had I *now* to fear? There entered three men, who introduced themselves, with perfect suavity, as officers of the police. A shriek had been heard by a neighbor during the night; suspicion of foul play had been aroused; information had been lodged at the police office, and they (the officers) had been deputed to search the premises.

I smiled,—for *what* had I to fear? I bade the gentlemen welcome. The shriek, I said, was my own in a dream. The old man, I mentioned, was absent in the country. I took my visitors all over the house. I bade them search—search *well.* I led them, at length, to *his* chamber. I showed them his treasures, secure, undisturbed. In the enthusiasm of my confidence, I brought chairs into the room, and desired them *here* to rest from their fatigues, while I myself, in the wild audacity of my perfect triumph, placed my own seat upon the very spot beneath which reposed the corpse of the victim.

The officers were satisfied. My *manner* had convinced them. I was singularly at ease. They sat, and while I answered cheerily, they chatted familiar things. But, ere long, I felt myself getting pale and wished them gone. My head ached, and I fancied a ringing in my ears: but still they sat and still chatted. The ringing became more distinct:—it continued and became more distinct: I talked more freely to get rid of the feeling: but it continued and gained definitiveness—until, at length, I found that the noise was *not* within my ears.

No doubt I now grew *very* pale;—but I talked more fluently, and with a heightened voice. Yet the sound increased—and what could I do? It was *a low, dull, quick sound—much such a sound as a watch makes when enveloped in cotton.* I gasped for breath—and yet the officers heard it not. I talked more quickly—more vehemently; but the noise steadily increased. I arose and argued about trifles, in a high key and with violent gesticulations, but the noise steadily increased. Why *would* they not be gone? I paced the floor to and fro with heavy strides, as if excited to fury by the observation of the men—but the noise steadily increased. Oh

God! what *could* I do? I foamed—I raved—I swore! I swung the chair upon which I had been sitting, and grated it upon the boards, but the noise arose over all and continually increased. It grew louder—louder—*louder!* And still the men chatted pleasantly, and smiled. Was it possible they heard not? Almighty God!—no, no! They heard!—they suspected!—they *knew!*—they were making a mockery of my horror!—this I thought, and this I think. But any thing was better than this agony! Any thing was more tolerable than this derision! I could bear those hypocritical smiles no longer! I felt that I must scream or die!—and now—again!—hark! louder! louder! louder! *louder!*—

"Villains!" I shrieked, "dissemble no more! I admit the deed!—tear up the planks!—here, here!—it is the beating of his hideous heart!"

SAMUEL L. CLEMENS

The Facts Concerning the Recent Carnival of Crime in Connecticut

I was feeling blithe, almost jocund. I put a match to my cigar, and just then the morning's mail was handed in. The first superscription I glanced at was in a handwriting that sent a thrill of pleasure through and through me. It was Aunt Mary's; and she was the person I loved and honored most in all the world, outside of my own household. She had been my boyhood's idol; maturity, which is fatal to so many enchantments, had not been able to dislodge her from her pedestal; no, it had only justified her right to be there, and placed her dethronement permanently among the impossibilities. To show how strong her influence over me was, I will observe that long after everybody else's "*do*-stop-smoking" had ceased to affect me in the slightest degree, Aunt Mary could still stir my torpid conscience into faint signs of life when she touched upon the matter. But all things have their limit, in this world. A happy day came at last, when even Aunt Mary's words could no longer move me. I was not merely glad to see that day arrive; I was more than glad—I was grateful; for when its sun had set, the one alloy that was able to mar my enjoyment of my aunt's society was gone. The remainder of her stay with us that winter was in every way a delight. Of course she pleaded with me just as earnestly as ever, after that blessed day, to quit my pernicious habit, but to no purpose whatever; the moment she opened the subject I at once became calmly, peacefully, contentedly indifferent—absolutely, adamantinely indifferent. Consequently the closing weeks of that memorable visit melted away as pleasantly as a dream, they were so freighted, for me, with tranquil satisfaction. I could not have enjoyed my pet vice more if my gentle tormentor had been a smoker herself, and an advocate of the practice. Well, the sight of her handwriting reminded me that I was getting very hungry to see her again. I easily guessed what I should find in her letter. I opened it. Good! just as I expected; she was coming! Coming this very day, too, and by the morning train; I might expect her any moment.

I said to myself, "I am thoroughly happy and content, now. If my most pitiless enemy could appear before me at this moment, I would freely right any wrong I may have done him."

Straightway the door opened, and a shrivelled, shabby dwarf entered. He was not more than two feet high. He seemed to be about forty years old. Every feature and every inch of him was a trifle out of shape; and so, while one could not put his finger upon any particular part and say, "This is a conspicuous deformity," the spectator perceived that this little person was a deformity as a whole,—a vague, general, evenly blended, nicely-adjusted deformity. There was a foxlike cunning in the face and the sharp little eyes, and also alertness and malice. And yet, this vile bit of human rubbish seemed to bear a sort of remote and ill-defined resemblance to me! It was dully perceptible in the mean form, the countenance, and even the clothes, gestures, manner, and attitudes of the creature. He was a far-fetched, dim suggestion of a burlesque upon me, a caricature of me in little. One thing about him struck me forcibly, and most unpleasantly: he was covered all over with a fuzzy, greenish mold, such as one sometimes sees upon mildewed bread. The sight of it was nauseating.

He stepped along with a chipper air, and flung himself into a doll's chair in a very free and easy way, without waiting to be asked. He tossed his hat into the waste basket. He picked up my old chalk pipe from the floor, gave the stem a wipe or two on his knee, filled the bowl from the tobacco-box at his side, and said to me in a tone of pert command,—

"Gimme a match!"

I blushed to the roots of my hair; partly with indignation, but mainly because it somehow seemed to me that this whole performance was very like an exaggeration of conduct which I myself had sometimes been guilty of in my intercourse with familiar friends,—but never, never with strangers, I observed to myself. I wanted to kick the pygmy into the fire, but some incomprehensible sense of being legally and legitimately under his authority forced me to obey his order. He applied the match to the pipe, took a contemplative whiff or two, and remarked, in an irritatingly familiar way,—

"Seems to me it's devilish odd weather for this time of year."

I flushed again, and in anger and humiliation as before; for the language was hardly an exaggeration of some that I have uttered in my day, and moreover was delivered in a tone of voice and with an exasperating drawl that had the seeming of a deliberate travesty of my style. Now there is nothing I am quite so sensitive about as a mocking imitation of my drawling infirmity of speech. I spoke up sharply and said,—

"Look here, you miserable ash-cat! you will have to give a little more attention to your manners, or I will throw you out of the window!"

The manikin smiled a smile of malicious content and security, puffed a whiff of smoke contemptuously toward me, and said, with a still more elaborate drawl,—

"Come—go gently, now; don't put on too many airs with your betters."

This cool snub rasped me all over, but it seemed to subjugate me, too, for a moment. The pygmy contemplated me awhile with his weasel eyes, and then said, in a peculiarly sneering way,—

"You turned a tramp away from your door this morning."

I said crustily,—

"Perhaps I did, perhaps I did n't. How do *you* know?"

"Well, I know. It is n't any matter *how* I know."

"Very well. Suppose I *did* turn a tramp away from the door—what of it?"

"Oh, nothing; nothing in particular. Only you lied to him."

"I *did n't!* That is, I—"

"Yes, but you did; you lied to him."

I felt a guilty pang,—in truth I had felt it forty times before that tramp had travelled a block from my door,—but still I resolved to make a show of feeling slandered; so I said,—

"This is a baseless impertinence. I said to the tramp—"

"There—wait. You were about to lie again. *I* know what you said to him. You said the cook was gone down town and there was nothing left from breakfast. Two lies. You knew the cook was behind the door, and plenty of provisions behind *her.*"

This astonishing accuracy silenced me; and it filled me with wondering speculations, too, as to how this cub could have got his information.

Of course he could have culled the conversation from the tramp, but by what sort of magic had he contrived to find out about the concealed cook? Now the dwarf spoke again:—

"It was rather pitiful, rather small, in you to refuse to read that poor young woman's manuscript the other day, and give her an opinion as to its literary value; and she had come so far, too, and *so* hopefully. Now *wasn't* it?"

I felt like a cur! And I had felt so every time the thing had recurred to my mind, I may as well confess. I flushed hotly and said,—

"Look here, have you nothing better to do than prowl around prying into other people's business? Did that girl tell you that?"

"Never mind whether she did or not. The main thing is, you did that contemptible thing. And you felt ashamed of it afterwards. Aha! you feel ashamed of it *now!*"

This with a sort of devilish glee. With fiery earnestness I responded,—

"I told that girl, in the kindest, gentlest way, that I could not consent to deliver judgment upon *any* one's manuscript, because an individual's verdict was worthless. It might underrate a work of high merit and lose it to the world, or it might overrate a trashy production and so open the way for its infliction upon the world. I said that the great public was the only tribunal competent to sit in judgment upon a literary effort, and therefore it must be best to lay it before that tribunal in the outset, since in the end it must stand or fall by that mighty court's decision any way."

"Yes, you said all that. So you did, you juggling, small-souled shuffler! And yet when the happy hopefulness faded out of that poor girl's face, when you saw her furtively slip beneath her shawl the scroll she had so patiently and honestly scribbled at,—so ashamed of her darling now, so proud of it before,—when you saw the gladness go out of her eyes and the tears come there, when she crept away so humbly who had come so—"

"Oh, peace! peace! peace! Blister your merciless tongue, have n't all these thoughts tortured me enough, without *your* coming here to fetch them back again?"

Remorse! remorse! It seemed to me that it would eat the very heart out of me! And yet that small fiend only sat there leering at me with joy and contempt, and placidly chuckling. Presently he began to speak again. Every sentence was an accusation, and every accusation a truth. Every clause was freighted with sarcasm and derision, every slow-dropping word burned like vitriol. The dwarf reminded me of times when I had flown at my children in anger and punished them for faults which a little inquiry would have taught me that others, and not they, had committed. He reminded me of how I had disloyally allowed old friends to be traduced in my hearing, and been too craven to utter a word in their defense. He reminded me of many dishonest things which I had done; of many which I had procured to be done by children and other irresponsible persons; of some which I had planned, thought upon, and longed to do, and been kept from the performance by fear of consequences only. With exquisite cruelty he recalled to my mind, item by item, wrongs and unkindnesses I had inflicted and humiliations I had put upon friends since dead, "who died thinking of those injuries, maybe, and grieving over them," he added, by way of poison to the stab.

"For instance," said he, "take the case of your younger brother, when you two were boys together, many a long year ago. He always lovingly trusted in you with a fidelity that your manifold treacheries were not able to shake. He followed you about like a dog, content to suffer wrong and abuse if he might only be with you; patient under these injuries so long as it was your hand that inflicted them. The latest picture you have of him in health and strength must be such a comfort to you! You pledged your honor that if he would let you blindfold him no harm should come to him; and then, giggling and choking over the rare fun of the joke, you led him to a brook thinly glazed with ice, and pushed him in; and how you did laugh! Man, you will never forget the gentle, reproachful look he gave you as he struggled shivering out, if you live a thousand years! Oho! you see it now, you see it *now!*"

"Beast, I have seen it a million times, and shall see it a million more! and may you rot away piecemeal, and suffer till doomsday what I suffer now, for bringing it back to me again!"

The dwarf chuckled contentedly, and went on with his accusing history of my career. I dropped into a moody, vengeful state, and suffered in silence under the merciless lash. At last this remark of his gave me a sudden rouse:—

"Two months ago, on a Tuesday, you woke up, away in the night, and fell to thinking, with shame, about a peculiarly mean and pitiful act of yours toward a poor ignorant Indian in the wilds of the Rocky Mountains in the winter of eighteen hundred and—"

"Stop a moment, devil! Stop! Do you mean to tell me that even my very *thoughts* are not hidden from you?"

"It seems to look like that. Did n't you think the thoughts I have just mentioned?"

"If I did n't, I wish I may never breathe again! Look here, friend—look me in the eye. Who *are* you?"

"Well, who do you think?"

"I think you are Satan himself. I think you are the devil."

"No."

"No? Then who *can* you be?"

"Would you really like to know?"

"*Indeed* I would."

"Well, I am your *Conscience!*"

In an instant I was in a blaze of joy and exultation. I sprang at the creature, roaring,—

"Curse you, I have wished a hundred million times that you were tangible, and that I could get my hands on your throat once! Oh, but I will wreak a deadly vengeance on—"

Folly! Lightning does not move more quickly than my Conscience did! He darted aloft so suddenly that in the moment my fingers clutched the empty air he was was already perched on the top of the high book-case, with his thumb at his nose in token of derision. I flung the poker at him, and missed. I fired the bootjack. In a blind rage I flew from place to place, and snatched and hurled any missile that came handy; the storm of books, inkstands, and chunks of coal gloomed the air and beat about the manikin's perch relentlessly, but all to no purpose; the nimble figure dodged every shot; and not only that, but burst into a cackle of sarcastic and triumphant laughter as I sat down exhausted. While I puffed and gasped with fatigue and excitement, my Conscience talked to this effect:—

"My good slave, you are curiously witless—no, I mean characteristically so. In truth, you are always consistent, always yourself, always an ass. Otherwise it must have occurred to you that if you attempted this murder with a sad heart and a heavy conscience, I would droop under the burdening influence instantly. Fool, I should have weighed a ton, and could not have budged from the floor; but instead, you are so cheerfully anxious to kill me that your *conscience is as light* as a feather; hence I am away up here out of your reach. I can almost respect a mere ordinary sort of fool; but *you*—pah!"

I would have given anything, then, to be heavy-hearted, so that I could get this person down from there and take his life, but I could no more be heavy-hearted over such a desire than I could have sorrowed over its accomplishment. So I could only look longingly up at my master, and rave at the ill-luck that denied me a heavy conscience the one only time that I had ever wanted such a thing in my life. By and by I got to musing over the hour's strange adventure, and of course my human curiosity began to work. I set myself to framing in my mind some questions for this fiend to answer. Just then one of my boys entered, leaving the door open behind him, and exclaimed,—

"My! what *has* been going on, here! The book-case is all one riddle of—"

I sprang up in consternation, and shouted,—

"Out of this! Hurry! Jump! Fly! Shut the door! Quick, or my Conscience will get away"

The door slammed to, and I locked it. I glanced up and was grateful, to the bottom of my heart, to see that my owner was still my prisoner. I said,—

"Hang you, I might have lost you! Children are the heedlessest creatures. But look here, friend, the boy did not seem to notice you at all; how is that?"

"For a very good reason. I am invisible to all but you."

I made mental note of that piece of information with a good deal of satisfaction. I could kill this miscreant now, if I got a chance, and no one would know it. But this very reflection made me so light-hearted that my Conscience could hardly keep his seat, but was like to float aloft toward the ceiling like a toy balloon. I said, presently,—

"Come, my Conscience, let us be friendly. Let us fly a flag of truce for a while. I am suffering to ask you some questions."

"Very well. Begin."

"Well, then, in the first place, why were you never visible to me before?"

"Because you never asked to see me before; that is, you never asked in the right spirit and the proper form before. You were just in the right spirit this time, and when you called for your most pitiless enemy I was that person by a very large majority, though you did not suspect it."

"Well, did that remark of mine turn you into flesh and blood?"

"No. It only made me visible to you. I am unsubstantial, just as other spirits are."

This remark prodded me with a sharp misgiving. If he was unsubstantial, how was I going to kill him? But I dissembled, and said persuasively,—

"Conscience, it is n't sociable of you to keep at such a distance. Come down and take another smoke."

This was answered with a look that was full of derision, and with this observation added:—

"Come where you can get at me and kill me? The invitation is declined with thanks."

"All right," said I to myself; "so it seems a spirit *can* be killed, after all; there will be one spirit lacking in this world, presently, or I lose my guess." Then I said aloud,—

"Friend—"

"There; wait a bit. I am not your friend, I am your enemy; I am not your equal, I am your master. Call me 'my lord,' if you please. You are too familiar."

"I don't like such titles. I am willing to call you *sir.* That is as far as—"

"We will have no argument about this. Just obey; that is all. Go on with your chatter."

"Very well, my lord,—since nothing but my lord will suit you,—I was going to ask you how long you will be visible to me?"

"Always!"

I broke out with strong indignation: "This is simply an outrage. That is what I think of it. You have dogged, and dogged, and *dogged* me, all the days of my life, invisible. That was misery enough; now to have such a looking things as you tagging after me like another shadow all the rest of my days is an intolerable prospect. You have my opinion, my lord; make the most of it."

"My lad, there was never so pleased a conscience in this world as I was when you made me visible. It gives me an inconceivable advantage. *Now,* I can look you straight in the eye, and call you names, and leer at you, jeer at you, sneer at you; and *you* know what eloquence there is in visible gesture and expression, more especially when the effect is heightened by audible speech. I shall always address your henceforth in your o-w-n s-n-i-v-e-l-i-n-g d-r-a-w-l—baby!"

I let fly with the coal-hod. No result. My lord said,—

"Come, come! Remember the flag of truce!"

"Ah, I forgot that. I will try to be civil; and *you* try it, too, for a novelty. The idea of a *civil* conscience! It is a good joke; an excellent joke. All the consciences *I* have ever heard of were nagging, badgering, fault-finding, execrable savages! Yes; and always in a sweat about some poor little insignificant trifle or other—destruction catch the lot of them, *I* say! I would trade mine for the small-pox and seven kinds of consumption, and be glad of the chance. Now tell me, why *is* it that a conscience can't haul a man over the coals once, for an offense, and then let him alone? Why is it that it wants to keep on pegging at him, day and night and night and day, week in and week out, forever and ever, about the same old thing? There is no sense in that, and no reason in it. I think a conscience that will act like that is meaner than the very dirt itself."

"Well, *we* like it; that suffices."

"Do you do it with the *honest intent* to improve a man?"

That question produced a sarcastic smile, and this reply:—

"No, sir. Excuse me. We do it simply because it is *'business.'* It is our trade. The *purpose* of it *is* to improve the man, but *we* are merely disinterested agents. We are appointed by authority, and have n't anything to say in the matter. We obey orders and leave the consequences where they belong. But I am willing to admit this much: we *do* crowd the orders a trifle when we get a chance, which is most of the time. We enjoy it. We are instructed to remind a man a few times of an error; and I don't mind acknowledging that we try to give pretty good measure. And when we get hold of a man of a peculiarly sensitive nature, oh, but we do haze him! I have known consciences to come all the way from China and Russia to see a person of that kind put through his paces, on a special occasion. Why, I knew a man of that sort who had accidentally crippled a mulatto baby; the news went abroad, and I wish you may never commit another sin if the consciences did n't flock from all over the earth to enjoy the fun and help his master exercise him. That man walked the floor in torture for forty-eight hours, without eating or sleeping, and then blew his brains out. The child was perfectly well again in three weeks."

"Well, you are a precious crew, not to put it too strong. I think I begin to see, now, why you have always been a trifle inconsistent with me. In your anxiety to get all the juice you can out of a sin, you make a man repent of it in three or four different ways. For instance, you found fault with me for lying to that tramp, and I suffered over that. But it was only yesterday that I told a tramp the square truth, to wit, that, it being regarded as bad citizenship to encourage vagrancy, I would give him nothing. What did you do *then?* Why, you made me say to myself, 'Ah, it would have been so much kinder and more blameless to ease him off with a little white lie, and send him away feeling that if he could not have bread, the gentle treatment was at least something to be grateful for!' Well, I suffered all day about *that.* Three days before, I had fed a tramp, and fed him freely, supposing it a virtuous act. Straight off you said, 'O false citizen, to have fed a tramp!' and I suffered as usual. I gave a tramp work; you object to it,—*after* the contract was made, of course; you never speak up beforehand. Next, I refused a tramp work; you objected to *that.* Next, I proposed to kill a tramp; you kept me awake all night, oozing remorse at every pore. Sure I was going to be right *this* time, I sent the next tramp away with my benediction; and I wish you may live as long as I do, if you did n't make me smart all night again because I did n't kill him. Is there *any* way of satisfying that malignant invention which is called a conscience?"

"Ha, ha! this is luxury! Go on!"

"But come, now, answer me that question. *Is* there any way?"

"Well, none that I propose to tell *you,* my son. Ass! I don't care *what* act you may turn your hand to, I can straightway whisper a word in your ear and make you think you have committed a dreadful meanness. It is my *business*—and my joy—to make you repent of *every*thing you do. If I have fooled away any opportunities it was not intentional; I beg to assure you it was not intentional."

"Don't worry; you have n't missed a trick that *I* know of. I never did a thing in all my life, virtuous or otherwise, that I did n't repent of within twenty-four hours. In church last Sunday I listened to a charity sermon. My first impulse was to give three hundred and fifty dollars; I repented of that and reduced it a hundred; repented of that and reduced it another hundred; repented of that and reduced it another hundred; repented of that and reduced the remaining fifty to twenty-five; repented of that and came down to fifteen; repented of that and dropped to two dollars and a half; when the plate came around at last, I repented once more and contributed ten cents. Well, when I got home, I did wish to goodness I had that ten cents back again! You never *did* let me get through a charity sermon without having something to sweat about."

"Oh, and I never shall, I never shall. You can always depend on me."

"I think so. Many and many 's the restless night I've wanted to take you by the neck. If I could only get hold of you now!"

"Yes, no doubt. But I am not an ass; I am only the saddle of an ass. But go on, go on. You entertain me more than I like to confess."

"I am glad of that. (You will not mind my lying a little, to keep in practice.) Look here; not to be too personal, I think you are about the shabbiest and most contemptible little shrivelled-up reptile that can be imagined. I am grateful enough that you are invisible to other people, for I should die with shame to be seen with such a mildewed monkey of a conscience as *you* are. Now if you were five or six feet high, and—"

"Oh, come! who is to blame?"

"*I* don't know."

"Why, you are; nobody else."

"Confound you, I was n't consulted about your personal appearance."

"I don't care, you had a good deal to do with it, nevertheless. When you were eight or nine years old, I was seven feet high and as pretty as a picture."

"I wish you had died young! So you have grown the wrong way, have you?"

"Some of us grow one way and some the other. You had a large conscience once; if you've a small conscience now, I reckon there are reasons for it. However, both of us are to blame, you and I. You see, you used to be conscientious about a great many things; morbidly so, I may say. It was a great many years ago. You probably do not remember it, now. Well, I took a great interest in my work, and I so enjoyed the anguish which certain pet sins of yours afflicted you with, that I kept pelting at you until I rather overdid the matter. You began to rebel. Of course I began to lose ground, then, and shrivel a little,—diminish in stature, get mouldy, and grow deformed. The more I weakened, the more stubbornly you fastened on to those particular sins; till at last the places on my person that represent those vices became as callous as shark skin. Take smoking, for instance. I played that card a little too long, and I lost. When people plead with you at this late day to quit that vice, that old callous place seems to enlarge and cover me all over like a shirt of mail. It exerts a mysterious, smothering effect; and presently I, your faithful hater, your devoted Conscience, go sound asleep! Sound? It is no name for it. I could n't hear it thunder at such a time. You have some few other vices—perhaps eighty, or maybe ninety—that affect me in much the same way."

"This is flattering; you must be asleep a good part of *y*our time."

"Yes, of late years. I should be asleep *all* the time, but for the help I get."

"Who helps you?"

"Other consciences. Whenever a person whose conscience I am acquainted with tires to plead with you about the vices you are callous to, I get my friend to give his client a pang concerning some villany of his own, and that shuts off his meddling and starts him off to hunt personal consolation. My field of usefulness is about trimmed down to tramps, budding authoresses, and that line of goods, now; but don't you worry—I'll harry you on *them* while they last! Just you put your trust in me."

"I think I can. But if you had only been good enough to mention these facts some thirty years ago, I should have turned my particular attention to sin, and I think that by this time I should not only have had you pretty permanently asleep on the entire list of human vices, but reduced to the size of a homœopathic pill, at that. That is about the style of conscience *I* am pining for. If I only had you shrunk down to a homœopathic pill, and could get my hands on you, would I put you in a glass case for a keepsake? No, sir. I would give you to a yellow dog! That is where *you* ought to be—you and all your tribe. You are not fit to be in society, in my opinion. Now another question. Do you know a good many consciences in this section?"

"Plenty of them."

"I would give anything to see some of them! Could you bring them here? And would they be visible to me?"

"Certainly not."

"I suppose I ought to have known that, without asking. But no matter, you can describe them. Tell me about my neighbor Thompson's conscience, please."

"Very well. I know him intimately; have known him many years. I knew him when he was eleven feet high and of a faultless figure. But he is very rusty and tough and misshapen, now, and hardly ever interests himself about anything. As to his present size—well, he sleeps in a cigar box."

"Likely enough. There are few smaller, meaner men in this region than Hugh Thompson. Do you know Robinson's conscience?"

"Yes. He is a shade under four and a half feet high; used to be a blonde; is a brunette, now, but still shapely and comely."

"Well, Robinson is a good fellow. Do you know Tom Smith's conscience?"

"I have known him from childhood. He was thirteen inches high, and rather sluggish, when he was two years old—as nearly all of us are, at that age. He is thirty-seven feet high, now, and the stateliest figure in America. His legs are still racked with growing-pains, but he has a good time, nevertheless. Never sleeps. He is the most active and energetic member of the New England Conscience Club; is president of it. Night and day you can find him pegging away at Smith, panting with his labor, sleeves rolled up, countenance all alive with enjoyment. He has got his victim splendidly dragooned, now. He can make poor Smith imagine that the most innocent little thing he does is an odious sin; and then he sets to work and almost tortures the soul out of him about it."

"Smith is the noblest man in all this section, and the purest; and yet is always breaking his heart because he cannot be good! Only a conscience *could* find pleasure in heaping agony upon a spirit like that. Do you know my Aunt Mary's conscience?"

"I have seen her at a distance, but am not acquainted with her. She lives in the open air altogether, because no door is large enough to admit her."

"I can believe that. Let me see. Do you know the conscience of that publisher who once stole some sketches of mine for a 'series' of his, and then left me to pay the law expenses I had to incur in order to choke him off?"

"Yes. He has a wide fame. He was exhibited, a month ago, with some other antiquities, for the benefit of a recent Member of the Cabinet's conscience, that was starving in exile. Tickets and fares were high, but I travelled for nothing by pretending to be the conscience of an editor, and got in for half price by representing myself to be the conscience of a clergyman. However, the publisher's conscience, which was to have been the main feature of the entertainment, was a failure—as an exhibition. He was there, but what of that? The management had provided a microscope with a magnifying power of only thirty thousand diameters, and so nobody got to see him, after all. There was great and general dissatisfaction, of course, but—"

Just here there was an eager footstep on the stair; I opened the door, and my Aunt Mary burst into the room. It was a joyful meeting, and a cheery bombardment of questions and answers concerning family matters ensued. By and by my aunt said,—

"But I am going to abuse you a little now. You promised me, the day I saw you last, that you would look after the needs of the poor family around the corner as faithfully as I had done it myself. Well, I found out by accident that you failed of your promise. *Was* that right?"

In simple truth, I never had thought of that family a second time! And now such a splintering pang of guilt shot through me! I glanced up at my Conscience. Plainly, my heavy heart was affecting him. His body was drooping forward; he seemed about to fall from the bookcase. My aunt continued:—

"And think how you have neglected my poor *protégée* at the almshouse, you dear, hard-hearted promise-breaker!" I blushed scarlet, and my tongue was tied. As the sense of my guilty negligence waxed sharper and stronger, my Conscience began to sway heavily back and forth; and when my aunt, after a little pause, said in a grieved tone, "Since you never once went to see her, maybe it will not distress you now to know that that poor child died, months ago, utterly friendless and forsaken!" my Conscience could no longer bear up under the weight of my sufferings, but tumbled headlong from his high perch and struck the floor with a dull, leaden thump. He lay there writhing with pain and quaking with apprehension, but straining every muscle in frantic efforts to get up. In a fever of expectancy I sprang to the door, locked it, placed my back against it, and bent a watchful gaze upon my struggling master. Already my fingers were itching to begin their murderous work.

"Oh, what *can* be the matter!" exclaimed my aunt, shrinking from me, and following with her frightened eyes the direction of mine. My breath was coming in short, quick gasps now, and my excitement was almost uncontrollable. My aunt cried out,—

"Oh, do not look so! You appall me! Oh, what can the matter be? What is it you see? Why do you stare so? Why do you work your fingers like that?"

"Peace, woman!" I said, in a hoarse whisper. "Look elsewhere; pay no attention to me; it is nothing—nothing. I am often this way. It will pass in a moment. It comes from smoking too much."

My injured lord was up, wild-eyed with terror, and trying to hobble toward the door. I could hardly breathe, I was so wrought up. My aunt wrung her hands, and said,—

"Oh, I knew how it would be; I knew it would come to this at last! Oh, I implore you to crush out that fatal habit while it may yet be time! You must not, you shall not be deaf to my supplications longer!" My struggling Conscience showed sudden signs of weariness! "Oh, promise me you will throw off this hateful slavery of tobacco!" My Conscience began to reel drowsily, and grope with his hands—enchanting spectacle! "I beg you, I beseech you, I implore you! Your reason is deserting you! There is madness in your eye! It flames with frenzy! Oh, hear me, hear me, and be saved! See, I plead with you on my very knees!" As she sank before me my Conscience reeled again, and then drooped languidly to the floor, blinking toward me a last supplication for mercy, with heavy eyes. "Oh, promise, or you are lost! Promise, and be redeemed! Promise! Promise and live!" With a long-drawn sigh my conquered Conscience closed his eyes and fell fast asleep!

With an exultant shout I sprang past my aunt, and in an instant I had my life-long foe by the throat. After so many years of waiting and longing, he was mine at last. I tore him to shreds and fragments. I rent the fragments to bits. I cast the bleeding rubbish into the fire, and drew into my nostrils the grateful incense of my burnt-offering. At last, and forever, my Conscience was dead!

I was a free man! I turned upon my poor aunt, who was almost petrified with terror, and shouted,—

"Out of this with your paupers, your charities, your reforms, your pestilent morals! You behold before you a man whose life-conflict is done, whose soul is at peace; a man whose heart is dead to sorrow, dead to suffering, dead to remorse; a man WITHOUT A CONSCIENCE! In my joy I spare you, though I could throttle you and never feel a pang! Fly!"

She fled. Since that day my life is all bliss. Bliss, unalloyed bliss. Nothing in all the world could persuade me to have a conscience again. I settled all my old outstanding scores, and began the world anew. I killed thirty-eight persons during the first two weeks—all of them on account of ancient grudges. I burned a dwelling that interrupted my view. I swindled a widow and some orphans out of their last cow, which is a very good one, though not thoroughbred, I believe. I have also committed scores of crimes, of various kinds, and have enjoyed my work exceedingly, whereas it would formerly have broken my heart and turned my hair gray, I have no doubt.

In conclusion I wish to state, by way of advertisement, that medical colleges desiring assorted tramps for scientific purposes, either by the gross, by cord measurement, or per ton, will do well to examine the lot in my cellar before purchasing elsewhere, as these were all selected and prepared by myself, and can be had at a low rate, because I wish to clear out my stock and get ready for the spring trade.

BRET HARTE

The Outcasts of Poker Flat

As Mr. John Oakhurst, gambler, stepped into the main street of Poker Flat on the morning of the twenty-third of November, 1850, he was conscious of a change in its moral atmosphere since the preceding night. Two or three men, conversing earnestly together, ceased as he approached, and exchanged significant glances. There was a Sabbath lull in the air, which, in a settlement unused to Sabbath influences, looked ominous.

Mr. Oakhurst's calm, handsome face betrayed small concern in these indications. Whether he was conscious of any predisposing cause, was another question. "I reckon they're after somebody," he reflected; "likely it's me." He returned to his pocket the handkerchief with which he had been whipping away the red dust of Poker Flat from his neat boots, and quietly discharged his mind of any further conjecture.

In point of fact, Poker Flat was "after somebody." It had lately suffered the loss of several thousand dollars, two valuable horses, and a prominent citizen. It was experiencing a spasm of virtuous reaction, quite as lawless and ungovernable as any of the acts that had provoked it. A secret committee had determined to rid the town of all improper persons. This was done permanently in regard of two men who were then hanging from the boughs of a sycamore in the gulch, and temporarily in the banishment of certain other objectionable characters. I regret to say that some of these were ladies. It is but due to the sex, however, to state that their impropriety was professional, and it was only in such easily established standards of evil that Poker Flat ventured to sit in judgment.

Mr. Oakhurst was right in supposing that he was included in this category. A few of the committee had urged hanging him as a possible example, and a sure method of reimbursing themselves from his pockets of the sums he had won from them. "It's agin justice," said Jim Wheeler, "to let this yer young man from Roaring Camp—an entire stranger—carry away our money." But a crude sentiment of equity residing in the breasts of those who had been fortunate enough to win from Mr. Oakhurst overruled this narrower local prejudice.

Mr. Oakhurst received his sentence with philosophic calmness, none the less coolly that he was aware of the hesitation of his judges. He was too much of a gambler not to accept Fate. With him life was at best an uncertain game, and he recognized the usual percentage in favor of the dealer.

A body of armed men accompanied the deported wickedness of Poker Flat to the outskirts of the settlement. Besides Mr. Oakhurst, who was known to be a coolly desperate man, and for whose intimidation the armed escort was intended, the expatriated party consisted of a young woman familiarly known as "The Duchess"; another, who had won the title of "Mother Shipton"; and "Uncle Billy," a suspected sluice-robber and confirmed drunkard. The cavalcade provoked no comments from the spectators, nor was any word uttered by the escort. Only, when the gulch which marked the uttermost limit of Poker Flat was reached, the leader spoke briefly and to the point. The exiles were forbidden to return at the peril of their lives.

As the escort disappeared, their pent-up feelings found vent in a few hysterical tears from the Duchess, some bad language from Mother Shipton, and a Parthian volley of expletives from Uncle Billy. The philosophic Oakhurst alone remained silent. He listened calmly to Mother Shipton's desire to cut somebody's heart out, to the repeated statements of the Duchess that she would die in the road, and to the alarming oaths that seemed to be bumped out of Uncle Billy as he rode forward. With the easy good-humor characteristic of his class, he insisted upon exchanging his own riding-horse, "Five Spot," for the sorry mule which the Duchess rode. But even this act did not draw the party into any closer sympathy. The young woman readjusted her somewhat draggled plumes with a feeble, faded coquetry; Mother Shipton eyed the possessor of "Five Spot" with malevolence, and Uncle Billy included the whole party in one sweeping anathema.

The road to Sandy Bar—a camp that, not having as yet experienced the regenerating influences of Poker Flat, consequently seemed to offer some invitation to the emigrants—lay over a steep mountain range. It was distant a day's severe travel. In that advanced season, the party soon passed out of the moist, temperate regions of the foot-hills into the dry, cold, bracing air of the Sierras. The trail was narrow and difficult. At noon the Duchess, rolling out of her saddle upon the ground, declared her intention of going no farther, and the party halted.

The spot was singularly wild and impressive. A wooded amphitheatre, surrounded on three sides by precipitous cliffs of naked granite, sloped gently toward the crest of another precipice that overlooked the valley. It was, undoubtedly, the most suitable spot for a camp, had camping been advisable. But Mr. Oakhurst knew that scarcely half the journey to Sandy Bar was accomplished, and the party were not equipped or provisioned for delay. This fact he pointed out to his companions curtly, with a philosophic commentary on the folly of "throwing up their hand before the game was played out." But they were furnished with liquor, which in this emergency stood them in place of food, fuel, rest, and prescience. In spite of his remonstrances, it was not long before they were more or less under its influence. Uncle Billy passed rapidly from a bellicose state into one of stupor, the Duchess became maudlin, and Mother Shipton snored. Mr. Oakhurst alone remained erect, leaning against a rock, calmly surveying them.

Mr. Oakhurst did not drink. It interfered with a profession which required coolness, impassiveness, and presence of mind, and, in his own language, he "could n't afford it." As he gazed at his recumbent fellow-exiles, the loneliness begotten of his pariah-trade, his habits of life, his very vices, for the first time seriously oppressed him. He bestirred himself in dusting his black clothes, washing his hands and face, and other acts characteristic of his studiously neat habits, and for a moment forgot his annoyance. The thought of deserting his weaker and more pitiable companions never perhaps occurred to him. Yet he could not help feeling the want of that excitement which, singularly enough, was most conducive to that calm equanimity for which he was notorious. He looked at the gloomy walls that rose a thousand feet sheer above the circling pines around him; at the sky, ominously clouded; at the valley below, already deepening into shadow. And, doing so, suddenly he heard his own name called.

A horseman slowly ascended the trail. In the fresh, open face of the new-comer Mr. Oakhurst recognized Tom Simson, otherwise known as "The Innocent" of Sandy Bar. He had met him some months before over a "little game," and had, with perfect equanimity, won the entire fortune—amounting to some forty dollars—of that guileless youth. After the game was finished, Mr. Oakhurst drew the youthful speculator behind the door and thus addressed him: "Tommy, you're a good little man, but you can't gamble worth a cent. Don't try it over again." He then handed him his money back, pushed him gently from the room, and so made a devoted slave of Tom Simson.

There was a remembrance of this in his boyish and enthusiastic greeting of Mr. Oakhurst. He had started, he said, to go to Poker Flat to seek his fortune. "Alone?" No, not exactly alone; in fact (a giggle), he had run away with Piney Woods. Did n't Mr. Oakhurst remember Piney? She that used to wait on the table at the Temperance House? They had been engaged a long time, but old Jake Woods had objected, and so they had run away, and were going to Poker Flat to be married, and here they were. And they were tired out, and how lucky it was they had found a place to camp and company. All this the Innocent delivered rapidly, while Piney, a stout, comely damsel of fifteen, emerged from behind the pine-tree, where she had been blushing unseen, and rode to the side of her lover.

Mr. Oakhurst seldom troubled himself with sentiment, still less with propriety; but he had a vague idea that the situation was not fortunate. He retained, however, his presence of mind sufficiently to kick Uncle Billy, who was about to say something, and Uncle Billy was sober enough to recognize in Mr. Oakhurst's kick a superior power that would not bear trifling. He then endeavored to dissuade Tom Simson from delaying further, but in vain. He even pointed out the fact that there was no provision, nor means of making a camp. But, unluckily, the Innocent met this objection by assuring the party that he was provided with an extra mule loaded with provisions, and by the discovery of a rude attempt at a log-house near the trail. "Piney can stay with Mrs. Oakhurst," said the Innocent, pointing to the Duchess, "and I can shift for myself."

Nothing but Mr. Oakhurst's admonishing foot saved Uncle Billy from bursting into a roar of laughter. As it was, he felt compelled to retire up the cañon until he could recover his gravity. There he confided the joke to the tall pine-trees, with many slaps of his leg, contortions of his face, and the usual profanity. But when he returned to the party, he found them seated by a fire—for the air had grown strangely chill and the sky overcast—in apparently amicable conversation. Piney was actually talking in an impulsive, girlish fashion to the Duchess, who was listening with an interest and animation she had not shown for many days. The Innocent was holding forth, apparently with equal effect, to Mr. Oakhurst and Mother Shipton, who was actually relaxing into amiability. "Is this yer a d—d picnic?" said Uncle Billy, with inward scorn, as he surveyed the sylvan group, the glancing firelight, and the tethered animals in the foreground. Suddenly an idea mingled with the alcoholic fumes that disturbed his brain. It was apparently of a jocular nature, for he felt impelled to slap his leg again and cram his fist into his mouth.

As the shadows crept slowly up the mountain, a slight breeze rocked the tops of the pine-trees, and moaned through their long and gloomy aisles. The ruined cabin, patched and covered with pine-boughs, was set apart for the ladies. As the lovers parted, they unaffectedly exchanged a kiss, so honest and sincere that it might have been heard above the swaying pines. The frail Duchess and the malevolent Mother Shipton were probably too stunned to remark upon this last evidence of simplicity, and so turned without a word to the hut. The fire was replenished, the men lay down before the door, and in a few minutes were asleep.

Mr. Oakhurst was a light sleeper. Toward morning he awoke benumbed and cold. As he stirred the dying fire, the wind, which was now blowing strongly, brought to his cheek that which caused the blood to leave it,—snow!

He started to his feet with the intention of awakening the sleepers, for there was no time to lose. But turning to where Uncle Billy had been lying, he found him gone. A suspicion leaped to his brain and a curse to his lips. He ran to the spot where the mules had been tethered; they were no longer there. The tracks were already rapidly disappearing in the snow.

The momentary excitement brought Mr. Oakhurst back to the fire with his usual calm. He did not waken the sleepers. The Innocent slumbered peacefully, with a smile on his good-humored, freckled face; the virgin Piney slept beside her frailer sisters as sweetly as though attended by celestial guardians, and Mr. Oakhurst, drawing his blanket over his shoulders, stroked his mustaches and waited for the dawn. It came slowly in a whirling mist of snow-flakes, that dazzled and confused the eye. What could be seen of the landscape appeared magically changed. He looked over the valley, and summed up the present and future in two words,—"snowed in!"

A careful inventory of the provisions, which, fortunately for the party, had been stored within the hut, and so escaped the felonious fingers of Uncle Billy, disclosed the fact that with care and prudence they might last ten days longer. "That is," said Mr. Oakhurst, *sotto voce* to the Innocent, "if you're willing to board us. If you ain't—and perhaps you'd better not—you can wait till Uncle Billy gets back with provisions." For some occult reason, Mr. Oakhurst could not bring himself to disclose Uncle Billy's rascality, and so offered the hypothesis that he had wandered from the camp and had accidentally stampeded the animals. He dropped a warning to the Duchess and Mother Shipton, who of course knew the facts of their associate's defection. "They'll find out the truth about us *all* when they find out anything," he added, significantly, "and there's no good frightening them now."

Tom Simson not only put all his worldly store at the disposal of Mr. Oakhurst, but seemed to enjoy the prospect of their enforced seclusion. "We'll have a good camp for a week, and then the snow'll melt, and we'll all go back together." The cheerful gayety of the young man, and Mr. Oakhurst's calm infected the others. The Innocent, with the aid of pine-boughs, extemporized a thatch for the roofless cabin, and the Duchess directed Piney in the rearrangement of the interior with a taste and tact that opened the blue eyes of that provincial maiden to their fullest extent. "I reckon now you're used to fine things at Poker Flat," said Piney. The Duchess turned away sharply to conceal something that reddened her cheeks through its professional tint, and Mother Shipton requested Piney not to "chatter." But when Mr. Oakhurst returned from a weary search for the trail, he heard the sound of happy laughter echoed from the rocks. He stopped in some alarm, and his thoughts first naturally reverted to the whiskey, which he had prudently *cachéd.* "And yet it don't somehow sound like whiskey," said the gambler. It was not until he caught sight of the blazing fire through the still-blinding storm and the group around it that he settled to the conviction that it was "square fun."

Whether Mr. Oakhurst had *cachéd* his cards with the whiskey as something debarred the free access of the community, I cannot say. It was certain that, in Mother Shipton's words, he "did n't say cards once" during that evening. Haply the time was beguiled by an accordion, produced somewhat ostentatiously by Tom Simson from his pack. Notwithstanding some difficulties attending the manipulation of this instrument, Piney Woods managed to pluck several reluctant melodies from its keys, to an accompaniment by the Innocent on a pair of bone castinets. But the crowning festivity of the evening was reached in a rude camp-meeting hymn, which the lovers, joining hands, sang with great earnestness and vociferation. I fear that a certain defiant tone and Covenanter's swing to its chorus, rather than any devotional quality, caused it speedily to infect the others, who at last joined in the refrain:—

"I'm proud to live in the service of the Lord,
And I'm bound to die in His army."

The pines rocked, the storm eddied and whirled above the miserable group, and the flames of their altar leaped heavenward, as if in token of the vow.

At midnight the storm abated, the rolling clouds parted, and the stars glittered keenly above the sleeping camp. Mr. Oakhurst, whose professional habits had enabled him to live on the smallest possible amount of sleep, in dividing the watch with Tom Simson, somehow managed to take upon himself the greater part of that duty. He excused himself to the Innocent, by saying that he had "often been a week without sleep." "Doing what?" asked Tom. "Poker!" replied Oakhurst, sententiously; "when a man gets a streak of luck, —nigger-luck,—he don't get tired. The luck gives in first. Luck," continued the gambler, reflectively, "is a mighty queer thing. All you know about it for certain is that it's bound to change. And it's finding out when it's going to change that makes you. We've had a streak of bad luck since we left Poker Flat,—you come along, and slap you get into it, too. If you can hold your cards right along you're all right. For," added the gambler, with cheerful irrelevance,—

" 'I'm proud to live in the service of the Lord,
And I'm bound to die in His army.' "

The third day came, and the sun, looking through the white-curtained valley, saw the outcasts divide their slowly decreasing store of provisions for the morning meal. It was one of the peculiarities of that mountain climate that its rays diffused a kindly warmth over the wintry landscape, as if in regretful commiseration of the past. But it revealed drift on drift of snow piled high around the hut,—a hopeless, uncharted, trackless sea of white lying below the rocky shores to which the castaways still clung. Through the marvellously clear air the smoke of the pastoral village of Poker Flat rose miles away. Mother Shipton saw it, and from a remote pinnacle of her rocky fastness, hurled in that direction a final malediction. It was her last vituperative attempt, and perhaps for that reason was invested with a certain degree of sublimity. It did her good, she privately informed the Duchess. "Just you go out there and cuss, and see." She then set herself to the task of amusing "the child," as she and the Duchess were pleased to call Piney. Piney was no chicken, but it was a soothing and original theory of the pair thus to account for the fact that she did n't swear and was n't improper.

When night crept up again through the gorges, the reedy notes of the accordion rose and fell in fitful spasms and long-drawn gasps by the flickering camp-fire. But music failed to fill entirely the aching void left by insufficient food, and a new diversion was proposed by Piney,—story-telling. Neither Mr. Oakhurst nor his female companions caring to relate their personal experiences, this plan would have failed, too, but for the Innocent. Some months before he had chanced upon a stray copy of Mr. Pope's ingenious translation of the Iliad. He now proposed to narrate the principal incidents of that poem—having thoroughly mastered the argument and fairly forgotten the words—in the current vernacular of Sandy Bar. And so for the rest of that night the Homeric demigods again walked the earth. Trojan bully and wily Greek wrestled in the winds, and the great pines in the cañon seemed to bow to the wrath of the son of Peleus. Mr. Oakhurst listened with quiet satisfaction. Most especially was he interested in the fate of "Ash-heels," as the Innocent persisted in denominating the "swift-footed Achilles."

So with small food and much of Homer and the accordion, a week passed over the heads of the outcasts. The sun again forsook them, and again from leaden skies the snow-flakes were sifted over the land. Day by day closer around them drew the snowy circle, until at last they looked from their prison over drifted walls of dazzling white, that towered twenty feet above their heads. It became more and more difficult to replenish their fires, even from the fallen trees beside them, now half hidden in the drifts. And yet no one complained. The lovers turned from the dreary prospect and looked into each other's eyes, and were happy. Mr. Oakhurst settled himself coolly to the losing game before him. The Duchess, more cheerful than she had been, assumed the care of Piney. Only Mother Shipton—once the strongest of the party—seemed to sicken and fade. At midnight on the tenth day she called Oakhurst to her side. "I'm going," she said, in a voice of querulous weakness, "but don't say anything about it. Don't waken the kids. Take the bundle from under my head and open it." Mr. Oakhurst did so. It contained Mother Shipton's rations for the last week, untouched. "Give 'em to the child," she said, pointing to the sleeping Piney. "You've starved yourself," said the gambler. "That's what they call it," said the woman, querulously, as she lay down again, and, turning her face to the wall, passed quietly away.

The accordion and the bones were put aside that day, and Homer was forgotten. When the body of Mother Shipton had been committed to the snow, Mr. Oakhurst took the Innocent aside, and showed him a pair of snow-shoes, which he had fashioned from the old pack-saddle. "There's one chance in a hundred to save her yet," he said, pointing to

Piney; "but it's there," he added, pointing toward Poker Flat. "If you can reach there in two days she's safe." "And you?" asked Tom Simson. "I'll stay here," was the curt reply.

The lovers parted with a long embrace. "You are not going, too?" said the Duchess, as she saw Mr. Oakhurst apparently waiting to accompany him. "As far as the cañon," he replied. He turned suddenly, and kissed the Duchess, leaving her pallid face aflame, and her trembling limbs rigid with amazement.

Night came, but not Mr. Oakhurst. It brought the storm again and the whirling snow. Then the Duchess, feeding the fire, found that some one had quietly piled beside the hut enough fuel to last a few days longer. The tears rose to her eyes, but she hid them from Piney.

The women slept but little. In the morning, looking into each other's faces, they read their fate. Neither spoke; but Piney, accepting the position of the stronger, drew near and placed her arm around the Duchess's waist. They kept this attitude for the rest of the day. That night the storm reached its greatest fury, and, rending asunder the protecting pines, invaded the very hut.

Toward morning they found themselves unable to feed the fire, which gradually died away. As the embers slowly blackened, the Duchess crept closer to Piney, and broke the silence of many hours: "Piney, can you pray?" "No, dear," said Piney, simply. The Duchess, without knowing exactly why, felt relieved, and, putting her head upon Piney's shoulder, spoke no more. And so reclining, the younger and purer pillowing the head of her soiled sister upon her virgin breast, they fell asleep.

The wind lulled as if it feared to waken them. Feathery drifts of snow, shaken from the long pine-boughs, flew like white-winged birds, and settled about them as they slept. The moon through the rifted clouds looked down upon what had been the camp. But all human stain, all trace of earthly travail, was hidden beneath the spotless mantle mercifully flung from above.

They slept all that day and the next, nor did they waken when voices and footsteps broke the silence of the camp. And when pitying fingers brushed the snow from their wan faces, you could scarcely have told from the equal peace that dwelt upon them, which was she that had sinned. Even the law of Poker Flat recognized this, and turned away, leaving them still locked in each other's arms.

But at the head of the gulch, on one of the largest pine-trees, they found the deuce of clubs pinned to the bark with a bowie-knife. It bore the following, written in pencil, in a firm hand:—

†

BENEATH THIS TREE

LIES THE BODY

OF

JOHN OAKHURST,

WHO STRUCK A STREAK OF BAD LUCK

ON THE 23D OF NOVEMBER, 1850,

AND

HANDED IN HIS CHECKS

ON THE 7TH DECEMBER, 1850.

↓

And pulseless and cold, with a Derringer by his side and a bullet in his heart, though still calm as in life, beneath the snow lay he who was at once the strongest and yet the weakest of the outcasts of Poker Flat.

AMBROSE BIERCE

Chickamauga

One sunny autumn afternoon a child strayed away from its rude home in a small field and entered a forest unobserved. It was happy in a new sense of freedom from control, happy in the opportunity of exploration and adventure; for this child's spirit, in bodies of its ancestors, had for thousands of years been trained to memorable feats of discovery and conquest—victories in battles whose critical moments were centuries, whose victors' camps were cities of hewn stone. From the cradle of its race it had conquered its way through two continents and passing a great sea had penetrated a third, there to be born to war and dominion as a heritage.

The child was a boy aged about six years, the son of a poor planter. In his younger manhood the father had been a soldier, had fought against naked savages and followed the flag of his country into the capital of a civilized race to the far South. In the peaceful life of a planter the warrior-fire survived; once kindled, it is never extinguished. The man loved military books and pictures and the boy had understood enough to make himself a wooden sword, though even the eye of his father would hardly have known it for what it was. This weapon he now bore bravely, as became the son of an heroic race, and pausing now and again in the sunny space of the forest assumed, with some exaggeration, the postures of aggression and defense that he had been taught by the engraver's art. Made reckless by the ease with which he overcame invisible foes attempting to stay his advance, he committed the common enough military error of pushing the pursuit to a dangerous extreme, until he found himself upon the margin of a wide but shallow brook, whose rapid waters barred his direct advance against the flying foe that had crossed with illogical ease. But the intrepid victor was not to be baffled; the spirit of the race which had passed the great sea burned unconquerable in that small breast and would not be denied. Finding a place where some bowlders in the bed of the stream lay but a step or a leap apart, he made his way across and fell again upon the rear-guard of his imaginary foe, putting all to the sword.

Now that the battle had been won, prudence required that he withdraw to his base of operations. Alas; like many a mightier conqueror, and like one, the mightiest, he could not

> curb the lust for war,
> Nor learn that tempted Fate will leave the loftiest star.

Advancing from the bank of the creek he suddenly found himself confronted with a new and more formidable enemy: in the path that he was following, sat, bolt upright, with ears erect and paws suspended before it, a rabbit! With a startled cry the child turned and fled, he knew not in what direction, calling with inarticulate cries for his mother, weeping, stumbling, his tender skin cruelly torn by brambles, his little heart beating hard with terror—breathless, blind with tears—lost in the forest! Then, for more than an hour, he wandered with erring feet through the tangled undergrowth, till at last, overcome by fatigue, he lay down in a narrow space between two rocks, within a few yards of the stream and still grasping his toy sword, no longer a weapon but a companion, sobbed himself to sleep. The wood birds sang merrily above his head; the squirrels, whisking their bravery of tail, ran barking from tree to tree, unconscious of the pity of it, and somewhere far away was a strange, muffled thunder, as if the partridges were drumming in celebration of nature's victory over the son of her immemorial enslavers. And back at the little plantation, where white men and black were hastily searching the fields and hedges in alarm, a mother's heart was breaking for her missing child.

Hours passed, and then the little sleeper rose to his feet. The chill of the evening was in his limbs, the fear of the gloom in his heart. But he had rested, and he no longer wept. With some blind instinct which impelled to action he struggled through the undergrowth about him and came to a more open ground—on his right the brook, to the left a gentle acclivity studded with infrequent trees; over all, the gathering gloom of twilight. A thin, ghostly mist rose along the water. It frightened and repelled him; instead of recrossing, in the direction whence he had come, he turned his back upon it, and went forward toward the dark inclosing wood. Suddenly he saw before him a strange moving object which he took to be some large animal—a dog, a pig—he could not name it; perhaps it was a bear. He had seen pictures of bears, but knew of nothing to their discredit and had vaguely wished to meet one. But something in form or movement of this object—something in the awkwardness of its approach—told him that it was not a bear, and curiosity was stayed by fear. He stood still and as it came slowly on gained courage every moment, for he saw that at least it had not the long, menacing ears of the rabbit. Possibly his impressionable mind was half conscious of something familiar in its shambling, awkward gait. Before it had approached near enough to resolve his doubts he saw that it was followed by another and another. To right and to left were many more; the whole open space about him was alive with them—all moving toward the brook.

They were men. They crept upon their hands and knees. They used their hands only, dragging their legs. They used their knees only, their arms hanging idle at their sides. They strove to rise to their feet, but fell prone in the attempt. They did nothing naturally, and nothing alike, save only to advance foot by foot in the same direction. Singly, in pairs and in little groups, they came on through the gloom, some halting now and again while others crept slowly past them, then resuming their movement. They came by dozens and by hundreds; as far on either hand as one could see in the deepening gloom they extended and the black wood behind them appeared to be inexhaustible. The very ground seemed in motion toward the creek. Occasionally one who had paused did not again go on, but lay motionless. He was dead. Some, pausing, made strange gestures with their hands, erected their arms and lowered them again, clasped their heads; spread their palms upward, as men are sometimes seen to do in public prayer.

Not all of this did the child note; it is what would have been noted by an elder observer; he saw little but that these were men, yet crept like babies. Being men, they were not terrible, though unfamiliarly clad. He moved among them freely, going from one to another and peering into their faces with childish curiosity. All their faces were singularly white and many were streaked and gouted with red. Something in this—something too, perhaps, in their grotesque attitudes and movements—reminded him of the painted clown whom he had seen last summer in the circus, and he laughed as he watched them. But on and ever on they crept, these maimed and bleeding men, as heedless as he of the dramatic contrast between his laughter and their own ghastly gravity. To him it was a merry spectacle. He had seen his father's negroes creep upon their hands and knees for his amusement—had ridden them so, "making believe" they were his horses. He now approached one of these crawling figures from behind and with an agile movement mounted it astride. The man sank upon his breast, recovered, flung the small boy fiercely to the ground as an unbroken colt might have done, then turned upon him a face that lacked a lower jaw—from the upper teeth to the throat was a great red gap fringed with hanging shreds of flesh and splinters of bone. The unnatural prominence of nose, the absence of chin, the fierce eyes, gave this man the appearance of a great bird of prey crimsoned in throat and breast by the blood of its quarry. The man rose to his knees, the child to his feet. The man shook his fist at the child; the child, terrified at last, ran to a tree near by, got upon the farther side of it and took a more serious view of the situation. And so the clumsy multitude dragged itself slowly and painfully along in hideous pantomime—moved forward down the slope like a swarm of great black beetles, with never a sound of going—in silence profound, absolute.

Instead of darkening, the haunted landscape began to brighten. Through the belt of trees beyond the brook shone a strange red light, the trunks and branches of the trees making a black lacework against it. It struck the creeping figures and gave them monstrous shadows, which caricatured their movements on the lit grass. It fell upon their faces, touching their whiteness with a ruddy tinge, accentuating the stains with which so many of them were freaked and maculated. It sparkled on buttons and bits of metal in their clothing. Instinctively the child turned toward the growing splendor and moved down the slope with his horrible companions; in a few moments had passed the foremost of the throng—not much of a feat, considering his advantages. He placed himself in the lead, his wooden sword still in hand, and solemnly directed the march, conforming his pace to theirs and occasionally turning as if to see that his forces did not straggle. Surely such a leader never before had such a following.

Scattered about upon the ground now slowly narrowing by the encroachment of this awful march to water, were certain articles to which, in the leader's mind, were coupled no significant associations: an occasional blanket, tightly rolled lengthwise, doubled and the ends bound together with a string; a heavy knapsack here, and there a broken rifle—such things, in short, as are found in the rear of retreating troops, the "spoor" of men flying from their hunters. Everywhere near the creek, which here had a margin of lowland, the earth was trodden into mud by the feet of men and horses. An observer of better experience in the use of his eyes would have noticed that these footprints pointed in both directions; the ground had been twice passed over—in advance and in retreat. A few hours before, these desperate, stricken men, with their more fortunate and now distant comrades, had penetrated the forest in thousands. Their successive battalions, breaking into swarms and re-forming in lines, had passed the child on every side—had almost trodden on him as he slept. The rustle and murmur of their march had not awakened him. Almost within a stone's throw of where he lay they had fought a battle; but all unheard by him were the roar of the musketry, the shock of the cannon, "the thunder of the captains and the shouting." He had slept through it all, grasping his little wooden sword with perhaps a tighter clutch in unconscious sympathy with his martial environment, but as heedless of the grandeur of the struggle as the dead who had died to make the glory.

The fire beyond the belt of woods on the farther side of the creek, reflected to earth from the canopy of its own smoke, was now suffusing the whole landscape. It transformed the sinuous line of mist to the vapor of gold. The water gleamed with dashes of red, and red, too, were many of the stones protruding above the surface. But that was blood; the less desperately wounded had stained them in crossing. On them, too, the child now crossed with eager steps; he was going to the fire. As he stood upon the farther bank he turned about to look at the companions of his march. The advance was arriving at the creek. The stronger had already drawn themselves to the brink and plunged their faces into the flood. Three or four who lay without motion appeared to have no heads. At this the child's eyes expanded with wonder; even his hospitable understanding could not accept a phenomenon implying such vitality as that. After slaking their thirst these men had not had the strength to back away from the water, nor to keep their heads above it. They were drowned. In rear of these, the open spaces of the forest showed the leader as many formless figures of his grim command as at first; but not nearly so many were in motion. He waved his cap for their encouragement and smilingly pointed with his weapon in the direction of the guiding light—a pillar of fire to this strange exodus.

Confident of the fidelity of his forces, he now entered the belt of woods, passed through it easily in the red illumination, climbed a fence, ran across a field, turning now and again to coquet with his responsive shadow, and so approached the blazing ruin of a dwelling. Desolation everywhere! In all the wide glare not a living thing was visible. He cared nothing for that; the spectacle pleased, and he danced with glee in imitation of the wavering flames. He ran about, collecting fuel, but every object that he found was too heavy for him to cast in from the distance to which the heat limited his approach. In despair he flung in his sword—a surrender to the superior forces of nature. His military career was at an end.

Shifting his position, his eyes fell upon some outbuildings which had an oddly familiar appearance, as if he had dreamed of them. He stood considering them with wonder, when suddenly the entire plantation, with its inclosing forest, seemed to turn as if upon a pivot. His little world swung half around; the points of the compass were reversed. He recognized the blazing building as his own home!

For a moment he stood stupefied by the power of the revelation, then ran with stumbling feet, making a half-circuit of the ruin. There, conspicuous in the light of the conflagration, lay the dead body of a woman—the white face turned upward, the hands thrown out and clutched full of grass, the clothing deranged, the long dark hair in tangles and full of clotted blood. The greater part of the forehead was torn away, and from the jagged hole the brain protruded, overflowing the temple, a frothy mass of gray, crowned with clusters of crimson bubbles—the work of a shell.

The child moved his little hands, making wild, uncertain gestures. He uttered a series of inarticulate and indescribable cries—something between the chattering of an ape and the gobbling of a turkey—a startling, soulless, unholy sound, the language of a devil. The child was a deaf mute.

Then he stood motionless, with quivering lips, looking down upon the wreck.

HENRY JAMES

THE MIDDLE YEARS

I

The April day was soft and bright, and poor Dencombe, happy in the conceit of reasserted strength, stood in the garden of the hotel, comparing, with a deliberation in which however there was still something of languor, the attractions of easy strolls. He liked the feeling of the south so far as you could have it in the north, he liked the sandy cliffs and the clustered pines, he liked even the colourless sea. "Bournemouth as a health-resort" had sounded like a mere advertisement, but he was thankful now for the commonest conveniences. The sociable country postman, passing through the garden, had just given him a small parcel which he took out with him, leaving the hotel to the right and creeping to a bench he had already haunted, a safe recess in the cliff. It looked to the south, to the tinted walls of the Island, and was protected behind by the sloping shoulder of the down. He was tired enough when he reached it, and for a moment was disappointed; he was better of course, but better, after all, than what? He should never again, as at one or two great moments of the past, be better than himself. The infinite of life was gone, and what remained of the dose a small glass scored like a thermometer by the apothecary. He sat and stared at the sea, which appeared all surface and twinkle, far shallower than the spirit of man. It was the abyss of human illusion that was the real, the tideless deep. He held his packet, which had come by book-post, unopened on his knee, liking, in the lapse of so many joys—his illness had made him feel his age—to know it was there, but taking for granted there could be no complete renewal of the pleasure, dear to young experience, of seeing one's self "just out." Dencombe, who had a reputation, had come out too often and knew too well in advance how he should look.

His postponement associated itself vaguely, after a little, with a group of three persons, two ladies and a young man, whom beneath him, straggling and seemingly silent, he could see move slowly together along the sands. The gentleman had his head bent over a book and was occasionally brought to a stop by the charm of this volume, which, as Dencombe could perceive even at a distance, had a cover alluringly red. Then his companions, going a little further, waited for him to come up, poking their parasols into the beach, looking around them at the sea and sky and clearly sensible of the beauty of the day. To these things the young man with the book was still more clearly indifferent; lingering, credulous, absorbed, he was an object of envy to an observer from whose connexion with literature all such artlessness had faded. One of the ladies was large and mature; the other had the spareness of comparative youth and of a social situation possibly inferior. The large lady carried back Dencombe's imagination to the age of crinoline; she wore a hat of the shape of a mushroom, decorated with a blue veil, and had the air, in her aggressive amplitude, of clinging to a vanished fashion or even a lost cause. Presently her companion produced from under the folds of a mantle a limp portable chair which she stiffened out and of which the large lady took possession. This act, and something in the movement of either party, at once characterised the performers—they performed for Dencombe's recreation—as opulent matron and humble dependent. Where moreover was the virtue of an approved novelist if one couldn't establish a relation between such figures? the clever theory for instance that the young man was the son of the opulent matron and that the humble dependent, the daughter of a clergyman or an officer, nourished a secret passion for him. Was that not visible from the way she stole behind her protectress to look back at him?—back to where he had let himself come to a full stop when his mother sat down to rest. His book was a novel, it had the catchpenny binding; so that while the romance of life stood neglected at his side he lost himself in that of the circulating library. He moved mechanically to where the sand was softer and ended by plumping down in it to finish his chapter at his ease. The humble dependent, discouraged by his remoteness, wandered with a martyred droop of the head in another direction, and the exorbitant lady, watching the waves, offered a confused resemblance to a flying-machine that had broken down.

When his drama began to fail Dencombe remembered that he had after all another pastime. Though such promptitude on the part of the publisher was rare he was already able to draw from its wrapper his "latest," perhaps his last. The cover of "The Middle Years" was duly meretricious, the smell of the fresh pages the very odour of sanctity; but for the moment he went no further—he had become conscious of a strange alienation. He had forgotten what his book was about. Had the assault of his old ailment, which he had so fallaciously come to Bournemouth to ward off, interposed utter blankness as to what had preceded it? He had finished the revision of proof before quitting London, but his subsequent fortnight in bed had passed the sponge over colour. He couldn't have chanted to himself a single sentence, couldn't have turned with curiosity or confidence to any particular page. His subject had already gone from him, leaving scarce a superstition behind. He uttered a low moan as he breathed the chill of this dark void, so desperately it seemed to represent the completion of a sinister process. The tears filled his mild eyes; something precious had passed away. This was the pang that had been sharpest during the last few years—the sense of ebbing time, of shrinking opportunity; and now he felt not so much that his last chance was going as that it was gone indeed. He had done all he should ever do, and yet hadn't done what he wanted. This was the laceration—that practically his career was over: it was as violent as a grip at his throat. He rose from his seat nervously—a creature hunted by a dread; then he fell back in his weakness and nervously opened his book. It was a single volume; he preferred single volumes and aimed at a rare compression. He began to read and, little by little, in this occupation, was pacified and reassured. Everything came back to him, but came back with a wonder, came back above all with a high and magnificent beauty. He read his own prose, he turned his own leaves, and had as he sat there with the spring sunshine on the page an emotion peculiar and intense. His career was over, no doubt, but it was over, when all was said, with *that.*

He had forgotten during his illness the work of the previous year; but what he had chiefly forgotten was that it was extraordinarily good. He dived once more into his story and was drawn down, as by a siren's hand, to where, in the dim underworld of fiction, the great glazed tank of art, strange silent subjects float. He recognised his motive and surrendered to his talent. Never probably had that talent, such as it was, been so fine. His difficulties were still there, but what was also there, to his perception, though probably, alas! to nobody's else, was the art that in most cases had surmounted them. In his surprised enjoyment of this ability he had a glimpse of a possible reprieve. Surely its force wasn't spent—there was life and service in it yet. It hadn't come to him easily, it had been backward and roundabout. It was the child of time, the nursling of delay; he had struggled and suffered for it, making sacrifices not to be counted, and now that it was really mature was it to cease to yield, to confess itself brutally beaten? There was an infinite charm for Dencombe in feeling as he had never felt before that diligence *vincit omnia.* The result produced in his little book was somehow a result beyond his conscious intention it was as if he had planted his genius, had trusted his method and they had grown up and flowered with this sweetness. If the achievement had been real, however, the process had been painful enough. What he saw so intensely today, what he felt as a nail driven in, was that only now, at the very last, had he come into possession. His development had been abnormally slow, almost grotesquely gradual. He had been hindered and retarded by experience, he had for long periods only groped his way. It had taken too much of his life to produce too little of his art. The art had come, but it had come after everything else. At such a rate a first existence was too short—long enough only to collect material; so that to fructify, to use the material, one should have a second age, an extension. This extension was what poor Dencombe sighed for. As he turned the last leaves of his volume he murmured "Ah for another go, ah for a better chance!"

The three persons drawing his attention to the sands had vanished and then reappeared; they had now wandered up a path, an artificial and easy ascent, which led to the top of the cliff. Dencombe's bench was halfway down, on a sheltered ledge, and the large lady, a massive heterogeneous person with bold black eyes and kind red cheeks, now took a few moments to rest. She wore dirty gauntlets and immense diamond earrings; at first she looked vulgar, but she contradicted this announcement in an agreeable off-hand tone. While her companions stood waiting for her she spread her skirts on the end of Dencombe's seat. The young man had gold spectacles, through which, with his finger still in his red-covered book, he glanced at the volume, bound in the same shade of the same colour, lying on the lap of the original occupant of the bench. After an instant Dencombe felt him struck with a resemblance; he had recognised the gilt stamp on the crimson cloth, was reading "The Middle Years" and now noted that somebody else had kept pace with him. The stranger was startled, possibly even a little ruffled, to find himself not the only person favoured with an early copy. The eyes of the two proprietors met a moment, and Dencombe borrowed amusement from the expression of those of his competitor, those, it might even be inferred, of his admirer. They confessed to some resentment—they seemed to say: "Hang it, has he got it *already?* Of course he's a brute of a reviewer!" Dencombe shuffled his copy out of sight while the opulent matron, rising from her repose, broke out: "I feel already the good of this air!"

"I can't say I do," said the angular lady. "I find myself quite let down."

"I find myself horribly hungry. At what time did you order luncheon?" her protectress pursued.

The young person put the question by. "Doctor Hugh always orders it."

"I ordered nothing today—I'm going to make you diet," said their comrade.

"Then I shall go home and sleep. *Qui dort dine!*"

"Can I trust you to Miss Vernham?" asked Doctor Hugh of his elder companion.

"Don't I trust *you?*" she archly enquired.

"Not too much!" Miss Vernham, with her eyes on the ground, permitted herself to declare. "You must come with us at least to the house," she went on while the personage on whom they appeared to be in attendance began to mount higher. She had got a little out of ear-shot; nevertheless Miss Vernham became, so far as Dencombe was concerned, less distinctly audible to murmur to the young man: "I don't think you realise all you owe the Countess!"

Absently, a moment, Doctor Hugh caused his gold-rimmed spectacles to shine at her. "Is that the way I strike you? I see—I see!"

"She's awfully good to us," continued Miss Vernham, compelled by the lapse of the other's motion to stand there in spite of his discussion of private matters. Of what use would it have been that Dencombe should be sensitive to shades hadn't he detected in that arrest a strange influence from the quiet old convalescent in the great tweed cape? Miss Vernham appeared suddenly to become aware of some such connexion, for she added in a moment: "If you want to sun yourself here you can come back after you've seen us home."

Doctor Hugh, at this, hesitated, and Dencombe, in spite of a desire to pass for unconscious, risked a covert glance at him. What his eyes met this time, as happened, was, on the part of the young lady, a queer stare, naturally vitreous, which made her remind him of some figure—he couldn't name it—in a play or a novel, some sinister governess or tragic old maid. She seemed to scan him, to challenge him, to say out of general spite: "What have you got to do with us?" At the same instant the rich humour of the Countess reached them from above: "Come, come, my little lambs; you should follow your old *bergère!*" Miss Vernham turned away for it, pursuing the ascent, and Doctor Hugh, after another mute appeal to Dencombe and a minute's evident demur, deposited his book on the bench as if to keep his place, or even as a gage of earnest return, and bounded without difficulty up the rougher part of the cliff.

Equally innocent and infinite are the pleasures of observation and the resources engendered by the trick of analysing life. It amused poor Dencombe, as he dawdled in his tepid air-bath, to believe himself awaiting a revelation of something at the back of a fine young mind. He looked hard at the book on the end of the bench, but wouldn't have touched it for the world. It served his purpose to have a theory that shouldn't be exposed to refutation. He already felt better of his melancholy; he had, according to his old formula, put his head at the window. A passing Countess could draw off the fancy when, like the elder of the ladies who had just retreated, she was as obvious as the giantess of a caravan. It was indeed general views that were terrible; short ones, contrary to an opinion sometimes expressed, were the refuge, were the remedy. Doctor Hugh couldn't possibly be anything but a reviewer who had understandings for early copies with publishers or with newspapers. He reappeared in a quarter of an hour with visible relief at finding Dencombe on the spot and the gleam of white teeth in an embarrassed but generous smile. He was perceptibly disappointed at the eclipse of the other copy of the book; it made a pretext the less for speaking to the quiet gentleman. But he spoke notwithstanding; he held up his own copy and broke out pleadingly: "*Do* say, if you have occasion to speak of it, that it's the best thing he has done yet!"

Dencombe responded with a laugh: "Done yet" was so amusing to him, made such a grand avenue of the future. Better still, the young man took *him* for a reviewer. He pulled out "The Middle Years" from under his cape, but instinctively concealed any telltale look of fatherhood. This was partly because a person was always a fool for insisting to others on his work. "Is that what you're going to say yourself?" he put to his visitor.

"I'm not quite sure I shall write anything. I don't, as a regular thing—I enjoy in peace. But it's awfully fine."

Dencombe just debated. If the young man had begun to abuse him he would have confessed on the spot to his identity, but there was no harm in drawing out any impulse to praise. He drew it out with such success that in a few moments his new acquaintance, seated by his side, was confessing candidly that the works of the author of the volumes before them were the only ones he could read a second time. He had come the day before from London, where a friend of his, a journalist had lent him his copy of the last, the copy sent to the office of the journal and already the subject of a "notice" which, as was pretended there—but one had to allow for "swagger"—had taken a full quarter of an hour to prepare. He intimated that he was ashamed for his friend, and in the case of a work demanding and repaying study, of such inferior manners; and with his fresh appreciation and his so irregular wish to express it, he speedily became for poor Dencombe a remarkable, a delightful apparition. Chance had brought the weary man of letters face to face with the greatest admirer in the new generation of whom it was supposable he might boast. The admirer in truth was mystifying, so rare a case was it to find a bristling young doctor—he looked like a German physiologist—enamoured of literary form. It was an accident, but happier than most accidents, so that Dencombe, exhilarated as well as confounded, spent half an hour in making his visitor talk while he kept himself quiet. He explained his premature possession of "The Middle Years" by an allusion to the friendship of the publisher, who, knowing he was at Bournemouth for his health, had paid him this graceful attention. He allowed he had been ill, for Doctor Hugh would infallibly have guessed it; he even went so far as to wonder if he mightn't look for some hygienic "tip" from a personage combining so bright an enthusiasm with a presumable knowledge of the remedies now in vogue. It would shake his faith a little perhaps to have to take a doctor seriously who could take *him* so seriously, but he enjoyed this gushing modern youth and felt with an acute pang that there would still be work to do in a world in which such odd combinations were presented. It wasn't true, what he had tried for renunciation's sake to believe, that all the combinations were exhausted. They weren't by any means—they were infinite: the exhaustion was in the miserable artist.

Doctor Hugh, an ardent physiologist, was saturated with the spirit of the age—in other words he had just taken his degree; but he was independent and various, he talked like a man who would have preferred to love literature best. He would fain have made fine phrases, but nature had denied him the trick. Some of the finest in "The Middle Years" had struck him inordinately, and he took the liberty of reading them to Dencombe in support of his plea. He grew vivid, in the balmy air, to his companion, for whose deep refreshment he seemed to have been sent; and was particularly ingenuous in describing how recently he had become acquainted, and how instantly infatuated, with the only man who had put flesh between the ribs of an art that was starving on superstitions. He hadn't yet written to him—he was deterred by a strain of respect. Dencombe at this moment rejoiced more inwardly than ever that he had never answered the photographers. His visitor's attitude promised him a luxury of intercourse, though he was sure a due freedom for Doctor Hugh would depend not a little on the Countess. He learned without delay what type of Countess was involved, mastering as well the nature of the tie that united the curious trio. The large lady, an Englishwoman by birth and the daughter of a celebrated baritone, whose taste *minus* his talent she had inherited, was the widow of a French nobleman and mistress of all that remained of the handsome fortune, the fruit of her father's earnings, that had constituted her dower. Miss Vernham, an odd creature but an accomplished pianist, was attached to her person at a salary. The Countess was generous, independent, eccentric; she travelled with her minstrel and her medical man. Ignorant and passionate she had nevertheless moments in which she was almost irresistible.

Dencombe saw her sit for her portrait in Doctor Hugh's free sketch, and felt the picture of his young friend's relation to her frame itself in his mind. This young friend, for a representative of the new psychology, was himself easily hypnotised, and if he became abnormally communicative it was only a sign of his real subjection. Dencombe did accordingly what he wanted with him, even without being known as Dencombe.

Taken ill on a journey in Switzerland the Countess had picked him up at an hotel, and the accident of his happening to please her had made her offer him, with her imperious liberality, terms that couldn't fail to dazzle a practitioner without patients and whose resources had been drained dry by his studies. It wasn't the way he would have proposed to spend his time, but it was time that would pass quickly, and meanwhile she was wonderfully kind. She exacted perpetual attention, but it was impossible not to like her. He gave details about his queer patient, a "type" if there ever was one, who had in connexion with her flushed obesity, and in addition to the morbid strain of a violent and aimless will, a grave organic disorder, but he came back to his loved novelist, whom he was so good as to pronounce more essentially a poet than many of those who went in for verse, with a zeal excited, as all his indiscretion had been excited, by the happy chance of Dencombe's sympathy and the coincidence of their occupation. Dencombe had confessed to a slight personal acquaintance with the author of "The Middle Years," but had not felt himself as ready as he could have wished when his companion, who had never yet encountered a being so privileged, began to be eager for particulars. He even divined in Doctor Hugh's eye at that moment a glimmer of suspicion. But the young man was too inflamed to be shrewd and repeatedly caught up the book to exclaim: "Did you notice this?" or "Weren't you immensely struck with that?" "There's a beautiful passage toward the end," he broke out; and again he laid his hand on the volume. As he turned the pages he came upon something else, while Dencombe saw him suddenly change colour. He had taken up as it lay on the bench Dencombe's copy instead of his own, and his neighbour at once guessed the reason of his start. Doctor Hugh looked grave an instant; then he said: "I see you've been altering the text!" Dencombe was a passionate corrector, a fingerer of style; the last thing he ever arrived at was a form final for himself. His ideal would have been to publish secretly, and then, on the published text, treat himself to the terrified revise, sacrificing always a first edition and beginning for posterity and even for the collectors, poor dears, with a second. This morning, in "The Middle Years," his pencil had pricked a dozen lights. He was amused at the effect of the young man's reproach; for an instant it made him change colour. He stammered at any rate ambiguously, then through a blur of ebbing consciousness saw Doctor Hugh's mystified eyes. He only had time to feel he was about to be ill again—that emotion, excitement, fatigue, the heat of the sun, the solicitation of the air, had combined to play him a trick, before, stretching out a hand to his visitor with a plaintive cry, he lost his senses altogether.

Later he knew he had fainted and that Doctor Hugh had got him home in a Bath-chair, the conductor of which, prowling within hail for custom, had happened to remember seeing him in the garden of the hotel. He had recovered his perception on the way, and had, in bed that afternoon, a vague recollection of Doctor Hugh's young face, as they went together, bent over him in a comforting laugh and expressive of something more than a suspicion of his identity. That identity was ineffaceable now, and all the more that he was rueful and sore. He had been rash, been stupid, had gone out too soon, stayed out too long. He oughtn't to have exposed himself to strangers, he ought to have taken his servant. He felt as if he had fallen into a hole too deep to descry any little patch of heaven. He was confused about the time that had passed—he pieced the fragments together. He had seen his doctor, the real one, the one who had treated him from the first and who had again been very kind. His servant was in and out on tiptoe, looking very wise after the fact. He said more than once something about the sharp young gentleman. The rest was vagueness in so far as it wasn't despair. The vagueness, however, justified itself by dreams, dozing anxieties from which he finally emerged to the consciousness of a dark room and a shaded candle.

"You'll be all right again—I know all about you now," said a voice near him that he felt to be young. Then his meeting with Doctor Hugh came back. He was too discouraged to joke about it yet, but made out after a little that the interest was intense for his visitor. "Of course I can't attend you professionally—you've got your own man, with whom I've talked and who's excellent," Doctor Hugh went on. "But you must let me come to see you as a good friend. I've just looked in before going to bed. You're doing beautifully, but it's a good job I was with you on the cliff. I shall come in early tomorrow. I want to do something for you. I want to do everything. You've done a tremendous lot for me." The young man held his hand, hanging over him, and poor Dencombe, weakly aware of this living pressure, simply lay there and accepted his devotion. He couldn't do anything less—he needed help too much.

The idea of the help he needed was very present to him that night, which he spent in a lucid stillness, an intensity of thought that constituted a reaction from his hours of stupor. He was lost, he was lost—he was lost if he couldn't be saved. He wasn't afraid of suffering, of death, wasn't even in love with life; but he had had a deep demonstration of desire. It came over him in the long quiet hours that only with "The Middle Years" had he taken his flight; only on that day, visited by soundless processions, had he recognised his kingdom. He had had a revelation of his range. What he dreaded was the idea that his reputation should stand on the unfinished. It wasn't with his past but with his future that it should properly be concerned. Illness and age rose before him like spectres with pitiless eyes: how was he to bribe such fates to give him the second chance? He had had the one chance that all men have—he had had the chance of life. He went to sleep again very late, and when he awoke Doctor Hugh was sitting at hand. There was already by this time something beautifully familiar in him.

"Don't think I've turned out your physician," he said; "I'm acting with his consent. He has been here and seen you. Somehow he seems to trust me. I told him how we happened to come together yesterday, and he recognises that I've a peculiar right."

Dencombe felt his own face pressing. "How have you squared the Countess?"

The young man blushed a little, but turned it off. "Oh never mind the Countess!"

"You told me she was very exacting."

Doctor Hugh had a wait. "So she is."

"And Miss Vernham's an *intrigante.*"

"How do you know that?"

"I know everything. One *has* to, to write decently!"

"I think she's mad," said limpid Doctor Hugh.

"Well, don't quarrel with the Countess—she's a present help to you."

"I don't quarrel," Doctor Hugh returned. "But I don't get on with silly women." Presently he added: "You seem very much alone."

"That often happens at my age. I've outlived, I've lost by the way."

Doctor Hugh faltered; then surmounting a soft scruple: "Whom have you lost?"

"Every one."

"Ah no," the young man breathed, laying a hand on his arm.

"I once had a wife—I once had a son. My wife died when my child was born, and my boy, at school, was carried off by typhoid."

"I wish I'd been there!" cried Doctor Hugh.

"Well—if you're here!" Dencombe answered with a smile that, in spite of dimness, showed how he valued being sure of his companion's whereabouts.

"You talk strangely of your age. You're not old."

"Hypocrite—so early!"

"I speak physiologically."

"That's the way I've been speaking for the last five years, and it's exactly what I've been saying to myself. It isn't till we *are* old that we begin to tell ourselves we're not."

"Yet I know I myself am young," Doctor Hugh returned.

"Not so well as I!" laughed his patient, whose visitor indeed would have established the truth in question by the honesty with which he changed the point of view, remarking that it must be one of the charms of age—at any rate in the case of high distinction—to feel that one has laboured and achieved. Doctor Hugh employed the common phrase about earning one's rest, and it made poor Dencombe for an instant almost angry. He recovered himself, however, to explain, lucidly enough, that if, ungraciously, he knew nothing of such a balm, it was doubtless because he had wasted inestimable years. He had followed literature from the first, but he had taken a lifetime to get abreast of her. Only today at last had he begun to *see,* so that all he had hitherto shown was a movement without a direction. He had ripened too late and was so clumsily constituted that he had had to teach himself by mistakes.

"I prefer your flowers then to other people's fruit, and your mistakes to other people's successes," said gallant Doctor Hugh. "It's for your mistakes I admire you."

"You're happy—you don't know," Dencombe answered.

Looking at his watch the young man had got up; he named the hour of the afternoon at which he would return. Dencombe warned him against committing himself too deeply, and expressed again all his dread of making him neglect the Countess—perhaps incur her displeasure.

"I want to be like you—I want to learn by mistakes!" Doctor Hugh laughed.

"Take care you don't make too grave a one! But do come back," Dencombe added with the glimmer of a new idea.

"You should have had more vanity!" His friend spoke as if he knew the exact amount required to make a man of letters normal.

"No, no—I only should have had more time. I want another go."

"Another go?"

"I want an extension."

"An extension?" Again Doctor Hugh repeated Dencombe's words, with which he seemed to have been struck.

"Don't you know?—I want to what they call 'live.' "

The young man, for good-bye, had taken his hand, which closed with a certain force. They looked at each other hard. "You *will live,*" said Doctor Hugh.

"Don't be superficial. It's too serious!"

"You *shall* live!" Dencombe's visitor declared, turning pale.

"Ah that's better!" And as he retired the invalid, with a troubled laugh, sank gratefully back.

All that day and all the following night he wondered if it mightn't be arranged. His doctor came again, his servant was attentive, but it was to his confident young friend that he felt himself mentally appeal. His collapse on the cliff was plausibly explained and his liberation, on a better basis, promised for the morrow; meanwhile, however, the intensity of his meditations kept him tranquil and made him indifferent. The idea that occupied him was none the less absorbing because it was a morbid fancy. Here was a clever son of the age, ingenious and ardent, who happened to have set him up for connoisseurs to worship. This servant of his altar had all the new learning in science and all the old reverence in faith; wouldn't he therefore put his knowledge at the disposal of his sympathy, his craft at the disposal of his love? Couldn't he be trusted to invent a remedy for a poor artist to whose art he had paid a tribute? If he couldn't the alternative was hard: Dencombe would have to surrender to silence unvindicated and undivined. The rest of the day and all the next he toyed in secret with this sweet futility. Who would work the miracle for him but the young man who could combine such lucidity with such passion? He thought of the fairy-tales of science and charmed himself into forgetting that he looked for a magic that was not of this world. Doctor Hugh was an apparition, and that placed him above the law. He came and went while his patient, who now sat up, followed him with supplicating eyes. The interest of knowing the great author had made the young man begin "The Middle Years" afresh and would help him to find a richer sense between its covers. Dencombe had told him what he "tried for"; with all his intelligence, on a first perusal, Doctor Hugh had failed to guess it. The baffled celebrity wondered then who in the world *would* guess it: he was amused once more at the diffused massive weight that could be thrown into the missing of an intention. Yet he wouldn't rail at the general mind today—consoling as that ever had been: the revelation of his own slowness had seemed to make all stupidity sacred.

Doctor Hugh, after a little, was visibly worried, confessing, on enquiry, to a source of embarrassment at home. "Stick to the Countess—don't mind me," Dencombe said repeatedly; for his companion was frank enough about the large lady's attitude. She was so jealous that she had fallen ill—she resented such a breach of allegiance. She paid so much for his fidelity that she must have it all: she refused him the right to other sympathies, charged him with scheming to make her die alone, for it was needless to point out how little Miss Vernham was a resource in trouble. When Doctor Hugh mentioned that the Countess would already have left Bournemouth if he hadn't kept her in bed, poor Dencombe held his arm tighter and said with decision: "Take her straight away." They had gone out together, walking back to the sheltered nook in which, the other day, they had met. The young man, who had given his companion a personal support, declared with emphasis that his conscience was clear—he could ride two horses at once. Didn't he dream for his future of a time when he should have to ride five hundred? Longing equally for virtue, Dencombe replied that in that golden age no patient would pretend to have contracted with him for his whole attention. On the part of the Countess wasn't such an avidity lawful? Doctor Hugh denied it, said there was no contract, but only a free understanding, and that a sordid servitude was impossible to a generous spirit; he liked moreover to talk about art, and that was the subject on which, this time, as they sat together on the sunny bench, he tried most to engage the author of "The Middle Years." Dencombe, soaring again a little on the weak wings of convalescence and still haunted by that happy notion of an organised rescue, found another strain of eloquence to plead the cause of a certain splendid "last manner," the very citadel, as it would prove, of his reputation, the stronghold into which his real treasure would be gathered. While his listener gave up the morning and the great still sea ostensibly waited he had a wondrous explanatory hour. Even for himself he was inspired as he told what his treasure would consist of; the precious metals he would dig from the mine, the jewels rare, strings of pearls, he would hang between the columns of his temple. He was wondrous for himself, so thick his convictions crowded, but still more wondrous for Doctor Hugh, who assured him none the less that the very pages he had just published were already encrusted with gems. This admirer, however, panted for the combinations to come and, before the face of the beautiful day, renewed to Dencombe his guarantee that his profession would hold itself responsible for such a life. Then he suddenly clapped his hand upon his watch-pocket and asked leave to absent himself for half an hour. Dencombe waited there for his return, but was at last recalled to the actual by the fall of a shadow across the ground. The shadow darkened into that of Miss Vernham, the young lady in attendance on the Countess; whom Dencombe, recognising her, perceived so clearly to have come to speak to him that he rose from his bench to acknowledge the civility. Miss Vernham indeed proved not particularly civil, she looked strangely agitated, and her type was now unmistakeable.

"Excuse me if I do ask," she said, "whether it's too much to hope that you may be induced to leave Doctor Hugh alone." Then before our poor friend, greatly disconcerted, could protest: "You ought to be informed that you stand in his light—that you may do him a terrible injury."

"Do you mean by causing the Countess to dispense with his services?"

"By causing her to disinherit him." Dencombe stared at this, and Miss Vernham pursued, in the gratification of seeing she could produce an impression: "It has depended on himself to come into something very handsome. He has had a grand prospect, but I think you've succeeded in spoiling it."

"Not intentionally, I assure you. Is there no hope the accident may be repaired?" Dencombe asked.

"She was ready to do anything for him. She takes great fancies, she lets herself go—it's her way. She has no relations, she's free to dispose of her money, and she's very ill," said Miss Vernham for a climax.

"I'm very sorry to hear it," Dencombe stammered.

"Wouldn't it be possible for you to leave Bournemouth? That's what I've come to see about."

He sank to his bench. "I'm very ill myself, but I'll try!"

Miss Vernham still stood there with her colourless eyes and the brutality of her good conscience. "Before it's too late, please!" she said; and with this she turned her back, in order, quickly, as if it had been a business to which she could spare but a precious moment, to pass out of his sight.

Oh yes, after this Dencombe was certainly very ill. Miss Vernham had upset him with her rough fierce news; it was the sharpest shock to him to discover what was at stake for a penniless young man of fine parts. He sat trembling on his bench, staring at the waste of waters, feeling sick with the directness of the blow. He was indeed too weak, too unsteady, too alarmed; but he would make the effort to get away, for he couldn't accept the guilt of interference and his honour was really involved. He would hobble home, at any rate, and then think what was to be done. He made his way back to the hotel and, as he went, had a characteristic vision of Miss Vernham's great motive. The Countess hated women of course—Dencombe was lucid about that; so the hungry pianist had no personal hopes and could only console herself with the bold conception of helping Doctor Hugh in order to marry him after he should get his money or else induce him to recognise her claim for compensation and buy her off. If she had befriended him at a fruitful crisis he would really, as a man of delicacy—and she knew what to think of that point—have to reckon with her.

At the hotel Dencombe's servant insisted on his going back to bed. The invalid had talked about catching a train and had begun with orders to pack; after which his racked nerves had yielded to a sense of sickness. He consented to see his physician, who immediately was sent for, but he wished it to be understood that his door was irrevocably closed to Doctor Hugh. He had his plan, which was so fine that he rejoiced in it after getting back to bed. Doctor Hugh, suddenly finding himself snubbed without mercy, would, in natural disgust and to the joy of Miss Vernham, renew his allegiance to the Countess. When his physician arrived Dencombe learned that he was feverish and that this was very wrong: he was to cultivate calmness and try, if possible, not to think. For the rest of the day he wooed stupidity; but there was an ache that kept him sentient, the probable sacrifice of his "extension," the limit of his course. His medical adviser was anything but pleased; his successive relapses were ominous. He charged this personage to put out a strong hand and take Doctor Hugh off his mind—it would contribute so much to his being quiet. The agitating name, in his room, was not mentioned again, but his security was a smothered fear, and it was not confirmed by the receipt, at ten o'clock that evening, of a telegram which his servant opened and read him and to which, with an address in London, the signature of Miss Vernham was attached. "Beseech you to use all influence to make our friend join us here in the morning. Countess much the worse for dreadful journey, but everything may still be saved." The two ladies had gathered themselves up and had been capable in the afternoon of a spiteful revolution. They had started for the capital, and if the elder one, as Miss Vernham had announced, was very ill, she had wished to make it clear that she was proportionately reckless. Poor Dencombe, who was not reckless and who only desired that everything should indeed be "saved," sent this missive straight off to the young man's lodging and had on the morrow the pleasure of knowing that he had quitted Bournemouth by an early train.

Two days later he pressed in with a copy of a literary journal in his hand. He had returned because he was anxious and for the pleasure of flourishing the great review of "The Middle Years." Here at least was something adequate—it rose to the occasion; it was an acclamation, a reparation, a critical attempt to place the author in the niche he had fairly won. Dencombe accepted and submitted; he made neither objection nor enquiry, for old complications had returned and he had had two dismal days. He was convinced not only that he should never again leave his bed, so that his young friend might pardonably remain, but that the demand he should make on the patience of beholders would be of the most moderate. Doctor Hugh had been to town, and he tried to find in his eyes some confession that the Countess was pacified and his legacy clinched; but all he could see there was the light of his juvenile joy in two or three of the phrases of the newspaper. Dencombe couldn't read them, but when his visitor had insisted on repeating them more than once he was able to shake an unintoxicated head. "Ah no—but they would have been true of what I *could* have done!"

"What people 'could have done' is mainly what they've in fact done," Doctor Hugh contended.

"Mainly, yes; but I've been an idiot!" Dencombe said.

Doctor Hugh did remain; the end was coming fast. Two days later his patient observed to him, by way of the feeblest of jokes, that there would now be no question whatever of a second chance. At this the young man stared; then he exclaimed: "Why it has come to pass—it has come to pass! The second chance has been the public's—the chance to find the point of view, to pick up the pearl!"

"Oh the pearl!" poor Dencombe uneasily sighed. A smile as cold as a winter sunset flickered on his drawn lips as he added: "The pearl is the unwritten—the pearl is the unalloyed, the *rest,* the lost!"

From that hour he was less and less present, heedless to all appearance of what went on round him. His disease was definitely mortal, of an action as relentless, after the short arrest that had enabled him to fall in with Doctor Hugh, as a leak in a great ship. Sinking steadily, though this visitor, a man of rare resources, now cordially approved by his physician, showed endless art in guarding him from pain, poor Dencombe kept no reckoning of favour or neglect, betrayed no symptom of regret or speculation. Yet toward the last he gave a sign of having noticed how for two days Doctor Hugh hadn't been in his room, a sign that consisted of his suddenly opening his eyes to put a question. Had he spent those days with the Countess?

"The Countess is dead," said Doctor Hugh. "I knew that in a particular contingency she wouldn't resist. I went to her grave."

Dencombe's eyes opened wider. "She left you 'something handsome'?"

The young man gave a laugh almost too light for a chamber of woe. "Never a penny. She roundly cursed me."

"Cursed you?" Dencombe wailed.

"For giving her up. I gave her up for *you.* I had to choose," his companion explained.

"You chose to let a fortune go?"

"I chose to accept, whatever they might be, the consequences of my infatuation," smiled Doctor Hugh. Then as a larger pleasantry: "The fortune be hanged! It's your own fault if I can't get your things out of my head."

The immediate tribute to his humour was a long bewildered moan; after which, for many hours, many days, Dencombe lay motionless and absent. A response so absolute, such a glimpse of a definite result and such a sense of credit, worked together in his mind and, producing a strange commotion, slowly altered and transfigured his despair. The sense of cold submersion left him—he seemed to float without an effort. The incident was extraordinary as evidence, and it shed an intenser light. At the last he signed to Doctor Hugh to listen and, when he was down on his knees by the pillow, brought him very near. "You've made me think it all a delusion."

"Not your glory, my dear friend," stammered the young man.

"Not my glory—what there is of it! It *is* glory—to have been tested, to have had our little quality and cast our little spell. The thing is to have made somebody care. You happen to be crazy of course, but that doesn't affect the law."

"You're a great success!" said Doctor Hugh, putting into his young voice the ring of a marriage-bell.

Dencombe lay taking this in; then he gathered strength to speak once more. "A second chance—*that's* the delusion. There never was to be but one. We work in the dark—we do what we can—we give what we have. Our doubt is our passion and our passion is our task. The rest is the madness of art."

"If you've doubted, if you've despaired, you've always 'done' it," his visitor subtly argued.

"We've done something or other," Dencombe conceded.

"Something or other is everything. It's the feasible. It's *you!*"

"Comforter!" poor Dencombe ironically sighed.

"But it's true," insisted his friend.

"It's true. It's frustration that doesn't count."

"Frustration's only life," said Doctor Hugh.

"Yes, it's what passes." Poor Dencombe was barely audible, but he had marked with the words the virtual end of his first and only chance.

GEORGE W. CABLE

Belles Demoiselles Plantation

The original grantee was Count—, assume the name to be De Charleu; the old Creoles never forgive a public mention. He was the French king's commissary. One day, called to France to explain the lucky accident of the commissariat having burned down with his account-books inside, he left his wife, a Choctaw Comptesse, behind.

Arrived at court, his excuses were accepted, and that tract granted him where afterwards stood Belles Demoiselles Plantation. A man cannot remember everything! In a fit of forgetfulness he married a French gentlewoman, rich and beautiful, and "brought her out." However, "All's well that ends well"; a famine had been in the colony, and the Choctaw Comptesse had starved, leaving nought but a half-caste orphan family lurking on the edge of the settlement, bearing our French gentlewoman's own new name, and being mentioned in Monsieur's will.

And the new Comptesse—she tarried but a twelvemonth, left Monsieur a lovely son, and departed, led out of this vain world by the swamp-fever.

From this son sprang the proud Creole family of De Charleu. It rose straight up, up, up, generation after generation, tall, branchless, slender, palm-like; and finally, in the time of which I am to tell, flowered with all the rare beauty of a century-plant, in Artemise, Innocente, Felicité, the twins Marie and Martha, Leontine and little Septima; the seven beautiful daughters for whom their home had been fitly named Belles Demoiselles.

The Count's grant had once been a long point, round which the Mississippi used to whirl, and seethe, and foam, that it was horrid to behold. Big whirlpools would open and wheel about in the savage eddies under the low bank, and close up again, and others open, and spin, and disappear. Great circles of muddy surface would boil up from hundreds of feet below, and gloss over, and seem to float away,—sink, come back again under water, and with only a soft hiss surge up again, and again drift off, and vanish. Every few minutes the loamy bank would tip down a great load of earth upon its besieger, and fall back a foot,—sometimes a yard,—and the writhing river would press after, until at last the Pointe was quite swallowed up, and the great river glided by in a majestic curve, and asked no more; the bank stood fast, the "caving" became a forgotten misfortune, and the diminished grant was a long, sweeping, willowy bend, rustling with miles of sugar-cane.

Coming up the Mississippi in the sailing craft of those early days, about the time one first could descry the white spires of the old St. Louis Cathedral, you would be pretty sure to spy, just over to your right under the levee, Belles Demoiselles Mansion, with its broad veranda and red painted cypress roof, peering over the embankment, like a bird in the nest, half hid by the avenue of willows which one of the departed De Charleus,—he that married a Marot,—had planted on the levee's crown.

The house stood unusually near the river, facing eastward, and standing four-square, with an immense veranda about its sides, and a flight of steps in front spreading broadly downward, as we open arms to a child. From the veranda nine miles of river were seen; and in their compass, near at hand, the shady garden full of rare and beautiful flowers; farther away broad fields of cane and rice, and the distant quarters of the slaves, and on the horizon everywhere a dark belt of cypress forest.

The master was old Colonel De Charleu,—Jean Albert Henri Joseph De Charleu-Marot, and "Colonel" by the grace of the first American governor. Monsieur,—he would not speak to any one who called him "Colonel,"—was a hoary-headed patriarch. His step was firm, his form erect, his intellect strong and clear, his countenance classic, serene, dignified, commanding, his manners courtly, his voice musical,—fascinating. He had had his vices,—all his life; but had borne them, as his race do, with a serenity of conscience and a cleanness of mouth that left no outward blemish on the surface of the gentleman. He had gambled in Royal street, drank hard in Orleans street, run his adversary through in the duelling-ground at Slaughter-house Point, and danced and quarreled at the St. Philippe-street-theatre quadroon balls. Even now, with all his courtesy and bounty, and a hospitality which seemed to be entertaining angels, he was bitter-proud and penurious, and deep down in his hard-finished heart loved nothing but himself, his name, and his motherless children. But these!—their ravishing beauty was all but excuse enough for the unbounded idolatry of their father. Against these seven goddesses he never rebelled. Had they even required him to defraud old De Carlos—

I can hardly say.

Old De Carlos was his extremely distant relative on the Choctaw side.

With this single exception, the narrow thread-like line of descent from the Indian wife, diminished to a mere strand by injudicious alliances, and deaths in the gutters of old New Orleans, was extinct. The name, by Spanish contact, had become De Carlos; but this one surviving bearer of it was known to all, and known only, as Ingin Charlie.

One thing I never knew a Creole to do. He will not utterly go back on the ties of blood, no matter what sort of knots those ties may be. For one reason, he is never ashamed of his or his father's sins; and for another,—he will tell you—he is "all heart"!

So the different heirs of the De Charleu estate had always strictly regarded the rights and interests of the De Carloses, especially their ownership of a block of dilapidated buildings in a part of the city, which had once been very poor property, but was beginning to be valuable. This block had much more than maintained the last De Carlos through a long and lazy lifetime, and, as his household consisted only of himself, and an aged and crippled negress, the inference was irresistible that he "had money." Old Charlie, though by *alias* an "Injin," was plainly a dark white man, about as old as Colonel De Charleu, sunk in the bliss of deep ignorance, shrewd, deaf, and, by repute at least, unmerciful.

The Colonel and he always conversed in English. This rare accomplishment, which the former had learned from his Scotch wife,—the latter from up-river traders,—they found an admirable medium of communication, answering, better than French could, a similar purpose to that of the stick which we fasten to the bit of one horse and breast-gear of another, whereby each keeps his distance. Once in a while, too, by way of jest, English found its way among the ladies of Belles Demoiselles, always signifying that their sire was about to have business with old Charlie.

Now a long standing wish to buy out Charlie troubled the Colonel. He had no desire to oust him unfairly; he was proud of being always fair; yet he did long to engross the whole estate under one title. Out of his luxurious idleness he had conceived this desire, and thought little of so slight an obstacle as being already somewhat in debt to old Charlie for money borrowed, and for which Belles Demoiselles was, of course, good, ten times over. Lots, buildings, rents, all, might as well be his, he thought, to give, keep, or destroy. "Had he but the old man's heritage. Ah! he might bring that into existence which his *belles demoiselles* had been begging for, 'since many years;' a home,—and such a home,—in the gay city. Here he should tear down this row of cottages, and make his garden wall; there that long rope-walk should give place to vine-covered arbors; the bakery yonder should make way for a costly conservatory; that wine warehouse should come down, and the mansion go up.

It should be the finest in the State. Men should never pass it, but they should say—'the palace of the De Charleus; a family of grand descent, a people of elegance and bounty, a line as old as France, a fine old man, and seven daughters as beautiful as happy; whoever dare attempt to marry there must leave his own name behind him!'

"The house should be of stones fitly set, brought down in ships from the land of 'les Yankees,' and it should have an airy belvedere, with a gilded image tip-toeing and shining on its peak, and from it you should see, far across the gleaming folds of the river, the red roof of Belles Demoiselles, the country-seat. At the big stone gate there should be a porter's lodge, and it should be a privilege even to see the ground."

Truly they were a family fine enough, and fancy-free enough to have fine wishes, yet happy enough where they were, to have had no wish but to live there always.

To those, who, by whatever fortune, wandered into the garden of Belles Demoiselles some summer afternoon as the sky was reddening towards evening, it was lovely to see the family gathered out upon the tiled pavement at the foot of the broad front steps, gaily chatting and jesting, with that ripple of laughter that comes so pleasingly from a bevy of girls. The father would be found seated in their midst, the center of attention and compliment, witness, arbiter, umpire, critic, by his beautiful children's unanimous appointment, but the single vassal, too, of seven absolute sovereigns.

Now they would draw their chairs near together in eager discussion of some new step in the dance, or the adjustment of some rich adornment. Now they would start about him with excited comments to see the eldest fix a bunch of violets in his button-hole. Now the twins would move down a walk after some unusual flower, and be greeted on their return with the high pitched notes of delighted feminine surprise.

As evening came on they would draw more quietly about their paternal center. Often their chairs were forsaken, and they grouped themselves on the lower steps, one above another, and surrendered themselves to the tender influences of the approaching night. At such an hour the passer on the river, already attracted by the dark figures of the broad-roofed mansion, and its woody garden standing against the glowing sunset, would hear the voices of the hidden group rise from the spot in the soft harmonies of an evening song; swelling clearer and clearer as the thrill of music warmed them into feeling, and presently joined by the deeper tones of the father's voice; then, as the daylight passed quite away, all would be still, and he would know that the beautiful home had gathered its nestlings under its wings.

And yet, for mere vagary, it pleased them not to be pleased.

"Arti!" called one sister to another in the broad hall, one morning,—mock amazement in her distended eyes,—"something is goin' to took place!"

"Comm-e-n-t?"—longdrawn perplexity.

"Papa is goin' to town!"

The news passed up stairs.

"Inno!"—one to another meeting in a doorway,—"something is goin' to took place!"

"Qu'est-ce-que c'est!"—vain attempt at gruffness.

"Papa is goin' to town!"

The unusual tidings were true. It was afternoon of the same day that the Colonel tossed his horse's bridle to his groom, and stepped up to old Charlie, who was sitting on his bench under a China-tree, his head, as was his fashion, bound in a Madras handkerchief. The "old man" was plainly under the effect of spirits, and smiled a deferential salutation without trusting himself to his feet.

"Eh, well Charlie!"—the Colonel raised his voice to suit his kinsman's deafness,—"how is those times with my friend Charlie?"

"Eh?" said Charlie, distractedly.

"Is that goin' well with my friend Charlie?"

"In de house,—call her,"—making a pretense of rising.

"Non, non! I don't want,"—the speaker paused to breathe—"ow is collection?"

"O!" said Charlie, "every day he make me more poorer!"

"What do you hask for it?" asked the planter indifferently, designating the house by a wave of his whip.

"Ask for w'at?" said Injin Charlie.

"De *house!* What you ask for it?"

"I don't believe," said Charlie.

"What you would *take* for it!" cried the planter.

"Wait for w'at?"

"What you would *take* for the whole block?"

"I don't want to sell him!"

"I'll give you *ten thousand dollah* for it."

"Ten t'ousand dollah for dis house? O, no, dat is no price. He is blame good old house,—dat old house." (Old Charlie and the Colonel never swore in presence of each other.) "Forty years dat old house didn't had to be paint! I easy can get fifty t'ousand dollah for dat old house."

"Fifty thousand picayunes; yes," said the colonel.

"She's a good house. Can make plenty money," pursued the deaf man.

"That's what make you so rich, eh, Charlie?"

"Non, I don't make nothing. Too blame clever, me, dat's de troub'. She's a good house,—make money fast like a steamboat,—make a barrel full in a week! Me, I lose money all de days. Too blame clever."

"Charlie!"

"Eh?"

"Tell me what you'll take?"

"Make? I don't make *nothing.* Too blame clever."

"What will you *take?"*

"Oh! I got enough already,—half drunk now."

"What will you take for the 'ouse?"

"You want to buy her?"

"I don't know,"—(shrug),—"may*be,*—if you sell it cheap."

"She's a bully old house."

There was a long silence. By and by old Charlie commenced—

"Old Injin Charlie is a low-down dog."

"Cest vrai, oui!" retorted the Colonel in an undertone.

"He's got Injin blood in him."

The Colonel nodded assent.

"But he's got some blame good blood, too, ain't it?"

The Colonel nodded impatiently.

"Bien! Old Charlie's Injin blood says, 'sell de house, Charlie, you blame old fool!' *Mais,* old Charlie's good blood says, 'Charlie! if you sell dat old house, Charlie, you low-down old dog, Charlie, what de Compte De Charleu make for you grace-gran'-muzzer, de dev' can eat you, Charlie, I don't care.' "

"But you'll sell it anyhow, won't you, old man?"

"No!" And the *no* rumbled off in muttered oaths like thunder out on the Gulf. The incensed old Colonel wheeled and started off.

"Curl!" [Colonel] said Charlie, standing up unsteadily.

The planter turned with an inquiring frown.

"I'll trade with you!" said Charlie.

The Colonel was tempted. " 'Ow'l you trade?" he asked.

"My house for yours!"

The old Colonel turned pale with anger. He walked very quickly back, and came close up to his kinsman.

"Charlie!" he said.

"Injin Charlie," with a tipsy nod.

But by this time self-control was returning. "Sell Belles Demoiselles to you?" he said in a high key, and then laughed "Ho, ho, ho!" and rode away.

A cloud, but not a dark one, overshadowed the spirits of Belles Demoiselles' plantation. The old master, whose beaming presence had always made him a shining Saturn, spinning and sparkling within the bright circle of his daughters, fell into musing fits, started out of frowning reveries, walked often by himself, and heard business from his overseer fretfully.

No wonder. The daughters knew his closeness in trade, and attributed to it his failure to negotiate for the Old Charlie buildings,—so to call them. They began to depreciate Belles Demoiselles. If a north wind blew, it was too cold to ride. If a shower had fallen, it was too muddy to drive. In the morning the garden was wet. In the evening the grasshopper was a burden. *Ennui* was turned into capital; every headache was interpreted a premonition of ague; and when the native exuberance of a flock of ladies without a want or a care burst out in laughter in the father's face, they spread their French eyes, rolled up their little hands, and with rigid wrists and mock vehemence vowed and vowed again that they only laughed at their misery, and should pine to death unless they could move to the sweet city. "O! the theater! O! Orleans Street! O! the masquerade! the Place d'Armes! the ball!" and they would call upon Heaven with French irreverence, and fall into each other's arms, and whirl down the hall singing a waltz, end with a grand collision and fall, and, their eyes streaming merriment, lay the blame on the slippery floor, that would some day be the death of the whole seven.

Three times more the fond father, thus goaded, managed, by accident,—business accident,—to see old Charlie and increase his offer; but in vain. He finally went to him formally.

"Eh?" said the deaf and distant relative. "For what you want him, eh? Why you don't stay where you halways be 'appy? Dis is a blame old rat-hole,—good for old Injin Charlie,—da's all. Why you don't stay where you be halways 'appy? Why you don't buy somewheres else?"

"That's none of your business," snapped the planter. Truth was, his reasons were unsatisfactory even to himself.

A sullen silence followed. Then Charlie spoke:

"Well, now, look here; I sell you old Charlie's house."

"*Bien!* and the whole block," said the Colonel.

"Hold on," said Charlie. "I sell you de 'ouse and de block. Den I go and git drunk, and go to sleep; de dev' comes along and says, 'Charlie! old Charlie, you blame low-down old dog, wake up! What you doin' here? Where's de 'ouse what Monsieur le Compte give your grace-granmuzzer? Don't you see dat fine gentyman, De Charleu, done gone and tore him down and make him over new, you blame old fool, Charlie, you low-down old Injin dog!' "

"I'll give you forty thousand dollars," said the Colonel.

"For de 'ouse?"

"For all."

The deaf man shook his head.

"Forty-five!" said the Colonel.

"What a lie? For what you tell me 'what a lie?' I don't tell you no lie."

"Non, non! I give you *forty-five!"* shouted the Colonel.

Charlie shook his head again.

"Fifty!"

He shook it again.

The figures rose and rose to—

"Seventy-five!"

The answer was an invitation to go away and let the owner alone, as he was, in certain specified respects, the vilest of living creatures, and no company for a fine gentyman.

The "fine gentyman" longed to blaspheme,—but before old Charlie!—in the name of pride, how could he? He mounted and started away.

"Tell you what I'll make wid you," said Charlie.

The other, guessing aright, turned back without dismounting, smiling.

"How much Belles Demoiselles hoes me now?" asked the deaf one.

"One hundred and eighty thousand dollars," said the Colonel, firmly.

"Yass," said Charlie. "I don't want Belles Demoiselles."

The old Colonel's quiet laugh intimated it made no difference either way.

"But me," continued Charlie, "me,—I'm got le Compte De Charleu's blood in me, any'ow,—a litt' bit, any'ow, ain't it?"

The Colonel nodded that it was.

"Bien! If I go out of dis place and don't go to Belles Demoiselles, de peoples will say,—day will say, 'Old Charlie he been all doze time tell a blame *lie!* He ain't no kin to his old grace-granmuzzer, not a blame bit! He don't got nary drop of De Charleu blood to save his blame low-down old Injin soul! No, sare! What I want wid money, den? No, sare? My place for yours!"

He turned to go into the house, just too soon to see the Colonel make an ugly whisk at him with his riding-whip. Then the Colonel, too, moved off.

Two or three times over, as he ambled homeward, laughter broke through his annoyance, as he recalled old Charlie's family pride and the presumption of his offer. Yet each time he could but think better of—not the offer to swap, but the preposterous ancestral loyalty. It was so much better than he could have expected from his "low-down" relative, and not unlike his own whim withal—the proposition which went with it was forgiven.

This last defeat bore so harshly on the master of Belles Demoiselles, that the daughters, reading chagrin in his face, began to repent. They loved their father as daughters can, and when they saw their pretended dejection harassing him seriously they restrained their complaints, displayed more than ordinary tenderness, and heroically and ostentatiously concluded there was no place like Belles Demoiselles. But the new mood touched him more than the old, and only refined his discontent. Here was a man, rich without the care of riches, free from any real trouble, happiness as native to his house as perfume to his garden, deliberately, as it were with premeditated malice, taking joy by the shoulder and bidding her be gone to town, whither he might easily have followed, only that the very same ancestral nonsense that kept Injin Charlie from selling the old place for twice its value prevented him from choosing any other spot for a city home.

But by and by the charm of nature and the merry hearts around him prevailed; the fit of exalted sulks passed off, and after a while the year flared up at Christmas, flickered, and went out.

New Year came and passed; the beautiful garden of Belles Demoiselles put on its spring attire; the seven fair sisters moved from rose to rose; the cloud of discontent had warmed into invisible vapor in the rich sunlight of family affection, and on the common memory the only scar of last year's wound was old Charlie's sheer impertinence in crossing the caprice of the De Charleus. The cup of gladness seemed to fill with the filling of the river.

How high it was! Its tremendous current rolled and tumbled and spun along, hustling the long funeral flotillas of drift,—and how near shore it came! Men were out day and night, watching the levee. On windy nights even the old Colonel took part, and grew light-hearted with occupation and excitement, as every minute the river threw a white arm over the levee's top, as though it would vault over. But all held fast, and, as the summer drifted in, the water sunk down into its banks and looked quite incapable of harm.

On a summer afternoon of uncommon mildness, old Colonel Jean Albert Henri Joseph De Charleu-Marot, being in a mood for reverie, slipped the custody of his feminine rulers and sought the crown of the levee, where it was his wont to promenade. Presently he sat upon a stone bench,—a favorite seat. Before him lay his broadspread fields; near by, his lordly mansion; and being still,—perhaps by female contact,—somewhat sentimental, he fell to musing on his past. It was hardly worthy to be proud of. All its morning was reddened with mad frolic, and far toward the meridian it was married with elegant rioting. Pride had kept him well nigh useless, and despised the honors won by valor; gaming had dimmed prosperity; death had taken his heavenly wife; voluptuous ease had mortgaged his lands; and yet his house still stood, his sweet-smelling fields were still fruitful, his name was fame enough; and yonder and yonder, among the trees and flowers, like angels walking in Eden, were the seven goddesses of his only worship.

Just then a slight sound behind him brought him to his feet. He cast his eyes anxiously to the outer edge of the little strip of bank between the levee's base and the river. There was nothing visible. He paused, with his ear toward the water, his face full of frightened expectation. Ha! There came a single plashing sound, like some great beast slipping into the river, and little waves in a wide semi-circle came out from under the bank and spread over the water!

"My God!"

He plunged down the levee and bounded through the low weeds to the edge of the bank. It was sheer, and the water about four feet below. He did not stand quite on the edge, but fell upon his knees a couple of yards away, wringing his hands, moaning and weeping, and staring through his watery eyes at a fine, long crevice just discernible under the matted grass, and curving outward on either hand toward the river.

"My God!" he sobbed aloud; "my God!" and even while he called, his God answered: the tough Bermuda grass stretched and snapped, the crevice slowly became a gape, and softly, gradually, with no sound but the closing of the water at last, a ton or more of earth settled into the boiling eddy and disappeared.

At the same instant a pulse of the breeze brought from the garden behind, the joyous, thoughtless laughter of the fair mistresses of Belles Demoiselles.

The old Colonel sprang up and clambered over the levee. Then forcing himself to a more composed movement, he hastened into the house and ordered his horse.

"Tell my children to make merry while I am gone," he left word. "I shall be back to-night," and the horse's hoofs clattered down a by-road leading to the city.

"Charlie," said the planter, riding up to a window, from which the old man's night-cap was thrust out, "what you say, Charlie,—my house for yours, eh, Charlie—what you say?"

"Ello!" said Charlie; "from where you come from dis time of to-night?"

"I come from the Exchange in St. Louis-street." (A small fraction of the truth.)

"What you want?" said matter-of-fact Charlie.

"I come to trade."

The low-down relative drew the worsted off his ears. "Oh! yass," he said with an uncertain air.

"Well, old man Charlie, what you say: my house for yours,—like you said,—eh, Charlie?"

"I dunno," said Charlie; "it's nearly mine now. Why you don't stay dare youse'f?"

"*Because I don't want!*" said the Colonel savagely. "Is dat reason enough for you? You better take me in de notion, old man, I tell you,—yes!"

Charlie never winced; but how his answer delighted the Colonel! Quoth Charlie:

"I don't care—I take him!—*mais,* possession give right off."

"Not the whole plantation, Charlie; only—"

"I don't care," said Charlie; "we easy can fix dat. *Mais,* what for you don't want to keep him? I don't want him. You better keep him."

"Don't you try to make no fool of me, old man," cried the planter.

"Oh, no!" said the other. "Oh, no! but you make a fool of yourself, ain't it?"

The dumbfounded Colonel stared; Charlie went on:

"Yass! Belles Demoiselles is more wort' dan tree block like dis one. I pass by dare since two weeks. Oh, pritty Belles Demoiselles! De cane was wave in de wind, de garden smell like a bouquet, de white-cap was jump up and down on de river; seven *belles demoiselles* was ridin' on horses. 'Pritty, pritty, pritty!' says old Charlie. Ah! *Monsieur le père,* 'ow 'appy, 'appy, 'appy!"

"Yass!" he continued—the Colonel still staring—"le Compte De Charleu have two familie. One was low-down Choctaw, one was high up *noblesse.* He give the low-down Choctaw dis old rat-hole; he give Belles Demoiselles to your gran-fozzer; and now you don't be *satisfait.* What I'll do wid Belles Demoiselles? She'll break me in two years, yass. And what you'll do wid old Charlie's house, eh? You'll tear her down and make you'se'f a blame old fool. I rather wouldn't trade!"

The planter caught a big breathful of anger, but Charlie went straight on:

"I rather wouldn't, *mais* I will do it for you;—just the same, like

Monsieur le Compte would say, 'Charlie, you old fool, I want to shange houses wid you.' "

So long as the Colonel suspected irony he was angry, but as Charlie seemed, after all, to be certainly in earnest, he began to feel conscious-stricken. He was by no means a tender man, but his lately-discovered misfortune had unhinged him, and this strange, undeserved, disinterested family fealty on the part of Charlie touched his heart. And should he still try to lead him into the pitfall he had dug? He hesitated;—no, he would show him the place by broad day-light, and if he chose to overlook the "caving bank," it would be his own fault;—a trade's a trade.

"Come," said the planter, "come at my house to-night; to-morrow we look at the place before breakfast, and finish the trade."

"For what?" said Charlie.

"Oh, because I got to come in town in the morning."

"I don't want," said Charlie. "How I'm goin' to come dere?"

"I git you a horse at the liberty stable."

"Well—anyhow—I don't care—I'll go." And they went.

When they had ridden a long time, and were on the road darkened by hedges of Cherokee rose, the Colonel called behind him to the "low-down" scion:

"Keep the road, old man."

"Eh?"

"Keep the road."

"Oh, yes; all right; I keep my word; we don't goin' to play no tricks, eh?"

But the Colonel seemed not to hear. His ungenerous design was beginning to be hateful to him. Not only old Charlie's unprovoked goodness was prevailing; the eulogy on Belles Demoiselles had stirred the depths of an intense love for his beautiful home. True, if he held to it, the caving of the bank, at its present fearful speed, would let the house into the river within three months; but were it not better to lose it so, than sell his birthright? Again,—coming back to the first thought,—to betray his own blood! It was only Injin Charlie; but had not the De Charleu blood just spoken out in him? Unconsciously he groaned.

After a time they struck a path approaching the plantation in the rear, and a little after, passing from behind a clump of live-oaks, they came in sight of the villa. It looked so like a gem, shining through its dark grove, so like a great glow-worm in the dense foliage, so significant of luxury and gayety, that the poor master, from an overflowing heart, groaned again.

"What?" asked Charlie.

The Colonel only drew his rein, and, dismounting mechanically, contemplated the sight before him. The high, arched doors and windows were thrown wide to the summer air; from every opening the bright light of numerous candelabra darted out upon the sparkling foliage of magnolia and bay, and here and there in the spacious verandas a colored lantern swayed in the gentle breeze. A sound of revel fell on the ear, the music of harps; and across one window, brighter than the rest, flitted, once or twice, the shadows of dancers. But oh! the shadows flitting across the heart of the fair mansion's master!

"Old Charlie," said he, gazing fondly at his house, "you and me is both old, eh?"

"Yass," said the stolid Charlie.

"And we has both been bad enough in our time, eh, Charlie?"

Charlie, surprised at the tender tone, repeated, "Yass."

"And you and me is mighty close?"

"Blame close, yass."

"But you never know me to cheat, old man!"

"No,"—impassively.

"And do you think I would cheat you now?"

"I dunno," said Charlie. "I don't believe."

"Well, old man, old man,"—his voice began to quiver,—"I shan't cheat you now. My God!—old man, I tell you—you better not make the trade!"

"Because for what?" asked Charlie in plain anger; but both looked quickly toward the house! The Colonel tossed his hands wildly in the air, rushed forward a step or two, and giving one fearful scream of agony and fright, fell forward on his face in the path. Old Charlie stood transfixed with horror. Belles Demoiselles, the realm of maiden beauty, the home of merriment, the house of dancing, all in the tremor and glow of pleasure, suddenly sunk, with one short, wild wail of terror—sunk, sunk, down, down, down, into the merciless, unfathomable flood of the Mississippi.

Twelve long months were midnight to the mind of the childless father; when they were only half gone, he took his bed; and every day, and every night, old Charlie, the "low-down," the "fool," watched him tenderly, tended him lovingly, for the sake of his name, his misfortunes, and his broken heart. No woman's step crossed the floor of the sick-chamber, whose western dormer-windows overpeered the dingy architecture of old Charlie's block; Charlie and a skilled physician, the one all interest, the other all gentleness, hope, and patience—these only entered by the door; but by the window came in a sweet-scented evergreen vine, transplanted from the caving bank of Belles Demoiselles. It caught the rays of sunset in its flowery net and let them softly in upon the sick man's bed; gathered the glancing beams of the moon at midnight, and often wakened the sleeper to look, with his mindless eyes, upon their pretty silver fragments strewn upon the floor.

By and by there seemed—there was—a twinkling dawn of returning reason. Slowly, peacefully, with an increase unseen from day to day, the light of reason came into the eyes, and speech became coherent; but withal there came a failing of the wrecked body, and the doctor said that monsieur was both better and worse.

One evening, as Charlie sat by the vine-clad window with his fireless pipe in his hand, the old Colonel's eyes fell full upon his own, and rested there.

"Charl—," he said with an effort, and his delighted nurse hastened to the bed-side and bowed his best ear. There was an unsuccessful effort or two, and then he whispered, smiling with sweet sadness,—

"We didn't trade."

The truth, in this case, was a secondary matter to Charlie; the main point was to give a pleasing answer. So he nodded his head decidedly, as who should say—"Oh yes, we did, it was a bonafide swap!" but when he saw the smile vanish, he tried the other expedient and shook his head with still more vigor, to signify that they had not so much as approached a bargain; and the smile returned.

Charlie wanted to see the vine recognized. He stepped backward to the window with a broad smile, shook the foliage, nodded and looked smart.

"I know," said the Colonel, with beaming eyes, "—many weeks."

The next day—

"Charl—"

The best ear went down.

"Send for a priest."

The priest came, and was alone with him a whole afternoon. When he left, the patient was very haggard and exhausted, but smiled and would not suffer the crucifix to be removed from his breast.

One more morning came. Just before dawn Charlie, lying on a pallet in the room, thought he was called, and came to the bedside.

"Old man," whispered the failing invalid, "is it caving yet?"

Charlie nodded.

"It won't pay you out."

"Oh dat makes not'ing," said Charlie. Two big tears rolled down his brown face. "Dat makes not'in."

The Colonel whispered once more:

"*Mes belles demoiselles!*—in paradise;—in the garden—I shall be with them at sunrise;" and so it was.

JOEL CHANDLER HARRIS

The Wonderful Tar-Baby Story

"Didn't the fox *never* catch the rabbit, Uncle Remus?" asked the little boy the next evening.

"He come mighty nigh it, honey, sho's you born—Brer Fox did. One day atter Brer Rabbit fool 'im wid dat calamus root, Brer Fox went ter wuk en got 'im some tar, en mix it wid some turkentime, en fix up a contrapshun w'at he call a Tar-Baby, en he tuck dish yer Tar-Baby en he sot 'er in de big road, en den he lay off in de bushes fer to see what de news wuz gwine ter be. En he didn't hatter wait long, needer, kaze bimeby here come Brer Rabbit pacin' down de road—lippity-clippity, clippity-lippity—dez ez sassy ez a jay-bird. Brer Fox, he lay low. Brer Rabbit come prancin' 'long twel he spy de Tar-Baby, en den he fotch up on his behime legs like he wuz 'stonished. De Tar-Baby, she sot dar, she did, en Brer Fox, he lay low.

" 'Mawnin'!' sez Brer Rabbit, sezee—'nice wedder dis mawnin',' sezee.

"Tar-Baby ain't sayin' nothin', en Brer Fox, he lay low.

" 'How duz yo' sym'tums seem ter segashuate?' sez Brer Rabbit, sezee.

"Brer Fox, he wink his eye slow, en lay low, en de Tar-Baby, she ain't sayin' nothin'.

" 'How you come on, den? Is you deaf?' sez Brer Rabbit, sezee. 'Kaze if you is, I kin holler louder,' sezee.

"Tar-Baby stay still, en Brer Fox, he lay low.

" 'You er stuck up, dat's w'at you is,' says Brer Rabbit, sezee, 'en I'm gwine ter kyore you, dat's w'at I'm a gwine ter do,' sezee.

"Brer Fox, he sorter chuckle in his stummick, he did, but Tar-Baby ain't sayin' nothin'.

" 'I'm gwine ter larn you how ter talk ter 'spectubble folks ef hit's de las' ack,' sez Brer Rabbit, sezee. 'Ef you don't take off dat hat en tell me howdy I'm gwine ter bus' you wide open,' sezee.

"Tar-Baby stay still, en Brer Fox, he lay low.

"Brer Rabbit keep on axin' 'im, en de Tar-Baby, she keep on sayin' nothin', twel present'y Brer Rabbit draw back wid his fis', he did, en blip he tuck 'er side er de head. Right dar's whar he broke his merlasses jug. His fis' stuck, en he can't pull loose. De tar hilt 'im. But Tar-Baby, she stay still, en Brer Fox, he lay low.

" 'Ef you don't lemme loose, I'll knock you agin,' sez Brer Rabbit, sezee, en wid dat he fotch 'er a swipe wid de udder han', en dat stuck. Tar-Baby, she ain't sayin' nothin', en Brer Fox, he lay low.

" 'Tu'n me loose, 'fo' I kick de natchul stuffin' outen you,' sez Brer Rabbit, sezee, but de Tar-Baby, she ain't sayin' nothin.' She des hilt on, en den Brer Rabbit lose de use er his feet in de same way. Brer Fox, he lay low. Den Brer Rabbit squall out dat ef de Tar-Baby don't tu'n 'im loose he butt 'en cranksided. En den he butted, en his head got stuck. Den Brer Fox, he sa'ntered fort', lookin' des ez innercent ez one er yo' mammy's mockin'-birds.

" 'Howdy, Brer Rabbit,' sez Brer Fox, sezee. 'You look sorter stuck up dis mawnin',' sezee, en den he rolled on de groun', en laughed en laughed twel he couldn't laugh no mo'. 'I speck you'll take dinner wid me dis time, Brer Rabbit. I done laid in some calamus root, en I ain't gwine ter take no skuse,' sez Brer Fox, sezee."

Here Uncle Remus paused, and drew a two-pound yam out of the ashes.

"Did the Fox eat the Rabbit?" asked the little boy to whom the story had been told.

"Dat's all de fur de tale goes," replied the old man. "He mought, en den again he moughtent. Some say Jedge B'ar come long en loosed 'im—some say he didn't. I hear Miss Sally callin'. You better run 'long."

How Mr. Rabbit Was Too Sharp for Mr. Fox

"Uncle Remus," said the little boy one evening, when he had found the old man with little or nothing to do, "did the Fox kill and eat the Rabbit when he caught him with the Tar-Baby?"

"Law, honey, ain't I tell you 'bout dat?" replied the old darkey, chuckling slyly. "I 'clar ter gracious I ought er tole you dat, but old man Nod wuz ridin on my eyeleds twel a leetle mo'n I'd a dis'member'd my own name, en den on to dat here come yo' mammy hollerin' atter you.

"W'at I tell you w'en I fus' begin? I tole you Brer Rabbit wuz a monstus soon creetur; leas'ways dat's w'at I laid out fer ter tell you. Well, den, honey, don't you go en make no udder calkalashuns, kaze in dem days Brer Rabbit en his fambly wuz at de head er de gang w'en enny racket wuz on han', en dar dey stayed. 'Fo' you begins fer ter wipe yo' eyes 'bout Brer Rabbit, you wait en see whar'bouts Brer Rabbit gwine ter fetch up at. But dat's needer yer ner dar.

"W'en Brer Fox fin' Brer Rabbit mixt up wid de Tar-Baby, he feel mighty good, en he roll on de groun' en laff. Bimeby he up'n say, sezee:

" 'Well, I speck I got you dis time, Brer Rabbit,' sezee; 'maybe I ain't, but I speck I is. You been runnin' roun' here sassin' atter me a mighty long time, but I speck you done come ter de een' er de row. You bin cuttin' up yo' capers en bouncin' roun' in dis neighborhood ontwel you come ter b'leeve yo'se'f de boss er de whole gang. En den you er allers somers whar you got no bizness,' sez Brer Fox, sezee. 'Who ax you fer ter come en strike up a 'quaintance wid dish yer Tar-Baby? En who stuck you up dar whar you iz? Nobody in de roun' worl'. You des tuck en jam yo'se'f on dat Tar-Baby widout waitin' fer enny invite,' sez Brer Fox, sezee, 'en dar you is, en dar you'll stay twel I fixes up a bresh-pile and fires her up, kaze I'm gwine ter bobbycue you dis day, sho,' sez Brer Fox, sezee.

"Den Brer Rabbit talk mighty 'umble.

" 'I don't keer w'at you do wid me, Brer Fox,' sezee, 'so you don't fling me in dat brier-patch. Roas' me, Brer Fox,' sezee, 'but don't fling me in dat brier-patch,' sezee.

" 'Hit's so much trouble fer ter kindle a fire,' sez Brer Fox, sezee, 'dat I speck I'll hatter hang you,' sezee.

" 'Hang me des ez high as you please, Brer Fox,' sez Brer Rabbit, sezee, 'but do fer de Lord's sake don't fling me in dat brier-patch,' sezee.

" 'I ain't got no string,' sez Brer Fox, sezee, 'en now I speck I'll hatter drown you,' sezee.

" 'Drown me des ez deep ez you please, Brer Fox,' sez Brer Rabbit, sezee, 'but don't fling me in dat brier-patch,' sezee.

" 'Dey ain't no water nigh,' sez Brer Fox, sezee, 'en now I speck I'll hatter skin you,' sezee.

" 'Skin me, Brer Fox,' sez Brer Rabbit, sezee, 'snatch out my eyeballs, t'ar out my years by de roots, en cut off my legs,' sezee, 'but do please, Brer Fox, don't fling me in dat brier-patch,' sezee.

"Co'se Brer Fox wanter hurt Brer Rabbit bad ez he kin, so he cotch 'im by de behime legs en slung 'im right in de middle er de brier-patch. Dar wuz a considerabul flutter whar Brer Rabbit struck de bushes, en Brer Fox sorter hang 'roun' fer ter see w'at wus gwine ter happen. Bimeby he hear somebody call 'im, en way up de hill he see Brer Rabbit settin' cross-legged on a chinkapin log koamin' de pitch out'n his ha'r wid a chip. Den Brer Fox know dat he bin swop off mighty bad. Brer

Rabbit wuz bleedzd fer ter fling back some er his sass, en he holler out:

" 'Bred en bawn in a brier-patch, Brer Fox—bred en bawn in a brier-patch!' en wid dat he skip out des ez lively ez a cricket in de embers."

SARAH ORNE JEWETT

A White Heron

I

The woods were already filled with shadows one June evening, just before eight o'clock, though a bright sunset still glimmered faintly among the trunks of the trees. A little girl was driving home her cow, a plodding, dilatory, provoking creature in her behavior, but a valued companion for all that. They were going away from the western light, and striking deep into the dark woods, but their feet were familiar with the path, and it was no matter whether their eyes could see it or not.

There was hardly a night the summer through when the old cow could be found waiting at the pasture bars; on the contrary, it was her greatest pleasure to hide herself away among the high huckleberry bushes, and though she wore a loud bell she had made the discovery that if one stood perfectly still it would not ring. So Sylvia had to hunt for her until she found her, and call Co'! Co'! with never an answering Moo, until her childish patience was quite spent. If the creature had not given good milk and plenty of it, the case would have seemed very different to her owners. Besides, Sylvia had all the time there was, and very little use to make of it. Sometimes in pleasant weather it was a consolation to look upon the cow's pranks as an intelligent attempt to play hide and seek, and as the child had no playmates she lent herself to this amusement with a good deal of zest. Though this chase had been so long that the wary animal herself had given an unusual signal of her whereabouts, Sylvia had only laughed when she came upon Mistress Moolly at the swamp side, and urged her affectionately homeward with a twig of birch leaves. The old cow was not inclined to wander farther, she even turned in the right direction for once as they left the pasture, and stepped along the road at a good pace. She was quite ready to be milked now, and seldom stopped to browse.

Sylvia wondered what her grandmother would say because they were so late. It was a great while since she had left home at half past five o'clock, but everybody knew the difficulty of making this errand a short one. Mrs. Tilley had chased the hornéd torment too many summer evenings herself to blame any one else for lingering, and was only thankful as she waited that she had Sylvia, nowadays, to give such valuable assistance. The good woman suspected that Sylvia loitered occasionally on her own account; there never was such a child for straying about out of doors since the world was made! Everybody said that it was a good change for a little maid who had tried to grow for eight years in a crowded manufacturing town, but, as for Sylvia herself, it seemed as if she never had been alive at all before she came to live at the farm. She thought often with wistful compassion of a wretched dry geranium that belonged to a town neighbor.

" 'Afraid of folks,' " old Mrs. Tilley said to herself, with a smile, after she had made the unlikely choice of Sylvia from her daughter's houseful of children, and was returning to the farm. " 'Afraid of folks,' they said! I guess she won't be troubled no great with 'em up to the old place!" When they reached the door of the lonely house and stopped to unlock it, and the cat came to purr loudly, and rub against them, a deserted pussy, indeed, but fat with young robins, Sylvia whispered that this was a beautiful place to live in, and she never should wish to go home.

The companions followed the shady woodroad, the cow taking slow steps, and the child very fast ones. The cow stopped long at the brook to drink, as if the pasture were not half a swamp, and Sylvia stood still and waited, letting her bare feet cool themselves in the shoal water, while the great twilight moths struck softly against her. She waded on through the brook as the cow moved away, and listened to the thrushes with a heart that beat fast with pleasure. There was a stirring in the great boughs overhead. They were full of little birds and beasts that seemed to be wide-awake, and going about their world, or else saying goodnight to each other in sleepy twitters. Sylvia herself felt sleepy as she walked along. However, it was not much farther to the house, and the air was soft and sweet. She was not often in the woods so late as this, and it made her feel as if she were a part of the gray shadows and the moving leaves. She was just thinking how long it seemed since she first came to the farm a year ago, and wondering if everything went on in the noisy town just the same as when she was there; the thought of the great red-faced boy who used to chase and frighten her made her hurry along the path to escape from the shadow of the trees.

Suddenly this little woods girl is horror stricken to hear a clear whistle not very far away. Not a bird's whistle, which would have a sort of friendliness, but a boy's whistle, determined, and somewhat aggressive. Sylvia left the cow to whatever sad fate might await her, and stepped discreetly aside into the bushes, but she was just too late. The enemy had discovered her, and called out in a very cheerful and persuasive tone, "Halloa, little girl, how far is it to the road?" and trembling Sylvia answered almost inaudibly, "A good ways."

She did not dare to look boldly at the tall young man, who carried a gun over his shoulder, but she came out of her bush and again followed the cow, while he walked alongside.

"I have been hunting for some birds," the stranger said kindly, "and I have lost my way, and need a friend very much. Don't be afraid," he added gallantly. "Speak up and tell me what your name is, and whether you think I can spend the night at your house, and go out gunning early in the morning."

Sylvia was more alarmed than before. Would not her grandmother consider her much to blame? But who could have foreseen such an accident as this? It did not appear to be her fault and she hung her head as if the stem of it were broken, but managed to answer "Sylvy," with much effort when her companion again asked her name.

Mrs. Tilley was standing in the doorway when the trio came into view. The cow gave a loud moo by way of explanation.

"Yes, you'd better speak up for yourself, you old trial! Where'd she tuck herself away this time, Sylvy?" Sylvia kept an awed silence; she knew by instinct that her grandmother did not comprehend the gravity of the situation. She must be mistaking the stranger for one of the farmer lads of the region.

The young man stood his gun beside the door, and dropped a heavy game-bag beside it; then he bade Mrs. Tilley good-evening, and repeated his wayfarer's story, and asked if he could have a night's lodging.

"Put me anywhere you like," he said. "I must be off early in the morning, before day; but I am very hungry, indeed. You can give me some milk at any rate, that's plain."

"Dear sakes, yes," responded the hostess, whose long slumbering hospitality seemed to be easily awakened. "You might fare better if you went out on the main road a mile or so, but you're welcome to what we've got. I'll milk right off, and you make yourself at home. You can sleep on husks or feathers," she proffered graciously. "I raised them all myself. There's good pasturing for geese just below here towards the ma'sh. Now step round and set a plate for the gentleman, Sylvy!" And Sylvia promptly stepped. She was glad to have something to do, and she was hungry herself.

It was a surprise to find so clean and comfortable a little dwelling in this New England wilderness. The young man had known the horrors of its most primitive housekeeping, and the dreary squalor of that level of society which does not rebel at the companionship of hens. This was the best thrift of an old-fashioned farmstead, though on such a small scale that it seemed like a hermitage. He listened eagerly to the old woman's quaint talk, he watched Sylvia's pale face and shining gray eyes with ever growing enthusiasm, and insisted that this was the best supper he had eaten for a month; then, afterward, the new-made friends sat down in the doorway together while the moon came up.

Soon it would be berry time, and Sylvia was a great help at picking. The cow was a good milker, though a plaguy thing to keep track of, the hostess gossiped frankly, adding presently that she had buried four children, so that Sylvia's mother, and a son (who might be dead) in California were all the children she had left. "Dan, my boy, was a great hand to go gunning," she explained sadly. "I never wanted for pa'tridges or gray squer'ls while he was to home. He's been a great wand'rer, I expect, and he's no hand to write letters. There, I don't blame him, I'd ha' seen the world myself if it had been so I could.

"Sylvia takes after him," the grandmother continued affectionately, after a minute's pause. "There ain't a foot o' ground she don't know her way over, and the wild creatur's counts her one o' themselves. Squer'ls she'll tame to come an' feed right out o' her hands, and all sorts o' birds. Last winter she got the jay birds to bangeing here, and I believe she'd 'a' scanted herself of her own meals to have plenty to throw out amongst 'em, if I hadn't kep' watch. Anything but crows, I tell her, I'm willin' to help support,—though Dan he went an' tamed one o' them that did seem to have reason same as folks. It was round here a good spell after he went away. Dan an' his father they didn't hitch,—but he never held up his head ag'in after Dan had dared him an' gone off."

The guest did not notice this hint of family sorrows in his eager interest in something else.

"So Sylvy knows all about birds, does she?" he exclaimed, as he looked round at the little girl who sat, very demure but increasingly sleepy, in the moonlight. "I am making a collection of birds myself. I have been at it ever since I was a boy." (Mrs. Tilley smiled.) "There are two or three very rare ones I have been hunting for these five years. I mean to get them on my own ground if they can be found."

"Do you cage 'em up?" asked Mrs. Tilley doubtfully, in response to this enthusiastic announcement.

"Oh, no, they're stuffed and preserved, dozens and dozens of them," said the ornithologist, "and I have shot or snared every one myself. I caught a glimpse of a white heron three miles from here on Saturday, and I have followed it in this direction. They have never been found in this district at all. The little white heron, it is," and he turned again to look at Sylvia with the hope of discovering that the rare bird was one of her acquaintances.

But Sylvia was watching a hop toad in the narrow footpath.

"You would know the heron if you saw it," the stranger continued eagerly. "A queer tall white bird with soft feathers and long thin legs. And it would have a nest perhaps in the top of a high tree, made of sticks, something like a hawk's nest."

Sylvia's heart gave a wild beat; she knew that strange white bird, and had once stolen softly near where it stood in some bright green swamp grass, away over at the other side of the woods. There was an open place where the sunshine always seemed strangely yellow and hot, where tall, nodding rushes grew, and her grandmother had warned her that she might sink in the soft black mud underneath and never be heard of more. Not far beyond were the salt marshes and beyond those was the sea, the sea which Sylvia wondered and dreamed about, but never had looked upon, though its great voice could often be heard above the noise of the woods on stormy nights.

"I can't think of anything I should like so much as to find that heron's nest," the handsome stranger was saying. "I would give ten dollars to anybody who could show it to me," he added desperately, "and I mean to spend my whole vacation hunting for it if need be. Perhaps it was only migrating, or had been chased out of its own region by some bird of prey."

Mrs. Tilley gave amazed attention to all this, but Sylvia still watched the toad, not divining, as she might have done at some calmer time, that the creature wished to get to its hole under the doorstep, and was much hindered by the unusual spectators at that hour of the evening. No amount of thought, that night, could decide how many wished-for treasures the ten dollars, so lightly spoken of, would buy.

The next day the young sportsman hovered about the woods, and Sylvia kept him company, having lost her first fear of the friendly lad, who proved to be most kind and sympathetic. He told her many things about the birds and what they knew and where they lived and what they did with themselves. And he gave her a jackknife, which she thought as great a treasure as if she were a desert islander. All day long he did not once make her troubled or afraid except when he brought down some unsuspecting singing creature from its bough. Sylvia would have liked him vastly better without his gun; she could not understand why he killed the very birds he seemed to like so much. But as the day waned, Sylvia watched the young man with loving admiration. She had never seen anybody so charming and delightful; the woman's heart, asleep in the child, was vaguely thrilled by a dream of love. Some premonition of that great power stirred and swayed these young foresters who traversed the solemn woodlands with soft-footed silent care. They stopped to listen to a bird's song; they pressed forward again eagerly, parting the branches,—speaking to each other rarely and in whispers; the young man going first and Sylvia following, fascinated, a few steps behind, with her gray eyes dark with excitement.

She grieved because the longed-for white heron was elusive, but she did not lead the guest, she only followed, and there was no such thing as speaking first. The sound of her own unquestioned voice would have terrified her,—it was hard enough to answer yes or no when there was need of that. At last evening began to fall, and they drove the cow together, and Sylvia smiled with pleasure when they came to the place where she heard the whistle and was afraid only the night before.

II

Half a mile from home, at the farther edge of the woods, where the land was highest, a great pine tree stood, the last of its generation. Whether it was left for a boundary mark, or for what reason, no one could say; the woodchoppers who had felled its mates were dead and gone long ago, and a whole forest of sturdy trees, pines and oaks and maples, had grown again. But the stately head of this old pine towered above them all and made a landmark for sea and shore miles and miles away. Sylvia knew it well. She had always believed that whoever climbed to the top of it could see the ocean; and the little girl had often laid her hand on the great rough trunk and looked up wistfully at those dark boughs that the wind always stirred, no matter how hot and still the air might be below. Now she thought of the tree with a new excitement, for why, if one climbed it at break of day, could not one see all the world, and easily discover whence the white heron flew, and mark the place, and find the hidden nest?

What a spirit of adventure, what wild ambition! What fancied triumph and delight and glory for the later morning when she could make known the secret! It was almost too real and too great for the childish heart to bear.

All night the door of the little house stood open, and the whippoorwills came and sang upon the very step. The young sportsman and his old hostess were sound asleep, but Sylvia's great design kept her broad awake and watching. She forgot to think of sleep. The short summer night seemed as long as the winter darkness, and at last when the whippoorwills ceased, and she was afraid the morning would after all come too soon, she stole out of the house and followed the pasture path through the woods, hastening toward the open ground beyond, listening with a sense of comfort and companionship to the drowsy twitter of a half-awakened bird, whose perch she had jarred in passing. Alas, if the great wave of human interest which flooded for the first time this dull little life should sweep away the satisfactions of an existence heart to heart with nature and the dumb life of the forest!

There was the huge tree asleep yet in the paling moonlight, and small and hopeful Sylvia began with utmost bravery to mount to the top of it, with tingling, eager blood coursing the channels of her whole frame, with her bare feet and fingers, that pinched and held like bird's claws to the monstrous ladder reaching up, up, almost to the sky itself. First she must mount the white oak tree that grew alongside, where she was almost lost among the dark branches and the green leaves heavy and wet with dew; a bird fluttered off its nest, and a red squirrel ran to and fro and scolded pettishly at the harmless housebreaker. Sylvia felt her way easily. She had often climbed there, and knew that higher still one of the oak's upper branches chafed against the pine trunk, just where its lower boughs were set close together. There, when she made the dangerous pass from one tree to the other, the great enterprise would really begin.

She crept out along the swaying oak limb at last, and took the daring step across into the old pine tree. The way was harder than she thought; she must reach far and hold fast, the sharp dry twigs caught and held her and scratched her like angry talons, the pitch made her thin little fingers clumsy and stiff as she went round and round the tree's great stem, higher and higher upward. The sparrows and robins in the woods below were beginning to wake and twitter to the dawn, yet it seemed much lighter there aloft in the pine tree, and the child knew that she must hurry if her project were to be of any use.

The tree seemed to lengthen itself out as she went up, and to reach farther and farther upward. It was like a great mainmast to the voyaging earth; it must truly have been amazed that morning through all its ponderous frame as it felt this determined spark of human spirit creeping and climbing from higher branch to branch. Who knows how steadily the least twigs held themselves to advantage this light, weak creature on her way! The old pine must have loved his new dependent. More than all the hawks, and bats, and moths, and even the sweet-voiced thrushes, was the brave, beating heart of the solitary gray-eyed child. And the tree stood still and held away the winds that June morning while the dawn grew bright in the east.

Sylvia's face was like a pale star, if one had seen it from the ground, when the last thorny bough was past, and she stood trembling and tired but wholly triumphant, high in the treetop. Yes, there was the sea with the dawning sun making a golden dazzle over it, and toward that glorious east flew two hawks with slow-moving pinions. How low they looked in the air from that height when before one had only seen them far up, and dark against the blue sky. Their gray feathers were as soft as moths; they seemed only a little way from the tree, and Sylvia felt as if she too could go flying away among the clouds. Westward, the woodlands and farms reached miles and miles into the distance; here and there were church steeples, and white villages; truly it was a vast and awesome world.

The birds sang louder and louder. At last the sun came up bewilderingly bright. Sylvia could see the white sails of ships out at sea, and the clouds that were purple and rose-colored and yellow at first began to fade away. Where was the white heron's nest in the sea of green branches, and was this wonderful sight and pageant of the world the only reward for having climbed to such a giddy height? Now look down again, Sylvia, where the green marsh is set among the shining birches and dark hemlocks; there where you saw the white heron once you will see him again; look, look! a white spot of him like a single floating feather comes up from the dead hemlock and grows larger, and rises, and comes close at last, and goes by the landmark pine with steady sweep of wing and outstretched slender neck and crested head. And wait! wait! do not move a foot or a finger, little girl, do not send an arrow of light and consciousness from your two eager eyes, for the heron has perched on a pine bough not far beyond yours, and cries, back to his mate on the nest, and plumes his feathers for the new day!

The child gives a long sigh a minute later when a company of shouting catbirds comes also to the tree, and vexed by their fluttering and lawlessness the solemn heron goes away. She knows his secret now, the wild, light, slender bird that floats and wavers, and goes back like an arrow presently to his home in the green world beneath. Then Sylvia, well satisfied, makes her perilous way down again, not daring to look far below the branch she stands on, ready to cry sometimes because her fingers ache and her lamed feet slip. Wondering over and over again what the stranger would say to her, and what he would think when she told him how to find his way straight to the heron's nest.

"Sylvy, Sylvy!" called the busy old grandmother again and again, but nobody answered, and the small husk bed was empty, and Sylvia had disappeared.

The guest waked from a dream, and remembering his day's pleasure hurried to dress himself that it might sooner begin. He was sure from the way the shy little girl looked once or twice yesterday that she had at least seen the white heron, and now she must really be persuaded to tell. Here she comes now, paler than ever, and her worn old frock is torn and tattered, and smeared with pine pitch. The grandmother and the sportsman stand in the door together and question her, and the splendid moment has come to speak of the dead hemlock tree by the green marsh.

But Sylvia does not speak after all, though the old grandmother fretfully rebukes her, and the young man's kind appealing eyes are looking straight in her own. He can make them rich with money; he has promised it, and they are poor now. He is so well worth making happy, and he waits to hear the story she can tell.

No, she must keep silence! What is it that suddenly forbids her and makes her dumb? Has she been nine years growing, and now, when the great world for the first time puts out a hand to her, must she thrust it aside for a bird's sake? The murmur of the pine's green branches is in her ears, she remembers how the white heron came flying through the golden air and how they watched the sea and the morning together, and Sylvia cannot speak; she cannot tell the heron's secret and give its life away.

Dear loyalty, that suffered a sharp pang as the guest went away disappointed later in the day, that could have served and followed him and loved him as a dog loves! Many a night Sylvia heard the echo of his whistle haunting the pasture path as she came home with the loitering cow. She forgot even her sorrow at the sharp report of his gun and the piteous sight of thrushes and sparrows dropping silent to the ground, their songs hushed and their pretty feathers stained and wet with blood. Were the birds better friends than their hunter might have been,—who can tell? Whatever treasures were lost to her, woodlands and summer time, remember! Bring your gifts and graces and tell your secrets to this lonely country child!

KATE CHOPIN

The Story of an Hour

Knowing that Mrs. Mallard was afflicted with a heart trouble, great care was taken to break to her as gently as possible the news of her husband's death.

It was her sister Josephine who told her, in broken sentences; veiled hints that revealed in half concealing. Her husband's friend Richards was there, too, near her. It was he who had been in the newspaper office when intelligence of the railroad disaster was received, with Brently Mallard's name leading the list of "killed." He had only taken the time to assure himself of its truth by a second telegram, and had hastened to forestall any less careful, less tender friend in bearing the sad message.

She did not hear the story as many women have heard the same, with a paralyzed inability to accept its significance. She wept at once, with sudden, wild abandonment, in her sister's arms. When the storm of grief had spent itself she went away to her room alone. She would have no one follow her.

There stood, facing the open window, a comfortable, roomy armchair. Into this she sank, pressed down by a physical exhaustion that haunted her body and seemed to reach into her soul.

She could see in the open square before her house the tops of trees that were all aquiver with the new spring life. The delicious breath of rain was in the air. In the street below a peddler was crying his wares. The notes of a distant song which some one was singing reached her faintly, and countless sparrows were twittering in the eaves.

There were patches of blue sky showing here and there through the clouds that had met and piled one above the other in the west facing her window.

She sat with her head thrown back upon the cushion of the chair, quite motionless, except when a sob came up into her throat and shook her, as a child who has cried itself to sleep continues to sob in its dreams.

She was young, with a fair, calm face, whose lines bespoke repression and even a certain strength. But now there was a dull stare in her eyes,

Luise

whose gaze was fixed away off yonder on one of those patches of blue sky. It was not a glance of reflection, but rather indicated a suspension of intelligent thought.

There was something coming to her and she was waiting for it, fearfully. What was it? She did not know; it was too subtle and elusive to name. But she felt it, creeping out of the sky, reaching toward her through the sounds, the scents, the color that filled the air.

Now her bosom rose and fell tumultuously. She was beginning to recognize this thing that was approaching to possess her, and she was striving to beat it back with her will—as powerless as her two white slender hands would have been.

When she abandoned herself a little whispered word escaped her slightly parted lips. She said it over and over under her breath: "free, free, free!" The vacant stare and the look of terror that had followed it went from her eyes. They stayed keen and bright. Her pulses beat fast, and the coursing blood warmed and relaxed every inch of her body.

She did not stop to ask if it were or were not a monstrous joy that held her. A clear and exalted perception enabled her to dismiss the suggestion as trivial.

She knew that she would weep again when she saw the kind, tender hands folded in death; the face that had never looked save with love upon her, fixed and gray and dead. But she saw beyond that bitter moment a long procession of years to come that would belong to her absolutely. And she opened and spread her arms out to them in welcome.

There would be no one to live for her during those coming years; she would live for herself. There would be no powerful will bending hers in that blind persistence with which men and women believe they have a right to impose a private will upon a fellow-creature. A kind intention or a cruel intention made the act seem no less a crime as she looked upon it in that brief moment of illumination.

And yet she had loved him—sometimes. Often she had not. What did it matter! What could love, the unsolved mystery, count for in face of this possession of self-assertion which she suddenly recognized as the strongest impulse of her being!

"Free! Body and soul free!" she kept whispering.

Josephine was kneeling before the closed door with her lips to the keyhole, imploring for admission. "Louise, open the door! I beg; open the door—you will make yourself ill. What are you doing, Louise? For heaven's sake open the door."

"Go away. I am not making myself ill." No; she was drinking in a very elixir of life through that open window.

Her fancy was running riot along those days ahead of her. Spring days, and summer days, and all sorts of days that would be her own. She breathed a quick prayer that life might be long. It was only yesterday she had thought with a shudder that life might be long.

She arose at length and opened the door to her sister's importunities. There was a feverish triumph in her eyes, and she carried herself unwittingly like a goddess of Victory. She clasped her sister's waist, and together they descended the stairs. Richards stood waiting for them at the bottom.

Someone was opening the front door with a latchkey. It was Brently Mallard who entered, a little travel-stained, composedly carrying his gripsack and umbrella. He had been far from the scene of accident, and did not even know there had been one. He stood amazed at Josephine's piercing cry; at Richards' quick motion to screen him from the view of his wife.

But Richards was too late.

When the doctors came they said she had died of heart disease—of joy that kills.

MARY E. WILKINS FREEMAN

Luella Miller

Close to the village street stood the one-story house in which Luella Miller, who had an evil name in the village, had dwelt. She had been dead for years, yet there were those in the village who, in spite of the clearer light which comes on a vantage-point from a long-past danger, half believed in the tale which they had heard from their childhood. In their hearts, although they scarcely would have owned it, was a survival of the wild horror and frenzied fear of their ancestors who had dwelt in the same age with Luella Miller. Young people even would stare with a shudder at the old house as they passed, and children never played around it as was their wont around an untenanted building. Not a window in the old Miller house was broken: the panes reflected the morning sunlight in patches of emerald and blue, and the latch of the sagging front door was never lifted, although no bolt secured it. Since Luella Miller had been carried out of it, the house had had no tenant except one friendless old soul who had no choice between that and the far-off shelter of the open sky. This old woman, who had survived her kindred and friends, lived in the house one week, then one morning no smoke came out of the chimney, and a body of neighbours, a score strong, entered and found her dead in her bed. There were dark whispers as to the cause of her death, and there were those who testified to an expression of fear so exalted that it showed forth the state of the departing soul upon the dead face. The old woman had been hale and hearty when she entered the house, and in seven days she was dead; it seemed that she had fallen a victim to some uncanny power. The minister talked in the pulpit with covert severity against the sin of superstition; still the belief prevailed. Not a soul in the village but would have chosen the almshouse rather than that dwelling. No vagrant, if he heard the tale, would seek shelter beneath that old roof, unhallowed by nearly half a century of superstitious fear.

There was only one person in the village who had actually known Luella Miller. That person was a woman well over eighty, but a marvel of vitality and unextinct youth. Straight as an arrow, with the spring of one recently let loose from the bow of life, she moved about the streets, and she always went to church, rain or shine. She had never married, and had lived alone for years in a house across the road from Luella Miller's.

This woman had none of the garrulousness of age, but never in all her life had she ever held her tongue for any will save her own, and she never spared the truth when she essayed to present it. She it was who bore testimony to the life, evil, though possibly wittingly or designedly so, of Luella Miller, and to her personal appearance. When this old woman spoke—and she had the gift of description, although her thoughts were clothed in the rude vernacular of her native village—one could seem to see Luella Miller as she had really looked. According to this woman, Lydia Anderson by name, Luella Miller had been a beauty of a type rather unusual in New England. She had been a slight, pliant sort of creature, as ready with a strong yielding to fate and as unbreakable as a willow. She had glimmering lengths of straight, fair hair, which she wore softly looped round a long, lovely face. She had blue eyes full of soft pleading, little slender, clinging hands, and a wonderful grace of motion and attitude.

"Luella Miller used to sit in a way nobody else could if they sat up and studied a week of Sundays," said Lydia Anderson, "and it was a sight to see her walk. If one of them willows over there on the edge of the brook could start up and get its roots free of the ground, and move off, it would go just the way Luella Miller used to. She had a green shot silk she used to wear, too, and a hat with green ribbon streamers, and a lace veil blowing across her face and out sideways, and a green ribbon flyin' from her waist. That was what she came out bride in when she married Erastus Miller. Her name before she was married was Hill. There was always a sight of "l's" in her name, married or single. Erastus Miller was good lookin', too, better lookin' than Luella. Sometimes I used to think that Luella wa'n't so handsome after all. Erastus just about worshiped her. I used to know him pretty well. He lived next door to me, and we went to school together. Folks used to say he was waitin' on me, but he wa'n't. I never thought he was except once or twice when he said things that some girls might have suspected meant somethin'. That was before Luella came here to teach the district school. It was funny how she came to get it, for folks said she hadn't any education, and that one of the big girls, Lottie Henderson, used to do all the teachin' for her, while she sat back and did embroidery work on a cambric pocket-handkerchief. Lottie Henderson was a real smart girl, a splendid scholar, and she just set her eyes by Luella, as all the girls did. Lottie would have made a real smart woman, but she died when Luella had been here about a year—just faded away and died: nobody knew what aided her. She dragged herself to that schoolhouse and helped Luella teach till the very last minute. The committee all knew how Luella didn't do much of the work herself, but they winked at it. It wa'n't long after Lottie died that Erastus married her. I always thought he hurried it up because she wa'n't fit to teach. One of the big boys used to help her after Lottie died, but he hadn't much government, and the school didn't do very well, and Luella might have had to give it up, for the committee couldn't have shut their eyes to things much longer. The boy that helped her was a real honest, innocent sort of fellow, and he was a good scholar, too. Folks said he overstudied, and that was the reason he was took crazy the year after Luella married, but I don't know. And I don't know what made Erastus Miller go into consumption of the blood the year after he was married: consumption wa'n't in his family. He just grew weaker and weaker, and went almost bent double when he tried to wait on Luella, and he spoke feeble, like an old man. He worked terrible hard till the last trying to save up a little to leave Luella. I've seen him out in the worst storms on a wood-sled—he used to cut and sell wood—and he was hunched up on top lookin' more dead than alive. Once I couldn't stand it: I went over and helped him pitch some wood on the cart—I was always strong in my arms. I wouldn't stop for all he told me to, and I guess he was glad enough for the help. That was only a week before he died. He fell on the kitchen floor while he was gettin' breakfast. He always got the breakfast and let Luella lay abed. He did all the sweepin' and the washin' and the ironin' and most of the cookin'. He couldn't bear to have Luella lift her finger, and she let him do for her. She lived like a queen for all the work she did. She didn't even do her sewin'. She said it made her shoulder ache to sew, and poor Erastus's sister Lily used to do all her sewin'. She wa'n't able to, either; she was never strong in her back, but she did it beautifully. She had to, to suit Luella, she was so dreadful particular. I never saw anythin' like the fagottin' and hem-stitchin' that Lily Miller did for Luella. She made all Luella's weddin' outfit, and that green silk dress, after Maria Babbit cut it. Maria she cut it for nothin', and she did a lot more cuttin' and fittin' for nothin' for Luella, too. Lily Miller went to live with Luella after Erastus died. She gave up her home, though she was real attached to it and wa'n't a mite afraid to stay alone. She rented it and she went to live with Luella right away after the funeral."

Then this old woman, Lydia Anderson, who remembered Luella Miller, would go on to relate the story of Lily Miller. It seemed that on the removal of Lily Miller to the house of her dead brother, to live with his widow, the village people first began to talk. This Lily Miller had been hardly past her first youth, and a most robust and blooming woman, rosy-cheeked, with curls of strong, black hair overshadowing round, candid temples and bright dark eyes. It was not six months after she had taken up her residence with her sister-in-law that her rosy colour faded and her pretty curves became wan hollows. White shadows began to show in the black rings of her hair, and the light died out of her eyes, her features sharpened, and there were pathetic lines at her mouth, which yet wore always an expression of utter sweetness and even happiness. She was devoted to her sister; there was no doubt that she loved her with her whole heart, and was perfectly content in her service. It was her sole anxiety lest she should die and leave her alone.

"The way Lily Miller used to talk about Luella was enough to make you mad and enough to make you cry," said Lydia Anderson. "I've been in there sometimes toward the last when she was too feeble to cook and carried her some blanc-mange or custard—somethin' I thought she might relish, and she'd thank me, and when I asked her how she was, say she felt better than she did yesterday, and asked me if I didn't think she looked better, dreadful pitiful, and say poor Luella had an awful time takin' care of her and doin' the work—she wa'n't strong enough to do anythin'—when all the time Luella wa'n't liftin' her finger and poor Lily didn't get any care except what the neighbours gave her, and Luella eat up everythin' that was carried in for Lily. I had it real straight that she did. Luella used to just sit and cry and do nothin'. She did act real fond of Lily, and she pined away considerable, too. There was those that thought she'd go into a decline herself. But after Lily died, her Aunt Abby Mixter came, and then Luella picked up and grew as fat and rosy as ever. But poor Aunt Abby begun to droop just the way Lily had, and I guess somebody wrote to her married daughter, Mrs. Sam Abbot, who lived in Barre, for she wrote her mother that she must leave right away and come and make her a visit, but Aunt Abby wouldn't go. I can see her now. She was a real good-lookin' woman, tall and large, with a big, square face and a high forehead that looked of itself kind of benevolent and good. She just tended out on Luella as if she had been a baby, and when her married daughter sent for her she wouldn't stir one inch. She'd always thought a lot of her daughter, too, but she said Luella needed her and her married daughter didn't. Her daughter kept writin' and writin', but it didn't do any good. Finally she came, and when she saw how bad her mother looked, she broke down and cried and all but went on her knees to have her come away. She spoke her mind out to Luella, too. She told her that she'd killed her husband and everybody that had anythin' to do with her, and she'd thank her to leave her mother alone. Luella went into hysterics, and Aunt Abby was so frightened that she called me after her daughter went. Mrs. Sam Abbot she went away fairly cryin' out loud in the buggy, the neighbours heard her, and well she might, for she never saw her mother again alive. I went in that night when Aunt Abby called for me, standin' in the door with her little green-checked shawl over her head. I can see her now. 'Do come over here, Miss Anderson,' she sung out, kind of gasping for breath. I didn't stop for anythin'. I put over as fast as I could, and when I got there, there was Luella laughin' and cryin' all together, and Aunt Abby trying to hush her, and all the time she herself was white as a sheet and shakin' so she could hardly stand. 'For the land sakes, Mrs. Mixter,' says I, 'you look worse than she does. You ain't fit to be up out of your bed.'

" 'Oh, there ain't anythin' the matter with me,' says she. Then she went on talkin' to Luella. 'There, there, don't, don't, poor little lamb,' says she. 'Aunt Abby is here. She ain't goin' away and leave you. Don't, poor little lamb.'

" 'Do leave her with me, Mrs. Mixter, and you get back to bed,' says I, for Aunt Abby had been layin' down considerable lately, though somehow she contrived to do the work.

" 'I'm well enough,' says she. 'Don't you think she had better have the doctor, Miss Anderson?'

" 'The doctor,' says I, 'I think *you* had better have the doctor. I think you need him much worse than some folks I could mention.' And I looked right straight at Luella Miller laughin' and cryin' and goin' on as if she was the centre of all creation. All the time she was actin' so—seemed as if she was too sick to sense anythin'—she was keepin' a sharp lookout as to how we took it out of the corner of one eye. I see her. You could never cheat me about Luella Miller. Finally I got real mad and I run home and I got a bottle of valerian I had, and I poured some boilin' hot water on a handful of catnip, and I mixed up that catnip tea with most half a wineglass of valerian, and I went with it over to Luella's. I marched right up to Luella, a-holdin' out of that cup, all smokin'. 'Now,' says I, 'Luella Miller, *'you swaller this!'*

" 'What is—what is it, oh, what is it?' she sort of screeches out. Then she goes off a-laughin' enough to kill.

" 'Poor lamb, poor little lamb,' says Aunt Abby, standin' over her, all kind of tottery, and tryin' to bathe her head with camphor.

" '*You swaller this right down,*' says I. And I didn't waste any ceremony. I just took hold of Luella Miller's chin and I tipped her head back, and I caught her mouth open with laughin', and I clapped that cup to her lips, and I fairly hollered at her: 'Swaller, swaller, swaller!' and she gulped it right down. She had to, and I guess it did her good. Anyhow, she stopped cryin' and laughin' and let me put her to bed, and she went to sleep like a baby inside of half an hour. That was more than poor Aunt Abby did. She lay awake all that night and I stayed with her, though she tried not to have me; said she wa'n't sick enough for watchers. But I stayed, and I made some good cornmeal gruel and I fed her a teaspoon every little while all night long. It seemed to me as if she was jest dyin' from bein' all wore out. In the mornin' as soon as it was light I run over to the Bisbees and sent Johnny Bisbee for the doctor. I told him to tell the doctor to hurry, and he come pretty quick. Poor Aunt Abby didn't seem to know much of anythin' when he got there. You couldn't hardly tell she breathed, she was so used up. When the doctor had gone, Luella came into the room lookin' like a baby in her ruffled nightgown. I can see her now. Her eyes were as blue and her face all pink and white like a blossom, and she looked at Aunt Abby in the bed sort of innocent and surprised. 'Why,' says she, 'Aunt Abby ain't got up yet?'

" 'No, she ain't,' says I, pretty short.

" 'I thought I didn't smell the coffee,' says Luella.

" 'Coffee,' says I. 'I guess if you have coffee this mornin' you'll make it yourself.'

" 'I never made the coffee in all my life,' says she, dreadful astonished. 'Erastus always made the coffee as long as he lived, and then Lily she made it, and then Aunt Abby made it. I don't believe I *can* make the coffee, Miss Anderson.'

" 'You can make it or go without, jest as you please,' says I.

" 'Ain't Aunt Abby goin' to get up?' says she.

" 'I guess she won't get up,' says I, 'sick as she is.' I was gettin' madder and madder. There was somethin' about that little pink-and-white thing standin' there and talkin' about coffee, when she had killed so many better folks than she was, and had jest killed another, that made me feel 'most as if I wished somebody would up and kill her before she had a chance to do any more harm.

" 'Is Aunt Abby sick?' says Luella, as if she was sort of aggrieved and injured.

" 'Yes,' says I, 'she's sick, and she's goin' to die, and then you'll be left alone, and you'll have to do for yourself and wait on yourself, or do without things.' I don't know but I was sort of hard, but it was the truth, and if I was any harder than Luella Miller had been I'll give up. I ain't never been sorry that I said it. Well, Luella, she up and had hysterics again at that, and I jest let her have 'em. All I did was to bundle her into the room on the other side of the entry where Aunt Abby couldn't hear her, if she wa'n't past it—I don't know but she was—and set her down hard in a chair and told her not to come back into the other room, and she minded. She had her hysterics in there till she got tired. When she found out that nobody was comin' to coddle her and do for her she stopped. At least I suppose she did. I had all I could do with poor Aunt Abby tryin' to keep the breath of life in her. The doctor had told me that she was dreadful low, and give me some very strong medicine to give to her in drops real often, and told me real particular about the nourishment. Well, I did as he told me real faithful till she wa'n't able to swaller any longer. Then I had her daughter sent for. I had begun to realize that she wouldn't last any time at all. I hadn't realized it before, though I spoke to Luella the way I did. The doctor he came, and Mrs. Sam Abbot, but when she got there it was too late; her mother was dead. Aunt Abby's daughter just give one look at her mother layin' there, then she turned sort of sharp and sudden and looked at me.

" 'Where is she?' says she, and I knew she meant Luella.

" 'She's out in the kitchen,' says I. 'She's too nervous to see folks die. She's afraid it will make her sick.'

"The Doctor he speaks up then. He was a young man. Old Doctor Park had died the year before, and this was a young fellow just out of college. 'Mrs. Miller is not strong,' says he, kind of severe, 'and she is quite right in not agitating herself.'

" 'You are another, young man; she's got her pretty claw on you,' thinks I, but I didn't say anythin' to him. I just said over to Mrs. Sam Abbot that Luella was in the kitchen, and Mrs. Sam Abbot she went out there, and I went, too, and I never heard anythin' like the way she talked to Luella Miller. I felt pretty hard to Luella myself, but this was more than I ever would have dared to say. Luella she was too scared to go into hysterics. She jest flopped. She seemed to jest shrink away to nothin' in that kitchen chair, with Mrs. Sam Abbot standin' over her and talkin' and tellin' her the truth. I guess the truth was most too much for her and no mistake, because Luella presently actually did faint away, and there wa'n't any sham about it, the way I always suspected there was about them hysterics. She fainted dead away and we had to lay her flat on the floor, and the Doctor he came runnin' out and he said somethin' about a weak heart dreadful fierce to Mrs. Sam Abbot, but she wa'n't a mite scared. She faced him jest as white as even Luella was layin' there lookin' like death and the Doctor feelin' of her pulse.

" 'Weak heart,' says she, 'weak heart; weak fiddlesticks! There ain't nothin' weak about that woman. She's got strength enough to hang onto other folks till she kills 'em. Weak? It was my poor mother that was weak: this woman killed her as sure as if she had taken a knife to her.'

"But the Doctor he didn't pay much attention. He was bendin' over Luella layin' there with her yellow hair all streamin' and her pretty pink-and-white face all pale, and her blue eyes like stars gone out, and he was holdin' onto her hand and smoothin' her forehead, and tellin' me to get the brandy in Aunt Abby's room, and I was sure as I wanted to be that Luella had got somebody else to hang onto, now Aunt Abby was gone, and I thought of poor Erastus Miller, and I sort of pitied the poor young Doctor, led away by a pretty face, and I made up my mind I'd see what I could do.

"I waited till Aunt Abby had been dead and buried about a month, and the Doctor was goin' to see Luella steady and folks were beginnin' to talk; then one evenin', when I knew the Doctor had been called out of town and wouldn't be round, I went over to Luella's. I found her all dressed up in a blue muslin with white polka dots on it, and her hair curled jest as pretty, and there wa'n't a young girl in the place could compare with her. There was somethin' about Luella Miller seemed to draw the heart right out of you, but she didn't draw it out of *me.* She was settin' rocking in the chair by her sittin'-room window, and Maria Brown had gone home. Maria Brown had been in to help her, or rather to do the work, for Luella wa'n't helped when she didn't do anythin'. Maria Brown was real capable and she didn't have any ties; she wa'n't married, and lived alone, so she'd offered. I couldn't see why she should do the work any more than Luella; she wa'n't any too strong; but she seemed to think she could and Luella seemed to think so, too, so she went over and did all the work—washed, and ironed, and baked, while Luella sat and rocked. Maria didn't live long afterward. She began to fade away just the same fashion the others had. Well, she was warned, but she acted real mad when folks said anythin': said Luella was a poor, abused woman, too delicate to help herself, and they'd ought to be ashamed, and if she died helpin' them that couldn't help themselves she would—and she did.

" 'I s'pose Maria has gone home,' says I to Luella, when I had gone in and sat down opposite her.

" 'Yes, Maria went half an hour ago, after she had got supper and washed the dishes,' says Luella, in her pretty way.

" 'I suppose she has got a lot of work to do in her own house to-night,' says I, kind of bitter, but that was all thrown away on Luella Miller. It seemed to her right that other folks that wa'n't any better able than she was herself should wait on her, and she couldn't get it through her head that anybody should think it *wa'n't* right.

" 'Yes,' says Luella, real sweet and pretty, 'yes, she said she had to do her washin' to-night. She has let it go for a fortnight along of comin' over here.'

" 'Why don't she stay home and do her washin' instead of comin' over here and doin' *your* work, when you are just as well able, and enough sight more so, than she is to do it?' says I.

"Then Luella she looked at me like a baby who has a rattle shook at it. She sort of laughed as innocent as you please. 'Oh, I can't do the work myself, Miss Anderson,' says she. 'I never did. Maria *has* to do it.'

"Then I spoke out: 'Has to do it!' says I. 'Has to do it!' She don't have to do it, either. Maria Brown has her own home and enough to live on. She ain't beholden to you to come over here and slave for you and kill herself.'

"Luella she jest set and stared at me for all the world like a doll-baby that was so abused that it was comin' to life.

" 'Yes,' says I, 'she's killin' herself. She's goin' to die just the way Erastus did, and Lily, and your Aunt Abby. You're killin' her jest as you did them. I don't know what there is about you, but you seem to bring a curse,' says I. 'You kill everybody that is fool enough to care anythin' about you and do for you.'

"She stared at me and she was pretty pale.

" 'And Maria ain't the only one you're goin' to kill,' says I. 'You're goin' to kill Doctor Malcom before you're done with him.'

"Then a red colour came flamin' all over her face. 'I ain't goin' to kill him, either,' says she, and she begun to cry.

" 'Yes, you *be!*' says I. Then I spoke as I had never spoke before. You see, I felt it on account of Erastus. I told her that she hadn't any business to think of another man after she'd been married to one that had died for her: that she was a dreadful woman; and she was, that's true enough, but sometimes I have wondered lately if she knew it—if she wa'n't like a baby with scissors in its hand cuttin' everybody without knowin' what it was doin'.

"Luella she kept gettin' paler and paler, and she never took her eyes off my face. There was somethin' awful about the way she looked at me and never spoke one word. After awhile I quit talkin' and I went home. I watched that night, but her lamp went out before nine o'clock, and when Doctor Malcom came drivin' past and sort of slowed up he see there wa'n't any light and he drove along. I saw her sort of shy out of meetin' the next Sunday, too, so he shouldn't go home with her, and I begun to think mebbe she did have some conscience after all. It was only a week after that that Maria Brown died—sort of sudden at the last, though everybody had seen it was comin'. Well, then there was a good deal of feelin' and pretty dark whispers. Folks said the days of witchcraft had come again, and they were pretty shy of Luella. She acted sort of offish to the Doctor and he didn't go there, and there wa'n't anybody to do anythin' for her. I don't know how she *did* get along. I wouldn't go in there and offer to help her—not because I was afraid of dyin' like the rest, but I thought she was just as well able to do her own work as I was to do it for her, and I thought it was about time that she did it and stopped killin' other folks. But it wa'n't very long before folks began to say that Luella herself was goin' into a decline jest the way her husband, and Lily, and Aunt Abby and the others had, and I saw myself that she looked pretty bad. I used to see her goin' past from the store with a bundle as if she could hardly crawl, but I remembered how Erastus used to wait and 'tend when he couldn't hardly put one foot before the other, and I didn't go out to help her.

"But at last one afternoon I saw the Doctor come drivin' up like mad with his medicine chest, and Mrs. Babbit came in after supper and said that Luella was real sick.

" 'I'd offer to go in and nurse her,' says she, 'but I've got my children to consider, and mebbe it ain't true what they say, but it's queer how many folks that have done for her have died.'

"I didn't say anythin', but I considered how she had been Erastus's wife and how he had set his eyes by her, and I made up my mind to go in the next mornin', unless she was better, and see what I could do; but the next mornin' I see her at the window, and pretty soon she came steppin' out as spry as you please, and a little while afterward Mrs. Babbit came in and told me that the Doctor had got a girl from out of town, a Sarah Jones, to come there, and she said she was pretty sure that the Doctor was goin' to marry Luella.

"I saw him kiss her in the door that night myself, and I knew it was true. The woman came that afternoon, and the way she flew around was a caution. I don't believe Luella had swept since Maria died. She swept and dusted, and washed and ironed; wet clothes and dusters and carpets were flyin' over there all day, and every time Luella set her foot out when the Doctor wa'n't there there was that Sarah Jones helpin' of her up and down the steps, as if she hadn't learned to walk.

"Well, everybody knew that Luella and the Doctor were goin' to be married, but it wa'n't long before they began to talk about his lookin' so poorly, jest as they had about the others; and they talked about Sarah Jones, too.

"Well, the Doctor did die, and he wanted to be married first, so as to leave what little he had to Luella, but he died before the minister could get there, and Sarah Jones died a week afterward.

"Well, that wound up everything for Luella Miller. Not another soul in the whole town would lift a finger for her. There got to be a sort of panic. Then she began to droop in good earnest. She used to have to go to the store herself, for Mrs. Babbit was afraid to let Tommy go for her, and I've seen her goin' past and stoppin' every two or three steps to rest. Well, I stood it as long as I could, but one day I see her comin' with her arms full and stoppin' to lean against the Babbit fence, and I run out and took her bundles and carried them to her house. Then I went home and never spoke one word to her though she called after me dreadful kind of pitiful. Well, that night I was taken sick with a chill, and I was sick as I wanted to be for two weeks. Mrs. Babbit had seen me run out to help Luella and she came in and told me I was goin' to die on account of it. I didn't know whether I was or not, but I considered I had done right by Erastus's wife.

"That last two weeks Luella she had a dreadful hard time, I guess. She was pretty sick, and as near as I could make out nobody dared go near her. I don't know as she was really needin' anythin' very much, for there was enough to eat in her house and it was warm weather, and she made out to cook a little flour gruel every day, I know, but I guess she had a hard time, she that had been so petted and done for all her life.

"When I got so I could go out, I went over there one morning. Mrs. Babbit had just come in to say she hadn't seen any smoke and she didn't know but it was somebody's duty to go in, but she couldn't help thinkin' of her children, and I got right up, though I hadn't been out of the house for two weeks, and I went in there, and Luella she was layin' on the bed, and she was dyin'.

"She lasted all that day and into the night. But I sat there after the new doctor had gone away. Nobody else dared to go there. It was about midnight that I left her for a minute to run home and get some medicine I had been takin', for I begun to feel rather bad.

"It was a full moon that night, and just as I started out of my door to cross the street back to Luella's, I stopped short, for I saw something."

Lydia Anderson at this juncture always said with a certain defiance that she did not expect to be believed, and then proceeded in a hushed voice:

"I saw what I saw, and I know I saw it, and I will swear on my death bed that I saw it. I saw Luella Miller and Erastus Miller, and Lily, and Aunt Abby, and Maria, and the Doctor, and Sarah, all goin' out of her door, and all but Luella shone white in the moonlight, and they were all helpin' her along till she seemed to fairly fly in the midst of them. Then it all disappeared. I stood a minute with my heart poundin', then I went over there. I thought of goin' for Mrs. Babbit, but I thought she'd be afraid. So I went alone, though I knew what had happened. Luella was layin' real peaceful, dead on her bed."

This was the story that the old woman, Lydia Anderson, told, but the sequel was told by the people who survived her, and this is the tale which has become folklore in the village.

Lydia Anderson died when she was eighty-seven. She had continued wonderfully hale and hearty for one of her years until about two weeks before her death.

One bright moonlight evening she was sitting beside a window in her parlour when she made a sudden exclamation, and was out of the house and across the street before the neighbour who was taking care of her could stop her. She followed as fast as possible and found Lydia Anderson stretched on the ground before the door of Luella Miller's deserted house, and she was quite dead.

The next night there was a red gleam of fire athwart the moonlight and the old house of Luella Miller was burned to the ground. Nothing is now left of it except a few old cellar stones and a lilac bush, and in summer a helpless trail of morning glories among the weeds, which might be considered emblematic of Luella herself.

CHARLOTTE PERKINS STETSON [GILMAN]

The Yellow Wallpaper

It is very seldom that mere ordinary people like John and myself secure ancestral halls for the summer.

A colonial mansion, a hereditary estate, I would say a haunted house, and reach the height of romantic felicity—but that would be asking too much of fate!

Still I will proudly declare that there is something queer about it.

Else, why should it be let so cheaply? And why have stood so long untenanted?

John laughs at me, of course, but one expects that in marriage.

John is practical in the extreme. He has no patience with faith, an intense horror of superstition, and he scoffs openly at any talk of things not to be felt and seen and put down in figures.

John is a physician, and *perhaps*—(I would not say it to a living soul, of course, but this is dead paper and a great relief to my mind—)*perhaps* that is one reason I do not get well faster.

You see he does not believe I am sick!

And what can one do?

If a physician of high standing, and one's own husband, assures friends and relatives that there is really nothing the matter with one but temporary nervous depression—a slight hysterical tendency—what is one to do?

My brother is also a physician, and also of high standing, and he says the same thing.

So I take phosphates or phosphites—whichever it is, and tonics, and journeys, and air, and exercise, and am absolutely forbidden to "work" until I am well again.

Personally, I disagree with their ideas.

Personally, I believe that congenial work, with excitement and change, would do me good.

But what is one to do?

I did write for a while in spite of them; but it *does* exhaust me a good deal—having to be so sly about it, or else meet with heavy opposition.

I sometimes fancy that in my condition if I had less opposition and more society and stimulus—but John says the very worst thing I can do is to think about my condition, and I confess it always makes me feel bad.

So I will let it alone and talk about the house.

The most beautiful place! It is quite alone, standing well back from the road, quite three miles from the village. It makes me think of English places that you read about, for there are hedges and walls and gates that lock, and lots of separate little houses for the gardeners and people.

There is a *delicious* garden! I never saw such a garden—large and shady, full of box-bordered paths, and lined with long grape-covered arbors with seats under them.

There were greenhouses, too, but they are all broken now.

There was some legal trouble, I believe, something about the heirs and co-heirs; anyhow, the place has been empty for years.

That spoils my ghostliness, I am afraid, but I don't care—there is something strange about the house—I can feel it.

I even said so to John one moonlight evening, but he said what I felt was a *draught,* and shut the window.

I get unreasonably angry with John sometimes. I'm sure I never used to be so sensitive. I think it is due to this nervous condition.

But John says if I feel so, I shall neglect proper self-control; so I take pains to control myself—before him, at least, and that makes me very tired.

I don't like our room a bit. I wanted one downstairs that opened on the piazza and had roses all over the window, and such pretty old-fashioned chintz hangings! but John would not hear of it.

He said there was only one window and not room for two beds, and no near room for him if he took another.

He is very careful and loving, and hardly lets me stir without special direction.

I have a schedule prescription for each hour in the day; he takes all care from me, and so I feel basely ungrateful not to value it more.

He said we came here solely on my account, that I was to have perfect rest and all the air I could get. "Your exercise depends on your strength, my dear," said he, "and your food somewhat on your appetite; but air you can absorb all the time." So we took the nursery at the top of the house.

It is a big, airy room, the whole floor nearly, with windows that look all ways, and air and sunshine galore. It was nursery first and then playroom and gymnasium, I should judge; for the windows are barred for little children, and there are rings and things in the walls.

The paint and paper look as if a boys' school had used it. It is stripped off—the paper—in great patches all around the head of my bed, about as far as I can reach, and in a great place on the other side of the room low down. I never saw a worse paper in my life. One of those sprawling, flamboyant patterns committing every artistic sin.

It is dull enough to confuse the eye in following, pronounced enough constantly to irritate and provoke study, and when you follow the lame uncertain curves for a little distance they suddenly commit suicide—plunge off at outrageous angles, destroy themselves in unheard-of contradictions.

The color is repellent, almost revolting; a smouldering unclean yellow, strangely faded by the slow-turning sunlight.

It is a dull yet lurid orange in some places, a sickly sulphur tint in others.

No wonder the children hated it! I should hate it myself if I had to live in this room long.

There comes John, and I must put this away,—he hates to have me write a word.

We have been here two weeks, and I haven't felt like writing before, since that first day.

I am sitting by the window now, up in this atrocious nursery, and there is nothing to hinder my writing as much as I please, save lack of strength.

John is away all day, and even some nights when his cases are serious.

I am glad my case is not serious!

But these nervous troubles are dreadfully depressing.

John does not know how much I really suffer. He knows there is no reason to suffer, and that satisfies him.

Of course it is only nervousness. It does weigh on me so not to do my duty in any way!

I meant to be such a help to John, such a real rest and comfort, and here I am a comparative burden already!

Nobody would believe what an effort it is to do what little I am able,—to dress and entertain, and order things.

It is fortunate Mary is so good with the baby. Such a dear baby!

And yet I *cannot* be with him, it makes me so nervous.

I suppose John never was nervous in his life. He laughs at me so about this wallpaper!

At first he meant to repaper the room, but afterward he said that I was letting it get the better of me, and that nothing was worse for a nervous patient than to give way to such fancies.

He said that after the wallpaper was changed it would be the heavy bedstead, and then the barred windows, and then that gate at the head of the stairs, and so on.

"You know the place is doing you good," he said, "and really, dear, I don't care to renovate the house just for a three months' rental."

"Then do let us go downstairs," I said. "There are such pretty rooms there."

Then he took me in his arms and called me a blessed little goose, and said he would go down cellar, if I wished, and have it whitewashed into the bargain.

But he is right enough about the beds and windows and things.

It is an airy and comfortable a room as anyone need wish, and, of course, I would not be so silly as to make him uncomfortable just for a whim.

I'm really getting quite fond of the big room, all but that horrid paper.

Out of one window I can see the garden, those mysterious deep-shaded arbors, the riotous old-fashioned flowers, and bushes and gnarly trees.

Out of another I get a lovely view of the bay and a little private wharf belonging to the estate. There is a beautiful shaded lane that runs down there from the house. I always fancy I see people walking in these numerous paths and arbors, but John has cautioned me not to give way to fancy in the least. He says that with my imaginative power and habit of story-making, a nervous weakness like mine is sure to lead to all manner of excited fancies, and that I ought to use my will and good sense to check the tendency. So I try.

I think sometimes that if I were only well enough to write a little it would relieve the press of ideas and rest me.

But I find I get pretty tired when I try.

It is so discouraging not to have any advice and companionship about my work. When I get really well, John says we will ask Cousin Henry and Julia down for a long visit; but he says he would as soon put fireworks in my pillow-case as to let me have those stimulating people about now.

I wish I could get well faster.

But I must not think about that. This paper looks to me as if it *knew* what a vicious influence it had!

There is a recurrent spot where the pattern lolls like a broken neck and two bulbous eyes stare at you upside down.

I get positively angry with the impertinence of it and the everlastingness. Up and down and sideways they crawl, and those absurd, unblinking eyes are everywhere. There is one place where two breadths didn't match, and the eyes go all up and down the line, one a little higher than the other.

I never saw so much expression in an inanimate thing before, and we all know how much expression they have! I used to lie awake as a child and get more entertainment and terror out of blank walls and plain furniture than most children could find in a toy-store.

I remember what a kindly wink the knobs of our big, old bureau used to have, and there was one chair that always seemed like a strong friend.

I used to feel that if any of the other things looked too fierce I could always hop into that chair and be safe.

The furniture in this room is no worse than inharmonious, however, for we had to bring it all from downstairs. I suppose when this was used as a playroom they had to take the nursery things out, and no wonder! I never saw such ravages as the children have made here.

The wallpaper, as I said before, is torn off in spots, and it sticketh closer than a brother—they must have had perseverance as well as hatred.

Then the floor is scratched and gouged and splintered, the plaster itself is dug out here and there, and this great heavy bed which is all we found in the room, looks as if it had been through the wars.

But I don't mind it a bit—only the paper.

There comes John's sister. Such a dear girl as she is, and so careful of me! I must not let her find me writing.

She is a perfect and enthusiastic housekeeper, and hopes for no better profession. I verily believe she thinks it is the writing which made me sick!

But I can write when she is out, and see her a long way off from these windows.

There is one that commands the road, a lovely shaded winding road, and one that just looks off over the country. A lovely country, too, full of great elms and velvet meadows.

This wallpaper has a kind of sub-pattern in a different shade, a particularly irritating one, for you can only see it in certain lights, and not clearly then.

But in the places where it isn't faded and where the sun is just so—I can see a strange, provoking, formless sort of figure that seems to skulk about behind that silly and conspicuous front design.

There's sister on the stairs!

Well, the Fourth of July is over! The people are all gone, and I am tired out. John thought it might do me good to see a little company, so we just had mother and Nellie and the children down for a week.

Of course I didn't do a thing. Jennie sees to everything now.

But it tired me all the same.

John says if I don't pick up faster he shall send me to Weir Mitchell in the fall.

But I don't want to go there at all. I had a friend who was in his hands once, and she says he is just like John and my brother, only more so!

Besides, it is such an undertaking to go so far.

I don't feel as if it was worth while to turn my hand over for anything, and I'm getting dreadfully fretful and querulous.

I cry at nothing, and cry most of the time.

Of course I don't when John is here, or anybody else, but when I am alone.

And I am alone a good deal just now. John is kept in town very often by serious cases, and Jennie is good and lets me alone when I want her to.

So I walk a little in the garden or down that lovely lane, sit on the porch under the roses, and lie down up here a good deal.

I'm getting really fond of the room in spite of the wallpaper. Perhaps *because* of the wallpaper.

It dwells in my mind so!

I lie here on this great immovable bed—it is nailed down, I believe—and follow that pattern about by the hour. It is as good as gymnastics, I assure you. I start, we'll say, at the bottom, down in the corner over there where it has not been touched, and I determine for the thousandth time that I *will* follow that pointless pattern to some sort of a conclusion.

I know a little of the principle of design, and I know this thing was not arranged on any laws of radiation, or alternation, or repetition, or symmetry, or anything else that I ever heard of.

It is repeated, of course, by the breadths, but not otherwise.

Looked at in one way each breadth stands alone, the bloated curves and flourishes—a kind of "debased Romanesque" with *delirium tremens*—go waddling up and down in isolated columns of fatuity.

But, on the other hand, they connect diagonally, and the sprawling outlines run off in great slanting waves of optic horror, like a lot of wallowing seaweeds in full chase.

The whole thing goes horizontally, too, at least it seems so, and I exhaust myself in trying to distinguish the order of its going in that direction.

They have used a horizontal breadth for a frieze, and that adds wonderfully to the confusion.

There is one end of the room where it is almost intact, and there, when the crosslights fade and the low sun shines directly upon it, I can almost fancy radiation after all,—the interminable grotesque seems to form around a common center and rush off in headlong plunges of equal distraction.

It makes me tired to follow it. I will take a nap I guess.

I don't know why I should write this.

I don't want to.

I don't feel able.

And I know John would think it absurd. But I *must* say what I feel and think in some way—it is such a relief!

But the effort is getting to be greater than the relief.

Half the time now I am awfully lazy, and lie down ever so much.

John says I mustn't lose my strength, and has me take cod liver oil and lots of tonics and things, to say nothing of ale and wine and rare meat.

Dear John! He loves me very dearly, and hates to have me sick. I tried to have a real earnest reasonable talk with him the other day, and tell him how I wish he would let me go and make a visit to Cousin Henry and Julia.

But he said I wasn't able to go, nor able to stand it after I got there; and I did not make out a very good case for myself, for I was crying before I had finished.

It is getting to be a great effort for me to think straight. Just this nervous weakness I suppose.

And dear John gathered me up in his arms, and just carried me upstairs and laid me on the bed, and sat by me and read to me till it tired my head.

He said I was his darling and his comfort and all he had, and that I must take care of myself for his sake, and keep well.

He says no one but myself can help me out of it, that I must use my will and self-control and not let any silly fancies run away with me.

There's one comfort, the baby is well and happy, and does not have to occupy this nursery with the horrid wallpaper.

If we had not used it, that blessed child would have! What a fortunate escape! Why, I wouldn't have a child of mine, an impressionable little thing, live in such a room for worlds.

I never thought of it before, but it is lucky that John kept me here after all, I can stand it so much easier than a baby, you see.

Of course I never mention it to them any more—I am too wise,—but I keep watch of it all the same.

There are things in that wallpaper that nobody knows about but me, or ever will.

Behind that outside pattern the dim shapes get clearer every day.

It is always the same shape, only very numerous.

And it is like a woman stooping down and creeping about behind that pattern. I don't like it a bit. I wonder—I begin to think—I wish John would take me away from here!

It is so hard to talk with John about my case, because he is so wise, and because he loves me so.

But I tried it last night.

It was moonlight. The moon shines in all around just as the sun does.

I hate to see it sometimes, it creeps so slowly, and always comes in by one window or another.

John was asleep and I hated to waken him, so I kept still and watched the moonlight on that undulating wallpaper till I felt creepy.

The faint figure behind seemed to shake the pattern, just as if she wanted to get out.

I got up softly and went to feel and see if the paper *did* move, and when I came back John was awake.

"What is it, little girl?" he said. "Don't go walking about like that—you'll get cold."

I thought it was a good time to talk, so I told him that I really was not gaining here, and that I wished he would take me away.

"Why, darling!" said he, "our lease will be up in three weeks, and I can't see how to leave before.

"The repairs are not done at home, and I cannot possibly leave town just now. Of course if you were in any danger, I could and would, but you really are better, dear, whether you can see it or not. I am a doctor, dear, and I know. You are gaining flesh and color, your appetite is better, I feel really much easier about you."

"I don't weigh a bit more," said I, "nor as much; and my appetite may be better in the evening when you are here, but it is worse in the morning when you are away!"

"Bless her little heart!" said he with a big hug, "she shall be as sick as she pleases! But now let's improve the shining hours by going to sleep, and talk about it in the morning!"

"And you won't go away?" I asked gloomily.

"Why, how can I, dear? It is only three weeks more and then we will take a nice little trip of a few days while Jennie is getting the house ready. Really dear you are better!"

"Better in body perhaps—" I began, and stopped short, for he sat up straight and looked at me with such a stern, reproachful look that I could not say another word.

"My darling," said he, "I beg of you, for my sake and for our child's sake, as well as for your own, that you will never for one instant let that idea enter your mind! There is nothing so dangerous, so fascinating, to a temperament like yours. It is a false and foolish fancy. Can you not trust me as a physician when I tell you so?"

So of course I said no more on that score, and we went to sleep before long. He thought I was asleep first, but I wasn't, and lay there for hours trying to decide whether that front pattern and the back pattern really did move together or separately.

On a pattern like this, by daylight, there is a lack of sequence, a defiance of law, that is a constant irritant to a normal mind.

The color is hideous enough, and unreliable enough, and infuriating enough, but the pattern is torturing.

You think you have mastered it, but just as you get well under way in following, it turns a back-somersault and there you are. It slaps you in the face, knocks you down, and tramples upon you. It is like a bad dream.

The outside pattern is a florid arabesque, reminding one of a fungus. If you can imagine a toadstool in joints, an interminable string of toadstools, budding and sprouting in endless convolutions—why, that is something like it.

That is, sometimes!

There is one marked peculiarity about this paper, a thing nobody seems to notice but myself, and that is that it changes as the light changes.

When the sun shoots in through the east window—I always watch for that first long, straight ray—it changes so quickly that I never can quite believe it.

That is why I watch it always.

By moonlight—the moon shines in all night when there is a moon—I wouldn't know it was the same paper.

At night in any kind of light, in twilight, candlelight, lamplight, and worst of all by moonlight, it becomes bars! The outside pattern, I mean, and the woman behind it is as plain as can be.

I didn't realize for a long time what the thing was that showed behind, that dim sub-pattern, but now I am quite sure it is a woman.

By daylight she is subdued, quiet. I fancy it is the pattern that keeps her so still. It is so puzzling. It keeps me quiet by the hour.

I lie down ever so much now. John says it is good for me, and to sleep all I can.

Indeed he started the habit by making me lie down for an hour after each meal.

It is a very bad habit I am convinced, for you see I don't sleep.

And that cultivates deceit, for I don't tell them I'm awake—O no!

The fact is I am getting a little afraid of John.

He seems very queer sometimes, and even Jennie has an inexplicable look.

It strikes me occasionally, just as a scientific hypothesis,—that perhaps it is the paper!

I have watched John when he did not know I was looking, and come into the room suddenly on the most innocent excuses, and I've caught him several times *looking at the paper!* And Jennie too. I caught Jennie with her hand on it once.

She didn't know I was in the room, and when I asked her in a quiet, a very quiet voice, with the most restrained manner possible, what she was doing with the paper—she turned around as if she had been caught stealing, and looked quite angry—asked me why I should frighten her so!

Then she said that the paper stained everything it touched, that she had found yellow smooches on all my clothes and John's, and she wished we would be more careful!

Did not that sound innocent? But I know she was studying that pattern, and I am determined that nobody shall find it out but myself!

Life is very much more exciting now than it used to be. You see I have something more to expect, to look forward to, to watch. I really do eat better, and am more quiet than I was.

John is so pleased to see me improve! He laughed a little the other day, and said I seemed to be flourishing in spite of my wallpaper.

I turned it off with a laugh. I had no intention of telling him it was *because* of the wallpaper—he would make fun of me. He might even want to take me away.

I don't want to leave now until I have found it out. There is a week more, and I think that will be enough.

I'm feeling so much better!

I don't sleep much at night, for it is so interesting to watch developments; but I sleep a good deal in the daytime.

In the daytime it is tiresome and perplexing.

There are always new shoots on the fungus, and new shades of yellow all over it. I cannot keep count of them, though I have tried conscientiously.

It is the strangest yellow, that wallpaper! It makes me think of all the yellow things I ever saw—not beautiful ones like buttercups, but old foul, bad yellow things.

But there is something else about that paper—the smell! I noticed it the moment we came into the room, but with so much air and sun it was not bad. Now we have had a week of fog and rain, and whether the windows are open or not, the smell is here.

It creeps all over the house.

I find it hovering in the dining-room, skulking in the parlor, hiding in the hall, lying in wait for me on the stairs.

It gets into my hair.

Even when I go to ride, if I turn my head suddenly and surprise it—there is that smell!

Such a peculiar odor, too! I have spent hours in trying to analyze it, to find what it smelled like.

It is not bad—at first, and very gentle, but quite the subtlest, most enduring odor I ever met.

In this damp weather it is awful, I wake up in the night and find it hanging over me.

It used to disturb me at first. I thought seriously of burning the house—to reach the smell.

But now I am used to it. The only thing I can think of that it is like is the *color* of the paper! A yellow smell.

There is a very funny mark on this wall, low down, near the mopboard. A streak that runs around the room. It goes behind every piece of furniture, except the bed, a long, straight, even *smooch,* as if it had been rubbed over and over.

I wonder how it was done and who did it, and what they did it for. Round and round and round—round and round and round—it makes me dizzy!

I really have discovered something at last.

Through watching so much at night, when it changes so, I have finally found out.

The front pattern *does* move—and no wonder! The woman behind shakes it!

Sometimes I think there are a great many women behind, and sometimes only one, and she crawls around fast, and her crawling shakes it all over.

Then in the very bright spots she keeps still, and in the very shady spots she just takes hold of the bars and shakes them hard.

And she is all the time trying to climb through. But nobody could climb through that pattern—it strangles so; I think that is why it has so many heads.

They get through, and then the pattern strangles them off and turns them upside down, and makes their eyes white!

If those heads were covered or taken off it would not be half so bad.

* * *

I think that woman gets out in the daytime!

And I'll tell you why—privately—I've seen her!

I can see her out of every one of my windows!

It is the same woman, I know, for she is always creeping, and most women do not creep by daylight.

I see her in that long shaded lane, creeping up and down. I see her in those dark grape arbors, creeping all around the garden.

I see her on that long road under the trees, creeping along, and when a carriage comes she hides under the blackberry vines.

I don't blame her a bit. It must be very humiliating to be caught creeping by daylight!

I always lock the door when I creep by daylight. I can't do it at night, for I know John would suspect something at once.

And John is so queer now, that I don't want to irritate him. I wish he would take another room! Besides, I don't want anybody to get that woman out at night but myself.

I often wonder if I could see her out of all the windows at once.

But, turn as fast as I can, I can only see out of one at one time.

And though I always see her, she *may* be able to creep faster than I can turn!

I have watched her sometimes away off in the open country, creeping as fast as a cloud shadow in a wind.

If only that top pattern could be gotten off from the under one! I mean to try it, little by little.

I have found out another funny thing, but I shan't tell it this time! It does not do to trust people too much.

There are only two more days to get this paper off, and I believe John is beginning to notice. I don't like the look in his eyes.

And I heard him ask Jennie a lot of professional questions about me. She had a very good report to give.

She said I slept a good deal in the daytime.

John knows I don't sleep very well at night, for all I'm so quiet!

He asked me all sorts of questions, too, and pretended to be very loving and kind.

As if I couldn't see through him!

Still, I don't wonder he acts so, sleeping under this paper for three months.

It only interests me, but I feel sure John and Jennie are secretly affected by it.

Hurrah! This is the last day, but it is enough. John is to stay in town over night, and won't be out until this evening.

Jennie wanted to sleep with me—the sly thing! but I told her I should undoubtedly rest better for a night all alone.

That was clever, for really I wasn't alone a bit! As soon as it was moonlight and that poor thing began to crawl and shake the pattern, I got up and ran to help her.

I pulled and she shook, I shook and she pulled, and before morning we had peeled off yards of that paper.

A strip about as high as my head and half around the room.

And then when the sun came and that awful pattern began to laugh at me, I declared I would finish it to-day!

We go away to-morrow, and they are moving all my furniture down again to leave things as they were before.

Jennie looked at the wall in amazement, but I told her merrily that I did it out of pure spite at the vicious thing.

She laughed and said she wouldn't mind doing it herself, but I must not get tired.

How she betrayed herself that time!

But I am here, and no person touches this paper but me,—not *alive!*

She tried to get me out of the room—it was too patent! But I said it was so quiet and empty and clean now that I believed I would lie down again and sleep all I could, and not to wake me even for dinner—I would call when I woke.

So now she is gone, and the servants are gone, and the things are gone, and there is nothing left but that great bedstead nailed down, with the canvas mattress we found on it.

We shall sleep downstairs to-night, and take the boat home to-morrow.

I quite enjoy the room, now it is bare again.

How those children did tear about here!

This bedstead is fairly gnawed!

But I must get to work.

I have locked the door and thrown the key down into the front path.

I don't want to go out, and I don't want to have anybody come in, till John comes.

I want to astonish him.

I've got a rope up here that even Jennie did not find. If that woman does get out, and tries to get away, I can tie her!

But I forgot I could not reach far without anything to stand on!

This bed will *not* move!

I tried to lift and push it until I was lame, and then I got so angry I bit off a little piece at one corner—but it hurt my teeth.

Then I peeled off all the paper I could reach standing on the floor. It sticks horribly and the pattern just enjoys it! All those strangled heads and bulbous eyes and waddling fungus growths just shriek with derision!

I am getting angry enough to do something desperate. To jump out of the window would be admirable exercise, but the bars are too strong even to try.

Besides I wouldn't do it. Of course not. I know well enough that a step like that is improper and might be misconstrued.

I don't like to *look* out of the windows even—there are so many of those creeping women, and they creep so fast.

I wonder if they all come out of that wallpaper as I did?

But I am securely fastened now by my well-hidden rope—you don't get *me* out in the road there!

I suppose I shall have to get back behind the pattern when it comes night, and that is hard!

It is so pleasant to be out in this great room and creep around as I please!

I don't want to go outside. I won't, even if Jennie asks me to.

For outside you have to creep on the ground, and everything is green instead of yellow.

But here I can creep smoothly on the floor, and my shoulder just fits in that long smooch around the wall, so I cannot lose my way.

Why there's John at the door!

It is no use, young man, you can't open it!

How he does call and pound!

Now he's crying for an axe.

It would be a shame to break down that beautiful door!

"John dear!" said I in the gentlest voice, "the key is down by the front steps, under a plantain leaf!"

That silenced him for a few moments.

Then he said—very quietly indeed, "Open the door, my darling!"

"I can't," said I. "The key is down by the front door under a plantain leaf!"

And then I said it again, several times, very gently and slowly, and said it so often that he had to go and see, and he got it of course, and came in. He stopped short by the door.

"What is the matter?" he cried. "For God's sake, what are you doing!"

I kept on creeping just the same, but I looked at him over my shoulder.

"I've got out at last," said I, "in spite of you and Jane? And I've pulled off most of the paper, so you can't put me back!"

Now why should that man have fainted? But he did, and right across my path by the wall, so that I had to creep over him every time!

O. HENRY

Mammon and the Archer

Old Anthony Rockwall, retired manufacturer and proprietor of Rockwall's Eureka Soap, looked out the library window of his Fifth Avenue mansion and grinned. His neighbour to the right—the aristocratic clubman, G. Van Schuylight Suffolk-Jones—came out to his waiting motor-car, wrinkling a contumelious nostril, as usual, at the Italian renaissance sculpture of the soap palace's front elevation.

"Stuck-up old statuette of nothing doing!" commented the ex-Soap King. "The Eden Musée'll get that old frozen Nesselrode yet if he don't watch out. I'll have this house painted red, white, and blue next summer and see if that'll make his Dutch nose turn up any higher."

And then Anthony Rockwall, who never cared for bells, went to the door of his library and shouted "Mike!" in the same voice that had once chipped off pieces of the welkin on the Kansas prairies.

"Tell my son," said Anthony to the answering menial, "to come in here before he leaves the house."

When young Rockwell entered the library the old man laid aside his newspaper, looked at him with a kindly grimness on his big, smooth, ruddy countenance, rumpled his mop of white hair with one hand and rattled the keys in his pocket with the other.

"Richard," said Anthony Rockwall, "what do you pay for the soap that you use?"

Richard, only six months home from college, was startled a little. He had not yet taken the measure of this sire of his, who was as full of unexpectedness as a girl at her first party.

"Six dollars a dozen, I think, dad."

"And your clothes?"

"I suppose about sixty dollars, as a rule."

"You're a gentleman," said Anthony, decidedly. "I've heard of these young bloods spending $24 a dozen for soap, and going over the hundred mark for clothes. You've got as much money to waste as any of 'em, and yet you stick to what's decent and moderate. Now I use the old Eureka—

not only for sentiment, but it's the purest soap made. Whenever you pay more than 10 cents a cake for soap you buy bad perfumes and labels. But 50 cents is doing very well for a young man in your generation, position and condition. As I said, you're a gentleman. They say it takes three generations to make one. They're off. Money'll do it as slick as soap grease. It's made you one. By hokey! it's almost made one of me. I'm nearly as impolite and disagreeable and ill-mannered as these two old knickerbocker gents on each side of me that can't sleep of nights because I bought in between 'em."

"There are some things that money can't accomplish," remarked young Rockwall, rather gloomily.

"Now, don't say that," said old Anthony, shocked. "I bet my money on money every time. I've been through the encyclopædia down to Y looking for something you can't buy with it; and I expect to have to take up the appendix next week. I'm for money against the field. Tell me something money won't buy."

"For one thing," answered Richard, rankling a little, "it won't buy one into the exclusive circles of society."

"Oho! won't it?" thundered the champion of the root of evil. "You tell me where your exclusive circles would be if the first Astor hadn't had the money to pay for his steerage passage over?"

Richard sighed.

"And that's what I was coming to," said the old man, less boisterously. "That's why I asked you to come in. There's something going wrong with you, boy. I've been noticing it for two weeks. Out with it. I guess I could lay my hands on eleven millions within twenty-four hours, besides the real estate. If it's your liver, there's the *Rambler* down in the bay, coaled, and ready to steam down to the Bahamas in two days."

"Not a bad guess, dad; you haven't missed it far."

"Ah," said Anthony, keenly; "what's her name?"

Richard began to walk up and down the library floor. There was enough comradeship and sympathy in this crude old father of his to draw his confidence.

"Why don't you ask her?" demanded old Anthony. "She'll jump at you. You've got the money and the looks, and you're a decent boy. Your hands are clean. You've got no Eureka soap on 'em. You've been to college, but she'll overlook that."

"I haven't had a chance," said Richard.

"Make one," said Anthony. "Take her for a walk in the park, or a straw ride, or walk home with her from church. Chance! Pshaw!"

"You don't know the social mill, dad. She's part of the stream that turns it. Every hour and minute of her time is arranged for days in advance. I must have that girl, dad, or this town is a blackjack swamp forevermore. And I can't write it—I can't do that."

"Tut!" said the old man. "Do you mean to tell me that with all the money I've got you can't get an hour or two of a girl's time for yourself?"

"I've put it off too late. She's going to sail for Europe at noon day after to-morrow for a two years' stay. I'm to see her alone tomorrow evening for a few minutes. She's at Larchmont now at her aunt's. I can't go there. But I'm allowed to meet her with a cab at the Grand Central Station to-morrow evening at the 8.30 train. We drive down Broadway to Wallack's at a gallop, where her mother and a box party will be waiting for us in the lobby. Do you think she would listen to a declaration from me during that six or eight minutes under those circumstances? No. And what chance would I have in the theatre or afterward? None. No, dad, this is one tangle that your money can't unravel. We can't buy one minute of time with cash; if we could, rich people would live longer. There's no hope of getting a talk with Miss Lantry before she sails."

"All right, Richard, my boy," said old Anthony, cheerfully. "You may run along down to your club now. I'm glad it ain't your liver. But don't forget to burn a few punk sticks in the joss house to the great god Mazuma from time to time. You say money won't buy time? Well, of course, you can't order eternity wrapped up and delivered at your residence for a price, but I've seen Father Time get pretty bad stone bruises on his heels when he walked through the gold diggings."

That night came Aunt Ellen, gentle, sentimental, wrinkled, sighing, oppressed by wealth, in to Brother Anthony at his evening paper, and began discourse on the subject of lovers' woes.

"He told me all about it," said Brother Anthony, yawning. "I told him my bank account was at his service. And then he began to knock money. Said money couldn't help. Said the rules of society couldn't be bucked for a yard by a team of ten-millionaires."

"Oh, Anthony," sighed Aunt Ellen, "I wish you would not think so much of money. Wealth is nothing where a true affection is concerned. Love is all-powerful. If he only had spoken earlier! She could not have refused our Richard. But now I fear it is too late. He will have no opportunity to address her. All your gold cannot bring happiness to your son."

At eight o'clock the next evening Aunt Ellen took a quaint old gold ring from a moth-eaten case and gave it to Richard.

"Wear it to-night, nephew," she begged. "Your mother gave it to me. Good luck in love she said it brought. She asked me to give it to you when you had found the one you loved."

Young Rockwall took the ring reverently and tried it on his smallest finger. It slipped as far as the second joint and stopped. He took it off and stuffed it into his vest pocket, after the manner of man. And then he 'phoned for his cab.

At the station he captured Miss Lantry out of the gabbing mob at eight thirty-two.

"We mustn't keep mamma and the others waiting," said she.

"To Wallack's Theatre as fast as you can drive!" said Richard, loyally.

They whirled up Forty-second to Broadway, and then down the white-starred lane that leads from the soft meadows of sunset to the rocky hills of morning.

At Thirty-fourth Street young Richard quickly thrust up the trap and ordered the cabman to stop.

"I've dropped a ring," he apologized, as he climbed out. "It was my mother's, and I'd hate to lose it. I won't detain you a minute—I saw where it fell."

In less than a minute he was back in the cab with the ring.

But within that minute a crosstown car had stopped directly in front of the cab. The cab-man tried to pass to the left, but a heavy express wagon cut him off. He tried the right and had to back away from a furniture van that had no business to be there. He tried to back out, but dropped his reins and swore dutifully. He was blockaded in a tangled mess of vehicles and horses.

One of those street blockades had occurred that sometimes tie up commerce and movement quite suddenly in the big city.

"Why don't you drive on?" said Miss Lantry impatiently. "We'll be late."

Richard stood up in the cab and looked around. He saw a congested flood of wagons, trucks, cabs, vans and street cars filling the vast space where Broadway, Sixth Avenue, and Thirty-fourth Street cross one another as a twenty-six inch maiden fills her twenty-two inch girdle. And still from all the cross streets they were hurrying and rattling toward the converging point at full speed, and hurling themselves into the straggling mass, locking wheels and adding their drivers' imprecations to the clamor. The entire traffic of Manhattan seemed to have jammed itself around them. The oldest New Yorker among the thousands of spectators that lined the sidewalks had not witnessed a street blockade of the proportions of this one.

"I'm very sorry," said Richard, as he resumed his seat, "but it looks as if we are stuck. They won't get this jumble loosened up in an hour. It was my fault. If I hadn't dropped the ring we—"

"Let me see the ring," said Miss Lantry. "Now that it can't be helped,

I don't care. I think theatres are stupid, anyway."

At 11 o'clock that night somebody tapped lightly on Anthony Rockwall's door.

"Come in," shouted Anthony, who was in a red dressing-gown, reading a book of piratical adventures.

Somebody was Aunt Ellen, looking like a gray-haired angel that had been left on earth by mistake.

"They're engaged, Anthony," she said, softly. "She has promised to marry our Richard. On their way to the theatre there was a street blockade, and it was two hours before their cab could get out of it.

"And oh, Brother Anthony, don't ever boast of the power of money again. A little emblem of true love—a little ring that symbolized unending and unmercenary affection—was the cause of our Richard finding his happiness. He dropped it in the street, and got out to recover it. And before they could continue the blockade occurred. He spoke to his love and won her there while the cab was hemmed in. Money is dross compared with true love, Anthony."

"All right," said old Anthony. "I'm glad the boy has got what he wanted. I told him I wouldn't spare any expense in the matter if—"

"But, Brother Anthony, what good could your money have done?"

"Sister," said Anthony Rockwall. "I've got my pirate in a devil of a scrape. His ship has just been scuttled, and he's too good a judge of the value of money to let drown. I wish you would let me go on with this chapter."

The story should end here. I wish it would as heartily as you who read it wish it did. But we must go to the bottom of the well for truth.

The next day a person with red hands and a blue polka-dot necktie, who called himself Kelly, called at Anthony Rockwall's house, and was at once received in the library.

"Well," said Anthony, reaching for his check-book, "it was a good bilin' of soap. Let's see—you had $5,000 in cash."

"I paid out $300 more of my own," said Kelly. "I had to go a little above the estimate. I got the express wagons and cabs mostly for $5; but the trucks and two-horse teams mostly raised me to $10. The motormen wanted $10, and some of the loaded teams $20. The cops struck me hardest—$50 I paid two, and the rest $20 and $25. But didn't it work beautiful. Mr. Rockwall? I'm glad William A. Brady wasn't onto that little outdoor vehicle mob scene. I wouldn't want William to break his heart with jealousy. And never a rehearsal, either! The boys was on time to the fraction of a second. It was two hours before a snake could get below Greeley's statue."

"Thirteen hundred—there you are, Kelly," said Anthony, tearing off a check. "Your thousand, and the $300 you were out. You don't despise money, do you, Kelly?"

"Me?" said Kelly. "I can lick the man that invented poverty."

Anthony called Kelly when he was at the door.

"You didn't notice," said he, "anywhere in the tie-up, a kind of a fat boy without any clothes on shooting arrows around with a bow, did you?"

"Why, no," said Kelly, mystified. "I didn't. If he was like you say, maybe the cops pinched him before I got there."

"I thought the little rascal wouldn't be on hand," chuckled Anthony. "Good-by, Kelly."

EDITH WHARTON

Pomegranate Seed

Charlotte Ashby paused on her doorstep. Dark had descended on the brilliancy of the March afternoon, and the grinding rasping street life of the city was at its highest. She turned her back on it, standing for a moment in the old-fashioned, marble-flagged vestibule before she inserted her key in the lock. The sash curtains drawn across the panes of the inner door softened the light within to a warm blur through which no details showed. It was the hour when, in the first months of her marriage to Kenneth Ashby, she had most liked to return to that quiet house in a street long since deserted by business and fashion. The contrast between the soulless roar of New York, its devouring blaze of lights, the oppression of its congested traffic, congested houses, lives, minds and this veiled sanctuary she called home, always stirred her profoundly. In the very heart of the hurricane she had found her tiny islet—or thought she had. And now, in the last months, everything was changed, and she always wavered on the doorstep and had to force herself to enter.

While she stood there she called up the scene within: the hall hung with old prints, the ladder-like stairs, and on the left her husband's long shabby library, full of books and pipes and worn armchairs inviting to meditation. How she had loved that room! Then, upstairs, her own drawing room, in which, since the death of Kenneth's first wife, neither furniture nor hangings had been changed, because there had never been money enough, but which Charlotte had made her own by moving furniture about and adding more books, another lamp, a table for the new reviews. Even on the occasion of her only visit to the first Mrs. Ashby—a distant, self-centered woman, whom she had known very slightly—she had looked about her with an innocent envy, feeling it to be exactly the drawing room she would have liked for herself; and now for more than a year it had been hers to deal with as she chose—the room to which she hastened back at dusk on winter days, where she sat reading by the fire, or answering notes at the pleasant roomy desk, or going over her step-children's copybooks, till she heard her husband's step.

Sometimes friends dropped in; sometimes—oftener—she was alone; and she liked that best, since it was another way of being with Kenneth, thinking over what he had said when they parted in the morning, imagining what he would say when he sprang up the stairs, found her by herself and caught her to him.

Now, instead of this, she thought of one thing only—the letter she might or might not find on the hall table. Until she had made sure whether or not it was there, her mind had no room for anything else. The letter was always the same—a square grayish envelope with "Kenneth Ashby, Esquire," written on it in bold but faint characters. From the first it had struck Charlotte as peculiar that anyone who wrote such a firm hand should trace the letters so lightly; the address was always written as though there were not enough ink in the pen, or the writer's wrist were too weak to bear upon it. Another curious thing was that, in spite of its masculine curves, the writing was so visibly feminine. Some hands are sexless, some masculine, at first glance; the writing on the gray envelope, for all its strength and assurance, was without doubt a woman's. The envelope never bore anything but the recipient's name; no stamp, no address. The letter was presumably delivered by hand—but by whose? No doubt it was slipped into the letter box, whence the parlormaid, when she closed the shutters and lit the lights, probably extracted it. At any rate, it was always in the evening, after dark, that Charlotte saw it lying there. She thought of the letter in the singular, as "it," because, though there had been several since her marriage—seven, to be exact—they were so alike in appearance that they had become merged in one another in her mind, become one letter, become "it."

The first had come the day after their return from their honeymoon—

a journey prolonged to the West Indies, from which they had returned to New York after an absence of more than two months. Reentering the house with her husband, late on the first evening—they had dined at his mother's—she had seen, alone on the hall table, the gray envelope. Her eye fell on it before Kenneth's, and her first thought was: "Why, I've seen that writing before"; but where she could not recall. The memory was just definite enough for her to identify the script whenever it looked up at her faintly from the same pale envelope; but on that first day she would have thought no more of the letter if, when her husband's glance lit on it, she had not chanced to be looking at him. It all happened in a flash—his seeing the letter, putting out his hand for it, raising it to his shortsighted eyes to decipher the faint writing, and then abruptly withdrawing the arm he had slipped through Charlotte's, and moving away to the hanging light, his back turned to her. She had waited—waited for a sound, an exclamation; waited for him to open the letter; but he had slipped it into his pocket without a word and followed her into the library. And there they had sat down by the fire and lit their cigarettes, and he had remained silent, his head thrown back broodingly against the armchair, his eyes fixed on the hearth, and presently had passed his hand over his forehead and said: "Wasn't it unusually hot at my mother's tonight? I've got a splitting head. Mind if I take myself off to bed?"

That was the first time. Since then Charlotte had never been present when he had received the letter. It usually came before he got home from his office, and she had to go upstairs and leave it lying there. But even if she had not seen it, she would have known it had come by the change in his face when he joined her—which, on those evenings, he seldom did before they met for dinner. Evidently, whatever the letter contained, he wanted to be by himself to deal with it; and when he reappeared he looked years older, looked emptied of life and courage, and hardly conscious of her presence. Sometimes he was silent for the rest of the evening; and if he spoke, it was usually to hint some criticism of her household arrangements, suggest some change in the domestic administration, to ask, a little nervously, if she didn't think Joyce's nursery governess was rather young and flighty, or if she herself always saw to it that Peter—whose throat was delicate—was properly wrapped up when he went to school. At such times Charlotte would remember the friendly warnings she had received when she became engaged to Kenneth Ashby: "Marrying a heartbroken widower! Isn't that rather risky? You know Elsie Ashby absolutely dominated him"; and how she had jokingly replied: "He may be glad of a little liberty for a change." And in this respect she had been right. She had needed no one to tell her, during the first months, that her husband was perfectly happy with her. When they came back from their protracted honeymoon the same friends said: "What have you done to Kenneth? He looks twenty years younger"; and this time she answered with careless joy: "I suppose I've got him out of his groove."

But what she noticed after the gray letters began to come was not so much his nervous tentative faultfinding—which always seemed to be uttered against his will—as the look in his eyes when he joined her after receiving one of the letters. The look was not unloving, not even indifferent; it was the look of a man who had been so far away from ordinary events that when he returns to familiar things they seem strange. She minded that more than the faultfinding.

Though she had been sure from the first that the handwriting on the gray envelope was a woman's, it was long before she associated the mysterious letters with any sentimental secret. She was too sure of her husband's love, too confident of filling his life, for such an idea to occur to her. It seemed far more likely that the letters—which certainly did not appear to cause him any sentimental pleasure—were addressed to the busy lawyer than to the private person. Probably they were from some tiresome client—women, he had often told her, were nearly always tiresome as clients—who did not want her letters opened by his secretary and therefore had them carried to his house. Yes; but in that case the unknown female must be unusually troublesome, judging from the effect her letters produced. Then again, though his professional discretion was exemplary, it was odd that he had never uttered an impatient comment, never remarked to Charlotte, in a moment of expansion, that there was a nuisance of a woman who kept badgering him about a case that had gone against her. He had made more than one semiconfidence of the kind—of course without giving names or details; but concerning this mysterious correspondent his lips were sealed.

There was another possibility: what is euphemistically called an "old entanglement." Charlotte Ashby was a sophisticated woman. She had few illusions about the intricacies of the human heart; she knew that there were often old entanglements. But when she had married Kenneth Ashby, her friends, instead of hinting at such a possibility, had said: "You've got your work cut out for you. Marrying a Don Juan is a sinecure to it. Kenneth's never looked at another woman since he first saw Elsie Corder. During all the years of their marriage he was more like an unhappy lover than a comfortably contented husband. He'll never let you move an armchair or change the place of a lamp; and whatever you venture to do, he'll mentally compare with what Elsie would have done in your place."

Except for an occasional nervous mistrust as to her ability to manage the children—a mistrust gradually dispelled by her good humor and the children's obvious fondness for her—none of these forebodings had come true. The desolate widower, of whom his nearest friends said that only his absorbing professional interests had kept him from suicide after his first wife's death, had fallen in love, two years later, with Charlotte Gorse, and after an impetuous wooing had married her and carried her off on a tropical honeymoon. And ever since he had been as tender and lover-like as during those first radiant weeks. Before asking her to marry him he had spoken to her frankly of his great love for his first wife and his despair after her sudden death; but even then he had assumed no stricken attitude, or implied that life offered no possibility of renewal. He had been perfectly simple and natural, and had confessed to Charlotte that from the beginning he had hoped the future held new gifts for him. And when, after their marriage, they returned to the house where his twelve years with his first wife had been spent, he had told Charlotte at once that he was sorry he couldn't afford to do the place over for her, but that he knew every woman had her own views about furniture and all sorts of household arrangements a man would never notice, and had begged her to make any changes she saw fit without bothering to consult him. As a result, she made as few as possible; but his way of beginning their new life in the old setting was so frank and unembarrassed that it put her immediately at her ease, and she was almost sorry to find that the portrait of Elsie Ashby, which used to hang over the desk in his library, had been transferred in their absence to the children's nursery. Knowing herself to be the indirect cause of this banishment, she spoke of it to her husband; but he answered: "Oh, I thought they ought to grow up with her looking down on them." The answer moved Charlotte, and satisfied her; and as the time went by she had to confess that she felt more at home in her house, more at ease and in confidence with her husband, since that long coldly beautiful face on the library wall no longer followed her with guarded eyes. It was as if Kenneth's love had penetrated to the secret she hardly acknowledged to her own heart—her passionate need to feel herself the sovereign even of his past.

With all this stored-up happiness to sustain her, it was curious that she had lately found herself yielding to a nervous apprehension. But there the apprehension was; and on this particular afternoon—perhaps because she was more tired than usual, or because of the trouble of finding a new cook or, for some other ridiculously trivial reason, moral or physical—she found herself unable to react against the feeling. Latch-key in hand, she looked back down the silent street to the whirl and illumination of the great thoroughfare beyond, and up at the sky already aflare with the city's nocturnal life. "Outside there," she thought, "skyscrapers, advertizements, telephones, wireless, airplanes, movies, motors, and all the rest of the twentieth century; and on the other side of the door something I can't explain, can't relate to them. Something as old as the world, as mysterious as life. . . . Nonsense! What am I worrying about? There hasn't been a letter for three months now—not since the day we came back from the country after Christmas. . . . Queer that they always seem to come after our holidays! . . . Why should I imagine there's going to be one tonight!"

No reason why, but that was the worst of it—one of the worst!—that there were days when she would stand there cold and shivering with the premonition of something inexplicable, intolerable, to be faced on the other side of the curtained panes; and when she opened the door and went in, there would be nothing; and on other days when she felt the same premonitory chill, it was justified by the sight of the gray envelope. So that ever since the last had come she had taken to feeling cold and premonitory every evening, because she never opened the door without thinking the letter might be there.

Well, she'd had enough of it: that was certain. She couldn't go on like that. If her husband turned white and had a headache on the days when the letter came, he seemed to recover afterward; but she couldn't. With her the strain had become chronic, and the reason was not far to seek. Her husband knew from whom the letter came and what was in it; he was prepared beforehand for whatever he had to deal with, and master of the situation, however bad; whereas she was shut out in the dark with her conjectures.

"I can't stand it! I can't stand it another day!" she exclaimed aloud, as she put her key in the lock. She turned the key and went in; and there, on the table, lay the letter.

II

She was almost glad of the sight. It seemed to justify everything, to put a seal of definiteness on the whole blurred business. A letter for her husband: a letter from a woman—no doubt another vulgar case of "old entanglement." What a fool she had been ever to doubt it, to rack her brains for less obvious explanations! She took up the envelope with a steady contemptuous hand, looked closely at the faint letters, held it against the light and just discerned the outline of the folded sheet within. She knew that now she would have no peace till she found out what was written on that sheet.

Her husband had not come in; he seldom got back from his office before half-past six or seven, and it was not yet six. She would have time to take the letter up to the drawing room, hold it over the tea kettle which at that hour always simmered by the fire in expectation of her return, solve the mystery and replace the letter where she had found it. No one would be the wiser, and her gnawing uncertainty would be over. The alternative, of course, was to question her husband; but to do that seemed even more difficult. She weighed the letter between thumb and finger, looked at it again under the light, started up the stairs with the envelope—and came down again and laid it on the table.

"No, I evidently can't," she said, disappointed.

What should she do, then? She couldn't go up alone to that warm welcoming room, pour out her tea, look over her correspondence, glance at a book or review—not with that letter lying below and the knowledge that in a little while her husband would come in, open it and turn into the library alone, as he always did on the days when the gray envelope came.

Suddenly she decided. She would wait in the library and see for herself; see what happened between him and the letter when they thought themselves unobserved. She wondered the idea had never occurred to her before. By leaving the door ajar, and sitting in the corner behind it, she could watch him unseen . . . . Well, then, she would watch him! She drew a chair into the corner, sat down, her eyes on the crack, and waited.

As far as she could remember, it was the first time she had ever tried to surprise another person's secret, but she was conscious of no compunction. She simply felt as if she were fighting her way through a stifling fog that she must at all costs get out of.

At length she heard Kenneth's latchkey and jumped up. The impulse to rush out and meet him had nearly made her forget why she was there; but she remembered in time and sat down again. From her post she covered the whole range of his movements—saw him enter the hall, draw the key from the door and take off his hat and overcoat. Then he turned to throw his gloves on the hall table, and at that moment he saw the envelope. The light was full on his face, and what Charlotte first noted there was a look of surprise. Evidently he had not expected the letter—had not thought of the possibility of its being there that day. But though he had not expected it, now that he saw it he knew well enough what it contained. He did not open it immediately, but stood motionless, the color slowly ebbing from his face. Apparently he could not make up his mind to touch it; but at length he put out his hand, opened the envelope, and moved with it to the light. In doing so he turned his back on Charlotte, and she saw only his bent head and slightly stooping shoulders. Apparently all the writing was on one page, for he did not turn the sheet but continued to stare at it for so long that he must have reread it a dozen times—or so it seemed to the woman breathlessly watching him. At length she saw him move; he raised the letter still closer to his eyes, as though he had not fully deciphered it. Then he lowered his head, and she saw his lips touch the sheet.

"Kenneth!" she exclaimed, and went on out into the hall.

The letter clutched in his hand, her husband turned and looked at her. "Where were you?" he said, in a low bewildered voice, like a man waked out of his sleep.

"In the library, waiting for you." She tried to steady her voice: "What's the matter! What's in that letter? You look ghastly."

Her agitation seemed to calm him, and he instantly put the envelope into his pocket with a slight laugh. "Ghastly? I'm sorry. I've had a hard day in the office—one or two complicated cases. I look dog-tired, I suppose."

"You didn't look tired when you came in. It was only when you opened that letter—"

He had followed her into the library, and they stood gazing at each other. Charlotte noticed how quickly he had regained his self-control; his profession had trained him to rapid mastery of face and voice. She saw at once that she would be at a disadvantage in any attempt to surprise his secret, but at the same moment she lost all desire to maneuver, to trick him into betraying anything he wanted to conceal. Her wish was still to penetrate the mystery, but only that she might help him to bear the burden it implied. "Even if it *is* another woman," she thought.

"Kenneth," she said, her heart beating excitedly, "I waited here on purpose to see you come in. I wanted to watch you while you opened that letter."

His face, which had paled, turned to dark red; then it paled again. "That letter? Why especially that letter?"

"Because I've noticed that whenever one of those letters comes it seems to have such a strange effect on you."

A line of anger she had never seen before came out between his eyes, and she said to herself: "The upper part of his face is too narrow; this is the first time I ever noticed it."

She heard him continue, in the cool and faintly ironic tone of the prosecuting lawyer making a point: "Ah, so you're in the habit of watching people open their letters when they don't know you're there?"

"Not in the habit. I never did such a thing before. But I had to find out what she writes to you, at regular intervals, in those gray envelopes."

He weighed this for a moment; then: "The intervals have not been regular," he said.

"Oh, I dare say you've kept a better account of the dates than I have," she retorted, her magnanimity vanishing at his tone. "All I know is that every time that woman writes to you—"

"Why do you assume it's a woman?"

"It's a woman's writing. Do you deny it?"

He smiled. "No, I don't deny it. I asked only because the writing is generally supposed to look more like a man's."

Charlotte passed this over impatiently. "And this woman—what does she write to you about?"

Again he seemed to consider a moment. "About business."

"Legal business?"

"In a way, yes. Business in general."

"You look after her affairs for her?"

"Yes."

"You've looked after them for a long time?"

"Yes. A very long time."

"Kenneth, dearest, won't you tell me who she is?"

"No. I can't." He paused, and brought out, as if with a certain hesitation: "Professional secrecy."

The blood rushed from Charlotte's heart to her temples. "Don't say that—don't!"

"Why not?"

"Because I saw you kiss the letter."

The effect of the words was so disconcerting that she instantly repented having spoken them. Her husband, who had submitted to her cross-questioning with a sort of contemptuous composure, as though he were humoring an unreasonable child, turned on her a face of terror and distress. For a minute he seemed unable to speak; then, collecting himself, with an effort, he stammered out: "The writing is very faint; you must have seen me holding the letter close to my eyes to try to decipher it."

"No; I saw you kissing it." He was silent. "Didn't I see you kissing it?"

He sank back into indifference. "Perhaps."

"Kenneth! You stand there and say that—to me?"

"What possible difference can it make to you? The letter is on business, as I told you. Do you suppose I'd lie about it? The writer is a very old friend whom I haven't seen for a long time."

"Men don't kiss business letters, even from women who are very old friends, unless they have been their lovers, and still regret them."

He shrugged his shoulders slightly and turned away, as if he considered the discussion at an end and were faintly disgusted at the turn it had taken.

"Kenneth!" Charlotte moved toward him and caught hold of his arm.

He paused with a look of weariness and laid his hand over hers. "Won't you believe me?" he asked gently.

"How can I? I've watched these letters come to you—for months now they've been coming. Ever since we came back from the West Indies—one of them greeted me the very day we arrived. And after each one of them I see their mysterious effect on you, I see you disturbed, unhappy, as if someone were trying to estrange you from me."

"No, dear; not that. Never!"

She drew back and looked at him with passionate entreaty. "Well, then, prove it to me, darling. It's so easy!"

He forced a smile. "It's not easy to prove anything to a woman who's once taken an idea into her head."

"You've only got to show me the letter."

His hand slipped from hers and he drew back and shook his head.

"You won't?"

"I can't."

"Then the woman who wrote it is your mistress."

"No, dear. No."

"Not now, perhaps. I suppose she's trying to get you back, and you're struggling, out of pity for me. My poor Kenneth!"

"I swear to you she never was my mistress."

Charlotte felt the tears rushing to her eyes. "Ah, that's worse, then—that's hopeless! The prudent ones are the kind that keep their hold on a man. We all know that." She lifted her hands and hid her face in them.

Her husband remained silent; he offered neither consolation nor denial, and at length, wiping away her tears, she raised her eyes almost timidly to his.

"Kenneth, think! We've been married such a short time. Imagine what you're making me suffer. You say you can't show me this letter. You refuse even to explain it."

"I've told you the letter is on business. I will swear to that too."

"A man will swear to anything to screen a woman. If you want me to believe you, at least tell me her name. If you'll do that, I promise you I won't ask to see the letter."

There was a long interval of suspense, during which she felt her heart beating against her ribs in quick admonitory knocks, as if warning her of the danger she was incurring.

"I can't," he said at length.

"Not even her name?"

"No."

"You can't tell me anything more?"

"No."

Again a pause; this time they seemed both to have reached the end of their arguments and to be helplessly facing each other across a baffling waste of incomprehension.

Charlotte stood breathing rapidly, her hands against her breast. She felt as if she had run a hard race and missed the goal. She had meant to move her husband and had succeeded only in irritating him; and this error of reckoning seemed to change him into a stranger, a mysterious incomprehensible being whom no argument or entreaty of hers could reach. The curious thing was that she was aware in him of no hostility or even impatience, but only of a remoteness, an inaccessibility, far more difficult to overcome. She felt herself excluded, ignored, blotted out of his life. But after a moment or two, looking at him more calmly, she saw that he was suffering as much as she was. His distant guarded face was drawn with pain; the coming of the gray envelope, though it always cast a shadow, had never marked him as deeply as this discussion with his wife.

Charlotte took heart; perhaps, after all, she had not spent her last shaft. She drew nearer and once more laid her hand on his arm. "Poor Kenneth! If you knew how sorry I am for you—"

She thought he winced slightly at this expression of sympathy, but he took her hand and pressed it.

"I can think of nothing worse than to be incapable of loving long," she continued, "to feel the beauty of a great love and to be too unstable to bear its burden."

He turned on her a look of wistful reproach. "Oh, don't say that of me. Unstable!"

She felt herself at last on the right tack, and her voice trembled with excitement as she went on: "Then what about me and this other woman? Haven't you already forgotten Elsie twice within a year?"

She seldom pronounced his first wife's name; it did not come naturally to her tongue. She flung it out now as if she were flinging some dangerous explosive into the open space between them, and drew back a step, waiting to hear the mine go off.

Her husband did not move; his expression grew sadder, but showed no resentment. "I have never forgotten Elsie," he said.

Charlotte could not repress a faint laugh. "Then, you poor dear, between the three of us—"

"There are not—" he began; and then broke off and put his hand to his forehead.

"Not what?"

"I'm sorry; I don't believe I know what I'm saying. I've got a blinding headache." He looked wan and furrowed enough for the statement to be true, but she was exasperated by his evasion.

"Ah, yes; the gray envelope headache!"

She saw the surprise in his eyes. "I'd forgotten how closely I've been watched," he said coldly. "If you'll excuse me, I think I'll go up and try an hour in the dark, to see if I can get rid of this neuralgia."

She wavered; then she said, with desperate resolution: "I'm sorry your head aches. But before you go I want to say that sooner or later this question must be settled between us. Someone is trying to separate us, and I don't care what it costs me to find out who it is." She looked him steadily in the eyes. "If it costs me your love, I don't care! If I can't have your confidence I don't want anything from you."

He still looked at her wistfully. "Give me time."

"Time for what? It's only a word to say."

"Time to show you that you haven't lost my love or my confidence."

"Well, I'm waiting."

He turned toward the door, and then glanced back hesitatingly. "Oh, do wait, my love," he said, and went out of the room.

She heard his tired step on the stairs and the closing of his bedroom door above. Then she dropped into a chair and buried her face in her folded arms. Her first movement was one of compunction; she seemed to herself to have been hard, unhuman, unimaginative. "Think of telling him that I didn't care if my insistence cost me his love! The lying rubbish!" She started up to follow him and unsay the meaningless words. But she was checked by a reflection. He had had his way, after all; he had eluded all attacks on his secret, and now he was shut up alone in his room, reading that other woman's letter.

III

She was still reflecting on this when the surprised parlormaid came in and found her. No, Charlotte said, she wasn't going to dress for dinner; Mr. Ashby didn't want to dine. He was very tired and had gone up to his room to rest; later she would have something brought on a tray to the drawing room. She mounted the stairs to her bedroom. Her dinner dress was lying on the bed, and at the sight the quiet routine of her daily life took hold of her and she began to feel as if the strange talk she had just had with her husband must have taken place in another world, between two beings who were not Charlotte Gorse and Kenneth Ashby, but phantoms projected by her fevered imagination. She recalled the year since her marriage—her husband's constant devotion: his persistent, almost too insistent tenderness; the feeling he had given her at times of being too eagerly dependent on her, too searchingly close to her, as if there were not air enough between her soul and his. It seemed preposterous, as she recalled all this, that a few moments ago she should have been accusing him of an intrigue with another woman! But, then, what—

Again she was moved by the impulse to go up to him, beg his pardon and try to laugh away the misunderstanding. But she was restrained by the fear of forcing herself upon his privacy. He was troubled and unhappy, oppressed by some grief or fear; and he had shown her that he wanted to fight out his battle alone. It would be wiser, as well as more generous, to respect his wish. Only, how strange, how unbearable, to be there, in the next room to his, and feel herself at the other end of the world! In her nervous agitation she almost regretted not having had the courage to open the letter and put it back on the hall table before he came in. At least she would have known what his secret was, and the bogy might have been laid. For she was beginning now to think of the mystery as something conscious, malevolent: a secret persecution before which he quailed, yet from which he could not free himself. Once or twice in his evasive eyes she thought she had detected a desire for help, an impulse of confession, instantly restrained and suppressed. It was as if he felt she could have helped him if she had known, and yet had been unable to tell her!

There flashed through her mind the idea of going to his mother. She was very fond of old Mrs. Ashby, a firm-fleshed clear-eyed old lady, with an astringent bluntness of speech which responded to the forthright and simple in Charlotte's own nature. There had been a tacit bond between them ever since the day when Mrs. Ashby Senior, coming to lunch for the first time with her new daughter-in-law, had been received by Charlotte downstairs in the library, and glancing up at the empty wall above her son's desk, had remarked laconically: "Elsie gone, eh?" adding, at Charlotte's murmured explanation: "Nonsense. Don't have her back. Two's company." Charlotte, at this reading of her thoughts, could hardly refrain from exchanging a smile of complicity with her mother-in-law; and it seemed to her now that Mrs. Ashby's almost uncanny directness might pierce to the core of this new mystery. But here again she hesitated, for the idea almost suggested a betrayal. What right had she to call in anyone, even so close a relation, to surprise a secret which her husband was trying to keep from her? "Perhaps, by and by, he'll talk to his mother of his own accord," she thought, and then ended: "But what does it matter? He and I must settle it between us."

She was still brooding over the problem when there was a knock on the door and her husband came in. He was dressed for dinner and seemed surprised to see her sitting there, with her evening dress lying unheeded on the bed.

"Aren't you coming down?"

"I thought you were not well and had gone to bed," she faltered.

He forced a smile. "I'm not particularly well, but we'd better go down." His face, though still drawn, looked calmer than when he had fled upstairs an hour earlier.

"There it is; he knows what's in the letter and has fought his battle out again, whatever it is," she reflected, "while I'm still in darkness." She rang and gave a hurried order that dinner should be served as soon as possible—just a short meal, whatever could be got ready quickly, as both she and Mr. Ashby were rather tired and not very hungry.

Dinner was announced, and they sat down to it. At first neither seemed able to find a word to say; then Ashby began to make conversation with an assumption of ease that was more oppressive than his silence. "How tired he is! How terribly overtired!" Charlotte said to herself, pursuing her own thoughts while he rambled on about municipal politics, aviation, and an exhibition of modern French painting, the health of an old aunt and the installing of the automatic telephone. "Good heavens, how tired he is!"

When they dined alone they usually went into the library after dinner, and Charlotte curled herself up on the divan with her knitting while he settled down in his armchair under the lamp and lit a pipe. But this evening, by tacit agreement, they avoided the room in which their strange talk had taken place, and went up to Charlotte's drawing room.

They sat down near the fire, and Charlotte said: "Your pipe?" after he had put down his hardly tasted coffee.

He shook his head. "No, not tonight."

"You must go to bed early; you look terribly tired. I'm sure they overwork you at the office."

"I suppose we all overwork at times."

She rose and stood before him with sudden resolution. "Well, I'm not going to have you use up your strength slaving in that way. It's absurd. I can see you're ill." She bent over him and laid her hand on his forehead. "My poor old Kenneth. Prepare to be taken away soon on a long holiday."

He looked up at her startled. "A holiday?"

"Certainly. Didn't you know I was going to carry you off at Easter? We're going to start in a fortnight on a month's voyage to somewhere or other. On any one of the big cruising steamers." She paused and bent closer, touching his forehead with her lips. "I'm tired, too, Kenneth."

He seemed to pay no heed to her last words, but sat, his hands on his knees, his head drawn back a little from her caress, and looked up at her with a stare of apprehension. "Again? My dear, we can't; I can't possibly go away."

"I don't know why you say 'again,' Kenneth; we haven't taken a real holiday this year."

"At Christmas we spend a week with the children in the country."

"Yes, but this time I mean away from the children, from servants, from the house. From everything that's familiar and fatiguing. Your mother will love to have Joyce and Peter with her."

He frowned and slowly shook his head. "No, dear; I can't leave them with my mother."

"Why, Kenneth, how absurd! She adores them. You didn't hesitate to leave them with her for over two months when we went to the West Indies."

He drew a deep breath and stood up uneasily. "That was different."

"Different? Why?"

"I mean, at that time I didn't realize—" He broke off as if to choose his words and then went on: "My mother adores the children, as you say. But she isn't always very judicious. Grandmothers always spoil children. And sometimes she talks before them without thinking." He turned to his wife with an almost pitiful gesture of entreaty. "Don't ask me to, dear."

Charlotte mused. It was true that the elder Mrs. Ashby had a fearless tongue, but she was the last woman in the world to say or hint anything before her grandchildren at which the most scrupulous parent could take offense. Charlotte looked at her husband in perplexity.

"I don't understand."

He continued to turn on her the same troubled and entreating gaze. "Don't try to," he muttered.

"Not try to?"

"Not now—not yet." He put up his hands and pressed them against his temples. "Can't you see that there's no use in insisting? I can't go away, no matter how much I might want to."

Charlotte still scrutinized him gravely. "The question is, *do* you want to?"

He returned her gaze for a moment; then his lips began to tremble, and he said, hardly above his breath: "I want—anything you want."

"And yet—"

"Don't ask me. I can't leave—I can't."

"You mean that you can't go away out of reach of those letters!"

Her husband had been standing before her in an uneasy half-hesitating attitude; now he turned abruptly away and walked once or twice up and down the length of the room, his head bent, his eyes fixed on the carpet.

Charlotte felt her resentfulness rising with her fears. "It's that," she persisted. "Why not admit it? You can't live without them."

He continued his troubled pacing of the room; then he stopped short, dropped into a chair and covered his face with his hands. From the shaking of his shoulders, Charlotte saw that he was weeping. She had never seen a man cry, except her father after her mother's death, when she was a little girl; and she remembered still how the sight had frightened her. She was frightened now; she felt that her husband was being dragged away from her into some mysterious bondage, and that she must use up her last atom of strength in the struggle for his freedom, and for hers.

"Kenneth—Kenneth!" she pleaded, kneeling down beside him. "Won't you listen to me? Won't you try to see what I'm suffering? I'm not unreasonable, darling, really not. I don't suppose I should ever have noticed the letters if it hadn't been for their effect on you. It's not my way to pry into other people's affairs; and even if the effect had been different—yes, yes, listen to me—if I'd seen that the letters made you happy, that you were watching eagerly for them, counting the days between their coming, that you wanted them, that they gave you something I haven't known how to give—why, Kenneth, I don't say I shouldn't have suffered from that, too; but it would have been in a different way, and I should have had the courage to hide what I felt, and the hope that someday you'd come to feel about me as you did about the writer of the letters. But what I can't bear is to see how you dread them, how they make you suffer, and yet how you can't live without them and won't go away lest you should miss one during your absence. Or perhaps," she added, her voice breaking into a cry of accusation—"perhaps it's because she's actually forbidden you to leave. Kenneth, you must answer me! Is that the reason? Is it because she's forbidden you that you won't go away with me?"

She continued to kneel at his side, and raising her hands, she drew his gently down. She was ashamed of her persistence, ashamed of uncovering that baffled disordered face, yet resolved that no such scruples should arrest her. His eyes were lowered, the muscles of his face quivered; she was making him suffer even more than she suffered herself. Yet this no longer restrained her.

"Kenneth, is it that? She won't let us go away together?"

Still he did not speak or turn his eyes to her, and a sense of defeat swept over her. After all, she thought, the struggle was a losing one. "You needn't answer. I see I'm right," she said.

Suddenly, as she rose, he turned and drew her down again. His hands caught hers and pressed them so tightly that she felt her rings cutting into her flesh. There was something frightening, convulsive in his hold; it was the clutch of a man who felt himself slipping over a precipice. He was staring up at her now as if salvation lay in the face she bent above him. "Of course we'll go away together. We'll go wherever you want," he said in a low confused voice; and putting his arm about her, he drew her close and pressed his lips on hers.

IV

Charlotte had said to herself: "I shall sleep tonight," but instead she sat before her fire into the small hours, listening for any sound that came from her husband's room. But he, at any rate, seemed to be resting after the tumult of the evening. Once or twice she stole to the door and in the faint light that came in from the street through his open window she saw him stretched out in heavy sleep—the sleep of weakness and exhaustion. "He's ill," she thought—"he's undoubtedly ill. And it's not overwork; it's this mysterious persecution."

She drew a breath of relief. She had fought through the weary fight and the victory was hers—at least for the moment. If only they could have started at once—started for anywhere! She knew it would be useless to ask him to leave before the holidays; and meanwhile the secret influence—as to which she was still so completely in the dark—would continue to work against her, and she would have to renew the struggle day after day till they started on their journey. But after that everything would be different. If once she could get her husband away under other skies, and all to herself, she never doubted her power to release him from the evil spell he was under. Lulled to quiet by the thought, she too slept at last.

When she woke, if was long past her usual hour, and she sat up in bed surprised and vexed at having overslept herself. She always liked to be down to share her husband's breakfast by the library fire; but a glance at the clock made it clear that he must have started long since for his office. To make sure, she jumped out of bed and went into his room, but it was empty. No doubt he had looked in on her before leaving, seen that she still slept, and gone downstairs without disturbing her; and their relations were sufficiently lover-like for her to regret having missed their morning hour.

She rang and asked if Mr. Ashby had already gone. Yes, nearly an hour ago, the maid said. He had given orders that Mrs. Ashby should not be waked and that the children should not come to her till she sent for them. . . . Yes, he had gone up to the nursery himself to give the order. All this sounded usual enough, and Charlotte hardly knew why she asked: "And did Mr. Ashby leave no other message?"

Yes, the maid said, he did; she was so sorry she'd forgotten. He'd told her, just as he was leaving, to say to Mrs. Ashby that he was going to see about their passages, and would she please be ready to sail tomorrow?

Charlotte echoed the woman's "Tomorrow," and sat staring at her incredulously. "Tomorrow—you're sure he said to sail tomorrow?"

"Oh, ever so sure, ma'am. I don't know how I could have forgotten to mention it."

"Well, it doesn't matter. Draw my bath, please." Charlotte sprang up, dashed through her dressing, and caught herself singing at her image in the glass as she sat brushing her hair. It made her feel young again to have scored such a victory. The other woman vanished to a speck on the horizon, as this one, who ruled the foreground, smiled back at the reflection of her lips and eyes. He loved her, then—he loved her as passionately as ever. He had divined what she had suffered, had understood that their happiness depended on their getting away at once, and finding each other again after yesterday's desperate groping in the fog. The nature of the influence that had come between them did not much matter to Charlotte now; she had faced the phantom and dispelled it. "Courage—that's the secret! If only people who are in love weren't always so afraid of risking their happiness by looking it in the eyes." As she brushed back her light abundant hair it waved electrically above her head, like the palms of victory. Ah, well, some women knew how to manage men, and some didn't—and only the fair—she gaily paraphrased—deserve the brave! Certainly she was looking very pretty.

The morning danced along like a cockleshell on a bright sea—such a sea as they would soon be speeding over. She ordered a particularly good dinner, saw the children off to their classes, had her trunks brought down, consulted with the maid about getting out summer clothes—for of course they would be heading for heat and sunshine—and wondered if she oughtn't to take Kenneth's flannel suits out of camphor. "But how absurd," she reflected, "that I don't yet know where we're going!" She looked at the clock, saw that it was close on noon and decided to call him up at his office. There was a slight delay; then she heard his secretary's voice saying that Mr. Ashby had looked in for a moment early, and left again almost immediately. . . . Oh, very well; Charlotte would ring up later. How soon was he likely to be back? The secretary answered that she couldn't tell; all they knew in the office was that when he left he had said he was in a hurry because he had to go out of town.

Out of town! Charlotte hung up the receiver and sat blankly gazing into new darkness. Why had he gone out of town? And where had he gone? And of all days, why should he have chosen the eve of their suddenly planned departure? She felt a faint shiver of apprehension. Of course he had gone to see that woman—no doubt to get her permission to leave. He was as completely in bondage as that; and Charlotte had been fatuous enough to see the palms of victory on her forehead. She burst into a laugh and, walking across the room, sat down again before her mirror. What a different face she saw! The smile on her pale lips seemed to mock the rosy vision of the other Charlotte. But gradually her color crept back. After all, she had a right to claim the victory, since her husband was doing what she wanted, not what the other woman exacted of him. It was natural enough, in view of his abrupt decision to leave the next day, that he should have arrangements to make, business matters to wind up; it was not even necessary to suppose that his mysterious trip was a visit to the writer of the letters. He might simply have gone to see a client who lived out of town. Of course they would not tell Charlotte at the office; the secretary had hesitated before imparting even such meager information as the fact of Mr. Ashby's absence. Meanwhile she would go on with her joyful preparations, content to learn later in the day to what particular island of the blest she was to be carried.

The hours wore on, or rather were swept forward on a rush of eager preparations. At last the entrance of the maid who came to draw the curtain roused Charlotte from her labors, and she saw to her surprise that the clock marked five. And she did not yet know where they were going the next day! She rang up her husband's office and was told that Mr. Ashby had not been there since the early morning. She asked for his partner, but the partner could add nothing to her information, for he himself, his suburban train having been behind time, had reached the office after Ashby had come and gone. Charlotte stood perplexed; then she decided to telephone to her mother-in-law. Of course Kenneth, on the eve of a month's absence, must have gone to see his mother. The mere fact that the children—in spite of his vague objections—would certainly have to be left with old Mrs. Ashby, made it obvious that he would have all sorts of matters to decide with her. At another time

Charlotte might have felt a little hurt at being excluded from their conference, but nothing mattered now but that she had won the day, that her husband was still hers and not another woman's. Gaily she called up Mrs. Ashby, heard her friendly voice, and began: "Well, did Kenneth's news surprise you? What do you think of our elopement?"

Almost instantly, before Mrs. Ashby could answer, Charlotte knew what her reply would be. Mrs. Ashby had not seen her son, she had had no word from him and did not know what her daughter-in-law meant. Charlotte stood silent in the intensity of her surprise. "But then, where *has* he been?" she thought. Then, recovering herself, she explained their sudden decision to Mrs. Ashby, and in doing so, gradually regained her own self-confidence, her conviction that nothing could ever again come between Kenneth and herself. Mrs. Ashby took the news calmly and approvingly. She, too, had thought that Kenneth looked worried and overtired, and she agreed with her daughter-in-law that in such cases change was the surest remedy. "I'm always so glad when he gets away. Elsie hated traveling; she was always finding pretexts to prevent his going anywhere. With you, thank goodness, it's different." Nor was Mrs. Ashby surprised at his not having had time to let her know of his departure. He must have been in a rush from the moment the decision was taken; but no doubt he'd drop in before dinner. Five minutes' talk was really all they needed. "I hope you'll gradually cure Kenneth of his mania for going over and over a question that could be settled in a dozen words. He never used to be like that, and if he carried the habit into his professional work he'd soon lose all his clients. . . . Yes, do come in for a minute, dear, if you have time; no doubt he'll turn up while you're here." The tonic ring of Mrs. Ashby's voice echoed on reassuringly in the silent room while Charlotte continued her preparations.

Toward seven the telephone rang, and she darted to it. Now she would know! But it was only from the conscientious secretary, to say that Mr. Ashby hadn't been back, or sent any word, and before the office closed she thought she ought to let Mrs. Ashby know. "Oh, that's all right. Thanks a lot!" Charlotte called out cheerfully, and hung up the receiver with a trembling hand. But perhaps by this time, she reflected, he was at his mother's. She shut her drawers and cupboards, put on her hat and coat and called up to the nursery that she was going out for a minute to see the children's grandmother.

Mrs. Ashby lived nearby, and during her brief walk through the cold spring dusk Charlotte imagined that every advancing figure was her husband's. But she did not meet him on the way, and when she entered the house she found her mother-in-law alone. Kenneth had neither telephoned nor come. Old Mrs. Ashby sat by her bright fire, her knitting needles flashing steadily through her active old hands, and her mere bodily presence gave reassurance to Charlotte. Yes, it was certainly odd that Kenneth had gone off for the whole day without letting any of them know; but, after all, it was to be expected. A busy lawyer held so many threads in his hands that any sudden change of plan would oblige him to make all sorts of unforeseen arrangements and adjustments. He might have gone to see some client in the suburbs and been detained there: his mother remembered his telling her that he had charge of the legal business of a queer old recluse somewhere in New Jersey, who was immensely rich but too mean to have a telephone. Very likely Kenneth had been stranded there.

But Charlotte felt her nervousness gaining on her. When Mrs. Ashby asked her at what hour they were sailing the next day and she had to say she didn't know—that Kenneth had simply sent her word he was going to take their passages—the uttering of the words again brought home to her the strangeness of the situation. Even Mrs. Ashby conceded that it was odd; but she immediately added that it only showed what a rush he was in.

"But, mother, it's nearly eight o'clock! He must realize that I've got to know when we're starting tomorrow."

"Oh, the boat probably doesn't sail till evening. Sometimes they have to wait till midnight for the tide. Kenneth's probably counting on that. After all, he has a level head."

Charlotte stood up. "It's not that. Something has happened to him."

Mrs. Ashby took off her spectacles and rolled up her knitting. "If you begin to let yourself imagine things—"

"Aren't you in the least anxious?"

"I never am till I have to be. I wish you'd ring for dinner, my dear. You'll stay and dine? He's sure to drop in here on his way home."

Charlotte called up her own house. No, the maid said, Mr. Ashby hadn't come in and hadn't telephoned. She would tell him as soon as he came that Mrs. Ashby was dining at his mother's. Charlotte followed her mother-in-law into the dining room and sat with parched throat before her empty plate, while Mrs. Ashby dealt calmly and efficiently with a short but carefully prepared repast. "You'd better eat something, child, or you'll be as bad as Kenneth. . . . Yes, a little more asparagus, please, Jane."

She insisted on Charlotte's drinking a glass of sherry and nibbling a bit of toast; then they returned to the drawing room, where the fire had been made up, and cushions in Mrs. Ashby's armchair shaken out and smoothed. How safe and familiar it all looked; and out there, somewhere in the uncertainty and mystery of the night, lurked the answer to the two women's conjectures, like an indistinguishable figure prowling on the threshold.

At last Charlotte got up and said: "I'd better go back. At this hour Kenneth will certainly go straight home."

Mrs. Ashby smiled indulgently. "It's not very late, my dear. It doesn't take two sparrows long to dine."

"It's after nine." Charlotte bent down to kiss her. "The fact is, I can't keep still."

Mrs. Ashby pushed aside her work and rested her two hands on the arms of her chair. "I'm going with you," she said, helping herself up.

Charlotte protested that it was too late, that it was not necessary, that she would call up as soon as Kenneth came in, but Mrs. Ashby had already rung for her maid. She was slightly lame, and stood resting on her stick while her wraps were brought. "If Mr. Kenneth turns up, tell him he'll find me at his own house," she instructed the maid as the two women got into the taxi which had been summoned. During the short drive Charlotte gave thanks that she was not returning home alone. There was something warm and substantial in the mere fact of Mrs. Ashby's nearness, something that corresponded with the clearness of her eyes and the texture of her fresh firm complexion. As the taxi drew up she laid her hand encouragingly on Charlotte's. "You'll see; there'll be a message."

The door opened at Charlotte's ring and the two entered. Charlotte's heart beat excitedly; the stimulus of her mother-in-law's confidence was beginning to flow through her veins.

"You'll see—you'll see," Mrs. Ashby repeated.

The maid who opened the door said no, Mr. Ashby had not come in, and there had been no message from him.

"You're sure the telephone's not out of order?" his mother suggested; and the maid said, well, it certainly wasn't half an hour ago; but she'd just go and ring up to make sure. She disappeared, and Charlotte turned to take off her hat and cloak. As she did so her eyes lit on the hall table, and there lay a gray envelope, her husband's name faintly traced on it. "Oh!" she cried out, suddenly aware that for the first time in months she had entered her house without wondering if one of the gray letters would be there.

"What is it, my dear?" Mrs. Ashby asked with a glance of surprise.

Charlotte did not answer. She took up the envelope and stood staring at it as if she could force her gaze to penetrate to what was within. Then an idea occurred to her. She turned and held out the envelope to her mother-in-law.

"Do you know that writing?" she asked.

Mrs. Ashby took the letter. She had to feel with her other hand for her eyeglasses, and when she had adjusted them she lifted the envelope to the light. "Why!" she exclaimed; and then stopped. Charlotte noticed that the letter shook in her usually firm hand. "But this is addressed to Kenneth," Mrs. Ashby said at length, in a low voice. Her tone seemed to imply that she felt her daughter-in-law's question to be slightly indiscreet.

"Yes, but no matter," Charlotte spoke with sudden decision. "I want to know—do you know the writing?"

Mrs. Ashby handed back the letter. "No," she said distinctly.

The two women had turned into the library. Charlotte switched on the electric light and shut the door. She still held the envelope in her hand.

"I'm going to open it," she announced.

She caught her mother-in-law's startled glance. "But, dearest—a letter not addressed to you? My dear, you can't!"

"As if I cared about that—now!" She continued to look intently at Mrs. Ashby. "This letter may tell me where Kenneth is."

Mrs. Ashby's glossy bloom was effaced by a quick pallor; her firm cheeks seemed to shrink and wither. "Why should it? What makes you believe—It can't possibly—"

Charlotte held her eyes steadily on that altered face. "Ah, then you *do* know the writing?" she flashed back.

"Know the writing? How should I? With all my son's correspondents. . . . What I do know is—" Mrs. Ashby broke off and looked at her daughter-in-law entreatingly, almost timidly.

Charlotte caught her by the wrist. "Mother! What do you know? Tell me! You must!"

"That I don't believe any good ever came of a woman's opening her husband's letters behind his back."

The words sounded to Charlotte's irritated ears as flat as a phrase culled from a book of moral axioms. She laughed impatiently and dropped her mother-in-law's wrist. "Is that all? No good can come of this letter, opened or unopened. I know that well enough. But whatever ill comes, I mean to find out what's in it." Her hands had been trembling as they held the envelope, but now they grew firm, and her voice also. She still gazed intently at Mrs. Ashby. "This is the ninth letter addressed in the same hand that has come for Kenneth since we've been married. Always these same gray envelopes. I've kept count of them because after each one he has been like a man who has had some dreadful shock. It takes him hours to shake off their effect. I've told him so. I've told him I must know from whom they come, because I can see they're killing him. He won't answer my questions; he says he can't tell me anything about the letters; but last night he promised to go away with me—to get away from them."

Mrs. Ashby, with shaking steps, had gone to one of the armchairs and sat down in it, her head drooping forward on her breast. "Ah," she murmured.

"So now you understand—"

"Did he tell you it was to get away from them?"

"He said, to get away—to get away. He was sobbing so that he could hardly speak. But I told him I knew that was why."

"And what did he say?"

"He took me in his arms and said he'd go wherever I wanted."

"Ah, thank God!" said Mrs. Ashby. There was a silence, during which she continued to sit with bowed head, and eyes averted from her daughter-in-law. At last she looked up and spoke. "Are you sure there have been as many as nine?"

"Perfectly. This is the ninth. I've kept count."

"And he has absolutely refused to explain?"

"Absolutely."

Mrs. Ashby spoke through pale contracted lips. "When did they begin to come? Do you remember?"

Charlotte laughed again. "Remember? The first one came the night we got back from our honeymoon."

"All that time?" Mrs. Ashby lifted her head and spoke with sudden energy. "Then—yes, open it."

The words were so unexpected that Charlotte felt the blood in her temples, and her hands began to tremble again. She tried to slip her finger under the flap of the envelope, but it was so tightly stuck that she had to hunt on her husband's writing table for his ivory letter opener. As she pushed about the familiar objects his own hands had so lately touched, they sent through her the icy chill emanating from the little personal effects of someone newly dead. In the deep silence of the room the tearing of the paper as she slit the envelope sounded like a human cry. She drew out the sheet and carried it to the lamp.

"Well?" Mrs. Ashby asked below her breath.

Charlotte did not move or answer. She was bending over the page with wrinkled brows, holding it nearer and nearer to the light. Her sight must be blurred, or else dazzled by the reflection of the lamplight on the smooth surface of the paper, for, strain her eyes as she would, she could discern only a few faint strokes, so faint and faltering as to be nearly undecipherable.

"I can't make it out," she said.

"What do you mean, dear?"

"The writing's too indistinct. . . . Wait."

She went back to the table and, sitting down close to Kenneth's reading lamp, slipped the letter under a magnifying glass. All this time she was aware that her mother-in-law was watching her intently.

"Well?" Mrs. Ashby breathed.

"Well, it's no clearer. I can't read it."

"You mean the paper is an absolute blank?"

"No, not quite. There is writing on it. I can make out something like 'mine'—oh, and 'come.' It might be 'come.' "

Mrs. Ashby stood up abruptly. Her face was even paler than before. She advanced to the table and, resting her two hands on it, drew a deep breath. "Let me see," she said, as if forcing herself to a hateful effort.

Charlotte felt the contagion of her whiteness. "She knows," she thought. She pushed the letter across the table. Her mother-in-law lowered her head over it in silence, but without touching it with her pale wrinkled hands.

Charlotte stood watching her as she herself, when she had tried to read the letter, had been watched by Mrs. Ashby. The latter fumbled for her glasses, held them to her eyes, and bent still closer to the outspread page, in order, as it seemed, to avoid touching it. The light of the lamp fell directly on her old face, and Charlotte reflected what depths of the unknown may lurk under the clearest and most candid lineaments. She had never seen her mother-in-law's features express any but simple and sound emotions—cordiality, amusement, a kindly sympathy; now and again a flash of wholesome anger. Now they seemed to wear a look of fear and hatred, of incredulous dismay and almost cringing defiance. It was as if the spirits warring within her had distorted her face to their own likeness. At length she raised her head. "I can't—I can't," she said in a voice of childish distress.

"You can't make it out either?"

She shook her head, and Charlotte saw two tears roll down her cheeks.

"Familiar as the writing is to you?" Charlotte insisted with twitching lips.

Mrs. Ashby did not take up the challenge. "I can make out nothing—nothing."

"But you do know the writing?"

Mrs. Ashby lifted her head timidly; her anxious eyes stole with a glance of apprehension around the quite familiar room. "How can I tell? I was startled at first. . . ."

"Startled by the resemblance?"

"Well, I thought—"

"You'd better say it out, mother! You knew at once it was *her* writing?"

"Oh, wait, my dear—wait."

"Wait for what?"

Mrs. Ashby looked up; her eyes, traveling slowly past Charlotte, were lifted to the blank wall behind her son's writing table.

Charlotte, following the glance, burst into a shrill laugh of accusation. "I needn't wait any longer! You've answered me now! You're looking straight at the wall where her picture used to hang!"

Mrs. Ashby lifted her hand with a murmur of warning. "Sh-h."

"Oh, you needn't imagine that anything can ever frighten me again!" Charlotte cried.

Her mother-in-law still leaned against the table. Her lips moved plaintively. "But we're going mad—we're both going mad. We both know such things are impossible."

Her daughter-in-law looked at her with a pitying stare. "I've known for a long time now that everything was possible."

"Even this?"

"Yes, exactly this."

"But this letter—after all, there's nothing in this letter—"

"Perhaps there would be to him. How can I tell? I remember his saying to me once that if you were used to a handwriting the faintest stroke of it became legible. Now I see what he meant. He *was* used to it."

"But the few strokes that I can make out are so pale. No one could possibly read that letter."

Charlotte laughed again. "I suppose everything's pale about a ghost," she said stridently.

"Oh, my child—my child—don't say it!"

"Why shouldn't I say it, when even the bare walls cry it out? What difference does it make if her letters are illegible to you and me? If even you can see her face on that blank wall, why shouldn't he read her writing on this blank paper? Don't you see that she's everywhere in this house, and the closer to him because to everyone else she's become invisible?" Charlotte dropped into a chair and covered her face with her hands. A turmoil of sobbing shook her from head to foot. At length a touch on her shoulder made her look up, and she saw her mother-in-law bending over her. Mrs. Ashby's face seemed to have grown still smaller and more wasted, but it had resumed its usual quiet look. Through all her tossing anguish, Charlotte felt the impact of that resolute spirit.

"Tomorrow—tomorrow. You'll see. There'll be some explanation tomorrow."

Charlotte cut her short. "An explanation? Who's going to give it, I wonder?"

Mrs. Ashby drew back and straightened herself heroically. "Kenneth himself will," she cried out in a strong voice. Charlotte said nothing, and the old woman went on: "But meanwhile we must act; we must notify the police. Now, without a moment's delay. We must do everything—everything."

Charlotte stood up slowly and stiffly; her joints felt as cramped as an old woman's. "Exactly as if we thought it could do any good to do anything?"

Resolutely Mrs. Ashby cried: "Yes!" and Charlotte went up to the telephone and unhooked the receiver.

STEPHEN CRANE

The Open Boat

A TALE INTENDED TO BE AFTER THE FACT: BEING THE EXPERIENCE OF FOUR MEN FROM THE SUNK STEAMER *Commodore*

I

None of them knew the color of the sky. Their eyes glanced level and were fastened upon the waves that swept toward them. These waves were of the hue of slate, save for the tops, which were of foaming white, and all of the men knew the colors of the sea. The horizon narrowed and widened, and dipped and rose, and at all times its edge was jagged with waves that seemed thrust up in points like rocks.

Many a man ought to have a bathtub larger than the boat which here rode upon the sea. These waves were most wrongfully and barbarously abrupt and tall, and each froth-top was a problem in small-boat navigation.

The cook squatted in the bottom, and looked with both eyes at the six inches of gunwale which separated him from the ocean. His sleeves were rolled over his fat forearms, and the two flaps of his unbuttoned vest dangled as he bent to bail out the boat. Often he said, "Gawd! that was a narrow clip." As he remarked it he invariably gazed eastward over the broken sea.

The oiler, steering with one of the two oars in the boat, sometimes raised himself suddenly to keep clear of water that swirled in over the stern. It was a thin little oar, and it seemed often ready to snap.

The correspondent, pulling at the other oar, watched the waves and wondered why he was there.

The injured captain, lying in the bow, was at this time buried in that profound dejection and indifference which comes, temporarily at least, to even the bravest and most enduring when, willy-nilly, the firm fails, the army loses, the ship goes down. The mind of the master of a vessel is rooted deep in the timbers of her, though he command for a day or a decade; and this captain had on him the stern impression of a scene in the grays of dawn of seven turned faces, and later a stump of a topmast with a white ball on it, that slashed to and fro at the waves, went low and lower, and down. Thereafter there was something strange in his voice. Although steady, it was deep with mourning, and of a quality beyond oration or tears.

"Keep'er a little more south, Billie," said he.

"A little more south, sir," said the oiler in the stern.

A seat in this boat was not unlike a seat upon a bucking broncho, and by the same token a broncho is not much smaller. The craft pranced and reared and plunged like an animal. As each wave came, and she rose for it, she seemed like a horse making at a fence outrageously high. The manner of her scramble over these walls of water is a mystic thing, and, moreover, at the top of them were ordinarily these problems in white water, the foam racing down from the summit of each wave requiring a new leap, and a leap from the air. Then, after scornfully bumping a crest, she would slide and race and splash down a long incline, and arrive bobbing and nodding in front of the next menace.

A singular disadvantage of the sea lies in the fact that after successfully surmounting one wave you discover that there is another behind it just as important and just as nervously anxious to do something effective in the way of swamping boats. In a ten-foot dinghy one can get an idea of the resources of the sea in the line of waves that is not probable to the average experience, which is never at sea in a dinghy. As each slaty wall of water approached, it shut all else from the view of the men in the boat, and it was not difficult to imagine that this particular wave was the final outburst of the ocean, the last effort of the grim water. There was a terrible grace in the move of the waves, and they came in silence, save for the snarling of the crests.

In the wan light the faces of the men must have been gray. Their eyes must have glinted in strange ways as they gazed steadily astern. Viewed from a balcony, the whole thing would, doubtless, have been weirdly picturesque. But the men in the boat had no time to see it, and if they had had leisure, there were other things to occupy their minds. The sun swung steadily up the sky, and they knew it was broad day because the color of the sea changed from slate to emerald-green streaked with amber lights, and the foam was like tumbling snow. The process of the breaking day was unknown to them. They were aware only of this effect upon the color of the waves that rolled toward them.

In disjointed sentences the cook and the correspondent argued as to the difference between a life-saving station and a house of refuge. The cook had said: "There's a house of refuge just north of the Mosquito Inlet Light, and as soon as they see us they'll come off in their boat and pick us up."

"As soon as who see us?" said the correspondent.

"The crew," said the cook.

"Houses of refuge don't have crews," said the correspondent. "As I understand them, they are only places where clothes and grub are stored for the benefit of shipwrecked people. They don't carry crews."

"Oh, yes, they do," said the cook.

"No, they don't," said the correspondent.

"Well, we're not there yet, anyhow," said the oiler, in the stern.

"Well," said the cook, "perhaps it's not a house of refuge that I'm thinking of as being near Mosquito Inlet Light; perhaps it's a life-saving station."

"We're not there yet," said the oiler in the stern.

II

As the boat bounced from the top of each wave the wind tore through the hair of the hatless men, and as the craft plopped her stern down again the spray slashed past them. The crest of each of these waves was a hill, from the top of which the men surveyed for a moment a broad tumultuous expanse, shining and wind-riven. It was probably splendid, it was probably glorious, this play of the free sea, wild with lights of emerald and white and amber.

"Bully good thing it's an on-shore wind," said the cook. "If not, where would we be? Wouldn't have a show."

"That's right," said the correspondent.

The busy oiler nodded his assent.

Then the captain, in the bow, chuckled in a way that expressed humor, contempt, tragedy, all in one. "Do you think we've got much of a show now, boys?" said he.

Whereupon the three were silent, save for a trifle of hemming and hawing. To express any particular optimism at this time they felt to be childish and stupid, but they all doubtless possessed this sense of the situation in their minds. A young man thinks doggedly at such times. On the other hand, the ethics of their condition was decidedly against any open suggestion of hopelessness. So they were silent.

"Oh, well," said the captain, soothing his children, "we'll get ashore all right."

But there was that in his tone which made them think; so the oiler quoth, "Yes! if this wind holds."

The cook was bailing. "Yes! if we don't catch hell in the surf."

Canton-flannel gulls flew near and far. Sometimes they sat down on the sea, near patches of brown seaweed that rolled over the waves with a movement like carpets on a line in a gale. The birds sat comfortably in groups, and they were envied by some in the dinghy, for the wrath of the sea was no more to them than it was to a covey of prairie chickens a thousand miles inland. Often they came very close and stared at the men with black bead-like eyes. At these times they were uncanny and sinister in their unblinking scrutiny, and the men hooted angrily at them, telling them to be gone. One came, and evidently decided to alight on the top of the captain's head. The bird flew parallel to the boat and did not circle, but made short sidelong jumps in the air in chicken fashion. His black eyes were wistfully fixed upon the captain's head. "Ugly brute," said the oiler to the bird. "You look as if you were made with a jackknife." The cook and the correspondent swore darkly at the creature. The captain naturally wished to knock it away with the end of the heavy painter, but he did not dare do it, because anything resembling an emphatic gesture would have capsized this freighted boat; and so, with his open hand, the captain gently and carefully waved the gull away. After it had been discouraged from the pursuit the captain breathed easier on account of his hair, and others breathed easier because the bird struck their minds at this time as being somehow gruesome and ominous.

In the meantime the oiler and the correspondent rowed; and also they rowed. They sat together in the same seat, and each rowed an oar. Then the oiler took both oars; then the correspondent took both oars, then the oiler; then the correspondent. They rowed and they rowed. The very ticklish part of the business was when the time came for the reclining one in the stern to take his turn at the oars. By the very last star of truth, it is easier to steal eggs from under a hen than it was to change seats in the dinghy. First the man in the stern slid his hand along the thwart and moved with care, as if he were of Sèvres. Then the man in the rowing-seat slid his hand along the other thwart. It was all done with the most extraordinary care. As the two sidled past each other, the whole party kept watchful eyes on the coming wave, and the captain cried: "Look out, now! Steady, there!"

The brown mats of seaweed that appeared from time to time were like islands, bits of earth. They were travelling, apparently, neither one way nor the other. They were, to all intents, stationary. They informed the men in the boat that it was making progress slowly toward the land.

The captain, rearing cautiously in the bow after the dinghy soared on a great swell, said that he had seen the lighthouse at Mosquito Inlet. Presently the cook remarked that he had seen it. The correspondent was at the oars then, and for some reason he too wished to look at the lighthouse; but his back was toward the far shore, and the waves were important, and for some time he could not seize an opportunity to turn his head. But at last there came a wave more gentle than the others, and when at the crest of it he swiftly scoured the western horizon.

"See it?" said the captain.

"No," said the correspondent, slowly; "I didn't see anything."

"Look again," said the captain. He pointed. "It's exactly in that direction."

At the top of another wave the correspondent did as he was bid, and this time his eyes chanced on a small, still thing on the edge of the swaying horizon. It was precisely like the point of a pin. It took an anxious eye to find a lighthouse so tiny.

"Think we'll make it, Captain?"

"If this wind holds and the boat don't swamp, we can't do much else," said the captain.

The little boat, lifted by each towering sea and splashed viciously by the crests, made progress that in the absence of seaweed was not apparent to those in her. She seemed just a wee thing wallowing, miraculously top up, at the mercy of five oceans. Occasionally a great spread of water, like white flames, swarmed into her.

"Bail her, cook," said the captain, serenely.

"All right, Captain," said the cheerful cook.

III

It would be difficult to describe the subtle brotherhood of men that was here established on the seas. No one said that it was so. No one mentioned it. But it dwelt in the boat, and each man felt it warm him. They were a captain, an oiler, a cook, and a correspondent, and they were friends—friends in a more curiously iron-bound degree than may be common. The hurt captain, lying against the water jar in the bow, spoke always in a low voice and calmly; but he could never command a more ready and swiftly obedient crew than the motley three of the dinghy. It was more than a mere recognition of what was best for the common safety. There was surely in it a quality that was personal and heart-felt. And after this devotion to the commander of the boat, there was this comradeship, that the correspondent, for instance, who had been taught to be cynical of men, knew even at the time was the best experience of his life. But no one said that it was so. No one mentioned it.

"I wish we had a sail," remarked the captain. "We might try my overcoat on the end of an oar, and give you two boys a chance to rest." So the cook and the correspondent held the mast and spread wide the overcoat; the oiler steered; and the little boat made good way with her new rig. Sometimes the oiler had to scull sharply to keep a sea from breaking into the boat, but otherwise sailing was a success.

Meanwhile the lighthouse had been growing slowly larger. It had now almost assumed color, and appeared like a little gray shadow on the sky. The man at the oars could not be prevented from turning his head rather often to try for a glimpse of this little gray shadow.

At last, from the top of each wave, the men in the tossing boat could see land. Even as the lighthouse was an upright shadow on the sky, this land seemed but a long black shadow on the sea. It certainly was thinner than paper. "We must be about opposite New Smyrna," said the cook, who had coasted this shore often in schooners. "Captain, by the way, I believe they abandoned that life-saving station there about a year ago."

"Did they?" said the captain.

The wind slowly died away. The cook and the correspondent were not now obliged to slave in order to hold high the oar. But the waves continued their old impetuous swooping at the dinghy, and the little craft, no longer underway, struggled woundily over them. The oiler or the correspondent took the oars again.

Shipwrecks are *apropos* of nothing. If men could only train for them and have them occur when the men had reached pink condition, there would be less drowning at sea. Of the four in the dinghy none had slept any time worth mentioning for two days and two nights previous to embarking in the dinghy, and in the excitement of clambering about the deck of a foundering ship they had also forgotten to eat heartily.

For these reasons, and for others, neither the oiler nor the correspondent was fond of rowing at this time. The correspondent wondered ingenuously how in the name of all that was sane could there be people who thought it amusing to row a boat. It was not an amusement; it was a diabolical punishment, and even a genius of mental aberrations could never conclude that it was anything but a horror to the muscles and a crime against the back. He mentioned to the boat in general how the amusement of rowing struck him, and the weary-faced oiler smiled in full sympathy. Previously to the foundering, by the way, the oiler had worked a double watch in the engine-room of the ship.

"Take her easy now, boys," said the captain. "Don't spend yourselves. If we have to run a surf you'll need all your strength, because we'll sure have to swim for it. Take your time."

Slowly the land arose from the sea. From a black line it became a line of black and a line of white—trees and sand. Finally the captain said that he could make out a house on the shore. "That's the house of refuge, sure," said the cook. "They'll see us before long, and come out after us."

The distant lighthouse reared high. "The keeper ought to be able to make us out now, if he's looking through a glass," said the captain. "He'll notify the life-saving people."

"None of those other boats could have got ashore to give word of this wreck," said the oiler, in a low voice, "else the life-boat would be out hunting us."

Slowly and beautifully the land loomed out of the sea. The wind came again. It had veered from the northeast to the southeast. Finally a new sound struck the ears of the men in the boat. It was the low thunder of the surf on the shore. "We'll never be able to make the lighthouse now," said the captain. "Swing her head a little more north, Billie."

"A little more north, sir," said the oiler.

Whereupon the little boat turned her nose once more down the wind, and all but the oarsman watched the shore grow. Under the influence of this expansion doubt and direful apprehension were leaving the minds of the men. The management of the boat was still most absorbing, but it could not prevent a quiet cheerfulness. In an hour, perhaps, they would be ashore.

Their backbones had become thoroughly used to balancing in the boat, and they now rode this wild colt of a dinghy like circus men. The correspondent thought that he had been drenched to the skin, but happening to feel in the top pocket of his coat, he found therein eight cigars. Four of them were soaked with sea-water; four were perfectly scatheless. After a search, somebody produced three dry matches; and thereupon the four waifs rode impudently in their little boat and, with an assurance of an impending rescue shining in their eyes, puffed at the big cigars, and judged well and ill of all men. Everybody took a drink of water.

IV

"Cook," remarked the captain, "there don't seem to be any signs of life about your house of refuge."

"No," replied the cook. "Funny they don't see us!"

A broad stretch of lowly coast lay before the eyes of the men. It was of low dunes topped with dark vegetation. The roar of the surf was plain, and sometimes they could see the white lip of a wave as it spun up the beach. A tiny house was blocked out black upon the sky. Southward, the slim lighthouse lifted its little gray length.

Tide, wind, and waves were swinging the dinghy northward. "Funny they don't see us," said the men.

The surf's roar was here dulled, but its tone was nevertheless thunderous and mighty. As the boat swam over the great rollers the men sat listening to this roar. "We'll swamp sure," said everybody.

It is fair to say here that there was not a life-saving station within twenty miles in either direction; but the men did not know this fact, and in consequence they made dark and opprobrious remarks concerning the eyesight of the nation's life-savers. Four scowling men sat in the dinghy and surpassed records in the invention of epithets.

"Funny they don't see us."

The light-heartedness of a former time had completely faded. To their sharpened minds it was easy to conjure pictures of all kinds of incompetency and blindness and, indeed, cowardice. There was the shore of the populous land, and it was bitter and bitter to them that from it came no sign.

"Well," said the captain, ultimately, "I suppose we'll have to make a try for ourselves. If we stay out here too long, we'll none of us have strength left to swim after the boat swamps."

And so the oiler, who was at the oars, turned the boat straight for the shore. There was a sudden tightening of muscles. There was some thinking.

"If we don't all get ashore," said the captain—"if we don't all get ashore, I suppose you fellows know where to send news of my finish?"

They then briefly exchanged some addresses and admonitions. As for the reflections of the men, there was a great deal of rage in them. Perchance they might be formulated thus: "If I am going to be drowned—if I am going to be drowned—if I am going to be drowned, why, in the name of the seven mad gods who rule the sea, was I allowed to come thus far and contemplate sand and trees? Was I brought here merely to have my nose dragged away as I was about to nibble the sacred cheese of life? It is preposterous. If this old ninny-woman, Fate, cannot do better than this, she should be deprived of the management of men's fortunes. She is an old hen who knows not her intention. If she has decided to drown me, why did she not do it in the beginning and save me all this trouble? The whole affair is absurd. . . . But no; she cannot mean to drown me. She dare not drown me. She cannot drown me. Not after all this work." Afterward the man might have had an impulse to shake his fist at the clouds. "Just you drown me, now, and then hear what I call you!"

The billows that came at this time were more formidable. They seemed always just about to break and roll over the little boat in a turmoil of foam. There was a preparatory and long growl in the speech of them. No mind unused to the sea would have concluded that the dinghy could ascend these sheer heights in time. The shore was still afar. The oiler was a wily surfman. "Boys," he said swiftly, "she won't live three minutes more, and we're too far out to swim. Shall I take her to sea again, Captain?"

"Yes; go ahead!" said the captain.

This oiler, by a series of quick miracles and fast and steady oarsmanship, turned the boat in the middle of the surf and took her safely to sea again.

There was a considerable silence as the boat bumped over the furrowed sea to deeper water. Then somebody in gloom spoke: "Well, anyhow, they must have seen us from the shore by now."

The gulls went in slanting flight up the wind toward the gray, desolate east. A squall, marked by dingy clouds and clouds brickred, like smoke from a burning building, appeared from the southeast.

"What do you think of those life-saving people? Ain't they peaches?"

"Funny they haven't seen us."

"Maybe they think we're out here for sport! Maybe they think we're fishin'. Maybe they think we're damned fools."

It was a long afternoon. A changed tide tried to force them southward, but wind and wave said northward. Far ahead, where coast-line, sea, and sky formed their mighty angle, there were little dots which seemed to indicate a city on the shore.

"St. Augustine?"

The captain shook his head. "Too near Mosquito Inlet."

And the oiler rowed, and then the correspondent rowed; then the oiler rowed. It was a weary business. The human back can become the seat of more aches and pains than are registered in books for the composite anatomy of a regiment. It is a limited area, but it can become the theater of innumerable muscular conflicts, tangles, wrenches, knots, and other comforts.

"Did you ever like to row, Billie?" asked the correspondent.

"No," said the oiler; "hang it!"

When one exchanged the rowing-seat for a place in the bottom of the boat, he suffered a bodily depression that caused him to be careless of everything save an obligation to wiggle one finger. There was cold sea-water swashing to and fro in the boat, and he lay in it. His head, pillowed on a thwart, was within an inch of the swirl of a wave-crest, and sometimes a particularly obstreperous sea came inboard and drenched him once more. But these matters did not annoy him. It is almost certain that if the boat had capsized he would have tumbled comfortably out upon the ocean as if he felt sure that it was a great soft mattress.

"Look! There's a man on the shore!"

"Where?"

"There! See 'im? See 'im?"

"Yes, sure! He's walking along."

"Now he's stopped. Look! He's facing us!"

"He's waving at us!"

"So he is! By thunder!"

"Ah, now we're all right! Now we're all right! There'll be a boat out here for us in half an hour."

"He's going on. He's running. He's going up to that house there."

The remote beach seemed lower than the sea, and it required a searching glance to discern the little black figure. The captain saw a floating stick, and they rowed to it. A bath towel was by some weird chance in the boat, and, tying this on the stick, the captain waved it. The oarsman did not dare turn his head, so he was obliged to ask questions.

"What's he doing now?"

"He's standing still again. He's looking, I think. . . . There he goes again—toward the house. . . . Now he's stopped again."

"Is he waving at us?"

"No, not now; he was, though."

"Look! There comes another man!"

"He's running."

"Look at him go, would you!"

"Why, he's on a bicycle. Now he's met the other man. They're both waving at us. Look!"

"There comes something up the beach."

"What the devil is that thing?"

"Why, it looks like a boat."

"Why, certainly, it's a boat."

"No; it's on wheels."

"Yes, so it is. Well, that must be the life-boat. They drag them along shore on a wagon."

"That's the life-boat, sure."

"No, by God, it's—it's an omnibus."

"I tell you it's a life-boat."

"It is not! It's an omnibus. I can see it plain. See? One of these big hotel omnibuses."

"By thunder, you're right. It's an omnibus, sure as fate. What do you suppose they are doing with an omnibus? Maybe they are going around collecting the life-crew, hey?"

"That's it, likely. Look! There's a fellow waving a little black flag. He's standing on the steps of the omnibus. There come those other two fellows. Now they're all talking together. Look at the fellow with the flag. Maybe he ain't waving it!"

"That ain't a flag, is it? That's his coat. Why, certainly, that's his coat."

"So it is; it's his coat. He's taken it off and is waving it around his head. But would you look at him swing it!"

"Oh, say, there isn't any life-saving station there. That's just a winter-resort hotel omnibus that has brought over some of the boarders to see us drown."

"What's that idiot with the coat mean? What's he signaling, anyhow?"

"It looks as if he were trying to tell us to go north. There must be a life-saving station up there."

"No; he thinks we're fishing. Just giving us a merry hand. See? Ah, there, Willie!"

"Well, I wish I could make something out of those signals. What do you suppose he means?"

"He don't mean anything; he's just playing."

"Well, if he'd just signal us to try the surf again, or to go to sea and wait, or go north, or go south, or go to hell, there would be some reason in it. But look at him! He just stands there and keeps his coat revolving like a wheel. The ass!"

"There come more people."

"Now there's quite a mob. Look! Isn't that a boat?"

"Where? Oh, I see where you mean. No, that's no boat."

"That fellow is still waving his coat."

"He must think we like to see him do that. Why don't he quit it? It don't mean anything."

"I don't know. I think he is trying to make us go north. It must be that there's a life-saving station there somewhere."

"Say, he ain't tired yet. Look at 'im wave!"

"Wonder how long he can keep that up. He's been revolving his coat ever since he caught sight of us. He's an idiot. Why aren't they getting men to bring a boat out? A fishing-boat—one of those big yawls—could come out here all right. Why don't he do something?"

"Oh, it's all right now."

"They'll have a boat out here for us in less than no time, now that they've seen us."

A faint yellow tone came into the sky over the low land. The shadows on the sea slowly deepened. The wind bore coldness with it, and the men began to shiver.

"Holy smoke!" said one, allowing his voice to express his impious mood, "if we keep on monkeying out here! If we've got to flounder out here all night!"

"Oh, we'll never have to stay here all night! Don't you worry. They've seen us now, and it won't be long before they'll come chasing out after us."

The shore grew dusky. The man waving a coat blended gradually into this gloom, and it swallowed in the same manner the omnibus and the group of people. The spray, when it dashed uproariously over the side, made the voyagers shrink and swear like men who were being branded.

"I'd like to catch the chump who waved the coat. I feel like socking him one, just for luck."

"Why? What did he do?"

"Oh, nothing, but then he seemed so damned cheerful."

In the meantime the oiler rowed, and then the correspondent rowed, and then the oiler rowed. Gray-faced and bowed forward, they mechanically, turn by turn, plied the leaden oars. The form of the lighthouse had vanished from the southern horizon, but finally a pale star appeared, just lifting from the sea. The streaked saffron in the west passed before the all-merging darkness, and the sea to the east was black. The land had vanished, and was expressed only by the low and drear thunder of the surf.

"If I am going to be drowned—if I am going to be drowned—if I am going to be drowned, why, in the name of the seven mad gods who rule the sea, was I allowed to come thus far and contemplate sand and trees? Was I brought here merely to have my nose dragged away as I was about to nibble the sacred cheese of life?"

The patient captain, drooped over the water-jar, was sometimes obliged to speak to the oarsman.

"Keep her head up! Keep her head up!"

"Keep her head up, sir." The voices were weary and low.

This was surely a quiet evening. All save the oarsman lay heavily and listlessly in the boat's bottom. As for him, his eyes were just capable of noting the tall black waves that swept forward in a most sinister silence, save for an occasional subdued growl of a crest.

The cook's head was on a thwart, and he looked without interest at the water under his nose. He was deep in other scenes. Finally he spoke. "Billie," he murmured, dreamfully, "what kind of pie do you like best?"

V

"Pie!" said the oiler and the correspondent, agitatedly. "Don't talk about those things, blast you!"

"Well," said the cook, "I was just thinking about ham sandwiches, and—"

A night on the sea in an open boat is a long night. As darkness settled finally, the shine of the light, lifting from the sea in the south, changed to full gold. On the northern horizon a new light appeared, a small bluish gleam on the edge of the waters. These two lights were the furniture of the world. Otherwise there was nothing but waves.

Two men huddled in the stern, and distances were so magnificent in the dinghy that the rower was enabled to keep his feet partly warm by thrusting them under his companions. Their legs indeed extended far under the rowing-seat until they touched the feet of the captain forward. Sometimes, despite the efforts of the tired oarsman, a wave came piling into the boat, an icy wave of the night, and the chilling water soaked them anew. They would twist their bodies for a moment and groan, and sleep the dead sleep once more, while the water in the boat gurgled about them as the craft rocked.

The plan of the oiler and the correspondent was for one to row until he lost the ability, and then arouse the other from his sea-water couch in the bottom of the boat.

The oiler plied the oars until his head drooped forward and the overpowering sleep blinded him; and he rowed yet afterward. Then he touched a man in the bottom of the boat, and called his name. "Will you spell me for a little while?" he said meekly.

"Sure, Billie," said the correspondent, awaking and dragging himself to a sitting position. They exchanged places carefully, and the oiler, cuddling down in the sea-water at the cook's side, seemed to go to sleep instantly.

The particular violence of the sea had ceased. The waves came without snarling. The obligation of the man at the oars was to keep the boat headed so that the tilt of the rollers would not capsize her, and to preserve her from filling when the crests rushed past. The black waves were silent and hard to be seen in the darkness. Often one was almost upon the boat before the oarsman was aware.

In a low voice the correspondent addressed the captain. He was not sure that the captain was awake, although this iron man seemed to be always awake. "Captain, shall I keep her making for that light north, sir?"

The same steady voice answered him. "Yes. Keep it about two points off the port bow."

The cook had tied a life-belt around himself in order to get even the warmth which this clumsy cork contrivance could donate, and he seemed almost stove-like when a rower, whose teeth invariably chattered wildly as soon as he ceased his labor, dropped down to sleep.

The correspondent, as he rowed, looked down at the two men sleeping underfoot. The cook's arm was around the oiler's shoulders, and, with their fragmentary clothing and haggard faces, they were the babes of the sea—a grotesque rendering of the old babes in the wood.

Later he must have grown stupid at his work, for suddenly there was a growling of water, and a crest came with a roar and a swash into the boat, and it was a wonder that it did not set the cook afloat in his life-belt. The cook continued to sleep, but the oiler sat up, blinking his eyes and shaking with the new cold.

"Oh, I'm awful sorry, Billie," said the correspondent, contritely.

"That's all right, old boy," said the oiler, and lay down again and was asleep.

Presently it seemed that even the captain dozed, and the correspondent thought that he was the one man afloat on all the ocean. The wind had a voice as it came over the waves, and it was sadder than the end.

There was a long, loud swishing astern of the boat, and a gleaming trail of phosphorescence, like blue flame, was furrowed on the black waters. It might have been made by a monstrous knife.

Then there came a stillness, while the correspondent breathed with open mouth and looked at the sea.

Suddenly there was another swish and another long flash of bluish light, and this time it was alongside the boat, and might almost have been reached with an oar. The correspondent saw an enormous fin speed like a shadow through the water, hurling the crystalline spray and leaving the long glowing trail.

The correspondent looked over his shoulder at the captain. His face was hidden, and he seemed to be asleep. He looked at the babes of the sea. They certainly were asleep. So, being bereft of sympathy, he leaned a little way to one side and swore softly into the sea.

But the thing did not then leave the vicinity of the boat. Ahead or astern, on one side or the other, at intervals long or short, fled the long sparkling streak, and there was to be heard the *whirroo* of the dark fin. The speed and power of the thing was greatly to be admired. It cut the water like a gigantic and keen projectile.

The presence of this biding thing did not affect the man with the same horror that it would if he had been a picnicker. He simply looked at the sea dully and swore in an undertone.

Nevertheless, it is true that he did not wish to be alone with the thing. He wished one of his companions to awake by chance and keep him company with it. But the captain hung motionless over the water-jar, and the oiler and the cook in the bottom of the boat were plunged in slumber.

VI

"If I am going to be drowned—if I am going to be drowned—if I am going to be drowned, why, in the name of the seven mad gods who rule the sea, was I allowed to come thus far and contemplate sand and trees?"

During this dismal night, it may be remarked that a man would conclude that it was really the intention of the seven mad gods to drown him, despite the abominable injustice of it. For it was certainly an abominable injustice to drown a man who had worked so hard, so hard. The man felt it would be a crime most unnatural. Other people had drowned at sea since galleys swarmed with painted sails, but still—

When it occurs to a man that nature does not regard him as important, and that she feels she would not maim the universe by disposing of him, he at first wishes to throw bricks at the temple, and he hates deeply the fact that there are no bricks and no temples. Any visible expression of nature would surely be pelleted with his jeers.

Then, if there be no tangible thing to hoot, he feels, perhaps, the desire to confront a personification and indulge in pleas, bowed to one knee, and with hands supplicant, saying, "Yes, but I love myself."

A high cold star on a winter's night is the word he feels that she says to him. Thereafter he knows the pathos of his situation.

The men in the dinghy had not discussed these matters, but each had, no doubt, reflected upon them in silence and according to his mind. There was seldom any expression upon their faces save the general one of complete weariness. Speech was devoted to the business of the boat.

To chime the notes of his emotion, a verse mysteriously entered the correspondent's head. He had even forgotten that he had forgotten this verse, but it suddenly was in his mind.

> A soldier of the Legion lay dying in Algiers;
> There was lack of woman's nursing,
> there was dearth of woman's tears;
> But a comrade stood beside him,
> and he took the comrade's hand,
> And he said, "I never more shall see
> my own, my native land."

In his childhood the correspondent had been made acquainted with the fact that a soldier of the Legion lay dying in Algiers, but he had never regarded it as important. Myriads of his schoolfellows had informed him of the soldier's plight, but the dinning had naturally ended by making him perfectly indifferent. He had never considered it his affair that a soldier of the Legion lay dying in Algiers, nor had it appeared to him as a matter for sorrow. It was less to him than the breaking of a pencil's point.

Now, however, it quaintly came to him as a human, living thing. It was no longer merely a picture of a few throes in the breast of a poet, meanwhile drinking tea and warming his feet at the grate; it was an actuality—stern, mournful, and fine.

The correspondent plainly saw the soldier. He lay on the sand with his feet out straight and still. While his pale left hand was upon his chest in an attempt to thwart the going of his life, the blood came between his fingers. In the far Algerian distance, a city of low square forms was set against a sky that was faint with the last sunset hues. The correspondent, plying the oars and dreaming of the slow and slower movements of the lips of the soldier, was moved by a profound and perfectly impersonal comprehension. He was sorry for the soldier of the Legion who lay dying in Algiers.

The thing which had followed the boat and waited had evidently grown bored at the delay. There was no longer to be heard the slash of the cutwater, and there was no longer the flame of the long trail. The light in the north still glimmered, but it was apparently no nearer to the boat. Sometimes the boom of the surf rang in the correspondent's ears, and he turned the craft seaward then and rowed harder. Southward, some one had evidently built a watch-fire on the beach. It was too low and too far to be seen, but it made a shimmering, roseate reflection upon the bluff in back of it, and this could be discerned from the boat. The wind came stronger, and sometimes a wave suddenly raged out like a mountain-cat, and there was to be seen the sheen and sparkle of a broken crest.

The captain, in the bow, moved on his water-jar and sat erect. "Pretty long night," he observed to the correspondent. He looked at the shore. "Those life-saving people take their time."

"Did you see that shark playing around?"

"Yes, I saw him. He was a big fellow, all right."

"Wish I had known you were awake."

Later the correspondent spoke into the bottom of the boat. "Billie!" There was a slow and gradual disentanglement. "Billie, will you spell me?"

"Sure," said the oiler.

As soon as the correspondent touched the cold, comfortable seawater in the bottom of the boat and had huddled close to the cook's life-belt he was deep in sleep, despite the fact that his teeth played all the popular airs. This sleep was so good to him that it was but a moment before he heard a voice call his name in a tone that demonstrated the last stages of exhaustion. "Will you spell me?"

"Sure, Billie."

The light in the north had mysteriously vanished, but the correspondent took his course from the wide-awake captain.

Later in the night they took the boat farther out to sea, and the captain directed the cook to take one oar at the stern and keep the boat facing the seas. He was to call out if he should hear the thunder of the surf. This plan enabled the oiler and the correspondent to get respite together. "We'll give those boys a chance to get into shape again," said the captain. They curled down and, after a few preliminary chatterings and trembles, slept once more the dead sleep. Neither knew they had bequeathed to the cook the company of another shark, or perhaps the same shark.

As the boat caroused on the waves, spray occasionally bumped over the side and gave them a fresh soaking, but this had no power to break their repose. The ominous slash of the wind and the water affected them as it would have affected mummies.

"Boys," said the cook, with the notes of every reluctance in his voice, "she's drifted in pretty close. I guess one of you had better take her to sea again." The correspondent, aroused, heard the crash of the toppled crests.

As he was rowing, the captain gave him some whiskey-and-water, and this steadied the chills out of him. "If I ever get ashore and anybody shows me even a photograph of an oar—"

At last there was a short conversation.

"Billie! . . . Billie, will you spell me?"

"Sure," said the oiler.

VII

When the correspondent again opened his eyes, the sea and the sky were each of the gray hue of the dawning. Later, carmine and gold was painted upon the waters. The morning appeared finally, in its splendor, with a sky of pure blue, and the sunlight flamed on the tips of the waves.

On the distant dunes were set many little black cottages, and a tall white windmill reared above them. No man, nor dog, nor bicycle appeared on the beach. The cottages might have formed a deserted village.

The voyagers scanned the shore. A conference was held in the boat. "Well," said the captain, "if no help is coming, we might better try a run through the surf right away. If we stay out here much longer we will be too weak to do anything for ourselves at all." The others silently acquiesced in this reasoning. The boat was headed for the beach. The correspondent wondered if none ever ascended the tall wind-tower, and if then they never looked seaward. This tower was a giant, standing with its back to the plight of the ants. It represented in a degree, to the correspondent, the serenity of nature amid the struggles of the individual—nature in the wind, and nature in the vision of men. She did not seem cruel to him then, nor beneficent, nor treacherous, nor wise. But she was indifferent, flatly indifferent. It is, perhaps, plausible that a man in this situation, impressed with the unconcern of the universe, should see the innumerable flaws of his life, and have them taste wickedly in his mind, and wish for another chance. A distinction between right and wrong seems absurdly clear to him, then, in this new ignorance of the grave-edge, and he understands that if he were given another opportunity he would mend his conduct and his words, and be better and brighter during an introduction or at a tea.

"Now, boys," said the captain, "she is going to swamp sure. All we can do is to work her in as far as possible, and then when she swamps, pile out and scramble for the beach. Keep cool now, and don't jump until she swamps sure."

The oiler took the oars. Over his shoulders he scanned the surf. "Captain," he said, "I think I'd better bring her about and keep her head-on to the seas and back her in."

"All right, Billie," said the captain. "Back her in." The oiler swung the boat then, and, seated in the stern, the cook and the correspondent were obliged to look over their shoulders to contemplate the lonely and indifferent shore.

The monstrous inshore rollers heaved the boat high until the men were again enabled to see the white sheets of water scudding up the slanted beach. "We won't get in very close," said the captain. Each time a man could wrest his attention from the rollers, he turned his glance toward the shore, and in the expression of the eyes during this contemplation there was a singular quality. The correspondent, observing the others, knew that they were not afraid, but the full meaning of their glances was shrouded.

As for himself, he was too tired to grapple fundamentally with the fact. He tried to coerce his mind into thinking of it, but the mind was dominated at this time by the muscles, and the muscles said they did not care. It merely occurred to him that if he should drown it would be a shame.

There were no hurried words, no pallor, no plain agitation. The men simply looked at the shore. "Now, remember to get well clear of the boat when you jump," said the captain.

Seaward the crest of a roller suddenly fell with a thunderous crash, and the long white comber came roaring down upon the boat.

"Steady now," said the captain. The men were silent. They turned their eyes from the shore to the comber and waited. The boat slid up the incline, leaped at the furious top, bounced over it, and swung down the long back of the wave. Some water had been shipped, and the cook bailed it out.

But the next crest crashed also. The tumbling, boiling flood of white water caught the boat and whirled it almost perpendicular. Water swarmed in from all sides. The correspondent had his hands on the gunwale at this time, and when the water entered at that place he swiftly withdrew his fingers, as if he objected to wetting them.

The little boat, drunken with this weight of water, reeled and snuggled deeper into the sea.

"Bail her out, cook! Bail her out!" said the captain.

"All right, Captain," said the cook.

"Now, boys, the next one will do for us sure," said the oiler. "Mind to jump clear of the boat."

The third wave moved forward, huge, furious, implacable. It fairly swallowed the dinghy, and almost simultaneously the men tumbled into the sea. A piece of life-belt had lain in the bottom of the boat, and as the correspondent went overboard he held this to his chest with his left hand.

The January water was icy, and reflected immediately that it was colder than he had expected to find it off the coast of Florida. This appeared to his dazed mind as a fact important enough to be noted at the time. The coldness of the water was sad; it was tragic. This fact was somehow mixed and confused with his opinion of his own situation, so that it seemed almost a proper reason for tears. The water was cold.

When he came to the surface he was conscious of little but the noisy water. Afterward he saw his companions in the sea. The oiler was ahead in the race. He was swimming strongly and rapidly. Off to the correspondent's left, the cook's great white and corked back bulged out of the water, and in the rear the captain was hanging with his one good hand to the keel of the overturned dinghy.

There is a certain immovable quality to a shore, and the correspondent wondered at it amid the confusion of the sea.

It seemed also very attractive; but the correspondent knew that it was a long journey, and he paddled leisurely. The piece of life-preserver lay under him, and sometimes he whirled down the incline of a wave as if he were on a hand-sled.

But finally he arrived at a place in the sea where travel was beset with difficulty. He did not pause swimming to inquire what manner of current had caught him, but there his progress ceased. The shore was set before him like a bit of scenery on a stage, and he looked at it and understood with his eyes each detail of it.

As the cook passed, much farther to the left, the captain was calling to him, "Turn over on your back, cook! Turn over on your back and use the oar."

"All right, sir." The cook turned on his back, and, paddling with an oar, went ahead as if he were a canoe.

Presently the boat also passed to the left of the correspondent, with the captain clinging with one hand to the keel. He would have appeared like a man raising himself to look over a board fence if it were not for the extraordinary gymnastics of the boat. The correspondent marvelled that the captain could still hold to it.

They passed on nearer to shore—the oiler, the cook, the captain—and following them went the water-jar, bouncing gaily over the seas.

The correspondent remained in the grip of this strange new enemy, a current. The shore, with its white slope of sand and its green bluff topped with little silent cottages, was spread like a picture before him. It was very near to him then, but he was impressed as one who, in a gallery, looks at a scene from Brittany or Algiers.

He thought: "I am going to drown? Can it be possible? Can it be possible? Can it be possible?" Perhaps an individual must consider his own death to be the final phenomenon of nature.

But later a wave perhaps whirled him out of this small deadly current, for he found suddenly that he could again make progress toward the shore. Later still he was aware that the captain, clinging with one hand to the keel of the dinghy, had his face turned away from the shore and toward him, and was calling his name. "Come to the boat! Come to the boat!"

In his struggle to reach the captain and the boat, he reflected that when one gets properly wearied drowning must really be a comfortable arrangement—a cessation of hostilities accompanied by a large degree of relief; and he was glad of it, for the main thing in his mind for some moments had been horror of the temporary agony; he did not wish to be hurt.

Presently he saw a man running along the shore. He was undressing with most remarkable speed. Coat, trousers, shirt, everything flew magically off him.

"Come to the boat!" called the captain.

"All right, Captain." As the correspondent paddled, he saw the captain let himself down to bottom and leave the boat. Then the correspondent performed his one little marvel of the voyage. A large wave caught him and flung him with ease and supreme speed completely over the boat and far beyond it. It struck him even then as an event in gymnastics and a true miracle of the sea. An overturned boat in the surf is not a plaything to a swimming man.

The correspondent arrived in water that reached only to his waist, but his condition did not enable him to stand for more than a moment. Each wave knocked him into a heap, and the undertow pulled at him.

Then he saw the man who had been running and undressing, and undressing and running, come bounding into the water. He dragged ashore the cook, and then waded toward the captain; but the captain waved him away and sent him to the correspondent. He was naked—naked as a tree in winter; but a halo was about his head, and he shone like a saint. He gave a strong pull, and a long drag, and a bully heave at the correspondent's hand. The correspondent, schooled in the minor formulae, said, "Thanks, old man." But suddenly the man cried, "What's that?" He pointed a swift finger. The correspondent said, "Go."

In the shallows, face downward, lay the oiler. His forehead touched sand that was periodically, between each wave, clear of the sea.

The correspondent did not know all that transpired afterward. When he achieved safe ground he fell, striking the sand with each particular part of his body. It was as if he had dropped from a roof, but the thud was grateful to him.

It seems that instantly the beach was populated with men with blankets, clothes, and flasks, and women with coffee-pots and all the remedies sacred to their minds. The welcome of the land to the men from the sea was warm and generous; but a still and dripping shape was carried slowly up the beach, and the land's welcome for it could only be the different and sinister hospitality of the grave.

When it came night, the white waves paced to and fro in the moonlight, and the wind brought the sound of the great sea's voice to the men on the shore, and they felt that they could then be interpreters.

WILLA CATHER

PAUL'S CASE

It was Paul's afternoon to appear before the faculty of the Pittsburgh High School to account for his various misdemeanours. He had been suspended a week ago, and his father had called at the Principal's office and confessed his perplexity about his son. Paul entered the faculty room suave and smiling. His clothes were a trifle outgrown, and the tan velvet on the collar of his open overcoat was frayed and worn; but for all that there was something of the dandy about him, and he wore an opal pin in his neatly knotted black four-in-hand, and a red carnation in his buttonhole. This latter adornment the faculty somehow felt was not properly significant of the contrite spirit befitting a boy under the ban of suspension.

Paul was tall for his age and very thin, with high, cramped shoulders and a narrow chest. His eyes were remarkable for a certain hysterical brilliancy, and he continually used them in a conscious, theatrical sort of way, peculiarly offensive in a boy. The pupils were abnormally large, as though he were addicted to belladonna, but there was a glassy glitter about them which that drug does not produce.

When questioned by the Principal as to why he was there, Paul stated, politely enough, that he wanted to come back to school. This was a lie, but Paul was quite accustomed to lying; found it, indeed, indispensable for overcoming friction. His teachers were asked to state their respective charges against him, which they did with such a rancour and aggrievedness as evinced that this was not a usual case. Disorder and impertinence were among the offences named, yet each of his instructors felt that it was scarcely possible to put into words the real cause of the trouble, which lay in a sort of hysterically defiant manner of the boy's; in the contempt which they all knew he felt for them, and which he seemingly made not the least effort to conceal. Once, when he had been making a synopsis of a paragraph at the blackboard, his English teacher had stepped to his side and attempted to guide his hand. Paul had started back with a shudder and thrust his hands violently behind him. The astonished woman could scarcely have been more hurt and embarrassed had he struck at her. The insult was so involuntary and definitely personal as to be unforgettable. In one way and another, he had made all his teachers, men and women alike, conscious of the same feeling of physical aversion. In one class he habitually sat with his hand shading his eyes; in another he always looked out of the window during the recitation; in another he made a running commentary on the lecture, with humorous intent.

His teachers felt this afternoon that his whole attitude was symbolized by his shrug and his flippantly red carnation flower, and they fell upon him without mercy, his English teacher leading the pack. He stood through it smiling, his pale lips parted over his white teeth. (His lips were continually twitching, and he had a habit of raising his eyebrows that was contemptuous and irritating to the last degree.) Older boys than Paul had broken down and shed tears under that ordeal, but his set smile did not once desert him, and his only sign of discomfort was the nervous trembling of the fingers that toyed with the buttons of his overcoat, and an occasional jerking of the other hand which held his hat. Paul was always smiling, always glancing about him, seeming to feel that people might be watching him and trying to detect something. This conscious expression, since it was as far as possible from boyish mirthfulness, was usually attributed to insolence or "smartness."

As the inquisition proceeded, one of his instructors repeated an impertinent remark of the boy's, and the Principal asked him whether he thought that a courteous speech to make to a woman. Paul shrugged his shoulders slightly and his eyebrows twitched.

"I don't know," he replied. "I didn't mean to be polite or impolite, either. I guess it's a sort of way I have, of saying things regardless."

The Principal asked him whether he didn't think that a way it would be well to get rid of. Paul grinned and said he guessed so. When he was told that he could go, he bowed gracefully and went out. His bow was like a repetition of the scandalous red carnation.

His teachers were in despair, and his drawing master voiced the feeling of them all when he declared there was something about the boy which none of them understood. He added: "I don't really believe that smile of his comes altogether from insolence; there's something sort of haunted about it. The boy is not strong, for one thing. There is something wrong about the fellow."

The drawing master had come to realize that, in looking at Paul, one saw only his white teeth and the forced animation of his eyes. One warm afternoon the boy had gone to sleep at his drawing-board, and his master had noted with amazement what a white, blue-veined face it was; drawn and wrinkled like an old man's about the eyes, the lips twitching even in his sleep.

His teachers left the building dissatisfied and unhappy; humiliated to have felt so vindictive toward a mere boy, to have uttered this feeling in cutting terms, and to have set each other on, as it were, in the grewsome game of intemperate reproach. One of them remembered having seen a miserable street cat set at bay by a ring of tormentors.

As for Paul, he ran down the hill whistling the Soldiers' Chorus from *Faust,* looking wildly behind him now and then to see whether some of his teachers were not there to witness his light-heartedness. As it was now late in the afternoon and Paul was on duty that evening as usher at Carnegie Hall, he decided that he would not go home to supper.

When he reached the concert hall the doors were not yet open. It was chilly outside, and he decided to go up into the picture gallery—always deserted at this hour—where there were some of Raffelli's gay studies of Paris streets and an airy blue Venetian scene or two that always exhilarated him. He was delighted to find no one in the gallery but the old guard, who sat in the corner, a newspaper on his knee, a black patch over one eye and the other closed. Paul possessed himself of the place and walked confidently up and down, whistling under his breath. After a while he sat down before a blue Rico and lost himself. When he bethought him to look at his watch, it was after seven o'clock, and he rose with a start and ran downstairs, making a face at Augustus Cæsar, peering out from the cast-room, and an evil gesture at the Venus of Milo as he passed her on the stairway.

When Paul reached the ushers' dressing-room half-a-dozen boys were there already, and he began excitedly to tumble into his uniform. It was one of the few that at all approached fitting, and Paul thought it very becoming—though he knew the tight, straight coat accentuated his narrow chest, about which he was exceedingly sensitive. He was always excited while he dressed, twanging all over to the tuning of the strings and the preliminary flourishes of the horns in the music-room; but tonight he seemed quite beside himself, and he teased and plagued the boys until, telling him that he was crazy, they put him down on the floor and sat on him.

Somewhat calmed by his suppression, Paul dashed out to the front of the house to seat the early comers. He was a model usher. Gracious and smiling he ran up and down the aisles. Nothing was too much trouble for him; he carried messages and brought programs as though it were his greatest pleasure in life, and all the people in his section thought him a charming boy, feeling that he remembered and admired them. As the house filled, he grew more and more vivacious and animated, and the colour came to his cheeks and lips. It was very much as though this were a great reception and Paul were the host. Just as the musicians came out to take their places, his English teacher arrived with checks for the seats which a prominent manufacturer had taken for the season. She betrayed some embarrassment when she handed Paul the tickets, and a *hauteur* which subsequently made her feel very foolish. Paul was startled for a moment, and had the feeling of wanting to put her out; what business had she here among all these fine people and gay colours? He looked her over and decided that she was not appropriately dressed and must be a fool to sit downstairs in such togs. The tickets had probably been sent her out of kindness, he reflected, as he put down a seat for her, and she had about as much right to sit there as he had.

When the symphony began Paul sank into one of the rear seats with a long sigh of relief, and lost himself as he had done before the Rico. It was not that symphonies, as such, meant anything in particular to Paul, but the first sigh of the instruments seemed to free some hilarious spirit within him; something that struggled there like the Genius in the bottle found by the Arab fisherman. He felt a sudden zest of life; the lights danced before his eyes and the concert hall blazed into unimaginable splendour. When the soprano soloist came on, Paul forgot even the nastiness of his teacher's being there, and gave himself up to the peculiar intoxication such personages always had for him. The soloist chanced to be a German woman, by no means in her first youth, and the mother of many children; but she wore a satin gown and a tiara, and she had that indefinable air of achievement, that world-shine upon her, which always blinded Paul to any possible defects.

After a concern was over, Paul was often irritable and wretched until he got to sleep,—and tonight he was even more than usually restless. He had the feeling of not being able to let down; of its being impossible to give up this delicious excitement which was the only thing that could be called living at all. During the last number he withdrew and, after hastily changing his clothes in the dressing-room, slipped out to the side door where the singer's carriage stood. Here he began pacing rapidly up and down the walk, waiting to see her come out.

Over yonder the Schenley, in its vacant stretch, loomed big and square through the fine rain, the windows of its twelve stories glowing like those of a lighted card-board house under a Christmas tree. All the actors and singers of any importance stayed there when they were in the city, and a number of the big manufacturers of the place lived there in the winter. Paul had often hung about the hotel, watching the people go in and out, longing to enter and leave school-masters and dull care behind him for ever.

At last the singer came out, accompanied by the conductor, who helped her into her carriage and closed the door with a cordial *auf wiedersehen,*—which set Paul to wondering whether she were not an old sweetheart of his. Paul followed the carriage over to the hotel, walking so rapidly as not to be far from the entrance when the singer alighted and disappeared behind the swinging glass doors which were opened by a negro in a tall hat and a long coat. In the moment that the door was ajar, it seemed to Paul that he, too, entered. He seemed to feel himself go after her up the steps, into the warm, lighted building, into an exotic, a tropical world of shiny, glistening surfaces and basking ease. He reflected upon the mysterious dishes that were brought into the dining-room, the green bottles in buckets of ice, as he had seen them in the supper party pictures of the Sunday supplement. A quick gust of wind brought the rain down with sudden vehemence, and Paul was startled to find that he was still outside in the slush of the gravel driveway; that his boots were letting in the water and his scanty overcoat was clinging wet about him; that the lights in front of the concert hall were out, and that the rain was driving in sheets between him and the orange glow of the windows above him. There it was, what he wanted—tangibly before him, like the fairy world of a Christmas pantomime; as the rain beat in his face, Paul wondered whether he were destined always to shiver in the black night outside, looking up at it.

He turned and walked reluctantly toward the car tracks. The end had to come sometime; his father in his night-clothes at the top of the stairs, explanations that did not explain, hastily improvised fictions that were forever tripping him up, his upstairs room and its horrible yellow wall-paper, the creaking bureau with the greasy plush collar-box, and over his painted wooden bed the pictures of George Washington and John

Calvin, and the framed motto, "Feed my Lambs," which had been worked in red worsted by his mother, whom Paul could not remember.

Half an hour later, Paul alighted from the Negley Avenue car and went slowly down one of the side streets off the main thoroughfare. It was a highly respectable street, where all the houses were exactly alike, and where business men of moderate means begot and reared large families of children, all of whom went to Sabbath-school and learned the shorter catechism, and were interested in arithmetic; all of whom were as exactly alike as their homes, and of a piece with the monotony in which they lived. Paul never went up Cordelia Street without a shudder of loathing. His home was next to the house of the Cumberland minister. He approached it tonight with the nerveless sense of defeat, the hopeless feeling of sinking back forever into ugliness and commonness that he had always had when he came home. The moment he turned into Cordelia Street he felt the waters close above his head. After each of these orgies of living, he experienced all the physical depression which follows a debauch; the loathing of respectable beds, of common food, of a house permeated by kitchen odours; a shuddering repulsion for the flavourless, colourless mass of every-day existence; a morbid desire for cool things and soft lights and fresh flowers.

The nearer he approached the house, the more absolutely unequal Paul felt to the sight of it all; his ugly sleeping chamber; the cold bath-room with the grimy zinc tub, the cracked mirror, the dripping spiggots; his father, at the top of the stairs, his hairy legs sticking out from his nightshirt, his feet thrust into carpet slippers. He was so much later than usual that there would certainly be inquiries and reproaches. Paul stopped short before the door. He felt that he could not be accosted by his father tonight; that he could not toss again on that miserable bed. He would not go in. He would tell his father that he had no car fare, and it was raining so hard he had gone home with one of the boys and stayed all night.

Meanwhile, he was wet and cold. He went around to the back of the house and tried one of the basement windows, found it open, raised it cautiously, and scrambled down the cellar wall to the floor. There he stood, holding his breath, terrified by the noise he had made; but the floor above him was silent, and there was no creak on the stairs. He found a soap-box, and carried it over to the soft ring of light that streamed from the furnace door, and sat down. He was horribly afraid of rats, so he did not try to sleep, but sat looking distrustfully at the dark, still terrified lest he might have awakened his father. In such reactions, after one of the experiences which made days and nights out of the dreary blanks of the calendar, when his senses were deadened, Paul's head was always singularly clear. Suppose his father had heard him getting in at the window and had come down and shot him for a burglar? Then, again, suppose his father had come down, pistol in hand, and he had cried out in time to save himself, and his father had been horrified to think how nearly he had killed him? Then, again, suppose a day should come when his father would remember that night, and wish there had been no warning cry to stay his hand? With this last supposition Paul entertained himself until daybreak.

The following Sunday was fine; the sodden November chill was broken by the last flash of autumnal summer. In the morning Paul had to go to church and Sabbath-school, as always. On seasonable Sunday afternoons the burghers of Cordelia Street usually sat out on their front "stoops," and talked to their neighbours on the next stoop, or called to those across the street in neighbourly fashion. The men sat placidly on gay cushions placed upon the steps that led down to the sidewalk, while the women, in their Sunday "waists," sat in rockers on the cramped porches, pretending to be greatly at their ease. The children played in the streets; there were so many of them that the place resembled the recreation grounds of a kindergarten. The men on the steps—all in their shirt sleeves, their vests unbuttoned—sat with their legs well apart, their stomachs comfortably protruding, and talked of the prices of things, or told anecdotes of the sagacity of their various chiefs and overlords. They occasionally looked over the multitude of squabbling children, listened affectionately to their high-pitched, nasal voices, smiling to see their own proclivities reproduced in their offspring, and interspersed their legends of the iron kings with remarks about their sons' progress at school, their grades in arithmetic, and the amounts they had saved in their toy banks.

On this last Sunday of November, Paul sat all the afternoon on the lowest step of his "stoop," staring into the street, while his sisters, in their rockers, were talking to the minister's daughters next door about how many shirt-waists they had made in the last week, and how many waffles some one had eaten at the last church supper. When the weather was warm, and his father was in a particularly jovial frame of mind, the girls made lemonade, which was always brought out in a red-glass pitcher, ornamented with forget-me-nots in blue enamel. This the girls thought very fine, and the neighbours joked about the suspicious colour of the pitcher.

Today Paul's father, on the top step, was talking to a young man who shifted a restless baby from knee to knee. He happened to be the young man who was daily held up to Paul as a model, and after whom it was his father's dearest hope that he would pattern. This young man was of a ruddy complexion, with a compressed, red mouth, and faded, near-sighted eyes, over which he wore thick spectacles, with gold bows that curved about his ears. He was clerk to one of the magnates of a great steel corporation, and was looked upon in Cordelia Street as a young man with a future. There was a story that, some five years ago—he was now barely twenty-six—he had been a trifle "dissipated," but in order to curb his appetites and save the loss of time and strength that a sowing of wild oats might have entailed, he had taken his chief's advice, oft reiterated to his employés, and at twenty-one had married the first woman whom he could persuade to share his fortunes. She happened to be an angular school-mistress, much older than he, who also wore thick glasses, and who had now borne him four children, all near-sighted, like herself.

The young man was relating how his chief, now cruising in the Mediterranean, kept in touch with all the details of the business, arranging his office hours on his yacht just as though he were at home, and "knocking off work enough to keep two stenographers busy." His father told, in turn, the plan his corporation was considering, of putting in an electric railway plant at Cairo. Paul snapped his teeth; he had an awful apprehension that they might spoil it all before he got there. Yet he rather liked to hear these legends of the iron kings, that were told and retold on Sundays and holidays; these stories of palaces in Venice, yachts on the Mediterranean, and high play at Monte Carlo appealed to his fancy, and he was interested in the triumphs of cash boys who had become famous, though he had no mind for the cash-boy stage.

After supper was over, and he had helped to dry the dishes, Paul nervously asked his father whether he could go to George's to get some help in his geometry, and still more nervously asked for car-fare. This latter request he had to repeat, as his father, on principle, did not like to hear requests for money, whether much or little. He asked Paul whether he could not go to some boy who lived nearer, and told him that he ought not to leave his school work until Sunday; but he gave him the dime. He was not a poor man, but he had a worthy ambition to come up in the world. His only reason for allowing Paul to usher was that he thought a boy ought to be earning a little.

Paul bounded upstairs, scrubbed the greasy odour of the dish-water from his hands with the ill-smelling soap he hated, and then shook over his fingers a few drops of violet water from the bottle he kept hidden in his drawer. He left the house with his geometry conspicuously under his arm, and the moment he got out of Cordelia Street and boarded a downtown car, he shook off the lethargy of two deadening days, and began to live again.

The leading juvenile of the permanent stock company which played at one of the downtown theatres was an acquaintance of Paul's, and the boy had been invited to drop in at the Sunday-night rehearsals whenever he could. For more than a year Paul had spent every available moment loitering about Charley Edwards's dressing-room. He had won a place among Edwards's following not only because the young actor, who could not afford to employ a dresser, often found him useful, but because he recognized in Paul something akin to what churchmen term "vocation."

It was at the theatre and at Carnegie Hall that Paul really lived; the rest was but a sleep and a forgetting. This was Paul's fairy tale, and it had for him all the allurement of a secret love. The moment he inhaled the gassy, painty, dusty odour behind the scenes, he breathed like a prisoner set free, and felt within him the possibility of doing or saying splendid, brilliant things. The moment the cracked orchestra beat out the overture from *Martha,* or jerked at the serenade from *Rigoletto,* all stupid and ugly things slid from him, and his senses were deliciously, yet delicately fired.

Perhaps it was because, in Paul's world, the natural nearly always wore the guise of ugliness, that a certain element of artificiality seemed to him necessary in beauty. Perhaps it was because his experience of life elsewhere was so full of Sabbath-school picnics, petty economies, wholesome advice as to how to succeed in life, and the unescapable odours of cooking, that he found this existence so alluring, these smartly-clad men and women so attractive, that he was so moved by these starry apple orchards that bloomed perennially under the lime-light.

It would be difficult to put it strongly enough how convincingly the stage entrance of that theatre was for Paul the actual portal of Romance. Certainly none of the company ever suspected it, least of all Charley Edwards. It was very like the old stories that used to float about London of fabulously rich Jews, who had subterranean halls, with palms, and fountains, and soft lamps, and richly apparelled women who never saw the disenchanting light of London day. So, in the midst of that smoke-palled city, enamoured of figures and grimy toil, Paul had his secret temple, his wishing-carpet, his bit of blue-and-white Mediterranean shore bathed in perpetual sunshine.

Several of Paul's teachers had a theory that his imagination had been perverted by garish fiction; but the truth was, he scarcely ever read at all. The books at home were not such as would either tempt or corrupt a youthful mind, and as for reading the novels that some of his friends urged upon him—well, he got what he wanted much more quickly from music; any sort of music, from an orchestra to a barrel organ. He needed only the spark, the indescribable thrill that made his imagination master of his senses, and he could make plots and pictures enough of his own.

It was equally true that he was not stage-struck—not, at any rate, in the usual acceptation of that expression. He had no desire to become an actor, any more than he had to become a musician. He felt no necessity to do any of these things; what he wanted was to see, to be in the atmosphere, float on the wave of it, to be carried out, blue league after blue league, away from everything.

After a night behind the scenes, Paul found the schoolroom more than ever repulsive; the bare floors and naked walls; the prosy men who never wore frock coats, or violets in their buttonholes; the women with their dull gowns, shrill voices, and pitiful seriousness about prepositions that govern the dative. He could not bear to have the other pupils think, for a moment, that he took these people seriously; he must convey to them that he considered it all trivial, and was there only by way of a joke, anyway. He had autograph pictures of all the members of the stock company which he showed his classmates, telling them the most incredible stories of his familiarity with these people, of his acquaintance with the soloists who came to Carnegie Hall, his suppers with them and the flowers he sent them. When these stories lost their effect, and his audience grew listless, he would bid all the boys good-bye, announcing that he was going to travel for awhile; going to Naples, to California, to Egypt. Then, next Monday, he would slip back, conscious and nervously smiling; his sister was ill, and he would have to defer his voyage until spring.

Matters went steadily worse with Paul at school. In the itch to let his instructors know how heartily he despised them, and how thoroughly he was appreciated elsewhere, he mentioned once or twice that he had no time to fool with theorems; adding—with a twitch of the eyebrows and a touch of that nervous bravado which so perplexed them—that he was helping the people down at the stock company; they were old friends of his.

The upshot of the matter was, that the Principal went to Paul's father, and Paul was taken out of school and put to work. The manager at Carnegie Hall was told to get another usher in his stead; the doorkeeper at the theatre was warned not to admit him to the house; and Charley Edwards remorsefully promised the boy's father not to see him again.

The members of the stock company were vastly amused when some of Paul's stories reached them—especially the women. They were hard-working women, most of them supporting indolent husbands or brothers, and they laughed rather bitterly at having stirred the boy to such fervid and florid inventions. They agreed with the faculty and with his father, that Paul's was a bad case.

The east-bound train was ploughing through a January snow-storm; the dull dawn was beginning to show grey when the engine whistled a mile out of Newark. Paul started up from the seat where he had lain curled in uneasy slumber, rubbed the breath-misted window glass with his hand, and peered out. The snow was whirling in curling eddies above the white bottom lands, and the drifts lay already deep in the fields and along the fences, while here and there the long dead grass and dried weed stalks protruded black above it. Lights shone from the scattered houses, and a gang of labourers who stood beside the track waved their lanterns.

Paul had slept very little, and he felt grimy and uncomfortable. He had made the all-night journey in a day coach because he was afraid if he took a Pullman he might be seen by some Pittsburgh business man who had noticed him in Denny & Carson's office. When the whistle woke him, he clutched quickly at his breast pocket, glancing about him with an uncertain smile. But the little, clay-bespattered Italians were still sleeping, the slatternly women across the aisle were in open-mouthed oblivion, and even the crumby, crying babies were for the nonce stilled. Paul settled back to struggle with his impatience as best he could.

When he arrived at the Jersey City station, he hurried through his breakfast, manifestly ill at ease and keeping a sharp eye about him. After he reached the Twenty-third Street station, he consulted a cabman, and had himself driven to a men's furnishing establishment which was just opening for the day. He spent upward of two hours there, buying with endless reconsidering and great care. His new street suit he put on in the fitting-room; the frock coat and dress clothes he had bundled into the cab with his new shirts. Then he drove to a hatter's and a shoe house. His next errand was at Tiffany's, where he selected silver mounted brushes and a scarf-pin. He would not wait to have his silver marked, he said. Lastly, he stopped at a trunk shop on Broadway, and had his purchases packed into varous travelling bags.

It was a little after one o'clock when he drove up to the Waldorf, and, after settling with the cabman, went into the office. He registered from Washington; said his mother and father had been abroad, and that he had come down to await the arrival of their steamer. He told his story plausibly and had no trouble, since he offered to pay for them in advance, in engaging his rooms; a sleeping-room, sitting-room and bath.

Not once, but a hundred times Paul had planned this entry into New York. He had gone over every detail of it with Charley Edwards, and in his scrap book at home there were pages of description about New York hotels, cut from the Sunday papers.

When he was shown to his sitting-room on the eighth floor, he saw at a glance that everything was as it should be; there was but one detail in his mental picture that the place did not realize, so he rang for the bell boy and sent him down for flowers. He moved about nervously until the boy returned, putting away his new linen and fingering it delightedly as he did so. When the flowers came, he put them hastily into water, and then tumbled into a hot bath. Presently he came out of his white bath-room, resplendent in his new silk underwear, and playing with the tassels of his red robe. The snow was whirling so fiercely outside his windows that he could scarcely see across the street; but within, the air was deliciously soft and fragrant. He put the violets and jonquils on the tabouret beside the couch, and threw himself down with a long sigh, covering himself with a Roman blanket. He was thoroughly tired; he had been in such haste, he had stood up to such a strain, covered so much ground in the last twenty-four hours, that he wanted to think how it had all come about. Lulled by the sound of the wind, the warm air, and the cool fragrance of the flowers, he sank into deep, drowsy retrospection.

It had been wonderfully simple; when they had shut him out of the theatre and concert hall, when they had taken away his bone, the whole thing was virtually determined. The rest was a mere matter of opportunity. The only thing that at all surprised him was his own courage—for he realized well enough that he had always been tormented by fear, a sort of apprehensive dread that, of late years, as the meshes of the lies he had told closed about him, had been pulling the muscles of his body tighter and tighter. Until now, he could not remember a time when he had not been dreading something. Even when he was a little boy, it was always there—behind him, or before, or on either side. There had always been the shadowed corner, the dark place into which he dared not look, but from which something seemed always to be watching him—and Paul had done things that were not pretty to watch, he knew.

But now he had a curious sense of relief, as though he had at last thrown down the gauntlet to the thing in the corner.

Yet it was but a day since he had been sulking in the traces; but yesterday afternoon that he had been sent to the bank with Denny & Carson's deposit, as usual—but this time he was instructed to leave the book to be balanced. There was above two thousand dollars in checks, and nearly a thousand in the bank notes which he had taken from the book and quietly transferred to his pocket. At the bank he had made out a new deposit slip. His nerves had been steady enough to permit of his returning to the office, where he had finished his work and asked for a full day's holiday tomorrow, Saturday, giving a perfectly reasonable pretext. The bank book, he knew, would not be returned before Monday or Tuesday, and his father would be out of town for the next week. From the time he slipped the bank notes into his pocket until he boarded the night train for New York, he had not known a moment's hesitation.

How astonishingly easy it had all been; here he was, the thing done; and this time there would be no awakening, no figure at the top of the stairs. He watched the snow flakes whirling by his window until he fell asleep.

When he awoke, it was four o'clock in the afternoon. He bounded up with a start; one of his precious days gone already! He spent nearly an hour in dressing, watching every stage of his toilet carefully in the mirror. Everything was quite perfect; he was exactly the kind of boy he had always wanted to be.

When he went downstairs, Paul took a carriage and drove up Fifth avenue toward the Park. The snow had somewhat abated; carriages and tradesmen's wagons were hurrying soundlessly to and fro in the winter twilight; boys in woollen mufflers were shovelling off the doorsteps; the avenue stages made fine spots of colour against the white street. Here and there on the corners whole flower gardens blooming behind glass windows, against which the snow flakes stuck and melted; violets, roses, carnations, lilies of the valley—somehow vastly more lovely and alluring that they blossomed thus unnaturally in the snow. The Park itself was a wonderful stage winter-piece.

When he returned, the pause of the twilight had ceased, and the tune of the streets had changed. The snow was falling faster, lights streamed from the hotels that reared their many stories fearlessly up into the storm, defying the raging Atlantic winds. A long, black stream of carriages poured down the avenue, intersected here and there by other streams, tending horizontally. There were a score of cabs about the entrance of this hotel, and his driver had to wait. Boys in livery were running in and out of the awning stretched across the sidewalk, up and down the red velvet carpet laid from the door to the street. Above, about, within it all, was the rumble and roar, the hurry and toss of thousands of human beings as hot for pleasure as himself, and on every side of him towered the glaring affirmation of the omnipotence of wealth.

The boy set his teeth and drew his shoulders together in a spasm of realization; the plot of all dramas, the text of all romances, the nerve-stuff of all sensations was whirling about him like the snow flakes. He burnt like a faggot in a tempest.

When Paul came down to dinner, the music of the orchestra floated up the elevator shaft to greet him. As he stepped into the thronged corridor, he sank back into one of the chairs against the wall to get his breath. The lights, the chatter, the perfumes, the bewildering medley of colour—he had, for a moment, the feeling of not being able to stand it. But only for a moment; these were his own people, he told himself. He went slowly about the corridors, through the writing-rooms, smoking-rooms, reception-rooms, as though he were exploring the chambers of an enchanted palace, built and peopled for him alone.

When he reached the dining-room he sat down at a table near a window. The flowers, the white linen, the many-coloured wine glasses, the gay toilettes of the women, the low popping of corks, the undulating repetitions of the *Blue Danube* from the orchestra, all flooded Paul's dream with bewildering radiance. When the roseate tinge of his champagne was added—that cold, precious, bubbling stuff that creamed and foamed in his glass—Paul wondered that there were honest men in the world at all. This was what all the world was fighting for, he reflected; this was what all the struggle was about. He doubted the reality of his past. Had he ever known a place called Cordelia Street, a place where fagged looking business men boarded the early car? Mere rivets in a machine they seemed to Paul,—sickening men, with combings of children's hair always hanging to their coats, and the smell of cooking in their clothes. Cordelia Street—Ah, that belonged to another time and country! Had he not always been thus, had he not sat here night after night, from as far back as he could remember, looking pensively over just such shimmering textures, and slowly twirling the stem of a glass like this one between his thumb and middle finger? He rather thought he had.

He was not in the least abashed or lonely. He had no especial desire to meet or to know any of these people; all he demanded was the right to look on and conjecture, to watch the pageant. The mere stage properties were all he contended for. Nor was he lonely later in the evening, in his loge at the Opera. He was entirely rid of his nervous misgivings, of his forced aggressiveness, of the imperative desire to show himself different from his surroundings. He felt now that his surroundings explained him. Nobody questioned the purple; he had only to wear it passively. He had only to glance down at his dress coat to reassure himself that here it would be impossible for anyone to humiliate him.

He found it hard to leave his beautiful sitting-room to go to bed that night, and sat long watching the raging storm from his turret window. When he went to sleep, it was with the lights turned on in his bedroom; partly because of his old timidity, and partly so that, if he should wake in the night, there would be no wretched moment of doubt, no horrible suspicion of yellow wall-paper, or of Washington and Calvin above his bed.

On Sunday morning the city was practically snowbound. Paul breakfasted late, and in the afternoon he fell in with a wild San Francisco boy, a freshman at Yale, who said he had run down for a "little flyer" over Sunday. The young man offered to show Paul the night side of the town, and the two boys went off together after dinner, not returning to the hotel until seven o'clock the next morning. They had started out in the confiding warmth of a champagne friendship, but their parting in the elevator was singularly cool. The freshman pulled himself together to make his train, and Paul went to bed. He awoke at two o'clock in the afternoon, very thirsty and dizzy, and rang for ice-water, coffee, and the Pittsburgh papers.

On the part of the hotel management, Paul excited no suspicion. There was this to be said for him, that he wore his spoils with dignity and in no way made himself conspicuous. His chief greediness lay in his ears and eyes, and his excesses were not offensive ones. His dearest pleasures were the grey winter twilights in his sitting-room; his quiet enjoyment of his flowers, his clothes, his wide divan, his cigarette and his sense of power. He could not remember a time when he had felt so at peace with himself. The mere release from the necessity of petty lying, lying every day and every day, restored his self-respect. He had never lied for pleasure, even at school; but to make himself noticed and admired, to assert his difference from other Cordelia Street boys; and he felt a good deal more manly, more honest, even, now that he had no need for boastful pretensions, now that he could, as his actor friends used to say, "dress the part." It was characteristic that remorse did not occur to him. His golden days went by without a shadow, and he made each as perfect as he could.

On the eighth day after his arrival in New York, he found the whole affair exploited in the Pittsburgh papers, exploited with a wealth of detail which indicated that local news of a sensational nature was at a low ebb. The firm of Denny & Carson announced that the boy's father had refunded the full amount of his theft, and that they had no intention of prosecuting. The Cumberland minister had been interviewed, and expressed his hope of yet reclaiming the motherless lad, and Paul's Sabbath-school teacher declared that she would spare no effort to that end. The rumour had reached Pittsburgh that the boy had been seen in a New York hotel, and his father had gone East to find him and bring him home.

Paul had just come in to dress for dinner; he sank into a chair, weak in the knees, and clasped his head in his hands. It was to be worse than jail, even; the tepid waters of Cordelia Street were to close over him finally and forever. The grey monotony stretched before him in hopeless, unrelieved years; Sabbath-school, Young People's Meeting, the yellow-papered room, the damp dish-towels; it all rushed back upon him with sickening vividness. He had the old feeling that the orchestra had suddenly stopped, the sinking sensation that the play was over. The sweat broke out on his face, and he sprang to his feet, looked about him with his white, conscious smile, and winked at himself in the mirror. With something of the childish belief in miracles with which he had so often gone to class, all his lessons unlearned, Paul dressed and dashed whistling down the corridor to the elevator.

He had no sooner entered the dining-room and caught the measure of the music, than his remembrance was lightened by his old elastic power of claiming the moment, mounting with it, and finding it all sufficient. The glare and glitter about him, the mere scenic accessories had again, and for the last time, their old potency. He would show himself that he was game, he would finish the thing splendidly. He doubted, more than ever, the existence of Cordelia Street, and for the first time he drank his wine recklessly. Was he not, after all, one of these fortunate beings? Was he not still himself, and in his own place? He drummed a nervous accompaniment to the music and looked about him, telling himself over and over that it had paid.

He reflected drowsily, to the swell of the violin and the chill sweetness of his wine, that he might have done it more wisely. He might have caught an outbound steamer and been well out of their clutches before now. But the other side of the world had seemed too far away and too uncertain then; he could not have waited for it; his need had been too sharp. If he had to choose over again, he would do the same thing tomorrow. He looked affectionately about the dining-room, now gilded with a soft mist. Ah, it had paid indeed!

Paul was awakened next morning by a painful throbbing in his head and feet. He had thrown himself across the bed without undressing, and had slept with his shoes on. His limbs and hands were lead heavy, and his tongue and throat were parched. There came upon him one of those fateful attacks of clear-headedness that never occurred except when he was physically exhausted and his nerves hung loose. He lay still and closed his eyes and let the tide of realities wash over him.

His father was in New York; "Stopping at some joint or other," he told himself. The memory of successive summers on the front stoop fell upon him like a weight of black water. He had not a hundred dollars left; and he knew now, more than ever, that money was everything, the wall that stood between all he loathed and all he wanted. The thing was winding itself up; he had thought of that on his first glorious day in New York, and had even provided a way to snap the thread. It lay on his dressing-table now; he had got it out last night when he came blindly up from dinner,—but the shiny metal hurt his eyes, and he disliked the look of it, anyway.

He rose and moved about with a painful effort, succumbing now and again to attacks of nausea. It was the old depression exaggerated; all the world had become Cordelia Street. Yet somehow he was not afraid of anything, was absolutely calm; perhaps because he had looked into the dark corner at last, and knew. It was bad enough, what he saw there; but somehow not so bad as his long fear of it had been. He saw everything clearly now. He had a feeling that he had made the best of it, that he had lived the sort of life he was meant to live, and for half an hour he sat staring at the revolver. But he told himself that was not the way, so he went downstairs and took a cab to the ferry.

When Paul arrived at Newark, he got off the train and took another cab, directing the driver to follow the Pennsylvania tracks out of the town. The snow lay heavy on the roadways and had drifted deep in the open fields. Only here and there the dead grass or dried weed stalks projected, singularly black, above it. Once well into the country, Paul dismissed the carriage and walked, floundering along the tracks, his mind a medley of irrelevant things. He seemed to hold in his brain an actual picture of everything he had seen that morning. He remembered every feature of both his drivers, the toothless old woman from whom he had bought the red flowers in his coat, the agent from whom he had got his ticket, and all of his fellow-passengers on the ferry. His mind, unable to cope with vital matters near at hand, worked feverishly and deftly at sorting and grouping these images. They made for him a part of the ugliness of the world, of the ache in his head, and the bitter burning on his tongue. He stooped and put a handful of snow into his mouth as he walked, but that, too, seemed hot. When he reached a little hillside, where the tracks ran through a cut some twenty feet below him, he stopped and sat down.

The carnations in his coat were drooping with the cold, he noticed; all their red glory over. It occurred to him that all the flowers he had seen in the show windows that first night must have gone the same way, long before this. It was only one splendid breath they had, in spite of their brave mockery at the winter outside the glass. It was a losing game in the end, it seemed, this revolt against the homilies by which the world is run. Paul took one of the blossoms carefully from his coat and scooped a little hole in the snow, where he covered it up. Then he dozed a while, from his weak condition, seeming insensible to the cold.

The sound of an approaching train woke him, and he started to his feet, remembering only his resolution, and afraid lest he should be too late. He stood watching the approaching locomotive, his teeth chattering, his lips drawn away from them in a frightened smile; once or twice he glanced nervously sidewise, as though he were being watched. When the right moment came, he jumped. As he fell, the folly of his haste occurred to him with merciless clearness, the vastness of what he had left undone. There flashed through his brain, clearer than ever before, the blue of Adriatic water, the yellow of Algerian sands.

He felt something strike his chest,—his body was being thrown swiftly through the air, on and on, immeasurably far and fast, while his limbs gently relaxed. Then, because the picture making mechanism was crushed, the disturbing visions flashed into black, and Paul dropped back into the immense design of things.

SHERWOOD ANDERSON

Death in the Woods

She was an old woman and lived on a farm near the town in which I lived. All country and small-town people have seen such old women, but no one knows much about them. Such an old woman comes into town driving an old worn-out horse or she comes afoot carrying a basket. She may own a few hens and have eggs to sell. She brings them in a basket and takes them to a grocer. There she trades them in. She gets some salt pork and some beans. Then she gets a pound or two of sugar and some flour.

Afterward she goes to the butcher's and asks for some dog meat. She may spend ten or fifteen cents, but when she does she asks for something. In my day the butchers gave liver to anyone who wanted to carry it away. In our family we were always having it. Once one of my brothers got a whole cow's liver at the slaughter-house near the fair-grounds. We had it until we were sick of it. It never cost a cent. I have hated the thought of it ever since.

The old farm woman got some liver and a soup bone. She never visited with anyone, and as soon as she got what she wanted she lit out for home. It made quite a load for such an old body. No one gave her a lift.

People drive right down a road and never notice an old woman like that.

There was such an old woman used to come into town past our house one summer and fall when I was sick with what was called inflammatory rheumatism. She went home later carrying a heavy pack on her back. Two or three large gaunt-looking dogs followed at her heels.

The old woman was nothing special. She was one of the nameless ones that hardly anyone knows, but she got into my thoughts. I have just suddenly now, after all these years, remembered her and what happened. It is a story. Her name was, I think, Grimes, and she lived with her husband and son in a small unpainted house on the bank of a small creek four miles from town.

The husband and son were a tough lot. Although the son was but twenty-one, he had already served a term in jail. It was whispered about that the woman's husband stole horses and ran them off to some other county. Now and then, when a horse turned up missing, the man had also disappeared. No one ever caught him. Once, when I was loafing at Tom Whitehead's livery barn, the man came there and sat on the bench in front. Two or three other men were there, but no one spoke to him. He sat for a few minutes and then got up and went away. When he was leaving he turned around and stared at the men. There was a look of defiance in his eyes. "Well, I have tried to be friendly. You don't want to talk to me. It has been so wherever I have gone in this town. If, some day, one of your fine horses turns up missing, well, then what?" He did not say anything actually. "I'd like to bust one of you on the jaw," was about what his eyes said. I remember how the look in his eyes made me shiver.

The old man belonged to a family that had had money once. His name was Grimes, Jake Grimes. It all comes back clearly now. His father, John Grimes, had owned a sawmill when the country was new and had made money. Then he got to drinking and running after women. When he died, there wasn't much left.

Jake blew in the rest. Pretty soon there wasn't any more lumber to cut and his land was nearly all gone.

He got his wife off a German farmer, for whom he went to work one June day in the wheat harvest. She was a young thing then and scared to death. You see, the farmer was up to something with the girl—she was, I think, a bound girl, and his wife had her suspicions. She took it out on the girl when the man wasn't around. Then, when the wife had to go off to town for supplies, the farmer got after her. She told young Jake that nothing really ever happened, but he didn't know whether to believe it or not.

He got her pretty easy himself, the first time he was out with her. He wouldn't have married her if the German farmer hadn't tried to tell him where to get off. He got her to go riding with him in his buggy one night when he was threshing on the place, and then he came for her the next Sunday night.

She managed to get out of the house without her employer's seeing, but when she was getting into the buggy he showed up. It was almost dark, and he just popped up suddenly at the horse's head. He grabbed the horse by the bridle and Jake got out his buggy whip.

They had it out all right! The German was a tough one. Maybe he didn't care whether his wife knew or not. Jake hit him over the face and shoulders with the buggy whip, but the horse got to acting up and he had to get out.

Then the two men went for it. The girl didn't see it. The horse started to run away and went nearly a mile down the road before the girl got him stopped. Then she managed to tie him to a tree beside the road. (I wonder how I know all this. It must have stuck in my mind from small-town tales when I was a boy.) Jake found her there after he got through with the German. She was huddled up in the buggy seat, crying, scared to death. She told Jake a lot of stuff, how the German had tried to get her, how he chased her once into the barn, how another time, when they happened to be alone in the barn together, he tore her dress open clear down the front. The German, she said, might have got her that time if he hadn't heard his old woman drive in at the gate. She had been off to town for supplies. Well, she would be putting the horse in the barn. The German managed to sneak off to the fields without his wife seeing. He told the girl he would kill her if she told. What could she do? She told a lie about ripping her dress in the barn when she was feeding the stock. I remember now that she was a bound girl and did not know where her father and mother were. Maybe she did not have any father. You know what I mean.

II

She married Jake and had a son and daughter but the daughter died.

Then she settled down to feed stock. That was her job. At the German's place she had cooked the food for the German and his wife. The wife was a strong woman with big hips and worked most of the time in the fields with her husband. She fed them and fed the cows in the barn, fed the pigs, the horses, and the chickens. Every moment of every day as a young girl was spent feeding something.

Then she married Jake Grimes and he had to be fed. She was a slight thing, and when she had been married for three or four years, and after the two children were born, her slender shoulders became stooped.

Jake always had a lot of big dogs around the house, that stood near the unused sawmill near the creek. He was always trading horses when he wasn't stealing something, and had a lot of poor bony ones about. Also, he kept three or four pigs and a cow. They were all pastured in the few acres left of the Grimes place and Jake did little.

He went into debt for a threshing outfit and ran it for several years, but it did not pay. People did not trust him. They were afraid he would steal the grain at night. He had to go a long way off to get work, and it cost too much to get there. In the winter he hunted and cut a little firewood, to be sold in some near-by town. When the boy grew up he was just like his father. They got drunk together. If there wasn't anything to eat in the house when they came home the old man gave his old woman a cut over the head. She had a few chickens of her own and had to kill one of them in a hurry. When they were all killed she wouldn't have any eggs to sell when she went to town, and then what would she do?

She had to scheme all her life about getting things fed, getting the pigs fed so they would grow fat and could be butchered in the fall. When they were butchered her husband took most of the meat off to town and sold it. If he did not do it first the boy did. They fought sometimes and when they fought the old woman stood aside trembling.

She had got the habit of silence anyway—that was fixed. Sometimes, when she began to look old—she wasn't forty yet—and when the husband and son were both off, trading horses or drinking or hunting or stealing, she went around the house and the barnyard muttering to herself.

How was she going to get everything fed?—that was her problem. The dogs had to be fed. There wasn't enough hay in the barn for the cow and the horses. If she didn't feed the chickens how could they lay eggs? Without eggs to sell how could she get things in town, things she had to have to keep the life of the farm going? Thank heaven, she did not have to feed her husband—in a certain way. That hadn't lasted long after their marriage and after the babies came. Where he went on his long trips she did not know. Sometimes he was gone from home for weeks, and after the boy grew up they went off together.

They left everything at home for her to manage and she had no money. She knew no one. No one ever talked to her in town. When it was winter she had to gather sticks of wood for her fire, had to try to keep the stock fed with very little grain.

The stock in the barn cried to her hungrily, the dogs followed her about. In the winter the hens laid few enough eggs. They huddled in the corners of the barn and she kept watching them. If a hen lays an egg in the barn in the winter and you do not find it, it freezes and breaks.

One day in winter the old woman went off to town with a few eggs and the dogs followed her. She did not get started until nearly three o'clock and the snow was heavy. She hadn't been feeling very well for several days and so she went muttering along, scantily clad, her shoulders stooped. She had an old grain bag in which she carried her eggs, tucked away down in the bottom. There weren't many of them, but in winter the price of eggs is up. She would get a little meat for the eggs, some salt pork, a little sugar, and some coffee, perhaps. It might be the butcher would give her a piece of liver.

When she had got to town and was trading in her eggs the dogs lay by the door outside. She did pretty well, got the things she needed, more than she had hoped. Then she went to the butcher and he gave her some liver and some dog meat.

It was the first time anyone had spoken to her in a friendly way for a long time. The butcher was alone in his shop when she went in and was annoyed by the thought of such a sick-looking old woman out on such a day. It was bitter cold and the snow, that had let up during the afternoon, was falling again. The butcher said something about her husband and her son, swore at them, and the old woman stared at him, a look of mild surprise in her eyes as he talked. He said that if either the husband or the son were going to get any of the liver or the heavy bones with scraps of meat hanging to them that he had put into the grain bag, he'd see him starve first.

Starve, eh? Well, things had to be fed. Men had to be fed, and the horses that weren't any good but maybe could be traded off, and the poor thin cow that hadn't given any milk for three months.

Horses, cows, pigs, dogs, men.

III

The old woman had to get back before darkness came if she could. The dogs followed at her heels, sniffing at the heavy grain bag she had fastened on her back. When she got to the edge of town she stopped by a fence and tied the bag on her back with a piece of rope she had carried in her dress pocket for just that purpose. That was an easier way to carry it. Her arms ached. It was hard when she had to crawl over fences, and once she fell over and landed in the snow. The dogs went frisking about. She had to struggle to get to her feet again, but she made it. The point of climbing over the fences was that there was a short cut over a hill and through a wood. She might have gone around by the road, but it was a mile farther that way. She was afraid she couldn't make it. And then, besides, the stock had to be fed. There was a little hay left, a little corn. Perhaps her husband and son would bring some home when they came. They had driven off in the only buggy the Grimes family had, a rickety thing, a rickety horse hitched to the buggy, two other rickety horses led by halters. They were going to trade horses, get a little money if they could. They might come home drunk. It would be well to have something in the house when they came back.

The son had an affair on with a woman at the county seat, fifteen miles away. She was a bad woman, a tough one. Once, in the summer, the son had brought her to the house. Both she and the son had been drinking. Jake Grimes was away and the son and his woman ordered the old woman about like a servant. She didn't mind much; she was used to it. Whatever happened, she never said anything. That was her way of getting along. She had managed that way when she was a young girl at the German's and ever since she had married Jake. That time her son brought his woman to the house they stayed all night, sleeping together just as though they were married. It hadn't shocked the old woman, not much. She had got past being shocked early in life.

With the pack on her back she went painfully along across an open field, wading in the deep snow, and got into the woods.

There was a path, but it was hard to follow. Just beyond the top of the hill, where the wood was thickest, there was a small clearing. Had someone once thought of building a house there? The clearing was as large as a building lot in town, large enough for a house and a garden. The path ran along the side of the clearing and when she got there the old woman sat down to rest at the foot of a tree.

It was a foolish thing to do. When she got herself placed, the pack against the tree's trunk, it was nice, but what about getting up again? She worried about that for a moment and then quietly closed her eyes.

She must have slept for a time. When you are about so cold you can't get any colder. The afternoon grew a little warmer and the snow came thicker than ever. Then after a time the weather cleared. The moon even came out.

There were four Grimes dogs that had followed Mrs. Grimes into town, all tall gaunt fellows. Such men as Jake Grimes and his son always keep just such dogs. They kick and abuse them, but they stay. The Grimes dogs, in order to keep from starving, had to do a lot of foraging for themselves, and they had been at it while the old woman slept with her back to the tree at the side of the clearing. They had been chasing rabbits in the woods and in adjoining fields, and in their ranging had picked up three other farm dogs.

After a time all the dogs came back to the clearing. They were excited about something. Such nights, cold and clear and with a moon, do things to dogs. It may be that some old instinct, come down from the time when they were wolves and ranged the woods in packs on winter nights, comes back into them.

The dogs in the clearing, before the old woman, had caught two or three rabbits and their immediate hunger had been satisfied. They began to play, running in circles in the clearing. Round and round they ran, each dog's nose at the tail of the next dog. In the clearing, under the snow-laden trees and under the wintry moon they made a strange picture, running thus silently, in a circle their running had beaten in the soft snow. The dogs made no sound. They ran around and around in the circle.

It may have been that the old woman saw them doing that before she died. She may have awakened once or twice and looked at the strange sight with dim old eyes.

She wouldn't be very cold now, just drowsy. Life hangs on a long time. Perhaps the old woman was out of her head. She may have dreamed of her girlhood, at the German's, and before that, when she was a child and before her mother lit out and left her.

Her dreams couldn't have been very pleasant. Not many pleasant things had happened to her. Now and then one of the Grimes dogs left the running circle and came to stand before her. The dog thrust his face close to her face. His red tongue was hanging out.

The running of the dogs may have been a kind of death ceremony. It may have been that the primitive instinct of the wolf, having been aroused in the dogs by the night and the running, made them somehow afraid.

"Now we are no longer wolves. We are dogs, the servants of men. Keep alive, man! When man dies we become wolves again."

When one of the dogs came to where the old woman sat with her back against the tree and thrust his nose close to her face he seemed satisfied and went back to run with the pack. All the Grimes dogs did it at some time during the evening, before she died. I knew all about it afterward, when I grew to be a man, because once in a wood on another winter night I saw a pack of dogs act just like that. The dogs were waiting for me to die as they had waited for the old woman that night when I was a child, but when it happened to me I was a young man and had no intention whatever of dying.

The old woman died softly and quietly. When she was dead and when one of the Grimes dogs had come to her and had found her dead all the dogs stopped running.

They gathered about her.

Well, she was dead now. She had fed the Grimes dogs when she was alive, what about now?

There was the pack on her back, the grain bag containing the piece of salt pork, the liver the butcher had given her, the dog meat, the soup bones. The butcher in town, having been suddenly overcome with a feeling of pity, had loaded her grain bag heavily. It had been a big haul for the old woman.

A big haul for the dogs now.

IV

One of the Grimes dogs sprang suddenly out from among the others and began worrying the pack on the old woman's back. Had the dogs really been wolves that one would have been the leader of the pack. What he did, all the others did.

All of them sank their teeth into the grain bag the old woman had fastened with ropes to her back.

They dragged the old woman's body out into the open clearing. The worn-out dress was quickly torn from her shoulders. When she was found, a day or two later, the dress had been torn from her body clear to the hips but the dogs had not touched her body. They had got the meat out of the grain bag, that was all. Her body was frozen stiff when it was found and the shoulders were so narrow and the body so slight that in death it looked like the body of some charming young girl.

Such things happened in towns of the Middle West, on farms near town, when I was a boy. A hunter out after rabbits found the old woman's body and did not touch it. Something, the beaten round path in the little snow-covered clearing, the silence of the place, the place where the dogs had worried the body trying to pull the grain bag away or tear it open—something startled the man and he hurried off to town.

I was in Main Street with one of my brothers, who was taking the afternoon papers to the stores. It was almost night.

The hunter came into a grocery and told his story. Then he went to a hardware shop and into a drug store. Men began to gather on the sidewalks. Then they started out along the road to the place in the wood.

My brother should have gone on about his business of distributing papers, but he didn't. Everyone was going to the woods. The undertaker went and the town marshal. Several men got on a dray and rode out to where the path left the road and went into the woods, but the horses weren't very sharply shod and slid about on the slippery roads. They made no better time than those of us who walked.

The town marshal was a large man whose leg had been injured in the Civil War. He carried a heavy cane and limped rapidly along the road. My brother and I followed at his heels, and as we went other men and boys joined the crowd.

It had grown dark by the time we got to where the old woman had left the road, but the moon had come out. The marshal was thinking there might have been a murder. He kept asking the hunter questions. The hunter went along with his gun across his shoulders, a dog following at his heels. It isn't often a rabbit hunter has a chance to be so conspicuous. He was taking full advantage of it, leading the procession with the town marshal. "I didn't see any wounds. She was a beautiful young girl. Her face was buried in the snow. No, I didn't know her." As a matter of fact, the hunter had not looked closely at the body. He had been frightened. She might have been murdered and someone might spring out from behind a tree and murder him too. In a woods, in the late afternoon, when the trees are all bare and there is white snow on the ground, when all is silent, something creepy steals over the mind and body. If something strange or uncanny has happened in the neighbourhood, all you think about is getting away from there as fast as you can.

The crowd of men and boys had got to where the old woman crossed the field and went, following the marshal and the hunter up the slight incline and into the woods.

My brother and I were silent. He had his bundle of papers in a bag slung across his shoulder. When he got back to town he would have to go on distributing his papers before he went home to supper. If I went along, as he had no doubt already determined I should, we would both be late. Either Mother or our younger sister would have to warm our supper.

Well, we would have something to tell. A boy did not get such a chance very often. It was lucky we just happened to go into the grocery when the hunter came in. The hunter was a country fellow. Neither of us had ever seen him before.

Now the crowd of men and boys had got to the clearing. Darkness comes quickly on such winter nights, but the full moon made everything clear. My brother and I stood near the trees beneath which the old woman had died.

She did not look old, lying there frozen in that light. One of the men turned her over in the snow and I saw everything. My body trembled with some strange mystical feeling, and so did my brother's. It might have been the cold.

Neither of us had ever seen a woman's body before. It may have been the snow, clinging to the frozen flesh, that made it look so white and lovely, so like marble. No woman had come with the party from town, but one of the men, he was the town blacksmith, took off his overcoat and spread it over her. Then he gathered her into his arms and started off to town, all the others following silently. At that time no one knew who she was.

V

I had seen everything, had seen the oval in the snow, like a miniature race track, where the dogs had run, had seen how the men were mystified, had seen the white, bare, young-looking shoulders, had heard the whispered comments of the men.

The men were simply mystified. They took the body to the undertaker's, and when the blacksmith, the hunter, the marshal, and several others had got inside, they closed the door. If Father had been there, perhaps he could have got in, but we boys couldn't.

I went with my brother to distribute the rest of his papers, and when we got home it was my brother who told the story.

I kept silent and went to bed early. It may have been I was not satisfied with the way he told it.

Later, in the town, I must have heard other fragments of the old woman's story. She was recognized the next day and there was an investigation.

The husband and son were found somewhere and brought to town, and there was an attempt to connect them with the woman's death, but it did not work. They had perfect enough alibis.

However, the town was against them. They had to get out. Where they went, I never heard.

I remember only the picture there in the forest, the men standing about, the naked, girlish-looking figure, face down in the snow, the tracks made by the running dogs, and the clear, cold winter sky above. White fragments of clouds were drifting across the sky. They went racing across the little open space among the trees.

The scene in the forest had become for me, without my knowing it, the foundation for the real story I am now trying to tell. The fragments, you see, had to be picked up slowly, long afterward.

Things happened. When I was a young man I worked on the farm of a German. The hired girl was afraid of her employer. The farmer's wife hated her.

I saw things at that place. Once, later, I had a half-uncanny, mystical sort of adventure with dogs in a forest on a clear, moonlit winter night. When I was a schoolboy, and on a summer day, I went with a boy friend out along a creek some miles from town and came to the house where the old woman had lived. No one had lived in the house since her death. The doors were broken from the hinges, the window lights were all broken. As the boy and I stood in the road outside, two dogs, just roving farm dogs, no doubt, came running around the corner of the house. The dogs were tall, gaunt fellows and came down to the fence and glared through at us, standing in the road.

The whole thing, the story of the old woman's death, was to me, as I grew older, like music heard from far off. The notes had to be picked up slowly one at a time. Something had to be understood.

The woman who died was one destined to feed animal life. Anyway, that is all she ever did. She was feeding animal life before she was born, as a child, as a young woman working on the farm of the German, after she married, when she grew old, and when she died. She fed animal life in cows, in chickens, in pigs, in horses, in dogs, in men. Her daughter had died in childhood, and with her one son she had no articulate relations. On the night when she died she was hurrying homeward, bearing on her body food for animal life.

She died in the clearing in the woods, and even after her death continued feeding animal life.

You see it is likely that, when my brother told the story, that night when we got home and my mother and sister sat listening, I did not think he got the point. He was too young and so was I. A thing so complete has its own beauty.

I shall not try to emphasize the point. I am only explaining why I was dissatisfied then, and have been ever since. I speak of that only that you may understand why I have been impelled to try to tell the simple story over again.

JACK LONDON

To Build a Fire

Day had broken cold and gray, exceedingly cold and gray, when the man turned aside from the main Yukon trail and climbed the high earth-bank, where a dim and little-travelled trail led eastward through the fat spruce timberland. It was a steep bank, and he paused for breath at the top, excusing the act to himself by looking at his watch. It was nine o'clock. There was no sun nor hint of sun, though there was not a cloud in the sky. It was a clear day, and yet there seemed an intangible pall over the face of things, a subtle gloom that made the day dark, and that was due to the absence of sun. This fact did not worry the man. He was used to the lack of sun. It had been days since he had seen the sun, and he knew that a few more days must pass before that cheerful orb, due south, would just peep above the sky line and dip immediately from view.

The man flung a look back along the way he had come. The Yukon lay a mile wide and hidden under three feet of ice. On top of this ice were as many feet of snow. It was all pure white, rolling in gentle undulations where the ice jams of the freeze-up had formed. North and south, as far as his eye could see, it was unbroken white, save for a dark hairline that curved and twisted from around the spruce-covered island to the south, and that curved and twisted away into the north, where it disappeared behind another spruce-covered island. This dark hairline was the trail—the main trail—that led south five hundred miles to the Chilcoot Pass, Dyea, and salt water; and that led north seventy miles to Dawson, and still on to the north a thousand miles to Nulato, and finally to St. Michael, on Bering Sea, a thousand miles and half a thousand more.

But all this—the mysterious, far-reaching hairline trail, the absence of sun from the sky, the tremendous cold, and the strangeness and weirdness of it all—made no impression on the man. It was not because he was long used to it. He was a newcomer in the land, a *chechaquo*, and this was his first winter. The trouble with him was that he was without imagination. He was quick and alert in the things of life, but only in the things, and not in the significances. Fifty degrees below zero meant eighty-odd degrees of frost. Such fact impressed him as being cold and uncomfortable, and that was all. It did not lead him to meditate upon his frailty as a creature of temperature, and upon man's frailty in general, able only to live within certain narrow limits of heat and cold; and from there on it did not lead him to the conjectural field of immortality and man's place in the universe. Fifty degrees below zero stood for a bite of frost that hurt and that must be guarded against by the use of mittens, ear flaps, warm moccasins, and thick socks. Fifty degrees below zero was to him just precisely fifty degrees below zero. That there should be anything more to it than that was a thought that never entered his head.

As he turned to go on, he spat speculatively. There was a sharp, explosive crackle that startled him. He spat again. And again, in the air, before it could fall to the snow, the spittle crackled. He knew that at fifty below spittle crackled on the snow, but this spittle had crackled in the air. Undoubtedly it was colder than fifty below—how much colder he did not know. But the temperature did not matter. He was bound for the old claim on the left fork of Henderson Creek, where the boys were already. They had come over across the divide from the Indian Creek country, while he had come the roundabout way to take a look at the possibilities of getting out logs in the spring from the islands in the Yukon. He would be in to camp by six o'clock; a bit after dark, it was true, but the boys would be there, a fire would be going, and a hot supper would be ready. As for lunch, he pressed his hand against the protruding bundle under his jacket. It was also under his shirt, wrapped up in a handkerchief and lying against the naked skin. It was the only way to keep the biscuits from freezing. He smiled agreeably to himself as he thought of those biscuits, each cut open and sopped in bacon grease, and each enclosing a generous slice of fried bacon.

He plunged in among the big spruce trees. The trail was faint. A foot of snow had fallen since the last sled had passed over, and he was glad he was without a sled, travelling light. In fact, he carried nothing but the lunch wrapped in the handkerchief. He was surprised, however, at the cold. It certainly was cold, he concluded, as he rubbed his numb nose and cheekbones with his mittened hand. He was a warm-whiskered man, but the hair on his face did not protect the high cheekbones and the eager nose that thrust itself aggressively into the frosty air.

At the man's heels trotted a dog, a big native husky, the proper wolf dog, gray-coated and without any visible or temperamental difference from its brother, the wild wolf. The animal was depressed by the tremendous cold. It knew that it was no time for travelling. Its instinct told it a truer tale than was told to the man by the man's judgment. In reality, it was not merely colder than fifty below zero; it was colder than sixty below, than seventy below. It was seventy-five below zero. Since the freezing point is thirty-two above zero, it meant that one hundred and seven degrees of frost obtained. The dog did not know anything about thermometers. Possibly in its brain there was no sharp consciousness of a condition of very cold such as was in the man's brain. But the brute had its instinct. It experienced a vague but menacing apprehension that subdued it and made it slink along at the man's heels, and that made it question eagerly every unwonted movement of the man as if expecting him to go into camp or to seek shelter somewhere and build a fire. The dog had learned fire, and it wanted fire, or else to burrow under the snow and cuddle its warmth away from the air.

The frozen moisture of its breathing had settled on its fur in a fine powder of frost, and especially were its jowls, muzzle, and eyelashes whitened by its crystalled breath. The man's red beard and mustache were likewise frosted, but more solidly, the deposit taking the form of ice and increasing with every warm, moist breath he exhaled. Also, the man was chewing tobacco, and the muzzle of ice held his lips so rigidly that he was unable to clear his chin when he expelled the juice. The result was that a crystal beard of the color and solidity of amber was increasing its length on his chin. If he fell down it would shatter itself, like glass, into brittle fragments. But he did not mind the appendage. It was the penalty all tobacco chewers paid in that country, and he had been out before in two cold snaps. They had not been so cold as this, he knew, but by the spirit thermometer at Sixty Mile he knew they had been registered at fifty below and at fifty-five.

He held on through the level stretch of woods for several miles, crossed a wide flat of nigger heads, and dropped down a bank to the frozen bed of a small stream. This was Henderson Creek, and he knew he was ten miles from the forks. He looked at his watch. It was ten o'clock. He was making four miles an hour, and he calculated that he would arrive at the forks at half-past twelve. He decided to celebrate that event by eating his lunch there.

The dog dropped in again at his heels, with a tail drooping discouragement, as the man swung along the creek bed. The furrow of the old sled trail was plainly visible, but a dozen inches of snow covered the marks of the last runners. In a month no man had come up or down that silent creek. The man held steadily on. He was not much given to thinking, and just then particularly he had nothing to think about save that he would eat lunch at the forks and that at six o'clock he would be in camp with the boys. There was nobody to talk to; and, had there been, speech would have been impossible because of the ice muzzle on his mouth. So he continued monotonously to chew tobacco and to increase the length of his amber beard.

Once in a while the thought reiterated itself that it was very cold and that he had never experienced such cold. As he walked along he rubbed his cheekbones and nose with the back of his mittened hand. He did this automatically, now and again changing hands. But, rub as he would, the instant he stopped his cheekbones were numb, and the following instant the end of his nose went numb. He was sure to frost his cheeks; he knew that, and experienced a pang of regret that he had not devised a nose strap of the sort Bud wore in cold snaps. Such a strap passed across the cheeks, as well, and saved them. But it didn't matter much, after all. What were frosted cheeks? A bit painful, that was all; they were never serious.

Empty as the man's mind was of thoughts, he was keenly observant, and he noticed the changes in the creek, the curves and bends and timber jams, and always he sharply noted where he placed his feet. Once, coming around a bend, he shied abruptly, like a startled horse, curved away from the place where he had been walking, and retreated several paces back along the trail. The creek he knew was frozen clear to the bottom—no creek could contain water in that arctic winter—but he knew also that there were springs that bubbled out from the hillsides and ran along under the snow and on top the ice of the creek. He knew that the coldest snaps never froze these springs, and he knew likewise their danger. They were traps. They hid pools of water under the snow that might be three inches deep, or three feet. Sometimes a skin of ice half an inch thick covered them, and in turn was covered by the snow. Sometimes there were alternate layers of water and ice skin, so that when one broke through he kept on breaking through for a while, sometimes wetting himself to the waist.

That was why he had shied in such panic. He had felt the give under his feet and heard the crackle of a snow-hidden ice skin. And to get his feet wet in such a temperature meant trouble and danger. At the very least it meant delay, for he would be forced to stop and build a fire, and under its protection to bare his feet while he dried his socks and moccasins. He stood and studied the creek bed and its banks, and decided that the flow of water came from the right. He reflected awhile, rubbing his nose and cheeks, then skirted to the left, stepping gingerly and testing the footing for each step. Once clear of the danger, he took a fresh chew of tobacco and swung along at his four-mile gait.

In the course of the next two hours he came upon several similar traps.

Usually the snow above the hidden pools had a sunken, candied appearance that advertised the danger. Once again, however, he had a close call; and once, suspecting danger, he compelled the dog to go on in front. The dog did not want to go. It hung back until the man shoved it forward, and then it went quickly across the white, unbroken surface. Suddenly it broke through, floundered to one side, and got away to firmer footing. It had wet its forefeet and legs, and almost immediately the water that clung to it turned to ice. It made quick efforts to lick the ice off its legs, then dropped down in the snow and began to bite out the ice that had formed between the toes. This was a matter of instinct. To permit the ice to remain would mean sore feet. It did not know this. It merely obeyed the mysterious prompting that arose from the deep crypts of its being. But the man knew, having achieved a judgment on the subject, and he removed the mitten from his right hand and helped tear out the ice particles. He did not expose his fingers more than a minute, and was astonished at the swift numbness that smote them. It certainly was cold. He pulled on the mitten hastily, and beat the hand savagely across his chest.

At twelve o'clock the day was at its brightest. Yet the sun was too far south on its winter journey to clear the horizon. The bulge of the earth intervened between it and Henderson Creek, where the man walked under a clear sky at noon and cast no shadow. At half-past twelve, to the minute, he arrived at the forks of the creek. He was pleased at the speed he had made. If he kept it up, he would certainly be with the boys by six. He unbuttoned his jacket and shirt and drew forth his lunch. The action consumed no more than a quarter of a minute, yet in that brief moment the numbness laid hold of the exposed fingers. He did not put the mitten on, but, instead, struck the fingers a dozen sharp smashes against his leg. Then he sat down on a snow-covered log to eat. The sting that followed upon the striking of his fingers against his leg ceased so quickly that he was startled. He had had no chance to take a bite of biscuit. He struck the fingers repeatedly and returned them to the mitten, baring the other hand for the purpose of eating. He tried to take a mouthful, but the ice muzzle prevented. He had forgotten to build a fire and thaw out. He chuckled at his foolishness, and as he chuckled he noted the numbness creeping into the exposed fingers. Also, he noted that the stinging which had first come to his toes when he sat down was already passing away. He wondered whether the toes were warm or numb. He moved them inside the moccasins and decided that they were numb.

He pulled the mitten on hurriedly and stood up. He was a bit frightened. He stamped up and down until the stinging returned into the feet.

It certainly was cold, was his thought. That man from Sulphur Creek had spoken the truth when telling how cold it sometimes got in the country. And he had laughed at him at the time! That showed one must not be too sure of things. There was no mistake about it, it *was* cold. He strode up and down, stamping his feet and threshing his arms, until reassured by the returning warmth. Then he got out matches and proceeded to make a fire. From the undergrowth, where high water of the previous spring had lodged a supply of seasoned twigs, he got his firewood. Working carefully from a small beginning, he soon had a roaring fire, over which he thawed the ice from his face and in the protection of which he ate his biscuits. For the moment the cold of space was outwitted. The dog took satisfaction in the fire, stretching out close enough for warmth and far enough away to escape being singed.

When the man had finished, he filled his pipe and took his comfortable time over a smoke. Then he pulled on his mittens, settled the ear flaps of his cap firmly about his ears, and took the creek trail up the left fork. The dog was disappointed and yearned back toward the fire. This man did not know cold. Possibly all the generations of his ancestry had been ignorant of cold, of real cold, of cold one hundred and seven degrees below freezing point. But the dog knew; all its ancestry knew, and it had inherited the knowledge. And it knew that it was not good to walk abroad in such fearful cold. It was the time to lie snug in a hole in the snow and wait for a curtain of cloud to be drawn across the face of outer space whence this cold came. On the other hand, there was no keen intimacy between the dog and the man. The one was the toil slave of the other, and the only caresses it had ever received were the caresses of the whip lash and of harsh and menacing throat sounds that threatened the whip lash. So the dog made no effort to communicate its apprehension to the man. It was not concerned in the welfare of the man; it was for its own sake that it yearned back toward the fire. But the man whistled, and spoke to it with the sound of whip lashes, and the dog swung in at the man's heels and followed after.

The man took a chew of tobacco and proceeded to start a new amber beard. Also, his moist breath quickly powdered with white his mustache, eyebrows, and lashes. There did not seem to be so many springs on the left fork of the Henderson, and for half an hour the man saw no signs of any. And then it happened. At a place where there were no signs, where the soft, unbroken snow seemed to advertise solidity beneath, the man broke through. It was not deep. He wet himself halfway to the knees before he floundered out to the firm crust.

He was angry, and cursed his luck aloud. He had hoped to get into camp with the boys at six o'clock, and this would delay him an hour, for he would have to build a fire and dry out his footgear. This was imperative at that low temperature—he knew that much; and he turned aside to the bank, which he climbed. On top, tangled in the underbrush about the trunks of several small spruce trees, was a high-water deposit of dry firewood—sticks and twigs, principally, but also larger portions of seasoned branches and fine, dry, last year's grasses. He threw down several large pieces on top of the snow. This served for a foundation and prevented the young flame from drowning itself in the snow it otherwise would melt. The flame he got by touching a match to a small shred of birch bark that he took from his pocket. This burned even more readily than paper. Placing it on the foundation, he fed the young flame with wisps of dry grass and with the tiniest dry twigs.

He worked slowly and carefully, keenly aware of his danger. Gradually, as the flame grew stronger, he increased the size of the twigs with which he fed it. He squatted in the snow, pulling the twigs out from their entanglement in the brush and feeding directly to the flame. He knew there must be no failure. When it is seventy-five below zero, a man must not fail in his first attempt to build a fire—that is, if his feet are wet. If his feet are dry, and he fails, he can run along the trail for half a mile and restore his circulation. But the circulation of wet and freezing feet cannot be restored by running when it is seventy-five below. No matter how fast he runs, the wet feet will freeze the harder.

All this the man knew. The old-timer on Sulphur Creek had told him about it the previous fall, and now he was appreciating the advice. Already all sensation had gone out of his feet. To build the fire he had been forced to remove his mittens, and the fingers had quickly gone numb. His pace of four miles an hour had kept his heart pumping blood to the surface of his body and to all the extremities. But the instant he stopped, the action of the pump eased down. The cold of space smote the unprotected tip of the planet, and he, being on that unprotected tip, received the full force of the blow. The blood of his body recoiled before it. The blood was alive, like the dog, and like the dog it wanted to hide away and cover itself up from the fearful cold. So long as he walked four miles an hour, he pumped that blood, willy-nilly, to the surface; but now it ebbed away and sank down into the recesses of his body. The extremities were the first to feel its absence. His wet feet froze the faster, and his exposed fingers numbed the faster, though they had not yet begun to freeze. Nose and cheeks were already freezing, while the skin of all his body chilled as it lost its blood.

But he was safe. Toes and nose and cheeks would be only touched by the frost, for the fire was beginning to burn with strength. He was feeding it with twigs the size of his finger. In another minute he would be able to feed it with branches the size of his wrist, and then he could remove his wet footgear, and, while it dried, he could keep his naked feet warm by the fire, rubbing them at first, of course, with snow. The fire was a success. He was safe. He remembered the advice of the old-timer on Sulphur Creek, and smiled. The old-timer had been very serious in laying down the law that no man must travel alone in the Klondike after fifty below. Well, here he was; he had had the accident; he was alone; and he had saved himself. Those old-timers were rather womanish, some of them, he thought. All a man had to do was to keep his head, and he was all right. Any man who was a man could travel alone. But it was surprising, the rapidity with which his cheeks and nose were freezing. And he had not thought his fingers could go lifeless in so short a time. Lifeless they were, for he could scarcely make them move together to grip a twig, and they seemed remote from his body and from him. When he touched a twig, he had to look and see whether or not he had hold of it. The wires were pretty well down between him and his finger ends.

All of which counted for little. There was the fire, snapping and crackling and promising life with every dancing flame. He started to untie his moccasins. They were coated with ice; the thick German socks were like sheaths of iron halfway to the knees; and the moccasin strings were like rods of steel all twisted and knotted as by some conflagration. For a moment he tugged with his numb fingers, then, realizing the folly of it, he drew his sheath knife.

But before he could cut the strings, it happened. It was his own fault or, rather, his mistake. He should not have built the fire under the spruce tree. He should have built it in the open. But it had been easier to pull the twigs from the brush and drop them directly on the fire. Now the tree under which he had done this carried a weight of snow on its boughs. No wind had blown for weeks, and each bough was fully freighted. Each time he had pulled a twig he had communicated a slight agitation to the tree—an imperceptible agitation, so far as he was concerned, but an agitation sufficient to bring about the disaster. High up in the tree one bough capsized its load of snow. This fell on the boughs beneath, capsizing them. This process continued, spreading out and involving the whole tree. It grew like an avalanche, and it descended without warning upon the man and the fire, and the fire was blotted out! Where it had burned was a mantle of fresh and disordered snow.

The man was shocked. It was as though he had just heard his own sentence of death. For a moment he sat and stared at the spot where the fire had been. Then he grew very calm. Perhaps the old-timer on Sulphur Creek was right. If he had only had a trail mate he would have been in no danger now. The trail mate could have built the fire. Well, it was up to him to build the fire over again, and this second time there must be no failure. Even if he succeeded, he would most likely lose some toes. His feet must be badly frozen by now, and there would be some time before the second fire was ready.

Such were his thoughts, but he did not sit and think them. He was busy all the time they were passing through his mind. He made a new foundation for a fire, this time in the open, where no treacherous tree could blot it out. Next he gathered dry grasses and tiny twigs from the high-water flotsam. He could not bring his fingers together to pull them out, but he was able to gather them by the handful. In this way he got many rotten twigs and bits of green moss that were undesirable, but it was the best he could do. He worked methodically, even collecting an armful of the larger branches to be used later when the fire gathered strength. And all the while the dog sat and watched him, a certain yearning wistfulness in its eye, for it looked upon him as the fire provider, and the fire was slow in coming.

When all was ready, the man reached in his pocket for a second piece of birch bark. He knew the bark was there, and, though he could not feel it with his fingers, he could hear its crisp rustling as he fumbled for it. Try as he would, he could not clutch hold of it. And all the time, in his consciousness, was the knowledge that each instant his feet were freezing. This thought tended to put him in a panic, but he fought against it and kept calm. He pulled on his mittens with his teeth, and threshed his arms back and forth, beating his hands with all his might against his sides. He did this sitting down, and he stood up to do it; and all the while the dog sat in the snow, its wolf brush of a tail curled around warmly over its forefeet, its sharp wolf ears pricked forward intently as it watched the man. And the man, as he beat and threshed with his arms and hands, felt a great surge of envy as he regarded the creature that was warm and secure in its natural covering.

After a time he was aware of the first faraway signals of sensation in his beaten fingers. The faint tingling grew stronger till it evolved into a stinging ache that was excruciating, but which the man hailed with satisfaction. He stripped the mitten from his right hand and fetched forth the birch bark. The exposed fingers were quickly going numb again. Next he brought out his bunch of sulphur matches. But the tremendous cold had already driven the life out of his fingers. In his effort to separate one match from the others, the whole bunch fell in the snow. He tried to pick it out of the snow, but failed. The dead fingers could neither touch nor clutch. He was very careful. He drove the thought of his freezing feet, and nose, and cheeks, out of his mind, devoting his whole soul to the matches. He watched, using the sense of vision in place of that of touch, and when he saw his fingers on each side the bunch, he closed them—that is, he willed to close them, for the wires were down, and the fingers did not obey. He pulled the mitten on the right hand, and beat it fiercely against his knee. Then, with both mittened hands, he scooped the bunch of matches, along with much snow, into his lap. Yet he was no better off.

After some manipulation he managed to get the bunch between the heels of his mittened hands. In this fashion he carried it to his mouth. The ice crackled and snapped when by a violent effort he opened his mouth. He drew the lower jaw in, curled the upper lip out of the way, and scraped the bunch with his upper teeth in order to separate a match. He succeeded in getting one, which he dropped on his lap. He was no better off. He could not pick it up. Then he devised a way. He picked it up in his teeth and scratched it on his leg. Twenty times he scratched before he succeeded in lighting it. As it flamed he held it with his teeth to the birch bark. But the burning brimstone went up his nostrils and into his lungs, causing him to cough spasmodically. The match fell into the snow and went out.

The old-timer on Sulphur Creek was right, he thought in the moment of controlled despair that ensued: after fifty below, a man should travel with a partner. He beat his hands, but failed in exciting any sensation. Suddenly he bared both hands, removing the mittens with his teeth. He caught the whole bunch between the heels of his hands. His arm muscles not being frozen enabled him to press the hand heels tightly against the matches. Then he scratched the bunch along his leg. It flared into flame, seventy sulphur matches at once! There was no wind to blow them out. He kept his head to one side to escape the strangling fumes, and held the blazing bunch to the birch bark. As he so held it, he became aware of sensation in his hand. His flesh was burning. He could smell it. Deep down below the surface he could feel it. The sensation developed into pain that grew acute. And still he endured it, holding the flame of the matches clumsily to the bark that would not light readily because his own burning hands were in the way, absorbing most of the flame.

At last, when he could endure no more, he jerked his hands apart. The blazing matches fell sizzling into the snow, but the birch bark was alight. He began laying dry grasses and the tiniest twigs on the flame. He could not pick and choose, for he had to lift the fuel between the heels of his hands. Small pieces of rotten wood and green moss clung to the twigs, and he bit them off as well as he could with his teeth. He cherished the flame carefully and awkwardly. It meant life, and it must not perish. The withdrawal of blood from the surface of his body now made him begin to shiver, and he grew more awkward. A large piece of green moss fell squarely on the little fire. He tried to poke it out with his fingers, but his shivering frame made him poke too far, and he disrupted the nucleus of the little fire, the burning grasses and tiny twigs separating and scattering. He tried to poke them together again, but in spite of the tenseness of the effort, his shivering got away with him, and the twigs were hopelessly scattered. Each twig gushed a puff of smoke and went out. The fire provider had failed. As he looked apathetically about him, his eyes chanced on the dog, sitting across the ruins of the fire from him, in the snow, making restless, hunching movements, slightly lifting one forefoot and then the other, shifting its weight back and forth on them with wistful eagerness.

The sight of the dog put a wild idea into his head. He remembered the tale of the man, caught in a blizzard, who killed a steer and crawled inside the carcass, and so was saved. He would kill the dog and bury his hands in the warm body until the numbness went out of them. Then he could build another fire. He spoke to the dog, calling it to him; but in his voice was a strange note of fear that frightened the animal, who had never known the man to speak in such way before. Something was the matter, and its suspicious nature sensed danger—it knew not what danger, but somewhere, somehow, in its brain arose an apprehension of the man. It flattened its ears down at the sound of the man's voice, and its restless, hunching movements and the liftings and shiftings of its forefeet became more pronounced; but it would not come to the man. He got on his hands and knees and crawled toward the dog. This unusual posture again excited suspicion, and the animal sidled mincingly away.

The man sat up in the snow for a moment and struggled for calmness. Then he pulled on his mittens, by means of his teeth, and got upon his feet. He glanced down at first in order to assure himself that he was really standing up, for the absence of sensation in his feet left him unrelated to the earth. His erect position in itself started to drive the webs of suspicion from the dog's mind; and when he spoke peremptorily, with the sound of whip lashes in his voice, the dog rendered its customary allegiance and came to him. As it came within reaching distance, the man lost his control. His arms flashed out to the dog, and he experienced genuine surprise when he discovered that his hands could not clutch, that there was neither bend nor feeling in the fingers. He had forgotten for the moment that they were frozen and that they were freezing more and more. All this happened quickly, and before the animal could get away, he encircled its body with his arms. He sat down in the snow, and in this fashion held the dog, while it snarled and whined and struggled.

But it was all he could do, hold its body encircled in his arms and sit there. He realized that he could not kill the dog. There was no way to do it. With his helpless hands he could neither draw nor hold his sheath knife nor throttle the animal. He released it, and it plunged wildly away, with tail between its legs, and still snarling. It halted forty feet away and surveyed him curiously, with ears sharply pricked forward.

The man looked down at his hands in order to locate them, and found them hanging on the ends of his arms. It struck him as curious that one should have to use his eyes in order to find out where his hands were. He began threshing his arms back and forth, beating the mittened hands against his sides. He did this for five minutes, violently, and his heart pumped enough blood up to the surface to put a stop to his shivering. But no sensation was aroused in the hands. He had an impression that they hung like weights on the ends of his arms, but when he tried to run the impression down, he could not find it.

A certain fear of death, dull and oppressive, came to him. This fear quickly became poignant as he realized that it was no longer a mere matter of freezing his fingers and toes, or of losing his hands and feet, but that it was a matter of life and death with the chances against him. This threw him into a panic, and he turned and ran up the creek bed along the old, dim trail. The dog joined in behind and kept up with him. He ran blindly, without intention, in fear such as he had never known in his life. Slowly, as he plowed and floundered through the snow, he began to see things again—the banks of the creek, the old timber jams, the leafless aspens, and the sky. The running made him feel better. He did not shiver. Maybe, if he ran on, his feet would thaw out; and, anyway, if he ran far enough, he would reach camp and the boys. Without doubt he would lose some fingers and toes and some of his face; but the boys would take care of him, and save the rest of him when he got there. And at the same time there was another thought in his mind that said he would never get to the camp and the boys; that it was too many miles away, that the freezing had too great a start on him, and that he would soon be stiff and dead. This thought he kept in the background and refused to consider. Sometimes it pushed itself forward and demanded to be heard, but he thrust it back and strove to think of other things.

It struck him as curious that he could run at all on feet so frozen that he could not feel them when they struck the earth and took the weight of his body. He seemed to himself to skim along above the surface, and to have no connection with the earth. Somewhere he had once seen a winged Mercury, and he wondered if Mercury felt as he felt when skimming over the earth.

His theory of running until he reached camp and the boys had one flaw in it: he lacked the endurance. Several times he stumbled, and finally he tottered, crumpled up, and fell. When he tried to rise, he failed. He must sit and rest, he decided, and next time he would merely walk and keep on going. As he sat and regained his breath, he noted that he was feeling quite warm and comfortable. He was not shivering, and it even seemed that a warm glow had come to his chest and trunk. And yet, when he touched his nose or cheeks, there was no sensation. Running would not thaw them out. Nor would it thaw out his hands and feet. Then the thought came to him that the frozen portions of his body must be extending. He tried to keep this thought down, to forget it, to think of something else; he was aware of the panicky feeling that it caused, and he was afraid of the panic. But the thought asserted itself, and persisted, until it produced a vision of his body totally frozen. This was too much, and he made another wild run along the trail. Once he slowed down to a walk, but the thought of the freezing extending itself made him run again.

And all the time the dog ran with him, at his heels. When he fell down a second time, it curled its tail over its forefeet and sat in front of him, facing him, curiously eager and intent. The warmth and security of the animal angered him, and he cursed it till it flattened down its ears appeasingly. This time the shivering came more quickly upon the man. He was losing in his battle with the frost. It was creeping into his body from all sides. The thought of it drove him on, but he ran no more than a hundred feet, when he staggered and pitched headlong. It was his last panic. When he had recovered his breath and control, he sat up and entertained in his mind the conception of meeting death with dignity. However, the conception did not come to him in such terms. His idea of it was that he had been making a fool of himself, running around like a chicken with its head cut off—such was the simile that occurred to him. Well, he was bound to freeze anyway, and he might as well take it decently. With this new-found peace of mind came the first glimmerings of drowsiness. A good idea, he thought, to sleep off to death. It was like taking an anesthetic. Freezing was not so bad as people thought. There were lots worse ways to die.

He pictured the boys finding his body next day. Suddenly he found himself with them, coming along the trail and looking for himself. And, still with them, he came around a turn in the trail and found himself lying in the snow. He did not belong with himself any more, for even then he was out of himself, standing with the boys and looking at himself in the snow. It certainly was cold, was his thought. When he got back to the States he could tell the folks what real cold was. He drifted on from this to a vision of the old-timer on Sulphur Creek. He could see him quite clearly, warm and comfortable, and smoking a pipe.

"You were right, old hoss; you were right," the man mumbled to the old-timer of Sulphur Creek.

Then the man drowsed off into what seemed to him the most comfortable and satisfying sleep he had ever known. The dog sat facing him and waiting. The brief day drew to a close in a long, slow twilight. There were no signs of a fire to be made, and, besides, never in the dog's experience had it known a man to sit like that in the snow and make no fire. As the twilight drew on, its eager yearning for the fire mastered it, and with a great lifting and shifting of forefeet, it whined softly, then flattened its ears down in anticipation of being chidden by the man. But the man remained silent. Later the dog whined loudly. And still later it crept close to the man and caught the scent of death. This made the animal bristle and back away. A little longer it delayed, howling under the stars that leaped and danced and shone brightly in the cold sky. Then it turned and trotted up the trail in the direction of the camp it knew, where were the other food providers and fire providers.

RING LARDNER

Champion

Midge Kelly scored his first knockout when he was seventeen. The knockee was his brother Connie, three years his junior and a cripple. The purse was a half dollar given to the younger Kelly by a lady whose electric had just missed bumping his soul from his frail little body.

Connie did not know Midge was in the house, else he never would have risked laying the prize on the arm of the least comfortable chair in the room, the better to observe its shining beauty. As Midge entered from the kitchen, the crippled boy covered the coin with his hand, but the movement lacked the speed requisite to escape his brother's quick eye.

"Watcha got there?" demanded Midge.

"Nothin'," said Connie.

"You're a one legged liar!" said Midge.

He strode over to his brother's chair and grasped the hand that concealed the coin.

"Let loose!" he ordered.

Connie began to cry.

"Let loose and shut up your noise," said the elder, and jerked his brother's hand from the chair arm.

The coin fell onto the bare floor. Midge pounced on it. His weak mouth widened in a triumphant smile.

"Nothin', huh?" he said. "All right, if it's nothin' you don't want it."

"Give that back," sobbed the younger.

"I'll give you a red nose, you little sneak! Where'd you steal it?"

"I didn't steal it. It's mine. A lady give it to me after she pretty near hit me with a car."

"It's a crime she missed you," said Midge.

Midge started for the front door. The cripple picked up his crutch, rose from his chair with difficulty, and, still sobbing, came toward Midge. The latter heard him and stopped.

"You better stay where you're at," he said.

"I want my money," cried the boy.

"I know what you want," said Midge.

Doubling up the fist that held the half dollar, he landed with all his strength on his brother's mouth. Connie fell to the floor with a thud, the crutch tumbling on top of him. Midge stood beside the prostrate form.

"Is that enough?" he said. "Or do you want this, too?"

And he kicked him in the crippled leg.

"I guess that'll hold you," he said.

There was no response from the boy on the floor. Midge looked at him a moment, then at the coin in his hand, and then went out into the street, whistling.

An hour later, when Mrs. Kelly came home from her day's work at Faulkner's Steam Laundry, she found Connie on the floor, moaning. Dropping on her knees beside him, she called him by name a score of times. Then she got up and, pale as a ghost, dashed from the house. Dr. Ryan left the Kelly abode about dusk and walked toward Halsted Street. Mrs. Dorgan spied him as he passed her gate.

"Who's sick, Doctor?" she called.

"Poor little Connie," he replied. "He had a bad fall."

"How did it happen?"

"I can't say for sure, Margaret, but I'd almost bet he was knocked down."

"Knocked down!" exclaimed Mrs. Dorgan.

"Why, who—?"

"Have you seen the other one lately?"

"Michael? No, not since mornin'. You can't be thinkin'——"

"I wouldn't put it past him, Margaret," said the doctor gravely. "The lad's mouth is swollen and cut, and his poor, skinny little leg is bruised. He surely didn't do it to himself and I think Helen suspects the other one."

"Lord save us!" said Mrs. Dorgan. "I'll run over and see if I can help."

"That's a good woman," said Doctor Ryan, and went on down the street.

Near midnight, when Midge came home, his mother was sitting at Connie's bedside. She did not look up.

"Well," said Midge, "what's the matter?"

She remained silent. Midge repeated his question.

"Michael, you know what's the matter," she said at length.

"I don't know nothin," said Midge.

"Don't lie to me, Michael. What did you do to your brother?"

"Nothin'."

"You hit him."

"Well, then, I hit him. What of it? It ain't the first time."

Her lips pressed tightly together, her face like chalk, Ellen Kelly rose from her chair and made straight for him. Midge backed against the door.

"Lay off'n me, Ma. I don't want to fight no woman."

Still she came on breathing heavily.

"Stop where you're at, Ma," he warned.

There was a brief struggle and Midge's mother lay on the floor before him.

"You ain't hurt, Ma. You're lucky I didn't land good. And I told you to lay off'n me."

"God forgive you, Michael!"

Midge found Hap Collins in the showdown game at the Royal.

"Come on out a minute," he said.

Hap followed him out on the walk.

"I'm leavin' town for a w'ile," said Midge.

"What for?"

"Well, we had a little run-in up to the house. The kid stole a half buck off'n me, and when I went after it he cracked me with his crutch. So I nailed him. And the old lady came at me with a chair and I took it off'n her and she fell down."

"How is Connie hurt?"

"Not bad."

"What are you runnin' away for?"

"Who the hell said I was runnin' away? I'm sick and tired o' gettin' picked on; that's all. So I'm leavin' for a w'ile and I want a piece o' money."

"I ain't only got six bits," said Happy.

"You're in bad shape, ain't you? Well, come through with it." Happy came through.

"You oughtn't to hit the kid," he said.

"I ain't astin' you who can I hit," snarled Midge. "You try to put somethin' over on me and you'll get the same dose. I'm goin' now."

"Go as far as you like," said Happy, but not until he was sure that Kelly was out of hearing.

Early the following morning, Midge boarded a train for Milwaukee. He had no ticket, but no one knew the difference. The conductor remained in the caboose.

On a night six months later, Midge hurried out of the "stage door" of the Star Boxing Club and made for Duane's saloon, two blocks away. In his pocket were twelve dollars, his reward for having battered up one Demon Dempsey through the six rounds of the first preliminary.

It was Midge's first professional engagement in the manly art. Also it was the first time in weeks that he had earned twelve dollars.

On the way to Duane's he had to pass Niemann's. He pulled his cap over his eyes and increased his pace until he had gone by. Inside Niemann's stood a trusting bartender, who for ten days had staked Midge to drinks and allowed him to ravage the lunch on a promise to come in and settle the moment he was paid for the "prelim."

Midge strode into Duane's and aroused the napping bartender by slapping a silver dollar on the festive board.

"Gimme a shot," said Midge.

The shooting continued until the wind-up at the Star was over and part of the fight crowd joined Midge in front of Duane's bar. A youth in the early twenties, standing next to young Kelly, finally summoned sufficient courage to address him.

"Wasn't you in the first bout?" he ventured.

"Yeh," Midge replied.

"My name's Hersch," said the other.

Midge received the startling information in silence.

"I don't want to butt in," continued Mr. Hersch, "but I'd like to buy you a drink."

"All right," said Midge, "but don't overstrain yourself."

Mr. Hersch laughed uproariously and beckoned to the bartender.

"You certainly gave that wop a trimmin' to-night," said the buyer of the drink, when they had been served. "I thought you'd kill him."

"I would if I hadn't let up," Midge replied. "I'll kill 'em all."

"You got the wallop all right," the other said admiringly.

"Have I got the wallop?" said Midge. "Say, I can kick like a mule. Did you notice them muscles in my shoulders?"

"Notice 'em? I couldn't help from noticin' 'em," said Hersch. "I says to the fella settin' alongside o' me, I says: 'Look at them shoulders! No wonder he can hit,' I says to him."

"Just let me land and it's good-by, baby," said Midge. "I'll kill 'em all."

The oral manslaughter continued until Duane's closed for the night. At parting, Midge and his new friend shook hands and arranged for a meeting the following evening.

For nearly a week the two were together almost constantly. It was Hersch's pleasant rôle to listen to Midge's modest revelations concerning himself, and to buy every time Midge's glass was empty. But there came an evening when Hersch regretfully announced that he must go home to supper.

"I got a date for eight bells," he confided. "I could stick till then, only I must clean up and put on the Sunday clo'es, 'cause she's the prettiest little thing in Milwaukee."

"Can't you fix it for two?" asked Midge.

"I don't know who to get," Hersch replied. "Wait, though. I got a sister and if she ain't busy, it'll be O.K. She's no bum for looks herself."

So it came about that Midge and Emma Hersch and Emma's brother and the prettiest little thing in Milwaukee foregathered at Wall's and danced half the night away. And Midge and Emma danced every dance together, for though every little onestep seemed to induce a new thirst of its own, Lou Hersch stayed too sober to dance with his own sister.

The next day, penniless at last in spite of his phenomenal ability to make someone else settle, Midge Kelly sought out Doc Hammond, matchmaker for the Star, and asked to be booked for the next show.

"I could put you on with Tracy for the next bout," said Doc.

"What's they in it?" asked Midge.

"Twenty if you cop," Doc told him.

"Have a heart," protested Midge. "Didn't I look good the other night?"

"You looked all right. But you aren't Freddie Welsh yet by a consid'able margin."

"I ain't scared of Freddie Welsh or none of 'em," said Midge.

"Well, we don't pay our boxers by the size of their chests," Doc said.

"I'm offerin' you this Tracy bout. Take it or leave it."

"All right; I'm on," said Midge, and he passed a pleasant afternoon at Duane's on the strength of his booking.

Young Tracy's manager came to Midge the night before the show.

"How do you feel about this go?" he asked.

"Me?" said Midge. "I feel all right. What do you mean, how do I feel?"

"I mean," said Tracy's manager, "that we're mighty anxious to win, 'cause the boy's got a chanct in Philly if he cops this one."

"What's your proposition?" asked Midge.

"Fifty bucks," said Tracy's manager.

"What do you think I am, a crook? Me lay down for fifty bucks. Not me!"

"Seventy-five, then," said Tracy's manager.

The market closed on eighty and the details were agreed on in short order. And the next night Midge was stopped in the second round by a terrific slap on the forearm.

This time Midge passed up both Niemann's and Duane's, having a sizable account at each place, and sought his refreshment at Stein's farther down the street.

When the profits of his deal with Tracy were gone, he learned, by first-hand information from Doc Hammond and the matchmakers at the other "clubs," that he was no longer desired for even the cheapest of preliminaries. There was no danger of his starving or dying of thirst while Emma and Lou Hersch lived. But he made up his mind, four months after his defeat by Young Tracy, that Milwaukee was not the ideal place for him to live.

"I can lick the best of 'em," he reasoned, "but there ain't no more chanct for me here. I can maybe go east and get on somewheres. And besides—"

But just after Midge had purchased a ticket to Chicago with the money he had "borrowed" from Emma Hersch "to buy shoes," a heavy hand was laid on his shoulders and he turned to face two strangers.

"Where are you goin', Kelly?" inquired the owner of the heavy hand.

"Nowheres," said Midge. "What the hell do you care?"

The other stranger spoke:

"Kelly, I'm employed by Emma Hersch's mother to see that you do right by her. And we want you to stay here till you've done it."

"You won't get nothin' but the worst of it, monkeying with me," said Midge.

Nevertheless, he did not depart for Chicago that night. Two days later, Emma Hersch became Mrs. Kelly, and the gift of the groom, when once they were alone, was a crushing blow on the bride's pale cheek.

Next morning, Midge left Milwaukee as he had entered it—by fast freight.

"They's no use kiddin' ourself any more," said Tommy Haley. "He might get down to thirty-seven in a pinch, but if he done below that a mouse could stop him. He's a welter; that's what he is and he knows it as well as I do. He's growed like a weed in the last six mont's. I told him, I says, 'If you don't quit growin' they won't be nobody for you to box, only Willard and them.' He says, 'Well, I wouldn't run away from Willard if I weighed twenty pounds more."

"He must hate himself," said Tommy's brother.

"I never seen a good one that didn't," said Tommy. "And Midge is a good one; don't make no mistake about that. I wisht we could of got Welsh before the kid growed so big. But it's too late now. I won't make no holler, though, if we can match him up with the Dutchman."

"Who do you mean?"

"Young Goetz, the welter champ. We mightn't not get so much dough for the bout itself, but it'd roll in afterward. What a drawin' card we'd be, 'cause the people pays their money to see the fella with the wallop, and that's Midge. And we'd keep the title just as long as Midge could make the weight."

"Can't you land no match with Goetz?"

"Sure, 'cause he needs the money. But I've went careful with the kid so far and look at the results I got! So what's the use of takin' a chanct? The kid's comin' every minute and Goetz is goin' back faster'n big Johnson did. I think we could lick him now; I'd bet my life on it. But six mont's from now they won't be no risk. He'll of licked hisself before that time. Then all as we'll have to do is sign up with him and wait for the referee to stop it. But Midge is so crazy to get at him now that I can't hardly hold him back."

The brothers Haley were lunching in a Boston hotel. Dan had come down from Holyoke to visit with Tommy and to watch the latter's protégé go twelve rounds, or less, with Bud Cross. The bout promised little in the way of a contest, for Midge had twice stopped the Baltimore youth and Bud's reputation for gameness was all that had earned him the date. The fans were willing to pay the price to see Midge's haymaking left, but they wanted to see it used on an opponent who would not jump out of the ring the first time he felt its crushing force. But Cross was such an opponent, and his willingness to stop boxing-gloves with his eyes, ears, nose and throat had long enabled him to escape the horrors of honest labor. A game boy was Bud, and he showed it in his battered, swollen, discolored face.

"I should think," said Dan Haley, "that the kid'd do whatever you tell him after all you done for him."

"Well," said Tommy, "he's took my dope pretty straight so far, but he's so sure of hisself that he can't see no reason for waitin'. He'll do what I say, though; he'd be a sucker not to."

"You got a contrac' with him?"

"No, I don't need no contrac'. He knows it was me that drug him out o' the gutter and he ain't goin' to turn me down now, when he's got the dough and bound to get more. Where'd he of been at if I hadn't listened to him when he first come to me? That's pretty near two years ago now, but it seems like last week. I was settin' in the s'loon acrost from the Pleasant Club in Philly, waitin' for McCann to count the dough and come over, when this little bum blowed in and tried to stand the house off for a drink. They told him nothin' doin' and to beat it out o' there, and then he seen me and come over to where I was settin' and ast me wasn't I a boxin' man and I told him who I was. Then he ast me for money to buy a shot and I told him to set down and I'd buy it for him.

"Then we got talkin' things over and he told me his name and told me about fightin' a couple o' prelims out to Milwaukee. So I says, 'Well, boy, I don't know how good or how rotten you are, but you won't never get nowheres trainin' on that stuff.' So he says he'd cut it out if he could get on in a bout and I says I would give him a chanct if he played square with me and didn't touch no more to drink. So we shook hands and I took him up to the hotel with me and give him a bath and the next day I bought him some clo'es. And I staked him to eats and sleeps for over six weeks. He had a hard time breakin' away from the polish, but finally I thought he was fit and I give him his chanct. He went on with Smiley Sayer and stopped him so quick that Smiley thought sure he was poisoned.

"Well, you know what he's did since. The only beatin' in his record was by Tracy in Milwaukee before I got hold of him, and he's licked Tracy three times in the last year.

"I've gave him all the best of it in a money way and he's got seven thousand bucks in cold storage. How's that for a kid that was in the gutter two years ago? And he'd have still more yet if he wasn't so nuts over clo'es and got to stop at the good hotels and so forth."

"Where's his home at?"

"Well, he ain't really got no home. He came from Chicago and his mother canned him out o' the house for bein' no good. She give him a raw deal, I guess, and he says he won't have nothin' to do with her unlest she comes to him first. She's got a pile o' money, he says, so he ain't worryin' about her."

The gentleman under discussion entered the café and swaggered to Tommy's table, while the whole room turned to look.

Midge was the picture of health despite a slightly colored eye and an ear that seemed to have no opening. But perhaps it was not his healthiness that drew all eyes. His diamond horse-shoe tie pin, his purple cross-striped shirt, his orange shoes and his light blue suit fairly screamed for attention.

"Where you been?" he asked Tommy. "I been lookin' all over for you."

"Set down," said his manager.

"No time," said Midge. "I'm goin' down to the w'arf and see 'em unload the fish."

"Shake hands with my brother Dan," said Tommy.

Midge shook with the Holyoke Haley.

"If you're Tommy's brother, you're O.K. with me," said Midge, and the brothers beamed with pleasure.

Dan moistened his lips and murmured an embarrassed reply, but it was lost on the young gladiator.

"Leave me take twenty," Midge was saying. "I prob'ly won't need it, but I don't like to be caught short."

Tommy parted with a twenty dollar bill and recorded the transaction in a small black book the insurance company had given him for Christmas.

"But," he said, "it won't cost you no twenty to look at them fish. Want me to go along?"

"No," said Midge hastily. "You and your brother here prob'ly got a lot to say to each other."

"Well," said Tommy, "don't take no bad money and don't get lost. And you better be back at four o'clock and lay down a w'ile."

"I don't need no rest to beat this guy," said Midge. "He'll do enough layin' down for the both of us."

And laughing even more than the jest called for, he strode out through the fire of admiring and startled glances.

The corner of Boylston and Tremont was the nearest Midge got to the wharf, but the lady awaiting him was doubtless a more dazzling sight than the catch of the luckiest Massachusetts fisherman. She could talk, too—probably better than the fish.

"O you Kid!" she said, flashing a few silver teeth among the gold. "O you fighting man!"

Midge smiled up at her.

"We'll go somewheres and get a drink," he said. "One won't hurt."

In New Orleans, five months after he had rearranged the map of Bud Cross for the third time, Midge finished training for his championship bout with the Dutchman.

Back in his hotel after the final workout, Midge stopped to chat with some of the boys from up north, who had made the long trip to see a champion dethroned, for the result of this bout was so nearly a foregone conclusion that even the experts had guessed it.

Tommy Haley secured the key and the mail and ascended to the Kelly suite. He was bathing when Midge came in, half hour later.

"Any mail?" asked Midge.

"There on the bed," replied Tommy from the tub.

Midge picked up the stack of letters and post-cards and glanced them over. From the pile he sorted out three letters and laid them on the table. The rest he tossed into the waste-basket. Then he picked up the three and sat for a few moments holding them, while his eyes gazed off into space. At length he looked again at the three unopened letters in his hand; then he put one in his pocket and tossed the other two at the basket. They missed their target and fell on the floor.

"Hell!" said Midge, and stooping over picked them up.

He opened one postmarked Milwaukee and read:

> DEAR HUSBAND:
>
> I have wrote to you so manny times and got no anser and I dont know if you ever got them, so I am writeing again in the hopes you will get this letter and anser. I dont like to bother you with my trubles and I would not only for the baby and I am not asking you should write to me but only send a little money and I am not asking for myself but the baby has not been well a day sence last Aug. and the dr. told me she cant live much longer unless I give her better food and thats impossible the way things are. Lou has not been working for a year and what I make dont hardly pay for the rent. I am not asking for you to give me any money, but only you should send what I loaned when convenient and I think it amts. to about $36.00. Please try and send that amt. and it will help me, but if you cant send the whole amt. try and send me something.
>
> Your wife,
>
> EMMA.

Midge tore the letter into a hundred pieces and scattered them over the floor.

"Money, money, money!" he said. "They must think I'm made o' money. I s'pose the old woman's after it too."

He opened his mother's letter:

> dear Michael Connie wonted me to rite and say you must beet the dutchman and he is sur you will and wonted me to say we wont you to rite and tell us about it, but I gess you havent no time to rite or we herd from you long beffore this but I wish you would rite jest a line or 2 boy becaus it wuld be better for Connie than a barl of medisin. It wuld help me to keep things going if you send me money now and then when you can spair it but if you cant send no money try and fine time to rite a letter onley a few lines and it will please Connie. jest think boy he hasent got out of bed in over 3 yrs. Connie says good luck.
>
> Your Mother,
> Ellen F. Kelly.

"I thought so," said Midge. "They're all alike."

The third letter was from New York. It read:

> HON:—This is the last letter you will get from me before your champ, but I will send you a telegram Saturday, but I can't say as much in a telegram as in a letter and I am writeing this to let you know I am thinking of you and praying for good luck.
>
> Lick him good hon and don't wait no longer than you have to and don't forget to wire me as soon as its over. Give him that little old left of yours on the nose hon and don't be afraid of spoiling his good looks because he couldn't be no homlier than he is. But don't let him spoil my baby's pretty face. You won't will you hon.
>
> Well hon I would give anything to be there and see it, but I guess you love Haley better than me or you wouldn't let him keep me away. But when your champ hon we can do as we please and tell Haley to go to the devil.
>
> Well hon I will send you a telegram Saturday and I almost forgot to tell you I will need some more money, a couple hundred say and you will have to wire it to me as soon as you get this. You will won't you hon.
>
> I will send you a telegram Saturday and remember hon I am pulling for you.
>
> Well good-by sweetheart and good luck. GRACE.

"They're all alike," said Midge. "Money, money, money."

Tommy Haley, shining from his ablutions, came in from the adjoining room.

"Thought you'd be layin' down," he said.

"I'm goin' to," said Midge, unbuttoning his orange shoes.

"I'll call you at six and you can eat up here without no bugs to pester you. I got to go down and give them birds their tickets."

"Did you hear from Goldberg?" asked Midge.

"Didn't I tell you? Sure; fifteen weeks at five hundred, if we win. And we can get a guarantee o' twelve thousand, with privileges either in New York or Milwaukee."

"Who with?"

"Anybody that'll stand up in front of you. You don't care who it is, do you?"

"Not me. I'll make 'em all look like a monkey."

"Well you better lay down a w'ile."

"Oh, say, wire two hundred to Grace for me, will you? Right away; the New York address."

"Two hundred! You just sent her three hundred last Sunday."

"Well, what the hell do you care?"

"All right, all right. Don't get sore about it. Anything else?"

"That's all," said Midge, and dropped onto the bed.

"And I want the deed done before I come back," said Grace as she rose from the table. "You won't fall down on me, will you, hon?"

"Leave it to me," said Midge. "And don't spend no more than you have to."

Grace smiled a farewell and left the café. Midge continued to sip his coffee and read his paper.

They were in Chicago and they were in the middle of Midge's first week in vaudeville. He had come straight north to reap the rewards of his glorious victory over the broken down Dutchman. A fortnight had been spent in learning his act, which consisted of a gymnastic exhibition and a ten minutes' monologue on the various excellences of Midge Kelly. And now he was twice daily turning 'em away from the Madison Theater.

His breakfast over and his paper read, Midge sauntered into the lobby and asked for his key. He then beckoned to a bell-boy, who had been hoping for that very honor.

"Find Haley, Tommy Haley," said Midge. "Tell him to come up to my room."

"Yes, sir, Mr. Kelly," said the boy, and proceeded to break all his former records for diligence.

Midge was looking out of his seventh-story window when Tommy answered the summons.

"What'll it be?" inquired his manager.

There was a pause before Midge replied.

"Haley," he said, "twenty-five per cent's a whole lot o' money."

"I guess I got it comin', ain't I?" said Tommy.

"I don't see how you figger it. I don't see where you're worth it to me."

"Well," said Tommy, "I didn't expect nothin' like this. I thought you was satisfied with the bargain. I don't want to beat nobody out o' nothin', but I don't see where you could have got anybody else that would of did all I done for you."

"Sure, that's all right," said the champion. "You done a lot for me in Philly. And you got good money for it, didn't you?"

"I ain't makin' no holler. Still and all, the big money's still ahead of us yet. And if it hadn't of been for me, you wouldn't of never got within grabbin' distance."

"Oh, I guess I could of went along all right," said Midge. "Who was it that hung that left on the Dutchman's jaw, me or you?"

"Yes, but you wouldn't been in the ring with the Dutchman if it wasn't for how I handled you."

"Well, this won't get us nowheres. The idear is that you ain't worth no twenty-five per cent now and it don't make no diff'rence what come off a year or two ago."

"Don't it?" said Tommy. "I'd say it made a whole lot of difference."

"Well, I say it don't and I guess that settles it."

"Look here, Midge," Tommy said, "I thought I was fair with you, but if you don't think so, I'm willin' to hear what you think is fair. I don't want nobody callin' me a Sherlock. Let's go down to business and sign up a contrac'. What's your figger?"

"I ain't namin' no figger," Midge replied. "I'm sayin' that twenty-five's too much. Now what are you willin' to take?"

"How about twenty?"

"Twenty's too much," said Kelly.

"What ain't too much?" asked Tommy.

"Well, Haley, I might as well give it to you straight. They ain't nothin' that ain't too much."

"You mean you don't want me at no figger?"

"That's the idear."

There was a minute's silence. Then Tommy Haley walked toward the door.

"Midge," he said, in a choking voice, "you're makin' a big mistake, boy. You can't throw down your best friends and get away with it. That damn woman will ruin you."

Midge sprang from his seat.

"You shut your mouth!" he stormed. "Get out o' here before they have to carry you out. You been spongin' off o' me long enough. Say one more word about the girl or about anything else and you'll get what the Dutchman got. Now get out!"

And Tommy Haley, having a very vivid memory of the Dutchman's face as he fell, got out.

Grace came in later, dropped her numerous bundles on the lounge and perched herself on the arm of Midge's chair.

"Well?" she said.

"Well," said Midge, "I got rid of him."

"Good boy!" said Grace. "And now I think you might give me that twenty-five per cent."

"Besides the seventy-five you're already gettin'?" said Midge.

"Don't be no grouch, hon. You don't look pretty when you're grouchy."

"It ain't my business to look pretty," Midge replied.

"Wait till you see how I look with the stuff I bought this mornin'!"

Midge glanced at the bundles on the lounge.

"There's Haley's twenty-five per cent," he said, "and then some."

The champion did not remain long without a manager. Haley's successor was none other than Jerome Harris, who saw in Midge a better meal ticket than his popular-priced musical show had been.

The contract, giving Mr. Harris twenty-five per cent of Midge's earnings, was signed in Detroit the week after Tommy Haley had heard his dismissal read. It had taken Midge just six days to learn that a popular actor cannot get on without the ministrations of a man who thinks, talks and means business. At first Grace objected to the new member of the firm, but when Mr. Harris had demanded and secured from the vaudeville people a one-hundred dollar increase in Midge's weekly stipend, she was convinced that the champion had acted for the best.

"You and my missus will have some great old times," Harris told Grace. "I'd of wired her to join us here, only I seen the Kid's bookin' takes us to Milwaukee next week, and that's where she is."

But when they were introduced in the Milwaukee hotel, Grace admitted to herself that her feeling for Mrs. Harris could hardly be called love at first sight. Midge, on the contrary, gave his new manager's wife the many times over and seemed loath to end the feast of his eyes.

"Some doll," he said to Grace when they were alone.

"Doll is right," the lady replied, "and sawdust where her brains ought to be."

"I'm li'ble to steal that baby," said Midge, and he smiled as he noted the effect of his words on his audience's face.

On Tuesday of the Milwaukee week the champion successfully defended his title in a bout that the newspapers never reported. Midge was alone in his room that morning when a visitor entered without knocking. The visitor was Lou Hersch.

Midge turned white at sight of him.

"What do you want?" he demanded.

"I guess you know," said Lou Hersch. "Your wife's starvin' to death and your baby's starvin' to death and I'm starvin' to death. And you're dirty with money."

"Listen," said Midge, "if it wasn't for you, I wouldn't never saw your sister. And, if you ain't man enough to hold a job, what's that to me? The best thing you can do is keep away from me."

"You give me a piece o' money and I'll go."

Midge's reply to the ultimatum was a straight right to his brother-in-law's narrow chest.

"Take that home to your sister."

And after Lou Hersch had picked himself up and slunk away, Midge thought: "It's lucky I didn't give him my left or I'd of croaked him. And if I'd hit him in the stomach, I'd of broke his spine."

There was a party after each evening performance during the Milwaukee engagement. The wine flowed freely and Midge had more of it than Tommy Haley ever would have permitted him. Mr. Harris offered no objection, which was possibly just as well for his own physical comfort.

In the dancing between drinks, Midge had his new manager's wife for a partner as often as Grace. The latter's face as she floundered round in the arms of the portly Harris, belied her frequent protestations that she was having the time of her life.

Several times that week, Midge thought Grace was on the point of starting the quarrel he hoped to have. But it was not until Friday night that she accommodated. He and Mrs. Harris had disappeared after the matinee and when Grace saw him again at the close of the night show, she came to the point at once.

"What are you tryin' to pull off?" she demanded.

"It's none o' your business, is it?" said Midge.

"You bet it's my business; mine and Harris's. You cut it short or you'll find out."

"Listen," said Midge, "have you got a mortgage on me or somethin'? You talk like we was married."

"We're goin' to be, too. And to-morrow's as good a time as any."

"Just about," Midge said. "You got as much chanct o' marryin' me to-morrow as the next day or next year and that ain't no chanct at all."

"We'll find out," said Grace.

"You're the one that's got somethin' to find out."

"What do you mean?"

"I mean I'm married already."

"You lie!"

"You think so, do you? Well, s'pose you go to this here address and get acquainted with my missus."

Midge scrawled a number on a piece of paper and handed it to her. She stared at it unseeingly.

"Well," said Midge. "I ain't kiddin' you. You go there and ask for Mrs. Michael Kelly, and if you don't find her, I'll marry you to-morrow before breakfast."

Still Grace stared at the scrap of paper. To Midge it seemed an age before she spoke again.

"You lied to me all this w'ile."

"You never ast me was I married. What's more, what the hell diff'-rence did it make to you? You got a split, didn't you? Better'n fifty-fifty."

He started away.

"Where you goin'?"

"I'm goin' to meet Harris and his wife."

"I'm goin' with you. You're not goin' to shake me now."

"Yes, I am, too," said Midge quietly. "When I leave town tomorrow night, you're going to stay here. And if I see where you're goin' to make a fuss, I'll put you in a hospital where they'll keep you quiet. You can get your stuff to-morrow mornin' and I'll slip you a hundred bucks. And then I don't want to see no more o' you. And don't try and tag along now or I'll have to add another K. O. to the old record."

When Grace returned to the hotel that night, she discovered that Midge and the Harrises had moved to another. And when Midge left town the following night, he was again without a manager, and Mr. Harris was without a wife.

Three days prior to Midge Kelly's ten-round bout with Young Milton in New York City, the sporting editor of *The News* assigned Joe Morgan to write two or three thousand words about the champion to run with a picture lay-out for Sunday.

Joe Morgan dropped in at Midge's training quarters Friday afternoon. Midge, he learned, was doing road work, but Midge's manager, Wallie Adams, stood ready and willing to supply reams of dope about the greatest fighter of the age.

"Let's hear what you've got," said Joe, "and then I'll try to fix up something."

So Wallie stepped on the accelerator of his imagination and shot away.

"Just a kid; that's all he is; a regular boy. Get what I mean? Don't know the meanin' o' bad habits. Never tasted liquor in his life and would prob'bly get sick if he smelled it. Clean livin' put him up where he's at. Get what I mean? And modest and unassumin' as a school girl. He's so quiet you wouldn't never know he was round. And he'd go to jail before he'd talk about himself.

"No job at all to get him in shape, 'cause he's always that way. The only trouble we have with him is gettin' him to light into these poor bums they match him up with. He's scared he'll hurt somebody. Get what I mean? He's tickled to death over this match with Milton, 'cause everybody says Milton can stand the gaff. Midge'll maybe be able to cut loose a little this time. But the last two bouts he had, the guys hadn't no business in the ring with him, and he was holdin' back all the w'ile for the fear he'd kill somebody. Get what I mean?"

"Is he married?" inquired Joe.

"Say, you'd think he was married to hear him rave about them kiddies he's got. His fam'ly's up in Canada to their summer home and Midge is wild to get up there with 'em. He thinks more o' that wife and them kiddies than all the money in the world. Get what I mean?"

"How many children has he?"

"I don't know, four or five, I guess. All boys and every one of 'em a dead ringer for their dad."

"Is his father living?"

"No, the old man died when he was a kid. But he's got a grand old mother and a kid brother out in Chi. They're the first ones he thinks about after a match, them and his wife and kiddies. And he don't forget to send the old woman a thousand bucks after every bout. He's going to buy her a new home as soon as they pay him off for this match."

"How about his brother? Is he going to tackle the game?"

"Sure, and Midge says he'll be a champion before he's twenty years old. They're a fightin' fam'ly and all of 'em honest and straight as a die. Get what I mean? A fella that I can't tell you his name come to Midge in Milwaukee onct and wanted him to throw a fight and Midge give him such a trimmin' in the street that he couldn't go on that night. That's the kind he is. Get what I mean?"

Joe Morgan hung around the camp until Midge and his trainers returned.

"One o' the boys from *The News,*" said Wallie by way of introduction. "I been givin' him your fam'ly hist'ry."

"Did he give you good dope?" he inquired.

"He's some historian," said Joe.

"Don't call me no names," said Wallie smiling. "Call us up if they's anything more you want. And keep your eyes on us Monday night. Get what I mean?"

The story in Sunday's *News* was read by thousands of lovers of the manly art. It was well written and full of human interest. Its slight inaccuracies went unchallenged, though three readers, besides Wallie Adams and Midge Kelly, saw and recognized them. The three were Grace, Tommy Haley and Jerome Harris and the comments they made were not for publication.

Neither the Mrs. Kelly in Chicago nor the Mrs. Kelly in Milwaukee knew that there was such a paper as the New York *News.* And even if they had known of it and that it contained two columns of reading matter about Midge, neither mother nor wife could have bought it. For *The News* on Sunday is a nickel a copy.

Joe Morgan could have written more accurately, no doubt, if instead of Wallie Adams, he had interviewed Ellen Kelly and Connie Kelly and Emma Kelly and Lou Hersch and Grace and Jerome Harris and Tommy Haley and Hap Collins and two or three Milwaukee bartenders.

But a story built on their evidence would never have passed the sporting editor.

"Suppose you can prove it," that gentleman would have said, "It wouldn't get us anything but abuse to print it. The people don't want to see him knocked. He's champion."

WILBUR DANIEL STEELE

The Man Who Saw Through Heaven

People have wondered (there being obviously no question of romance involved) how I could ever have allowed myself to be let in for the East African adventure of Mrs. Diana in search of her husband. There were several reasons. To begin with, the time and effort and money weren't mine; they were the property of the wheel of which I was but a cog, the Society through which Diana's life had been insured, along with the rest of that job-lot of missionaries. The "letting in" was the firm's. In the second place, the wonderers have not counted on Mrs. Diana's capacity for getting things done for her. Meek and helpless. Yes, but God was on her side. Too meek, too helpless to move mountains herself, if those who happened to be handy didn't move them for her then her God would know the reason why. Having dedicated her all to making straight the Way, why should her neighbour cavil at giving a little? The writer for one, a colonial governor general for another, railway magnates, insurance managers, *safari* leaders, the ostrich-farmer of Ndua, all these and a dozen others in their turns have felt the hundred-ton weight of her thin-lipped meekness—have seen her in metaphor sitting grimly on the doorsteps of their souls.

A third reason lay in my own troubled conscience. Though I did it in innocence, I can never forget that it was I who personally conducted Diana's party to the observatory on that fatal night in Boston before it sailed. Had it not been for that kindly intentioned "hunch" of mine, the astounded eye of the Reverend Hubert Diana would never have gazed through the floor of Heaven, and he would never have undertaken to measure the Infinite with the foot-rule of his mind.

It all started so simply. My boss at the shipping-and-insurance office gave me the word in the morning. "Bunch of missionaries for the *Platonic* to-morrow. They're on our hands in a way. Show 'em the town." It wasn't so easy when you think of it: one male and seven females on their way to the heathen; though it was easier in Boston than it might have been in some other towns. The evening looked the simplest. My friend Krum was at the Observatory that semester; there at least I was sure their sensibilities would come to no harm.

On the way out in the street car, seated opposite to Diana and having to make conversation, I talked of Krum and of what I knew of his work with the spiral nebulæ. Having to appear to listen, Diana did so (as all day long) with a vaguely indulgent smile. He really hadn't time for me. That night his life was exalted as it had never been, and would perhaps never be again. To'morrow's sailing, the actual fact of leaving all to follow Him, held his imagination in thrall. Moreover, he was a bridegroom of three days with his bride beside him, his nerves at once assuaged and thrilled. No, but more. As if a bride were not enough, arrived in Boston, he had found himself surrounded by a very galaxy of womanhood gathered from the four corners; already within hours one felt the chaste tentacles of their feminine dependence curling about the party's unique man; already their contacts with the world of their new lives began to be made through him; already they saw in part through his eyes. I wonder what he would have said if I had told him he was a little drunk.

In the course of the day I think I had got him fairly well. As concerned his Church he was at once an asset and a liability. He believed its dogma as few still did, with a simplicity, "the old-time religion." He was born that kind. Of the stuff of the fanatic, the reason he was not a fanatic was that, curiously impervious to little questionings, he had never been aware that his faith was anywhere attacked. A self-educated man, he had accepted the necessary smattering facts of science with a serene indulgence, as simply so much further proof of what the Creator could do when He put His Hand to it. Nor was he conscious of any conflict between these facts and the fact that there existed a substantial Heaven, geographically up, and a substantial Hot Place, geographically down.

So, for his Church, he was an asset in these days. And so, and for the same reason, he was a liability. The Church must after all keep abreast of the times. For home consumption, with modern congregations, especially urban ones, a certain streak of "healthy" skepticism is no longer amiss in the pulpit; it makes people who read at all more comfortable in their pews. A man like Hubert Diana is more for the cause than a hundred. But what to do with him? Well, such things arrange themselves. There's the Foreign Field. The blacker the heathen the whiter the light they'll want, and the solider the conception of a God the Father enthroned in a Heaven of which the sky above them is the visible floor.

And that, at bottom, was what Hubert Diana believed. Accept as he would with the top of his brain the fact of a spherical earth zooming through space, deep in his heart he knew that the world lay flat from modern Illinois to ancient Palestine, and that the sky above it, blue by day and by night festooned with guiding stars for wise men, was the nether side of a floor on which the resurrected trod. . . .

I shall never forget the expression of his face when he realized he was looking straight through it that night. In the quiet dark of the dome I saw him remove his eye from the eye-piece of the telescope up there on the staging and turn it in the ray of a hooded bulb on the demon's keeper, Krum.

"What's that, Mr. Krum? I didn't get you!"

"I say, that particular cluster you're looking at——"

"This star, you mean?"

"You'd have to count awhile to count the stars describing their orbits in that 'star,' Mr. Diana. But what I was saying—have you ever had the wish I used to have as a boy—that you could actually look back into the past? With your own two eyes?"

Diana spoke slowly. He didn't know it, but it had already begun to happen; he was already caught. "I have often wished, Mr. Krum, that I might actually look back into the time of our Lord. Actually. Yes."

Krum grunted. He was young. "We'd have to pick a nearer neighbour than *Messier 79* then. The event you see when you put your eye to that lens is happening much too far in the past. The light-waves thrown off by that particular cluster on the day, say, of the Crucifixion—*you* won't live to see them. They've hardly started yet—a mere twenty centuries on their way—leaving them something like eight hundred and thirty centuries yet to come before they reach the earth."

Diana laughed the queerest catch of a laugh. "And—and there—there won't be any earth here, then, to welcome them."

"*What?*" It was Krum's turn to look startled. So for a moment the two faces remained in confrontation, the one, as I say, startled, the other exuding visibly little sea-green globules of sweat. It was Diana that caved in first, his voice hardly louder than a whisper.

"W-w-will there?"

None of us suspected the enormousness of the thing that had happened in Diana's brain. Krum shrugged his shoulders and snapped his fingers. Deliberately. *Snap!* "What's a thousand centuries or so in the cosmic reckoning?" He chuckled. "We're just beginning to get out among 'em with *Messier,* you know. In the print room, Mr. Diana, I can show you photographs of clusters to which, if you cared to go, travelling at the speed of light——"

The voice ran on; but Diana's eye had gone back to the eye-piece, and his affrighted soul had reëntered the big black tube sticking its snout out of the slit in the iron hemisphere. . . . "At the speed of light!" . . . That unsuspected, that wildly chance-found chink in the armour of his philosophy! The body is resurrected and it ascends to Heaven instantaneously. At what speed must it be borne to reach instantaneously that city beyond the ceiling of the sky? At a speed inconceivable, mystical. At, say (as he had often said to himself), *the speed of light.* . . . And now, hunched there in the trap that had caught him, black rods, infernal levers and wheels, he was aware of his own eye passing vividly through unpartitioned emptiness, *eight hundred and fifty centuries at the speed of light!*

"And still beyond these," Krum was heard, "we begin to come into the regions of the spiral nebulæ. We've some interesting photographs in the print room, if you've the time."

The ladies below were tired of waiting. One had "lots of packing to do." The bride said, "Yes, I do think we should be getting along. Hubert, dear, if you're ready——"

The fellow actually jumped. It's lucky he didn't break anything. His face looked greener and dewier than ever amid the contraptions above. "If you—you and the ladies, Cora—wouldn't mind—if Mr.—Mr.—(he'd mislaid my name) would see you back to the hotel——" Meeting silence, he began to expostulate. "I feel that this is a rich experience. I'll follow shortly; I know the way."

In the car going back into the city Mrs. Diana set at rest the flutterings of six hearts. Being unmarried, they couldn't understand men as she did. When I think of that face of hers, to which I was destined to grow only too accustomed in the weary, itchy days of the trek into Kavirondoland, with its slightly tilted nose, its irregular pigmentation, its easily inflamed lids, and long moist cheeks, like a hunting dog, glorying in weariness, it seems incredible that a light of coyness could have found lodgment there. But that night it did. She sat serene among her virgins.

"You don't know Bert. You wait; he'll get a perfectly wonderful sermon out of all that to-night, Bert will."

Krum was having a grand time with his neophyte. He would have stayed up all night. Immured in the little print room crowded with files and redolent of acids, he conducted his disciple "glassy-eyed" through the dim frontiers of space, holding before him one after another the likenesses of universes sister to our own, islanded in immeasurable vacancy, curled like glimmering crullers on their private Milky Ways, and hiding in their wombs their myriad "coal-pockets," star-dust fœtuses of which—their quadrillion years accomplished—their litters of new suns would be born, to bear their planets, to bear their moons in turn.

"And beyond these?"

Always, after each new feat of distance, it was the same. "And beyond?" Given an ell, Diana surrendered to a pop-eyed lust for nothing less than light-years. "And still beyond?"

"Who knows?"

"The mind quits. For if there's no end to these nebulæ——"

"But supposing there is?"

"An end? But, Mr. Krum, in the very idea of an ending——"

"An end to what we might call this particular category of magnitudes. Eh?"

"I don't get that."

"Well, take this—take the opal in your ring there. The numbers and distances inside that stone may conceivably be to themselves as staggering as ours to us in our own system. Come! that's not so far-fetched. What are we learning about the structure of the atom? A nucleus (call it a sun) revolved about in eternal orbits by electrons (call them planets, worlds). Infinitesimal; but after all, what are bigness and littleness but matters of comparison? To eyes on one of those electrons (don't be too sure there aren't any) its tutelary sun may flame its way across a heaven a comparative ninety million miles away. Impossible for them to conceive of a boundary to their billions of atomic systems, molecular universes. In that category of magnitudes its diameter is infinity; once it has made the leap into our category and become an opal it is merely a quarter of an inch. That's right, Mr. Diana, you may well stare at it: between *now* and *now* ten thousand histories may have come and gone down there. . . . And just so the diameter of our own cluster of universes, going over into another category, may be——"

"May be a—a ring—a little stone—in a—a—a—ring."

Krum was tickled by the way the man's imagination jumped and engulfed it.

"Why not? That's as good a guess as the next. A ring, let's say, worn carelessly on the—well, say the tentacle—of some vast organism—some inchoate creature hobnobbing with its cloudy kind in another system of universes—which in turn——"

It is curious that none of them realized next day that they were dealing with a stranger, a changed man. Why he carried on, why he capped that night of cosmic debauch by shaving, eating an unremarkable breakfast, packing his terrestrial toothbrush and collars, and going up the gangplank in tow of his excited convoy to sail away, is beyond explanation—unless it was simply that he was in a daze.

It wasn't until four years later that I was allowed to know what had happened on that ship, and even then the tale was so disjointed, warped, and opinionated, so darkly seen in the mirror of Mrs. Diana's orthodoxy, that I had almost to guess what it was *really* all about.

"When Hubert turned irreligious. . . ." That phrase, recurrent on her tongue in the meanderings of the East African quest to which we were by then committed, will serve to measure her understanding. Irreligious! Good Lord! But from that sort of thing I had to reconstruct the drama. Evening after evening beside her camp fire (appended to the Mineral Survey Expedition Toward Uganda through the kindness—actually the worn-down surrender—of the Protectorate government) I lingered awhile before joining the merrier engineers, watched with fascination the bumps growing under the mosquitoes on her forehead, and listened to the jargon of her mortified meekness and her scandalized faith.

There had been a fatal circumstance, it seems, at the very outset. If Diana could but have been seasick, as the rest of them were (horribly), all might still have been well. In the misery of desired death, along with the other contents of a heaving midriff, he might have brought up the assorted universes of which he had been led too rashly to partake. But he wasn't. As if his wife's theory was right, as if Satan was looking out for him, he was spared to prowl the swooping decks immune. Four days and nights alone. Time enough to digest and assimilate into his being beyond remedy that lump of whirling magnitudes and to feel himself surrendering with a strange new ecstasy to the drunkenness of liberty.

Such liberty! Given Diana's type, it is hard to imagine it adequately. The abrupt, complete removal of the toils of reward and punishment; the withdrawal of the surveillance of an all-seeing, all-knowing Eye; the windy assurance of being responsible for nothing, important to no one, no longer (as the police say) "wanted"! It must have been beautiful in those few days of its first purity, before it began to be discoloured by his contemptuous pity for others, the mask of his inevitable loneliness and his growing fright.

The first any of them knew of it—even his wife—was in mid-voyage, the day the sea went down and the seven who had been sick came up. There seemed an especial Providence in the calming of the waters; it was Sunday morning and Diana had been asked to conduct the services.

He preached on the text: "For of such is the kingdom of Heaven."

"If our concept of God means anything it means a God *all*-mighty, Creator of *all* that exists, Director of the *infinite,* cherishing in His Heaven the saved souls of *all space and all time.*"

Of course; amen. And wasn't it nice to feel like humans again, and real sunshine pouring up through the lounge ports from an ocean suddenly grown kind. . . . But—then—*what* was Diana *saying?*

Mrs. Diana couldn't tell about it coherently even after a lapse of fifty months. Even in a setting as remote from that steamer's lounge as the equatorial bush, the ember-reddened canopy of thorn trees, the meandering camp fires, the chant and tramp somewhere away of Kikuyu porters dancing in honour of an especial largesse of fat zebra meat—even here her memory of that impious outburst was too vivid, too aghast.

"It was Hubert's look! The way he stared at us! As if you'd said he was licking his chops! . . . That *'Heaven'* of his!"

It seems they hadn't waked up to what he was about until he had the dimensions of his sardonic Paradise irreparably drawn in. The final haven of all right souls. Not alone the souls released from this our own tiny earth. In the millions of solar systems we see as stars how many millions of satellites must there be upon which at some time in their histories conditions suited to organic life subsist? Uncounted hordes of wheeling populations! Of men? God's creatures at all events, a portion of them reasoning. Weirdly shaped, perhaps, but what of that? And that's only to speak of our own inconsiderable cluster of universes. That's to say nothing of other systems of magnitudes, where God's creatures are to our world what we are to the world's in the atoms in our finger-rings. (He had shaken *his,* here, in their astounded faces.) And all these, all the generations of these enormous and microscopic beings harvested through a time beside which the life-span of our earth is as a second in a million centuries: all these brought to rest for an eternity to which time itself is a watch-tick—all crowded to rest pell-mell, thronged, serried, packed, packed to suffocation in layers unnumbered light-years deep. This must needs be our concept of Heaven if God is the God of the Whole. If, on the other hand——

The other hand was the hand of the second officer, the captain's delegate at divine worship that Sabbath day. He at last had "come to."

I don't know whether it was the same day or the next; Mrs. Diana was too vague. But here's the picture. Seven women huddled in the large stateroom on B-deck, conferring in whispers, aghast, searching one another's eyes obliquely even as they bowed their heads in prayer for some light—and of a sudden the putting back of the door and the in-marching of the Reverend Hubert. . . .

As Mrs. Diana tried to tell me, "You understand, don't you, he had just taken a bath? And he hadn't—he had forgotten to——"

Adam-innocent there he stood. Not a stitch. But I don't believe for a minute it was a matter of forgetting. In the high intoxication of his soul-release, already crossed (by the second officer) and beginning to show his zealot claws, he needed some gesture stunning enough to witness to his separation, his unique rightness, his contempt of match-flare civilizations and infinitesimal taboos.

But I can imagine that stateroom scene: the gasps, the heads colliding in aversion, and Diana's six weedy feet of birthday-suit towering in the shadows, and ready to sink through the deck, I'll warrant, now the act was irrevocable, but still grimly carrying it off.

"And if, on the other hand, you ask me to bow down before a God peculiar to this one earth, this one grain of dust lost among the giants of space, watching its sparrows fall, profoundly interested in a speck called Palestine no bigger than the quadrillionth part of one of the atoms in the ring here on my finger——"

Really scared by this time, one of the virgins shrieked. It was altogether too close quarters with a madman.

Mad? Of course there was the presumption: "Crazy as a loon." Even legally it was so adjudged at the *Platonic's* first port-of-call, Algiers, where, when Diana escaped ashore and wouldn't come back again, he had to be given over to the workings of the French Law. I talked with the magistrate myself some forty months later, when, "let in" for the business as I have told, I stopped there on my way out.

"But what would you?" were his words. "We must live in the world as the world lives, is it not? Sanity? Sanity is what? Is it, for example, an intellectual clarity, a balanced perception of the realities? Naturally, speaking out of court, your friend was of a sanity—of a sanity, sir——" Here the magistrate made with thumb and fingers the gesture only the French can make for a thing that is matchless, a beauty, a transcendent instance of any kind. He himself was Gallic, rational. Then, with a lift of shoulder, "But what would you? We must live in the world that seems."

Diana, impounded in Algiers for deportation, escaped. What, after all, are the locks and keys of this pinchbeck category of magnitudes? More remarkable still, there in Arab Africa, he succeeded in vanishing from the knowledge and pursuit of men. And of women. His bride, now that their particular mission had fallen through, was left to decide whether to return to America or to go on with two of the company, the Misses Brookhart and Smutts, who were bound for a school in Smyrna. In the end she followed the latter course. It was there, nearly four years later, that I was sent to join her by an exasperated and worn-out Firm.

By that time she knew again where her husband-errant was—or where at least, from time to time in his starry dartings over this our mote of dust, he had been heard of, spoken to, seen.

Could we but have a written history of those years of his apostolic vagabondage, a record of the towns in which he was jailed or from which he was kicked out, of the ports in which he starved, of the ships on which he stowed away, presently to reveal himself in proselyting ardour, denouncing the earthlings, the fatelings, the dupes of bugaboo, meeting scoff with scoff, preaching the new revelation red-eyed, like an angry prophet. Or was it, more simply, like a man afraid?

Was that the secret, after all, of his prodigious restlessness? Had it anything in common with the swarming of those pale worms that flee the Eye of the Infinite around the curves of the stone you pick up in a field? Talk of the man without a country! What of the man without a universe?

It is curious that I never suspected his soul's dilemma until I saw the first of his mud-sculptures in the native village of Ndua in the province of Kasuma in British East. Here it was, our objective attained, we parted company with the government *safari* and shifted the burden of Way-straightening to the shoulders of Major Wyeside, the ostrich-farmer of the neighbourhood.

While still on the *safari* I had put to Mrs. Diana a question that had bothered me: "Why on earth should your husband ever have chosen this particular neck of the woods to land up in? Why Kavirondoland?"

"It was here we were coming at the time Hubert turned irreligious, to found a mission. It's a coincidence, isn't it?"

And yet I would have sworn Diana hadn't a sense of humour about him anywhere. But perhaps it *wasn't* an ironic act. Perhaps it was simply that, giving up the struggle with a society blinded by "a little learning" and casting about for a virgin field, he had remembered this.

"I supposed he was a missionary," Major Wyeside told us with a flavour of indignation. "I went on that. I let him live here—six or seven months of it—while he was learning the tongue. I was a bit nonplussed, to put it mildly, when I discovered what he was up to."

What things Diana had been up to the Major showed us in one of the huts in the native kraal—a round dozen of them, modelled in mud and baked. Blackened blobs of mud, that's all. Likenesses of nothing under the sun, fortuitous masses sprouting haphazard tentacles, only two among them showing pustules that might have been experimental heads. . . . The ostrich-farmer saw our faces.

"Rum, eh? Of course I realized the chap was anything but fit. A walking skeleton. Nevertheless, whatever it is about these beasties, there's not a nigger in the village has dared set foot inside this hut since Diana left. You can see for yourselves it's about to crash. There's another like it he left at Suki, above here. Taboo, no end!"

So Diana's "hunch" had been right. He had found his virgin field indeed, fit soil for his cosmic fright. A religion in the making, here before our eyes.

"This was at the very last before he left," Wyeside explained. "He took to making these mud-pies quite of a sudden; the whole lot within a fortnight's time. Before that he had simply talked, harangued. He would sit here in the doorway of an evening with the niggers squatted around and harangue 'em by the hour. I knew something of it through my house-boys. The most amazing rot. All about the stars to begin with, as if these black baboons could half grasp *astronomy!* But that seemed all proper. Then there was talk about a something a hundred times as big and powerful as the world, sun, moon, and stars put together—some perfectly enormous stupendous awful being—but knowing how mixed the boys can get, it still seemed all regular—simply the parson's way of getting at the notion of an Almighty God. But no, they insisted, there wasn't any God. That's the point, they said; there *is no* God. . . . Well, that impressed me as a go. That's when I decided to come down and get the rights of this star-swallowing monstrosity the beggar was feeding my labour on. And here he sat in the doorway with one of these beasties—here it is, this one—waving it furiously in the niggers' benighted faces. And do you know what he'd done?—you can see the mark here still on this wabble-leg, this tentacle-business—he had taken off a ring he had and screwed it on just here. His finger ring, my word of honour! And still, if you'll believe it, I didn't realize he was just daft. Not until he spoke to me. 'I find,' he was good enough to enlighten me, 'I find I have to make it somehow concrete.' . . . 'Make what?' . . . 'Our wearer.' . . . 'Our *what, where?*' . . . 'In the following category.' . . . His actual words, honour bright. I was going to have him sent down-country where he could be looked after. He got ahead of me though. He cleared out. When I heard he'd turned up at Suki I ought, I suppose, to have attended to it. But I was having trouble with leopards. And you know how things go."

From there we went to Suki, the Major accompanying. It was as like Ndua as one flea to its brother, a stockade inclosing round houses of mud, wattles, and thatch, and full of naked heathen. The Kavirondo are the nakedest of all African peoples and, it is said, the most moral. It put a great strain on Mrs. Diana; all that whole difficult anxious time, as it were detachedly, I could see her itching to get them into Mother Hubbards and cast-off Iowa pants.

Here, too, as the Major had promised, we found a holy of holies, rather a dreadful of dreadfuls, "taboo no end," its shadows cluttered with the hurlothrumbos of Diana's artistry. What puzzled me was their number. Why this appetite for experimentation? There was an uncertainty; one would think its effect on potential converts would be bad. Here, as in Ndua, Diana had contented himself at first with words and skyward gesticulations. Not for so long, however. Feeling the need of giving his concept of the cosmic "wearer" a substance much earlier, he had shut himself in with the work, literally—a fever of creation. We counted seventeen of the nameless "blobs," all done, we were told, in the seven days and nights before their maker had again cleared out. The villagers would hardly speak of him; only after spitting, their eyes averted, and in an undertone, would they mention him: "He of the Ring." Thereafter we were to hear of him only as "He of the Ring."

Leaving Suki, Major Wyeside turned us over (thankfully, I warrant) to a native who told us his name was Charlie Kamba. He had spent some years in Nairobi, running for an Indian outfitter, and spoke English remarkably well. It was from him we learned, quite casually, when our modest eight-load *safari* was some miles on its way, that the primary object of our coming was non-existent. Hubert Diana was dead.

Dead nearly five weeks—a moon and a little—and buried in the mission church at Tara Hill.

Mission church! There was a poser for us. *Mission church?*

Well, then, Charlie Kamba gave us to know that he was paraphrasing in a large way suitable to our habits of thought. We shouldn't have understood *his* informant's "wizard house" or "house of the effigy."

I will say for Mrs. Diana that in the course of our halt of lugubrious amazement she shed tears. That some of them were not tears of unrealized relief it would be hardly natural to believe. She had desired loyally to find her husband, but when she should have found him—what? This problem, sturdily ignored so long, was now removed.

Turn back? Never! Now it would seem the necessity for pressing forward was doubled. In the scrub-fringed ravine of our halt the porters resumed their loads, the dust stood up again, the same caravan moved on. But how far it was now from being the same.

From that moment it took on, for me at least, a new character. It wasn't the news especially; the fact that Diana was dead had little to do with it. Perhaps it was simply that the new sense of something aimfully and cumulatively dramatic in our progress had to have a beginning, and that moment would do as well as the next.

Six villages: M'nann, Leika, Leikapo, Shamba, Little Tara, and Tara, culminating in the apotheosis of Tara Hill. Six stops for the night on the road it had cost Diana as many months to cover in his singular pilgrimage to his inevitable goal. Or in his flight to it. Yes, his stampede. Now the pipers at that four-day orgy of liberty on the *Platonic's* decks were at his heels for their pay. Now that his strength was failing, the hosts of loneliness were after him, creeping out of their dreadful magnitudes, the hounds of space. Over all that ground it seemed to me we were following him not by the world of hearsay but, as one follows a wounded animal making for its earth, by the droppings of his blood.

Our progress had taken on a pattern; it built itself with a dramatic artistry; it gathered suspense. As though it were a story at its most breathless places "continued in our next," and I a reader forgetting the road's weariness, the dust, the torment of insects never escaped, the inadequate food, I found myself hardly able to keep from running on ahead to reach the evening's village, to search out the inevitable repository of images left by the white stranger who had come and tarried there awhile and gone again.

More concrete and ever more concrete. The immemorial compromise with the human hunger for a symbol to see with the eyes, touch with the hands. Hierarchy after hierarchy of little mud effigies—one could see the necessity pushing the man. Out of the protoplasmic blobs of Ndua,

Suki, even M'nann, at Leikapo Diana's concept of infinity (so pure in that halcyon epoch at sea), of categories nested within categories like Japanese boxes, of an overcreature wearing our cosmos like a trinket, unawares, had become a mass with legs to stand on and a real head. The shards scattered about in the filth of the hut there (as if in violence of despair) were still monstrosities, but with a sudden stride of concession their monstrousness was the monstrousness of lizard and turtle and crocodile. At Shamba there were dozens of huge-footed birds.

It is hard to be sure in retrospect, but I do believe that by the time we reached Little Tara I began to see the thing as a whole—the fœtus, working out slowly, blindly, but surely, its evolution in the womb of fright. At Little Tara there was a change in the character of the exhibits; their numbers had diminished, their size had grown. There was a boar with tusks and a bull the size of a dog with horns, and on a tusk and on a horn an indentation left by a ring.

I don't believe Mrs. Diana got the thing at all. Toward the last she wasn't interested in the huts of relics; at Little Tara she wouldn't go near the place; she was "too tired." It must have been pretty awful, when you think of it, even if all she saw in them was the mud-pie play of a man reverted to a child.

There was another thing at Little Tara quite as momentous as the jump to boar and bull. Here at last a mask had been thrown aside. Here there had been no pretense of proselyting, no astronomical lectures, no doorway harangues. Straightway he had arrived (a fabulous figure already, long heralded), he had commandeered a house and shut himself up in it and there, mysterious, assiduous, he had remained three days and nights, eating nothing, but drinking gallons of the foul water they left in gourds outside his curtain of reeds. No one in the village had ever seen what he had done and left there. Now, candidly, those labours were for himself alone.

Here at last in Tara the moment of that confession had overtaken the fugitive. It was he, ill with fever and dying of nostalgia—not these naked black baboon men seen now as little more than blurs—who had to give the Beast of the Infinite a name and a shape. And more and more, not only a shape, but a *shapeliness.* From the instant when, no longer able to live alone with nothingness, he had given it a likeness in Ndua mud, and perceived that it was intolerable and fled its face, the turtles and distorted crocodiles of Leikapo and the birds of Shamba had become inevitable, and no less inevitable the Little Tara boar and bull. Another thing grows plain in retrospect: the reason why, done to death (as all the way they reported him) he couldn't die. He didn't dare to. Didn't dare to close his eyes.

It was at Little Tara we first heard of him as "Father Witch," a name come back, we were told, from Tara, where he had gone. I had heard it pronounced several times before it suddenly obtruded from the native context as actually two English words. That was what made it queer. It was something they must have picked up by rote, uncomprehending; something then they could have had from no lips but his own. When I repeated it after them with a better accent they pointed up toward the north, saying "Tara! Tara!"—their eagerness mingled with awe.

I shall never forget Tara as we saw it, after our last blistering scramble up a gorge, situated in the clear air on a slope belted with cedars. A mid-African stockade left by some blunder in an honest Colorado landscape, or a newer and bigger Vermont. Here at the top of our journey, black savages, their untidy *shambas,* the very Equator, all these seemed as incongruous as a Gothic cathedral in a Congo marsh. I wonder if Hubert Diana knew whither his instinct was guiding him on the long road of his journey here to die. . . .

He had died and he was buried, not in the village, but about half a mile distant, on the ridge; this we were given to know almost before we had arrived. There was no need to announce ourselves, the word of our coming had outrun us; the populace was at the gates.

"Our Father Witch! Our Father Witch!" They knew what we were after; the funny parrot-wise English stood out from the clack and clatter of their excited speech. "Our Father Witch! Ay! Ay!" With a common eagerness they gesticulated at the hilltop beyond the cedars.

Certainly here was a change. No longer the propitiatory spitting, the averted eyes, the uneasy whispering allusion to him who had passed that way: here in Tara they would shout him from the housetops, with a kind of civic pride.

We learned the reason for this on our way up the hill. It was because they were his chosen, the initiate.

We made the ascent immediately, against the village's advice. It was near evening; the return would be in the dark; it was bad lion country; wouldn't to-morrow morning do? . . . No, it wouldn't do the widow. Her face was set. . . . And so, since we were resolved to go, the village went with us, armed with spears and rattles and drums. Charlie Kamba walked beside us, sifting the information a hundred were eager to give.

These people were proud, he said, because their wizard was more powerful than all the wizards of all the other villages "in the everywhere together." If he cared to he could easily knock down all the other villages in the "everywhere," destroying all the people and all the cattle. If he cared to he could open his mouth and swallow the sky and the stars. But

Tara he had chosen. Tara he would protect. He made their mealies to grow and their cattle to multiply.

I protested, "But he is *dead* now!"

Charlie Kamba made signs of deprecation. I discerned that he was far from clear about the thing himself.

Yes, he temporized, this Father Witch was dead, quite dead. On the other hand, he was up there. On the other hand, he would never die. He was longer than for ever. Yes, quite true, he was dead and buried under the pot.

I gave it up. "How did he die?"

Well, he came to this village of Tara very suffering, very sick. The dead man who walked. His face was very sad. Very eaten. Very frightened. He came to this hill. So he lived here for two full moons, very hot, very eaten, very dead. These men made him a house as he commanded them, also a stockade. In the house he was very quiet, very dead, making magic two full moons. Then he came out and they that were waiting saw him. He had made the magic, and the magic had made him well. His face was kind. He was happy. He was full fed. He was full fed, these men said, without any eating. Yes, they carried up to him very fine food, because they were full of wonder and some fear, but he did not eat any of it. Some water he drank. So, for two days and the night between them, he continued sitting in the gate of the stockade, very happy, very full fed. He told these people very much about their wizard, who is bigger than everywhere and longer than for ever and can, if he cares to, swallow the sky and stars. From time to time, however, ceasing to talk to these people, he got to his knees and talked in his own strange tongue to Our Father Witch, his eyes held shut. When he had done this just at sunset of the second day he fell forward on his face. So he remained that night. The next day these men took him into the house and buried him under the pot. On the other hand, Our Father Witch is longer than for ever. He remains there still. . . .

The first thing I saw in the hut's interior was the earthen pot at the northern end, wrong-side-up on the ground. I was glad I had preceded Mrs. Diana. I walked across and sat down on it carelessly, hoping so that her afflicted curiosity might be led astray. It gave me the oddest feeling, though, to think of what was there beneath my nonchalant sitting-portion—aware as I was of the Kavirondo burial of a great man—up to the neck in mother earth, and the rest of him left out in the dark of the pot for the undertakings of the ants. I hoped his widow wouldn't wonder about that inverted vessel of clay.

I needn't have worried. Her attention was arrested otherwheres. I shall not forget the look of her face, caught above me in the red shaft of sundown entering the western door, as she gazed at the last and the largest of the Reverend Hubert Diana's gods. That long, long cheek of hers, buffeted by sorrow, startled now, and mortified. Not till that moment, I believe, had she comprehended the steps of mud images she had been following for what they were, the steps of idolatry.

For my part, I wasn't startled. Even before we started up the hill, knowing that her husband had dared to die here, I could have told her pretty much what she would find.

This overlord of the cosmic categories that he had fashioned (at last) in his own image sat at the other end of the red-streaked house upon a bench—a throne?—of mud. Diana had been no artist. An ovoid two-eyed head, a cylindrical trunk, two arms, two legs, that's all. But indubitably man, man-size. Only one finger of one of the hands had been done with much care. It wore an opal, a two-dollar stone from Mexico, set in a silver ring. This was the hand that was lifted, and over it the head was bent.

I've said Diana was no artist. I'll take back the words. The figure was crudeness itself, but in the relation between that bent head and that lifted hand there was something which was something else. A sense of scrutiny one would have said no genius of mud could ever have conveyed. An attitude of interest centered in that bauble, intense and static, breathless and eternal all in one—penetrating to its bottom atom, to the last electron, to a hill upon it, and to a two-legged mite about to die. Marking (yes, I'll swear to the incredible) the sparrow's fall.

The magic was made. The road that had commenced with the blobs of Ndua—the same that commenced with our hairy ancestors listening to the night wind in their caves—was run.

And from here Diana, of a sudden happy, of a sudden looked after, "full fed," had walked out——

But no; I couldn't stand that mortified sorrow on the widow's face any longer. She had to be made to see. I said it aloud:

"From here, Mrs. Diana, your husband walked out——"

"He had sunk to idolatry. *Idolatry!*"

"To the bottom, yes. And come up its whole history again. And from here he walked out into the sunshine to kneel and talk with 'Our Father Which——' "

She got it. She caught it. I wish you could have seen the light going up those long, long cheeks as she got it:

"Our Father which art in Heaven, Hallowed be Thy Name!"

We went down hill in the darkness, convoyed by a vast rattling of gourds and beating of goat-hide drums.

CONRAD AIKEN

Silent Snow, Secret Snow

Just why it should have happened, or why it should have happened just when it did, he could not, of course, possibly have said; nor perhaps would it even have occurred to him to ask. The thing was above all a secret, something to be preciously concealed from Mother and Father; and to that very fact it owed an enormous part of its deliciousness. It was like a peculiarly beautiful trinket to be carried unmentioned in one's trouser pocket—a rare stamp, an old coin, a few tiny gold links found trodden out of shape on the path in the park, a pebble of carnelian, a seashell distinguishable from all others by an unusual spot or stripe—and, as if it were any one of these, he carried around with him everywhere a warm and persistent and increasingly beautiful sense of possession. Nor was it only a sense of possession—it was also a sense of protection. It was as if, in some delightful way, his secret gave him a fortress, a wall behind which he could retreat into heavenly seclusion. This was almost the first thing he had noticed about it—apart from the oddness of the thing itself—and it was this that now again, for the fiftieth time, occurred to him, as he sat in the little schoolroom. It was the half-hour for geography. Miss Buell was revolving with one finger, slowly, a huge terrestrial globe which had been placed on her desk. The green and yellow continents passed and repassed, questions were asked and answered, and now the little girl in front of him, Deirdre, who had a funny little constellation of freckles on the back of her neck, exactly like the Big Dipper, was standing up and telling Miss Buell that the equator was the line that ran round the middle.

Miss Buell's face, which was old and grayish and kindly, with gray stiff curls beside the cheeks, and eyes that swam very brightly, like little minnows, behind thick glasses, wrinkled itself into a complication of amusements.

"Ah! I see. The earth is wearing a belt, or a sash. Or someone drew a line round it!"

"Oh no—not that—I mean——"

In the general laughter, he did not share, or only a very little. He was thinking about the Arctic and Antarctic regions, which of course, on the globe, were white. Miss Buell was now telling them about the tropics, the jungles, the steamy heat of equatorial swamps, where the birds and butterflies, and even the snakes, were like living jewels. As he listened to these things, he was already, with a pleasant sense of half-effort, putting his secret between himself and the words. Was it really an effort at all? For effort implied something voluntary, and perhaps even something one did not especially want; whereas this was distinctly pleasant, and came almost of its own accord. All he needed to do was to think of that morning, the first one, and then of all the others——

But it was all so absurdly simple! It had amounted to so little. It was nothing, just an idea—and just why it should have become so wonderful, so permanent, was a mystery—a very pleasant one, to be sure, but also, in an amusing way, foolish. However, without ceasing to listen to Miss Buell, who had now moved up to the north temperate zones, he deliberately invited his memory of the first morning. It was only a moment or two after he had waked up—or perhaps the moment itself. But was there, to be exact, an exact moment? Was one awake all at once? or was it gradual? Anyway, it was after he had stretched a lazy hand up toward the headrail, and yawned, and then relaxed again among his warm covers, all the more grateful on a December morning, that the thing had happened. Suddenly, for no reason, he had thought of the postman, he remembered the postman. Perhaps there was nothing so odd in that. After all, he heard the postman almost every morning in his life—his heavy boots could be heard clumping round the corner at the top of the little cobbled hill-street, and then, progressively nearer, progressively louder, the double knock at each door, the crossings and re-crossings of the street, till finally the clumsy steps came stumbling across to the very door, and the tremendous knock came which shook the house itself.

(Miss Buell was saying, "Vast wheat-growing areas in North America and Siberia."

Deirdre had for the moment placed her left hand across the back of her neck.)

But on this particular morning, the first morning, as he lay there with his eyes closed, he had for some reason *waited* for the postman. He wanted to hear him come round the corner. And that was precisely the joke—he never did. He never came. He never had come—*round the corner*—again. For when at last the steps *were* heard, they had already, he was quite sure, come a little down the hill, to the first house; and even so, the steps were curiously different—they were softer, they had a new secrecy about them, they were muffled and indistinct; and while the rhythm of them was the same, it now said a new thing—it said peace, it said remoteness, it said cold, it said sleep. And he had understood the situation at once—nothing could have seemed simpler—there had been snow in the night, such as all winter he had been longing for; and it was this which had rendered the postman's first footsteps inaudible, and the later ones faint. Of course! How lovely! And even now it must be snowing—it was going to be a snowy day—the long white ragged lines were drifting and sifting across the street, across the faces of the old houses, whispering and hushing, making little triangles of white in the corners between cobblestones, seething a little when the wind blew them over the ground to a drifted corner; and so it would be all day, getting deeper and deeper and silenter and silenter.

(Miss Buell was saying, "Land of perpetual snow.")

All this time, of course (while he lay in bed), he had kept his eyes closed, listening to the nearer progress of the postman, the muffled footsteps thumping and slipping on the snow-sheathed cobbles; and all the other sounds—the double knocks, a frosty far-off voice or two, a bell ringing thinly and softly as if under a sheet of ice—had the same slightly abstracted quality, as if removed by one degree from actuality—as if everything in the world had been insulated by snow. But when at last, pleased, he opened his eyes, and turned them toward the window, to see for himself this long-desired and now so clearly imagined miracle—what he saw instead was brilliant sunlight on a roof; and when, astonished, he jumped out of bed and stared down into the street, expecting to see the cobbles obliterated by the snow, he saw nothing but the bare bright cobbles themselves.

Queer, the effect this extraordinary surprise had had upon him—all the following morning he had kept with him a sense as of snow falling about him, a secret screen of new snow between himself and the world. If he had not dreamed such a thing—and how could he have dreamed it while awake?—how else could one explain it? In any case, the delusion had been so vivid as to affect his entire behavior. He could not now remember whether it was on the first or the second morning—or was it even the third?—that his mother had drawn attention to some oddness in his manner.

"But my darling"—she had said at the breakfast table—"what has come over you? You don't seem to be listening. . . ."

And how often that very thing had happened since!

(Miss Buell was now asking if anyone knew the difference between the North Pole and the Magnetic Pole. Deirdre was holding up her flickering brown hand, and he could see the four white dimples that marked the knuckles.)

Perhaps it hadn't been either the second or third morning—or even the fourth or fifth. How could he be sure? How could he be sure just when the delicious *progress* had become clear? Just when it had really *begun?* The intervals weren't very precise. . . . All he now knew was, that at some point or other—perhaps the second day, perhaps the sixth—he had noticed that the presence of the snow was a little more insistent, the sound of it clearer; and, conversely, the sound of the postman's footsteps more indistinct. Not only could he not hear the steps come round the corner, he could not even hear them at the first house. It was below the first house that he heard them; and then, a few days later, it was below the second house that he heard them; and a few days later again, below the third. Gradually, gradually, the snow was becoming heavier, the sound of its seething louder, the cobblestones more and more muffled. When he found, each morning, on going to the window, after the ritual of listening, that the roofs and cobbles were as bare as ever, it made no difference. This was, after all, only what he had expected. It was even what pleased him, what rewarded him: the thing was his own, belonged to no one else. No one else knew about it, not even his mother and father. There, outside, were the bare cobbles; and here, inside, was the snow. Snow growing heavier each day, muffling the world, hiding the ugly, and deadening increasingly—above all—the steps of the postman.

"But, my darling"—she had said at the luncheon table—"what has come over you? You don't seem to listen when people speak to you. That's the third time I've asked you to pass your plate. . . ."

How was one to explain this to Mother? or to Father? There was, of course, nothing to be done about it: nothing. All one could do was to laugh embarrassedly, pretend to be a little ashamed, apologize, and take a sudden and somewhat disingenuous interest in what was being done or said. The cat had stayed out all night. He had a curious swelling on his left cheek—perhaps somebody had kicked him, or a stone had struck him. Mrs. Kempton was or was not coming to tea. The house was going to be housecleaned, or "turned out," on Wednesday instead of Friday. A new lamp was provided for his evening work—perhaps it was eyestrain which accounted for this new and so peculiar vagueness of his—Mother was looking at him with amusement as she said this, but with something else as well. A new lamp? A new lamp. Yes, Mother, No, Mother, Yes, Mother. School is going very well. The geometry is very easy. The history is very dull. The geography is very interesting—particularly when it takes one to the North Pole. Why the North Pole? Oh, well, it would be fun to be an explorer. Another Peary or Scott or Shackleton. And then abruptly he found his interest in the talk at an end, stared at the pudding on his plate, listened, waited, and began once more—ah, how heavenly, too, the first beginnings—to hear or feel—for could he actually hear it?—the silent snow, the secret snow.

(Miss Buell was telling them about the search for the Northwest Passage, about Hendrik Hudson, the *Half Moon.*)

This had been, indeed, the only distressing feature of the new experience; the fact that it so increasingly had brought him into a kind of mute misunderstanding, or even conflict, with his father and mother. It was as if he were trying to lead a double life. On the one hand, he had to be Paul Hasleman, and keep up the appearance of being that person—dress, wash, and answer intelligently when spoken to—; on the other, he had to explore this new world which had been opened to him. Nor could there be the slightest doubt—not the slightest—that the new world was the profounder and more wonderful of the two. It was irresistible. It was miraculous. Its beauty was simply beyond anything—beyond speech as beyond thought—utterly incommunicable. But how then, between the two worlds, of which he was thus constantly aware, was he to keep a balance? One must get up, one must go to breakfast, one must talk with Mother, go to school, do one's lessons—and, in all this, try not to appear too much of a fool. But if all the while one was also trying to extract the full deliciousness of another and quite separate existence, one which could not easily (if at all) be spoken of—how was one to manage? How was one to explain? Would it be safe to explain? Would it be absurd? Would it merely mean that he would get into some obscure kind of trouble?

These thoughts came and went, came and went, as softly and secretly as the snow; they were not precisely a disturbance, perhaps they were even a pleasure; he liked to have them; their presence was something almost palpable, something he could stroke with his hand, without closing his eyes, and without ceasing to see Miss Buell and the schoolroom and the globe and the freckles on Deirdre's neck; nevertheless he did in a sense cease to see, or to see the obvious external world, and substituted for this vision the vision of snow, the sound of snow, and the slow, almost soundless, approach of the postman. Yesterday, it had been only at the sixth house that the postman had become audible; the snow was much deeper now, it was falling more swiftly and heavily, the sound of its seething was more distinct, more soothing, more persistent. And this morning, it had been—as nearly as he could figure—just above the seventh house—perhaps only a step or two above; at most, he had heard two or three footsteps before the knock had sounded. . . . And with each such narrowing of the sphere, each nearer approach of the limit at which the postman was first audible, it was odd how sharply was increased the amount of illusion which had to be carried into the ordinary business of daily life. Each day, it was harder to get out of bed, to go to the window, to look out at the—as always—perfectly empty and snowless street. Each day it was more difficult to go through the perfunctory motions of greeting Mother and Father at breakfast, to reply to their questions, to put his books together and go to school. And at school, how extraordinarily hard to conduct with success simultaneously the public life and the life that was secret! There were times when he longed—positively ached—to tell everyone about it—but *was* it absurd?—and more importantly by a sense of mysterious power in his very secrecy. Yes; it must be kept secret. That, more and more, became clear. At whatever cost to himself, whatever pain to others——

(Miss Buell looked straight at him, smiling, and said, "Perhaps we'll ask Paul. I'm sure Paul will come out of his daydream long enough to be able to tell us. Won't you, Paul?" He rose slowly from his chair, resting one hand on the brightly varnished desk, and deliberately stared through the snow toward the blackboard. It was an effort, but it was amusing to make it. "Yes," he said slowly, "it was what we now call the Hudson River. This he thought to be the Northwest Passage. He was disappointed." He sat down again, and as he did so Deirdre half turned in her chair and gave him a shy smile, of approval and admiration.)

At whatever pain to others.

This part of it was very puzzling, very puzzling. Mother was very nice, and so was Father. Yes, that was all true enough. He wanted to be nice to them, to tell them everything—and yet, was it really wrong of him to want to have a secret place of his own?

At bed-time, the night before, Mother had said, "If this goes on, my lad, we'll have to see a doctor, we will! We can't have our boy—" But what was it she had said? "Live in another world"? "Live so far away"? The word "far" had been in it, he was sure, and then Mother had taken up a magazine again and laughed a little, but with an expression which wasn't mirthful. He had felt sorry for her. . . .

The bell rang for dismissal. The sound came to him through long curved parallels of falling snow. He saw Deirdre rise, and had himself risen almost as soon—but not quite as soon—as she.

II

On the walk homeward, which was timeless, it pleased him to see through the accompaniment, or counterpoint, of snow, the items of mere externality on his way. There were many kinds of brick in the sidewalks, and laid in many kinds of pattern. The garden walls, too, were various, some of wooden palings, some of plaster, some of stone. Twigs of bushes leaned over the walls: the little hard green winter-buds of lilac, on gray stems, sheathed and fat; other branches very thin and fine and black and desiccated. Dirty sparrows huddled in the bushes, as dull in color as dead fruit left in leafless trees. A single starling creaked on a weather vane. In the gutter, beside a drain, was a scrap of torn and dirty newspaper, caught in a little delta of filth; the word ECZEMA appeared in large capitals, and below it was a letter from Mrs. Amelia D. Cravath, 2100 Pine Street, Forth Worth, Texas, to the effect that after being a sufferer for years she had been cured by Caley's Ointment. In the little delta, beside the fan-shaped and deeply runneled continent of brown mud, were lost twigs, descended from their parent trees, dead matches, a rusty horse-chestnut burr, a small concentration of eggshell, a streak of yellow sawdust which had been wet and now was dry and congealed, a brown pebble, and a broken feather. Farther on was a cement sidewalk, ruled into geometrical parallelograms, with a brass inlay at one end commemorating the contractors who had laid it, and, halfway across, an irregular and random series of dog-tracks, immortalized in synthetic stone. He knew these well, and always stepped on them; to cover the little hollows with his own foot had always been a queer pleasure; today he did it once more, but perfunctorily and detachedly, all the while thinking of something else. That was a dog, a long time ago, who had made a mistake and walked on the cement while it was still wet. He had probably wagged his tail, but that hadn't been recorded. Now, Paul Hasleman, aged twelve, on his way home from school, crossed the same river, which in the meantime had frozen into rock. Homeward through the snow, the snow falling in bright sunshine. Homeward?

Then came the gateway with the two posts surmounted by egg-shaped stones which had been cunningly balanced on their ends, as if by Columbus, and mortared in the very act of balance; a source of perpetual wonder. On the brick wall just beyond, the letter H had been stenciled, presumably for some purpose. H? H.

The green hydrant, with a little green-painted chain attached to the brass screw-cap.

The elm tree, with the great gray wound in the bark, kidney-shaped, into which he always put his hand—to feel the cold but living wood. The injury, he had been sure, was due to the gnawings of a tethered horse. But now it deserved only a passing palm, a merely tolerant eye. There were more important things. Miracles. Beyond the thoughts of trees, mere elms. Beyond the thoughts of sidewalks, mere stone, mere brick, mere cement. Beyond the thoughts even of his own shoes, which trod these sidewalks obediently, bearing a burden—far above—of elaborate mystery. He watched them. They were not very well polished; he had neglected them, for a very good reason: they were one of the many parts of the increasing difficulty of the daily return to daily life, the morning struggle. To get up, having at last opened one's eyes, to go to the window, and discover no snow, to wash, to dress, to descend the curving stairs to breakfast—

At whatever pain to others, nevertheless, one must persevere in severance, since the incommunicability of the experience demanded it. It was desirable, of course, to be kind to Mother and Father, especially as they seemed to be worried, but it was also desirable to be resolute. If they should decide—as appeared likely—to consult the doctor, Doctor Howells, and have Paul inspected, his heart listened to through a kind of dictaphone, his lungs, his stomach—well, that was all right. He would go through with it. He would give them answer for question, too—perhaps such answers as they hadn't expected? No. That would never do. For the secret world must, at all costs, be preserved.

The bird-house in the apple tree was empty—it was the wrong time of year for wrens. The little round black door had lost its pleasure. The wrens were enjoying other houses, other nests, remoter trees. But this too was a notion which he only vaguely and grazingly entertained—as if, for the moment, he merely touched an edge of it; there was something further on, which was already assuming a sharper importance; something which already teased at the corners of his eyes, teasing also at the corner of his mind. It was funny to think that he so wanted this, so awaited it—and yet found himself enjoying this momentary dalliance with the bird-house, as if for a quite deliberate postponement and enhancement of the approaching pleasure. He was aware of his delay, of his smiling and detached and now almost uncomprehending gaze at the little bird-house; he knew what he was going to look at next: it was his own little cobbled hill-street, his own house, the little river at the bottom of the hill, the grocer's shop with the cardboard man in the window—and now, thinking of all this, he turned his head, still smiling, and looking quickly right and left through the snow-laden sunlight.

And the mist of snow, as he had foreseen, was still on it—a ghost of snow falling in the bright sunlight, softly and steadily floating and turning and pausing, soundlessly meeting the snow that covered, as with a transparent mirage, the bare bright cobbles. He loved it—he stood still and loved it. Its beauty was paralyzing—beyond all words, all experience, all dream. No fairy story he had ever read could be compared with it—none had ever given him this extraordinary combination of ethereal loveliness with a something else, unnameable, which was just faintly and deliciously terrifying. What was this thing? As he thought of it, he looked upward toward his own bedroom window, which was open—and it was as if he looked straight into the room and saw himself lying half awake in his bed. There he was—at this very instant he was still perhaps actually there—more truly there than standing here at the edge of the cobbled hill-street, with one hand lifted to shade his eyes against the snow-sun. Had he indeed ever left his room, in all this time? since that very first morning? Was the whole progress still being enacted there, was it still the same morning, and himself not yet wholly awake? And even now, had the postman not yet come round the corner? . . .

This idea amused him, and automatically, as he thought of it, he turned his head and looked toward the top of the hill. There was, of course, nothing there—nothing and no one. The street was empty and quiet. And all the more because of its emptiness it occurred to him to count the houses—a thing which, oddly enough, he hadn't before thought of doing. Of course, he had known there weren't many—many, that is, on his own side of the street, which were the ones that figured in the postman's progress—but nevertheless it came as something of a shock to find that there were precisely *six,* above his own house—his own house was the seventh.

Six!

Astonished, he looked at his own house—looked at the door, on which was the number thirteen—and then realized that the whole thing was exactly and logically and absurdly what he ought to have known. Just the same, the realization gave him abruptly, and even a little frighteningly, a sense of hurry. He was being hurried—he was being rushed. For—he knit his brow—he couldn't be mistaken—it was just above the *seventh* house, his *own* house, that the postman had first been audible this very morning. But in that case—in that case—did it mean that tomorrow he would hear nothing? The knock he had heard must have been the knock of their own door. Did it mean—and this was an idea which gave him a really extraordinary feeling of surprise—that he would never hear the postman again?—that tomorrow morning the postman would already have passed the house, in a snow so deep as to render his footsteps completely inaudible? That he would have made his approach down the snow-filled street so soundlessly, so secretly, that he, Paul Hasleman, there lying in bed, would not have waked in time, or waking, would have heard nothing?

But how could that be? Unless even the knocker should be muffled in the snow—frozen tight, perhaps? . . . But in that case——

A vague feeling of disappointment came over him; a vague sadness as if he felt himself deprived of something which he had long looked forward to, something much prized. After all this, all this beautiful progress, the slow delicious advance of the postman through the silent and secret snow, the knock creeping closer each day, and the footsteps nearer, the audible compass of the world thus daily narrowed, narrowed, narrowed, as the snow soothingly and beautifully encroached and deepened, after all this, was he to be defrauded of the one thing he had so wanted—to be able to count, as it were, the last two or three solemn footsteps, as they finally approached his own door? Was it all going to happen, at the end, so suddenly? or indeed, had it already happened? with no slow and subtle gradations of menace, in which he could luxuriate?

He gazed upward again, toward his own window which flashed in the sun; and this time almost with a feeling that it would be better if he *were* still in bed, in that room; for in that case this must still be the first morning, and there would be six more mornings to come—or, for that matter, seven or eight or nine—how could he be sure?—or even more.

III

After supper, the inquisition began. He stood before the doctor, under the lamp, and submitted silently to the usual thumpings and tappings.

"Now will you please say 'Ah!'?"

"Ah!"

"Now again, please, if you don't mind."

"Ah."

"Say it slowly, and hold it if you can—"

"Ah-h-h-h-h-h—"

"Good."

How silly all this was. As if it had anything to do with his throat! Or his heart, or lungs!

Relaxing his mouth, of which the corners, after all this absurd stretching, felt uncomfortable, he avoided the doctor's eyes, and stared toward the fireplace, past his mother's feet (in gray slippers) which projected from the green chair, and his father's feet (in brown slippers) which stood neatly side by side on the hearth rug.

"Hm. There is certainly nothing wrong there . . .?"

He felt the doctor's eyes fixed upon him, and, as if merely to be polite, returned the look, but with a feeling of justifiable evasiveness.

"Now, young man, tell me—do you feel all right?"

"Yes, sir, quite all right."

"No headaches? no dizziness?"

"No, I don't think so."

"Let me see. Let's get a book, if you don't mind—yes, thank you, that will do splendidly—and now, Paul, if you'll just read it, holding it as you would normally hold it—"

He took the book and read:

"And another praise have I to tell for this the city our mother, the gift of a great god, a glory of the land most high; the might of horses, the might of young horses, the might of the sea. . . . For thou, son of Cronus, our lord Poseidon, hath throned herein this pride, since in these roads first thou didst show forth the curb that cures the rage of steeds. And the shapely oar, apt to men's hands, hath a wondrous speed on the brine, following the hundred-footed Nereids. . . . O land that art praised above all lands, now is it for thee to make those bright praises seen in deeds."

He stopped, tentatively, and lowered the heavy book.

"No—as I thought—there is certainly no superficial sign of eye-strain."

Silence thronged the room, and he was aware of the focused scrutiny of the three people who confronted him. . . .

"We could have his eyes examined—but I believe it is something else."

"What could it be?" That was his father's voice.

"It's only this curious absent-mindedness—" This was his mother's voice.

In the presence of the doctor, they both seemed irritatingly apologetic.

"I believe it is something else. Now Paul—I would like very much to ask you a question or two. You will answer them, won't you—you know I'm an old, old friend of yours, eh? That's right! . . ."

His back was thumped twice by the doctor's fat fist—then the doctor was grinning at him with false amiability, while with one fingernail he was scratching the top button of his waistcoat. Beyond the doctor's shoulder was the fire, the fingers of flame making light prestidigitation against the sooty fireback, the soft sound of their random flutter the only sound.

"I would like to know—is there anything that worries you?"

The doctor was again smiling, his eyelids low against the little black pupils, in each of which was a tiny white bead of light. Why answer him? why answer him at all? "At whatever pain to others"—but it was all a nuisance, this necessity for resistance, this necessity for attention; it was as if one had been stood up on a brilliantly lighted stage, under a great round blaze of spotlight; as if one were merely a trained seal, or a performing dog, or a fish, dipped out of an aquarium and held up by the tail. It would serve them right if he were merely to bark or growl. And meanwhile, to miss these last few precious hours, these hours of which each minute was more beautiful than the last, more menacing—! He still looked, as if from a great distance, at the beads of light in the doctor's eyes, at the fixed false smile, and then, beyond, once more at his mother's slippers, his father's slippers, the soft flutter of the fire. Even here, even amongst these hostile presences, and in this arranged light, he could see the snow, he could hear it—it was in the corners of the room, where the shadow was deepest, under the sofa, behind the half-opened door which led to the dining room. It was gentler here, softer, its seethe the quietest of whispers, as if, in deference to a drawing room, it had quite deliberately put on its "manners"; it kept itself out of sight, obliterated itself, but distinctly with an air of saying, "Ah, but just wait! Wait till we are alone together! Then I will begin to tell you something new! Something white! something cold! something sleepy! something of cease, and peace, and the long bright curve of space! Tell them to go away. Banish them. Refuse to speak. Leave them, go upstairs to your room, turn out the light and get into bed—I will go with you, I will be waiting for you, I will tell you a better story than Little Kay of the Skates, or The Snow Ghost—I will surround your bed, I will close the windows, pile a deep drift against the door, so that none will ever again be able to enter. Speak to them! . . ." It seemed as if the little hissing voice came from a slow white spiral of falling flakes in the corner by the front window—but he could not be sure. He felt himself smiling, then, and said to the doctor, but without looking at him, looking beyond him still—

"Oh no, I think not—"

"But are you sure, my boy?"

His father's voice came softly and coldly then—the familiar voice of silken warning.

"You needn't answer at once, Paul—remember we're trying to help you—think it over and be quite sure, won't you?"

He felt himself smiling again, at the notion of being quite sure. What a joke! As if he weren't so sure that reassurance was no longer necessary, and all this cross-examination a ridiculous farce, a grotesque parody! What could they know about it? these gross intelligences, these humdrum minds so bound to the usual, the ordinary? Impossible to tell them about it! Why, even now, even now, with the proof so abundant, so formidable, so imminent, so appallingly present here in this very room, could they believe it?—could even his mother believe it? No—it was only too plain that if anything were said about it, the merest hint given, they would be incredulous—they would laugh—they would say "Absurd!"—think things about him which weren't true. . . .

"Why no, I'm not worried—why should I be?"

He looked then straight at the doctor's low-lidded eyes, looked from one of them to the other, from one bead of light to the other, and gave a little laugh.

The doctor seemed to be disconcerted by this. He drew back in his chair, resting a fat white hand on either knee. The smile faded slowly from his face.

"Well, Paul!" he said, and paused gravely, "I'm afraid you don't take this quite seriously enough. I think you perhaps don't quite realize—don't quite realize—" He took a deep quick breath and turned, as if helplessly, at a loss for words, to the others. But Mother and Father were both silent—no help was forthcoming.

"You must surely know, be aware, that you have not been quite yourself, of late? Don't you know that? . . ."

It was amusing to watch the doctor's renewed attempt at a smile, a queer disorganized look, as of confidential embarrassment.

"I feel all right, sir," he said, and again gave the little laugh.

"And we're trying to help you." The doctor's tone sharpened.

"Yes, sir, I know. But why? I'm all right. I'm just *thinking,* that's all."

His mother made a quick movement forward, resting a hand on the back of the doctor's chair.

"Thinking?" she said. "But my dear, about what?"

This was a direct challenge—and would have to be directly met. But before he met it, he looked again into the corner by the door, as if for reassurance. He smiled again at what he saw, at what he heard. The little spiral was still there, still softly whirling, like the ghost of a white kitten chasing the ghost of a white tail, and making as it did so the faintest of whispers. It was all right! If only he could remain firm, everything was going to be all right.

"Oh, about anything, about nothing—*you* know the way you do!"

"You mean—daydreaming?"

"Oh, no—thinking!"

"But thinking about *what?*"

"Anything."

He laughed a third time—but this time, happening to glance upward toward his mother's face, he was appalled at the effect his laughter seemed to have upon her. Her mouth had opened in an expression of horror. . . . This was too bad! Unfortunate! He had known it would cause pain, of course—but he hadn't expected it to be quite so bad as this. Perhaps—perhaps if he just gave them a tiny gleaming hint——?

"About the snow," he said.

"What on earth?" This was his father's voice. The brown slippers came a step nearer on the hearth-rug.

"But my dear, what do you mean?" This was his mother's voice.

The doctor merely stared.

"Just *snow,* that's all. I like to think about it."

"Tell us about it, my boy."

"But that's all it is. There's nothing to tell. *You* know what snow is?"

This he said almost angrily, for he felt that they were trying to corner him. He turned sideways so as no longer to face the doctor, and the better to see the inch of blackness between the window-sill and the lowered curtain—the cold inch of beckoning and delicious night. At once he felt better, more assured.

"Mother—can I go to bed, now, please? I've got a headache."

"But I thought you said——"

"It's just come. It's all these questions—! Can I, mother?"

"You can go as soon as the doctor has finished."

"Don't you think this thing ought to be gone into thoroughly, and *now?*" This was Father's voice. The brown slippers again came a step nearer, the voice was the well-known "punishment" voice, resonant and cruel.

"Oh, what's the use, Norman——"

Quite suddenly, everyone was silent. And without precisely facing them, nevertheless he was aware that all three of them were watching him with an extraordinary intensity—staring hard at him—as if he had done something monstrous, or was himself some kind of monster. He could hear the soft irregular flutter of the flames; the cluck-click-cluck-click of the clock; far and faint, two sudden spurts of laughter from the kitchen, as quickly cut off as begun; a murmur of water in the pipes; and then, the silence seemed to deepen, to spread out, to become world-long and world-wide, to become timeless and shapeless, and to center inevitably and rightly, with a slow and sleepy but enormous concentration of all power, on the beginning of a new sound. What this new sound was going to be, he knew perfectly well. It might begin with a hiss, but it would end with a roar—there was no time to lose—he must escape. It mustn't happen here——

Without another word, he turned and ran up the stairs.

IV

Not a moment too soon. The darkness was coming in long white waves. A prolonged sibilance filled the night—a great seamless seethe of wild influence went abruptly across it—a cold low humming shook the windows. He shut the door and flung off his clothes in the dark. The bare black floor was like a little raft tossed in waves of snow, almost overwhelmed, washed under whitely, up again, smothered in curled billows of feather. The snow was laughing; it spoke from all sides at once; it pressed closer to him as he ran and jumped exulting into his bed.

"Listen to us!" it said. "Listen! We have come to tell you the story we told you about. You remember? Lie down. Shut your eyes, now—you will no longer see much—in this white darkness who could see, or want to see? We will take the place of everything. . . . Listen——"

A beautiful varying dance of snow began at the front of the room, came forward and then retreated, flattened out toward the floor, then rose fountain-like to the ceiling, swayed, recruited itself from a new stream of flakes which poured laughing in through the humming window, advanced again, lifted long white arms. It said peace, it said remoteness, it said cold—it said——

But then a gash of horrible light fell brutally across the room from the opening door—the snow drew back hissing—something alien had come into the room—something hostile. This thing rushed at him, clutched at him, shook him—and he was not merely horrified, he was filled with such a loathing as he had never known. What was this? this cruel disturbance? this act of anger and hate? It was as if he had to reach up a hand toward another world for any understanding of it—an effort of which he was only barely capable. But of that other world he still remembered just enough to know the exorcising words. They tore themselves from his other life suddenly——

"Mother! Mother! Go away! I hate you!"

And with that effort, everything was solved, everything became all right: the seamless hiss advanced once more, the long white wavering lines rose and fell like enormous whispering sea-waves, the whisper becoming louder, the laughter more numerous.

"Listen!" it said. "We'll tell you the last, the most beautiful and secret story—shut your eyes—it is a very small story—a story that gets smaller and smaller—it comes inward instead of opening like a flower—it is a flower becoming a seed—a little cold seed—do you hear? we are leaning closer to you——"

The hiss was now becoming a roar—the whole world was a vast moving screen of snow—but even now it said peace, it said remoteness, it said cold, it said sleep.

KATHERINE ANNE PORTER

Theft

She had the purse in her hand when she came in. Standing in the middle of the floor, holding her bathrobe around her and trailing a damp towel in one hand, she surveyed the immediate past and remembered everything clearly. Yes, she had opened the flap and spread it out on the bench after she had dried the purse with her handkerchief.

She had intended to take the Elevated, and naturally she looked in her purse to make certain she had the fare, and was pleased to find forty cents in the coin envelope. She was going to pay her own fare, too, even if Camilo did have the habit of seeing her up the steps and dropping a nickel in the machine before he gave the turnstile a little push and sent her through it with a bow. Camilo by a series of compromises had managed to make effective a fairly complete set of smaller courtesies, ignoring the larger and more troublesome ones. She had walked with him to the station in a pouring rain, because she knew he was almost as poor as she was, and when he insisted on a taxi, she was firm and said, "You know it simply will not do." He was wearing a new hat of a pretty biscuit shade, for it never occurred to him to buy anything of a practical color; he had put it on for the first time and the rain was spoiling it. She kept thinking, "But this is dreadful, where will he get another?" She compared it with Eddie's hats that always seemed to be precisely seven years old and as if they had been quite purposely left out in the rain, and yet they sat with a careless and incidental rightness on Eddie. But Camilo was far different; if he wore a shabby hat it would be merely shabby on him, and he would lose his spirits over it. If she had not feared Camilo would take it badly, for he insisted on the practice of his little ceremonies up to the point he had fixed for them, she would have said to him as they left Thora's house, "Do go home. I can surely reach the station by myself."

"It is written that we must be rained upon tonight," said Camilo, "so let it be together."

At the foot of the platform stairway she staggered slightly—they were both nicely set up on Thora's cocktails—and said: "At least, Camilo, do me the favor not to climb these stairs in your present state, since for you it is only a matter of coming down again at once, and you'll certainly break your neck."

He made three quick bows, he was Spanish, and leaped off through the rainy darkness. She stood watching him, for he was a very graceful young man, thinking that tomorrow morning he would gaze soberly at his spoiled hat and soggy shoes and possibly associate her with his misery. As she watched, he stopped at the far corner and took off his hat and hid it under his overcoat. She felt she had betrayed him by seeing, because he would have been humiliated if he thought she even suspected him of trying to save his hat.

Roger's voice sounded over her shoulder above the clang of the rain falling on the stairway shed, wanting to know what she was doing out in the rain at this time of night, and did she take herself for a duck? His long, imperturbable face was streaming with water, and he tapped a bulging spot on the breast of his buttoned-up overcoat: "Hat," he said. "Come on, let's take a taxi."

She settled back against Roger's arm which he laid around her shoulders, and with the gesture they exchanged a glance full of long amiable associations, then she looked through the window at the rain changing the shapes of everything, and the colors. The taxi dodged in and out between the pillars of the Elevated, skidding slightly on every curve, and she said: "The more it skids the calmer I feel, so I really must be drunk."

"You must be," said Roger. "This bird is a homicidal maniac, and I could do with a cocktail myself this minute."

They waited on the traffic at Fortieth Street and Sixth Avenue, and three boys walked before the nose of the taxi. Under the globes of light they were cheerful scarecrows, all very thin and all wearing very seedy snappy-cut suits and gay neckties. They were not very sober either, and they stood for a moment wobbling in front of the car, and there was an argument going on among them. They leaned toward each other as if they were getting ready to sing, and the first one said: "When I get married it won't be jus' for getting married, I'm gonna marry for *love,* see?" and the second one said, "Aw, gwan and tell that stuff to *her,* why n't yuh?" and the third one gave a kind of hoot, and said, "Hell, dis guy? Wot the hell's he got?" and the first one said: "Aaah, shurrup yuh mush, I got plenty." Then they all squealed and scrambled across the street beating the first one on the back and pushing him around.

"Nuts," commented Roger, "pure nuts."

Two girls went skittering by in short transparent raincoats, one green, one red, their heads tucked against the drive of the rain. One of them was saying to the other, "Yes, I know all about *that.* But what about me? You're always so sorry for *him* . . ." and they ran on with their little pelican legs flashing back and forth.

The taxi backed up suddenly and leaped forward again, and after a while Roger said: "I had a letter from Stella today, and she'll be home on the twenty-sixth, so I suppose she's made up her mind and it's all settled."

"I had a sort of letter today too," she said, "making up my mind for me. I think it is time for you and Stella to do something definite."

When the taxi stopped on the corner of West Fifty-third Street, Roger said, "I've just enough if you'll add ten cents," so she opened her purse and gave him a dime, and he said, "That's beautiful, that purse."

"It's a birthday present," she told him, "and I like it. How's your show coming?"

"Oh, still hanging on, I guess. I don't go near the place. Nothing sold yet. I mean to keep right on the way I'm going and they can take it or leave it. I'm through with the argument."

"It's absolutely a matter of holding out, isn't it?"

"Holding out's the tough part."

"Good night, Roger."

"Good night, you should take aspirin and push yourself into a tub of hot water, you look as though you're catching cold."

"I will."

With the purse under her arm she went upstairs, and on the first landing Bill heard her step and poked his head out with his hair tumbled and his eyes red, and he said: "For Christ's sake, come in and have a drink with me. I've had some bad news."

"You're perfectly sopping," said Bill, looking at her drenched feet. They had two drinks, while Bill told how the director had thrown his play out after the cast had been picked over twice, and had gone through three rehearsals. "I said to him, 'I didn't say it was a masterpiece, I said it would make a good show.' And he said, "It just doesn't *play,* do you see? It needs a doctor.' So I'm stuck, absolutely stuck," said Bill, on the edge of weeping again. "I've been crying," he told her, "in my cups." And he went on to ask her if she realized his wife was ruining him with her extravagance. "I send her ten dollars every week of my unhappy life, and I don't really have to. She threatens to jail me if I don't, but she can't do it. God, let her try it after the way she treated me! She's no right to alimony and she knows it. She keeps on saying she's got to have it for the baby and I keep on sending it because I can't bear to see anybody suffer. So I'm way behind on the piano and the victrola, both—"

"Well, this is a pretty rug, anyhow," she said.

Bill stared at it and blew his nose. "I got it at Ricci's for ninety-five dollars," he said. "Ricci told me it once belonged to Marie Dressler, and cost fifteen hundred dollars, but there's a burnt place on it, under the divan. Can you beat that?"

"No," she said. She was thinking about her empty purse and that she could not possibly expect a check for her latest review for another three days, and her arrangement with the basement restaurant could not last much longer if she did not pay something on account. "It's no time to speak of it," she said, "but I've been hoping you would have by now that fifty dollars you promised for my scene in the third act. Even if it doesn't play. You were to pay me for the work anyhow out of your advance."

"Weeping Jesus," said Bill, "you, too?" He gave a loud sob, or hiccough, in his moist handkerchief. "Your stuff was no better than mine, after all. Think of that."

"But you got something for it," she said. "Seven hundred dollars."

Bill said, "Do me a favor, will you? Have another drink and forget about it. I can't, you know I can't, I would if I could, but you know the fix I'm in."

"Let it go, then," she found herself saying almost in spite of herself. She had meant to be quite firm about it. They drank again without speaking, and she went to her apartment on the floor above.

There, she now remembered distinctly, she had taken the letter out of the purse before she spread the purse out to dry.

She had sat down and read the letter over again: but there were phrases that insisted on being read many times, they had a life of their own separate from the others, and when she tried to read past and around them, they moved with the movement of her eyes, and she could not escape them . . . "thinking about you more than I mean to . . . yes, I even talk about you . . . why were you so anxious to destroy . . . even if I could see you now I would not . . . not worth all this abominable . . . the end . . ."

Carefully she tore the letter into narrow strips and touched a lighted match to them in the coal grate.

Early the next morning she was in the bathtub when the janitress knocked and then came in, calling out that she wished to examine the radiators before she started the furnace going for the winter. After moving about the room for a few minutes, the janitress went out, closing the door very sharply.

She came out of the bathroom to get a cigarette from the package in the purse. The purse was gone. She dressed and made coffee, and sat by the window while she drank it. Certainly the janitress had taken the purse, and certainly it would be impossible to get it back without a great deal of ridiculous excitement. Then let it go. With this decision of her mind, there rose coincidentally in her blood a deep almost murderous anger. She set the cup carefully in the center of the table, and walked steadily downstairs, three long flights and a short hall and a steep short flight into the basement, where the janitress, her face streaked with coal dust, was shaking up the furnace. "Will you please give me back my purse? There isn't any money in it. It was a present, and I don't want to lose it."

The janitress turned without straightening up and peered at her with hot flickering eyes, a red light from the furnace reflected in them. "What do you mean, your purse?"

"The gold cloth purse you took from the wooden bench in my room," she said. "I must have it back."

"Before God I never laid eyes on your purse, and that's the holy truth," said the janitress.

"Oh, well then, keep it," she said, but in a very bitter voice; "keep it if you want it so much." And she walked away.

She remembered how she had never locked a door in her life, on some principle of rejection in her that made her uncomfortable in the ownership of things, and her paradoxical boast before the warnings of her friends, that she had never lost a penny by theft; and she had been pleased with the bleak humility of this concrete example designed to illustrate and justify a certain fixed, otherwise baseless and general faith which ordered the movements of her life without regard to her will in the matter.

In this moment she felt that she had been robbed of an enormous number of valuable things, whether material or intangible: things lost or broken by her own fault, things she had forgotten and left in houses when she moved: books borrowed from her and not returned, journeys she had planned and had not made, words she had waited to hear spoken to her and had not heard, and the words she had meant to answer with; bitter alternatives and intolerable substitutes worse than nothing, and yet inescapable: the long patient suffering of dying friendships and the dark inexplicable death of love—all that she had had, and all that she had missed, were lost together, and were twice lost in this landslide of remembered losses.

The janitress was following her upstairs with the purse in her hand and the same deep red fire flickering in her eyes. The janitress thrust the purse towards her while they were still a half dozen steps apart, and said: "Don't never tell on me. I musta been crazy. I get crazy in the head sometimes, I swear I do. My son can tell you."

She took the purse after a moment, and the janitress went on: "I got a niece who is going on seventeen, and she's a nice girl and I thought I'd give it to her. She needs a pretty purse. I musta been crazy; I thought maybe you wouldn't mind, you leave things around and don't seem to notice much."

She said: "I missed this because it was a present to me from someone . . ."

The janitress said: "He'd get you another if you lost this one. My niece is young and needs pretty things, we oughta give the young ones a chance. She's got young men after her maybe will want to marry her. She oughta have nice things. She needs them bad right now. You're a grown woman, you've had your chance, you ought to know how it is!"

She held the purse out to the janitress saying: "You don't know what you're talking about. Here, take it, I've changed my mind. I really don't want it."

The janitress looked up at her with hatred and said: "I don't want it either now. My niece is young and pretty, she don't need fixin' up to be pretty, she's young and pretty anyhow! I guess you need it worse than she does!"

"It wasn't really yours in the first place," she said, turning away. "You mustn't talk as if I had stolen it from you."

"It's not from me, it's from her you're stealing it," said the janitress, and went back downstairs.

She laid the purse on the table and sat down with the cup of chilled coffee, and thought: I was right not to be afraid of any thief but myself, who will end by leaving me nothing.

JAMES M. CAIN

The Baby in the Icebox

Of course there was plenty pieces in the paper about what happened out at the place last summer, but they got it all mixed up, so I will now put down how it really was, and 'specially the beginning of it, so you will see it is not no lies in it.

Because when a guy and his wife begin to play leapfrog with a tiger, like you might say, and the papers put in about that part and not none of the stuff that started it off, and then one day say X marks the spot and next day say it wasn't really no murder but don't tell you what it was, why, I don't blame people if they figure there was something funny about it or maybe that somebody ought to be locked up in the booby hatch. But there wasn't no booby hatch to this, nothing but plain onriness and a dirty rat getting it in the neck where he had it coming to him, as you will see when I get the first part explained right.

Things first begun to go sour between Duke and Lura when they put the cats in. They didn't need no cats. They had a combination auto camp, filling station, and lunchroom out in the country a ways, and they got along all right. Duke run the filling station, and got me in to help him, and Lura took care of the lunchroom and shacks. But Duke wasn't satisfied. Before he got this place he had raised rabbits, and one time he had bees, and another time canary birds, and nothing would suit him now but to put in some cats to draw trade. Maybe you think that's funny, but out here in California they got every kind of a farm there is, from kangaroos to alligators, and it was just about the idea that a guy like Duke would think up. So he begun building a cage, and one day he showed up with a truckload of wildcats.

I wasn't there when they unloaded them. It was two or three cars waiting and I had to gas them up. But soon as I got a chance I went back there to look things over. And believe me, they wasn't pretty. The guy that sold Duke the cats had went away about five minutes before, and Duke was standing outside the cage and he had a stick of wood in his hand with blood on it. Inside was a dead cat. The rest of them was on a shelf, that had been built for them to jump on, and every one of them was snarling at Duke.

I don't know if you ever saw a wildcat, but they are about twice as big as a house cat, brindle gray, with tufted ears and a bobbed tail. When they set and look at you they look like a owl, but they wasn't setting and looking now. They was marching around, coughing and spitting, their eyes shooting red and green fire, and it was a ugly sight, 'specially with that bloody dead one down on the ground. Duke was pale, and the breath was whistling through his nose, and it didn't take no doctor to see he was scared to death.

"You better bury that cat," he says to me. "I'll take care of the cars."

I looked through the wire and he grabbed me. "Look out!" he says. "They'd kill you in a minute."

"In that case," I says, "how do I get the cat out?"

"You'll have to get a stick," he says, and shoves off.

I was pretty sore, but I begun looking around for a stick. I found one, but when I got back to the cage Lura was there. "How did that happen?" she says.

"I don't know," I says, "but I can tell you this much: If there's any more of them to be buried around here, you can get somebody else to do it. My job is to fix flats, and I'm not going to be no cat undertaker."

She didn't have nothing to say to that. She just stood there while I was trying the stick, and I could hear her toe snapping up and down in the sand, and from that I knowed she was choking it back, what she really thought, and didn't think no more of this here cat idea than I did.

The stick was too short. "My," she says, pretty disagreeable, "that looks terrible. You can't bring people out here with a thing like that in there."

"All right," I snapped back. "Find me a stick."

She didn't make no move to find no stick. She put her hand on the gate. "Hold on," I says. "Them things are nothing to monkey with."

"Huh," she says. "All they look like to me is a bunch of cats."

There was a kennel back of the cage, with a drop door on it, where they was supposed to go at night. How you got them back there was bait them with food, but I didn't know that then. I yelled at them, to drive them back in there, but nothing happened. All they done was yell back. Lura listened to me awhile, and then she gave a kind of gasp like she couldn't stand it no longer, opened the gate, and went in.

Now believe me, that next was a bad five minutes, because she wasn't hard to look at, and I hated to think of her getting mauled up by them babies. But a guy would of had to of been blind if it didn't show him that she had a way with cats. First thing she done, when she got in, she stood still, didn't make no sudden motions or nothing, and begun to talk to them. Not no special talk. Just "Pretty pussy, what's the matter, what they been doing to you?"—like that. Then she went over to them.

They slid off, on their bellies, to another part of the shelf. But she kept after them, and got her hand on one, and stroked him on the back. Then she got ahold of another one, and pretty soon she had give them all a pat. Then she turned around, picked up the dead cat by one leg, and come out with him. I put him on the wheelbarrow and buried him.

Now, why was it that Lura kept it from Duke how easy she had got the cat out and even about being in the cage at all? I think it was just because she didn't have the heart to show him up to hisself how silly he looked. Anyway, at supper that night, she never said a word. Duke, he was nervous and excited and told all about how the cats had jumped at him and how he had to bean one to save his life, and then he give a long spiel about cats and how fear is the only thing they understand, so you would of thought he was Martin Johnson just back from the jungle or something.

But it seemed to me the dishes was making quite a noise that night, clattering around on the table, and that was funny, because one thing you could say for Lura was: she was quiet and easy to be around. So when Duke, just like it was nothing at all, asks me by the way how did I get the cat out, I heared my mouth saying, "With a stick," and not nothing more. A little bird flies around and tells you, at a time like that. Lura let it pass. Never said a word. And if you ask me, Duke never did find out how easy she could handle the cats, and that ain't only guesswork, but on account of something that happened a little while afterward, when we got the mountain lion.

A mountain lion is a cougar, only out here they call them a mountain lion. Well, one afternoon about five o'clock this one of ours squat down on her hunkers and set up the worst squalling you ever listen to. She kept it up all night, so you wanted to go out and shoot her, and next morning at breakfast Duke come running in and says come on out and look what happened. So we went out there, and there in the cage with her was the prettiest he mountain lion you ever seen in your life. He was big, probably weighed a hundred and fifty pounds, and his coat was a pearl gray so glossy it looked like a pair of new gloves, and he had a spot of white on his throat. Sometimes they have white.

"He come down from the hills when he heard her call last night," says Duke, "and he got in there somehow. Ain't it funny? When they hear that note nothing can stop them."

"Yeah," I says. "It's love."

"That's it," says Duke. "Well, we'll be having some little ones soon. Cheaper'n buying them."

After he had went off to town to buy the stuff for the day, Lura sat down to the table with me. "Nice of you," I says, "to let Romeo in last night."

"Romeo?" she says.

"Yes, Romeo. That's going to be papa of twins soon, out in the lion cage."

"Oh," she says, "didn't he get in there himself?"

"He did not. If she couldn't get out, how could he get in?"

All she give me at that time was a dead pan. Didn't know nothing about it at all. Fact of the matter, she made me a little sore. But after she brung me my second cup of coffee she kind of smiled. "Well?" she says. "You wouldn't keep two loving hearts apart, would you?"

So things was, like you might say, a little gritty, but they got a whole lot worse when Duke come home with Rajah, the tiger. Because by that time he had told so many lies that he begun to believe them hisself, and put on all the airs of a big animal trainer. When people come out on Sundays, he would take a black snake whip and go in with the mountain lions and wildcats, and snap it at them, and they would snarl and yowl and Duke acted like he was doing something. Before he went in, he would let the people see him strapping on a big six-shooter, and Lura got sorer by the week.

For one thing, he looked so silly. She couldn't see nothing to going in with the cats, and 'specially she couldn't see no sense in going in with a whip, a six-shooter, and a ten-gallon hat like them cow people wears. And for another thing, it was bad for business. In the beginning, when Lura would take the customers' kids out and make out the cat had their finger, they loved it, and they loved it still more when the little mountain lions come and they had spots and would push up their ears to be scratched. But when Duke started that stuff with the whip it scared them to death, and even the fathers and mothers was nervous, because there was the gun and they didn't know what would happen next. So business begun to fall off.

And then one afternoon he put down a couple of drinks and figured it was time for him to go in there with Rajah. Now it had took Lura one minute to tame Rajah. She was in there sweeping out his cage one morning when Duke was away, and when he started sliding around on his belly he got a bucket of water in the face, and that was that. From then on he was her cat. But what happened when Duke tried to tame him was awful. The first thing I knew what he was up to was when he made a speech to the people from the mountain lion cage telling them not to go away yet, there was more to come. And when he come out he headed over to the tiger.

"What's the big idea?" I says. "What you up to now?"

"I'm going in with that tiger," he says. "It's got to be done, and I might as well do it now."

"Why has it got to be done?" I says.

He looked at me like as though he pitied me.

"I guess there's a few things about cats you don't know yet," he says. "You got a tiger on your hands, you got to let him know who's boss, that's all."

"Yeah?" I says. "And who is boss?"

"You see that?" he says, and cocks his finger at his face.

"See what?" I says.

"The human eye," he says. "The human eye, that's all. A cat's afraid of it. And if you know your business, you'll keep him afraid of it. That's all I'll use, the human eye. But, of course, just for protection, I've got these too."

"Listen, sweetheart," I says to him. "If you give me a choice between the human eye and a Bengal tiger, which one I got the most fear of, you're going to see a guy getting a shiner every time. If I was you, I'd lay off that cat."

He didn't say nothing: hitched up his holster, and went in. He didn't even get a chance to unlimber his whip. That tiger, soon as he saw him, begun to move around in a way that made your blood run cold. He didn't make for Duke first, you understand. He slid over, and in a second he was between Duke and the gate. That's one thing about a tiger you better not forget if you ever meet one. He can't work examples in arithmetic, but when it comes to the kinds of brains that mean meat, he's the brightest boy in the class and then some. He's born knowing more about cutting off a retreat than you'll ever know, and his legs do it for him, just automatic, so his jaws will be free for the main business of the meeting.

Duke backed away, and his face was awful to see. He was straining every muscle to keep his mouth from sliding down in his collar. His left hand fingered the whip a little, and his right pawed around, like he had some idea of drawing the gun. But the tiger didn't give him time to make up his mind what his idea was, if any.

He would slide a few feet on his belly, then get up and trot a step or two, then slide on his belly again. He didn't make no noise, you understand. He wasn't telling Duke, "Please go away"; he meant to kill him, and a killer don't generally make no more fuss than he has to. So for a few seconds you could even hear Duke's feet sliding over the floor. But all of a sudden a kid begun to whimper, and I come to my senses. I run around to the back of the cage, because that was where the tiger was crowding him, and I yelled at him.

"Duke!" I says. "In his kennel! Quick!"

He didn't seem to hear me. He was still backing, and the tiger was still coming. A woman screamed. The tiger's head went down, he crouched on the ground, and tightened every muscle. I knew what that meant. Everybody knew what it meant, and 'specially Duke knew what it meant. He made a funny sound in his throat, turned, and ran.

That was when the tiger sprung. Duke had no idea where he was going, but when he turned he fell through the trapdoor and I snapped it down. The tiger hit it so hard I thought it would split. One of Duke's legs was out, and the tiger was on it in a flash, but all he got on that grab was the sole of Duke's shoe. Duke got his leg in somehow and I jammed the door down tight.

It was a sweet time at supper that night. Lura didn't see this here, because she was busy in the lunchroom when it happened, but them people had talked on their way out, and she knowed all about it. What she said was plenty. And Duke, what do you think he done? He passed it off like it wasn't nothing at all. "Just one of them things you got to expect," he says. And then he let on he knowed what he was doing all the time, and the only lucky part of it was that he didn't have to shoot a valuable animal like Rajah was. "Keep cool, that's the main thing," he says. "A thing like that can happen now and then, but never let a animal see you excited."

I heard him, and I couldn't believe my ears, but when I looked at Lura I jumped. I think I told you she wasn't hard to look at. She was a kind of medium size, with a shape that would make a guy leave his happy home, sunburned all over, and high cheekbones that give her eyes a funny slant. But her eyes was narrowed down to slits, looking at Duke, and they shot green where the light hit them, and it come over me all of a sudden that she looked so much like Rajah, when he was closing in on Duke in the afternoon, that she could of been his twin sister.

Next off, Duke got it in his head he was such a big cat man now that he had to go up in the hills and do some trapping. Bring in his own stuff, he called it.

I didn't pay much attention to it at the time. Of course, he never brought in no stuff, except a couple of raccoons that he probably bought down the road for two dollars, but Duke was the kind of a guy that every once in a while has to sit on a rock and fish, so when he loaded up the flivver and blew, it wasn't nothing you would get excited about. Maybe I didn't really care what he was up to, because it was pretty nice, running the place with Lura with him out of the way, and I didn't ask no questions. But it was more to it than cats or 'coons or fish, and Lura knowed it, even if I didn't.

Anyhow, it was while he was away on one of them trips of his that Wild Bill Smith, the Texas Tornado, showed up. Bill was a snake doctor. He had a truck, with his picture painted on it, and two or three boxes of old rattlesnakes with their teeth pulled out, and he sold snake oil that would cure what ailed you, and a Indian herb medicine that would do the same. He was a fake, but he was big and brown and had white teeth, and I guess he really wasn't no bad guy. The first I seen of him was when he drove up in his truck, and told me to gas him up and look at his tires. He had a bum differential that made a funny rattle, but he said never mind and went over to the lunchroom.

He was there a long time, and I thought I better let him know his car was ready. When I went over there, he was setting on a stool with a sheepish look on his face, rubbing his hand. He had a snake ring on one finger, with two red eyes, and on the back of his hand was red streaks. I knew what that meant. He had started something and Lura had fixed him. She had a pretty arm, but a grip like iron, that she said come from milking cows when she was a kid. What she done when a guy got fresh was take hold of his hand and squeeze it so the bones cracked, and he generally changed his mind.

She handed him his check without a word, and I told him what he owed on the car, and he paid up and left.

"So you settled his hash, hey?" I says to her.

"If there's one thing gets on my nerves," she says, "it's a man that starts something the minute he gets in the door."

"Why didn't you yell for me?"

"Oh, I didn't need no help."

But the next day he was back, and after I filled up his car I went over to see how he was behaving. He was setting at one of the tables this time, and Lura was standing beside him. I saw her jerk her hand away quick, and he give me the bright grin a man has when he's got something he wants to cover up. He was all teeth. "Nice day," he says. "Great weather you have in this country."

"So I hear," I says. "Your car's ready."

"What I owe you?" he says.

"Dollar twenty."

He counted it out and left.

"Listen," says Lura, "we weren't doing anything when you come in. He was just reading my hand. He's a snake doctor, and knows about the zodiac."

"Oh, wasn't we?" I says. "Well, wasn't we nice!"

"What's it to you?" she says.

"Nothing," I snapped at her. I was pretty sore.

"He says I was born under the sign of Yin," she says. You would of thought it was a piece of news fit to put in the paper.

"And who is Yin?" I says.

"It's Chinese for tiger," she says.

"Then bite yourself off a piece of raw meat," I says, and slammed out of there. We didn't have no nice time running the joint *that* day.

Next morning he was back. I kept away from the lunchroom, but I took a stroll and seen them back there with the tigers. We had hauled a tree in there by that time for Rajah to sharpen his claws on, and she was setting on that. The tiger had his head in her lap, and Wild Bill was looking through the wire. He couldn't even draw his breath. I didn't go near enough to hear what they was saying. I went back to the car and begin blowing the horn.

He was back quite a few times after that, in between while Duke was away. Then one night I heard a truck drive up. I knowed that truck by its rattle. And it was daylight before I heard it go away.

Couple weeks after that, Duke come running over to me at the filling station. "Shake hands with me," he says, "I'm going to be a father."

"Gee," I says, "that's great!"

But I took good care he wasn't around when I mentioned it to Lura.

"Congratulations," I says. "Letting Romeos into the place seems to be about the best thing you do."

"What do you mean?" she says.

"Nothing," I says. "Only I heard him drive up that night. Look like to me the moon was under the sign of Cupid. Well, it's nice if you can get away with it."

"Oh," she says.

"Yeah," I says. "A fine double cross you thought up. I didn't know they tried that any more."

She set and looked at me, and then her mouth begin to twitch and her eyes filled with tears. She tried to snuffle them up but it didn't work. "It's not any double cross," she says. "That night I never went out there. And I never let anybody in. I was supposed to go away with him that night, but—"

She broke off and begin to cry. I took her in my arms. "But then you found this out?" I says. "Is that it?" She nodded her head. It's awful to have a pretty woman in your arms that's crying over somebody else.

From then on, it was terrible. Lura would go along two or three days pretty well, trying to like Duke again on account of the baby coming, but then would come a day when she looked like some kind of a hex, with her eyes all sunk in so you could hardly see them at all, and not a word out of her.

Them bad days, anyhow when Duke wasn't around, she would spend with the tiger. She would set and watch him sleep, or maybe play with him, and he seemed to like it as much as she did. He was young when we got him, and mangy and thin, so you could see his slats. But now he was about six years old, and had been fed good, so he had got his growth, and his coat was nice, and I think he was the biggest tiger I ever seen. A tiger, when he is really big, is a lot bigger than a lion, and sometimes when Rajah would be rubbing around Lura, he looked more like a mule than a cat.

His shoulders come up above her waist, and his head was so big it would cover both legs when he put it in her lap. When his tail would go sliding past her it looked like some kind of a constrictor snake. His teeth were something to make you lie awake nights. A tiger has the biggest teeth of any cat, and Rajah's must have been four inches long, curved like a cavalry sword, and ivory white. They were the most murderous-looking fangs I ever set eyes on.

When Lura went to the hospital it was a hurry call, and she didn't even have time to get her clothes together. Next day Duke had to pack her bag, and he was strutting around, because it was a boy, and Lura had named him Ron. But when he come out with the bag he didn't have much of a strut. "Look what I found," he says to me, and fishes something out of his pocket. It was the snake ring.

"Well?" I says. "They sell them in any ten-cent store."

"H'm," he says, and kind of weighed the ring in his hand. That afternoon, when he come back, he says: "Ten-cent store, hey? I took it to a jeweler today, and he offered me two hundred dollars for it."

"You ought to sold it," I says. "Maybe save you bad luck."

Duke went away again right after Lura come back, and for a little while things was all right. She was crazy about the little boy, and I thought he was pretty cute myself, and we got along fine. But then Duke come back and at lunch one day he made a crack about the ring. Lura didn't say nothing, but he kept at it, and pretty soon she wheeled on him.

"All right," she says. "There was another man around here, and I loved him. He give me that ring, and it meant that he and I belonged to each other. But I didn't go with him, and you know why I didn't. For Ron's sake, I've tried to love you again, and maybe I can yet, God knows. A woman can do some funny things if she tries. But that's where we're at now. That's right where we're at. And if you don't like it, you better say what you're going to do."

"When was this?" says Duke.

"It was quite a while ago. I told you I give him up, and I give him up for keeps."

"It was just before you knowed about Ron, wasn't it?" he says.

"Hey," I cut in. "That's no way to talk."

"Just what I thought," he says, not paying no attention to me. "Ron. That's a funny name for a kid. I thought it was funny, right off when I heard it. Ron. Ron. That's a laugh, ain't it?"

"That's a lie," she says. "That's a lie, every bit of it. And it's not the only lie you've been getting away with around here. Or think you have. Trapping up in the hills, hey? And what do you trap?"

But she looked at me and choked it back. I begun to see that the cats wasn't the only things had been gumming it up.

"All right," she wound up. "Say what you're going to do. Go on. Say it!"

But he didn't.

"Ron," he cackles, "that's a hot one," and walks out.

Next day was Saturday, and he acted funny all day. He wouldn't speak to me or Lura, and once or twice I heard him mumbling to himself. Right after supper he says to me, "How are we on oil?"

"All right," I says. "The truck was around yesterday."

"You better drive in and get some," he says. "I don't think we got enough."

"Enough?" I says. "We got enough for two weeks."

"Tomorrow is Sunday," he says, "and there'll be a big call for it. Bring out a hundred gallon and tell them to put it on the account."

By that time I would give in to one of his nutty ideas rather than have an argument with him, and besides, I never tumbled that he was up to anything. So I wasn't there for what happened next, but I got it out of Lura later, so here is how it was:

Lura didn't pay much attention to the argument about the oil, but washed up the supper dishes, and then went in the bedroom to make sure everything was all right with the baby. When she come out she left the door open, so she could hear if he cried. The bedroom was off the sitting room, because these here California houses don't have but one floor, and all the rooms connect. Then she lit the fire, because it was cool, and sat there watching it burn. Duke come in, walked around, and then went out back. "Close the door," she says to him. "I'll be right back," he says.

So she sat looking at the fire, she didn't know how long, maybe five minutes, maybe ten minutes. But pretty soon she felt the house shake. She thought maybe it was a earthquake, and looked at the pictures, but they was all hanging straight. Then she felt the house shake again. She listened, but it wasn't no truck outside that would cause it, and it wouldn't be no state-road blasting or nothing like that at that time of night. Then she felt it shake again, and this time it shook in a regular movement, one, two, three, four, like that. And then all of a sudden she knew what it was, why Duke had acted so funny all day, why he had sent me off for the oil, why he had left the door open, and all the rest of it. There was five hundred pound of cat walking through the house, and Duke had turned him loose to kill her.

She turned around, and Rajah was looking at her, not five foot away. She didn't do nothing for a minute, just set there thinking what a boob Duke was to figure on the tiger doing his dirty work for him, when all the time she could handle him easy as a kitten, only Duke didn't know it. Then she spoke. She expected Rajah to come and put his head in her lap, but he didn't. He stood there and growled, and his ears flattened back. That scared her, and she thought of the baby. I told you a tiger has that kind of brains. It no sooner went through her head about the baby than Rajah knowed she wanted to get to that door, and he was over there before she could get out of the chair.

He was snarling in a regular roar now, but he hadn't got a whiff of the baby yet, and he was still facing Lura. She could see he meant business. She reached in the fireplace, grabbed a stick that was burning bright, and walked him down with it. A tiger is afraid of fire, and she shoved it right in his eyes. He backed past the door, and she slid in the bedroom. But he was right after her, and she had to hold the stick at him with one hand and grab her baby with the other.

But she couldn't get out. He had her cornered, and he was kicking up such a awful fuss she knowed the stick wouldn't stop him long. So she dropped it, grabbed up the baby's covers, and threw them at his head. They went wild but they saved her just the same. A tiger, if you throw something at him with a human smell, will generally jump on it and bite at it before he does anything else, and that's what he done now. He jumped so hard the rug went out from under him, and while he was scrambling to his feet she shot past him with the baby and pulled the door shut after her.

She run in my room, got a blanket, wrapped the baby in it, and run out to the electric icebox. It was the only thing around the place that was steel. Soon as she opened the door she knowed why she couldn't do nothing with Rajah. His meat was in there; Duke hadn't fed him. She pulled the meat out, shoved the baby in, cut off the current, and closed the door. Then she picked up the meat and went around the outside of the house to the window of the bedroom. She could see Rajah in there, biting at the top of the door, where a crack of light showed through. He reached to the ceiling. She took a grip on the meat and drove at the screen with it. It give way, and the meat went through. He was on it before it hit the floor.

Next thing was to give him time to eat. She figured she could handle him once he got something in his belly. She went back to the sitting room. And in there, kind of peering around, was Duke. He had his gun strapped on, and one look at his face was all she needed to know she hadn't made no mistake about why the tiger was loose.

"Oh," he says, kind of foolish, and then walked back and closed the door. "I meant to come back sooner, but I couldn't help looking at the night. You got no idea how beautiful it is. Stars is bright as anything."

"Yeah," she says. "I noticed."

"Beautiful," he says. "Beautiful."

"Was you expecting burglars or something?" she says, looking at the gun.

"Oh, that," he says. "No. Cat's been kicking up a fuss. I put it on, case I have to go back there. Always like to have it handy."

"The tiger," she says. "I thought I heard him, myself."

"Loud," says Duke. "Awful loud."

He waited. She waited. She wasn't going to give him the satisfaction of opening up first. But just then there come a growl from the bedroom, and the sound of bones cracking. A tiger acts awful sore when he eats. "What's that?" says Duke.

"I wonder," says Lura. She was hell-bent on making him spill it first.

They both looked at each other, and then there was more growls, and more sound of cracking bones. "You better go in there," says Duke, soft and easy, with the sweat standing out on his forehead and his eyes shining bright as marbles. "Something might be happening to Ron."

"Do you know what I think it is?" says Lura.

"What's that?" says Duke. His breath was whistling through his nose like it always done when he got excited.

"I think it's that tiger you sent in here to kill me," says Lura. "So you could bring in that woman you been running around with for over a year. That redhead that raises rabbit fryers on the Ventura road. That cat you been trapping!"

"And 'stead of getting you he got Ron," says Duke. "Little Ron! Oh my, ain't that tough? Go in there, why don't you? Ain't you got no mother love? Why don't you call up his pappy, get him in there? What's the matter? Is he afraid of a cat?"

Lura laughed at him. "All right," she says. "Now you go." With that she took hold of him. He tried to draw the gun, but she crumpled up his hand like a piece of wet paper and the gun fell on the floor. She bent him back on the table and beat his face in for him. Then she picked him up, dragged him to the front door, and threw him out. He run off a little ways. She come back and saw the gun. She picked it up, went to the door again, and threw it after him. "And take that peashooter with you," she says.

That was where she made her big mistake. When she turned to go back to the house, he shot, and that was the last she knew for a while.

Now, for what happened next, it wasn't nobody there, only Duke and the tiger, but after them state cops got done fitting it all together, combining the ruins and all, it wasn't no trouble to tell how it was, anyway most of it, and here's how they figured it out:

Soon as Duke seen Lura fall, right there in front of the house, he knowed he was up against it. So the first thing he done was run to where she was and put the gun in her hand to make it look like she had shot herself. That was where he made *his* mistake, because if he had kept the gun he might of had a chance. Then he went inside to telephone, and what he said was, soon as he got hold of the state police: "For God's sake come out here quick. My wife has went crazy and throwed the baby to the tiger and shot herself and I'm all alone in the house with him and—*oh, my God, here he comes!*"

Now that last was something he didn't figure on saying. So far as he knowed, the tiger was in the room, having a nice meal off his son, so everything was hotsy-totsy. But what he didn't know was that that piece of burning firewood that Lura had dropped had set the room on fire and on account of that the tiger had got out. How did he get out? We never did quite figure that out. But this is how I figure it, and one man's guess is good as another's:

The fire started near the window, we knew that much. That was where Lura dropped the stick, right next to the cradle, and that was where a guy coming down the road in a car first seen the flames. And what I think is that soon as the tiger got his eye off the meat and seen the fire, he begun to scramble away from it, just wild. And when a wild tiger hits a beaverboard wall, he goes through, that's all. While Duke was telephoning, Rajah come through the wall like a clown through a hoop, and the first thing he seen was Duke, at the telephone, and Duke wasn't no friend, not to Rajah he wasn't.

Anyway, that's how things was when I got there with the oil. The state cops was a little ahead of me, and I met the ambulance with Lura in it, coming down the road seventy mile an hour, but just figured there had been a crash up the road, and didn't know nothing about it having Lura in it. And when I drove up, there was plenty to look at all right. The house was in flames, and the police was trying to get in, but couldn't get nowheres near it on account of the heat, and about a hundred cars parked all around, with people looking, and a gasoline pumper cruising up and down the road, trying to find a water connection somewhere they could screw their hose to.

But inside the house was the terrible part. You could hear Duke screaming, and in between Duke was the tiger. And both of them was screams of fear, but I think the tiger was worse. It is a awful thing to hear a animal letting out a sound like that. It kept up about five minutes after I got there, and then all of a sudden you couldn't hear nothing but the tiger. And then in a minute that stopped.

There wasn't nothing to do about the fire. In a half hour the whole place was gone, and they was combing the ruins for Duke. Well, they found him. And in his head was four holes, two on each side, deep. We measured them fangs of the tiger. They just fit.

Soon as I could I run in to the hospital. They had got the bullet out by that time, and Lura was laying in bed all bandaged around the head, but there was a guard over her, on account of what Duke said over the telephone. He was a state cop. I sat down with him, and he didn't like it none. Neither did I. I knowed there was something funny about it, but what broke your heart was Lura, coming out of the ether. She would groan and mutter and try to say something so hard it would make your head ache. After a while I got up and went in the hall. But then I see the state cop shoot out of the room and line down the hall as fast as he could go. At last she had said it. The baby was in the electric icebox. They found him there, still asleep and just about ready for his milk. The fire had blackened up the outside, but inside it was as cool and nice as a new bathtub.

Well, that was about all. They cleared Lura, soon as she told her story, and the baby in the icebox proved it. Soon as she got out of the hospital she got a offer from the movies, but 'stead of taking it she come out to the place and her and I run it for a while, anyway the filling-station end, sleeping in the shacks and getting along nice. But one night I heard a rattle from a bum differential, and I never even bothered to show up for breakfast the next morning.

I often wish I had. Maybe she left me a note.

ANITA LOOS

Liquor Makes You Smart

Well, Dorothy and I were spending a delightful winter at Palm Beach but we decided that society gets on a girl's nerves. So we decided to get away from everything and take a trip to Cuba. I telegraphed my husband at New York to send us the money but he became economical and said stay where we were.

So, then, we counted up our money and we had enough fare to get to Cuba, but we did not have so much left to pay high price hotel bills.

But I am always of the optamistic nature. So I said, "Lets go anyway and maybe everything will all turn out for the best." Dorothy said, "If you are game to face the sheriff of Cuba, I guess I can take a chance." So, then we went to Cuba.

But when we got there I had to realize that Cuba is no city for a girl like Dorothy. Because Dorothy makes friends very, very easily. And Cuban gentlemen on the street do even more. So insted of pretending that she did not notice them like I always do, Dorothy would pass remarks right back, even if they did not understand the English landguage. And it only encouraged them, so by the time we would get back to our hotel it was practically a parade. And speaking to an officer does less than no good because Havanan policemen go even longer lengths than gentlemen in a business suit.

So I told Dorothy if she did not stop I would insist on spending all our time in bars where we would be with Americans. So Dorothy said that was a threat that could not make her quale. So, then, we went to the most famous bar at Cuba, called Sloppy Joes. And it was given the nickname of Sloppy Joes bar by a big Congressman's wife who was at Cuba quite a few years ago and seemed to notice that the gentleman called Joe who ran it was not so well groomed. So he has not done anything about it since, and he is practically an example of what happens to gentlemen who stop grooming. But his bar is really a delightful spot.

I mean the walls are full of more different kind of bottles than any spot in the world. And Americans can sit there and drink their choice and gaze at bottles that they have not seen for years. And some of the bottles they have never seen at all, so that it is practically like a wonderful old libery full of unusual books. And if we Americans would improve our time at Sloppy Joes bar by reading all the labels it would be an education. But most Americans who sit in bars do not want to learn anything. And Dorothy says, "What American could read after he hit Sloppy Joes anyway?"

So I ordered a cute drink of foreign emported liquor out of a quaint bottle, but Dorothy did nothing but drink large size glasses of beer and hold conversations with bartenders. And I finally had to realize that even Sloppy Joes bar was no place for a girl like Dorothy. So when we got back to our hotel I told Dorothy that I would not stay in Cuba with a girl like her unless we spent more time with the upper classes.

Then it turned out that Dorothy had met quite a lot of delightful native gentlemen of the upper classes that very morning in the Union Club of Havana, which is a male club for gentlemen only. But Dorothy went in because she thought it was a hotel and she was looking for a bar as usual. So quite a few of the Havanan gentlemen she met in the Union

Club tried to make her see her mistake, but they did it in the Havanan landguage so Dorothy did not understand them until she reached the third floor where she met one who was quite educated in English.

But by the time she learned of her mistake she had made dozens of dozens of Cuban gentlemen friends, because there is nothing that a Cuban enjoys more than the acquaintance of we American girls. So by the time Dorothy started back and got to the main floor going out, she had collected practically a whole deck of calling cards from Cuban gentlemen.

So Dorothy told me to cut the deck, and she would call up the loser and give him an introduction to me. So I asked Dorothy how she would be able to talk to him on the telephone if he did not know the English landguage. But Dorothy said that all a girl had to do in Havana was to say "Sevilla Biltmore Hotel" over the telephone in a female American voice and the Havanan would be there by the shortest possible direct root.

I told Dorothy not to call them up until tea time when we were ready. Because it was only 2 oclock and we had to go shopping. But Dorothy said "Let him come and wait. What is time to a Cuban?" So she called him up. And he was in the lobby of the Sevilla Biltmore by the time we got downstairs.

So Dorothy said lets take him shopping but I said No, because we were only going to a wholesale Phillipinos to buy perfume which is very very cheap in Havana and I do not like to take gentlemen shopping for small size nicknacks and give them a false sense of values. So we left him sitting in the lobby. But when we got back to the hotel we were quite late from loitering and we did not know if he would still be there. But we did not really care so much because Cuban gentlemen who are wealthy are quite prolific at Havana on account of all of the sugar that comes out of the sugar cane. So it is always easy to find another.

But he was still sitting in the lobby and when Dorothy came up he was quite delighted. So then Dorothy introduced him to me and he was even more delighted because girls of the blonde coloring are quite novel to a Cuban.

So we sat down to have delicious Backardi cocktails and he started breaking out into Cuban. Whenever I hold a conversation with some gentleman in his own landguage I like to always be on the safe side when he stops to wait for an answer. So I always give a smile and say yes. Because I think that politeness comes first. But after a little while Dorothy began to get quite restless. And finally she could not stand it any longer. So Dorothy got up from the table and said, "I'm going to hunt up an interperator, because the last time you said yes, I think you promised him something illegal." I told Dorothy to hurry back because girls are not really safe with Cubans even in a lobby.

So Dorothy went over to a table full of American gentlemen who were of the gambling profession. I mean Dorothy had met one of them in an elevator so she knew that she would be among friends. So she asked them if one of them knew the native landguage and would be an interperator and protect two American girls from a Cuban who looked like he was full of evil intentions.

There was one gambler there who was of practically no social position. I mean he did not even make use of a name, but only went by the nickname of the Frisco Flash. So he told Dorothy he would interperate for us because he understood several Cuban words and what he did not understand he could fake. So when I saw Dorothy start to bring him over to the table, I was quite delighted because he was of the middle age generation and looked quite fatherly. And he and Dorothy arrived at the table just in time to save me from having to give a Cuban a push.

But when he sat down, instead of interperating other peoples thoughts, he started right in to tell us how famous he was all over the world for his motto, which was

"Any man from any land
At any game that he can name
For any amount that he can count."

So I really began to be nervous and I told him that I thought he was quite dangerous and I would be afraid to leave my Cuban gentleman friend alone with anyone like he. So he said "That's all right girlie. I pay my commissions and you'll get your 10 per cent." So I did not make any reply to such a mersenary remark but I held my dignity. So then he went on to tell Dorothy that he could always tell by the look on a "sucker's" face what he was good for in dollars and cents. So he looked over my Cuban friends expression and he said it would be about $30,000. And I really have to admire his training, after all, because that was what it turned out to be.

Then we all decided to go to the Gambling Casino for dinner. So Dorothy and I went to our rooms to dress and we had quite a little quarrel. Because I told Dorothy that I did not seem to care for an interperator who not only made his living at cards, but could not even talk Cuban. But Dorothy said I should have reverants for the elder generation that had to use cards because my own game might go out of date some time. So then I only gave Dorothy a look, because the law of nature always teaches that the feeling gentlemen have for girls goes on forever. But then I decided that if it was going to be rivalery between an elderly gambler and I over a Cuban, we would see who got 10 per cent at the finish.

When we went downstairs to meet our escorts they were in the barroom of the hotel playing dice and my Cuban gentleman friend had won practically every time, which made him feel very very good.

So we all went to the National Casino of Gambling for dinner and it is really very very unusual to see a gambling Casino with policemen at all of the doorways to protect the gamblers, insted of visa versa as policemen do in America. I mean in America policemen are always smashing in the door with an axe. So life in Cuba is really much more restful.

And the Casino at Cuba is very very beautiful with quite a lot of Art, and marbel statuary and windows that look out on the scenery, which is quite novel because in Casinos at America all the windows have to have blinds to cover it up.

So after we had quite a delicious dinner we all went into the gambling rooms and my Cuban gentleman friend bought Dorothy and I $100 worth of checks each to gamble with. So of course Dorothy gambled with them. But I do not believe in gambling. So I put my checks in my hand bag, because our Cuban gentleman friend was very very busy gambling himself so he did not notice what we were doing.

When he came over to Dorothy and I to buy us some more checks, I could not tell him I was apposed to gambling on account of not being able to talk Cuban. So when it came time to go back to our hotel Dorothy had lost everything, but all I had to do was to cash in my checks for $500. And I think that is the only refined way girls can act at Casinos and hold their dignity.

But the Frisco Flash did not gamble either, because he said he was apposed to any kind of gambling which could not be controlled. So he spent the evening holding a conversation with a croupier to see what he could find out about our Cuban friend. And this croupier knew the histry of Havana so he told him that our Cuban friend could never get any money from his family, but he had just sold some horses for $30,000 and had it in cash.

On the way home I became quite indignent at our interperator because he made an engagement with my Cuban aquaintence to come up to his room and play a game of piquay, which was the only game of cards the Cuban gentleman knew how to play. So the Frisco Flash told Dorothy that when she saw him in the lobby in the morning he hoped she would show proper respect due a newly rich man. So we said good-night, but after they started away he had an afterthought and he came back and got Dorothy off on one side and said, "Say how does that game of piquay go, anyway?" Dorothy did not know but the Flash told her not to worry because he was always prepared for any emergency.

So Dorothy said, "Good luck. Don't let him freeze his fingers on a cold deck." But the Frisco Flash answered back with another one of his mottos which was

"A good horse never stumbles
And a sucker never tumbles."

And the last Dorothy and I saw of them they were going down the hall into the room of the Frisco Flash which was nothing but a gambling den in disguise.

So then we went to our room and we had quite a little quarrel. Because I told Dorothy that she should not mix the upper classes with the lower classes in our aquaintenceship, especially when one of them was likely to take all the money away from the other one and practically spoil everybody's enjoyment. But then Dorothy said why didn't I study the Flash's methods and learn something new. And I told Dorothy that I did not see what anybody could learn from someone who had to sit up all night and work hard to win money at a game he did not know.

Well, when Dorothy and I went down in the lobby in the morning, the Frisco Flash was sitting at a table drinking champagne alone to celebrate winning $30,000 at piquay. And he had $15,000 of it right in his pocket, because that was all of the cash the Cuban had the night before. So he asked us to sit down and have a bottle of champagne and celebrate to. But I told him I did not care to drink, because I had a luncheon engagement with my Cuban gentleman friend and I did not want my brains to be unstrung. So then he said that I was foolish because liquor makes you smart. So then Dorothy said that she always noticed that liquor made her smart to. So they had a few drinks.

And the more drinks they had, the more smart they decided they were becoming. And Dorothy finally got to feeling so smart that she made a suggestion that they go out to the Casino and win back the money she had lost because she said that if the Flash added his smartness to her smartness they would wipe out the joint. But the Flash could not go, because he had an engagement to meet his Cuban aquaintence and get the rest of the $30,000. And he was afraid to leave him loose around Havana with all that cash when he had such an open hearted Cuban nature.

So Dorothy and the Flash had some more champagne and Dorothy finally got to feeling so smart that she said she had decided she could buck the Casino single handed. So she started off alone with all of the money she had in the world.

Then the Flash had more champagne and decided that he ought to do something more than a commission for a little girl like I who had brought him all that good luck. So I told him that if he really wanted to do something he could do it at the jewelry shop next door.

So we went into the jewelry shop and he was feeling so full of exileration that he told me to select my own choice. So my own choice turned out to be quite a cute bracelet for $10,000. So he paid the money and we went back to the lobby to wait for the Cuban to arrive and pay the Flash his $15,000.

Finally our Cuban aquaintence came in and he brought a gentleman friend of his own along to be his interperator, because of the ineficiency of the Flash in talking Cuban.

Then the Flash ordered some more champagne and while they were all drinking it I really began to feel very very sorry that my Cuban aquaintence had to give up $15,000 more to a gambler that I had really been responsible for introducing to him. So while they were all drinking champagne I began to think up ideas.

I finally thought up one and I opened my pocketbook and I took out my box from the jewelers with the bracelet in it and I showed it to the Cuban gentlemen. So they admired it very very much and finally my Cuban aquaintence asked his interperator to ask me where I got it. So then I told the interperator to tell him that the jewelry store next door sent it in to me on approval, but it was much too expensive for a girl like I to pay for, so I would have to send it back.

So then quite a look of askance seemed to come into the countenance of the Frisco Flash. And he kept right on looking at me and looking at me. So then my Cuban aquaintence wanted to know how much the bracelet cost. So I said it cost $15,000. So when my Cuban aquaintence heard it he took out his wallit and he started in to count his $15,000 out. And by that time the expression on the face of the Frisco Flash seemed to be practically paralized.

So my Cuban aquaintence gave me the money to pay for my bracelet and I thanked him very very much, because, after all, it was all he had. But he promised the Flash that he would get $15,000 for him as soon as he could ask for it from his family. So then the Flash said, "Gentlemen, if you will pardon me, I'll pay my respects to this little lady and go out for air." So he kissed my hand with reverants and went away.

Finally Dorothy arrived back from the Gambling Casino and I had to lend her $3 of my money to pay for her taxicab.

Then we all had luncheon, but at luncheon I decided that I had really seen enough of Cuba because when an honest interperator got to interperating my Cuban aquaintence it turned out that he was nothing but a bore. So we told them we would see them at dinner, but we really took a boat at 4 oclock for Miami and the next morning we were quite delighted to be back where a girl speaks her own landguage and knows what is going on around her.

DOROTHY PARKER

The Standard of Living

Annabel and Midge came out of the tea room with the arrogant slow gait of the leisured, for their Saturday afternoon stretched ahead of them. They had lunched, as was their wont, on sugar, starches, oils, and butter-fats. Usually they ate sandwiches of spongy new white bread greased with butter and mayonnaise; they ate thick wedges of cake lying wet beneath ice cream and whipped cream and melted chocolate gritty with nuts. As alternates, they ate patties, sweating beads of inferior oil, containing bits of bland meat bogged in pale, stiffening sauce; they ate pastries, limber under rigid icing, filled with an indeterminate yellow sweet stuff, not still solid, not yet liquid, like salve that has been left in the sun. They chose no other sort of food, nor did they consider it. And their skin was like the petals of wood anemones, and their bellies were as flat and their flanks as lean as those of young Indian braves.

Annabel and Midge had been best friends almost from the day that Midge had found a job as stenographer with the firm that employed Annabel. By now, Annabel, two years longer in the stenographic department, had worked up to the wages of eighteen dollars and fifty cents a week; Midge was still at sixteen dollars. Each girl lived at home with her family and paid half her salary to its support.

The girls sat side by side at their desks, they lunched together every noon, together they set out for home at the end of the day's work. Many of their evenings and most of their Sundays were passed in each other's company. Often they were joined by two young men, but there was no steadiness to any such quartet; the two young men would give place, unlamented, to two other young men, and lament would have been inappropriate, really, since the newcomers were scarcely distinguishable from their predecessors. Invariably the girls spent the fine idle hours of their hot-weather Saturday afternoons together. Constant use had not worn ragged the fabric of their friendship.

They looked alike, though the resemblance did not lie in their features. It was in the shape of their bodies, their movements, their style, and their adornments. Annabel and Midge did, and completely, all that young office workers are besought not to do. They painted their lips and their nails, they darkened their lashes and lightened their hair, and scent seemed to shimmer from them. They wore thin, bright dresses, tight over their breasts and high on their legs, and tilted slippers, fancifully strapped. They looked conspicuous and cheap and charming.

Now, as they walked across to Fifth Avenue with their skirts swirled by the hot wind, they received audible admiration. Young men grouped lethargically about newsstands awarded them murmurs, exclamations, even—the ultimate tribute—whistles. Annabel and Midge passed without the condescension of hurrying their pace; they held their heads higher and set their feet with exquisite precision, as if they stepped over the necks of peasants.

Always the girls went to walk on Fifth Avenue on their free afternoons, for it was the ideal ground for their favorite game. The game could be played anywhere, and, indeed, was, but the great shop windows stimulated the two players to their best form.

Annabel had invented the game; or rather she had evolved it from an old one. Basically, it was no more than the ancient sport of what-would-you-do-if-you-had-a-million dollars? But Annabel had drawn a new set of rules for it, had narrowed it, pointed it, made it stricter. Like all games, it was the more absorbing for being more difficult.

Annabel's version went like this: You must suppose that somebody dies and leaves you a million dollars, cool. But there is a condition to the bequest. It is stated in the will that you must spend every nickel of the money on yourself.

There lay the hazard of the game. If, when playing it, you forgot, and listed among your expenditures the rental of a new apartment for your family, for example, you lost your turn to the other player. It was astonishing how many—and some of them among the experts, too—would forfeit all their innings by such slips.

It was essential, of course, that it be played in passionate seriousness. Each purchase must be carefully considered and, if necessary, supported by argument. There was no zest to playing wildly. Once Annabel had introduced the game to Sylvia, another girl who worked in the office. She explained the rules to Sylvia and then offered her the gambit "What would be the first thing you'd do?" Sylvia had not shown the decency of even a second of hesitation. "Well," she said, "the first thing I'd do, I'd go out and hire somebody to shoot Mrs. Gary Cooper, and then . . ." So it is to be seen that she was no fun.

But Annabel and Midge were surely born to be comrades, for Midge played the game like a master from the moment she learned it. It was she who added the touches that made the whole thing cozier. According to Midge's innovations, the eccentric who died and left you the money was not anybody you loved, or, for the matter of that, anybody you even knew. It was somebody who had seen you somewhere and had thought, "That girl ought to have lots of nice things. I'm going to leave her a million dollars when I die." And the death was to be neither untimely nor painful. Your benefactor, full of years and comfortably ready to depart, was to slip softly away during sleep and go right to heaven. These embroideries permitted Annabel and Midge to play their game in the luxury of peaceful consciences.

Midge played with a seriousness that was not only proper but extreme. The single strain on the girls' friendship had followed an announcement once made by Annabel that the first thing she would buy with her million dollars would be a silver-fox coat. It was as if she had struck Midge across the mouth. When Midge recovered her breath, she cried that she couldn't imagine how Annabel could do such a thing—silver-fox coats were common! Annabel defended her taste with the retort that they were not common, either. Midge then said that they were so. She added that everybody had a silver-fox coat. She went on, with perhaps a slight loss of head, to declare that she herself wouldn't be caught dead in silver fox.

For the next few days, though the girls saw each other as constantly, their conversation was careful and infrequent, and they did not once play their game. Then one morning, as soon as Annabel entered the office, she came to Midge and said that she had changed her mind. She would not buy a silver-fox coat with any part of her million dollars. Immediately on receiving the legacy, she would select a coat of mink.

Midge smiled and her eyes shone. "I think," she said, "you're doing absolutely the right thing."

Now, as they walked along Fifth Avenue, they played the game anew. It was one of those days with which September is repeatedly cursed; hot and glaring, with slivers of dust in the wind. People drooped and shambled, but the girls carried themselves tall and walked a straight line, as befitted young heiresses on their afternoon promenade. There was no longer need for them to start the game at its formal opening. Annabel went direct to the heart of it.

"All right," she said. "So you've got this million dollars. So what would be the first thing you'd do?"

"Well, the first thing I'd do," Midge said, "I'd get a mink coat." But she said it mechanically, as if she were giving the memorized answer to an expected question.

"Yes," Annabel said, "I think you ought to. The terribly dark kind of mink." But she, too, spoke as if by rote. It was too hot; fur, no matter how dark and sleek and supple, was horrid to the thoughts.

They stepped along in silence for a while. Then Midge's eye was caught by a shop window. Cool, lovely gleamings were there set off by chaste and elegant darkness.

"No," Midge said, "I take it back. I wouldn't get a mink coat the first thing. Know what I'd do? I'd get a string of pearls. Real pearls."

Annabel's eyes turned to follow Midge's.

"Yes," she said, slowly. "I think that's kind of a good idea. And it would make sense, too. Because you can wear pearls with anything."

Together they went over to the shop window and stood pressed against it. It contained but one object—a double row of great, even pearls clasped by a deep emerald around a little pink velvet throat.

"What do you suppose they cost?" Annabel said.

"Gee, I don't know," Midge said. "Plenty, I guess."

"Like a thousand dollars?" Annabel said.

"Oh, I guess like more," Midge said. "On account of the emerald."

"Well, like ten thousand dollars?" Annabel said.

"Gee, I wouldn't even know," Midge said.

The devil nudged Annabel in the ribs. "Dare you to go in and price them," she said.

"Like fun!" Midge said.

"Dare you," Annabel said.

"Why, a store like this wouldn't even be open this afternoon," Midge said.

"Yes, it is so, too," Annabel said. "People just came out. And there's a doorman on. Dare you."

"Well," Midge said. "But you've got to come too."

They tendered thanks, icily, to the doorman for ushering them into the shop. It was cool and quiet, a broad, gracious room with paneled walls and soft carpet. But the girls wore expressions of bitter disdain, as if they stood in a sty.

A slim, immaculate clerk came to them and bowed. His neat face showed no astonishment at their appearance.

"Good afternoon," he said. He implied that he would never forget it if they would grant him the favor of accepting his soft-spoken greeting.

"Good afternoon," Annabel and Midge said together, and in like freezing accents.

"Is there something—?" the clerk said.

"Oh, we're just looking," Annabel said. It was as if she flung the words down from a dais.

The clerk bowed.

"My friend and myself merely happened to be passing," Midge said, and stopped, seeming to listen to the phrase. "My friend here and myself," she went on, "merely happened to be wondering how much are those pearls you've got in your window."

"Ah, yes," the clerk said. "The double rope. That is two hundred and fifty thousand dollars, Madam."

"I see," Midge said.

The clerk bowed. "An exceptionally beautiful necklace," he said. "Would you care to look at it?"

"No, thank you," Annabel said.

"My friend and myself merely happened to be passing," Midge said.

They turned to go; to go, from their manner, where the tumbrel awaited them. The clerk sprang ahead and opened the door. He bowed as they swept by him.

The girls went on along the Avenue and disdain was still on their faces.

"Honestly!" Annabel said. "Can you imagine a thing like that?"

"Two hundred and fifty thousand dollars!" Midge said. "That's a quarter of a million dollars right there!"

"He's got his nerve!" Annabel said.

They walked on. Slowly the disdain went, slowly and completely as if drained from them, and with it went the regal carriage and tread. Their shoulders dropped and they dragged their feet; they bumped against each other, without notice or apology, and caromed away again. They were silent and their eyes were cloudy.

Suddenly Midge straightened her back, flung her head high, and spoke, clear and strong.

"Listen, Annabel," she said. "Look. Suppose there was this terribly rich person, see? You don't know this person, but this person has seen you somewhere and wants to do something for you. Well, it's a terribly old person, see? And so this person dies, just like going to sleep, and leaves you ten million dollars. Now, what would be the first thing you'd do?"

JAMES THURBER

The Unicorn in the Garden

Once upon a sunny morning a man who sat in a breakfast nook looked up from his scrambled eggs to see a white unicorn with a gold horn quietly cropping the roses in the garden. The man went up to the bedroom where his wife was still asleep and woke her. "There's a unicorn in the garden," he said. "Eating roses." She opened one unfriendly eye and looked at him. "The unicorn is a mythical beast," she said, and turned her back on him. The man walked slowly downstairs and out into the garden. The unicorn was still there; he was now browsing among the tulips. "Here, unicorn," said the man, and he pulled up a lily and gave it to him. The unicorn ate it gravely. With a high heart, because there was a unicorn in his garden, the man went upstairs and roused his wife again. "The unicorn," he said, "ate a lily." His wife sat up in bed and looked at him, coldly. "You are a booby," she said, "and I am going to have you put in the booby-hatch." The man, who had never liked the words "booby" and "booby-hatch," and who liked them even less on a shining morning when there was a unicorn in the garden, thought for a moment. "We'll see about that," he said. He walked over to the door. "He has a golden horn in the middle of his forehead," he told her. Then he went back to the garden to watch the unicorn; but the unicorn had gone away. The man sat down among the roses and went to sleep.

As soon as the husband had gone out of the house, the wife got up and dressed as fast as she could. She was very excited and there was a gloat in her eye. She telephoned the police and she telephoned a psychiatrist; she told them to hurry to her house and bring a strait-jacket. When the police and the psychiatrist arrived they sat down in chairs and looked at her, with great interest. "My husband," she said, "saw a unicorn this morning." The police looked at the psychiatrist and the psychiatrist looked at the police. "He told me it ate a lily," she said. The psychiatrist looked at the police and the police looked at the psychiatrist. "He told me it had a golden horn in the middle of its forehead," she said. At a solemn signal from the psychiatrist, the police leaped from their chairs and seized the wife. They had a hard time subduing her, for she put up a terrific struggle, but they finally subdued her. Just as they got her into the strait-jacket, the husband came back into the house.

"Did you tell your wife you saw a unicorn?" asked the police. "Of course not," said the husband. "The unicorn is a mythical beast." "That's all I wanted to know," said the psychiatrist. "Take her away. I'm sorry, sir, but your wife is as crazy as a jay bird." So they took her away, cursing and screaming, and shut her up in an institution. The husband lived happily ever after.

Moral: Don't count your boobies until they are hatched.

JEAN TOOMER

Becky

Becky was the white woman who had two Negro sons. She's dead; they've gone away. The pines whisper to Jesus. The Bible flaps its leaves with an aimless rustle on her mound.

Becky had one Negro son. Who gave it to her? Damn buck nigger, said the white folks' mouths. She wouldnt tell. Common, God-forsaken, insane white shameless wench, said the white folks' mouths. Her eyes were sunken, her neck stringy, her breasts fallen, till then. Taking their words, they filled her, like a bubble rising—then she broke. Mouth setting in a twist that held her eyes, harsh, vacant, staring. . . . Who gave it to her? Low-down nigger with no self-respect, said the black folks' mouths. She wouldnt tell. Poor Catholic poor-white crazy woman, said the black folks' mouths. White folks and black folks built her cabin, fed her and her growing baby, prayed secretly to God who'd put His cross upon her and cast her out.

When the first was born, the white folks said they'd have no more to do with her. And black folks, they too joined hands to cast her out. . . . The pines whispered to Jesus. . . . The railroad boss said not to say he said it, but she could live, if she wanted to, on the narrow strip of land between the railroad and the road. John Stone, who owned the lumber and the bricks, would have shot the man who told he gave the stuff to Lonnie Deacon, who stole out there at night and built the cabin. A single room held down to earth. . . . O fly away to Jesus. . . . by a leaning chimney. . . .

Six trains each day rumbled past and shook the ground under her cabin. Fords, and horse- and mule-drawn buggies went back and forth along the road. No one ever saw her. Trainmen, and passengers who'd heard about her, threw out papers and food. Threw out little crumpled slips of paper scribbled with prayers, as they passed her eye-shaped piece of sandy ground. Ground islandized between the road and railroad track. Pushed up where a blue-sheen God with listless eyes could look at it. Folks from the town took turns, unknown, of course, to each other, in bringing corn and meat and sweet potatoes. Even sometimes snuff. . . . O thank y Jesus. . . . Old David Georgia, grinding cane and boiling syrup, never went her way without some sugar sap. No one ever saw her. The boy grew up and ran around. When he was five years old as folks reckoned it, Hugh Jourdon saw him carrying a baby. "Becky has another son," was what the whole town knew. But nothing was said, for the part of man that says things to the likes of that had told itself that if there was a Becky, that Becky now was dead.

The two boys grew. Sullen and cunning. . . . O pines, whisper to Jesus; tell Him to come and press sweet Jesus-lips against their lips and eyes. . . . It seemed as though with those two big fellows there, there could be no room for Becky. The part that prayed wondered if perhaps she'd really died, and they had buried her. No one dared ask. They'd beat and cut a man who meant nothing at all in mentioning that they lived along the road. White or colored? No one knew, and least of all themselves. They drifted around from job to job. We, who had cast out their mother because of them, could we take them in? They answered black and white folks by shooting up two men and leaving town. "Godam the white folks; godam the niggers," they shouted as they left town. Becky? Smoke curled up from her chimney; she must be there. Trains passing shook the ground. The ground shook the leaning chimney. Nobody noticed it. A creepy feeling came over all who saw that thin wraith of smoke and felt the trembling of the ground. Folks began to take her food again. They quit it soon because they had a fear. Becky if dead might be a hant, and if alive—it took some nerve even to mention it. . . . O pines, whisper to Jesus. . .

It was Sunday. Our congregation had been visiting at Pulverton, and were coming home. There was no wind. The autumn sun, the bell from Ebenezer Church, listless and heavy. Even the pines were stale, sticky, like the smell of food that makes you sick. Before we turned the bend of the road that would show us the Becky cabin, the horses stopped stock-still, pushed back their ears, and nervously whinnied. We urged, then whipped them on. Quarter of a mile away thin smoke curled up from the leaning chimney. . . . O pines, whisper to Jesus. . . . Goose-flesh came on my skin though there still was neither chill nor wind. Eyes left their sockets for the cabin. Ears burned and throbbed. Uncanny eclipse! fear closed my mind. We were just about to pass. . . . Pines shout to Jesus! . . . the ground trembled as a ghost train rumbled by. The chimney fell into the cabin. Its thud was like a hollow report, ages having passed since it went off. Barlo and I were pulled out of our seats. Dragged to the door that had swung open. Through the dust we saw the bricks in a mound upon the floor. Becky, if she was there, lay under them. I thought I heard a groan. Barlo, mumbling something, threw his Bible on the pile. (No one has ever touched it.) Somehow we got away. My buggy was still on the road. The last thing that I remember was whipping old Dan like fury; I remember nothing after that—that is, until I reached town and folks crowded round to get the true word of it.

F. SCOTT FITZGERALD

The Bridal Party

There was the usual insincere little note saying: "I wanted you to be the first to know." It was a double shock to Michael, announcing, as it did, both the engagement and the imminent marriage; which, moreover, was to be held, not in New York, decently and far away, but here in Paris under his very nose, if that could be said to extend over the Protestant Episcopal Church of the Holy Trinity, Avenue George-Cinq. The date was two weeks off, early in June.

At first Michael was afraid and his stomach felt hollow. When he left the hotel that morning, the *femme de chambre,* who was in love with his fine, sharp profile and his pleasant buoyancy, scented the hard abstraction that had settled over him. He walked in a daze to his bank, he bought a detective story at Smith's on the Rue de Rivoli, he sympathetically stared for a while at a faded panorama of the battlefields in a tourist-office window and cursed a Greek tout who followed him with a half-displayed packet of innocuous post cards warranted to be very dirty indeed.

But the fear stayed with him, and after a while he recognized it as the fear that now he would never be happy. He had met Caroline Dandy when she was seventeen, possessed her young heart all through her first season in New York, and then lost her, slowly, tragically, uselessly, because he had no money and could make no money; because, with all the energy and good will in the world, he could not find himself; because, loving him still, Caroline had lost faith and begun to see him as something pathetic, futile and shabby, outside the great, shining stream of life toward which she was inevitably drawn.

Since his only support was that she loved him, he leaned weakly on that; the support broke, but still he held on to it and was carried out to sea and washed up on the French coast with its broken pieces still in his hands. He carried them around with him in the form of photographs and packets of correspondence and a liking for a maudlin popular song called *Among My Souvenirs.* He kept clear of other girls, as if Caroline would somehow know it and reciprocate with a faithful heart. Her note informed him that he had lost her forever.

It was a fine morning. In front of the shops in the Rue de Castiglione, proprietors and patrons were on the sidewalk gazing upward for the Graf Zeppelin, shining and glorious, symbol of escape and destruction—of escape, if necessary, through destruction—glided in the Paris sky. He heard a woman say in French that it would not her astonish if that commenced to let fall the bombs. Then he heard another voice, full of husky laughter, and the void in his stomach froze. Jerking about, he was face to face with Caroline Dandy and her fiancé.

"Why, Michael! Why, we were wondering where you were. I asked at the Guaranty Trust, and Morgan and Company, and finally sent a note to the National City——"

Why didn't they back away? Why didn't they back right up walking backward down the Rue de Castiglione, across the Rue de Rivoli, through the Tuileries Gardens, still walking backward as fast as they could till they grew vague and faded out across the river?

"This is Hamilton Rutherford, my fiancé."

"We've met before."

"At Pat's, wasn't it?"

"And last spring in the Ritz Bar."

"Michael, where have you been keeping yourself?"

"Around here." This agony. Previews of Hamilton Rutherford flashed before his eyes—a quick series of pictures, sentences. He remembered hearing that he had bought a seat in 1920 for a hundred and twenty-five thousand of borrowed money, and just before the break sold it for more than half a million. Not handsome like Michael, but vitally attractive, confident, authoritative, just the right height over Caroline there—Michael had always been too short for Caroline when they danced.

Rutherford was saying: "No, I'd like it very much if you'd come to the bachelor dinner. I'm taking the Ritz Bar from nine o'clock on. Then right after the wedding there'll be a reception and breakfast at the Hotel George-Cinq."

"And, Michael, George Packman is giving a party day after tomorrow at Chez Victor, and I want you to be sure and come. And also to tea Friday at Jebby West's; she'd want to have you if she knew where you were. What's your hotel, so we can send you an invitation? You see, the reason we decided to have it over here is because mother has been sick in a nursing home here and the whole clan is in Paris. Then Hamilton's mother's being here too——"

The entire clan; they had always hated him, except her mother; always discouraged his courtship. What a little counter he was in this game of families and money! Under his hat his brow sweated with the humiliation of the fact that for all his misery he was worth just exactly so many invitations. Frantically he began to mumble something about going away.

Then it happened—Caroline saw deep into him, and Michael knew that she saw. She saw through to his profound woundedness, and something quivered inside her, died out along the curve of her mouth and in her eyes. He had moved her. All the unforgettable impulses of first love had surged up once more; their hearts had in some way touched across two feet of Paris sunlight. She took her fiancé's arm suddenly, as if to steady herself with the feel of it.

They parted. Michael walked quickly for a minute; then he stopped, pretending to look in a window, and saw them farther up the street, walking fast into the Place Vendôme, people with much to do.

He had things to do also—he had to get his laundry.

"Nothing will ever be the same again," he said to himself. "She will never be happy in her marriage and I will never be happy at all any more."

The two vivid years of his love for Caroline moved back around him like years in Einstein's physics. Intolerable memories arose—of rides in the Long Island moonlight; of a happy time at Lake Placid with her cheeks so cold there, but warm just underneath the surface; of a despairing afternoon in a little café on Forty-eighth Street in the last sad months when their marriage had come to seem impossible.

"Come in," he said aloud.

The concierge with a telegram; brusque because Mr. Curly's clothes were a little shabby. Mr. Curly gave few tips; Mr. Curly was obviously a *petit client.*

Michael read the telegram.

"An answer?" the concierge asked.

"No," said Michael, and then, on an impulse: "Look."

"Too bad—too bad," said the concierge. "Your grandfather is dead."

"Not too bad," said Michael. "It means that I come into a quarter of a million dollars."

Too late by a single month; after the first flush of the news his misery was deeper than ever. Lying awake in bed that night, he listened endlessly to the long caravan of a circus moving through the street from one Paris fair to another.

When the last van had rumbled out of hearing and the corners of the furniture were pastel blue with the dawn, he was still thinking of the look in Caroline's eyes that morning—the look that seemed to say: "Oh, why couldn't you have done something about it? Why couldn't you have been stronger, made me marry you? Don't you see how sad I am?"

Michael's fist clenched.

"Well, I won't give up till the last moment," he whispered. "I've had all the bad luck so far, and maybe it's turned at last. One takes what one can get, up to the limit of one's strength, and if I can't have her, at least she'll go into this marriage with some of me in her heart."

II

Accordingly he went to the party at Chez Victor two days later, upstairs and into the little salon off the bar where the party was to assemble for cocktails. He was early; the only other occupant was a tall lean man of fifty. They spoke.

"You waiting for George Packman's party?"

"Yes. My name's Michael Curly."

"My name's——"

Michael failed to catch the name. They ordered a drink, and Michael supposed that the bride and groom were having a gay time.

"Too much so," the other agreed, frowning. "I don't see how they stand it. We all crossed on the boat together; five days of that crazy life and then two weeks of Paris. You"—he hesitated, smiling faintly—"you'll excuse me for saying that your generation drinks too much."

"Not Caroline."

"No, not Caroline. She seems to take only a cocktail and a glass of champagne, and then she's had enough, thank God. But Hamilton drinks too much and all this crowd of young people drink too much. Do you live in Paris?"

"For the moment," said Michael.

"I don't like Paris. My wife—that is to say, my ex-wife, Hamilton's mother—lives in Paris."

"You're Hamilton Rutherford's father?"

"I have that honor. And I'm not denying that I'm proud of what he's done; it was just a general comment."

"Of course."

Michael glanced up nervously as four people came in. He felt suddenly that his dinner coat was old and shiny; he had ordered a new one that morning. The people who had come in were rich and at home in their richness with one another—a dark, lovely girl with a hysterical little laugh whom he had met before; two confident men whose jokes referred invariably to last night's scandal and tonight's potentialities, as if they had important rôles in a play that extended indefinitely into the past and the future. When Caroline arrived, Michael had scarcely a moment of her, but it was enough to note that, like all the others, she was strained and tired. She was pale beneath her rouge; there were shadows under her eyes. With a mixture of relief and wounded vanity, he found himself placed far from her and at another table; he needed a moment to adjust himself to his surroundings. This was not like the immature set in which he and Caroline had moved; the men were more than thirty and had an air of sharing the best of this world's good. Next to him was Jebby West, whom he knew; and, on the other side, a jovial man who immediately began to talk to Michael about a stunt for the bachelor dinner: They were going to hire a French girl to appear with an actual baby in her arms, crying: "Hamilton, you can't desert me now!" The idea seemed stale and unamusing to Michael, but its originator shook with anticipatory laughter.

Farther up the table there was talk of the market—another drop today, the most appreciable since the crash; people were kidding Rutherford about it: "Too bad, old man. You better not get married, after all."

Michael asked the man on his left, "Has he lost a lot?"

"Nobody knows. He's heavily involved, but he's one of the smartest young men in Wall Street. Anyhow, nobody ever tells you the truth."

It was a champagne dinner from the start, and toward the end it reached a pleasant level of conviviality, but Michael saw that all these people were too weary to be exhilarated by any ordinary stimulant; for weeks they had drunk cocktails before meals like Americans, wines and brandies like Frenchmen, beer like Germans, whiskey-and-soda like the English, and as they were no longer in the twenties, this preposterous *mélange,* that was like some gigantic cocktail in a nightmare, served only to make them temporarily less conscious of the mistakes of the night before. Which is to say that it was not really a gay party; what gayety existed was displayed in the few who drank nothing at all.

But Michael was not tired, and the champagne stimulated him and made his misery less acute. He had been away from New York for more than eight months and most of the dance music was unfamiliar to him, but at the first bars of the "Painted Doll", to which he and Caroline had moved through so much happiness and despair the previous summer, he crossed to Caroline's table and asked her to dance.

She was lovely in a dress of thin ethereal blue, and the proximity of her crackly yellow hair, of her cool and tender gray eyes, turned his body clumsy and rigid; he stumbled with their first step on the floor. For a moment it seemed that there was nothing to say; he wanted to tell her about his inheritance, but the idea seemed abrupt unprepared for.

"Michael, it's so nice to be dancing with you again."

He smiled grimly.

"I'm so happy you came," she continued. "I was afraid maybe you'd be silly and stay away. Now we can be just good friends and natural together. Michael, I want you and Hamilton to like each other."

The engagement was making her stupid; he had never heard her make such a series of obvious remarks before.

"I could kill him without a qualm," he said pleasantly, "but he looks like a good man. He's fine. What I want to know is, what happens to people like me who aren't able to forget?"

As he said this he could not prevent his mouth from drooping suddenly, and glancing up, Caroline saw, and her heart quivered violently, as it had the other morning.

"Do you mind so much, Michael?"

"Yes."

For a second as he said this, in a voice that seemed to have come up from his shoes, they were not dancing; they were simply clinging together. Then she leaned away from him and twisted her mouth into a lovely smile.

"I didn't know what to do at first, Michael. I told Hamilton about you—that I'd cared for you an awful lot—but it didn't worry him, and he was right. Because I'm over you now—yes, I am. And you'll wake up some sunny morning and be over me just like that."

He shook his head stubbornly.

"Oh, yes. We weren't for each other. I'm pretty flighty, and I need somebody like Hamilton to decide things. It was that more than the question of—of——"

"Of money." Again he was on the point of telling her what had happened, but again something told him it was not the time.

"Then how do you account for what happened when we met the other day," he demanded helplessly—"what happened just now? When we just pour toward each other like we used to—as if we were one person, as if the same blood was flowing through both of us?"

"Oh, don't," she begged him. "You mustn't talk like that; everything's decided now. I love Hamilton with all my heart. It's just that I remember certain things in the past and I feel sorry for you—for us—for the way we were."

Over her shoulder, Michael saw a man come toward them to cut in. In a panic he danced her away, but inevitably the man came on.

"I've got to see you alone, if only for a minute," Michael said quickly. "When can I?"

"I'll be at Jebby West's tea tomorrow," she whispered as a hand fell politely upon Michael's shoulder.

But he did not talk to her at Jebby West's tea. Rutherford stood next to her, and each brought the other into all conversations. They left early. The next morning the wedding cards arrived in the first mail.

Then Michael, grown desperate with pacing up and down his room, determined on a bold stroke; he wrote to Hamilton Rutherford, asking him for a rendezvous the following afternoon. In a short telephone communication Rutherford agreed, but for a day later than Michael had asked. And the wedding was only six days away.

They were to meet in the bar of the Hotel Jena. Michael knew what he would say: "See here, Rutherford, do you realize the responsibility you're taking in going through with this marriage? Do you realize the harvest of trouble and regret you're sowing in persuading a girl into something contrary to the instincts of her heart?" He would explain that the barrier between Caroline and himself had been an artificial one and was now removed, and demand that the matter be put up to Caroline frankly before it was too late.

Rutherford would be angry, conceivably there would be a scene, but Michael felt that he was fighting for his life now.

He found Rutherford in conversation with an older man, whom Michael had met at several of the wedding parties.

"I saw what happened to most of my friends," Rutherford was saying, "and I decided it wasn't going to happen to me. It isn't so difficult; if you take a girl with common sense, and tell her what's what, and do your stuff damn well, and play decently square with her, it's a marriage. If you stand for any nonsense at the beginning, it's one of these arrangements—within five years the man gets out, or else the girl gobbles him up and you have the usual mess."

"Right!" agreed his companion enthusiastically. "Hamilton, boy, you're right."

Michael's blood boiled slowly.

"Doesn't it strike you," he inquired coldly, "that your attitude went out of fashion about a hundred years ago?"

"No, it didn't," said Rutherford pleasantly, but impatiently. "I'm as modern as anybody. I'd get married in an aeroplane next Saturday if it'd please my girl."

"I don't mean that way of being modern. You can't take a sensitive woman——"

"Sensitive? Women aren't so darn sensitive. It's fellows like you who are sensitive; it's fellows like you they exploit—all your devotion and kindness and all that. They read a couple of books and see a few pictures because they haven't got anything else to do, and then they say they're finer in grain than you are, and to prove it they take the bit in their teeth and tear off for a fare-you-well—just about as sensitive as a fire horse."

"Caroline happens to be sensitive," said Michael in a clipped voice.

At this point the other man got up to go; when the dispute about the check had been settled and they were alone, Rutherford leaned back to Michael as if a question had been asked him.

"Caroline's more than sensitive," he said. "She's got sense."

His combative eyes, meeting Michael's, flickered with a gray light. "This all sounds pretty crude to you, Mr. Curly, but it seems to me that the average man nowadays just asks to be made a monkey of by some woman who doesn't even get any fun out of reducing him to that level. There are darn few men who possess their wives any more, but I am going to be one of them."

To Michael it seemed time to bring the talk back to the actual situation: "Do you realize the responsibility you're taking?"

"I certainly do," interrupted Rutherford. "I'm not afraid of responsibility. I'll make the decisions—fairly, I hope, but anyhow they'll be final."

"What if you didn't start right?" said Michael impetuously. "What if your marriage isn't founded on mutual love?"

"I think I see what you mean," Rutherford said, still pleasant. "And since you've brought it up, let me say that if you and Caroline had married, it wouldn't have lasted three years. Do you know what your affair was founded on? On sorrow. You got sorry for each other. Sorrow's a lot of fun for most women and for some men, but it seems to me that a marriage ought to be based on hope." He looked at his watch and stood up.

"I've got to meet Caroline. Remember, you're coming to the bachelor dinner day after tomorrow."

Michael felt the moment slipping away. "Then Caroline's personal feelings don't count with you?" he demanded fiercely.

"Caroline's tired and upset. But she has what she wants, and that's the main thing."

"Are you referring to yourself?" demanded Michael incredulously.

"Yes."

"May I ask how long she's wanted you?"

"About two years." Before Michael could answer, he was gone.

During the next two days Michael floated in an abyss of helplessness. The idea haunted him that he had left something undone that would sever this knot drawn tighter under his eyes. He phoned Caroline, but she insisted that it was physically impossible for her to see him until the day before the wedding, for which day she granted him a tentative rendezvous. Then he went to the bachelor dinner, partly in fear of an evening alone at his hotel, partly from a feeling that by his presence at that function he was somehow nearer to Caroline, keeping her in sight.

The Ritz Bar had been prepared for the occasion by French and American banners and by a great canvas covering one wall, against which the guests were invited to concentrate their proclivities in breaking glasses.

At the first cocktail, taken at the bar, there were many slight spillings from many trembling hands, but later, with the champagne, there was a rising tide of laughter and occasional bursts of song.

Michael was surprised to find what a difference his new dinner coat, his new silk hat, his new, proud linen made in his estimate of himself; he felt less resentment toward all these people for being so rich and assured. For the first time since he had left college he felt rich and assured himself; he felt that he was part of all this, and even entered into the scheme of Johnson, the practical joker, for the appearance of the woman betrayed, now waiting tranquilly in the room across the hall.

"We don't want to go too heavy," Johnson said, "because I imagine Ham's had a pretty anxious day already. Did you see Fullman Oil's sixteen points off this morning?"

"Will that matter to him?" Michael asked, trying to keep the interest out of his voice.

"Naturally. He's in heavily; he's always in everything heavily. So far he's had luck; anyhow, up to a month ago."

The glasses were filled and emptied faster now, and men were shouting at one another across the narrow table. Against the bar a group of ushers was being photographed, and the flash light surged through the room in a stifling cloud.

"Now's the time," Johnson said. "You're to stand by the door, remember, and we're both to try and keep her from coming in—just till we get everybody's attention."

He went on out into the corridor, and Michael waited obediently by the door. Several minutes passed. Then Johnson reappeared with a curious expression on his face.

"There's something funny about this."

"Isn't the girl there?"

"She's there all right, but there's another woman there, too; and it's nobody we engaged either. She wants to see Hamilton Rutherford, and she looks as if she had something on her mind."

They went out into the hall. Planted firmly in a chair near the door sat an American girl a little the worse for liquor, but with a determined expression on her face. She looked up at them with a jerk of her head.

"Well, j'tell him?" she demanded. "The name is Marjorie Collins, and he'll know it. I've come a long way, and I want to see him now and quick, or there's going to be more trouble than you ever saw." She rose unsteadily to her feet.

"You go in and tell Ham," whispered Johnson to Michael. "Maybe he'd better get out. I'll keep her here."

Back at the table, Michael leaned close to Rutherford's ear and, with a certain grimness, whispered:

"A girl outside named Marjorie Collins says she wants to see you. She looks as if she wanted to make trouble."

Hamilton Rutherford blinked and his mouth fell ajar; then slowly the lips came together in a straight line and he said in a crisp voice:

"Please keep her there. And send the head barman to me right away."

Michael spoke to the barman, and then, without returning to the table, asked quietly for his coat and hat. Out in the hall again, he passed Johnson and the girl without speaking and went out into the Rue Cambon. Calling a cab, he gave the address of Caroline's hotel.

His place was beside her now. Not to bring bad news, but simply to be with her when her house of cards came falling around her head.

Rutherford had implied that he was soft—well, he was hard enough not to give up the girl he loved without taking advantage of every chance within the pale of honor. Should she turn away from Rutherford, she would find him there.

She was in; she was surprised when he called, but she was still dressed and would be down immediately. Presently she appeared in a dinner gown, holding two blue telegrams in her hand. They sat down in armchairs in the deserted lobby.

"But, Michael, is the dinner over?"

"I wanted to see you, so I came away."

"I'm glad." Her voice was friendly, but matter-of-fact. "Because I'd just phoned your hotel that I had fittings and rehearsals all day tomorrow. Now we can have our talk after all."

"You're tired," he guessed. "Perhaps I shouldn't have come."

"No. I was waiting up for Hamilton. Telegrams that may be important. He said he might go on somewhere, and that may mean any hour, so I'm glad I have someone to talk to."

Michael winced at the impersonality in the last phrase.

"Don't you care when he gets home?"

"Naturally," she said, laughing, "but I haven't got much say about it, have I?"

"Why not?"

"I couldn't start by telling him what he could and couldn't do."

"Why not?"

"He wouldn't stand for it."

"He seems to want merely a housekeeper," said Michael ironically.

"Tell me about your plans, Michael," she asked quickly.

"My plans? I can't see any future after the day after tomorrow. The only real plan I ever had was to love you."

Their eyes brushed past each other's, and the look he knew so well was staring out at him from hers. Words flowed quickly from his heart:

"Let me tell you just once more how well I've loved you, never wavering for a moment, never thinking of another girl. And now when I think of all the years ahead without you, without any hope, I don't want to live, Caroline darling. I used to dream about our home, our children, about holding you in my arms and touching your face and hands and hair that used to belong to me, and now I just can't wake up."

Caroline was crying softly. "Poor Michael—poor Michael." Her hand reached out and her fingers brushed the lapel of his dinner coat. "I was so sorry for you the other night. You looked so thin, and as if you needed a new suit and somebody to take care of you." She sniffled and looked more closely at his coat. "Why, you've got a new suit! And a new silk hat! Why, Michael, how swell!" She laughed, suddenly cheerful through her tears. "You must have come into money, Michael; I never saw you so well turned out."

For a moment, at her reaction, he hated his new clothes.

"I have come into money," he said. "My grandfather left me about a quarter of a million dollars."

"Why, Michael," she cried, "how perfectly swell! I can't tell you how glad I am. I've always thought you were the sort of person who ought to have money."

"Yes, just too late to make a difference."

The revolving door from the street groaned around and Hamilton Rutherford came into the lobby. His face was flushed, his eyes were restless and impatient.

"Hello, darling; hello, Mr. Curly." He bent and kissed Caroline. "I broke away for a minute to find out if I had any telegrams. I see you've got them there." Taking them from her, he remarked to Curly, "That was an odd business there in the bar, wasn't it? Especially as I understand some of you had a joke fixed up in the same line." He opened one of the telegrams, closed it and turned to Caroline with the divided expression of a man carrying two things in his head at once.

"A girl I haven't seen for two years turned up," he said. "It seemed to be some clumsy form of blackmail, for I haven't and never have had any sort of obligation toward her whatever."

"What happened?"

"The head barman had a Sûreté Générale man there in ten minutes and it was settled in the hall. The French blackmail laws make ours look like a sweet wish, and I gather they threw a scare into her that she'll remember. But it seems wiser to tell you."

"Are you implying that I mentioned the matter?" said Michael stiffly.

"No," Rutherford said slowly. "No, you were just going to be on hand. And since you're here, I'll tell you some news that will interest you even more."

He handed Michael one telegram and opened the other.

"This is in code," Michael said.

"So is this. But I've got to know all the words pretty well this last week. The two of them together mean that I'm due to start life all over."

Michael saw Caroline's face grow a shade paler, but she sat quiet as a mouse.

"It was a mistake and I stuck to it too long," continued Rutherford. "So you see I don't have all the luck, Mr. Curly. By the way, they tell me you've come into money."

"Yes," said Michael.

"There we are, then." Rutherford turned to Caroline. "You understand, darling, that I'm not joking or exaggerating. I've lost almost every cent I had and I'm starting life over."

Two pairs of eyes were regarding her—Rutherford's noncommittal and unrequiring, Michael's hungry, tragic, pleading. In a minute she had raised herself from the chair and with a little cry thrown herself into Hamilton Rutherford's arms.

"Oh, darling," she cried, "what does it matter! It's better; I like it better, honestly I do! I want to start that way; I want to! Oh please don't worry or be sad even for a minute!"

"All right, baby," said Rutherford. His hand stroked her head gently for a moment; then he took his arm from around her.

"I promised to join the party for an hour," he said. "So I'll say good night, and I want you to go to bed soon and get a good sleep. Good night, Mr. Curly. I'm sorry to have let you in for all these financial matters."

But Michael had already picked up his hat and cane. "I'll go along with you," he said.

III

It was such a fine morning. Michael's cutaway hadn't been delivered, so he felt rather uncomfortable passing before the cameras and moving-picture machines in front of the little church on the Avenue George-Cinq.

It was such a clean, new church that it seemed unforgivable not to be dressed properly, and Michael, white and shaky after a sleepless night, decided to stand in the rear. From there he looked at the back of Hamilton Rutherford, and the lacy, filmy back of Caroline, and the fat back of George Packman, which looked unsteady, as if it wanted to lean against the bride and groom.

The ceremony went on for a long time under the gay flags and pennons overhead, under the thick beams of June sunlight slanting down through the tall windows upon the well-dressed people.

As the procession, headed by the bride and groom, started down the aisle, Michael realized with alarm he was just where everyone would dispense with their parade stiffness, become informal and speak to him.

So it turned out. Rutherford and Caroline spoke first to him; Rutherford grim with the strain of being married, and Caroline lovelier than he had ever seen her, floating all softly down through the friends and relatives of her youth, down through the past and forward to the future by the sunlit door.

Michael managed to murmur, "Beautiful, simply beautiful," and then other people passed and spoke to him—old Mrs. Dandy, straight from her sickbed and looking remarkably well, or carrying it off like the very fine old lady she was; and Rutherford's father and mother, ten years divorced, but walking side by side and looking made for each other and proud. Then all Caroline's sisters and their husbands and her little nephews in Eton suits, and then a long parade, all speaking to Michael because he was still standing paralyzed just at that point where the procession broke.

He wondered what would happen now. Cards had been issued for a reception at the George-Cinq; an expensive enough place, heaven knew. Would Rutherford try to go through with that on top of those disastrous telegrams? Evidently, for the procession outside was streaming up there through the June morning, three by three and four by four. On the corner the long dresses of girls, five abreast, fluttered many-colored in the wind. Girls had become gossamer again, perambulatory flora; such lovely fluttering dresses in the bright noon wind.

Michael needed a drink; he couldn't face that reception line without a drink. Diving into a side doorway of the hotel, he asked for the bar, whither a *chasseur* led him through half a kilometer of new American-looking passages.

But—how did it happen?—the bar was full. There were ten—fifteen men and two—four girls, all from the wedding, all needing a drink. There were cocktails and champagne in the bar; Rutherford's cocktails and champagne, as it turned out, for he had engaged the whole bar and the ballroom and the two great reception rooms and all the stairways leading up and down, and windows looking out over the whole square block of Paris. By and by Michael went and joined the long, slow drift of the receiving line. Through a flowery mist of "Such a lovely wedding," "My dear, you were simply lovely," "You're a lucky man, Rutherford" he passed down the line. When Michael came to Caroline, she took a single step forward and kissed him on the lips, but he felt no contact in the kiss; it was unreal and he floated on away from it. Old Mrs. Dandy, who had always liked him, held his hand for a minute and thanked him for the flowers he had sent when he heard she was ill.

"I'm so sorry not to have written; you know, we old ladies are grateful for——" The flowers, the fact that she had not written, the wedding—Michael saw that they all had the same relative importance to her now; she had married off five other children and seen two of the marriages go to pieces, and this scene, so poignant, so confusing to Michael, appeared to her simply a familiar charade in which she had played her part before.

A buffet luncheon with champagne was already being served at small tables and there was an orchestra playing in the empty ballroom. Michael sat down with Jebby West; he was still a little embarrassed at not wearing a morning coat, but he perceived now that he was not alone in the omission and felt better. "Wasn't Caroline divine?" Jebby West said. "So entirely self-possessed. I asked her this morning if she wasn't a little nervous at stepping off like this. And she said, 'Why should I be? I've been after him for two years, and now I'm just happy, that's all.' "

"It must be true," said Michael gloomily.

"What?"

"What you just said."

He had been stabbed, but, rather to his distress, he did not feel the wound.

He asked Jebby to dance. Out on the floor, Rutherford's father and mother were dancing together.

"It makes me a little sad, that," she said. "Those two hadn't met for years; both of them were married again and she divorced again. She went to the station to meet him when he came over for Caroline's wedding, and invited him to stay at her house in the Avenue du Bois with a whole lot of other people, perfectly proper, but he was afraid his wife would hear about it and not like it, so he went to a hotel. Don't you think that's sort of sad?"

An hour or so later Michael realized suddenly that it was afternoon. In one corner of the ballroom an arrangement of screens like a moving-picture stage had been set up and photographers were taking official pictures of the bridal party. The bridal party, still as death and pale as wax under the bright lights, appeared, to the dancers circling the modulated semidarkness of the ballroom, like those jovial or sinister groups that one comes upon in The Old Mill at an amusement park.

After the bridal party had been photographed, there was a group of the ushers; then the bridesmaids, the families, the children. Later, Caroline, active and excited, having long since abandoned the repose implicit in her flowing dress and great bouquet, came and plucked Michael off the floor.

"Now we'll have them take one of just old friends." Her voice implied that this was best, most intimate of all. "Come here, Jebby, George—not you, Hamilton; this is just my friends—Sally——"

A little after that, what remained of formality disappeared and the hours flowed easily down the profuse stream of champagne. In the modern fashion, Hamilton Rutherford sat at the table with his arm about an old girl of his and assured his guests, which included not a few bewildered but enthusiastic Europeans, that the party was not nearly at an end; it was to reassemble at Zelli's after midnight. Michael saw Mrs. Dandy, not quite over her illness, rise to go and become caught in polite group after group, and he spoke of it to one of her daughters, who thereupon forcibly abducted her mother and called her car. Michael felt very considerate and proud of himself after having done this, and drank much more champagne.

"It's amazing," George Packman was telling him enthusiastically. "This show will cost Ham about five thousand dollars, and I understand they'll be just about his last. But did he countermand a bottle of champagne or a flower? Not he! He happens to have it—that young man. Do you know that T. G. Vance offered him a salary of fifty thousand dollars a year ten minutes before the wedding this morning? In another year he'll be back with the millionaires."

The conversation was interrupted by a plan to carry Rutherford out on communal shoulders—a plan which six of them put into effect, and then stood in the four-o'clock sunshine waving good-by to the bride and groom. But there must have been a mistake somewhere, for five minutes later Michael saw both bride and groom descending the stairway to the reception, each with a glass of champagne held defiantly on high.

"This is our way of doing things," he thought. "Generous and fresh and free; a sort of Virginia-plantation hospitality, but at a different pace now, nervous as a ticker tape."

Standing unself-consciously in the middle of the room to see which was the American ambassador, he realized with a start that he hadn't really thought of Caroline for hours. He looked about him with a sort of alarm, and then he saw her across the room, very bright and young, and radiantly happy. He saw Rutherford near her, looking at her as if he could never look long enough, and as Michael watched them they seemed to recede as he had wished them to do that day in the Rue de Castiglione—recede and fade off into joys and griefs of their own, into the years that would take the toll of Rutherford's fine pride and Caroline's young, moving beauty; fade far away, so that now he could scarcely see them, as if they were shrouded in something as misty as her white, billowing dress.

Michael was cured. The ceremonial function, with its pomp and its revelry, had stood for a sort of initiation into a life where even his regret could not follow them. All the bitterness melted out of him suddenly and the world reconstituted itself out of the youth and happiness that was all around him, profligate as the spring sunshine. He was trying to remember which one of the bridesmaids he had made a date to dine with tonight as he walked forward to bid Hamilton and Caroline Rutherford good-by.

WILLIAM FAULKNER

Wash

Sutpen stood above the pallet bed on which the mother and child lay. Between the shrunken planking of the wall the early sunlight fell in long pencil strokes, breaking upon his straddled legs and upon the riding whip in his hand, and lay across the still shape of the mother, who lay looking up at him from still, inscrutable, sullen eyes, the child at her side wrapped in a piece of dingy though clean cloth. Behind them an old Negro woman squatted beside the rough hearth where a meager fire smoldered.

"Well, Milly," Sutpen said, "too bad you're not a mare. Then I could give you a decent stall in the stable."

Still the girl on the pallet did not move. She merely continued to look up at him without expression, with a young, sullen, inscrutable face still pale from recent travail. Sutpen moved, bringing into the splintered pencils of sunlight the face of a man of sixty. He said quietly to the squatting Negress, "Griselda foaled this morning."

"Horse or mare?" the Negress said.

"A horse. A damned fine colt. . . . What's this?" He indicated the pallet with the hand which held the whip.

"That un's a mare, I reckon."

"Hah," Sutpen said. "A damned fine colt. Going to be the spit and image of old Rob Roy when I rode him North in '61. Do you remember?"

"Yes, Marster."

"Hah." He glanced back towards the pallet. None could have said if the girl still watched him or not. Again his whip hand indicated the pallet. "Do whatever they need with whatever we've got to do it with." He went out, passing out the crazy doorway and stepping down into the rank weeds (there yet leaned rusting against the corner of the porch the scythe which Wash had borrowed from him three months ago to cut them with) where his horse waited, where Wash stood holding the reins.

When Colonel Sutpen rode away to fight the Yankees, Wash did not go. "I'm looking after the Kernel's place and niggers," he would tell all who asked him and some who had not asked—a gaunt, malaria-ridden man with pale, questioning eyes, who looked about thirty-five, though it was known that he had not only a daughter but an eight-year-old granddaughter as well. This was a lie, as most of them—the few remaining men between eighteen and fifty—to whom he told it, knew, though there were some who believed that he himself really believed it, though even these believed that he had better sense than to put it to the test with Mrs. Sutpen or the Sutpen slaves. Knew better or was just too lazy and shiftless to try it, they said, knowing that his sole connection with the Sutpen plantation lay in the fact that for years now Colonel Sutpen had allowed him to squat in a crazy shack on a slough in the river bottom on the Sutpen place, which Sutpen had built for a fishing lodge in his bachelor days and which had since fallen in dilapidation from disuse, so that now it looked like an aged or sick wild beast crawled terrifically there to drink in the act of dying.

The Sutpen slaves themselves heard of his statement. They laughed. It was not the first time they had laughed at him, calling him white trash behind his back. They began to ask him themselves, in groups, meeting him in the faint road which led up from the slough and the old fish camp, "Why ain't you at de war, white man?"

Pausing, he would look about the ring of black faces and white eyes and teeth behind which derision lurked. "Because I got a daughter and family to keep," he said. "Git out of my road, niggers."

"Niggers?" they repeated; "niggers?" laughing now. "Who him, calling us niggers?"

"Yes," he said. "I ain't got no niggers to look after my folks if I was gone."

"Nor nothing else but dat shack down yon dat Cunnel wouldn't *let* none of us live in."

Now he cursed them; sometimes he rushed at them, snatching up a stick from the ground while they scattered before him, yet seeming to surround him still with that black laughing, derisive, evasive, inescapable, leaving him panting and impotent and raging. Once it happened in the very back yard of the big house itself. This was after bitter news had come down from the Tennessee mountains and from Vicksburg, and Sherman had passed through the plantation, and most of the Negroes had followed him. Almost everything else had gone with the Federal troops, and Mrs. Sutpen had sent word to Wash that he could have the scuppernongs ripening in the arbor in the back yard. This time it was a house servant, one of the few Negroes who remained; this time the Negress had to retreat up the kitchen steps, where she turned. "Stop right dar, white man. Stop right whar you is. You ain't never crossed dese steps whilst Cunnel here, and you ain't ghy' do hit now."

This was true. But there was this of a kind of pride: he had never tried to enter the big house, even though he believed that if he had, Sutpen would have received him, permitted him. "But I ain't going to give no black nigger the chance to tell me I can't go nowhere," he said to himself. "I ain't even going to give Kernel the chance to have to cuss a nigger on my account." This, though he and Sutpen had spent more than one afternoon together on those rare Sundays when there would be no company in the house. Perhaps his mind knew that it was because Sutpen had nothing else to do, being a man who could not bear his own company. Yet the fact remained that the two of them would spend whole afternoons in the scuppernong arbor, Sutpen in the hammock and Wash squatting against a post, a pail of cistern water between them, taking drink for drink from the same demijohn. Meanwhile on weekdays he would see the fine figure of the man—they were the same age almost to a day, though neither of them (perhaps because Wash had a grandchild while Sutpen's son was a youth in school) ever thought of himself as being so—on the fine figure of the black stallion, galloping about the plantation. For that moment his heart would be quiet and proud. It would seem to him that that world in which Negroes, whom the Bible told him had been created and cursed by God to be brute and vassal to all men of white skin, were better found and housed and even clothed than he and his; that world in which he sensed always about him mocking echoes of black laughter was but a dream and an illusion, and that the actual world was this one across which his own lonely apotheosis seemed to gallop on the black thoroughbred, thinking how the Book said also that all men were created in the image of God and hence all men made the same image in God's eyes at least; so that he could say, as though speaking of himself, "A fine proud man. If God Himself was to come down and ride the natural earth, that's what He would aim to look like."

Sutpen returned in 1865, on the black stallion. He seemed to have aged ten years. His son had been killed in action the same winter in which his wife had died. He returned with his citation for gallantry from the hand of General Lee to a ruined plantation, where for a year now his daughter had subsisted partially on the meager bounty of the man to whom fifteen years ago he had granted permission to live in that tumbledown fishing camp whose very existence he had at the time forgotten. Wash was there to meet him, unchanged: still gaunt, still ageless, with his pale, questioning gaze, his air diffident, a little servile, a little familiar. "Well, Kernel," Wash said, "they kilt us but they ain't whupped us yit, air they?"

That was the tenor of their conversation for the next five years. It was inferior whiskey which they drank now together from a stoneware jug, and it was not in the scuppernong arbor. It was in the rear of the little store which Sutpen managed to set up on the highroad: a frame shelved room where, with Wash for clerk and porter, he dispensed kerosene and staple foodstuffs and stale gaudy candy and cheap beads and ribbons to Negroes or poor whites of Wash's own kind, who came afoot or on gaunt mules to haggle tediously for dimes and quarters with a man who at one time could gallop (the black stallion was still alive; the stable in which his jealous get lived was in better repair than the house where the master himself lived) for ten miles across his own fertile land and who had led troops gallantly in battle; until Sutpen in fury would empty the store, close and lock the doors from the inside. Then he and Wash would repair to the rear and the jug. But the talk would not be quiet now, as when Sutpen lay in the hammock, delivering an arrogant monologue while Wash squatted guffawing against his post. They both sat now, though Sutpen had the single chair while Wash used whatever box or keg was handy, and even this for just a little while, because soon Sutpen would reach that stage of impotent and furious undefeat in which he would rise, swaying and plunging, and declare again that he would take his pistol and the black stallion and ride single-handed into Washington and kill Lincoln, dead now, and Sherman, now a private citizen. "Kill them!" he would shout. "Shoot them down like the dogs they are—"

"Sho, Kernel; sho, Kernel," Wash would say, catching Sutpen as he fell. Then he would commandeer the first passing wagon or, lacking that, he would walk the mile to the nearest neighbor and borrow one and return and carry Sutpen home. He entered the house now. He had been doing so for a long time, taking Sutpen home in whatever borrowed wagon might be, talking him into locomotion with cajoling murmurs as though he were a horse, a stallion himself. The daughter would meet them and hold open the door without a word. He would carry his burden through the once white formal entrance, surmounted by a fanlight imported piece by piece from Europe and with a board now nailed over a missing pane, across a velvet carpet from which all nap was now gone, and up a formal stairs, now but a fading ghost of bare boards between two strips of fading paint, and into the bedroom. It would be dusk by now, and he would let his burden sprawl onto the bed and undress it and then he would sit quietly in a chair beside. After a time the daughter would come to the door. "We're all right now," he would tell her. "Don't you worry none, Miss Judith."

Then it would become dark, and after a while he would lie down on the floor beside the bed, though not to sleep, because after a time—sometimes before midnight—the man on the bed would stir and groan and then speak. "Wash?"

"Hyer I am, Kernel. You go back to sleep. We ain't whupped yit, air we? Me and you kin do hit."

Even then he had already seen the ribbon about his granddaughter's waist. She was now fifteen, already mature, after the early way of her kind. He knew where the ribbon came from; he had been seeing it and its kind daily for three years, even if she had lied about where she got it, which she did not, at once bold, sullen, and fearful. "Sho now," he said. "Ef Kernel wants to give hit to you, I hope you minded to thank him."

His heart was quiet, even when he saw the dress, watching her secret, defiant, frightened face when she told him that Miss Judith, the daughter, had helped her to make it. But he was quite grave when he approached Sutpen after they closed the store that afternoon, following the other to the rear.

"Get the jug," Sutpen directed.

"Wait," Wash said. "Not yit for a minute."

Neither did Sutpen deny the dress. "What about it?" he said.

But Wash met his arrogant stare; he spoke quietly. "I've knowed you for going on twenty years. I ain't never yit denied to do what you told me to do. And I'm a man nigh sixty. And she ain't nothing but a fifteen-year-old gal."

"Meaning that I'd harm a girl? I, a man as old as you are?"

"If you was ara other man, I'd say you was as old as me. And old or no old, I wouldn't let her keep that dress nor nothing else that come from your hand. But you are different."

"How different?" But Wash merely looked at him with his pale, questioning, sober eyes. "So that's why you are afraid of me?"

Now Wash's gaze no longer questioned. It was tranquil, serene. "I ain't afraid. Because you air brave. It ain't that you were a brave man at one minute or day of your life and got a paper to show hit from General Lee. But you air brave, the same as your air alive and breathing. That's where hit's different. Hit don't need no ticket from nobody to tell me that. And I know that whatever you handle or tech, whether hit's a regiment of men or a ignorant gal or just a hound dog, that you will make hit right."

Now it was Sutpen who looked away, turning suddenly, brusquely. "Get the jug," he said sharply.

"Sho, Kernel," Wash said.

So on that Sunday dawn two years later, having watched the Negro midwife, which he had walked three miles to fetch, enter the crazy door beyond which his granddaughter lay wailing, his heart was still quiet though concerned. He knew what they had been saying—the Negroes in cabins about the land, the white men who loafed all day long about the store, watching quietly the three of them: Sutpen, himself, his granddaughter with her air of brazen and shrinking defiance as her condition became daily more and more obvious, like three actors that came and went upon a stage. "I know what they say to one another," he thought. "I can almost hyear them: *Wash Jones has fixed old Sutpen at last. Hit taken him twenty years, but he has done hit at last.*"

It would be dawn after a while, though not yet. From the house, where the lamp shone dim beyond the warped door-frame, his granddaughter's voice came steadily as though run by a clock, while thinking went slowly and terrifically, fumbling, involved somehow with a sound of galloping hooves, until there broke suddenly free in mid-gallop the fine proud figure of the man on the fine proud stallion, galloping; and then that at which thinking fumbled, broke free too and quite clear, not in justification nor even explanation, but as the apotheosis, lonely, explicable, beyond all fouling by human touch: "He is bigger than all them Yankees that kilt his son and his wife and taken his niggers and ruined his land, bigger than this hyer durn country that he fit for and that has denied him into keeping a little country store; bigger than the denial which hit helt to his lips like the bitter cup in the Book. And how could I have lived this nigh to him for twenty years without being teched and changed by him? Maybe I ain't as big as him and maybe I ain't done none of the galloping. But at least I done been drug along. Me and him kin do hit, if so be he will show me what he aims for me to do."

Then it was dawn. Suddenly he could see the house, and the old Negress in the door looking at him. Then he realized that his granddaughter's voice had ceased. "It's a girl," the Negress said. "You can go tell him if you want to." She reentered the house.

"A girl," he repeated; "a girl"; in astonishment, hearing the galloping hooves, seeing the proud galloping figure emerge again. He seemed to watch it pass, galloping through avatars which marked the accumulation of years, time, to the climax where it galloped beneath a brandished saber and a shot-torn flag rushing down a sky in color like thunderous sulphur, thinking for the first time in his life that perhaps Sutpen was an old man like himself. "Gittin a gal," he thought in that astonishment; then he thought with the pleased surprise of a child: "Yes, sir. Be dawg if I ain't lived to be a great-grandpaw after all."

He entered the house. He moved clumsily, on tiptoe, as if he no longer lived there, as if the infant which had just drawn breath and cried in light had dispossessed him, be it of his own blood too though it might. But even above the pallet he could see little save the blur of his granddaughter's exhausted face. Then the Negress squatting at the hearth spoke, "You better gawn tell him if you going to. Hit's daylight now."

But this was not necessary. He had no more than turned the corner of the porch where the scythe leaned which he had borrowed three months ago to clear away the weeds through which he walked, when Sutpen himself rode up on the old stallion. He did not wonder how Sutpen had got the word. He took it for granted that this was what had brought the other out at this hour on Sunday morning, and he stood while the other dismounted, and he took the reins from Sutpen's hand, an expression on his gaunt face almost imbecile with a kind of weary triumph, saying, "Hit's a gal, Kernel. I be dawg if you ain't as old as I am—" until Sutpen passed him and entered the house. He stood there with the reins in his hand and heard Sutpen cross the floor to the pallet. He heard what Sutpen said, and something seemed to stop dead in him before going on.

The sun was now up, the swift sun of Mississippi latitudes, and it seemed to him that he stood beneath a strange sky, in a strange scene, familiar only as things are familiar in dreams, like the dreams of falling to one who has never climbed. "I kain't have heard what I thought I heard," he thought quietly. "I know I kain't." Yet the voice, the familiar voice which had said the words was still speaking, talking now to the old Negress about a colt foaled that morning. "That's why he was up so early," he thought. "That was hit. Hit ain't me and mine. Hit ain't even hisn that got him outen bed."

Sutpen emerged. He descended into the weeds, moving with that heavy deliberation which would have been haste when he was younger. He had not yet looked full at Wash. He said, "Dicey will stay and tend to her. You better—" Then he seemed to see Wash facing him and paused. "What?" he said.

"You said—" To his own ears Wash's voice sounded flat and ducklike, like a deaf man's. "You said if she was a mare, you could give her a good stall in the stable."

"Well?" Sutpen said. His eyes widened and narrowed, almost like a man's fists flexing and shutting, as Wash began to advance towards him, stooping a little. Very astonishment kept Sutpen still for the moment, watching that man whom in twenty years he had no more known to make any motion save at command than he had the horse which he rode. Again his eyes narrowed and widened; without moving he seemed to rear suddenly upright. "Stand back," he said suddenly and sharply. "Don't you touch me."

"I'm going to tech you, Kernel," Wash said in that flat, quiet, almost soft voice, advancing.

Sutpen raised the hand which held the riding whip; the old Negress peered around the crazy door with her black gargoyle face of a worn gnome. "Stand back, Wash," Sutpen said. Then he struck. The old Negress leaped down into the weeds with the agility of a goat and fled. Sutpen slashed Wash again across the face with the whip, striking him to his knees. When Wash rose and advanced once more he held in his hands the scythe which he had borrowed from Sutpen three months ago and which Sutpen would never need again.

When he reëntered the house his granddaughter stirred on the pallet bed and called his name fretfully. "What was that?" she said.

"What was what, honey?"

"That ere racket out there."

"'Twarn't nothing," he said gently. He knelt and touched her hot forehead clumsily. "Do you want ara thing?"

"I want a sup of water," she said querulously. "I been laying here wanting a sup of water a long time, but don't nobody care enough to pay me no mind."

"Sho now," he said soothingly. He rose stiffly and fetched the dipper of water and raised her head to drink and laid her back and watched her turn to the child with an absolutely stonelike face. But a moment later he saw that she was crying quietly. "Now, now," he said, "I wouldn't do that. Old Dicey says hit's a right fine gal. Hit's all right now. Hit's all over now. Hit ain't no need to cry now."

But she continued to cry quietly, almost sullenly, and he rose again and stood uncomfortably above the pallet for a time, thinking as he had thought when his own wife lay so and then his daughter in turn: "Women. Hit's a mystry to me. They seem to want em, and yit when they git em they cry about hit. Hit's a mystry to me. To ara man." Then he moved away and drew a chair up to the window and sat down.

Through all that long, bright, sunny forenoon he sat at the window, waiting. Now and then he rose and tiptoed to the pallet. But his granddaughter slept now, her face sullen and calm and weary, the child in the crook of her arm. Then he returned to the chair and sat again, waiting, wondering why it took them so long, until he remembered that it was Sunday. He was sitting there at mid-afternoon when a half-grown white boy came around the corner of the house upon the body and gave a choked cry and looked up and glared for a mesmerized instant at Wash in the window before he turned and fled. Then Wash rose and tiptoed again to the pallet.

The granddaughter was awake now, wakened perhaps by the boy's cry without hearing it. "Milly," he said, "air you hungry?" She didn't answer, turning her face away. He built up the fire on the hearth and cooked the food which he had brought home the day before: fatback it was, and cold corn pone; he poured water into the stale coffee pot and heated it. But she would not eat when he carried the plate to her, so he ate himself, quietly, alone, and left the dishes as they were and returned to the window.

Now he seemed to sense, feel, the men who would be gathering with horses and guns and dogs—the curious, and the vengeful: men of Sutpen's own kind, who had made the company about Sutpen's table in the time when Wash himself had yet to approach nearer to the house than the scuppernong arbor—men who had also shown the lesser ones how to fight in battle, who maybe also had signed papers from the generals saying that they were among the first of the brave; who had also galloped in the old days arrogant and proud on the fine horses across the fine plantations—symbols also of admiration and hope; instruments too of despair and grief.

That was whom they would expect him to run from. It seemed to him that he had no more to run from than he had to run to. If he ran, he would merely be fleeing one set of bragging and evil shadows for another just like them, since they were all of a kind throughout all the earth which he knew, and he was old, too old to flee far even if he were to flee. He could never escape them, no matter how much or how far he ran: a man going on sixty could not run that far. Not far enough to escape beyond the boundaries of earth where such men lived, set the order and the rule of living. It seemed to him that he now saw for the first time, after five years, how it was that Yankees or any other living armies had managed to whip them: the gallant, the proud, the brave; the acknowledged and chosen best among them all to carry courage and honor and pride. Maybe if he had gone to the war with them he would have discovered them sooner. But if he had discovered them sooner, what would he have done with his life since? How could he have borne to remember for five years what his life had been before?

Now it was getting toward sunset. The child had been crying; when he went to the pallet he saw his granddaughter nursing it, her face still bemused, sullen, inscrutable. "Air you hungry yit?" he said.

"I don't want nothing."

"You ought to eat."

This time she did not answer at all, looking down at the child. He returned to his chair and found that the sun had set. "Hit kain't be much longer," he thought. He could feel them quite near now, the curious and the vengeful. He could even seem to hear what they were saying about him, the undercurrent of believing beyond the immediate fury: *Old Wash Jones he come a tumble at last. He thought he had Sutpen, but Sutpen fooled him. He thought he had Kernel where he would have to marry the gal or pay up. And Kernel refused.* "But I never expected that, Kernel!" he cried aloud, catching himself at the sound of his own voice, glancing quickly back to find his granddaughter watching him.

"Who you talking to now?" she said.

"Hit ain't nothing. I was just thinking and talked out before I knowed hit."

Her face was becoming indistinct again, again a sullen blur in the twilight. "I reckon so. I reckon you'll have to holler louder than that before he'll hear you, up yonder at that house. And I reckon you'll need to do more than holler before you get him down here too."

"Sho now," he said. "Don't you worry none." But already thinking was going smoothly on: "You know I never. You know how I ain't never expected or asked nothing from ara living man but what I expected from you. And I never asked that. I didn't think hit would need. I said, *I don't need to. What need has a fellow like Wash Jones to question or doubt the man that General Lee himself says in a handwrote ticket that he was brave?* Brave," he thought. "Better if nara one of them had never rid back home in '65"; thinking *Better if his kind and mine too had never drawn the breath of life on this earth. Better that all who remain of us be blasted from the face of earth than that another Wash Jones should see his whole life shredded from him and shrivel away like a dried shuck thrown onto the fire.*

He ceased, became still. He heard the horses, suddenly and plainly; presently he saw the lantern and the movement of men, the glint of gun barrels, in its moving light. Yet he did not stir. It was quite dark now, and he listened to the voices and the sounds of underbrush as they surrounded the house. The lantern itself came on; its light fell upon the quiet body in the weeds and stopped, the horses tall and shadowy. A man descended and stooped in the lantern light, above the body. He held a pistol; he rose and faced the house. "Jones," he said.

"I'm here," Wash said quietly from the window. "That you, Major?"

"Come out."

"Sho," he said quietly. "I just want to see to my granddaughter."

"We'll see to her. Come on out."

"Sho, Major. Just a minute."

"Show a light. Light your lamp."

"Sho. In just a minute." They could hear his voice retreat into the house, though they could not see him as he went swiftly to the crack in the chimney where he kept the butcher knife: the one thing in his slovenly life and house in which he took pride, since it was razor sharp. He approached the pallet, his granddaughter's voice:

"Who is it? Light the lamp, grandpaw."

"Hit won't need no light, honey. Hit won't take but a minute," he said, kneeling, fumbling toward her voice, whispering now. "Where air you?"

"Right here," she said fretfully. "Where would I be? What is . . ." His hand touched her face. "What is . . . Grandpaw! Grand. . . ."

"Jones!" the sheriff said. "Come out of there!"

"In just a minute, Major," he said. Now he rose and moved swiftly. He knew where in the dark the can of kerosene was, just as he knew that it was full, since it was not two days ago that he had filled it at the store and held it there until he got a ride home with it, since the five gallons were heavy. There were still coals on the hearth; besides, the crazy building itself was like tinder: the coals, the hearth, the walls exploding in a single blue glare. Against it the waiting men saw him in a wild instant springing toward them with the lifted scythe before the horses reared and whirled. They checked the horses and turned them back toward the glare, yet still in wild relief against it the gaunt figure ran toward them with the lifted scythe.

"Jones!" the sheriff shouted; "stop! Stop, or I'll shoot. Jones! *Jones!*" Yet still the gaunt, furious figure came on against the glare and roar of the flames. With the scythe lifted, it bore down upon them, upon the wild glaring eyes of the horses and the swinging glints of gun barrels, without any cry, any sound.

ERNEST HEMINGWAY

Hills Like White Elephants

The hills across the valley of the Ebro were long and white. On this side there was no shade and no trees and the station was between two lines of rails in the sun. Close against the side of the station there was the warm shadow of the building and a curtain, made of strings of bamboo beads, hung across the open door into the bar, to keep out flies. The American and the girl with him sat at a table in the shade, outside the building. It was very hot and the express from Barcelona would come in forty minutes. It stopped at this junction for two minutes and went on to Madrid.

"What should we drink?" the girl asked. She had taken off her hat and put it on the table.

"It's pretty hot," the man said.

"Let's drink beer."

"Dos cervezas," the man said into the curtain.

"Big ones?" a woman asked from the doorway.

"Yes. Two big ones."

The woman brought two glasses of beer and two felt pads. She put the felt pads and the beer glasses on the table and looked at the man and the girl. The girl was looking off at the line of hills. They were white in the sun and the country was brown and dry.

"They look like white elephants," she said.

"I've never seen one," the man drank his beer.

"No, you wouldn't have."

"I might have," the man said. "Just because you say I wouldn't have doesn't prove anything."

The girl looked at the bead curtain. "They've painted something on it," she said. "What does it say?"

"Anis de Toro. It's a drink."

"Could we try it?"

The man called "Listen" through the curtain. The woman came out from the bar.

"Four reales."

"We want two Anis del Toro."

"With water?"

"Do you want it with water?"

"I don't know," the girl said. "Is it good with water?"

"It's all right."

"You want them with water?" asked the woman.

"Yes, with water."

"It tastes like licorice," the girl said and put the glass down.

"That's the way with everything."

"Yes," said the girl. "Everything tastes of licorice. Especially all the things you've waited so long for, like absinthe."

"Oh, cut it out."

"You started it," the girl said. "I was being amused. I was having a fine time."

"Well, let's try and have a fine time."

"All right. I was trying. I said the mountains looked like white elephants. Wasn't that bright?"

"That was bright."

"I wanted to try this new drink. That's all we do, isn't it—look at things and try new drinks?"

"I guess so."

The girl looked across at the hills.

"They're lovely hills," she said. "They don't really look like white elephants. I just meant the coloring of their skin through the trees."

"Should we have another drink?"

"All right."

The warm wind blew the bead curtain against the table.

"The beer's nice and cool," the man said.

"It's lovely," the girl said.

"It's really an awfully simple operation, Jig," the man said. "It's not really an operation at all."

The girl looked at the ground the table legs rested on.

"I know you wouldn't mind it, Jig. It's really not anything. It's just to let the air in."

The girl did not say anything.

"I'll go with you and I'll stay with you all the time. They just let the air in and then it's all perfectly natural."

"Then what will we do afterward?"

"We'll be fine afterward. Just like we were before."

"What makes you think so?"

"That's the only thing that bothers us. It's the only thing that's made us unhappy."

The girl looked at the bead curtain, put her hand out and took hold of two of the strings of beads.

"And you think then we'll be all right and be happy."

"I know we will. You don't have to be afraid. I've known lots of people that have done it."

"So have I," said the girl. "And afterward they were all so happy."

"Well," the man said, "if you don't want to you don't have to. I wouldn't have you do it if you didn't want to. But I know it's perfectly simple."

"And you really want to?"

"I think it's the best thing to do. But I don't want you to do it if you don't really want to."

"And if I do it you'll be happy and things will be like they were and you'll love me?"

"I love you now. You know I love you."

"I know. But if I do it, then it will be nice again if I say things are like white elephants, and you'll like it?"

"I'll love it. I love it now but I just can't think about it. You know how I get when I worry."

"If I do it you won't ever worry?"

"I won't worry about that because it's perfectly simple."

"Then I'll do it. Because I don't care about me."

"What do you mean?"

"I don't care about me."

"Well, I care about you."

"Oh, yes. But I don't care about me. And I'll do it and then everything will be fine."

"I don't want you to do it if you feel that way."

The girl stood up and walked to the end of the station. Across, on the other side, were fields of grain and trees along the banks of the Ebro. Far away, beyond the river, were mountains. The shadow of a cloud moved across the field of grain and she saw the river through the trees.

"And we could have all this," she said. "And we could have everything and every day we make it more impossible."

"What did you say?"

"I said we could have everything."

"We can have everything."

"No, we can't."

"We can have the whole world."

"No, we can't."

"We can go everywhere."

"No, we can't. It isn't ours any more."

"It's ours."

"No, it isn't. And once they take it away, you never get it back."

"But they haven't taken it away."

"We'll wait and see."

"Come on back in the shade," he said. "You mustn't feel that way."

"I don't feel any way," the girl said. "I just know things."

"I don't want you to do anything that you don't want to do——"

"Nor that isn't good for me," she said. "I know. Could we have another beer?"

"All right. But you've got to realize——"

"I realize," the girl said. "Can't we maybe stop talking?"

They sat down at the table and the girl looked across at the hills on the dry side of the valley and the man looked at her and at the table.

"You've got to realize," he said, "that I don't want you to do it if you don't want to. I'm perfectly willing to go through with it if it means anything to you."

"Doesn't it mean anything to you? We could get along."

"Of course it does. But I don't want anybody but you. I don't want any one else. And I know it's perfectly simple."

"Yes, you know it's perfectly simple."

"It's all right for you to say that, but I do know it."

"Would you do something for me now?"

"I'd do anything for you."

"Would you please please please please please please please stop talking?"

He did not say anything but looked at the bags against the wall of the station. There were labels on them from all the hotels where they had spent nights.

"But I don't want you to," he said, "I don't care anything about it."

"I'll scream," the girl said.

The woman came out through the curtains with two glasses of beer and put them down on the damp felt pads. "The train comes in five minutes," she said.

"What did she say?" asked the girl.

"That the train is coming in five minutes."

The girl smiled brightly at the woman, to thank her.

"I'd better take the bags over to the other side of the station," the man said. She smiled at him.

"All right. Then come back and we'll finish the beer."

He picked up the two heavy bags and carried them around the station to the other tracks. He looked up the tracks but could not see the train. Coming back, he walked through the barroom, where people waiting for the train were drinking. He drank an Anis at the bar and looked at the people. They were all waiting reasonably for the train. He went out through the bead curtain. She was sitting at the table and smiled at him.

"Do you feel better?" he asked.

"I feel fine," she said. "There's nothing wrong with me. I feel fine."

ZORA NEALE HURSTON

The Eatonville Anthology

I. THE PLEADING WOMAN

Mrs. Tony Roberts is the pleading woman. She just loves to ask for things. Her husband gives her all he can take and scrape, which is considerably more than most wives get for their housekeeping, but she goes from door to door begging for things.

She starts at the store. "Mist' Clarke," she sing-songs in a high keening voice, "gimme lil' piece uh meat tuh boil a pot uh greens wid. Lawd knows me an' mah chillen is so hongry! Hits uh SHAME! Tony don't fee-ee-eee-ed me!"

Mr. Clarke knows that she has money and that her larder is well stocked, for Tony Roberts is the best provider on his list. But her keening annoys him and he rises heavily. The pleader at his elbow shows all the joy of a starving man being seated at a feast.

"Thass right Mist' Clarke. De Lawd loveth de cheerful giver. Gimme jes' a lil' piece 'bout dis big (indicating the width of her hand) an' de Lawd'll bless yuh."

She follows this angel-on-earth to his meat tub and superintends the cutting, crying out in pain when he refuses to move the knife over just a teeny bit mo'.

Finally, meat in hand, she departs, remarking on the meanness of some people who give a piece of salt meat only two-fingers wide when they were plainly asked for a hand-wide piece. Clarke puts it down to Tony's account and resumes his reading.

With the slab of salt pork as a foundation, she visits various homes until she has collected all she wants for the day. At the Piersons for instance: "Sister Pierson, plee-ee-ease gimme uh han'ful uh collard greens fuh me an' mah po' chillen! 'Deed, me an' mah children is so hongry. Tony doan' fee-ee-eed me!"

Mrs. Pierson picks a bunch of greens for her, but she springs away from them as if they were poison. "Lawd a mussy, Mis' Pierson, you ain't gonna gimme dat lil' eye-full uh greens fuh me an' mah chillen, is you?

Don't be so graspin'; Gawd won't bless yuh. Gimme uh han'full mo'. Lawd, some folks is got everything, an' theys jes' as gripin' an stingy!"

Mrs. Pierson raises the ante, and the pleading woman moves on to the next place, and on and on. The next day, it commences all over.

II. TURPENTINE LOVE

Jim Merchant is always in good humor—even with his wife. He says he fell in love with her at first sight. That was some years ago. She has had all her teeth pulled out, but they still get along splendidly.

He says the first time he called on her he found out that she was subject to fits. This didn't cool his love, however. She had several in his presence.

One Sunday, while he was there, she had one, and her mother tried to give her a dose of turpentine to stop it. Accidentally, she spilled it in her eye and it cured her. She never had another fit, so they got married and have kept each other in good humor ever since.

III.

Becky Moore has eleven children of assorted colors and sizes. She has never been married, but that is not her fault. She has never stopped any of the fathers of her children from proposing, so if she has no father for her children it's not her fault. The men round about are entirely to blame.

The other mothers of the town are afraid that it is catching. They won't let their children play with hers.

IV. TIPPY

Sykes Jones' family all shoot craps. The most interesting member of the family—also fond of bones, but another kind—is Tippy, the Jones' dog.

He is so thin, that it amazes one that he lives at all. He sneaks into village kitchens if the housewives are careless about the doors and steals meats, even off the stoves. He also sucks eggs.

For these offenses he has been sentenced to death dozens of times, and the sentences executed upon him, only they didn't work. He has been fed bluestone, strychnine, nux vomica, even an entire Peruna bottle beaten up. It didn't fatten him, but it didn't kill him. So Eatonville has resigned itself to the plague of Tippy, reflecting that it has erred in certain matters and is being chastened.

In spite of all the attempts upon his life, Tippy is still willing to be friendly with anyone who will let him.

V. THE WAY OF A MAN WITH A TRAIN

Old Man Anderson lived seven or eight miles out in the country from Eatonville. Over by Lake Apopka. He raised feed-corn and cassava and went to market with it two or three times a year. He bought all of his victuals wholesale so he wouldn't have to come to town for several months more.

He was different from citybred folks. He had never seen a train. Everybody laughed at him for even the smallest child in Eatonville had either been to Maitland or Orlando and watched a train go by. On Sunday afternoons all of the young people of the village would go over to Maitland, a mile away, to see Number 35 whizz southward on its way to Tampa and wave at the passengers. So we looked down on him a little. Even we children felt superior in the presence of a person so lacking in worldly knowledge.

The grown-ups kept telling him he ought to go see a train. He always said he didn't have time to wait so long. Only two trains a day passed through Maitland. But patronage and ridicule finally had its effect and Old Man Anderson drove in one morning early. Number 78 went north to Jacksonville at 10:20. He drove his light wagon over in the woods beside the railroad below Maitland, and sat down to wait. He began to fear that his horse would get frightened and run away with the wagon. So he took him out and led him deeper into the grove and tied him securely. Then he returned to his wagon and waited some more. Then he remembered that some of the train-wise villagers had said the engine belched fire and smoke. He had better move his wagon out of danger. It might catch fire. He climbed down from the seat and placed himself between the shafts to draw it away. Just then 78 came thundering over the trestle spouting smoke, and suddenly began blowing for Maitland. Old Man Anderson became so frightened he ran away with the wagon through the woods and tore it up worse than the horse ever could have done. He doesn't know yet what a train looks like, and says he doesn't care.

VI. COON TAYLOR

Coon Taylor never did any real stealing. Of course, if he saw a chicken or a watermelon he'd take it. The people used to get mad but they never could catch him. He took so many melons from Joe Clarke that he set up in the melon patch one night with his shotgun loaded with rock salt. He was going to fix Coon. But he was tired. It is hard work being a mayor, postmaster, storekeeper and everything. He dropped asleep sitting on a stump in the middle of the patch. So he didn't see Coon when he came. Coon didn't see him either, that is, not at first. He knew the stump was there, however. He had opened many of Clarke's juicy Florida Favorite on it. He selected his fruit, walked over to the stump and burst the melon on it. That is, he thought it was the stump until it fell over with a yell. Then he knew it was no stump and departed hastily from those parts. He had cleared the fence when Clarke came to, as it were. So the charge of rock-salt was wasted on the desert air.

During the sugar-cane season, he found he couldn't resist Clarke's soft green cane, but Clarke did not go to sleep this time. So after he had cut six of eight stalks by the moonlight, Clarke rose up out of the cane strippings with his shotgun and made Coon sit right down and chew up the last one of them on the spot. And the next day he made Coon leave his town for three months.

VII. VILLAGE FICTION

Joe Lindsay is said by Lum Boger to be the largest manufacturer of prevarications in Eatonville; Brazzle (late owner of the world's leanest and meanest mule) contends that his business is the largest in the state and his wife holds that he is the biggest liar in the world.

Exhibit A—He claims that while he was in Orlando one day he saw a doctor cut open a woman, remove everything—liver, lights and heart included—clean each of them separately; the doctor then washed out the empty woman, dried her out neatly with a towel and replaced the organs so expertly that she was up and about her work in a couple of weeks.

VIII.

Sewell is a man who lives all to himself. He moves a great deal. So often, that 'Lige Moseley says his chickens are so used to moving that every time he comes out into his backyard the chickens lie down and cross their legs, ready to be tied up again.

He is baldheaded; but he says he doesn't mind that, because he wants as little as possible between him and God.

IX.

Mrs. Clarke is Joe Clarke's wife. She is a soft-looking, middle-aged woman, whose bust and stomach are always holding a get-together.

She waits on the store sometimes and cries every time he yells at her which he does every time she makes a mistake, which is quite often. She calls her husband "Jody." They say he used to beat her in the store when he was a young man, but he is not so impatient now. He can wait until he goes home.

She shouts in Church every Sunday and shakes the hand of fellowship with everybody in the Church with her eyes closed, but somehow always misses her husband.

X.

Mrs. McDuffy goes to Church every Sunday and always shouts and tells her "determination." Her husband always sits in the back row and beats her as soon as they get home. He says there's no sense in her shouting, as big a devil as she is. She just does it to slur him. Elijah Moseley asked her why she didn't stop shouting, seeing she always got a beating about it. She says she can't "squinch the sperrit." Then Elijah asked Mr. McDuffy to stop beating her, seeing that she was going to shout anyway. He answered that she just did it for spite and that his fist was just as hard as her head. He could last just as long as she. So the village let the matter rest.

XI. DOUBLE-SHUFFLE

Back in the good old days before the World War, things were very simple in Eatonville. People didn't fox-trot. When the town wanted to put on its Sunday clothes and wash behind the ears, it put on a "break-down." The daring younger set would two-step and waltz, but the good church members and the elders stuck to the grand march. By rural canons dancing is wicked, but one is not held to have danced until the feet have been crossed. Feet don't get crossed when one grand marches.

At elaborate affairs the organ from the Methodist church was moved up to the hall and Lizzimore, the blind man presided. When informal gatherings were held, he merely played his guitar assisted by any volunteer with mouth organs or accordions.

Among white people the march is as mild as if it had been passed on by Volstead. But it still has a kick in Eatonville. Everybody happy, shining eyes, gleaming teeth. Feet dragged 'shhlap, shhlap! to beat out the time. No orchestra needed. Round and round! Back again, parse-me-la! shlap! shlap! Strut! Strut! Seaboard! Shlap! Shalp! Tiddy bumm! Mr. Clarke in the lead with Mrs. Moseley.

It's too much for some of the young folks. Double shuffling commences. Buck and wing. Lizzimore about to break his guitar. Accordion doing contortions. People fall back against the walls, and let the soloist have it, shouting as they clap the old, old double shuffle songs.

'Me an' mah honey got two mo' days
Two mo' days tuh do de buck'

Sweating bodies, laughing mouths, grotesque faces, feet drumming fiercely. Deacons clapping as hard as the rest.

Great big nigger, black as tar
Trying tuh git tuh hebben on uh 'lectric car.

Some love cabbage, some love kale
But I love a gal wid a short skirt tail.

Long tall angel—steppin' down,
Long white robe an' starry crown.

'Ah would not marry uh black gal (bumm bumm!)
Tell yuh de reason why
Every time she comb her hair
She make de goo-goo eye.

Would not marry a yaller gal (bumm bumm!)
Tell yuh de reason why
Her neck so long an' stringy
Ahm 'fraid she'd never die.

Would not marry uh preacher
Tell yuh de reason why
Every time he comes tuh town
He makes de chicken fly.

When the buck dance was over, the boys would give the floor to the girls and they would parse-me-la with a slye eye out of the corner to see if anybody was looking who might "have them up in church" on conference night. Then there would be more dancing. Then Mr. Clarke would call for everybody's best attention and announce that *'freshments was served! Every gent'man would please take his lady by the arm and scorch her right up to de table fur a treat!*

Then the men would stick their arms out with a flourish and ask their ladies: "You lak chicken? Well, then, take a wing." And the ladies would take the proffered "wings" and parade up to the long table and be served. Of course most of them had brought baskets in which were heaps of jointed and fried chicken, two or three kinds of pies, cakes, potato pone and chicken purlo. The hall would separate into happy groups about the baskets until time for more dancing.

But the boys and girls got scattered about during the war, and now they dance the fox-trot by a brand new piano. They do waltz and two-step still, but no one now considers it good form to lock his chin over his partner's shoulder and stick out behind. One night just for fun and to humor the old folks, they danced, that is, they grand marched, but everyone picked up their feet. *Bah!!*

XII. THE HEAD OF THE NAIL

Daisy Taylor was the town vamp. Not that she was pretty. But sirens were all but non-existent in the town. Perhaps she was forced to it by circumstances. She was quite dark, with little bushy patches of hair squatting over her head. These were held down by shingle-nails often. No one knows whether she did this for artistic effect or for lack of hairpins, but there they were shining in the little patches of hair when she got all dressed for the afternoon and came up to Clarke's store to see if there was any mail for her.

It was seldom that anyone wrote to Daisy, but she knew that the men of the town, would be assembled there by five o'clock, and some one could usually be induced to buy her some soda water or peanuts.

Daisy flirted with married men. There were only two single men in town. Lum Boger, who was engaged to the assistant schoolteacher, and Hiram Lester, who had been off to school at Tuskegee and wouldn't look at a person like Daisy. In addition to other drawbacks, she was pigeon-toed and her petticoat was always showing so perhaps he was justified. There was nothing else to do except flirt with married men.

This went on for a long time. First one wife and then another complained of her, or drove her from the preserves by threat.

But the affair with Crooms was the most prolonged and serious. He was even known to have bought her a pair of shoes.

Mrs. Laura Crooms was a meek little woman who took all of her troubles crying, and talked a great deal of leaving things in the hands of God.

The affair came to a head one night in orange picking time. Crooms was over at Oneido picking oranges. Many fruit pickers move from one town to the other during the season.

The *town* was collected at the store-postoffice as is customary on Saturday nights. The *town* has had its bath and with its week's pay in pocket fares forth to be merry. The men tell stories and treat the ladies to soda-water, peanuts and peppermint candy.

Daisy was trying to get treats, but the porch was cold to her that night.

"Ah don't keer if you don't treat me. What's a dirty lil nickel?" She flung this at Walter Thomas. "The everloving Mister Crooms will gimme anything atall Ah wants."

"You better shet up yo' mouf talking 'bout Albert Crooms. Heah his wife comes right now."

Daisy went akimbo. "Who? Me! Ah don't keer whut Laura Crooms think. If she ain't a heavy hip-ted Mama enough to keep him, she don't need to come crying to me."

She stood making goo-goo eyes as Mrs. Crooms walked upon the porch. Daisy laughed loud, made several references to Albert Crooms, and when she saw the mail-bag come in from Maitland she said, "Ah better go in an' see if Ah ain't got a letter from Oneido."

The more Daisy played the game of getting Mrs. Crooms' goat, the better she liked it. She ran in and out of the store laughing until she could scarcely stand. Some of the people present began to talk to Mrs. Crooms—to egg her on to halt Daisy's boasting, but she was for leaving it all in the hands of God. Walter Thomas kept on after Mrs. Crooms until she stiffened and resolved to fight. Daisy was inside when she came to this resolve and never dreamed anything of the kind could happen. She had gotten hold of an envelope and came laughing and shouting, "Oh, Ah can't stand to see Oneido lose!"

There was a box of ax-handles on display on the porch, propped up against the door jamb. As Daisy stepped upon the porch, Mrs. Crooms leaned the heavy end of one of those handles heavily upon her head. She staggered from the porch to the ground and the timid Laura, fearful of a counter-attack, struck again and Daisy toppled into the town ditch. There was not enough water in there to do more than muss her up. Every time she tried to rise, down would come that ax-handle again. Laura was fighting a scared fight. With Daisy thoroughly licked, she retired to the store porch and left her fallen enemy in the ditch. But Elijah Moseley, who was some distance down the street when the trouble began arrived as the victor was withdrawing. He rushed up and picked Daisy out of the mud and began feeling her head.

"Is she hurt much?" Joe Clarke asked from the doorway.

"I don't know," Elijah answered. "I was just looking to see if Laura had been lucky enough to hit one of those nails on the head and drive it in."

Before a week was up, Daisy moved to Orlando. There in a wider sphere, perhaps, her talents as a vamp were appreciated.

XIII. PANTS AND CAL'LINE

Sister Cal'line Potts was a silent woman. Did all of her laughing down inside, but did the thing that kept the town in an uproar of laughter. It was the general opinion of the village that Cal'line would do anything she had a mind to. And she had a mind to do several things.

Mitchell Potts, her husband, had a weakness for women. No one ever believed that she was jealous. She did things to the women, surely. But most any townsman would have said that she did them because she liked the novel situation and the queer things she could bring out of it.

Once he took up with Delphine—called Mis' Pheeny by the town. She lived on the outskirts on the edge of the piney woods. The town winked and talked. People don't make secrets of such things in villages. Cal'line went about her business with her thin black lips pursed tight as ever, and her shiny black eyes unchanged.

"Dat devil of a Cal'line's got somethin' up her sleeve!" The town smiled in anticipation.

"Delphine is too big a cigar for her to smoke. She ain't crazy," said some as the weeks went on and nothing happened. Even Pheeny herself would give an extra flirt to her over-starched petticoats as she rustled into church past her on Sundays.

Mitch Potts said furthermore, that he was tired of Cal'line's foolishness. She had to stay where he put her. His African soupbone (arm) was too strong to let a woman run over him. 'Nough was 'nough. And he did some fancy cussing, and he was the fanciest cusser in the county.

So the town waited and the longer it waited, the odds changed slowly from the wife to the husband.

One Saturday, Mitch knocked off work at two o'clock and went over to Maitland. He came back with a rectangular box under his arm and kept straight on out to the barn to put it away. He ducked around the corner of the house, but even so, his wife glimpsed the package. Very much like a shoe-box. So!

He put on the kettle and took a bath. She stood in her bare feet at the ironing board and kept on ironing. He dressed. It was about five o'clock but still very light. He fiddled around outside. She kept on with her ironing. As soon as the sun got red, he sauntered out to the barn, got the parcel and walked away down the road, past the store and out into the piney woods. As soon as he left the house, Cal'line slipped on her shoes without taking time to don stockings, put on one of her husband's old Stetsons, worn and floppy, slung the axe over her shoulder and followed in his wake. He was hailed cheerily as he passed the sitters on the store porch and answered smiling sheepishly and passed on. Two minutes later passed his wife, silently, unsmiling, and set the porch to giggling and betting.

An hour passed perhaps. It was dark. Clarke had long ago lighted the swinging kerosene lamp inside.

XIV.

Once 'way back yonder before the stars fell all the animals used to talk just like people. In them days dogs and rabbits was the best of friends—even tho both of them was stuck on the same gal—which was Miss Nancy Coon. She had the sweetest smile and the prettiest striped and bushy tail to be found anywhere.

They both run their legs nigh off trying to win her for themselves—fetching nice ripe persimmons and such. But she never give one or the other no satisfaction.

Finally one night Mr. Dog popped the question right out. "Miss Coon," he says, "Ma'am, also Ma'am which would you ruther be—a lark flyin' or a dove a settin'?"

Course Miss Nancy she blushed and laughed a little and hid her face behind her bushy tail for a spell. Then she said sorter shy like, "I does love yo' sweet voice, brother dawg—but—I ain't jes' exactly set my mind yit."

Her and Mr. Dog set on a spell, when up comes hopping Mr. Rabbit wid his tail fresh washed and his whiskers shining. He got right down to business and asked Miss Coon to marry him, too.

"Oh, Miss Nancy," he says, "Ma'am, also Ma'am, if you'd see me settin' straddle of a mud-cat leadin' a minnow, what would you think? Ma'am also Ma'am?" Which is a out and out proposal as everybody knows.

"Youse awful nice, Brother Rabbit and a beautiful dancer, but you cannot sing like Brother Dog. Both you uns come back next week to gimme time for to decide."

They both left arm-in-arm. Finally Mr. Rabbit says to Mr. Dog. "Taint no use in me going back—she ain't gwinter have me. So I mought as well give up. She loves singing, and I ain't got nothing but a squeak."

"Oh, don't talk that a way," says Mr. Dog, tho' he is glad Mr. Rabbit can't sing none.

"Thass all right, Brer Dog. But if I had a sweet voice like you got, I'd have it worked on and make it sweeter."

"How! How! How!" Mr. Dog cried, jumping up and down.

"Lemme fix it for you, like I do for Sister Lark and Sister Mockingbird."

"When? Where?" asked Mr. Dog, all excited. He was figuring that if he could sing just a little better Miss Coon would be bound to have him.

"Just you meet me t'morrer in de huckleberry patch," says the rabbit and off they both goes to bed.

The dog is there on time next day and after a while the rabbit comes loping up.

"Mawnin', Brer Dawg," he says kinder chippy like. "Ready to git yo' voice sweetened?"

"Sholy, sholy, Brer Rabbit. Let's we all hurry about it. I wants tuh serenade Miss Nancy from the piney woods tuh night."

"Well, den, open yo' mouf and poke out yo' tongue," says the rabbit.

No sooner did Mr. Dog poke out his tongue than Mr. Rabbit split it with a knife and ran for all he was worth to a hollow stump and hid hisself.

The dog has been mad at the rabbit ever since.

Anybody who don't believe it happened, just look at the dog's tongue and he can see for himself where the rabbit slit it right up the middle.

Stepped on a tin, mah story ends.

LANGSTON HUGHES

Slave on the Block

They were people who went in for Negroes—Michael and Anne—the Carraways. But not in the social-service, philanthropic sort of way, no. They saw no use in helping a race that was already too charming and naive and lovely for words. Leave them unspoiled and just enjoy them,

Michael and Anne felt. So they went in for the Art of Negroes—the dancing that had such jungle life about it, the songs that were so simple and fervent, the poetry that was so direct, so real. They never tried to influence that art, they only bought it and raved over it, and copied it. For they were artists, too.

In their collection they owned some Covarrubias originals. Of course Covarrubias wasn't a Negro, but how he caught the darky spirit! They owned all the Robeson records and all the Bessie Smith. And they had a manuscript of Countee Cullen's. They saw all the plays with or about Negroes, read all the books, and adored the Hall Johnson Singers. They had met Doctor DuBois, and longed to meet Carl Van Vechten. Of course they knew Harlem like their own backyard, that is, all the speakeasies and night clubs and dance halls, from the Cotton Club and the ritzy joints where Negroes couldn't go themselves, down to places like the Hot Dime, where white folks couldn't get in—unless they knew the man. (And tipped heavily.)

They were acquainted with lots of Negroes, too—but somehow the Negroes didn't seem to like them very much. Maybe the Carraways gushed over them too soon. Or maybe they looked a little like poor white folks, although they were really quite well off. Or maybe they tried too hard to make friends, dark friends, and the dark friends suspected something. Or perhaps their house in the Village was too far from Harlem, or too hard to find, being back in one of those queer and expensive little side streets that had once been alleys before the art invasion came. Anyway, occasionally, a furtive Negro might accept their invitation for tea, or cocktails; and sometimes a lesser Harlem celebrity or two would decorate their rather slow parties; but one seldom came back for more. As much as they loved Negroes, Negroes didn't seem to love Michael and Anne.

But they were blessed with a wonderful colored cook and maid—until she took sick and died in her room in their basement. And then the most marvellous ebony boy walked into their life, a boy as black as all the Negroes they'd ever known put together.

"He *is* the jungle," said Anne when she saw him.

"He's 'I Couldn't Hear Nobody Pray,' " said Michael.

For Anne thought in terms of pictures: she was a painter. And Michael thought in terms of music: he was a composer for the piano. And they had a most wonderful idea of painting pictures and composing music that went together, and then having a joint "concert-exhibition" as they would call it. Her pictures and his music. The Carraways, a sonata and a picture, a fugue and a picture. It would be lovely, and such a novelty, people would have to like it. And many of their things would be Negro. Anne had painted their maid six times. And Michael had composed several themes based on the spirituals, and on Louis Armstrong's jazz. Now here was this ebony boy. The essence in the flesh.

They had nearly missed the boy. He had come, when they were out, to gather up the things the cook had left, and take them to her sister in Jersey. It seems that he was the late cook's nephew. The new colored maid had let him in and given him the two suitcases of poor dear Emma's belongings, and he was on his way to the Subway. That is, he was in the hall, going out just as the Carraways, Michael and Anne, stepped in. They could hardly see the boy, it being dark in the hall, and he being dark, too.

"Hello," they said. "Is this Emma's nephew?"

"Yes'm," said the maid. "Yes'm."

"Well, come in," said Anne, "and let us see you. We loved your aunt so much. She was the best cook we ever had."

"You don't know where *I* could get a job, do you?" said the boy. This took Michael and Anne back a bit, but they rallied at once. So charming and naive to ask right away for what he wanted.

Anne burst out, "You know, I think I'd like to paint you."

Michael said, "Oh, I say now, that would be lovely! He's so utterly Negro."

The boy grinned.

Anne said, "Could you come back tomorrow?"

And the boy said, "Yes, indeed. I sure could."

The upshot of it was that they hired him. They hired him to look after the garden, which was just about as big as Michael's grand piano—only a little square behind the house. You know those Village gardens. Anne sometimes painted it. And occasionally they set the table there for four on a spring evening. Nothing grew in the garden really, practically nothing. But the boy said he could plant things. And they had to have some excuse to hire him.

The boy's name was Luther. He had come from the South to his relatives in Jersey, and had had only one job since he got there, shining shoes for a Greek in Elizabeth. But the Greek fired him because the boy wouldn't give half his tips over to the proprietor.

"I never heard of a job where I had to pay the boss, instead of the boss paying me," said Luther. "Not till I got here."

"And then what did you do?" said Anne.

"Nothing. Been looking for a job for the last four months."

"Poor boy," said Michael; "poor, dear boy."

"Yes," said Anne. "You must be hungry." And they called the cook to give him something to eat.

Luther dug around in the garden a little bit that first day, went out and bought some seeds, came back and ate some more. They made a place for him to sleep in the basement by the furnace. And the next day Anne started to paint him, after she'd bought the right colors.

"He'll be good company for Mattie," they said. "She claims she's afraid to stay alone at night when we're out, so she leaves." They suspected, though, that Mattie just liked to get up to Harlem. And they thought right. Mattie was not as settled as she looked. Once out, with the Savoy open until three in the morning, why come home? That was the way Mattie felt.

In fact, what happened was that Mattie showed Luther where the best and cheapest hot spots in Harlem were located. Luther hadn't even set foot in Harlem before, living twenty-eight miles away, as he did, in Jersey, and being a kind of quiet boy. But the second night he was there Mattie said, "Come on, let's go. Working for white folks all day, I'm tired. They needn't think I was made to answer telephones all night." So out they went.

Anne noticed that most mornings Luther would doze almost as soon as she sat him down to pose, so she eventually decided to paint Luther asleep. "The Sleeping Negro," she would call it. Dear, natural childlike people, they would sleep anywhere they wanted to. Anyway, asleep, he kept still and held the pose.

And he *was* an adorable Negro. Not tall, but with a splendid body. And a slow and lively smile that lighted up his black, black face, for his teeth were very white, and his eyes, too. Most effective in oil and canvas. Better even than Emma had been. Anne could stare at him at leisure when he was asleep. One day she decided to paint him nude, or at least half nude. A slave picture, that's what she would do. The market at New Orleans for a background. And call it "The Boy on the Block."

So one morning when Luther settled down in his sleeping pose, Anne said, "No," she had finished that picture. She wanted to paint him now representing to the full the soul and sorrow of his people. She wanted to paint him as a slave about to be sold. And since slaves in warm climates had no clothes, would he please take off his shirt.

Luther smiled a sort of embarrassed smile and took off his shirt.

"Your undershirt, too," said Anne. But it turned out that he had on a union suit, so he had to go out and change altogether. He came back and mounted the box that Anne said would serve just then for a slave block, and she began to sketch. Before luncheon Michael came in, and went into rhapsodies over Luther on the box without a shirt, about to be sold into slavery. He said he must put him into music right now. And he went to the piano and began to play something that sounded like

Deep River in the jaws of a dog, but Michael said it was a modern slave plaint, 1850 in terms of 1933. Vieux Carré remembered on 135th Street. Slavery in the Cotton Club.

Anne said, "It's too marvellous!" And they painted and played till dark, with rest periods in between for Luther. Then they all knocked off for dinner. Anne and Michael went out later to one of Lew Leslie's new shows. And Luther and Mattie said, "Thank God!" and got dressed up for Harlem.

Funny, they didn't like the Carraways. They treated them nice and paid them well. "But they're too strange," said Mattie, "they makes me nervous."

"They is mighty funny," Luther agreed.

They didn't understand the vagaries of white folks, neither Luther nor Mattie, and they didn't want to be bothered trying.

"I does my work," said Mattie. "After that I don't want to be painted, or asked to sing songs, nor nothing like that."

The Carraways often asked Luther to sing, and he sang. He knew a lot of southern worksongs and reels, and spirituals and ballads.

> "Dear Ma, I'm in hard luck:
> Three days since I et,
> And the stamp on this letter's
> Gwine to put me in debt."

The Carraways allowed him to neglect the garden altogether. About all Luther did was pose and sing. And he got tired of that.

Indeed, both Luther and Mattie became a bit difficult to handle as time went on. The Carraways blamed it on Mattie. She had got hold of Luther. She was just simply spoiling a nice simple young boy. She was old enough to know better. Mattie was in love with Luther.

At least, he slept with her. The Carraways discovered this one night about one o'clock when they went to wake Luther up (the first time they'd ever done such a thing) and ask him if he wouldn't sing his own marvellous version of John Henry for a man who had just come from Saint Louis and was sailing for Paris tomorrow. But Luther wasn't in his own bed by the furnace. There was a light in Mattie's room, so Michael knocked softly. Mattie said, "Who's that?" And Michael poked his head in, and here were Luther and Mattie in bed together!

Of course, Anne condoned them. "It's so simple and natural for Negroes to make love." But Mattie, after all, was forty if she was a day. And Luther was only a kid. Besides Anne thought that Luther had been ever so much nicer when he first came than he was now. But from so many nights at the Savoy, he had become a marvellous dancer, and he was teaching Anne the Lindy Hop to Cab Calloway's records. Besides, her picture of "The Boy on the Block" wasn't anywhere near done. And he did take pretty good care of the furnace. So they kept him. At least, Anne kept him, although Michael said he was getting a little bored with the same Negro always in the way.

For Luther had grown a bit familiar lately. He smoked up all their cigarettes, drank their wine, told jokes on them to their friends, and sometimes even came upstairs singing and walking about the house when the Carraways had guests in who didn't share their enthusiasm for Negroes, natural or otherwise.

Luther and Mattie together were a pair. They quite frankly lived with one another now. Well, let that go. Anne and Michael prided themselves on being different; artists, you know, and liberal-minded people—maybe a little scatter-brained, but then (secretly, they felt) that came from genius. They were not ordinary people, bothering about the liberties of others. Certainly, the last thing they would do would be to interfere with the delightful simplicity of Negroes.

But Mattie must be giving Luther money and buying him clothes. He was really dressing awfully well. And on her Thursday afternoons off she would come back loaded down with packages. As far as the Carraways could tell, they were all for Luther.

And sometimes there were quarrels drifting up from the basement. And often, all too often, Mattie had moods. Then Luther would have moods. And it was pretty awful having two dark and glowering people around the house. Anne couldn't paint and Michael couldn't play.

One day, when she hadn't seen Luther for three days, Anne called downstairs and asked him if he wouldn't please come up and take off his shirt and get on the box. The picture was almost done. Luther came dragging his feet upstairs and humming:

"Before I'd be a slave
I'd be buried in ma grave
And go home to my Jesus
And be free."

And that afternoon he let the furnace go almost out.

That was the state of things when Michael's mother (whom Anne had never liked) arrived from Kansas City to pay them a visit. At once neither Mattie nor Luther liked her either. She was a mannish old lady, big and tall, and inclined to be bossy. Mattie, however, did spruce up her service, cooked delicious things, and treated Mrs. Carraway with a great deal more respect than she did Anne.

"I never play with servants," Mrs. Carraway had said to Michael, and Mattie must have heard her.

But Luther, he was worse than ever. Not that he did anything wrong, Anne thought, but the way he did things! For instance, he didn't need to sing now all the time, especially since Mrs. Carraway had said she didn't like singing. And certainly not songs like "You Rascal, You."

But all things end! With the Carraways and Luther it happened like this: One forenoon, quite without a shirt (for he expected to pose) Luther came sauntering through the library to change the flowers in the vase. He carried red roses. Mrs. Carraway was reading her morning scripture from the Health and Life.

"Oh, good morning," said Luther. "How long are you gonna stay in this house?"

"I never liked familiar Negroes," said Mrs. Carraway, over her nose glasses.

"Huh!" said Luther. "That's too bad! I never liked poor white folks."

Mrs. Carraway screamed, a short loud, dignified scream. Michael came running in bathrobe and pyjamas. Mrs. Carraway grew tall. There was a scene. Luther talked. Michael talked. Anne appeared.

"Never, never, never," said Mrs. Carraway, "have I suffered such impudence from servants—and a nigger servant—in my own son's house."

"Mother, Mother, Mother," said Michael. "Be calm. I'll discharge him." He turned on the nonchalant Luther. "Go!" he said, pointing toward the door. "Go, go!"

"Michael," Anne cried, "I haven't finished 'The Slave on the Block.' " Her husband looked nonplussed. For a moment he breathed deeply.

"Either he goes or I go," said Mrs. Carraway, firm as a rock.

"He goes," said Michael with strength from his mother.

"Oh!" cried Anne. She looked at Luther. His black arms were full of roses he had brought to put in the vases. He had on no shirt. "Oh!" His body was ebony.

"Don't worry 'bout me!" said Luther. "I'll go."

"Yes, we'll go," boomed Mattie from the doorway, who had come up from below, fat and belligerent. "We've stood enough foolery from you white folks! Yes, we'll go. Come on, Luther."

What could she mean, "stood enough"? What had they done to them, Anne and Michael wondered. They had tried to be kind. "Oh!"

"Sneaking around knocking on our door at night," Mattie went on. "Yes, we'll go. Pay us! Pay us! Pay us!" So she remembered the time they had come for Luther at night. That was it.

"I'll pay you," said Michael. He followed Mattie out.

Anne looked at her black boy.

"Good-bye," Luther said. "You fix the vases."

He handed her his armful of roses, glanced impudently at old Mrs. Carraway and grinned—grinned that wide, beautiful, white-toothed grin that made Anne say when she first saw him, "He looks like the jungle." Grinned, and disappeared in the dark hall, with no shirt on his back.

"Oh," Anne moaned distressfully, "my 'Boy on the Block'!"

"Huh!" snorted Mrs. Carraway.

ERSKINE CALDWELL

Kneel to the Rising Sun

A shiver went through Lonnie. He drew his hand away from his sharp chin, remembering what Clem had said. It made him feel now as if he were committing a crime by standing in Arch Gunnard's presence and allowing his face to be seen.

He and Clem had been walking up the road together that afternoon on their way to the filling station when he told Clem how much he needed rations. Clem stopped a moment to kick a rock out of the road, and said that if you worked for Arch Gunnard long enough, your face would be sharp enough to split the boards for your own coffin.

As Lonnie turned away to sit down on an empty box beside the gasoline pump, he could not help wishing that he could be as unafraid of Arch Gunnard as Clem was. Even if Clem was a Negro, he never hesitated to ask for rations when he needed something to eat; and when he and his family did not get enough, Clem came right out and told Arch so. Arch stood for that, but he swore that he was going to run Clem out of the county the first chance he got.

Lonnie knew without turning around that Clem was standing at the corner of the filling station with two or three other Negroes and looking at him, but for some reason he was unable to meet Clem's eyes.

Arch Gunnard was sitting in the sun, honing his jackknife blade on his boot top. He glanced once or twice at Lonnie's hound, Nancy, who was lying in the middle of the road waiting for Lonnie to go home.

"That your dog, Lonnie?"

Jumping with fear, Lonnie's hand went to his chin to hide the lean face that would accuse Arch of short-rationing.

Arch snapped his fingers and the hound stood up, wagging her tail. She waited to be called.

"Mr. Arch, I—"

Arch called the dog. She began crawling towards them on her belly, wagging her tail a little faster each time Arch's fingers snapped. When she was several feet away, she turned over on her back and lay on the ground with her four paws in the air.

Dudley Smith and Jim Weaver, who were lounging around the filling station, laughed. They had been leaning against the side of the building, but they straightened up to see what Arch was up to.

Arch spat some more tobacco juice on his boot top and whetted the jackknife blade some more.

"What kind of a hound dog is that, anyway, Lonnie?" Arch said. "Looks like to me it might be a ketch hound."

Lonnie could feel Clem Henry's eyes boring into the back of his head. He wondered what Clem would do if it had been his dog Arch Gunnard was snapping his fingers at and calling like that.

"His tail's way too long for a coon hound or a bird dog, ain't it, Arch?" somebody behind Lonnie said, laughing out loud.

Everybody laughed then, including Arch. They looked at Lonnie, waiting to hear what he was going to say to Arch.

"Is he a ketch hound, Lonnie?" Arch said, snapping his finger again.

"Mr. Arch, I—"

"Don't be ashamed of him, Lonnie, if he don't show signs of turning out to be a bird dog or a foxhound. Everybody needs a hound around the house that can go out and catch pigs and rabbits when you are in a hurry for them. A ketch hound is a mighty respectable animal. I've known the time when I was mighty proud to own one."

Everybody laughed.

Arch Gunnard was getting ready to grab Nancy by the tail. Lonnie sat up, twisting his neck until he caught a glimpse of Clem Henry at the other corner of the filling station. Clem was staring at him with unmistakable meaning, with the same look in his eyes he had had that afternoon when he said that nobody who worked for Arch Gunnard ought to stand for short-rationing. Lonnie lowered his eyes. He could not figure out how a Negro could be braver than he was. There were a lot of times like that when he would have given anything he had to be able to jump into Clem's shoes and change places with him.

"The trouble with this hound of yours, Lonnie, is that he's too heavy on his feet. Don't you reckon it would be a pretty slick little trick to lighten the load some, being as how he's a ketch hound to begin with?"

Lonnie remembered then what Clem Henry had said he would do if Arch Gunnard ever tried to cut off his dog's tail. Lonnie knew, and Clem knew, and everybody else knew, that that would give Arch the chance he was waiting for. All Arch asked, he had said, was for Clem Henry to overstep his place just one little half inch, or to talk back to him with just one little short word, and he would do the rest. Everybody knew what Arch meant by that, especially if Clem did not turn and run. And Clem had not been known to run from anybody, after fifteen years in the country.

Arch reached down and grabbed Nancy's tail while Lonnie was wondering about Clem. Nancy acted as if she thought Arch were playing some kind of a game with her. She turned her head around until she could reach Arch's hand to lick it. He cracked her on the bridge of the nose with the end of the jackknife.

"He's a mighty playful dog, Lonnie," Arch said, catching up a shorter grip on the tail, "but his wagpole is way too long for a dog his size, especially when he wants to be a ketch hound."

Lonnie swallowed hard.

"Mr. Arch, she's a mighty fine rabbit tracker. I—"

"Shucks, Lonnie," Arch said, whetting the knife blade on the dog's tail, "I ain't ever seen a hound in all my life that needed a tail that long to hunt rabbits with. It's way too long for just a common, ordinary, everyday ketch hound."

Lonnie looked up hopefully at Dudley Smith and the others. None of them offered any help. It was useless for him to try to stop Arch, because Arch Gunnard would let nothing stand in his way when once he had set his head on what he wished to do. Lonnie knew that if he should let himself show any anger or resentment, Arch would drive him off the farm before sundown that night. Clem Henry was the only person there who would help him, but Clem . . .

The white men and the Negroes at both corners of the filling station waited to see what Lonnie was going to do about it. All of them hoped he would put up a fight for his hound. If anyone ever had the nerve to stop Arch Gunnard from cutting off a dog's tail, it might put an end to it. It was plain, though, that Lonnie, who was one of Arch's sharecroppers, was afraid to speak up. Clem Henry might; Clem was the only one who might try to stop Arch, even if it meant trouble. And all of them knew that Arch would insist on running Clem out of the country, or filling him full of lead.

"I reckon it's all right with you, ain't it, Lonnie?" Arch said. "I don't seem to hear no objections."

Clem Henry stepped forward several paces, and stopped.

Arch laughed, watching Lonnie's face, and jerked Nancy to her feet. The hound cried out in pain and surprise, but Arch made her be quiet by kicking her in the belly.

Lonnie winced. He could hardly bear to see anybody kick his dog like that.

"Mr. Arch, I . . ."

A contraction in his throat almost choked him for several moments, and he had to open his mouth wide and fight for breath. The other white men around him were silent. Nobody liked to see a dog kicked in the belly like that.

Lonnie could see the other end of the filling station from the corner of his eye. He saw a couple of Negroes go up behind Clem and grasp his overalls. Clem spat on the ground, between outspread feet, but he did not try to break away from them.

"Being as how I don't hear no objections, I reckon it's all right to go ahead and cut it off," Arch said, spitting.

Lonnie's head went forward and all he could see of Nancy was her hind feet. He had come to ask for a slab of sowbelly and some molasses, or something. Now he did not know if he could ever bring himself to ask for rations, no matter how much hungrier they became at home.

"I always make it a habit of asking a man first," Arch said. "I wouldn't want to go ahead and cut off a tail if a man had any objections. That wouldn't be right. No, sir, it just wouldn't be fair and square."

Arch caught a shorter grip on the hound's tail and placed the knife blade on it two or three inches from the rump. It looked to those who were watching as if his mouth were watering, because tobacco juice began to trickle down the corners of his lips. He brought up the back of his hand and wiped his mouth.

A noisy automobile came plowing down the road through the deep red dust. Everyone looked up as it passed in order to see who was in it.

Lonnie glanced at it, but he could not keep his eyes raised. His head fell downward once more until he could feel his sharp chin cutting into his chest. He wondered then if Arch had noticed how lean his face was.

"I keep two or three ketch hounds around my place," Arch said, honing the blade on the tail of the dog as if it were a razor strop until his actions brought smiles to the faces of the men grouped around him, "but I never could see the sense of a ketch hound having a long tail. It only gets in their way when I send them out to catch a pig or a rabbit for my supper."

Pulling with his left hand and pushing with his right, Arch Gunnard docked the hound's tail as quickly and as easily as if he were cutting a willow switch in the pasture to drive the cows home with. The dog sprang forward with the release of her tail until she was far beyond Arch's reach, and began howling so loud she could be heard half a mile away. Nancy stopped once and looked back at Arch, and then she sprang to the middle of the road and began leaping and twisting in circles. All that time she was yelping and biting at the bleeding stub of her tail.

Arch leaned backward and twirled the severed tail in one hand while he wiped the jackknife blade on his boot sole. He watched Lonnie's dog chasing herself around in circles in the red dust.

Nobody had anything to say then. Lonnie tried not to watch his dog's agony, and he forced himself to keep from looking at Clem Henry. Then, with his eyes shut, he wondered why he had remained on Arch Gunnard's plantation all those past years, sharecropping for a mere living on short rations, and becoming leaner and leaner all the time. He knew then how true it was what Clem had said about Arch's sharecroppers' faces becoming sharp enough to hew their own coffins. His hands went to his chin before he knew what he was doing. His hand dropped when he had felt the bones of jaw and the exposed tendons of his cheeks.

As hungry as he was, he knew that even if Arch did give him some rations then, there would not be nearly enough for them to eat for the following week. Hatty, his wife, was already broken down from hunger and work in the fields, and his father, Mark Newsome, stone-deaf for the past twenty years, was always asking him why there was never enough food in the house for them to have a solid meal. Lonnie's head fell forward a little more, and he could feel his eyes becoming damp.

The pressure of his sharp chin against his chest made him so uncomfortable that he had to raise his head at last in order to ease the pain of it.

The first thing he saw when he looked up was Arch Gunnard twirling Nancy's tail in his left hand. Arch Gunnard had a trunk full of dogs' tails at home. He had been cutting off tails ever since anyone could remember, and during all those years he had accumulated a collection of which he was so proud that he kept the trunk locked and the key tied around his neck on a string. On Sunday afternoons when the preacher came to visit, or when a crowd was there to loll on the front porch and swap stories, Arch showed them off, naming each tail from memory just as well as if he had had a tag on it.

Clem Henry had left the filling station and was walking alone down the road towards the plantation. Clem Henry's house was in a cluster of Negro cabins below Arch's big house, and he had to pass Lonnie's house to get there. Lonnie was on the verge of getting up and leaving when he saw Arch looking at him. He did not know whether Arch was looking at his lean face, or whether he was watching to see if he were going to get up and go down the road with Clem.

The thought of leaving reminded him of his reason for being there. He had to have some rations before suppertime that night, no matter how short they were.

"Mr. Arch, I . . ."

Arch stared at him for a moment, appearing as if he had turned to listen to some strange sound unheard of before that moment.

Lonnie bit his lips, wondering if Arch was going to say anything about how lean and hungry he looked. But Arch was thinking about something else. He slapped his hand on his leg and laughed out loud.

"I sometimes wish niggers had tails," Arch said, coiling Nancy's tail into a ball and putting it into his pocket. "I'd a heap rather cut off nigger tails than dog tails. There'd be more to cut, for one thing."

Dudley Smith and somebody else behind them laughed for a brief moment. The laughter died out almost as suddenly as it had risen.

The Negroes who had heard Arch shuffled their feet in the dust and moved backwards. It was only a few minutes until not one was left at the filling station. They went up the road behind the red wooden building until they were out of sight.

Arch got up and stretched. The sun was getting low, and it was no longer comfortable in the October air. "Well, I reckon I'll be getting on home to get me some supper," he said.

He walked slowly to the middle of the road and stopped to look at Nancy retreating along the ditch.

"Nobody going my way?" he asked. "What's wrong with you, Lonnie? Going home to supper, ain't you?"

"Mr. Arch, I . . ."

Lonnie found himself jumping to his feet. His first thought was to ask for the sowbelly and molasses, and maybe some corn meal; but when he opened his mouth, the words refused to come out. He took several steps forward and shook his head. He did not know what Arch might say or do if he said "No."

"Hatty'll be looking for you," Arch said, turning his back and walking off.

He reached into his hip pocket and took out Nancy's tail. He began twirling it as he walked down the road towards the big house in the distance.

Dudley Smith went inside the filling station, and the others walked away.

After Arch had gone several hundred yards, Lonnie sat down heavily on the box beside the gas pump from which he had got up when Arch spoke to him. He sat down heavily, his shoulders drooping, his arms falling between his outspread legs.

Lonnie did not know how long his eyes had been closed, but when he opened them, he saw Nancy lying between his feet, licking the docked tail. While he watched her, he felt the sharp point of his chin cutting into his chest again. Presently the door behind him was slammed shut, and a minute later he could hear Dudley Smith walking away from the filling station on his way home.

II

Lonnie had been sleeping fitfully for several hours when he suddenly found himself wide awake. Hatty shook him again. He raised himself on his elbow and tried to see into the darkness of the room. Without knowing what time it was, he was able to determine that it was still nearly two hours until sunrise.

"Lonnie," Hatty said again, trembling in the cold night air, "Lonnie, your pa ain't in the house."

Lonnie sat upright in bed.

"How do you know he ain't?" he said.

"I've been lying here wide awake ever since I got in bed, and I heard him when he went out. He's been gone all that time."

"Maybe he just stepped out for a while," Lonnie said, turning and trying to see through the bedroom window.

"I know what I'm saying, Lonnie," Hatty insisted. "Your pa's been gone a heap too long."

Both of them sat without a sound for several minutes while they listened for Mark Newsome.

Lonnie got up and lit a lamp. He shivered while he was putting on his shirt, overalls, and shoes. He tied his shoelaces in hard knots because he couldn't see in the faint light. Outside the window it was almost pitch-dark, and Lonnie could feel the damp October air blowing against his face.

"I'll go help look," Hatty said, throwing the covers off and starting to get up.

Lonnie went to the bed and drew the covers back over her and pushed her back into place.

"You try to get some sleep, Hatty," he said; "you can't stay awake the whole night. I'll go bring Pa back."

He left Hatty, blowing out the lamp, and stumbled through the dark hall, feeling his way to the front porch by touching the wall with his hands. When he got to the porch, he could still barely see any distance ahead, but his eyes were becoming more accustomed to the darkness. He waited a minute, listening.

Feeling his way down the steps into the yard, he walked around the corner of the house and stopped to listen again before calling his father.

"Oh, Pa!" he said loudly. "Oh, Pa!"

He stopped under the bedroom window when he realized what he had been doing.

"Now that's a fool thing for me to be out here doing," he said, scolding himself. "Pa couldn't hear it thunder."

He heard a rustling of the bed.

"He's been gone long enough to get clear to the crossroads, or more," Hatty said, calling through the window.

"Now you lay down and try to get a little sleep, Hatty," Lonnie told her. "I'll bring him back in no time."

He could hear Nancy scratching fleas under the house, but he knew she was in no condition to help look for Mark. It would be several days before she recovered from the shock of losing her tail.

"He's been gone a long time," Hatty said, unable to keep still.

"That don't make no difference," Lonnie said. "I'll find him sooner or later. Now you go on to sleep like I told you, Hatty."

Lonnie walked towards the barn, listening for some sound. Over at the big house he could hear the hogs grunting and squealing, and he wished they would be quiet so he could hear other sounds. Arch Gunnard's dogs were howling occasionally, but they were not making any more noise than they usually did at night, and he was accustomed to their howling.

Lonnie went to the barn, looking inside and out. After walking around the barn, he went into the field as far as the cotton shed. He knew it was useless, but he could not keep from calling his father time after time.

"Oh, Pa!" he said, trying to penetrate the darkness.

He went farther into the field.

"Now, what in the world could have become of Pa?" he said, stopping and wondering where to look next.

After he had gone back to the front yard, he began to feel uneasy for the first time. Mark had not acted any more strangely during the past week than he ordinarily did, but Lonnie knew he was upset over the way

Arch Gunnard was giving out short rations. Mark had even said that, at the rate they were being fed, all of them would starve to death inside another three months.

Lonnie left the yard and went down the road towards the Negro cabins. When he got to Clem's house, he turned in and walked up the path to the door. He knocked several times and waited. There was no answer, and he rapped louder.

"Who's that?" he heard Clem say from bed.

"It's me," Lonnie said. "I've got to see you a minute, Clem. I'm out in the front yard."

He sat down and waited for Clem to dress and come outside. While he waited, he strained his ears to catch any sound that might be in the air. Over the fields towards the big house he could hear the fattening hogs grunt and squeal.

Clem came out and shut the door. He stood on the doorsill a moment speaking to his wife in bed, telling her he would be back and not to worry.

"Who's that?" Clem said, coming down into the yard.

Lonnie got up and met Clem halfway.

"What's the trouble?" Clem asked then, buttoning up his overall jumper.

"Pa's not in his bed," Lonnie said, "and Hatty says he's been gone from the house most all night. I went out in the field, and all around the barn, but I couldn't find a trace of him anywhere."

Clem then finished buttoning his jumper and began rolling a cigarette. He walked slowly down the path to the road. It was still dark, and it would be at least an hour before dawn made it any lighter.

"Maybe he was too hungry to stay in bed any longer," Clem said. "When I saw him yesterday, he said he was so shrunk up and weak he didn't know if he could last much longer. He looked like his skin and bones couldn't shrivel much more."

"I asked Arch last night after suppertime for some rations—just a little piece of sowbelly and some molasses. He said he'd get around to letting me have some the first thing this morning."

"Why don't you tell him to give you full rations or none?" Clem said. "If you knew you wasn't going to get none at all, you could move away and find a better man to sharecrop for, couldn't you?"

"I've been loyal to Arch Gunnard for a long time now," Lonnie said. "I'd hate to haul off and leave him like that."

Clem looked at Lonnie, but he did not say anything more just then. They turned up the road towards the driveway that led up to the big house. The fattening hogs were still grunting and squealing in the pen, and one of Arch's hounds came down a cotton row beside the driveway to smell their shoes.

"Them fattening hogs always get enough to eat," Clem said. "There's not a one of them that don't weigh seven hundred pounds right now, and they're getting bigger every day. Besides taking all that's thrown to them, they make a lot of meals off the chickens that get in there to peck around."

Lonnie listened to the grunting of the hogs as they walked up the driveway towards the big house.

"Reckon we'd better get Arch up to help look for Pa?" Lonnie said. "I'd hate to wake him up, but I'm scared Pa might stray off into the swamp and get lost for good. He couldn't hear it thunder, even. I never could find him back there in all that tangle if he got into it."

Clem said something under his breath and went on towards the barn and hog pen. He reached the pen before Lonnie got there.

"You'd better come here quick," Clem said, turning around to see where Lonnie was.

Lonnie ran to the hog pen. He stopped and climbed halfway up the wooden-and-wire sides of the fence. At first he could see nothing, but gradually he was able to see the moving mass of black fattening hogs on the other side of the pen. They were biting and snarling at each other like a pack of hungry hounds turned loose on a dead rabbit.

Lonnie scrambled to the top of the fence, but Clem caught him and pulled him back.

"Don't go in that hog pen that way," he said. "Them hogs will tear you to pieces, they're that wild. They're fighting over something."

Both of them ran around the corner of the pen and got to the side where the hogs were. Down under their feet on the ground Lonnie caught a glimpse of a dark mass splotched with white. He was able to see it for a moment only, because one of the hogs trampled over it.

Clem opened and closed his mouth several times before he was able to say anything at all. He clutched at Lonnie's arm, shaking him.

"That looks like it might be your pa," he said. "I swear before goodness, Lonnie, it does look like it."

Lonnie still could not believe it. He climbed to the top of the fence and began kicking his feet at the hogs, trying to drive them away. They paid no attention to him.

While Lonnie was perched there, Clem had gone to the wagon shed, and he ran back with two singletrees he had somehow managed to find there in the dark. He handed one to Lonnie, poking it at him until Lonnie's attention was drawn from the hogs long enough to take it.

Clem leaped over the fence and began swinging the singletree at the hogs. Lonnie slid down beside him, yelling at them. One hog turned on Lonnie and snapped at him, and Clem struck it over the back of the neck with enough force to drive it off momentarily.

By then Lonnie was able to realize what had happened. He ran to the mass of hogs, kicking them with his heavy stiff shoes and striking them on their heads with the iron-tipped singletree. Once he felt a stinging sensation, and looked down to see one of the hogs biting the calf of his leg. He had just enough time to hit the hog and drive it away before his leg was torn. He knew most of his overall leg had been ripped away, because he could feel the night air on his bare wet calf.

Clem had gone ahead and had driven the hogs back. There was no other way to do anything. They were in a snarling circle around them, and both of them had to keep the singletrees swinging back and forth all the time to keep the hogs off. Finally Lonnie reached down and got a grip on Mark's leg. With Clem helping, Lonnie carried his father to the fence and lifted him over to the other side.

They were too much out of breath for a while to say anything, or to do anything else. The snarling, fattening hogs were at the fence, biting the wood and wire, and making more noise than ever.

While Lonnie was searching in his pockets for a match, Clem struck one. He held the flame close to Mark Newsome's head.

They both stared unbelievingly, and then Clem blew out the match. There was nothing said as they stared at each other in the darkness.

Clem walked several steps away, and turned and came back beside Lonnie.

"It's him, though," Clem said, sitting down on the ground. "It's him, all right."

"I reckon so," Lonnie said. He could think of nothing else to say then.

They sat on the ground, one on each side of Mark, looking at the body. There had been no sign of life in the body beside them since they had first touched it. The face, throat, and stomach had been completely devoured.

"You'd better go wake up Arch Gunnard," Clem said after a while.

"What for?" Lonnie said. "He can't help none now. It's too late for help."

"Makes no difference," Clem insisted. "You'd better go wake him up and let him see what there is to see. If you wait till morning, he might take it into his head to say the hogs didn't do it. Right now is the time to get him up so he can see what his hogs did."

Clem turned around and looked at the big house. The dark outline against the dark sky made him hesitate.

"A man who short-rations tenants ought to have to sit and look at that till it's buried."

Lonnie looked at Clem fearfully. He knew Clem was right, but he was scared to hear a Negro say anything like that about a white man.

"You oughtn't talk like that about Arch," Lonnie said. "He's in bed asleep. He didn't have a thing to do with it. He didn't have no more to do with it than I did."

Clem laughed a little, and threw his singletree on the ground between his feet. After letting it lie there a little while, he picked it up and began beating the ground with it.

Lonnie got to his feet slowly. He had never seen Clem act like that before, and he did not know what to think about it. He left without saying anything and walked stiffly to the house in the darkness to wake up Arch Gunnard.

III

Arch was hard to wake up. And even after he was awake, he was in no hurry to get up. Lonnie was standing outside the bedroom window, and Arch was lying in bed six or eight feet away. Lonnie could hear him toss and grumble.

"Who told you to come and wake me up in the middle of the night?" Arch said.

"Well, Clem Henry's out here, and he said maybe you'd like to know about it."

Arch tossed around on the bed, flailing the pillow with his fists.

"You tell Clem Henry I said that one of these days he's going to find himself turned inside out, like a coat sleeve."

Lonnie waited doggedly. He knew Clem was right in insisting that Arch ought to wake up and come out there to see what had happened. Lonnie was afraid to go back to the barnyard and tell Clem that Arch was not coming. He did not know, but he had a feeling that Clem might go into the bedroom and drag Arch out of bed. He did not like to think of anything like that taking place.

"Are you still out there, Lonnie?" Arch shouted.

"I'm right here, Mr. Arch. I—"

"If I wasn't so sleepy, I'd come out there and take a stick and—I don't know what I wouldn't do!"

Lonnie met Arch at the back step. On the way out to the hog pen Arch did not speak to him. Arch walked heavily ahead, not even waiting to see if Lonnie was coming. The lantern that Arch was carrying cast long flat beams of yellow light over the ground; and when they got to where Clem was waiting beside Mark's body, the Negro's face shone in the night like a highly polished plowshare.

"What was Mark doing in my hog pen at night, anyway?" Arch said, shouting at them both.

Neither Clem nor Lonnie replied. Arch glared at them for not answering. But no matter how many times he looked at them, his eyes returned each time to stare at the torn body of Mark Newsome on the ground at his feet.

"There's nothing to be done now," Arch said finally. "We'll just have to wait till daylight and send for the undertaker." He walked a few steps away. "Looks like you could have waited till morning in the first place. There wasn't no sense in getting me up."

He turned his back and looked sideways at Clem. Clem stood up and looked him straight in the eyes.

"What do you want, Clem Henry?" he said. "Who told you to be coming around my house in the middle of the night? I don't want niggers coming here except when I send for them."

"I couldn't stand to see anybody eaten up by the hogs, and not do anything about it," Clem said.

"You mind your own business," Arch told him. "And when you talk to me, take off your hat, or you'll be sorry for it. It wouldn't take much to make me do you up the way you belong."

Lonnie backed away. There was a feeling of uneasiness around them. That was how trouble between Clem and Arch always began. He had seen it start that way dozens of times before. As long as Clem turned and went away, nothing happened, but sometimes he stayed right where he was and talked up to Arch just as if he had been a white man, too.

Lonnie hoped it would not happen this time. Arch was already mad enough about being waked up in the middle of the night, and Lonnie knew there was no limit to what Arch would do when he got good and mad at a Negro. Nobody had ever seen him kill a Negro, but he had said he had, and he told people that he was not scared to do it again.

"I reckon you know how he came to get eaten up by the hogs like that," Clem said, looking straight at Arch.

Arch whirled around.

"Are you talking to me . . .?"

"I asked you that," Clem stated.

"God damn you, yellow-blooded . . ." Arch yelled.

He swung the lantern at Clem's head. Clem dodged, but the bottom of it hit his shoulder, and it was smashed to pieces. The oil splattered on the ground, igniting in the air from the flaming wick. Clem was lucky not to have it splash on his face and overalls.

"Now, look here . . ." Clem said.

"You yellow-blooded nigger," Arch said, rushing at him. "I'll teach you to talk back to me. You've got too big for your place for the last time. I've been taking too much from you, but I ain't doing it no more."

"Mr. Arch, I . . ." Lonnie said, stepping forward partly between them. No one heard him.

Arch stood back and watched the kerosene flicker out on the ground.

"You know good and well why he got eaten up by the fattening hogs," Clem said, standing his ground. "He was so hungry he had to get up out of bed in the middle of the night and come up here in the dark trying to find something to eat. Maybe he was trying to find the smokehouse. It makes no difference, either way. He's been on short rations like everybody else working on your place, and he was so old he didn't know where else to look for food except in your smokehouse. You know good and well that's how he got lost up here in the dark and fell in the hog pen."

The kerosene had died out completely. In the last faint flare, Arch had reached down and grabbed up the singletree that had been lying on the ground where Lonnie had dropped it.

Arch raised the singletree over his head and struck with all his might at Clem. Clem dodged, but Arch drew back again quickly and landed a blow on his arm just above the elbow before Clem could dodge it. Clem's arm dropped to his side, dangling lifelessly.

"You God-damn yellow-blooded nigger!" Arch shouted. "Now's your time, you black bastard! I've been waiting for the chance to teach you your lesson. And this's going to be one you won't never forget."

Clem felt the ground with his feet until he had located the other singletree. He stooped down and got it. Raising it, he did not try to hit Arch, but held it in front of him so he could ward off Arch's blows at his head. He continued to stand his ground, not giving Arch an inch.

"Drop that singletree," Arch said.

"I won't stand here and let you beat me like that," Clem protested.

"By God, that's all I want to hear," Arch said, his mouth curling. "Nigger, your time has come, by God!"

He swung once more at Clem, but Clem turned and ran towards the barn. Arch went after him a few steps and stopped. He threw aside the singletree and turned and ran back to the house.

Lonnie went to the fence and tried to think what was best for him to do. He knew he could not take sides with a Negro, in the open, even if Clem had helped him, and especially after Clem had talked to Arch in the way he wished he could himself. He was a white man, and to save his life he could not stand to think of turning against Arch, no matter what happened.

Presently a light burst through one of the windows of the house, and he heard Arch shouting at his wife to wake her up.

When he saw Arch's wife go to the telephone, Lonnie realized what was going to happen. She was calling up the neighbors and Arch's friends. They would not mind getting up in the night when they found out what was going to take place.

Out behind the barn he could hear Clem calling him. Leaving the yard, Lonnie felt his way out there in the dark.

"What's the trouble, Clem?" he said.

"I reckon my time has come," Clem said. "Arch Gunnard talks that way when he's good and mad. He talked just like he did that time he carried Jim Moffin off to the swamp—and Jim never came back."

"Arch wouldn't do anything like that to you, Clem," Lonnie said excitedly, but he knew better.

Clem said nothing.

"Maybe you'd better strike out for the swamps till he changes his mind and cools off some," Lonnie said. "You might be right, Clem."

Lonnie could feel Clem's eyes burning into him.

"Wouldn't be no sense in that, if you'd help me," Clem said. "Wouldn't you stand by me?"

Lonnie trembled as the meaning of Clem's suggestion became clear to him. His back was to the side of the barn, and he leaned against it while sheets of black and white passed before his eyes.

"Wouldn't you stand by me?" Clem asked again.

"I don't know what Arch would say to that," Lonnie told him haltingly.

Clem walked away several paces. He stood with his back to Lonnie while he looked across the field towards the quarter where his home was.

"I could go in that little patch of woods out there and stay till they get tired of looking for me," Clem said, turning around to see Lonnie.

"You'd better go somewhere," Lonnie said uneasily. "I know Arch Gunnard. He's hard to handle when he makes up his mind to do something he wants to do. I couldn't stop him an inch. Maybe you'd better get clear out of the country, Clem."

"I couldn't do that, and leave my family down there across the field," Clem said.

"He's going to get you if you don't."

"If you'd only sort of help me out a little, he wouldn't. I would only have to go and hide out in that little patch of woods over there a while.

Looks like you could do that for me, being as how I helped you find your pa when he was in the hog pen."

Lonnie nodded, listening for sounds from the big house. He continued to nod at Clem while Clem was waiting to be assured.

"If you're going to stand up for me," Clem said, "I can just go over there in the woods and wait till they get it off their minds. You won't be telling them where I'm at, and you could say I struck out for the swamp. They wouldn't ever find me without bloodhounds."

"That's right," Lonnie said, listening for sounds of Arch's coming out of the house. He did not wish to be found back there behind the barn where Arch could accuse him of talking to Clem.

The moment Lonnie replied, Clem turned and ran off into the night. Lonnie went after him a few steps, as if he had suddenly changed his mind about helping him, but Clem was lost in the darkness by then.

Lonnie waited for a few minutes, listening to Clem crashing through the underbrush in the patch of woods a quarter of a mile away. When he could hear Clem no longer, he went around the barn to meet Arch.

Arch came out of the house carrying his double-barreled shotgun and the lantern he had picked up in the house. His pockets were bulging with shells.

"Where is that damn nigger, Lonnie?" Arch asked him. "Where'd he go to?"

Lonnie opened his mouth, but no words came out.

"You know which way he went, don't you?"

Lonnie again tried to say something, but there were no sounds. He jumped when he found himself nodding his head to Arch.

"Mr. Arch, I—"

"That's all right, then," Arch said. "That's all I need to know now, Dudley Smith and Tom Hawkins and Frank and Dave Howard and the rest will be here in a minute, and you can stay right here so you can show us where he's hiding out."

Frantically Lonnie tried to say something. Then he reached for Arch's sleeve to stop him, but Arch had gone.

Arch ran around the house to the front yard. Soon a car came racing down the road, its headlights lighting up the whole place, hog pen and all. Lonnie knew it was probably Dudley Smith, because his was the first house in that direction, only half a mile away. While he was turning into the driveway, several other automobiles came into sight, both up the road and down it.

Lonnie trembled. He was afraid Arch was going to tell him to point out where Clem had gone to hide. Then he knew Arch would tell him. He had promised Clem he would not do that. But try as he might, he could not make himself believe that Arch Gunnard would do anything more than whip Clem.

Clem had not done anything that called for lynching. He had not raped a white woman, he had not shot at a white man; he had only talked back to Arch, with his hat on. But Arch was mad enough to do anything; he was mad enough at Clem not to stop at anything short of lynching.

The whole crowd of men was swarming around him before he realized it. And there was Arch clutching his arm and shouting into his face.

"Mr. Arch, I—"

Lonnie recognized every man in the feeble dawn. They were excited, and they looked like men on the last lap of an all-night fox-hunting party. Their shotguns and pistols were held at their waist, ready for the kill.

"What's the matter with you, Lonnie?" Arch said, shouting into his ear. "Wake up and say where Clem Henry went to hide out. We're ready to go get him."

Lonnie remembered looking up and seeing Frank Howard dropping yellow twelve-gauge shells into the breech of his gun. Frank bent forward so he could hear Lonnie tell Arch where Clem was hiding.

"You ain't going to kill Clem this time, are you, Mr. Arch?" Lonnie asked.

"Kill him?" Dudley Smith repeated. "What do you reckon I've been waiting all this time for if it wasn't for a chance to get Clem. That nigger has had it coming to him ever since he came to this county. He's a bad nigger, and it's coming to him."

"It wasn't exactly Clem's fault," Lonnie said. "If Pa hadn't come up here and fell in the hog pen, Clem wouldn't have had a thing to do with it. He was helping me, that's all."

"Shut up, Lonnie," somebody shouted at him. "You're so excited you don't know what you're saying. You're taking up for a nigger when you talk like that."

People were crowding around him so tightly he felt as if he were being squeezed to death. He had to get some air, get his breath, get out of the crowd.

"That's right," Lonnie said.

He heard himself speak, but he did not know what he was saying.

"But Clem helped me find Pa when he got lost looking around for something to eat."

"Shut up, Lonnie," somebody said again. "You damn fool, shut up!"

Arch grabbed his shoulder and shook him until his teeth rattled. Then Lonnie realized what he had been saying.

"Now, look here, Lonnie," Arch shouted. "You must be out of your head, because you know good and well you wouldn't talk like a nigger-lover in your right mind."

"That's right," Lonnie said, trembling all over. "I sure wouldn't want to talk like that."

He could still feel the grip on his shoulder where Arch's strong fingers had hurt him.

"Did Clem go to the swamp, Lonnie?" Dudley Smith said. "Is that right, Lonnie?"

Lonnie tried to shake his head; he tried to nod his head. Then Arch's fingers squeezed his thin neck. Lonnie looked at the men wild-eyed.

"Where's Clem hiding, Lonnie?" Arch demanded, squeezing.

Lonnie went three or four steps towards the barn. When he stopped, the men behind him pushed forward again. He found himself being rushed behind the barn and beyond it.

"All right, Lonnie," Arch said. "Now which way?"

Lonnie pointed towards the patch of woods where the creek was. The swamp was in the other direction.

"He said he was going to hide out in that little patch of woods along the creek over there, Mr. Arch," Lonnie said. "I reckon he's over there now."

Lonnie felt himself being swept forward, and he stumbled over the rough ground trying to keep from being knocked down and trampled upon. Nobody was talking, and everyone seemed to be walking on tiptoes. The gray light of early dawn was increasing enough both to hide them and to show the way ahead.

Just before they reached the fringe of the woods, the men separated, and Lonnie found himself a part of the circle that was closing in on Clem.

Lonnie was alone, and there was nobody to stop him, but he was unable to move forward or backward. It began to be clear to him what he had done.

Clem was probably up a tree somewhere in the woods ahead, but by that time he had been surrounded on all sides. If he should attempt to break and run, he would be shot down like a rabbit.

Lonnie sat down on a log and tried to think what to do. The sun would be up in a few more minutes, and as soon as it came up, the men would close in on the creek and Clem. He would have no chance at all among all those shotguns and pistols.

Once or twice he saw the flare of a match through the underbrush where some of the men were lying in wait. A whiff of cigarette smoke struck his nostrils, and he found himself wondering if Clem could smell it wherever he was in the woods.

There was still no sound anywhere around him, and he knew that Arch Gunnard and the rest of the men were waiting for the sun, which would in a few minutes come up behind him in the east.

It was light enough by that time to see plainly the rough ground and the tangled underbrush and the curling bark on the pine trees.

The men had already begun to creep forward, guns raised as if stalking a deer. The woods were not large, and the circle of men would be able to cover it in a few minutes at the rate they were going forward. There was still a chance that Clem had slipped through the circle before dawn broke, but Lonnie felt that he was still there. He began to feel then that Clem was there because he himself had placed him there for the men to find more easily.

Lonnie found himself moving forward, drawn into the narrowing circle. Presently he could see the men all around him in dim outline. Their eyes were searching the heavy green pine tops as they went forward from tree to tree.

"Oh, Pa!" he said in a hoarse whisper. "Oh, Pa!"

He went forward a few steps, looking into the bushes and up into the treetops. When he saw the other men again, he realized that it was not Mark Newsome being sought. He did not know what had made him forget like that.

The creeping forward began to work into the movement of Lonnie's body. He found himself springing forward on his toes, and his body was leaning in that direction. It was like creeping up on a rabbit when you did not have a gun to hunt with.

He forgot again what he was doing there. The springing motion in his legs seemed to be growing stronger with each step. He bent forward so far he could almost touch the ground with his fingertips. He could not stop now. He was keeping up with the circle of men.

The fifteen men were drawing closer and closer together. The dawn had broken enough to show the time on the face of a watch. The sun was beginning to color the sky above.

Lonnie was far in advance of anyone else by then. He could not hold himself back. The strength in his legs was more than he could hold in check.

He had for so long been unable to buy shells for his gun that he had forgotten how much he liked to hunt.

The sound of the men's steady creeping had become a rhythm in his ears.

"Here's the bastard!" somebody shouted, and there was a concerted crashing through the dry underbrush. Lonnie dashed forward, reaching the tree almost as quickly as anyone else.

He could see everybody with guns raised, and far into the sky above the sharply outlined face of Clem Henry gleamed in the rising sun. His body was hugging the slender top of the pine.

Lonnie did not know who was the first to fire, but the rest of the men did not hesitate. There was a deafening roar as the shotguns and revolvers flared and smoked around the trunk of the tree.

He closed his eyes; he was afraid to look again at the face above. The firing continued without break. Clem hugged the tree with all his might, and then, with the faraway sound of splintering wood, the top of the tree and Clem came crashing through the lower limbs to the ground. The body, sprawling and torn, landed on the ground with a thud that stopped Lonnie's heart for a moment.

He turned, clutching for the support of a tree, as the firing began once more. The crumpled body was tossed time after time, like a sackful of kittens being killed with an automatic shotgun, as charges of lead were fired into it from all sides. A cloud of dust rose from the ground and drifted overhead with the choking odor of burned powder.

Lonnie did not remember how long the shooting lasted. He found himself running from tree to tree, clutching at the rough pine bark, stumbling wildly towards the cleared ground. The sky had turned from gray to red when he emerged in the open, and as he ran, falling over the hard clods in the plowed field, he tried to keep his eyes on the house ahead.

Once he fell and found it almost impossible to rise again to his feet. He struggled to his knees, facing the round red sun. The warmth gave him the strength to rise to his feet, and he muttered unintelligibly to himself. He tried to say things he had never thought to say before.

When he got home, Hatty was waiting for him in the yard. She had heard the shots in the woods, and she had seen him stumbling over the hard clods in the field, and she had seen him kneeling there looking straight into the face of the sun. Hatty was trembling as she ran to Lonnie to find out what the matter was.

Once in his own yard, Lonnie turned and looked for a second over his shoulder. He saw the men climbing over the fence at Arch Gunnard's. Arch's wife was standing on the back porch, and she was speaking to them.

"Where's your pa, Lonnie?" Hatty said. "And what in the world was all that shooting in the woods for?" Lonnie stumbled forward until he had reached the front porch. He fell upon the steps.

"Lonnie, Lonnie!" Hatty was saying. "Wake up and tell me what in the world is the matter. I've never seen the like of all that's going on."

"Nothing," Lonnie said. "Nothing."

"Well, if there's nothing the matter, can't you go up to the big house and ask for a little piece of streak-of-lean? We ain't got a thing to cook for breakfast. Your pa's going to be hungrier than ever after being up walking around all night."

"What?" Lonnie said, his voice rising to a shout as he jumped to his feet.

"Why, I only said go up to the big house and get a little piece of streak-of-lean, Lonnie. That's all I said."

He grabbed his wife about the shoulders.

"Meat?" he yelled, shaking her roughly.

"Yes," she said, pulling away from him in surprise. "Couldn't you go ask Arch Gunnard for a little bit of streak-of-lean?"

Lonnie slumped down again on the steps, his hands falling between his outspread legs and his chin falling on his chest.

"No," he said almost inaudibly. "No. I ain't hungry."

ISAAC BASHEVIS SINGER

Gimpel the Fool

I

I am Gimpel the fool. I don't think myself a fool. On the contrary. But that's what folks call me. They gave me the name while I was still in school. I had seven names in all: imbecile, donkey, flax-head, dope, glump, ninny, and fool. The last name stuck. What did my foolishness consist of? I was easy to take in. They said, "Gimpel, you know the rabbi's wife has been brought to childbed?" So I skipped school. Well, it turned out to be a lie. How was I supposed to know? She hadn't had a big belly. But I never looked at her belly. Was that really so foolish? The gang laughed and hee-hawed, stomped and danced and chanted a good-night prayer. And instead of the raisins they give when a woman's lying in, they stuffed my hand full of goat turds. I was no weakling. If I slapped someone he'd see all the way to Cracow. But I'm really not a slugger by nature. I think to myself: Let it pass. So they take advantage of me.

I was coming home from school and heard a dog barking. I'm not afraid of dogs, but of course I never want to start up with them. One of them may be mad, and if he bites there's not a Tartar in the world who can help you. So I made tracks. Then I looked around and saw the whole market place wild with laughter. It was no dog at all but Wolf-Leib the Thief. How was I supposed to know it was he? It sounded like a howling bitch.

When the pranksters and leg-pullers found that I was easy to fool, every one of them tried his luck with me. "Gimpel, the Czar is coming to Frampol; Gimpel, the moon fell down in Turbeen; Gimpel, little Hodel Furpiece found a treasure behind the bathhouse." And I like a golem believed everyone. In the first place, everything is possible, as it is written in the Wisdom of the Fathers, I've forgotten just how. Second, I had to believe when the whole town came down on me! If I ever dared to say, "Ah, you're kidding!" there was trouble. People got angry. "What do you mean! You want to call everyone a liar?" What was I to do? I believed them, and I hope at least that did them some good.

I was an orphan. My grandfather who brought me up was already bent toward the grave. So they turned me over to a baker, and what a time they gave me there! Every woman or girl who came to bake a batch of noodles had to fool me at least once. "Gimpel, there's a fair in heaven; Gimpel, the rabbi gave birth to a calf in the seventh month; Gimpel, a cow flew over the roof and laid brass eggs." A student from the yeshiva came once to buy a roll, and he said, "You, Gimpel, while you stand here scraping with your baker's shovel the Messiah has come. The dead have arisen." "What do you mean?" I said. "I heard no one blowing the ram's horn!" He said, "Are you deaf?" And all began to cry, "We heard it, we heard!" Then in came Rietze the Candle-dipper and called out in her hoarse voice, "Gimpel, your father and mother have stood up from the grave. They're looking for you."

To tell the truth, I knew very well that nothing of the sort had happened, but all the same, as folks were talking, I threw on my wool vest and went out. Maybe something had happened. What did I stand to lose by looking? Well, what a cat music went up! And then I took a vow to believe nothing more. But that was no go either. They confused me so that I didn't know the big end from the small.

I went to the rabbi to get some advice. He said, "It is written, better to be a fool all your days than for one hour to be evil. You are not a fool. They are the fools. For he who causes his neighbor to feel shame loses Paradise himself." Nevertheless the rabbi's daughter took me in. As I left the rabbinical court she said, "Have you kissed the wall yet?" I said, "No; what for?" She answered, "It's the law; you've got to do it after every visit." Well, there didn't seem to be any harm in it. And she burst out laughing. It was a fine trick. She put one over on me, all right.

I wanted to go off to another town, but then everyone got busy matchmaking, and they were after me so they nearly tore my coat tails off. They talked at me and talked until I got water on the ear. She was no chaste maiden, but they told me she was virgin pure. She had a limp, and they said it was deliberate, from coyness. She had a bastard, and they told me the child was her little brother. I cried, "You're wasting your time. I'll never marry that whore." But they said indignantly, "What a way to talk! Aren't you ashamed of yourself? We can take you to the rabbi and have you fined for giving her a bad name." I saw then that I wouldn't escape them so easily and I thought: They're set on making me their butt. But when you're married the husband's the master, and if that's all right with her it's agreeable to me too. Besides, you can't pass through life unscathed, nor expect to.

I went to her clay house, which was built on the sand, and the whole gang, hollering and chorusing, came after me. They acted like bear-baiters. When we came to the well they stopped all the same. They were afraid to start anything with Elka. Her mouth would open as if it were on a hinge, and she had a fierce tongue. I entered the house. Lines were strung from wall to wall and clothes were drying. Barefoot she stood by the tub, doing the wash. She was dressed in a worn hand-me-down gown of plush. She had her hair put up in braids and pinned across her head. It took my breath away, almost, the reek of it all.

Evidently she knew who I was. She took a look at me and said, "Look who's here! He's come, the drip. Grab a seat."

I told her all; I denied nothing. "Tell me the truth," I said, "are you really a virgin, and is that mischievous Yechiel actually your little brother? Don't be deceitful with me, for I'm an orphan."

"I'm an orphan myself," she answered, "and whoever tries to twist you up, may the end of his nose take a twist. But don't let them think they can take advantage of me. I want a dowry of fifty guilders, and let them take up a collection besides. Otherwise they can kiss my you-know-what." She was very plainspoken. I said, "It's the bride and not the groom who gives a dowry." Then she said, "Don't bargain with me. Either a flat 'yes' or a flat 'no'—Go back where you came from."

I thought: No bread will ever be baked from *this* dough. But ours is not a poor town. They consented to everything and proceeded with the wedding. It so happened that there was a dysentery epidemic at the time. The ceremony was held at the cemetery gates, near the little corpse-washing hut. The fellows got drunk. While the marriage contract was being drawn up I heard the most pious high rabbi ask, "Is the bride a widow or a divorced woman?" And the sexton's wife answered for her, "Both a widow and divorced." It was a black moment for me. But what was I to do, run away from under the marriage canopy?

There was singing and dancing. An old granny danced opposite me, hugging a braided white *chalah.* The master of revels made a "God 'a mercy" in memory of the bride's parents. The schoolboys threw burrs, as on Tishe b'Av fast day. There were a lot of gifts after the sermon: a noodle board, a kneading trough, a bucket, brooms, ladles, household articles galore. Then I took a look and saw two strapping young men carrying a crib. "What do we need this for?" I asked. So they said, "Don't rack your brains about it. It's all right, it'll come in handy." I realized I was going to be rooked. Take it another way though, what did I stand to lose? I reflected: I'll see what comes of it. A whole town can't go altogether crazy.

2

At night I came where my wife lay, but she wouldn't let me in. "Say, look here, is this what they married us for?" I said. And she said, "My monthly has come." "But yesterday they took you to the ritual bath, and that's afterward, isn't it supposed to be?" "Today isn't yesterday," said she, "and yesterday's not today. You can beat it if you don't like it." In short, I waited.

Not four months later she was in childbed. The townsfolk hid their laughter with their knuckles. But what could I do? She suffered intolerable pains and clawed at the walls. "Gimpel," she cried, "I'm going. Forgive me!" The house filled with women. They were boiling pans of water. The screams rose to the welkin.

The thing to do was to go to the House of Prayer to repeat Psalms, and that was what I did.

The townsfolk liked that, all right. I stood in a corner saying Psalms and prayers, and they shook their heads at me. "Pray, pray!" they told me. "Prayer never made any woman pregnant." One of the congregation put a straw to my mouth and said, "Hay for the cows." There was something to that too, by God!

She gave birth to a boy. Friday at the synagogue the sexton stood up before the Ark, pounded on the reading table, and announced, "The wealthy Reb Gimpel invites the congregation to a feast in honor of the birth of a son." The whole House of Prayer rang with laughter. My face was flaming. But there was nothing I could do. After all, I *was* the one responsible for the circumcision honors and rituals.

Half the town came running. You couldn't wedge another soul in. Women brought peppered chick-peas, and there was a keg of beer from the tavern. I ate and drank as much as anyone, and they all congratulated me. Then there was a circumcision, and I named the boy after my father, may he rest in peace. When all were gone and I was left with my wife alone, she thrust her head through the bed-curtain and called me to her.

"Gimpel," said she, "why are you silent? Has your ship gone and sunk?"

"What shall I say?" I answered. "A fine thing you've done to me! If my mother had known of it she'd have died a second time."

She said, "Are you crazy, or what?"

"How can you make such a fool," I said, "of one who should be the lord and master?"

"What's the matter with you?" she said. "What have you taken it into your head to imagine?"

I saw that I must speak bluntly and openly. "Do you think this is the way to use an orphan?" I said. "You have borne a bastard."

She answered, "Drive this foolishness out of your head. The child is yours."

"How can he be mine?" I argued. "He was born seventeen weeks after the wedding."

She told me then that he was premature. I said, "Isn't he a little too premature?" She said, she had had a grandmother who carried just as short a time and she resembled this grandmother of hers as one drop of water does another. She swore to it with such oaths that you would have believed a peasant at the fair if he had used them. To tell the plain truth, I didn't believe her; but when I talked it over next day with the schoolmaster he told me that the very same thing had happened to Adam and Eve. Two they went up to bed, and four they descended.

"There isn't a woman in the world who is not the granddaughter of Eve," he said.

That was how it was; they argued me dumb. But then, who really knows how such things are?

I began to forget my sorrow. I loved the child madly, and he loved me too. As soon as he saw me he'd wave his little hands and want me to pick him up, and when he was colicky I was the only one who could pacify him. I bought him a little bone teething ring and a little gilded cap. He was forever catching the evil eye from someone, and then I had to run to get one of those abracadabras for him that would get him out of it. I worked like an ox. You know how expenses go up when there's an infant in the house. I don't want to lie about it; I didn't dislike Elka either, for that matter. She swore at me and cursed, and I couldn't get enough of her. What strength she had! One of her looks could rob you of the power of speech. And her orations! Pitch and sulphur, that's what they were full of, and yet somehow also full of charm. I adored her every word. She gave me bloody wounds though.

In the evening I brought her a white loaf as well as a dark one, and also poppyseed rolls I baked myself. I thieved because of her and swiped everything I could lay hands on: macaroons, raisins, almonds, cakes. I hope I may be forgiven for stealing from the Saturday pots the women left to warm in the baker's oven. I would take out scraps of meat, a chunk of pudding, a chicken leg or head, a piece of tripe, whatever I could nip quickly. She ate and became fat and handsome.

I had to sleep away from home all during the week, at the bakery. On Friday nights when I got home she always made an excuse of some sort. Either she had heartburn, or a stitch in the side, or hiccups, or headaches. You know what women's excuses are. I had a bitter time of it. It was rough. To add to it, this little brother of hers, the bastard, was growing bigger. He'd put lumps on me, and when I wanted to hit back she'd open her mouth and curse so powerfully I saw a green haze floating before my eyes. Ten times a day she threatened to divorce me. Another man in my place would have taken French leave and disappeared. But I'm the type that bears it and says nothing. What's one to do? Shoulders are from God, and burdens too.

One night there was a calamity in the bakery; the oven burst, and we almost had a fire. There was nothing to do but go home, so I went home. Let me, I thought, also taste the joy of sleeping in bed in mid-week. I didn't want to wake the sleeping mite and tiptoed into the house. Coming in, it seemed to me that I heard not the snoring of one but, as it were, a double snore, one a thin enough snore and the other like the snoring of a slaughtered ox. Oh, I didn't like that! I didn't like it at all. I went up to the bed, and things suddenly turned black. Next to Elka lay a man's form. Another in my place would have made an uproar, and enough noise to rouse the whole town, but the thought occurred to me that I might wake the child. A little thing like that—why frighten a little swallow, I thought. All right then, I went back to the bakery and stretched out on a sack of flour and till morning I never shut an eye. I shivered as if I had had malaria. "Enough of being a donkey," I said to myself. "Gimpel isn't going to be a sucker all his life. There's a limit even to the foolishness of a fool like Gimpel."

In the morning I went to the rabbi to get advice, and it made a great commotion in the town. They sent the beadle for Elka right away. She came, carrying the child. And what do you think she did? She denied it, denied everything, bone and stone! "He's out of his head," she said. "I know nothing of dreams or divinations." They yelled at her, warned her, hammered on the table, but she stuck to her guns: it was a false accusation, she said.

The butchers and the horse-traders took her part. One of the lads from the slaughterhouse came by and said to me, "We've got our eye on you, you're a marked man." Meanwhile the child started to bear down and soiled itself. In the rabbinical court there was an Ark of the Covenant, and they couldn't allow that, so they sent Elka away.

I said to the rabbi, "What shall I do?"

"You must divorce her at once," said he.

"And what if she refuses?" I asked.

He said, "You must serve the divorce. That's all you'll have to do."

I said, "Well, all right, Rabbi. Let me think about it."

"There's nothing to think about," said he. "You mustn't remain under the same roof with her."

"And if I want to see the child?" I asked.

"Let her go, the harlot," said he, "and her brood of bastards with her."

The verdict he gave was that I mustn't even cross her threshold—never again, as long as I should live.

During the day it didn't bother me so much. I thought: It was bound to happen, the abscess had to burst. But at night when I stretched out upon the sacks I felt it all very bitterly. A longing took me, for her and for the child. I wanted to be angry, but that's my misfortune exactly, I don't have it in me to be really angry. In the first place—this was how my thoughts went—there's bound to be a slip sometimes. You can't live without errors. Probably that lad who was with her led her on and gave her presents and what not, and women are often long on hair and short on sense, and so he got around her. And then since she denies it so, maybe I was only seeing things? Hallucinations do happen. You see a figure or a mannikin or something, but when you come up closer it's nothing, there's not a thing there. And if that's so, I'm doing her an injustice. And when I got so far in my thoughts I started to weep. I sobbed so that I wet the flour where I lay. In the morning I went to the rabbi and told him that I had made a mistake. The rabbi wrote on with his quill, and he said that if that were so he would have to reconsider the whole case. Until he had finished I wasn't to go near my wife, but I might send her bread and money by messenger.

3

Nine months passed before all the rabbis could come to an agreement. Letters went back and forth. I hadn't realized that there could be so much erudition about a matter like this.

Meanwhile Elka gave birth to still another child, a girl this time. On the Sabbath I went to the synagogue and invoked a blessing on her. They called me up to the Torah, and I named the child for my mother-in-law—may she rest in peace. The louts and loudmouths of the town who came into the bakery gave me a going over. All Frampol refreshed its spirits because of my trouble and grief. However, I resolved that I would always believe what I was told. What's the good of *not* believing? Today it's your wife you don't believe; tomorrow it's God Himself you won't take stock in.

By an apprentice who was her neighbor I sent her daily a corn or a wheat loaf, or a piece of pastry, rolls or bagels, or, when I got the chance, a slab of pudding, a slice of honeycake, or wedding strudel—whatever came my way. The apprentice was a goodhearted lad, and more than once he added something on his own. He had formerly annoyed me a lot, plucking my nose and digging me in the ribs, but when he started to be a visitor to my house he became kind and friendly. "Hey, you, Gimpel," he said to me, "you have a very decent little wife and two fine kids. You don't deserve them."

"But the things people say about her," I said.

"Well, they have long tongues," he said, "and nothing to do with them but babble. Ignore it as you ignore the cold of last winter."

One day the rabbi sent for me and said, "Are you certain, Gimpel, that you were wrong about your wife?"

I said, "I'm certain."

"Why, but look here! You yourself saw it."

"It must have been a shadow," I said.

"The shadow of what?"

"Just of one of the beams, I think."

"You can go home then. You owe thanks to the Yanover rabbi. He found an obscure reference in Maimonides that favored you."

I seized the rabbi's hand and kissed it.

I wanted to run home immediately. It's no small thing to be separated for so long a time from wife and child. Then I reflected: I'd better go back to work now, and go home in the evening. I said nothing to anyone, although as far as my heart was concerned it was like one of the Holy Days. The women teased and twitted me as they did every day, but my thought was: Go on, with your loose talk. The truth is out, like the oil upon the water. Maimonides says it's right, and therefore it is right!

At night, when I had covered the dough to let it rise, I took my share of bread and a little sack of flour and started homeward. The moon was full and the stars were glistening, something to terrify the soul. I hurried onward, and before me darted a long shadow. It was winter, and a fresh snow had fallen. I had a mind to sing, but it was growing late and I didn't want to wake the householders. Then I felt like whistling, but I remembered that you don't whistle at night because it brings the demons out. So I was silent and walked as fast as I could.

Dogs in the Christian yards barked at me when I passed, but I thought: Bark your teeth out! What are you but mere dogs? Whereas I am a man, the husband of a fine wife, the father of promising children.

As I approached the house my heart started to pound as though it were the heart of a criminal. I felt no fear, but my heart went thump! thump! Well, no drawing back. I quietly lifted the latch and went in. Elka was asleep. I looked at the infant's cradle. The shutter was closed, but the moon forced its way through the cracks. I saw the newborn child's face and loved it as soon as I saw it—immediately—each tiny bone.

Then I came nearer to the bed. And what did I see but the apprentice lying there beside Elka. The moon went out all at once. It was utterly black, and I trembled. My teeth chattered. The bread fell from my hands, and my wife waked and said, "Who is that, ah?"

I muttered, "It's me."

"Gimpel?" she asked. "How come you're here? I thought it was forbidden."

"The rabbi said," I answered and shook as with a fever.

"Listen to me, Gimpel," she said, "go out to the shed and see if the goat's all right. It seems she's been sick." I have forgotten to say that we had a goat. When I heard she was unwell I went into the yard. The nannygoat was a good little creature. I had a nearly human feeling for her.

With hesitant steps I went up to the shed and opened the door. The goat stood there on her four feet. I felt her everywhere, drew her by the horns, examined her udders, and found nothing wrong. She had probably eaten too much bark. "Good night, little goat," I said. "Keep well." And the little beast answered with a "Maa" as though to thank me for the good will.

I went back. The apprentice had vanished.

"Where," I asked, "is the lad?"

"What lad?" my wife answered.

"What do you mean?" I said. "The apprentice. You were sleeping with him."

"The things I have dreamed this night and the night before," she said, "may they come true and lay you low, body and soul! An evil spirit has taken root in you and dazzles your sight." She screamed out, "You hateful creature! You moon calf! You spook! You uncouth man! Get out, or I'll scream all Frampol out of bed!"

Before I could move, her brother sprang out from behind the oven and struck me a blow on the back of the head. I thought he had broken my neck. I felt that something about me was deeply wrong, and I said, "Don't make a scandal. All that's needed now is that people should accuse me of raising spooks and *dybbuks.*" For that was what she had meant. "No one will touch bread of my baking."

In short, I somehow calmed her.

"Well," she said, "that's enough. Lie down, and be shattered by wheels."

Next morning I called the apprentice aside. "Listen here, brother!" I said. And so on and so forth. "What do you say?" He stared at me as though I had dropped from the roof or something.

"I swear," he said, "you'd better go to an herb doctor or some healer. I'm afraid you have a screw loose, but I'll hush it up for you." And that's how the thing stood.

To make a long story short, I lived twenty years with my wife. She bore me six children, four daughters and two sons. All kinds of things happened, but I neither saw nor heard. I believed, and that's all. The rabbi recently said to me, "Belief in itself is beneficial. It is written that a good man lives by his faith."

Suddenly my wife took sick. It began with a trifle, a little growth upon the breast. But she evidently was not destined to live long; she had no years. I spent a fortune on her. I have forgotten to say that by this time I had a bakery of my own and in Frampol was considered to be something of a rich man. Daily the healer came, and every witch doctor in the neighborhood was brought. They decided to use leeches, and after that to try cupping. They even called a doctor from Lublin, but it was too late. Before she died she called me to her bed and said, "Forgive me, Gimpel."

I said, "What is there to forgive? You have been a good and faithful wife."

"Woe, Gimpel!" she said. "It was ugly how I deceived you all these years. I want to go clean to my Maker, and so I have to tell you that the children are not yours."

If I had been clouted on the head with a piece of wood it couldn't have bewildered me more.

"Whose are they?" I asked.

"I don't know," she said. "There were a lot . . . but they're not yours." And as she spoke she tossed her head to the side, her eyes turned glassy, and it was all up with Elka. On her whitened lips there remained a smile.

I imagined that, dead as she was, she was saying, "I deceived Gimpel. That was the meaning of my brief life."

4

One night, when the period of mourning was done, as I lay dreaming on the flour sacks, there came the Spirit of Evil himself and said to me, "Gimpel, why do you sleep?"

I said, "What should I be doing? Eating *kreplach?*"

"The whole world deceives you," he said, "and you ought to deceive the world in your turn."

"How can I deceive all the world?" I asked him.

He answered, "You might accumulate a bucket of urine every day and at night pour it into the dough. Let the sages of Frampol eat filth."

"What about the judgment in the world to come?" I said.

"There is no world to come," he said. "They've sold you a bill of goods and talked you into believing you carried a cat in your belly. What nonsense!"

"Well then," I said, "and is there a God?"

He answered, "There is no God either."

"What," I said, "*is* there, then?"

"A thick mire."

He stood before my eyes with a goatish beard and horn, long-toothed, and with a tail. Hearing such words, I wanted to snatch him by the tail, but I tumbled from the flour sacks and nearly broke a rib. Then it happened that I had to answer the call of nature, and, passing, I saw the risen dough, which seemed to say to me, "Do it!" In brief, I let myself be persuaded.

At dawn the apprentice came. We kneaded the bread, scattered caraway seeds on it, and set it to bake. Then the apprentice went away, and I was left sitting in the little trench by the oven, on a pile of rags. Well, Gimpel, I thought, you've revenged yourself on them for all the shame they've put on you. Outside the frost glittered, but it was warm beside the oven. The flames heated my face. I bent my head and fell into a doze.

I saw in a dream, at once, Elka in her shroud. She called to me, "What have you done, Gimpel?"

I said to her, "It's all your fault," and started to cry.

"You fool!" she said. "You fool! Because I was false is everything false too? I never deceived anyone but myself. I'm paying for it all, Gimpel. They spare you nothing here."

I looked at her face. It was black; I was startled and waked, and remained sitting dumb. I sensed that everything hung in the balance. A false step now and I'd lose Eternal Life. But God gave me His help. I seized the long shovel and took out the loaves, carried them into the yard, and started to dig a hole in the frozen earth.

My apprentice came back as I was doing it. "What are you doing boss?" he said, and grew pale as a corpse.

"I know what I'm doing," I said, and I buried it all before his very eyes.

Then I went home, took my hoard from its hiding place, and divided it among the children. "I saw your mother tonight," I said. "She's turning black, poor thing."

They were so astounded they couldn't speak a word.

"Be well," I said, "and forget that such a one as Gimpel ever existed." I put on my short coat, a pair of boots, took the bag that held my prayer shawl in one hand, my stock in the other, and kissed the *mezzuzah.* When people saw me in the street they were greatly surprised.

"Where are you going?" they said.

I answered, "Into the world." And so I departed from Frampol.

I wandered over the land, and good people did not neglect me. After many years I became old and white; I heard a great deal, many lies and falsehoods, but the longer I lived the more I understood that there were really no lies. Whatever doesn't really happen is dreamed at night. It happens to one if it doesn't happen to another, tomorrow if not today, or a century hence if not next year. What difference can it make? Often I heard tales of which I said, "Now this is a thing that cannot happen." But before a year had elapsed I heard that it actually had come to pass somewhere.

Going from place to place, eating at strange tables, it often happens that I spin yarns—improbable things that could never have happened—about devils, magicians, windmills, and the like. The children run after me, calling, "Grandfather, tell us a story." Sometimes they ask for particular stories, and I try to please them. A fat young boy once said to me, "Grandfather, it's the same story you told us before." The little rogue, he was right.

So it is with dreams too. It is many years since I left Frampol, but as soon as I shut my eyes I am there again. And whom do you think I see? Elka. She is standing by the washtub, as at our first encounter, but her face is shining and her eyes are as radiant as the eyes of a saint, and she speaks outlandish words to me, strange things. When I wake I have forgotten it all. But while the dream lasts I am comforted. She answers all my queries, and what comes out is that all is right. I weep and implore, "Let me be with you." And she consoles me and tells me to be patient. The time is nearer than it is far. Sometimes she strokes and kisses me and weeps upon my face. When I awaken I feel her lips and taste the salt of her tears.

No doubt the world is entirely an imaginary world, but it is only once removed from the true world. At the door of the hovel where I lie, there stands the plank on which the dead are taken away. The gravedigger Jew has his spade ready. The grave waits and the worms are hungry; the shrouds are prepared—I carry them in my beggar's sack. Another *shnorrer* is waiting to inherit my bed of straw. When the time comes I will go joyfully. Whatever may be there, it will be real, without complication, without ridicule, without deception. God be praised: there even Gimpel cannot be deceived.

JOHN O'HARA

Over the River and Through the Wood

Mr. Winfield's hat and coat and bag were in the hall of his flat, and when the man downstairs phoned to tell him the car was waiting, he was all ready. He went downstairs and said hello to Robert, the giant Negro chauffeur, and handed Robert the bag, and followed him out to the car. For the first time he knew that he and his granddaughter were not to make the trip alone, for there were two girls with Sheila, and she introduced them: "Grandfather, I'd like to have you meet my friends. This is Helen Wales, and this is Kay Farnsworth. My grandfather, Mr. Winfield." The names meant nothing to Mr. Winfield. What did mean something was that he was going to have to sit on the strapontin, or else sit outside with Robert, which was no good. Not that Robert wasn't all right, as chauffeurs go, but Robert was wearing a raccoon coat, and Mr. Winfield had no raccoon coat. So it was sit outside and freeze or sit on the little seat inside.

Apparently it made no difference to Sheila. He got inside, and when he closed the door behind him, she said, "I wonder what's keeping Robert?"

"He's strapping my bag on that thing in the back," said Mr. Winfield. Sheila obviously was not pleased by the delay, but in a minute or two they got under way, and Mr. Winfield rather admired the way Sheila carried on her conversation with her two friends and at the same time routed and rerouted Robert so that they were out of the city in no time. To Mr. Winfield it was pleasant and a little like old times to have the direction and the driving done for you. Not that he ever drove himself anymore, but when he hired a car, he always had to tell the driver just where to turn and where to go straight. Sheila knew.

The girls were of an age, and the people they talked about were referred to by first names only. Ted, Bob, Gwen, Jean, Mary, Liz. Listening with some care, Mr. Winfield discovered that school acquaintances and boys whom they knew slightly were mentioned by their last names.

Sitting where he was, he could not watch the girls' faces, but he formed his opinions of the Misses Wales and Farnsworth. Miss Wales supplied every other word when Sheila was talking. She was the smallest of the three girls, and the peppy kind. Miss Farnsworth looked out of the window most of the time, and said hardly anything. Mr. Winfield could see more of her face, and he found himself asking, "I wonder if that child really likes anybody." Well, that was one way to be. Make the world show *you.* You could get away with it, too, if you were as attractive as Miss Farnsworth. The miles streamed by and the weather got colder, and Mr. Winfield listened and soon understood that he was not expected to contribute to the conversation.

"We stop here," said Sheila. It was Danbury, and they came to a halt in front of the old hotel. "Wouldn't you like to stop here, Grandfather?" He understood then that his daughter had told Sheila to stop here; obediently and with no dignity he got out. When he returned to the car, the three girls were finishing their cigarettes, and as he climbed back in the car, he noticed how Miss Farnsworth had been looking at him and continued to look at him, almost as though she were making a point of not helping him—although he wanted no help. He wasn't really an *old* man, an *old man.* Sixty-five.

The interior of the car was filled with cigarette smoke, and Miss

Farnsworth asked Mr. Winfield if he'd mind opening a window. He opened it. Then Sheila said one window didn't make any difference; open both windows, just long enough to let the smoke get out. "My! That air feels good," said Miss Wales. Then: "But what about you, Mr. Winfield? You're in a terrible draught there." He replied, for the first use of his voice thus far, that he did not mind. And at that moment the girls thought they saw a car belonging to a boy they knew, and they were in Sheffield, just over the Massachusetts line, before Miss Farnsworth realized that the windows were open and creating a terrible draught. She realized it when the robe slipped off her leg, and she asked Mr. Winfield if he would mind closing the window. But he was unable to get the crank started; his hands were so cold there was no strength in them. "We'll be there soon," said Sheila. Nevertheless, she closed the windows, not even acknowledging Mr. Winfield's shamed apologies.

He had to be first out of the car when they arrived at the house in Lenox, and it was then that he regretted having chosen the strapontin. He started to get out of the car, but when his feet touched the ground, the hardpacked frozen cinders of the driveway flew up at him. His knees had no strength in them, and he stayed there on the ground for a second or two, trying to smile it off. Helpful Robert—almost too helpful; Mr. Winfield wasn't that old—jumped out of the car and put his hands in Mr. Winfield's armpits. The girls were frightened, but it seemed to Mr. Winfield that they kept looking toward the library window, as though they were afraid Sheila's mother would be there and blaming them for his fall. If they only knew. . . .

"You go on in, Grandfather, if you're sure you're all right," said Sheila. "I have to tell Robert about the bags."

"I'm all right," said Mr. Winfield. He went in, and hung up his coat and hat in the clothes closet under the stairs. A telephone was there, and in front of the telephone a yellow card of numbers frequently called. Mr. Winfield recognized only a few of the names, but he guessed there was an altogether different crowd of people coming up here these days. Fifteen years make a difference, even in a place like Lenox. Yes, it was fifteen years since he had been up here in the summertime. These trips, these annual trips for Thanksgiving, you couldn't tell anything about the character of the place from these trips. You never saw anybody but your own family and, like today, their guests.

He went out to the darkened hall and Ula, the maid, jumped in fright. "Ugh. Oh. It's you, Mr. Winfield. You like to scare me."

"Hello, Ula. Glad to see you're still holding the fort. Where's Mrs. Day?"

"Upstairs, I think. . . . Here she is now," said Ula.

His daughter came down the steps; her hand on the banister was all he could see at first. "Is that you, Father? I thought I heard the car."

"Hello, Mary," he said. At the foot of the stairs they went through the travesty of a kiss that both knew so well. He leaned forward so that his head was above her shoulder. To Ula, a good Catholic, it must have looked like the kiss of peace. *"Pax tibi,"* Mr. Winfield felt like saying, but he said, "Where have you—"

"Father! You're freezing!" Mrs. Day tried very hard to keep the vexation out of her tone.

"It was a cold ride," he said. "This time of year. We had snow flurries between Danbury and Sheffield, but the girls enjoyed it."

"You go right upstairs and have a bath, and I'll send up—what would you like? Tea? Chocolate? Coffee?"

He was amused. The obvious thing would be to offer him a drink, and it was so apparent that she was talking fast to avoid that. "I think cocoa would be fine, but you'd better have a real drink for Sheila and her friends."

"Now, why do you take that tone, Father? You could have a drink if you wanted it, but you're on the wagon, aren't you?"

"Still on it. Up there with the driver."

"Well, and besides, liquor doesn't warm you up the same way something hot does. I'll send up some chocolate. I've put you in your old room, of course. You'll have to share the bathroom with one of Sheila's friends, but that's the best I could do. Sheila wasn't even sure she was coming till the very last minute."

"I'll be all right. It sounds like—I didn't bring evening clothes."

"We're not dressing."

He went upstairs. His room, the room itself, was just about the same; but the furniture was rearranged, his favorite chair not where he liked it best, but it was a good house; you could tell it was being lived in, *this year,* today, tomorrow. Little touches, ashtrays, flowers. It seemed young and white, cool with a warm breath, comfortable—and absolutely strange to him and, more especially, he to it. Whatever of the past this house had held, it was gone now. He sat in the chair and lit a cigarette. In a wave, in a lump, in a gust, the old thoughts came to him. Most of the year they were in the back of his mind, but up here Mr. Winfield held a sort of annual review of far-off, but never-out-of-sight regrets. This house, it used to be his until Mary's husband bought it. A good price, and in 1921 he certainly needed the money. He needed everything, and today he had an income from the money he got for this house, and that was about all. He remembered the day Mary's husband came to him and said, "Mr. Winfield, I hate to have to be the one to do this, but Mary—Mary doesn't—well, she thinks you weren't very nice to Mrs. Winfield. I don't know anything about it myself, of course, but that's what Mary thinks. I expected, naturally, I thought you'd come and live with us now that Mrs. Winfield has died, but—well, the point is, I know you've lost a lot of money, and also I happen to know about Mrs. Winfield's will. So I'm prepared to make you a pretty good offer, strictly legitimate based on current values, for the house in Lenox. I'll pay the delinquent taxes myself and give you a hundred and fifty thousand dollars for the house and grounds. That ought to be enough to pay off your debts and give you a fairly decent income. And, uh, I happen to have a friend who knows Mr. Harding quite well. Fact, he sees the President informally one night a week, and I know he'd be only too glad, if you were interested . . ."

He remembered how that had tempted him. Harding might have fixed it so he could go to London, where Enid Walter was. But even then it was too late. Enid had gone back to London because he didn't have the guts to divorce his wife, and the reason he wouldn't divorce his wife was that he wanted to "protect" Mary, and Mary's standing, and Mary's husband's standing, and Mary's little daughter's standing; and now he was "protecting" them all over again, by selling his house so that he would not become a family charge—protecting the very same people from the embarrassment of a poor relation. "You can have the house," he told Day. "It's worth that much, but no more, and I'm grateful to you for not offering me more. About a political job, I think I might like to go to California this winter. I have some friends out there I haven't seen in years." He had known that that was exactly what Mary and her husband wanted, so he'd gone.

There was a knock on the door. It was Ula with a tray. "Why two cups, Ula?" he said.

"Oh. Di put two cups? So I did. I'm just so used to putting two cups." She had left the door open behind her, and as she arranged the things on the marble-topped table he saw Sheila and the two other girls, standing and moving in the hall.

"This is your room, Farnie," said Sheila. "You're down this way, Helen. Remember what I told you, Farnie. Come on, Helen."

"Thank you, Ula," he said. She went out and closed the door, and he stood for a moment, contemplating the chocolate, then poured out a cup and drank it. It made him a little thirsty, but it was good and warming, and Mary was right; it was better than a drink. He poured out another cup and nibbled on a biscuit. He had an idea: Miss Farnsworth might like some. He admired that girl. She had spunk. He bet she knew what she wanted, or seemed to, and no matter how unimportant were the things she wanted, they were the things she wanted, and not someone else. She could damn well thank the Lord, too, that she was young enough to have a whack at whatever she wanted, and not have to wait the way he had. That girl would make up her mind about a man or a fortune or a career, and by God she would attain whatever it was. If she found, as she surely would find, that nothing ever was enough, she'd at least find it out in time; and early disillusionment carried a compensatory philosophical attitude, which in a hard girl like this one would take nothing from her charm. Mr. Winfield felt her charm, and began regarding her as the most interesting person he had met in many dull years. It would be fun to talk to her, to sound her out and see how far she had progressed toward, say, ambition or disillusionment. It would be fun to do, and it would be just plain nice of him, as former master of this house, to invite her to have a cup of cocoa with him. Good cocoa.

He made his choice between going out in the hall and knocking on her door, and knocking on her door to the bathroom. He decided on the second procedure because he didn't want anyone to see him knocking on her door. So he entered the bathroom and tapped on the door that led to her room. "In a minute," he thought he heard her say. But then he knew he must have been wrong. It sounded more like "Come in." He hated people who knocked on doors and had to be told two or three times to come in, and it would make a bad impression if he started the friendship that way.

He opened the door, and immediately he saw how right he had been in thinking she had said "In a minute." For Miss Farnsworth was standing in the middle of the room, standing there all but nude. Mr. Winfield instantly knew that this was the end of any worthwhile life he had left. There was cold murder in the girl's eyes, and loathing and contempt and the promise of the thought his name forever would evoke. She spoke to him: "Get out of here, you dirty old man."

He returned to his room and his chair. Slowly he took a cigarette out of his case, and did not light it. He did everything slowly. There was all the time in the world, too much of it, for him. He knew it would be hours before he would begin to hate himself. For a while he would just sit there and plan his own terror.

TESS SLESINGER

White on Black

One of the private schools attended by the "nice" children of the West Side some twenty years ago followed not only the liberal practice of mixing rich and poor, Gentile and Jew, but made a point also of including Negroes. Not many, of course—just enough so that when the eye of a visiting parent roved down the rows of pink and white faces collected for the Harvest Festival or the Easter Play, it stumbled complacently here and there—perhaps three or four times in all the auditorium—on an equally scrubbed black one sticking out like a solitary violet in a bed of primroses. For, except in the case of two sisters, or of a brother and sister, these black children never made friends among themselves, seldom even to the extent of choosing seats side by side in assemblies.

I suppose that the effect upon the rest of us was, as it was intended to be, on the whole good. It must have taught us well-bred little boys and girls at the least the untruth of the common slander that Negroes have an unpleasant odor; for certainly none of the Wilsons and Whites and Washingtons in our school ever smelt of anything but soap. And we were brought up, through weekly ethics lessons and the influence of the inevitable elderly lady teacher who had never got Harriet Beecher Stowe out of her mind, to the axiom that all men were created equal.

The few scattered colored children in clean clothes, then, contributed practically to our liberal education. But what effect we, in our more than clean, our often luxurious clothes and with our pink and white faces, had in turn upon them, it is impossible for one of us to judge. Although I can tell you today what has happened since to a number of my old schoolmates, even to those in whom I have long ceased to be interested, and although I run every year across gossip concerning still others, none of us has any idea what happened to our colored classmates. Some of them left school before the high-school years were over; some of them were graduated and stood at our elbows with their rolled-up diplomas; but all of them have equally dropped out of our common knowledge since. Where are they now? Did they drift back to Harlem, those Wilsons and Washingtons and Whites? How do they look back upon their ten years' interlude with white children? I cannot imagine. But I remember vividly the school careers of the two who were in my class.

The Wilsons, brother and sister, joined us in the sixth grade. Paul was exquisitely made, his face chiselled and without fault; a pair of delicately dilated nostrils at the end of a short fine nose, and an aureole of dim black curls. Elizabeth was bigger, coarser, more negroid; darker, her lips were thick, her nose less perfect; but still she was a beautiful child, luxuriously made, and promising to develop into a type of the voluptuous Negro woman at her best. Elizabeth was older than Paul; but her brain, like her nose, was less sharp, and both were put into the same class.

For the first week or two our kind teachers paid them the surplus attention which was always extended to Negro, or crippled, or poverty-stricken children. They suggested that Paul be chosen when the boys were choosing up sides; they asked the girls to take Elizabeth as partner. The children stood off from them no more than they stood off from any newcomers. We were not adultly snobbish; we merely glared at all newcomers in our world until they should prove themselves worthy. But by the end of the month, there was no longer any question of choosing Paul: Paul himself was the chooser and the permanently chosen; likewise Elizabeth was besieged with requests for the seats on either side of her in assembly, and it became an honor to have a seat in the same row; and the teachers turned around, and were given rather to suppressing the colored Wilsons than to bringing them out.

For after a certain natural humility had worn off, Paul and Elizabeth were not merely taken into the group; they took over the group. Including the faculty. They were a smashing success. For one thing, they feared nothing; furthermore, they proved marvelous athletes; and they were born leaders. Electing Paul to the captaincy of the basketball team was a mere formality; even if he hadn't richly deserved it, he would have permitted no one else to hold it. Elizabeth was as strong as a horse, less skillful, less graceful than he, but easily outshining, by her animal strength and fearlessness, all the white girls in the class. Beside their athletic prowess, which alone would have won them popularity in a class of eleven-year-olds, both of them were gifted with an over-powering jubilancy and a triumphant bullying wit, which inevitably made them czars.

They ruled the class with a rod of iron, chose their intimates, played with them, dropped them, and patronized the teachers. Their power spread to politics; by the end of the first year Paul was president of the class, and Elizabeth, who could not spell, secretary. Their class-meetings were masterpieces of irreverent wit and bedlam, subtly dominated by the tacitly authoritative Paul. The teachers turned over to them the difficult business of controlling the class after recess, and Paul, in his double capacity of legal president and illegal czar, easily succeeded where they had long failed. Even his sister, who was no small power among the girls, feared and adored him. If her authority was for one moment questioned, she had only to say, "I'll call Paul. . . ."

I remember myself—and probably not a few others of the dazzled little white girls did the same in secret—going home to dream about marrying Paul and taking Elizabeth to live with us. I remember a moment of certainly unprecedented and of almost unsurpassed voluptuous pleasure on an occasion when Paul, twisting his wiry body into one of those marvelous knots from which he unrolled himself to shoot a basket, stretched so far that his shirt left his trousers and revealed a few inches of coffee-colored skin glistening with sweat, which caused me to gasp with delight. We girls chose to play against the boys of the class rather than among ourselves, and I was surely not the only girl who had voted favorably for the pure delight of being tossed on the ground and swung round the hips by the jubilant Paul, who had, beside his lovely body and fierce little nostrils, not the slightest inhibition.

For two years the noisy Wilsons demoralized the entire class into a raucous group that was never tired of wrestling, playing basketball, shouting jokes, and merrily defying the teachers. Not even the famous Seventh Grade Trouble, which involved the Wilsons as central figures, subdued them. Not even the visit, upon that terrifying occasion, of their mother. All of us made a point of walking past the principal's office to view Mrs. Wilson, who sat there, dressed in black and with her face held low and ashamed as though she were the culprit herself. We whispered afterward, among ourselves, of what a lady Mrs. Wilson was; we had never before seen a colored lady.

The high-school years loomed ahead. We were to be joined by another section of the same grade, and we were determined to maintain our solidarity with Paul at our head. Our reputation as a champion class had preceded us; but with it, we soon noticed, a reputation for rowdiness. Paul was instantly elected captain of the basketball team. But he was just nosed out of the presidency by a white boy belonging to the other section, who must have gained some treacherous votes from among our own. Although the other boy occupied the chair, Paul managed, for half a year, to bully even the new section into slowly waning submission to the last echoes of his power.

Elizabeth's popularity remained limited to the girls in our own old section. The others adopted her at first as a novelty, but they had not been trained to her loud hearty jokes and her powerful wrestling, and soon tired of her and left her to her old companions. These dwindled slowly, as we girls gained consciousness of our status as girls and wished to dissociate ourselves from anything rowdy. Of course it was our fault—we could have pushed Elizabeth forward and remained loyal to her—but we had so many things to think of in those days. And I think something of the sort was bound to happen to Elizabeth anyway; she did not have the native personality to warrant and sustain the unlimited popularity which had fallen on her partly because of her strength and partly because she was her brother's sister. There was a quiet girl in our class, less mature than the rest of us—who were, in that first year of high-school, more fiercely mature than some of us are today, which is ten years later. This girl, Diana, fastened upon Elizabeth as a chum, and from now on the curious pair were inseparable.

I remember the early days when it became the thing for the boys to take the girls to the corner soda-store after basketball games, and for each boy to treat one girl to a fudge sundae. We couldn't help noticing that the boys, so eager to rough-house with Elizabeth in the classroom, hesitated among themselves as to which should treat her, and that the same one never treated her twice. We noticed too, that the soda-clerk stared at the dark blemish in our small white group. Elizabeth never seemed to notice anything; she developed a habit of kidding the soda-clerk in a loud professional voice, and soon our indignation was shifted to her, and we told her to lower her voice and not fool around with soda-clerks. Toward the end of the year Diana and Elizabeth dissociated themselves from our group, and began to occupy a little table by themselves in a corner. Here they would sit and pretend to be alone, and we could hear them giggling and whispering happily. Paul, of course, was still too young and too "manly" ever to join these parties.

In the course of that first year in high-school many things beside the soda-parties happened to us. Wrestling between boys and girls was outlawed, the girls began to loop their hair in buns over the ears, and the boys began to appear in navy-blue long trousers.

I remember Paul in his first longies. Instead of navy-blue, he appeared in a sleek suit of light Broadway tan, nicely nipped in at the waist, which harmonized with his clear mocha skin and showed off his dapper little figure to perfection. But it didn't quite fit in our school. I noticed that day, standing in line behind him to buy lunch tickets, that he wore brand new shoes: they were long and very pointed, and polished a brilliant ochre; they were button shoes, with cloth tops; they squeaked like nothing else in the world. I remember staring at them, and wondering where I had seen shoes like those before: was it in the elevator at home?

We were so grown-up that year that instead of shooting baskets in the twenty-minute recess that followed lunch, we got one girl to play the piano and the rest of us danced. Only about half of the boys were bold enough to dance; Paul still belonged to the group which stood in a corner and laughed and imitated their bolder friends, waiting for younger girls to be imported into the high-school department next year. With one boy to every pair of girls, it was not surprising that Elizabeth danced more than half of her dances with her friend Diana. The rest of us paired off with our girl-friends equally often.

But for no reason that anyone could see, Elizabeth's friends still diminished week by week. She had occasional spurts of her old popularity, but these were chiefly occasioned by reaction against some more stable idol, who would soon be restored to her post. Elizabeth's one permanent friend was Diana, the quiet little blonde girl who had no other friends. As far as I know, Diana was the only girl who ever invited Elizabeth to her house, and it was rumored that Diana was the only one who had seen the inside of the Wilson house, but Diana could be made neither to say whether it was true, nor what it was like if she had seen it. As for the rest of us, we were a little uncomfortable about omitting Elizabeth at afternoon parties at our homes; but somebody's mother settled it for us by saying that she thought it would be an unkindness to the little colored girl to invite her to a home where there would be none of her own people. This conflicted, of course, with the lesson of our ethics classes, but we were thirteen-going-on-fourteen, and we had too much to think about, so we let it go at that.

Meanwhile Paul, who had remained captain all the first year, failed to be elected for the second. Some of his classmates started propaganda to the effect that, while still their best player, he was no good as a captain, and they self-righteously elected the second-best player in his stead. Paul took out his anger in refusing to coöperate with the team, and developed into a poor sport, that worst of anathemas in school, successfully hogging the ball so that no one else had a chance. The epithet poor sport began to be whispered about the classroom, and when class elections for the second year were held, Paul was not even nominated for an office. Our section had sworn to stand by him when we had suffered defeat at the beginning of the year, but when the time came we simply sat and held our tongues, and elected another boy from the hostile section.

When the Wilsons returned for the second year after vacation, they looked a little different to us. Paul had turned into something resembling an uptown beau, and Elizabeth's face had grown coarser. Elizabeth joined her friend Diana at once, and their companionship remained unbroken. Paul, however, held in considerably less esteem, remained aloof, making no effort to regain his lost popularity, and pursued his way sullenly and almost defiantly among us. He met our reproaches with indifference.

That year evening dances broke out among us. For the sake of girls who might never be asked, there was a rule that everyone must come unescorted and unescorting. It was easy enough, of course, to break the rule. Most of the girls came regularly attended by boys from the upper classes. Elizabeth came the first few times with her brother, which was as good as coming unattended. Paul stood in a corner with the stags; Elizabeth sat with the other girls who had come unattended or attended by brothers, looking very dark and strange in her short-sleeved light dresses, and accepted gratefully her few opportunities to dance.

There began to be whispers among us of what we would do if Paul asked one of us to come to a dance with him, or offered a treat to a soda. We admitted to feeling uncomfortable at the thought of being seen on the street with him. At the same time we realized that what we were contemplating was horribly unfair. But Evelyn—Evelyn, who led our class in social matters because at fourteen she wore rouge and baby French heels—said, "School is school; it's not the World; it's not our Real Lives," and we let it go at that. As we had tacitly adopted policies toward Elizabeth, we now officially adopted one toward Paul; we were to be extra nice to him, but not in the way that one treats a boy; and we were to dance with him when he asked us, but very kindly refused his invitations to escort us anywhere outside the school walls. Fortunately for our peace of mind, ethics lessons were that year changed to weekly lessons in elocution for the girls, and public speaking for the boys.

But none of us was given the chance to refuse him. So far as I know, he never asked a girl to go anywhere with him, never left the stag-line at our Friday night dances, and after the first half-dozen, he never even came with Elizabeth. He scrupulously avoided even the careless physical contacts in the elevator, of which the other boys took modest advantage. Also, when we followed our policy of being nice to him in school, we found ourselves politely ignored. Paul grew increasingly sullen, even occasionally rude, and one girl reported that he had passed her on the street and pretended not to see her, neglecting to lift his elegant tan felt hat.

In the middle of that year Elizabeth's friend Diana was withdrawn from the school by her parents and sent to a boarding-school in the

South, rumor said to get her away from the black girl and teach her a proper sense of color.

With her friend gone, Elizabeth picked up smaller fry and dazzled them, because, unlike Paul, she seemed to want never to be alone. But even with these she learned to disappear at the school door, or at most to walk no further with a white classmate than the end of the school block. There, making some excuse about having to hurry, or going in another direction, she would dash away with a good-humored smile. I remember watching her running away from us once and wondering to what strange world she disappeared every day after school.

Of course, not one of the nice girls in our school would have dreamed of hurting Elizabeth's feelings by suggesting that she leave us on the street, but there must have been some hesitating on the corner before Elizabeth so effectively learned that her position with her white schoolmates ended with the school door. Or could it have been that dark lady, who had sat in the principal's office with her head lowered as though she were the culprit, that time of the Seventh Grade Trouble? But no matter, we were in our third year of high-school now, and had forgotten the seventh grade as we had forgotten the famous trouble, and were used now to seeing our dark classmate hurry off after school and run down the long block, leaving us standing on the corner, discussing our this and that, which was so awfully important to us. . . .

In the third year of high-school, Paul simply did not appear. We were, I suppose, faintly relieved, in so far as we thought about him at all. He removed, after all, such uncomfortable questions as playing other schools with a Negro on our first team. And our own old section, our merry, rowdy section, of which Paul had once been undisputed king, had imperceptibly melted away, the boundary line was wavery, our old loyalty vague, a thing of the past; Paul, so far as he was anything in our minds, was a memory belonging to our lost section. When we asked Elizabeth what had happened to him, she told us he was going to another school because he didn't like girls and considered our private school sissy. She carried it off rather well, I think. One or two of us suggested that he might have been fired, because we all knew that his work had gone off badly in that last year.

Elizabeth herself, in those last two years, toned down considerably. Her prowess in studies had never been great, and she seemed now to be devoting more time to them. Her athletic ability had not lived up to its promise, because she had been after all primarily interested in roughneck play, and seemed unable or unwilling to tame her strength and spirits into rules and skill. She abandoned the bright colors she had worn as a child, and came to school in neat and modest dresses. She dropped without reluctance into the common order of students, learned to toady as she had once been toadied to, and managed to keep up a decent sober reputation which ensured her a mild amount of companionship, restricted, of course, to within the school walls. On committees Elizabeth volunteered for unpleasant jobs and carried them out cheerfully and efficiently. She grew generous and sweet-tempered, and a little like a servant; and like a servant, she was thanked for her services and forgotten.

Paul had dropped out of our existence.

The last time I saw either of them was at our graduation dance. Elizabeth had long ago given up coming alone to our dances, but she came, of course, to this one, looking rather too burly and black in the prescribed white dress, with bare arms which hung like bones from her ungainly shoulders. She was the whole of the committee on refreshments, and all during the first part of the evening she stood behind a table with her diploma tucked on a rack over her head—nobody from her family had come to see her be graduated—and cheerfully dispensed sandwiches and ice-cream.

Everybody was mingling proudly in the big assembly room, waiting for the chairs to be removed for dancing; everybody was very nice to Elizabeth and even took down her address as a matter of form, but in the rush of taking addresses that really meant something and comparing notes about future colleges, she was forgotten, and if it hadn't been for a teacher who came to her rescue, she might have been completely alone. When the dancing began, the teacher led her away from the buffet table with her arm around her, to bring her to the row of chairs where girls sat waiting for partners.

Some of us must have had compunctions—I know I did—floating by her in our partners' arms, for on that night the least popular girl had achieved a faithful escort, if only by importing boys from classes below who felt it an honor to be there at all. But none of us felt badly enough to urge our partners to leave us and dance with Elizabeth. Later one or two boys danced a waltz with her, because a waltz was the least difficult thing to sacrifice. She sat all evening and talked cheerfully to the teacher. She looked uncomplaining, as though she had quietly learned her place. She even seemed to enjoy watching the rest of us dance.

The evening broke up on a high-note of "See you again," "Don't forget," and "Oh, the most marvelous time!" and I remember emerging from the dance-room in a fever of happiness, walking on winged feet. I pushed my way through the gay crowd outside the door. Somebody tapped me on the arm: "Miss!" I turned and saw, for the first time in three years, Paul Wilson, the king of our old section! I smiled eagerly, delighted to see him again. "Why Paul!" I exclaimed, holding out my hand.

He was as beautiful as he had been three years before, but his face was different, hardened perhaps, so that the dapper tan clothes he wore made him cheap and flashy. He still wore pointed button shoes with cloth tops. He was standing by the wall with his hat pulled down over his eyes. "Why, Paul!" I said.

He looked up, caught my eye, and shifted his away as though he had failed to recognize me. He looked down at the floor and spoke in a low voice. "Miss, would you mind finding my sister Elizabeth Wilson inside and say her brother is waiting for her?" He stuck his hands suddenly into his pockets with something of his old sullen gesture.

I remember turning from him with an overpowering sense of guilt to spare him embarrassment, and going back with tears burning my eyes to find Elizabeth. I left him standing there against the wall, with his hat over his eyes, snubbing his former classmates, while they passed their former god and leader, some of them too happy to distinguish his features under that hat, others no doubt turning from him to prevent his embarrassment, and even, on that happy night, to spare themselves. . . . This should have been his graduation.

EUDORA WELTY

Why I Live at the P.O.

I was getting along fine with Mama, Papa-Daddy and Uncle Rondo until my sister Stella-Rondo just separated from her husband and came back home again. Mr. Whitaker! Of course I went with Mr. Whitaker first, when he first appeared here in China Grove, taking "Pose Yourself" photos, and Stella-Rondo broke us up. Told him I was one-sided. Bigger on one side than the other, which is a deliberate, calculated falsehood: I'm the same. Stella-Rondo is exactly twelve months to the day younger than I am and for that reason she's spoiled.

She's always had anything in the world she wanted and then she'd throw it away. Papa-Daddy gave her this gorgeous Add-a-Pearl necklace when she was eight years old and she threw it away playing baseball when she was nine, with only two pearls.

So as soon as she got married and moved away from home the first thing she did was separate! From Mr. Whitaker! This photographer with the popeyes she said she trusted. Came home from one of those towns up in Illinois and to our complete surprise brought this child of two.

Mama said she like to made her drop dead for a second. "Here you had this marvelous blonde child and never so much as wrote your mother a word about it," says Mama. "I'm thoroughly ashamed of you." But of course she wasn't.

Stella-Rondo just calmly takes off this *hat,* I wish you could see it. She says, "Why, Mama, Shirley-T.'s adopted, I can prove it."

"How?" says Mama, but all I says was, "H'm!" There I was over the hot stove, trying to stretch two chickens over five people and a completely unexpected child into the bargain, without one moment's notice.

"What do you mean—'H'm!'?" says Stella-Rondo, and Mama says, "I heard that, Sister."

I said that oh, I didn't mean a thing, only that whoever Shirley-T. was, she was the spit-image of Papa-Daddy if he'd cut off his beard, which of course he'd never do in the world. Papa-Daddy's Mama's papa and sulks.

Stella-Rondo got furious! She said, "Sister, I don't need to tell you you got a lot of nerve and always did have and I'll thank you to make no future reference to my adopted child whatsoever."

"Very well," I said. "Very well, very well. Of course I noticed at once she looks like Mr. Whitaker's side too. That frown. She looks like a cross between Mr. Whitaker and Papa-Daddy."

"Well, all I can say is she isn't."

"She looks exactly like Shirley Temple to me," says Mama, but Shirley-T. just ran away from her.

So the first thing Stella-Rondo did at the table was turn Papa-Daddy against me.

"Papa-Daddy," she says. He was trying to cut up his meat. "Papa-Daddy!" I was taken completely by surprise. Papa-Daddy is about a million years old and's got this long-long beard. "Papa-Daddy, Sister says she fails to understand why you don't cut off your beard."

So Papa-Daddy l-a-y-s down his knife and fork! He's real rich. Mama says he is, he says he isn't. So he says, "Have I heard correctly? You don't understand why I don't cut off my beard?"

"Why," I says, "Papa-Daddy, of course I understand, I did not say any such of a thing, the idea!"

He says, "Hussy!"

I says, "Papa-Daddy, you know I wouldn't any more want you to cut off your beard than the man in the moon. It was the farthest thing from my mind! Stella-Rondo sat there and made that up while she was eating breast of chicken."

But he says, "So the postmistress fails to understand why I don't cut off my beard. Which job I got you through my influence with the government. 'Bird's nest'—is that what you call it?"

Not that it isn't the next to smallest P.O. in the entire state of Mississippi.

I says, "Oh, Papa-Daddy," I says, "I didn't say any such of a thing, I never dreamed it was a bird's nest, I have always been grateful though this is the next to smallest P.O. in the state of Mississippi, and I do not enjoy being referred to as a hussy by my own grandfather."

But Stella-Rondo says, "Yes, you did say it too. Anybody in the world could of heard you, that had ears."

"Stop right there," says Mama, looking at *me*.

So I pulled my napkin straight back through the napkin ring and left the table.

As soon as I was out of the room Mama says, "Call her back, or she'll starve to death," but Papa-Daddy says, "This is the beard I started growing on the Coast when I was fifteen years old." He would of gone on till nightfall if Shirley-T. hadn't lost the Milky Way she ate in Cairo.

So Papa-Daddy says, "I am going out and lie in the hammock, and you can all sit here and remember my words: I'll never cut off my beard as long as I live, even one inch, and I don't appreciate it in you at all." Passed right by me in the hall and went straight out and got in the hammock.

It would be a holiday. It wasn't five minutes before Uncle Rondo suddenly appeared in the hall in one of Stella-Rondo's flesh-colored kimonos, all cut on the bias, like something Mr. Whitaker probably thought was gorgeous.

"Uncle Rondo!" I says. "I didn't know who that was! Where are you going?"

"Sister," he says, "get out of my way, I'm poisoned."

"If you're poisoned stay away from Papa-Daddy," I says. "Keep out of the hammock. Papa-Daddy will certainly beat you on the head if you come within forty miles of him. He thinks I deliberately said he ought to cut off his beard after he got me the P.O., and I've told him and told him and told him, and he acts like he just don't hear me. Papa-Daddy must of gone stone deaf."

"He picked a fine day to do it then," says Uncle Rondo, and before you could say "Jack Robinson" flew out in the yard.

What he'd really done, he'd drunk another bottle of that prescription. He does it every single Fourth of July as sure as shooting, and it's horribly expensive. Then he falls over in the hammock and snores. So he insisted on zigzagging right on out to the hammock, looking like a half-wit.

Papa-Daddy woke up with this horrible yell and right there without moving an inch he tried to turn Uncle Rondo against me. I heard every word he said. Oh, he told Uncle Rondo I didn't learn to read till I was eight years old and he didn't see how in the world I ever got the mail put up at the P.O., much less read it all, and he said if Uncle Rondo could only fathom the lengths he had gone to to get me that job! And he said on the other hand he thought Stella-Rondo had a brilliant mind and deserved credit for getting out of town. All the time he was just lying there swinging as pretty as you please and looping out his beard, and poor Uncle Rondo was *pleading* with him to slow down the hammock, it was making him as dizzy as a witch to watch it. But that's what Papa-Daddy likes about a hammock. So Uncle Rondo was too dizzy to get turned against me for the time being. He's Mama's only brother and is a good case of a one-track mind. Ask anybody. A certified pharmacist.

Just then I heard Stella-Rondo raising the upstairs window. While she was married she got this peculiar idea that it's cooler with the windows shut and locked. So she has to raise the window before she can make a soul hear her outdoors.

So she raises the window and says, *"Oh!"* You would have thought she was mortally wounded.

Uncle Rondo and Papa-Daddy didn't even look up, but kept right on with what they were doing. I had to laugh.

I flew up the stairs and threw the door open! I says, "What in the wide world's the matter, Stella-Rondo? You mortally wounded?"

"No," she says, "I am not mortally wounded but I wish you would do me the favor of looking out that window there and telling me what you see."

So I shade my eyes and look out the window.

"I see the front yard," I says.

"Don't you see any human beings?" she says.

"I see Uncle Rondo trying to run Papa-Daddy out of the hammock," I says. "Nothing more. Naturally, it's so suffocating-hot in the house, with all the windows shut and locked, everybody who cares to stay in their right mind will have to go out and get in the hammock before the Fourth of July is over."

"Don't you notice anything different about Uncle Rondo?" asks Stella-Rondo.

"Why, no, except he's got on some terrible-looking flesh-colored contraption I wouldn't be found dead in, is all I can see," I says.

"Never mind, you won't be found dead in it, because it happens to be part of my trousseau, and Mr. Whitaker took several dozen photographs of me in it," says Stella-Rondo. "What on earth could Uncle Rondo *mean* by wearing part of my trousseau out in the broad open daylight without saying so much as 'Kiss my foot,' *knowing* I only got home this morning after my separation and hung my negligee up on the bathroom door, just as nervous as I could be?"

"I'm sure I don't know, and what do you expect me to do about it?" I says. "Jump out the window?"

"No, I expect nothing of the kind. I simply declare that Uncle Rondo looks like a fool in it, that's all," she says. "It makes me sick to my stomach."

"Well, he looks as good as he can," I says. "As good as anybody in reason could." I stood up for Uncle Rondo, please remember. And I said to Stella-Rondo, "I think I would do well not to criticize so freely if I were you and came home with a two-year-old child I had never said a word about, and no explanation whatever about my separation."

"I asked you the instant I entered this house not to refer one more time to my adopted child, and you gave me your word of honor you would not," was all Stella-Rondo would say, and started pulling out every one of her eyebrows with some cheap Kress tweezers.

So I merely slammed the door behind me and went down and made some green-tomato pickle. Somebody had to do it. Of course Mama had turned both the Negroes loose; she always said no earthly power could hold one anyway on the Fourth of July, so she wouldn't even try. It turned out that Jaypan fell in the lake and came within a very narrow limit of drowning.

So Mama trots in. Lifts up the lid and says, "H'm! Not very good for your Uncle Rondo in his precarious condition, I must say. Or poor little adopted Shirley-T. Shame on you!"

That made me tired. I says, "Well, Stella-Rondo had better thank her lucky stars it was her instead of me came trotting in with that very peculiar-looking child. Now if it had been me that trotted in from Illinois and brought a peculiar-looking child of two, I shudder to think of the reception I'd of got, much less controlled the diet of an entire family."

"But you must remember, Sister, that you were never married to Mr. Whitaker in the first place and didn't go up to Illinois to live," says Mama, shaking a spoon in my face. "If you had I would of been just as overjoyed to see you and your little adopted girl as I was to see Stella-Rondo, when you wound up with your separation and came on back home."

"You would not," I says.

"Don't contradict me, I would," says Mama.

But I said she couldn't convince me though she talked till she was blue in the face. Then I said, "Besides, you know as well as I do that that child is not adopted."

"She most certainly is adopted," says Mama, stiff as a pocker.

I says, "Why, Mama, Stella-Rondo had her just as sure as anything in this world, and just too stuck up to admit it."

"Why, Sister," said Mama. "Here I thought we were going to have a pleasant Fourth of July, and you start right out not believing a word your own baby sister tells you!"

"Just like Cousin Annie Flo. Went to her grave denying the facts of life," I remind Mama.

"I told you if you ever mentioned Annie Flo's name I'd slap your face," says Mama, and slaps my face.

"All right, you wait and see," I says.

"I," says Mama, "*I* prefer to take my children's word for anything when it's humanly possible." You ought to see Mama, she weighs two hundred pounds and has real tiny feet.

Just then something perfectly horrible occurred to me.

"Mama," I says, "can that child talk?" I simply had to whisper! "Mama, I wonder if that child can be—you know—in any way? Do you realize," I says, "that she hasn't spoken one single, solitary word to a human being up to this minute? This is the way she looks," I says, and I looked like this.

Well, Mama and I just stood there and stared at each other. It was horrible!

"I remember well that Joe Whitaker frequently drank like a fish," says Mama. "I believed to my soul he drank *chemicals.*" And without another word she marches to the foot of the stairs and calls Stella-Rondo.

"Stella-Rondo? O-o-o-o-o! Stella-Rondo!"

"What?" says Stella-Rondo from upstairs. Not even the grace to get up off the bed.

"Can that child of yours talk?" asks Mama.

Stella-Rondo says, "Can she what?"

"Talk! Talk!" says Mama. "Burdyburdyburdyburdy!"

So Stella-Rondo yells back, "Who says she can't talk?"

"Sister says so," says Mama.

"You didn't have to tell me, I know whose word of honor don't mean a thing in this house," says Stella-Rondo.

And in a minute the loudest Yankee voice I ever heard in my life yells out, "OE'm Pop-OE the Sailor-r-r-r Ma-a-an!" and then somebody jumps up and down in the upstairs hall. In another second the house would of fallen down.

"Not only talks, she can tap-dance!" calls Stella-Rondo. "Which is more than some people I won't name can do."

"Why, the little precious darling thing!" Mama says, so surprised. "Just as smart as she can be!" Starts talking baby talk right there. Then she turns on me. "Sister, you ought to be thoroughly ashamed! Run upstairs this instant and apologize to Stella-Rondo and Shirley-T."

"Apologize for what?" I says. "I merely wondered if the child was normal, that's all. Now that she's proved she is, why, I have nothing further to say."

But Mama just turned on her heel and flew out, furious. She ran right upstairs and hugged the baby. She believed it was adopted. Stella-Rondo hadn't done a thing but turn her against me from upstairs while I stood there helpless over the hot stove. So that made Mama, Papa-Daddy and the baby all on Stella-Rondo's side.

Next, Uncle Rondo.

I must say that Uncle Rondo has been marvelous to me at various times in the past and I was completely unprepared to be made to jump out of my skin, the way it turned out. Once Stella-Rondo did something perfectly horrible to him—broke a chain letter from Flanders Field—and he took the radio back he had given her and gave it to me. Stella-Rondo was furious! For six months we all had to call her Stella instead of Stella-Rondo, or she wouldn't answer. I always thought Uncle Rondo had all the brains of the entire family. Another time he sent me to Mammoth Cave, with all expenses paid.

But this would be the day he was drinking that prescription, the Fourth of July.

So at supper Stella-Rondo speaks up and says she thinks Uncle Rondo ought to try to eat a little something. So finally Uncle Rondo said he would try a little cold biscuits and ketchup, but that was all. So *she* brought it to him.

"Do you think it wise to disport with ketchup in Stella-Rondo's flesh-colored kimono?" I says. Trying to be considerate! If Stella-Rondo couldn't watch out for her trousseau, somebody had to.

"Any objections?" asks Uncle Rondo, just about to pour out all the ketchup.

"Don't mind what she says, Uncle Rondo," says Stella-Rondo. "Sister has been devoting this solid afternoon to sneering out my bedroom window at the way you look."

"What's that?" says Uncle Rondo. Uncle Rondo has got the most terrible temper in the world. Anything is liable to make him tear the house down if it comes at the wrong time.

So Stella-Rondo says, "Sister says, 'Uncle Rondo certainly does look like a fool in that pink kimono!' "

Do you remember who it was really said that?

Uncle Rondo spills out all the ketchup and jumps out of his chair and tears off the kimono and throws it down on the dirty floor and puts his foot on it. It had to be sent all the way to Jackson to the cleaners and re-pleated.

"So that's your opinion of your Uncle Rondo, is it?" he says. "I look like a fool, do I? Well, that's the last straw. A whole day in this house with nothing to do, and then to hear you come out with a remark like that behind my back!"

"I didn't say any such of a thing, Uncle Rondo," I says, "and I'm not saying who did, either. Why, I think you look all right. Just try to take care of yourself and not talk and eat at the same time," I says. "I think you better go lie down."

"Lie down my foot," says Uncle Rondo. I ought to of known by that he was fixing to do something perfectly horrible.

So he didn't do anything that night in the precarious state he was in—just played Casino with Mama and Stella-Rondo and Shirley-T. and gave Shirley-T. a nickel with a head on both sides. It tickled her nearly to death, and she called him "Papa." But at 6:30 A.M. the next morning, he threw a whole five-cent package of some unsold one-inch firecrackers from the store as hard as he could into my bedroom and they every one went off. Not one bad one in the string. Anybody else, there'd be one that wouldn't go off.

Well, I'm just terribly susceptible to noise of any kind, the doctor has always told me I was the most sensitive person he had ever seen in his whole life, and I was simply prostrated. I couldn't eat! People tell me they heard it as far as the cemetery, and old Aunt Jep Patterson, that had been holding her own so good, thought it was Judgment Day and she was going to meet her whole family. It's usually so quiet here.

And I'll tell you it didn't take me any longer than a minute to make up my mind what to do. There I was with the whole entire house on

Stella-Rondo's side and turned against me. If I have anything at all I have pride.

So I just decided I'd go straight down to the P.O. There's plenty of room there in the back, I says to myself.

Well! I made no bones about letting the family catch on to what I was up to. I didn't try to conceal it.

The first thing they knew, I marched in where they were all playing Old Maid and pulled the electric oscillating fan out by the plug, and everything got real hot. Next I snatched the pillow I'd done the needlepoint on right off the davenport from behind Papa-Daddy. He went "Ugh!" I beat Stella-Rondo up the stairs and finally found my charm bracelet in her bureau drawer under a picture of Nelson Eddy.

"So that's the way the land lies," says Uncle Rondo. There he was, piecing on the ham. "Well, Sister, I'll be glad to donate my army cot if you got any place to set it up, providing you'll leave right this minute and let me get some peace." Uncle Rondo was in France.

"Thank you kindly for the cot and 'peace' is hardly the word I would select if I had to resort to firecrackers at 6:30 A.M. in a young girl's bedroom," I says back to him. "And as to where I intend to go, you seem to forget my position as postmistress of China Grove, Mississippi," I says. "I've always got the P.O."

Well, that made them all sit up and take notice.

I went out front and started digging up some four-o'clocks to plant around the P.O.

"Ah-ah-ah!" says Mama, raising the window. "Those happen to be my four-o'clocks. Everything planted in that star is mine. I've never known you to make anything grow in your life."

"Very well," I says. "But I take the fern. Even you, Mama, can't stand there and deny that I'm the one watered that fern. And I happen to know where I can send in a box top and get a packet of one thousand mixed seeds, no two the same kind, free."

"Oh, where?" Mama wants to know.

But I says, "Too late. You 'tend to your house, and I'll 'tend to mine. You hear things like that all the time if you know how to listen to the radio. Perfectly marvelous offers. Get anything you want free."

So I hope to tell you I marched in and got that radio, and they could of all bit a nail in two, especially Stella-Rondo, that it used to belong to, and she well knew she couldn't get it back, I'd sue for it like a shot. And I very politely took the sewing-machine motor I helped pay the most on to give Mama for Christmas back in 1929, and a good big calendar, with the first-aid remedies on it. The thermometer and the

Hawaiian ukulele certainly were rightfully mine, and I stood on the step-ladder and got all my watermelon-rind preserves and every fruit and vegetable I'd put up, every jar. Then I began to pull the tacks out of the bluebird wall vases on the archway to the dining room.

"Who told you you could have those, Miss Priss?" says Mama, fanning as hard as she could.

"I bought 'em and I'll keep track of 'em," I says. "I'll tack 'em up one on each side the post-office window, and you can see 'em when you come to ask me for your mail, if you're so dead to see 'em."

"Not I! I'll never darken the door to that post office again if I live to be a hundred," Mama says. "Ungrateful child! After all the money we spent on you at the Normal."

"Me either," says Stella-Rondo. "You can just let my mail lie there and *rot,* for all I care. I'll never come and relieve you of a single, solitary piece."

"I should worry," I says. "And who you think's going to sit down and write you all those big fat letters and postcards, by the way? Mr. Whitaker? Just because he was the only man ever dropped down in China Grove and you got him—unfairly—is he going to sit down and write you a lengthy correspondence after you come home giving no rhyme nor reason whatsoever for your separation and no explanation for the presence of that child? I may not have your brilliant mind, but I fail to see it."

So Mama says, "Sister, I've told you a thousand times that Stella-Rondo simply got homesick, and this child is far too big to be hers," and she says, "Now, why don't you all just sit down and play Casino?"

Then Shirley-T. sticks out her tongue at me in this perfectly horrible way. She has no more manners than the man in the moon. I told her she was going to cross her eyes like that some day and they'd stick.

"It's too late to stop me now," I says. "You should have tried that yesterday. I'm going to the P.O. and the only way you can possibly see me is to visit me there."

So Papa-Daddy says, "You'll never catch me setting foot in that post office, even if I should take a notion into my head to write a letter some place." He says, "I won't have you reachin' out of that little old window with a pair of shears and cuttin' off any beard of mine. I'm too smart for you!"

"We all are," says Stella-Rondo.

But I said, "If you're so smart, where's Mr. Whitaker?"

So then Uncle Rondo says, "I'll thank you from now on to stop reading all the orders I get on postcards and telling everybody in China

Grove what you think is the matter with them," but I says, "I draw my own conclusions and will continue in the future to draw them." I says, "If people want to write their inmost secrets on penny postcards, there's nothing in the wide world you can do about it, Uncle Rondo."

"And if you think we'll ever *write* another postcard you're sadly mistaken," says Mama.

"Cutting off your nose to spite your face then," I says. "But if you're all determined to have no more to do with the U.S. mail, think of this: What will Stella-Rondo do now, if she wants to tell Mr. Whitaker to come after her?"

"Wah!" says Stella-Rondo. I knew she'd cry. She had a conniption fit right there in the kitchen.

"It will be interesting to see how long she holds out," I says. "And now—I am leaving."

"Good-bye," says Uncle Rondo.

"Oh, I declare," says Mama, "to think that a family of mine should quarrel on the Fourth of July, or the day after, over Stella-Rondo leaving old Mr. Whitaker and having the sweetest little adopted child! It looks like we'd all be glad!"

"Wah!" says Stella-Rondo, and has a fresh conniption fit.

"*He* left *her*—you mark my words," I says. "That's Mr. Whitaker. I know Mr. Whitaker. After all, I knew him first. I said from the beginning he'd up and leave her. I foretold every single thing that's happened."

"Where did he go?" asks Mama.

"Probably to the North Pole, if he knows what's good for him," I says.

But Stella-Rondo just bawled and wouldn't say another word. She flew to her room and slammed the door.

"Now look what you've gone and done, Sister," says Mama. "You go apologize."

"I haven't got time, I'm leaving," I says.

"Well, what are you waiting around for?" asks Uncle Rondo.

So I just picked up the kitchen clock and marched off, without saying "Kiss my foot" or anything, and never did tell Stella-Rondo good-bye.

There was a girl going along on a little wagon right in front.

"Girl," I says, "come help me haul these things down the hill, I'm going to live in the post office."

Took her nine trips in her express wagon. Uncle Rondo came out on the porch and threw her a nickel.

And that's the last I've laid eyes on any of my family or my family laid eyes on me for five solid days and nights. Stella-Rondo may be telling the most horrible tales in the world about Mr. Whitaker, but I haven't heard them. As I tell everybody, I draw my own conclusions.

But oh, I like it here. It's ideal, as I've been saying. You see, I've got everything cater-cornered, the way I like it. Hear the radio? All the war news. Radio, sewing machine, book ends, ironing board and that great big piano lamp—peace, that's what I like. Butter-bean vines planted all along the front where the strings are.

Of course, there's not much mail. My family are naturally the main people in China Grove, and if they prefer to vanish from the face of the earth, for all the mail they get or the mail they write, why, I'm not going to open my mouth. Some of the folks here in town are taking up for me and some turned against me. I know which is which. There are always people who will quit buying stamps just to get on the right side of Papa-Daddy.

But here I am, and here I'll stay. I want the world to know I'm happy.

And if Stella-Rondo should come to me this minute, on bended knees, and *attempt* to explain the incidents of her life with Mr. Whitaker, I'd simply put my fingers in both my ears and refuse to listen.

JOHN CHEEVER

The Swimmer

It was one of those midsummer Sundays when everyone sits around saying, "I *drank* too much last night." You might have heard it whispered by the parishioners leaving church, heard it from the lips of the priest himself, struggling with his cassock in the *vestiarium,* heard it from the golf links and the tennis courts, heard it from the wildlife preserve where the leader of the Audubon group was suffering from a terrible hangover. "I *drank* too much," said Donald Westerhazy. "We all *drank* too much," said Lucinda Merrill. "It must have been the wine," said Helen Westerhazy. "I *drank* too much of that claret."

This was at the edge of the Westerhazys' pool. The pool, fed by an artesian well with a high iron content, was a pale shade of green. It was a fine day. In the west there was a massive stand of cumulus cloud so like a city seen from a distance—from the bow of an approaching ship—that it might have had a name. Lisbon. Hackensack. The sun was hot. Neddy Merrill sat by the green water, one hand in it, one around a glass of gin. He was a slender man—he seemed to have the especial slenderness of youth—and while he was far from young he had slid down his banister that morning and given the bronze backside of Aphrodite on the hall table a smack, as he jogged toward the smell of coffee in his dining room. He might have been compared to a summer's day, particularly the last hours of one, and while he lacked a tennis racket or a sail bag the impression was definitely one of youth, sport, and clement weather. He had been swimming and now he was breathing deeply, stertorously as if he could gulp into his lungs the components of that moment, the heat of the sun, the intenseness of his pleasure. It all seemed to flow into his chest. His own house stood in Bullet Park, eight miles to the south, where his four beautiful daughters would have had their lunch and might be playing tennis. Then it occurred to him that by taking a dogleg to the southwest he could reach his home by water.

His life was not confining and the delight he took in this observation could not be explained by its suggestion of escape. He seemed to see, with a cartographer's eye, that string of swimming pools, that quasi-subterranean stream that curved across the county. He had made a discovery, a contribution to modern geography; he would name the stream Lucinda after his wife. He was not a practical joker nor was he a fool but he was determinedly original and had a vague and modest idea of himself as a legendary figure. The day was beautiful and it seemed to him that a long swim might enlarge and celebrate its beauty.

He took off a sweater that was hung over his shoulders and dove in. He had an inexplicable contempt for men who did not hurl themselves into pools. He swam a choppy crawl, breathing either with every stroke or every fourth stroke and counting somewhere well in the back of his mind the one-two one-two of a flutter kick. It was not a serviceable stroke for long distances but the domestication of swimming had saddled the sport with some customs and in his part of the world a crawl was customary. To be embraced and sustained by the light green water was less a pleasure, it seemed, than the resumption of a natural condition, and he would have liked to swim without trunks, but this was not possible, considering his project. He hoisted himself up on the far curb—he never used the ladder—and started across the lawn. When Lucinda asked where he was going he said he was going to swim home.

The only maps and charts he had to go by were remembered or imaginary but these were clear enough. First there were the Grahams, the Hammers, the Lears, the Howlands, and the Crosscups. He would cross Ditmar Street to the Bunkers and come, after a short portage, to the Levys, the Welchers, and the public pool in Lancaster. Then there were the Hallorans, the Sachses, the Biswangers, Shirley Adams, the Gilmartins, and the Clydes. The day was lovely, and that he lived in a world so generously supplied with water seemed like a clemency, a beneficence. His heart was high and he ran across the grass. Making his way home by an uncommon route gave him the feeling that he was a pilgrim, an explorer, a man with a destiny, and he knew that he would find friends all along the way; friends would line the banks of the Lucinda River.

He went through a hedge that separated the Westerhazys' land from the Grahams', walked under some flowering apple trees, passed the shed that housed their pump and filter, and came out at the Grahams' pool. "Why, Neddy," Mrs. Graham said, "what a marvelous surprise. I've been trying to get you on the phone all morning. Here, let me get you a drink." He saw then, like any explorer, that the hospitable customs and traditions of the natives would have to be handled with diplomacy if he was ever going to reach his destination. He did not want to mystify or seem rude to the Grahams nor did he have the time to linger there. He swam the length of their pool and joined them in the sun and was rescued, a few minutes later, by the arrival of two carloads of friends from Connecticut. During the uproarious reunions he was able to slip away. He went down by the front of the Grahams' house, stepped over a thorny hedge, and crossed a vacant lot to the Hammers'. Mrs. Hammer, looking up from her roses, saw him swim by although she wasn't quite sure who it was. The Lears heard him splashing past the open windows of their living room. The Howlands and the Crosscups were away. After leaving the Howlands' he crossed Ditmar Street and started for the Bunkers', where he could hear, even at that distance, the noise of a party.

The water refracted the sound of voices and laughter and seemed to suspend it in midair. The Bunkers' pool was on a rise and he climbed some stairs to a terrace where twenty-five or thirty men and women were drinking. The only person in the water was Rusty Towers, who floated there on a rubber raft. Oh, how bonny and lush were the banks of the Lucinda River! Prosperous men and women gathered by the sapphire-colored waters while caterer's men in white coats passed them cold gin. Overhead a red de Haviland trainer was circling around and around and around in the sky with something like the glee of a child in a swing. Ned felt a passing affection for the scene, a tenderness for the gathering, as if it was something he might touch. In the distance he heard thunder. As soon as Enid Bunker saw him she began to scream: "Oh, look who's here! What a marvelous surprise! When Lucinda said that you couldn't come I thought I'd *die.*" She made her way to him through the crowd, and when they had finished kissing she led him to the bar, a progress that was slowed by the fact that he stopped to kiss eight or ten other women and shake the hands of as many men. A smiling bartender he had seen at a hundred parties gave him a gin and tonic and he stood by the bar for a moment, anxious not to get stuck in any conversation that would delay his voyage. When he seemed about to be surrounded he dove in and swam close to the side to avoid colliding with Rusty's raft. At the far end of the pool he bypassed the Tomlinsons with a broad smile and jogged up the garden path. The gravel cut his feet but this was the only unpleasantness. The party was confined to the pool, and as he went toward the house he heard the brilliant, watery sound of voices fade, heard the noise of a radio from the Bunkers' kitchen, where someone was listening to a ball game. Sunday afternoon. He made his way through the parked cars and down the grassy border of their driveway to Alewives Lane. He did not want to be seen on the road in his bathing trunks but there was no traffic and he made the short distance to the Levys' driveway, marked with a PRIVATE PROPERTY sign and a green tube for *The New York Times.* All the doors and windows of the big house were open but there were no signs of life; not even a dog barked. He went around the side of the house to the pool and saw that the Levys had only recently left. Glasses and bottles and dishes of nuts were on a table at the deep end, where there was a bathhouse or gazebo, hung with Japanese lanterns. After swimming the pool he got himself a glass and poured a drink. It was his fourth or fifth drink and he had swum nearly half the length of the Lucinda River. He felt tired, clean, and pleased at that moment to be alone; pleased with everything.

It would storm. The stand of cumulus cloud—that city—had risen and darkened, and while he sat there he heard the percussiveness of thunder again. The de Haviland trainer was still circling overhead and it seemed to Ned that he could almost hear the pilot laugh with pleasure in the afternoon; but when there was another peal of thunder he took off for home. A train whistle blew and he wondered what time it had gotten to be. Four? Five? He thought of the provincial station at that hour, where a waiter, his tuxedo concealed by a raincoat, a dwarf with some flowers wrapped in newspaper, and a woman who had been crying would be waiting for the local. It was suddenly growing dark; it was that moment when the pin-headed birds seem to organize their song into some acute and knowledgeable recognition of the storm's approach. Then there was a fine noise of rushing water from the crown of an oak at his back, as if a spigot there had been turned. Then the noise of fountains came from the crowns of all the tall trees. Why did he love storms, what was the meaning of his excitement when the door sprang open and the rain wind fled rudely up the stairs, why had the simple task of shutting the windows of an old house seemed fitting and urgent, why did the first watery notes of a storm wind have for him the unmistakable sound of good news, cheer, glad tidings? Then there was an explosion, a smell of cordite, and rain lashed the Japanese lanterns that Mrs. Levy had bought in Kyoto the year before last, or was it the year before that?

He stayed in the Levys' gazebo until the storm had passed. The rain had cooled the air and he shivered. The force of the wind had stripped a maple of its red and yellow leaves and scattered them over the grass and the water. Since it was midsummer the tree must be blighted, and yet he felt a peculiar sadness at this sign of autumn. He braced his shoulders, emptied his glass, and started for the Welchers' pool. This meant crossing the Lindleys' riding ring and he was surprised to find it overgrown with grass and all the jumps dismantled. He wondered if the Lindleys had sold their horses or gone away for the summer and put them out to board. He seemed to remember having heard something about the Lindleys and their horses but the memory was unclear. On he went, barefoot through the wet grass, to the Welchers', where he found their pool was dry.

This breach in his chain of water disappointed him absurdly, and he felt like some explorer who seeks a torrential headwater and finds a dead stream. He was disappointed and mystified. It was common enough to go away for the summer but no one ever drained his pool. The Welchers had definitely gone away. The pool furniture was folded, stacked, and covered with a tarpaulin. The bathhouse was locked. All the windows of the house were shut, and when he went around to the driveway in front he saw a FOR SALE sign nailed to a tree. When had he last heard from the Welchers—when, that is, had he and Lucinda last regretted an invitation to dine with them? It seemed only a week or so ago. Was his memory failing or had he so disciplined it in the repression of unpleasant facts that he had damaged his sense of the truth? Then in the distance he heard the sound of a tennis game. This cheered him, cleared away all his apprehensions and let him regard the overcast sky and the cold air with indifference. This was the day that Neddy Merrill swam across the county. That was the day! He started off then for his most difficult portage.

Had you gone for a Sunday afternoon ride that day you might have seen him, close to naked, standing on the shoulders of Route 424, waiting for a chance to cross. You might have wondered if he was the victim of foul play, had his car broken down, or was he merely a fool. Standing barefoot in the deposits of the highway—beer cans, rags, and blowout patches—exposed to all kinds of ridicule, he seemed pitiful. He had known when he started that this was a part of his journey—it had been on his maps—but confronted with the lines of traffic, worming through the summery light, he found himself unprepared. He was laughed at, jeered at, a beer can was thrown at him, and he had no dignity or humor to bring to the situation. He could have gone back, back to the Westerhazys', where Lucinda would still be sitting in the sun. He had signed nothing, vowed nothing, pledged nothing, not even to himself. Why, believing as he did, that all human obduracy was susceptible to common sense, was he unable to turn back? Why was he determined to complete his journey even if it meant putting his life in danger? At what point had this prank, this joke, this piece of horseplay become serious? He could not go back, he could not even recall with any clearness the green water at the Westerhazys', the sense of inhaling the day's components, the friendly and relaxed voices saying that they had *drunk* too much. In the space of an hour, more or less, he had covered a distance that made his return impossible.

An old man, tooling down the highway at fifteen miles an hour, let him get to the middle of the road, where there was a grass divider. Here he was exposed to the ridicule of the northbound traffic, but after ten or fifteen minutes he was able to cross. From here he had only a short walk to the Recreation Center at the edge of the village of Lancaster, where there were some handball courts and a public pool.

The effect of the water on voices, the illusion of brilliance and suspense, was the same here as it had been at the Bunkers' but the sounds here were louder, harsher, and more shrill, and as soon as he entered the crowded enclosure he was confronted with regimentation. "ALL SWIMMERS MUST TAKE A SHOWER BEFORE USING THE POOL. ALL SWIMMERS MUST USE THE FOOTBATH, ALL SWIMMERS MUST WEAR THEIR IDENTIFICATION DISKS." He took a shower, washed his feet in a cloudy and bitter solution, and made his way to the edge of the water. It stank of chlorine and looked to him like a sink. A pair of lifeguards in a pair of towers blew police whistles at what seemed to be regular intervals and abused the swimmers through a public address system. Neddy remembered the sapphire water at the Bunkers' with longing and thought that he might contaminate himself—damage his own prosperousness and charm—by swimming in this murk, but he reminded himself that he was an explorer, a pilgrim, and that this was merely a stagnant bend in the Lucinda River. He dove, scowling with distaste, into the chlorine and had to swim with his head above water to avoid collisions, but even so he was bumped into, splashed, and jostled. When he got to the shallow end both lifeguards were shouting at him: "Hey, you, you without the identification disk, get outa the water." He did, but they had no way of pursuing him and he went through the reek of suntan oil and chlorine out through the hurricane fence and passed the handball courts. By crossing the road he entered the wooded part of the Halloran estate. The woods were not cleared and the footing was treacherous and difficult until he reached the lawn and the clipped beech hedge that encircled their pool.

The Hallorans were friends, an elderly couple of enormous wealth who seemed to bask in the suspicion that they might be Communists. They were zealous reformers but they were not Communists, and yet when they were accused, as they sometimes were, of subversion, it seemed to gratify and excite them. Their beech hedge was yellow and he guessed this had been blighted like the Levys' maple. He called hullo, hullo, to warn the Hallorans of his approach, to palliate his invasion of their privacy. The Hallorans, for reasons that had never been explained to him, did not wear bathing suits. No explanations were in order, really. Their nakedness was a detail in their uncompromising zeal for reform and he stepped politely out of his trunks before he went through the opening in the hedge.

Mrs. Halloran, a stout woman with white hair and a serene face, was reading the *Times.* Mr. Halloran was taking beech leaves out of the water with a scoop. They seemed not surprised or displeased to see him. Their pool was perhaps the oldest in the country, a fieldstone rectangle, fed by a brook. It had no filter or pump and its waters were the opaque gold of the stream.

"I'm swimming across the county," Ned said.

"Why, I didn't know one could," exclaimed Mrs. Halloran.

"Well, I've made it from the Westerhazys'," Ned said. "That must be about four miles."

He left his trunks at the deep end, walked to the shallow end, and swam this stretch. As he was pulling himself out of the water he heard Mrs. Halloran say, "We've been *terribly* sorry to hear about all your misfortunes, Neddy."

"My misfortunes?" Ned asked. "I don't know what you mean."

"Why, we heard that you'd sold the house and that your poor children . . ."

"I don't recall having sold the house," Ned said, "and the girls are at home."

"Yes," Mrs. Halloran sighed. "Yes . . ." Her voice filled the air with an unseasonable melancholy and Ned spoke briskly. "Thank you for the swim."

"Well, have a nice trip," said Mrs. Halloran.

Beyond the hedge he pulled on his trunks and fastened them. They were loose and he wondered if, during the space of an afternoon, he could have lost some weight. He was cold and he was tired and the naked Hallorans and their dark water had depressed him. The swim was too much for his strength but how could he have guessed this, sliding down the banister that morning and sitting in the Westerhazys' sun? His arms were lame. His legs felt rubbery and ached at the joints. The worst of it was the cold in his bones and the feeling that he might never be warm again. Leaves were falling down around him and he smelled wood smoke on the wind. Who would be burning wood at this time of year?

He needed a drink. Whiskey would warm him, pick him up, carry him through the last of his journey, refresh his feeling that it was original and valorous to swim across the county. Channel swimmers took brandy. He needed a stimulant. He crossed the lawn in front of the Hallorans' house and went down a little path to where they had built a house for their only daughter, Helen, and her husband, Eric Sachs. The Sachses' pool was small and he found Helen and her husband there.

"Oh, *Neddy,*" Helen said. "Did you lunch at Mother's?"

"Not *really,*" Ned said. "I *did* stop to see your parents." This seemed to be explanation enough. "I'm terribly sorry to break in on you like this but I've taken a chill and I wonder if you'd give me a drink."

"Why, I'd *love* to," Helen said, "but there hasn't been anything in this house to drink since Eric's operation. That was three years ago."

Was he losing his memory, had his gift for concealing painful facts let him forget that he had sold his house, that his children were in trouble, and that his friend had been ill? His eyes slipped from Eric's face to his abdomen, where he saw three pale, sutured scars, two of them at least a foot long. Gone was his navel, and what, Neddy thought, would the roving hand, bed-checking one's gifts at 3 A.M., make of a belly with no navel, no link to birth, this breach in the succession?

"I'm sure you can get a drink at the Biswangers'," Helen said. "They're having an enormous do. You can hear it from here. Listen!"

She raised her head and from across the road, the lawns, the gardens, the woods, the fields, he heard again the brilliant noise of voices over water. "Well, I'll get wet," he said, still feeling that he had no freedom of choice about his means of travel. He dove into the Sachses' cold water and, gasping, close to drowning, made his way from one end of the pool to the other. "Lucinda and I want *terribly* to see you," he said over his shoulder, his face set toward the Biswangers'. "We're sorry it's been so long and we'll call you *very* soon."

He crossed some fields to the Biswangers' and the sounds of revelry there. They would be honored to give him a drink, they would be happy to give him a drink. The Biswangers invited him and Lucinda for dinner four times a year, six weeks in advance. They were always rebuffed and yet they continued to send out their invitations, unwilling to comprehend the rigid and undemocratic realities of their society. They were the sort of people who discussed the price of things at cocktails, exchanged market tips during dinner, and after dinner told dirty stories to mixed company. They did not belong to Neddy's set—they were not even on Lucinda's Christmas-card list. He went toward their pool with feelings of indifference, charity, and some unease, since it seemed to be getting dark and these were the longest days of the year. The party when he joined it was noisy and large. Grace Biswanger was the kind of hostess who asked the optometrist, the veterinarian, the real-estate dealer, and the dentist. No one was swimming and the twilight, reflected on the water of the pool, had a wintry gleam. There was a bar and he started for this. When Grace Biswanger saw him she came toward him, not affectionately as he had every right to expect, but bellicosely.

"Why, this party has everything," she said loudly, "including a gate crasher."

She could not deal him a social blow—there was no question about this and he did not flinch. "As a gate crasher," he asked politely, "do I rate a drink?"

"Suit yourself," she said. "You don't seem to pay much attention to invitations."

She turned her back on him and joined some guests, and he went to the bar and ordered a whiskey. The bartender served him but he served him rudely. His was a world in which the caterer's men kept the social score, and to be rebuffed by a part-time barkeep meant that he had suffered some loss of social esteem. Or perhaps the man was new and uninformed. Then he heard Grace at his back say: "They went for broke overnight—nothing but income—and he showed up drunk one Sunday and asked us to loan him five thousand dollars. . . ." She was always talking about money. It was worse than eating your peas off a knife. He dove into the pool, swam its length and went away.

The next pool on his list, the last but two, belonged to his old mistress, Shirley Adams. If he had suffered any injuries at the Biswangers' they would be cured here. Love—sexual roughhouse in fact—was the supreme elixir, the pain killer, the brightly colored pill that would put the spring back into his step, the joy of life in his heart. They had had an affair last week, last month, last year. He couldn't remember. It was he who had broken it off, his was the upper hand, and he stepped through the gate of the wall that surrounded her pool with nothing so considered as self-confidence. It seemed in a way to be his pool, as the lover, particularly the illicit lover, enjoys the possessions of his mistress with an authority unknown to holy matrimony. She was there, her hair the color of brass, but her figure, at the edge of the lighted, cerulean water, excited in him no profound memories. It had been, he thought, a lighthearted affair, although she had wept when he broke it off. She seemed confused to see him and he wondered if she was still wounded. Would she, God forbid, weep again?

"What do you want?" she asked.

"I'm swimming across the county."

"Good Christ. Will you ever grow up?"

"What's the matter?"

"If you've come here for money," she said, "I won't give you another cent."

"You could give me a drink."

"I could but I won't. I'm not alone."

"Well, I'm on my way."

He dove in and swam the pool, but when he tried to haul himself up onto the curb he found that the strength in his arms and shoulders had gone, and he paddled to the ladder and climbed out. Looking over his shoulder he saw, in the lighted bathhouse, a young man. Going out onto the dark lawn he smelled chrysanthemums or marigolds—some stubborn autumnal fragrance—on the night air, strong as gas. Looking overhead he saw that the stars had come out, but why should he seem to see Andromeda, Cepheus, and Cassiopeia? What had become of the constellations of midsummer? He began to cry.

It was probably the first time in his adult life that he had ever cried, certainly the first time in his life that he had ever felt so miserable, cold, tired, and bewildered. He could not understand the rudeness of the caterer's barkeep or the rudeness of a mistress who had come to him on her knees and showered his trousers with tears. He had swum too long, he had been immersed too long, and his nose and his throat were sore from the water. What he needed then was a drink, some company, and some clean, dry clothes, and while he could have cut directly across the road to his home he went on to the Gilmartins' pool. Here, for the first time in his life, he did not dive but went down the steps into the icy water and swam a hobbled sidestroke that he might have learned as a youth. He staggered with fatigue on his way to the Clydes' and paddled the length of their pool, stopping again and again with his hand on the curb to rest. He climbed up the ladder and wondered if he had the strength to get home. He had done what he wanted, he had swum the county, but he was so stupefied with exhaustion that his triumph seemed vague. Stooped, holding on to the gateposts for support, he turned up the driveway of his own house.

The place was dark. Was it so late that they had all gone to bed? Had Lucinda stayed at the Westerhazys' for supper? Had the girls joined her there or gone someplace else? Hadn't they agreed, as they usually did on Sunday, to regret all their invitations and stay at home? He tried the garage doors to see what cars were in but the doors were locked and rust came off the handles onto his hands. Going toward the house, he saw that the force of the thunderstorm had knocked one of the rain gutters loose. It hung down over the front door like an umbrella rib, but it could be fixed in the morning. The house was locked, and he thought that the stupid cook or the stupid maid must have locked the place up until he remembered that it had been some time since they had employed a maid or a cook. He shouted, pounded on the door, tried to force it with his shoulder, and then, looking in at the windows, saw that the place was empty.

TILLIE OLSEN

I Stand Here Ironing

I stand here ironing, and what you asked me moves tormented back and forth with the iron.

"I wish you would manage the time to come in and talk with me about your daughter. I'm sure you can help me understand her. She's a youngster who needs help and whom I'm deeply interested in helping."

"Who needs help." Even if I came, what good would it do? You think because I am her mother I have a key, or that in some way you could use me as a key? She has lived for nineteen years. There is all that life that has happened outside of me, beyond me.

And when is there time to remember, to sift, to weigh, to estimate, to total? I will start and there will be an interruption and I will have to gather it all together again. Or I will become engulfed with all I did or did not do, with what should have been and what cannot be helped.

She was a beautiful baby. The first and only one of our five that was beautiful at birth. You do not guess how new and uneasy her tenancy in her now-loveliness. You did not know her all those years she was thought homely, or see her poring over her baby pictures, making me tell her over and over how beautiful she had been—and would be, I would tell her—and was now, to the seeing eye. But the seeing eyes were few or nonexistent. Including mine.

I nursed her. They feel that's important nowadays. I nursed all the children, but with her, with all the fierce rigidity of first motherhood, I did like the books then said. Though her cries battered me to trembling and my breasts ached with swollenness, I waited till the clock decreed.

Why do I put that first? I do not even know if it matters, or if it explains anything.

She was a beautiful baby. She blew shining bubbles of sound. She loved motion, loved light, loved color and music and textures. She would lie on the floor in her blue overalls patting the surface so hard in ecstasy her hands and feet would blur. She was a miracle to me, but when she was eight months old I had to leave her daytimes with the woman downstairs to whom she was no miracle at all, for I worked or looked for work and for Emily's father, who "could no longer endure" (he wrote in his good-bye note) "sharing want with us."

I was nineteen. It was the pre-relief, pre-WPA world of the depression. I would start running as soon as I got off the streetcar, running up the stairs, the place smelling sour, and awake or asleep to startle awake, when she saw me she would break into a clogged weeping that could not be comforted, a weeping I can hear yet.

After a while I found a job hashing at night so I could be with her days, and it was better. But it came to where I had to bring her to his family and leave her.

It took a long time to raise the money for her fare back. Then she got chicken pox and I had to wait longer. When she finally came, I hardly knew her, walking quick and nervous like her father, looking like her father, thin, and dressed in a shoddy red that yellowed her skin and glared at the pockmarks. All the baby loveliness gone.

She was two. Old enough for nursery school they said, and I did not know then what I know now—the fatigue of the long day, and the lacerations of group life in nurseries that are only parking places for children.

Except that it would have made no diffrence if I had known. It was the only place there was. It was the only way we could be together, the only way I could hold a job.

And even without knowing, I knew. I knew the teacher that was evil because all these years it has curdled into my memory, the little boy hunched in the corner, her rasp, "why aren't you outside, because Alvin hits you? that's no reason, go out, scaredy." I knew Emily hated it even if she did not clutch and implore "don't go Mommy" like the other children, mornings.

She always had a reason why we should stay home. Momma, you look sick, Momma. I feel sick. Momma, the teachers aren't there today, they're sick. Momma, we can't go, there was a fire there last night. Momma, it's a holiday today, no school, they told me.

But never a direct protest, never rebellion. I think of our others in their three-, four-year-oldness—the explosions, the tempers, the denunciations, the demands—and I feel suddenly ill. I put the iron down. What in me demanded that goodness in her? And what was the cost, the cost to her of such goodness?

The old man living in the back once said in his gentle way: "You should smile at Emily more when you look at her." What *was* in my face when I looked at her? I loved her. There were all the acts of love.

It was only with the others I remembered what he said, and it was the face of joy, and not of care or tightness or worry I turned to them—too late for Emily. She does not smile easily, let alone almost always as her brothers and sisters do. Her face is closed and sombre, but when she wants, how fluid. You must have seen it in her pantomimes, you spoke of her rare gift for comedy on the stage that rouses a laughter out of the audience so dear they applaud and applaud and do not want to let her go.

Where does it come from, that comedy? There was none of it in her when she came back to me that second time, after I had had to send her away again. She had a new daddy now to learn to love, and I think perhaps it was a better time.

Except when we left her alone nights, telling ourselves she was old enough.

"Can't you go some other time, Mommy, like tomorrow?" she would ask. "Will it be just a little while you'll be gone? Do you promise?"

The time we came back, the front door open, the clock on the floor in the hall. She rigid awake. "It wasn't just a little while. I didn't cry. Three times I called you, just three times, and then I ran downstairs to open the door so you could come faster. The clock talked loud. I threw it away, it scared me what it talked."

She said the clock talked loud again that night I went to the hospital to have Susan. She was delirious with the fever that comes before red measles, but she was fully conscious all the week I was gone and the week after we were home when she could not come near the new baby or me.

She did not get well. She stayed skeleton thin, not wanting to eat, and night after night she had nightmares. She would call for me, and I would rouse from exhaustion to sleepily call back: "You're all right, darling, go to sleep, it's just a dream," and if she still called, in a sterner voice, "now go to sleep, Emily, there's nothing to hurt you." Twice, only twice, when I had to get up for Susan anyhow, I went in to sit with her.

Now when it is too late (as if she would let me hold and comfort her like I do the others) I get up and go to her at once at her moan or restless stirring. "Are you awake, Emily? Can I get you something?" And the answer is always the same: "No, I'm all right, go back to sleep, Mother."

They persuaded me at the clinic to send her away to a convalescent home in the country where "she can have the kind of food and care you can't manage for her, and you'll be free to concentrate on the new baby." They still send children to that place. I see pictures on the society page of sleek young women planning affairs to raise money for it, or dancing at the affairs, or decorating Easter eggs or filling Christmas stockings for the children.

They never have a picture of the children so I do not know if the girls still wear those gigantic red bows and the ravaged looks on the every other Sunday when parents can come to visit "unless otherwise notified"—as we were notified the first six weeks.

Oh it is a handsome place, green lawns and tall trees and fluted flower beds. High up on the balconies of each cottage the children stand, the girls in their red bows and white dresses, the boys in white suits and giant red ties. The parents stand below shrieking up to be heard and the children shriek down to be heard, and between them the invisible wall "Not To Be Contaminated by Parental Germs or Physical Affection."

There was a tiny girl who always stood hand in hand with Emily. Her parents never came. One visit she was gone. "They moved her to Rose Cottage" Emily shouted in explanation. "They don't like you to love anybody here."

She wrote once a week, the labored writing of a seven-year-old. "I am fine. How is the baby. If I write my leter nicely I will have a star. Love." There never was a star. We wrote every other day, letters she could never hold or keep but only hear read—once. "We simply do not have room for children to keep any personal possessions," they patiently explained when we pieced one Sunday's shrieking together to plead how much it would mean to Emily, who loved so to keep things, to be allowed to keep her letters and cards.

Each visit she looked frailer. "She isn't eating," they told us.

(They had runny eggs for breakfast or mush with lumps, Emily said later, I'd hold it in my mouth and not swallow. Nothing ever tasted good, just when they had chicken.)

It took us eight months to get her released home, and only the fact that she gained back so little of her seven lost pounds convinced the social worker.

I used to try to hold and love her after she came back, but her body would stay stiff, and after a while she'd push away. She ate little. Food sickened her, and I think much of life too. Oh she had physical lightness and brightness, twinkling by on skates, bouncing like a ball up and down up and down over the jump rope, skimming over the hill; but these were momentary.

She fretted about her appearance, thin and dark and foreign-looking at a time when every little girl was supposed to look or thought she should look a chubby blonde replica of Shirley Temple. The doorbell sometimes rang for her, but no one seemed to come and play in the house or be a best friend. Maybe because we moved so much.

There was a boy she loved painfully through two school semesters. Months later she told me how she had taken pennies from my purse to buy him candy. "Licorice was his favorite and I brought him some every day, but he still liked Jennifer better'n me. Why, Mommy?" The kind of question for which there is no answer.

School was a worry to her. She was not glib or quick in a world where glibness and quickness were easily confused with ability to learn. To her overworked and exasperated teachers she was an overconscientious "slow learner" who kept trying to catch up and was absent entirely too often.

I let her be absent, though sometimes the illness was imaginary. How different from my now-strictness about attendance with the others. I wasn't working. We had a new baby, I was home anyhow. Sometimes, after Susan grew old enough, I would keep her home from school, too, to have them all together.

Mostly Emily had asthma, and her breathing, harsh and labored, would fill the house with a curiously tranquil sound. I would bring the two old dresser mirrors and her boxes of collections to her bed. She would select beads and single earrings, bottle tops and shells, dried flowers and pebbles, old postcards and scraps, all sorts of oddments; then she and Susan would play Kingdom, setting up landscapes and furniture, peopling them with action.

Those were the only times of peaceful companionship between her and Susan. I have edged away from it, that poisonous feeling between them, that terrible balancing of hurts and needs I had to do between the two, and did so badly, those earlier years.

Oh there are conflicts between the others too, each one human, needing, demanding, hurting, taking—but only between Emily and Susan, no, Emily toward Susan that corroding resentment. It seems so obvious on the surface, yet it is not obvious. Susan, the second child, Susan, golden- and curly-haired and chubby, quick and articulate and assured, everything in appearance and manner Emily was not; Susan, not able to resist Emily's precious things, losing or sometimes clumsily breaking them; Susan telling jokes and riddles to company for applause while Emily sat silent (to say to me later: that was *my* riddle, Mother, I told it to Susan); Susan, who for all the five years' difference in age was just a year behind Emily in developing physically.

I am glad for that slow physical development that widened the difference between her and her contemporaries, though she suffered over it. She was too vulnerable for that terrible world of youthful competition, of preening and parading, of constant measuring of yourself against every other, of envy, "If I had that copper hair," "If I had that skin. . . ." She tormented herself enough about not looking like the others, there was enough of the unsureness, the having to be conscious of words before you speak, the constant caring—what are they thinking of me? without having it all magnified by the merciless physical drives.

Ronnie is calling. He is wet and I change him. It is rare there is such a cry now. That time of motherhood is almost behind me when the ear is not one's own but must always be racked and listening for the child cry, the child call. We sit for a while and I hold him, looking out over the city spread in charcoal with its soft aisles of light. "*Shoogily,*" he breathes and curls closer. I carry him back to bed, asleep. *Shoogily.* A funny word, a family word, inherited from Emily, invented by her to say: *comfort.*

In this and other ways she leaves her seal, I say aloud. And startle at my saying it. What do I mean? What did I start to gather together, to try and make coherent? I was at the terrible, growing years. War years. I do not remember them well. I was working, there were four smaller ones now, there was not time for her. She had to help be a mother, and housekeeper, and shopper. She had to set her seal. Mornings of crisis and near hysteria trying to get lunches packed, hair combed, coats and shoes found, everyone to school or Child Care on time, the baby ready for transportation. And always the paper scribbled on by a smaller one, the book looked at by Susan then mislaid, the homework not done. Running out to that huge school where she was one, she was lost, she was a drop;

suffering over the unpreparedness, stammering and unsure in her classes.

There was so little time left at night after the kids were bedded down. She would struggle over books, always eating (it was in those years she developed her enormous appetite that is legendary in our family) and I would be ironing, or preparing food for the next day, or writing V-mail to Bill, or tending the baby. Sometimes, to make me laugh, or out of her despair, she would imitate happenings or types at school.

I think I said once: "Why don't you do something like this in the school amateur show?" One morning she phoned me at work, hardly understandable through the weeping: "Mother, I did it. I won, I won; they gave me first prize; they clapped and clapped and wouldn't let me go."

Now suddenly she was Somebody, and as imprisoned in her difference as she had been in anonymity.

She began to be asked to perform at other high schools, even in colleges, then at city and statewide affairs. The first one we went to, I only recognized her that first moment when thin, shy, she almost drowned herself into the curtains. Then: Was this Emily? The control, the command, the convulsing and deadly clowning, the spell, then the roaring, stamping audience, unwilling to let this rare and precious laughter out of their lives.

Afterwards: You ought to do something about her with a gift like that—but without money or knowing how, what does one do? We have left it all to her, and the gift has as often eddied inside, clogged and clotted, as been used and growing.

She is coming. She runs up the stairs two at a time with her light graceful step, and I know she is happy tonight. Whatever it was that occasioned your call did not happen today.

"Aren't you ever going to finish the ironing, Mother? Whistler painted his mother in a rocker. I'd have to paint mine standing over an ironing board." This is one of her communicative nights and she tells me everything and nothing as she fixes herself a plate of food out of the icebox.

She is so lovely. Why did you want me to come in at all? Why were you concerned? She will find her way.

She starts up the stairs to bed. "Don't get me up with the rest in the morning." "But I thought you were having midterms." "Oh, those," she comes back in, kisses me, and says quite lightly, "in a couple of years when we'll all be atom-dead they won't matter a bit."

She has said it before. She *believes* it. But because I have been dredging the past, and all that compounds a human being is so heavy and meaningful in me, I cannot endure it tonight.

I will never total it all. I will never come in to say: She was a child seldom smiled at. Her father left me before she was a year old. I had to work her first six years when there was work, or I sent her home and to his relatives. There were years she had care she hated. She was dark and thin and foreign-looking in a world where the prestige went to blondeness and curly hair and dimples, she was slow where glibness was prized. She was a child of anxious, not proud, love. We were poor and could not afford for her the soil of easy growth. I was a young mother, I was a distracted mother. There were the other children pushing up, demanding. Her younger sister seemed all that she was not. There were years she did not want me to touch her. She kept too much in herself, her life was such she had to keep too much in herself. My wisdom came too late. She has much to her and probably nothing will come of it. She is a child of her age, of depression, of war, of fear.

Let her be. So all that is in her will not bloom—but in how many does it? There is still enough left to live by. Only help her to know—help make it so there is cause for her to know—that she is more than this dress on the ironing board, helpless before the iron.

IRWIN SHAW

The Eighty-Yard Run

The pass was high and wide and he jumped for it, feeling it slap flatly against his hands, as he shook his hips to throw off the halfback who was diving at him. The center floated by, his hands desperately brushing Darling's knee as Darling picked his feet up high and delicately ran over a blocker and an opposing linesman in a jumble on the ground near the scrimmage line. He had ten yards in the clear and picked up speed, breathing easily, feeling his thigh pads rising and falling against his legs, listening to the sound of cleats behind him, pulling away from them, watching the other backs heading him off toward the sideline, the whole picture, the men closing in on him, the blockers fighting for position, the ground he had to cross, all suddenly clear in his head, for the first time in his life not a meaningless confusion of men, sounds, speed. He smiled a little to himself as he ran, holding the ball lightly in front of him with his two hands, his knees pumping high, his hips twisting in the almost girlish run of a back in a broken field. The first halfback came at him and he fed him his leg, then swung at the last moment, took the shock of the man's shoulder without breaking stride, ran right through him, his cleats biting securely into the turf. There was only the safety man now, coming warily at him, his arms crooked, hands spread. Darling tucked the ball in, spurted at him, driving hard, hurling himself along, his legs pounding, knees high, all two hundred pounds bunched into controlled attack. He was sure he was going to get past the safety man. Without thought, his arms and legs working beautifully together, he headed right for the safety man, stiff-armed him, feeling blood spurt instantaneously from the man's nose onto his hand, seeing his face go awry, head turned, mouth pulled to one side. He pivoted away, keeping the arm locked, dropping the safety man as he ran easily toward the goal line, with the drumming of cleats diminishing behind him.

How long ago? It was autumn then, and the ground was getting hard because the nights were cold and leaves from the maples around the stadium blew across the practice fields in gusts of wind, and the girls were beginning to put polo coats over their sweaters when they came to watch practice in the afternoon. . . . Fifteen years. Darling walked slowly over the same ground in the spring twilight, in his neat shoes, a man of thirty-five dressed in a double-breasted suit, ten pounds heavier in the fifteen years, but not fat, with the years between 1925 and 1940 showing in his face.

The coach was smiling quietly to himself and the assistant coaches were looking at each other with pleasure the way they always did when one of the second stringers suddenly did something fine, bringing credit to them, making their $2,000 a year a tiny bit more secure.

Darling trotted back, smiling, breathing deeply but easily, feeling wonderful, not tired, though this was the tail end of practice and he'd run eighty yards. The sweat poured off his face and soaked his jersey and he liked the feeling, the warm moistness lubricating his skin like oil. Off in a corner of the field some players were punting and the smack of leather against the ball came pleasantly through the afternoon air. The freshmen were running signals on the next field and the quarterback's sharp voice, the pound of the eleven pairs of cleats, the "Dig, now *dig!*" of the coaches, the laughter of the players all somehow made him feel happy as he trotted back to midfield, listening to the applause and shouts of the students along the sidelines, knowing that after that run the coach would have to start him Saturday against Illinois.

Fifteen years, Darling thought, remembering the shower after the workout, the hot water steaming off his skin and the deep soapsuds and all the young voices singing with the water streaming down and towels going and managers running in and out and the sharp sweet smell of oil of wintergreen and everybody clapping him on the back as he dressed and Packard, the captain, who took being captain very seriously, coming over to him and shaking his hand and saying, "Darling, you're going to go places in the next two years."

The assistant manager fussed over him, wiping a cut on his leg with alcohol and iodine, the little sting making him realize suddenly how fresh and whole and solid his body felt. The manager slapped a piece of adhesive tape over the cut, and Darling noticed the sharp clean white of the tape against the ruddiness of the skin, fresh from the shower.

He dressed slowly, the softness of his shirt and the soft warmth of his wool socks and his flannel trousers a reward against his skin after the harsh pressure of the shoulder harness and thigh and hip pads. He drank three glasses of cold water, the liquid reaching down coldly inside of him, soothing the harsh dry places in his throat and belly left by the sweat and running and shouting of practice.

Fifteen years.

The sun had gone down and the sky was green behind the stadium and he laughed quietly to himself as he looked at the stadium, rearing above the trees, and knew that on Saturday when the 70,000 voices roared as the team came running out onto the field, part of that enormous salute would be for him. He walked slowly, listening to the gravel crunch satisfactorily under his shoes in the still twilight, feeling his clothes swing lightly against his skin, breathing the thin evening air, feeling the wind move softly in his damp hair, wonderfully cool behind his ears and at the nape of his neck.

Louise was waiting for him at the road, in her car. The top was down and he noticed all over again, as he always did when he saw her, how pretty she was, the rough blonde hair and the large, inquiring eyes and the bright mouth, smiling now.

She threw the door open. "Were you good today?" she asked.

"Pretty good," he said. He climbed in, sank luxuriously into the soft leather, stretched his legs far out. He smiled, thinking of the eighty yards. "Pretty damn good."

She looked at him seriously for a moment, then scrambled around, like a little girl, kneeling on the seat next to him, grabbed him, her hands along his ears, and kissed him as he sprawled, head back, on the seat cushion. She let go of him, but kept her head close to his, over his. Darling reached up slowly and rubbed the back of his hand against her cheek, lit softly by a street lamp a hundred feet away. They looked at each other, smiling.

Louise drove down to the lake and they sat there silently, watching the moon rise behind the hills on the other side. Finally he reached over, pulled her gently to him, kissed her. Her lips grew soft, her body sank into his, tears formed slowly in her eyes. He knew, for the first time, that he could do whatever he wanted with her.

"Tonight," he said. "I'll call for you at seven-thirty. Can you get out?"

She looked at him. She was smiling, but the tears were still full in her eyes. "All right," she said. "I'll get out. How about you? Won't the coach raise hell?"

Darling grinned. "I got the coach in the palm of my hand," he said. "Can you wait till seven-thirty?"

She grinned back at him. "No," she said.

They kissed and she started the car and they went back to town for dinner. He sang on the way home.

Christian Darling, thirty-five years old, sat on the frail spring grass, greener now than it ever would be again on the practice field, looked thoughtfully up at the stadium, a deserted ruin in the twilight. He had started on the first team that Saturday and every Saturday after that for the next two years, but it had never been as satisfactory as it should have been. He never had broken away, the longest run he'd ever made was thirty-five yards, and that in a game that was already won, and then that kid had come up from the third team, Diederich, a blank-faced German kid from Wisconsin, who ran like a bull, ripping lines to pieces Saturday after Saturday, plowing through, never getting hurt, never changing his expression, scoring more points, gaining more ground than all the rest of the team put together, making everybody's All-American, carrying the ball three times out of four, keeping everybody else out of the headlines. Darling was a good blocker and he spent his Saturday afternoons working on the big Swedes and Polacks who played tackle and end for Michigan, Illinois, Purdue, hurling into huge pile-ups, bobbing his head wildly to elude the great raw hands swinging like meat-cleavers at him as he went charging in to open up holes for Diederich coming through like a locomotive behind him. Still, it wasn't so bad. Everybody liked him and he did his job and he was pointed out on the campus and boys always felt important when they introduced their girls to him at their proms, and Louise loved him and watched him faithfully in the games, even in the mud, when your own mother wouldn't know you, and drove him around in her car keeping the top down because she was proud of him and wanted to show everybody that she was Christian

Darling's girl. She bought him crazy presents because her father was rich, watches, pipes, humidors, an icebox for beer for his room, curtains, wallets, a fifty-dollar dictionary.

"You'll spend every cent your old man owns," Darling protested once when she showed up at his rooms with seven different packages in her arms and tossed them onto the couch.

"Kiss me," Louise said, "and shut up."

"Do you want to break your poor old man?"

"I don't mind. I want to buy you presents."

"Why?"

"It makes me feel good. Kiss me. I don't know why. Did you know that you're an important figure?"

"Yes," Darling said gravely.

"When I was waiting for you at the library yesterday two girls saw you coming and one of them said to the other, 'That's Christian Darling. He's an important figure.' "

"You're a liar."

"I'm in love with an important figure."

"Still, why the hell did you have to give me a forty-pound dictionary?"

"I wanted to make sure," Louise said, "that you had a token of my esteem. I want to smother you in tokens of my esteem."

Fifteen years ago.

They'd married when they got out of college. There'd been other women for him, but all casual and secret, more for curiosity's sake, and vanity, women who'd thrown themselves at him and flattered him, a pretty mother at a summer camp for boys, an old girl from his home town who'd suddenly blossomed into a coquette, a friend of Louise's who had dogged him grimly for six months and had taken advantage of the two weeks that Louise went home when her mother died. Perhaps Louise had known, but she'd kept quiet, loving him completely, filling his rooms with presents, religiously watching him battling with the big Swedes and Polacks on the line of scrimmage on Saturday afternoons, making plans for marrying him and living with him in New York and going with him there to the night clubs, the theaters, the good restaurants, being proud of him in advance, tall, white-teethed, smiling, large, yet moving lightly, with an athlete's grace, dressed in evening clothes, approvingly eyed by magnificently dressed and famous women in theater lobbies, with Louise adoringly at his side.

Her father, who manufactured inks, set up a New York office for Darling to manage and presented him with three hundred accounts, and they lived on Beekman Place with a view of the river with fifteen thousand dollars a year between them, because everybody was buying everything in those days, including ink. They saw all the shows and went to all the speakeasies and spent their fifteen thousand dollars a year and in the afternoons Louise went to the art galleries and the matinees of the more serious plays that Darling didn't like to sit through and Darling slept with a girl who danced in the chorus of *Rosalie* and with the wife of a man who owned three copper mines. Darling played squash three times a week and remained as solid as a stone barn and Louise never took her eyes off him when they were in the same room together, watching him with a secret, miser's smile, with a trick of coming over to him in the middle of a crowded room and saying gravely, in a low voice, "You're the handsomest man I've ever seen in my whole life. Want a drink?"

Nineteen twenty-nine came to Darling and to his wife and father-in-law, the maker of inks, just as it came to everyone else. The father-in-law waited until 1933 and then blew his brains out and when Darling went to Chicago to see what the books of the firm looked like he found out all that was left were debts and three or four gallons of unbought ink.

"Please, Christian," Louise said, sitting in their neat Beekman Place apartment, with a view of the river and prints of paintings by Dufy and Braque and Picasso on the wall, "please, why do you want to start drinking at two o'clock in the afternoon?"

"I have nothing else to do," Darling said, putting down his glass, emptied of its fourth drink. "Please pass the whisky."

Louise filled his glass. "Come take a walk with me," she said. "We'll walk along the river."

"I don't want to walk along the river," Darling said, squinting intensely at the prints of paintings by Dufy, Braque and Picasso.

"We'll walk along Fifth Avenue."

"I don't want to walk along Fifth Avenue."

"Maybe," Louise said gently, "you'd like to come with me to some art galleries. There's an exhibition by a man named Klee. . . ."

"I don't want to go to any art galleries. I want to sit here and drink Scotch whisky," Darling said. "Who the hell hung those goddam pictures up on the wall?"

"I did," Louise said.

"I hate them."

"I'll take them down," Louise said.

"Leave them there. It gives me something to do in the afternoon. I can hate them." Darling took a long swallow. "Is that the way people paint these days?"

"Yes, Christian. Please don't drink any more."

"Do you like painting like that?"

"Yes, dear."

"Really?"

"Really."

Darling looked carefully at the prints once more. "Little Louise Tucker. The middle-western beauty. I like pictures with horses in them. Why should you like pictures like that?"

"I just happen to have gone to a lot of galleries in the last few years . . ."

"Is that what you do in the afternoon?"

"That's what I do in the afternoon," Louise said.

"I drink in the afternoon."

Louise kissed him lightly on the top of his head as he sat there squinting at the pictures on the wall, the glass of whisky held firmly in his hand. She put on her coat and went out without saying another word. When she came back in the early evening, she had a job on a woman's fashion magazine.

They moved downtown and Louise went out to work every morning and Darling sat home and drank and Louise paid the bills as they came up. She made believe she was going to quit work as soon as Darling found a job, even though she was taking over more responsibility day by day at the magazine, interviewing authors, picking painters for the illustrations and covers, getting actresses to pose for pictures, going out for drinks with the right people, making a thousand new friends whom she loyally introduced to Darling.

"I don't like your hat," Darling said, once, when she came in in the evening and kissed him, her breath rich with Martinis.

"What's the matter with my hat, Baby?" she asked, running her fingers through his hair. "Everybody says it's very smart."

"It's too damned smart," he said. "It's not for you. It's for a rich, sophisticated woman of thirty-five with admirers."

Louise laughed. "I'm practicing to be a rich, sophisticated woman of thirty-five with admirers," she said. He stared soberly at her. "Now, don't look so grim, Baby. It's still the same simple little wife under the hat." She took the hat off, threw it into a corner, sat on his lap. "See? Homebody Number One."

"Your breath could run a train," Darling said, not wanting to be mean, but talking out of boredom, and sudden shock at seeing his wife curiously a stranger in a new hat, with a new expression in her eyes under the little brim, secret, confident, knowing.

Louise tucked her head under his chin so he couldn't smell her breath. "I had to take an author out for cocktails," she said. "He's a boy from the Ozark Mountains and he drinks like a fish. He's a Communist."

"What the hell is a Communist from the Ozarks doing writing for a woman's fashion magazine?"

Louise chuckled. "The magazine business is getting all mixed up these days. The publishers want to have a foot in every camp. And anyway, you can't find an author under seventy these days who isn't a Communist."

"I don't think I like you to associate with all those people, Louise," Darling said. "Drinking with them."

"He's a very nice, gentle boy," Louise said. "He reads Ernest Dowson."

"Who's Ernest Dowson?"

Louise patted his arm, stood up, fixed her hair. "He's an English poet."

Darling felt that somehow he had disappointed her. "Am I supposed to know who Ernest Dowson is?"

"No, dear. I'd better go in and take a bath."

After she had gone, Darling went over to the corner where the hat was lying and picked it up. It was nothing, a scrap of straw, a red flower, a veil, meaningless on his big hand, but on his wife's head a signal of something . . . big city, smart and knowing women drinking and dining with men other than their husbands, conversation about things a normal man wouldn't know much about, Frenchmen who painted as though they used their elbows instead of brushes, composers who wrote whole symphonies without a single melody in them, writers who knew all about politics and women who knew all about writers, the movement of the proletariat, Marx, somehow mixed up with five-dollar dinners and the best-looking women in America and fairies who made them laugh and half-sentences immediately understood and secretly hilarious and wives who called their husbands "Baby." He put the hat down, a scrap of straw and a red flower, and a little veil. He drank some whisky straight and went into the bathroom where his wife was lying deep in her bath, singing to herself and smiling from time to time like a little girl, paddling the water gently with her hands, sending up a slight spicy fragrance from the bath salts she used.

He stood over her, looking down at her. She smiled up at him, her eyes half closed, her body pink and shimmering in the warm, scented water. All over again, with all the old suddenness, he was hit deep inside him with the knowledge of how beautiful she was, how much he needed her.

"I came in here," he said, "to tell you I wish you wouldn't call me 'Baby.' "

She looked up at him from the bath, her eyes quickly full of sorrow, half-understanding what he meant. He knelt and put his arms around her, his sleeves plunged heedlessly in the water, his shirt and jacket soaking wet as he clutched her wordlessly, holding her crazily tight, crushing her breath from her, kissing her desperately, searchingly, regretfully.

He got jobs after that, selling real estate and automobiles, but somehow, although he had a desk with his name on a wooden wedge on it, and he went to the office religiously at nine each morning, he never managed to sell anything and he never made any money.

Louise was made assistant editor, and the house was always full of strange men and women who talked fast and got angry on abstract subjects like mural painting, novelists, labor unions. Negro short-story writers drank Louise's liquor, and a lot of Jews, and big solemn men with scarred faces and knotted hands who talked slowly but clearly about picket lines and battles with guns and leadpipe at mine-shaft-heads and in front of factory gates. And Louise moved among them all, confidently, knowing what they were talking about, with opinions that they listened to and argued about just as though she were a man. She knew everybody, condescended to no one, devoured books that Darling had never heard of, walked along the streets of the city, excited, at home, soaking in all the million tides of New York without fear, with constant wonder.

Her friends liked Darling and sometimes he found a man who wanted to get off in the corner and talk about the new boy who played fullback for Princeton, and the decline of the double wing-back, or even the state of the stock market, but for the most part he sat on the edge of things, solid and quiet in the high storm of words. "The dialectics of the situation . . . The theater has been given over to expert jugglers . . . Picasso? What man has a right to paint old bones and collect ten thousand dollars for them? . . . I stand firmly behind Trotsky . . . Poe was the last American critic. When he died they put lilies on the grave of American criticism. I don't say this because they panned my last book, but . . ."

Once in a while he caught Louise looking soberly and consideringly at him through the cigarette smoke and the noise and he avoided her eyes and found an excuse to get up and go into the kitchen for more ice or to open another bottle.

"Come on," Cathal Flaherty was saying, standing at the door with a girl, "you've got to come down and see this. It's down on Fourteenth Street, in the old Civic Repertory, and you can only see it on Sunday nights and I guarantee you'll come out of the theater singing." Flaherty was a big young Irishman with a broken nose who was the lawyer for a longshoreman's union, and he had been hanging around the house for six months on and off, roaring and shutting everybody else up when he got in an argument. "It's a new play, *Waiting for Lefty;* it's about taxi-drivers."

"Odets," the girl with Flaherty said. "It's by a guy named Odets."

"I never heard of him," Darling said.

"He's a new one," the girl said.

"It's like watching a bombardment," Flaherty said. "I saw it last Sunday night. You've got to see it."

"Come on, Baby," Louise said to Darling, excitement in her eyes already. "We've been sitting in the Sunday *Times* all day, this'll be a great change."

"I see enough taxi-drivers every day," Darling said, not because he meant that, but because he didn't like to be around Flaherty, who said things that made Louise laugh a lot and whose judgment she accepted on almost every subject. "Let's go to the movies."

"You've never seen anything like this before," Flaherty said. "He wrote this play with a baseball bat."

"Come on," Louise coaxed, "I bet it's wonderful."

"He has long hair," the girl with Flaherty said. "Odets. I met him at a party. He's an actor. He didn't say a goddam thing all night."

"I don't feel like going down to Fourteenth Street," Darling said, wishing Flaherty and his girl would get out. "It's gloomy."

"Oh, hell!" Louise said loudly. She looked coolly at Darling, as though she'd just been introduced to him and was making up her mind about him, and not very favorably. He saw her looking at him, knowing there was something new and dangerous in her face and he wanted to say something, but Flaherty was there and his damned girl, and anyway, he didn't know what to say.

"I'm going," Louise said, getting her coat. "I don't think Fourteenth Street is gloomy."

"I'm telling you," Flaherty was saying, helping her on with her coat, "it's the Battle of Gettysburg in Brooklynese."

"Nobody could get a word out of him," Flaherty's girl was saying as they went through the door. "He just sat there all night."

The door closed. Louise hadn't said good night to him. Darling walked around the room four times, then sprawled out on the sofa, on top of the Sunday *Times.* He lay there for five minutes looking at the ceiling, thinking of Flaherty walking down the street talking in that booming voice, between the girls, holding their arms.

Louise had looked wonderful. She'd washed her hair in the afternoon and it had been very soft and light and clung close to her head as she stood there angrily putting her coat on. Louise was getting prettier every year, partly because she knew by now how pretty she was, and made the most of it.

"Nuts," Darling said, standing up. "Oh, nuts."

He put on his coat and went down to the nearest bar and had five drinks off by himself in a corner before his money ran out.

The years since then had been foggy and downhill. Louise had been nice to him, and in a way, loving and kind, and they'd fought only once, when he said he was going to vote for Landon. ("Oh, Christ," she'd said, "doesn't *anything* happen inside your head? Don't you read the papers? The penniless Republican!") She'd been sorry later and apologized for hurting him, but apologized as she might to a child. He'd tried hard, had gone grimly to the art galleries, the concert halls, the bookshops, trying to gain on the trail of his wife, but it was no use. He was bored, and none of what he saw or heard or dutifully read made much sense to him and finally he gave it up. He had thought, many nights as he ate dinner alone, knowing that Louise would come home late and drop silently into bed without explanation, of getting a divorce, but he knew the loneliness, the hopelessness, of not seeing her again would be too much to take. So he was good, completely devoted, ready at all times to go any place with her, do anything she wanted. He even got a small job, in a broker's office and paid his own way, bought his own liquor.

Then he'd been offered the job of going from college to college as a tailor's representative. "We want a man," Mr. Rosenberg had said, "who as soon as you look at him, you say, 'There's a university man.' " Rosenberg had looked approvingly at Darling's broad shoulders and well-kept waist, at his carefully brushed hair and his honest, wrinkle-less face. "Frankly, Mr. Darling, I am willing to make you a proposition. I have inquired about you, you are favorably known on your old campus, I understand you were in the backfield with Alfred Diederich."

Darling nodded. "Whatever happened to him?"

"He is walking around in a cast for seven years now. An iron brace. He played professional football and they broke his neck for him."

Darling smiled. That, at least, had turned out well.

"Our suits are an easy product to sell, Mr. Darling," Rosenberg said. "We have a handsome, custom-made garment. What has Brooks Brothers got that we haven't got? A name. No more."

"I can make fifty, sixty dollars a week," Darling said to Louise that night. "And expenses. I can save some money and then come back to New York and really get started here."

"Yes, Baby," Louise said.

"As it is," Darling said carefully, "I can make it back here once a month, and holidays and the summer. We can see each other often."

"Yes, Baby." He looked at her face, lovelier now at thirty-five than it had ever been before, but fogged over now as it had been for five years with a kind of patient, kindly, remote boredom.

"What do you say?" he asked. "Should I take it?" Deep within him he hoped fiercely, longingly, for her to say, "No, Baby, you stay right here," but she said, as he knew she'd say, "I think you'd better take it."

He nodded. He had to get up and stand with his back to her, looking out the window, because there were things plain on his face that she had never seen in the fifteen years she'd known him. "Fifty dollars is a lot of money," he said. "I never thought I'd ever see fifty dollars again." He laughed. Louise laughed, too.

Christian Darling sat on the frail green grass of the practice field. The shadow of the stadium had reached out and covered him. In the distance the lights of the university shone a little mistily in the light haze of evening. Fifteen years. Flaherty even now was calling for his wife, buying her a drink, filling whatever bar they were in with that voice of his and that easy laugh. Darling half-closed his eyes, almost saw the boy fifteen years ago reach for the pass, slip the halfback, go skittering lightly down the field, his knees high and fast and graceful, smiling to himself because he knew he was going to get past the safety man. That was the high point, Darling thought, fifteen years ago, on an autumn afternoon, twenty years old and far from death, with the air coming easily into his lungs, and a deep feeling inside him that he could do anything, knock over anybody, outrun whatever had to be outrun. And the shower after and the three glasses of water and the cool night air on his damp head and Louise sitting hatless in the open car with a smile and the first kiss she ever really meant. The high point, an eighty-yard run in the practice, and a girl's kiss and everything after that a decline. Darling laughed. He had practiced the wrong thing, perhaps. He hadn't practiced for 1929 and New York City and a girl who would turn into a woman. Somewhere, he thought, there must have been a point where she moved up to me, was even with me for a moment, when I could have held her hand, if I'd known, held tight, gone with her. Well, he'd never known. Here he was on a playing field that was fifteen years away and his wife was in another city having dinner with another and better man, speaking with him a different, new language, a language nobody had ever taught him.

Darling stood up, smiled a little, because if he didn't smile he knew the tears would come. He looked around him. This was the spot. O'Connor's pass had come sliding out just to here . . . the high point. Darling put up his hands, felt all over again the flat slap of the ball. He shook his hips to throw off the halfback, cut back inside the center, picked his knees high as he ran gracefully over two men jumbled on the ground at the line of scrimmage, ran easily, gaining speed, for ten yards, holding the ball lightly in his two hands, swung away from the halfback diving at him, ran, swinging his hips in the almost girlish manner of a back in a broken field, tore into the safety man, his shoes drumming heavily on the turf, stiff-armed, elbow locked, pivoted, raced lightly and exultantly for the goal line.

It was only after he had sped over the goal line and slowed to a trot that he saw the boy and girl sitting together on the turf, looking at him wonderingly.

He stopped short, dropping his arms. "I . . ." he said, gasping a little, though his condition was fine and the run hadn't winded him. "I—once I played here."

The boy and the girl said nothing. Darling laughed embarrassedly, looked hard at them sitting there, close to each other, shrugged, turned and went toward his hotel, the sweat breaking out on his face and running down into his collar.

JEROME WEIDMAN

My Father Sits in the Dark

My father has a peculiar habit. He is fond of sitting in the dark, alone. Sometimes I come home very late. The house is dark. I let myself in quietly because I do not want to disturb my mother. She is a light sleeper. I tiptoe into my room and undress in the dark. I go to the kitchen for a drink of water. My bare feet make no noise. I step into the room and almost trip over my father. He is sitting in a kitchen chair, in his pajamas, smoking his pipe.

'Hello, Pop,' I say.

'Hello, son.'

'Why don't you go to bed, Pa?'

'I will,' he says.

But he remains there. Long after I am asleep I feel sure that he is still sitting there, smoking.

Many times I am reading in my room. I hear my mother get the house ready for the night. I hear my kid brother go to bed. I hear my sister come in. I hear her do things with jars and combs until she, too, is quiet. I know she has gone to sleep. In a little while I hear my mother say good night to my father. I continue to read. Soon I become thirsty. (I drink a lot of water.) I go to the kitchen for a drink. Again I almost stumble across my father. Many times it startles me. I forget about him. And there he is—smoking, sitting, thinking.

'Why don't you go to bed, Pop?'

'I will, son.'

But he doesn't. He just sits there and smokes and thinks. It worries me. I can't understand it. What can he be thinking about? Once I asked him.

'What are you thinking about, Pa?'

'Nothing,' he said.

Once I left him there and went to bed. I awoke several hours later. I was thirsty. I went to the kitchen. There he was. His pipe was out. But he sat there, staring into a corner of the kitchen. After a moment I became accustomed to the darkness. I took my drink. He still sat and stared. His eyes did not blink. I thought he was not even aware of me. I was afraid.

'Why don't you go to bed, Pop?'

'I will, son,' he said. 'Don't wait up for me.'

'But,' I said, 'you've been sitting here for hours. What's wrong? What are you thinking about?'

'Nothing, son,' he said. 'Nothing. It's just restful. That's all.'

The way he said it was convincing. He did not seem worried. His voice was even and pleasant. It always is. But I could not understand it. How could it be restful to sit alone in an uncomfortable chair far into the night, in darkness?

What can it be?

I review all the possibilities. It can't be money. I know that. We haven't much, but when he is worried about money he makes no secret of it. It can't be his health. He is not reticent about that either. It can't be the health of anyone in the family. We are a bit short on money, but we are long on health. (Knock wood, my mother would say.) What can it be? I am afraid I do not know. But that does not stop me from worrying.

Maybe he is thinking of his brothers in the old country. Or of his mother and two step-mothers. Or of his father. But they are all dead. And he would not brood about them like that. I say brood, but it is not really true. He does not brood. He does not even seem to be thinking. He looks too peaceful, too, well not contented, just too peaceful, to be brooding. Perhaps it is as he says. Perhaps it is restful. But it does not seem possible. It worries me.

If I only knew what he thinks about. If I only knew that he thinks at all. I might not be able to help him. He might not even need help. It may be as he says. It may be restful. But at least I would not worry about it.

Why does he just sit there, in the dark? Is his mind failing? No, it can't be. He is only fifty-three. And he is just as keen-witted as ever. In fact, he is the same in every respect. He still likes beet soup. He still reads the second section of the *Times* first. He still wears wing collars. He still believes that Debs could have saved the country and that T.R. was a tool of the moneyed interests. He is the same in every way. He does not even look older than he did five years ago. Everybody remarks about that. Well-preserved, they say. But he sits in the dark, alone, smoking, staring straight ahead of him, unblinking, into the small hours of the night.

If it is as he says, if it is restful, I will let it go at that. But suppose it is not. Suppose it is something I cannot fathom. Perhaps he needs help. Why doesn't he speak? Why doesn't he frown or laugh or cry? Why doesn't he do something? Why does he just sit there?

Finally I become angry. Maybe it is just my unsatisfied curiosity. Maybe I *am* a bit worried. Anyway, I become angry.

'Is something wrong, Pop?'

'Nothing, son. Nothing at all.'

But this time I am determined not to be put off. I am angry.

'Then why do you sit here all alone, thinking, till late?'

'It's restful, son. I like it.'

I am getting nowhere. Tomorrow he will be sitting there again. I will be puzzled. I will be worried. I will not stop now. I am angry.

'Well, what do you *think* about, Pa? Why do you just sit here? What's worrying you? What do you think about?'

'Nothing's worrying me, son. I'm all right. It's just restful. That's all. Go to bed, son.'

My anger has left me. But the feeling of worry is still there. I must get an answer. It seems so silly. Why doesn't he tell me? I have a funny feeling that unless I get an answer I will go crazy. I am insistent.

'But what do you *think* about, Pa? What is it?'

'Nothing, son. Just things in general. Nothing special. Just things.'

I can get no answer.

It is very late. The street is quiet and the house is dark. I climb the steps softly, skipping the ones that creak. I let myself in with my key and tiptoe into my room. I remove my clothes and remember that I am thirsty. In my bare feet I walk to the kitchen. Before I reach it I know he is there.

I can see the deeper darkness of his hunched shape. He is sitting in the same chair, his elbows on his knees, his cold pipe in his teeth, his unblinking eyes staring straight ahead. He does not seem to know I am there. He did not hear me come in. I stand quietly in the doorway and watch him.

Everything is quiet, but the night is full of little sounds. As I stand there motionless I begin to notice them. The ticking of the alarm clock on the icebox. The low hum of an automobile passing many blocks away. The swish of papers moved along the street by the breeze. A whispering rise and fall of sound, like low breathing. It is strangely pleasant.

The dryness in my throat reminds me. I step briskly into the kitchen.

'Hello, Pop,' I say.

'Hello, son,' he says. His voice is low and dreamlike. He does not change his position or shift his gaze.

I cannot find the faucet. The dim shadow of light that comes through the window from the street lamp only makes the room seem darker. I reach for the short chain in the center of the room. I snap on the light.

He straightens up with a jerk, as though he has been struck. 'What's the matter, Pop?' I ask.

'Nothing,' he says. 'I don't like the light.'

'What's the matter with the light?' I say. 'What's wrong?'

'Nothing,' he says. 'I don't like the light.'

I snap the light off. I drink my water slowly. I must take it easy, I say to myself. I must get to the bottom of this.

'Why don't you go to bed? Why do you sit here so late in the dark?'

'It's nice,' he says. 'I can't get used to lights. We didn't have lights when I was a boy in Europe.'

My heart skips a beat and I catch my breath happily. I begin to think I understand. I remember the stories of his boyhood in Austria. I see the wide-beamed *kretchma,* with my grandfather behind the bar. It is late, the customers are gone, and he is dozing. I see the bed of glowing coals, the last of the roaring fire. The room is already dark, and growing darker. I see a small boy, crouched on a pile of twigs at one side of the huge fireplace, his starry gaze fixed on the dull remains of the dead flames. The boy is my father.

I remember the pleasure of those few moments while I stood quietly in the doorway watching him.

'You mean there's nothing wrong? You just sit in the dark because you like it, Pop?' I find it hard to keep my voice from rising in a happy shout.

'Sure,' he says. 'I can't think with the light on.'

I set my glass down and turn to go back to my room. 'Good night, Pop,' I say.

'Good night,' he says.

Then I remember. I turn back. 'What do you think about, Pop?' I ask.

His voice seems to come from far away. It is quiet and even again. 'Nothing,' he says softly. 'Nothing special.'

BERNARD MALAMUD

Idiots First

The thick ticking of the tin clock stopped. Mendel, dozing in the dark, awoke in fright. The pain returned as he listened. He drew on his cold embittered clothing, and wasted minutes sitting at the edge of the bed.

"Isaac," he ultimately sighed.

In the kitchen, Isaac, his astonished mouth open, held six peanuts in his palm. He placed each on the table. "One . . . two . . . nine."

He gathered each peanut and appeared in the doorway. Mendel, in loose hat and long overcoat, still sat on the bed. Isaac watched with small eyes and ears, thick hair graying the sides of his head.

"Schlaf," he nasally said.

"No," muttered Mendel. As if stifling he rose. "Come, Isaac."

He wound his old watch though the sight of the stopped mechanism nauseated him.

Isaac wanted to hold it to his ear.

"No, it's late." Mendel put the watch carefully away. In the drawer he found the little paper bag of crumpled ones and fives and slipped it into his overcoat pocket. He helped Isaac on with his coat.

Isaac looked at one dark window, then at the other. Mendel stared at both blank windows.

They went slowly down the darkly lit stairs, Mendel first, Isaac watching the moving shadows on the wall. To one long shadow he offered a peanut.

"Hungrig."

In the vestibule the old man gazed through the thin glass. The November night was cold and bleak. Opening the door, he cautiously thrust his head out. Though he saw nothing he quickly shut the door.

"Ginzburg, that he came to see me yesterday," he whispered in Isaac's ear.

Isaac sucked air.

"You know who I mean?"

Isaac combed his chin with his fingers.

"That's the one, with the black whiskers. Don't talk to him or go with him if he asks you."

Isaac moaned.

"Young people he don't bother so much," Mendel said in afterthought.

It was suppertime and the street was empty, but the store windows dimly lit their way to the corner. They crossed the deserted street and went on. Isaac, with a happy cry, pointed to the three golden balls. Mendel smiled but was exhausted when they got to the pawnshop.

The pawnbroker, a red-bearded man with black horn-rimmed glasses, was eating a whitefish at the rear of the store. He craned his head, saw them, and settled back to sip his tea.

In five minutes he came forward, patting his shapeless lips with a large white handkerchief.

Mendel, breathing heavily, handed him the worn gold watch. The pawnbroker, raising his glasses, screwed in his eyepiece. He turned the watch over once. "Eight dollars."

The dying man wet his cracked lips. "I must have thirty-five."

"So go to Rothschild."

"Cost me myself sixty."

"In 1905." The pawnbroker handed back the watch. It had stopped ticking. Mendel wound it slowly. It ticked hollowly.

"Isaac must go to my uncle that he lives in California."

"It's a free country," said the pawnbroker.

Isaac, watching a banjo, snickered.

"What's the matter with him?" the pawnbroker asked.

"So let be eight dollars," muttered Mendel, "but where will I get the rest till tonight?"

"How much for my hat and coat?" he asked.

"No sale." The pawnbroker went behind the cage and wrote out a ticket. He locked the watch in a small drawer but Mendel still heard it ticking.

In the street he slipped the eight dollars into the paper bag, then searched in his pockets for a scrap of writing. Finding it, he strained to read the address by the light of the street lamp.

As they trudged to the subway, Mendel pointed to the sprinkled sky.

"Isaac, look how many stars are tonight."

"Eggs," said Isaac.

"First we will go to Mr. Fishbein, after we will eat."

They got off the train in upper Manhattan and had to walk several blocks before they located Fishbein's house.

"A regular palace," Mendel murmured, looking forward to a moment's warmth.

Isaac stared uneasily at the heavy door of the house.

Mendel rang. The servant, a man with long sideburns, came to the door and said Mr. and Mrs. Fishbein were dining and could see no one.

"He should eat in peace but we will wait till he finishes."

"Come back tomorrow morning. Tomorrow morning Mr. Fishbein will talk to you. He don't do business or charity at this time of the night."

"Charity I am not interested—"

"Come back tomorrow."

"Tell him it's life or death—"

"Whose life or death?"

"So if not his, then mine."

"Don't be such a big smart aleck."

"Look me in my face," said Mendel, "and tell me if I got time till tomorrow morning?"

The servant stared at him, then at Isaac, and reluctantly let them in.

The foyer was a vast high-ceilinged room with many oil paintings on the walls, voluminous silken draperies, a thick flowered rug on the floor, and a marble staircase.

Mr. Fishbein, a paunchy bald-headed man with hairy nostrils and small patent-leather feet, ran lightly down the stairs, a large napkin tucked under a tuxedo coat button. He stopped on the fifth step from the bottom and examined his visitors.

"Who comes on Friday night to a man that he has guests to spoil him his supper?"

"Excuse me that I bother you, Mr. Fishbein," Mendel said. "If I didn't come now I couldn't come tomorrow."

"Without more preliminaries, please state your business. I'm a hungry man."

"Hungrig," wailed Isaac.

Fishbein adjusted his pince-nez. "What's the matter with him?"

"This is my son Isaac. He is like this all his life."

Isaac mewled.

"I am sending him to California."

"Mr. Fishbein don't contribute to personal pleasure trips."

"I am a sick man and he must go tonight on the train to my Uncle Leo."

"I never give to unorganized charity," Fishbein said, "but if you are hungry I will invite you downstairs in my kitchen. We having tonight chicken with stuffed derma."

"All I ask is thirty-five dollars for the train to my uncle in California. I have already the rest."

"Who is your uncle? How old a man?"

"Eighty-one years, a long life to him."

Fishbein burst into laughter. "Eighty-one years and you are sending him this halfwit."

Mendel, flailing both arms, cried, "Please, without names."

Fishbein politely conceded.

"Where is open the door there we go in the house," the sick man said. "If you will kindly give me thirty-five dollars, God will bless you. What is thirty-five dollars to Mr. Fishbein? Nothing. To me, for my boy, is everything."

Fishbein drew himself up to his tallest height.

"Private contributions I don't make—only to institutions. This is my fixed policy."

Mendel sank to his creaking knees on the rug.

"Please, Mr. Fishbein, if not thirty-five, give maybe twenty."

"Levinson!" Fishbein angrily called.

The servant with the long sideburns appeared at the top of the stairs.

"Show this party where is the door—unless he wishes to partake food before leaving the premises."

"For what I got chicken won't cure it," Mendel said.

"This way if you please," said Levinson, descending.

Isaac assisted his father up.

"Take him to an institution," Fishbein advised over the marble balustrade. He ran quickly up the stairs and they were at once outside, buffeted by winds.

The walk to the subway was tedious. The wind blew mournfully. Mendel, breathless, glanced furtively at shadows. Isaac, clutching his peanuts in his frozen fist, clung to his father's side. They entered a small park to rest for a minute on a stone bench under a leafless two-branched tree. The thick right branch was raised, the thin left one hung down. A very pale moon rose slowly. So did a stranger as they approached the bench.

"Gut yuntif," he said hoarsely.

Mendel, drained of blood, waved his wasted arms. Isaac yowled sickly. Then a bell chimed and it was only ten. Mendel let out a piercing anguished cry as the bearded stranger disappeared into the bushes. A policeman came running and, though he beat the bushes with his nightstick, could turn up nothing. Mendel and Isaac hurried out of the little park. When Mendel glanced back the dead tree had its thin arm raised, the thick one down. He moaned.

They boarded a trolley, stopping at the home of a former friend, but he had died years ago. On the same block they went into a cafeteria and ordered two fried eggs for Isaac. The tables were crowded except where a heavyset man sat eating soup with kasha. After one look at him they left in haste, although Isaac wept.

Mendel had another address on a slip of paper but the house was too far away, in Queens, so they stood in a doorway shivering.

What can I do, he frantically thought, in one short hour?

He remembered the furniture in the house. It was junk but might bring a few dollars. "Come, Isaac." They went once more to the pawnbroker's to talk to him, but the shop was dark and an iron gate—rings and gold watches glinting through it—was drawn tight across his place of business.

They huddled behind a telephone pole, both freezing. Isaac whimpered.

"See the big moon, Isaac. The whole sky is white."

He pointed but Isaac wouldn't look.

Mendel dreamed for a minute of the sky lit up, long sheets of light in all directions. Under the sky, in California, sat Uncle Leo drinking tea with lemon. Mendel felt warm but woke up cold.

Across the street stood an ancient brick synagogue.

He pounded on the huge door but no one appeared. He waited till he had breath and desperately knocked again. At last there were footsteps within, and the synagogue door creaked open on its massive brass hinges.

A darkly dressed sexton, holding a dripping candle, glared at them.

"Who knocks this time of night with so much noise on the synagogue door?"

Mendel told the sexton his troubles. "Please, I would like to speak to the rabbi."

"The rabbi is an old man. He sleeps now. His wife won't let you see him. Go home and come back tomorrow."

"To tomorrow I said goodbye already. I am a dying man."

Though the sexton seemed doubtful he pointed to an old wooden house next door. "In there he lives." He disappeared into the synagogue with his lit candle casting shadows around him.

Mendel, with Isaac clutching his sleeve, went up the wooden steps and rang the bell. After five minutes a big-faced, gray-haired, bulky woman came out on the porch with a torn robe thrown over her nightdress. She emphatically said the rabbi was sleeping and could not be waked.

But as she was insisting, the rabbi himself tottered to the door. He listened a minute and said, "Who wants to see me let them come in."

They entered a cluttered room. The rabbi was an old skinny man with bent shoulders and a wisp of white beard. He wore a flannel nightgown and black skullcap; his feet were bare.

"Vey is mir," his wife muttered. "Put on shoes or tomorrow comes sure pneumonia." She was a woman with a big belly, years younger than her husband. Staring at Isaac, she turned away.

Mendel apologetically related his errand. "All I need is thirty-five dollars."

"Thirty-five?" said the rabbi's wife. "Why not thirty-five thousand? Who has so much money? My husband is a poor rabbi. The doctors take away every penny."

"Dear friend," said the rabbi, "if I had I would give you."

"I got already seventy," Mendel said, heavy-hearted. "All I need more is thirty-five."

"God will give you," said the rabbi.

"In the grave," said Mendel. "I need tonight. Come, Isaac."

"Wait," called the rabbi.

He hurried inside, came out with a fur-lined caftan, and handed it to Mendel.

"Yascha," shrieked his wife, "not your new coat!"

"I got my old one. Who needs two coats for one old body?"

"Yascha, I am screaming—"

"Who can go among poor people, tell me, in a new coat?"

"Yascha," she cried, "what can this man do with your coat? He needs tonight the money. The pawnbrokers are asleep."

"So let him wake them up."

"No." She grabbed the coat from Mendel.

He held onto a sleeve, wrestling her for the coat. Her I know, Mendel thought. "Shylock," he muttered. Her eyes glittered.

The rabbi groaned and tottered dizzily. His wife cried out as Mendel yanked the coat from her hands.

"Run," cried the rabbi.

"Run, Isaac."

They ran out of the house and down the steps.

"Stop, you thief," called the rabbi's wife.

The rabbi pressed both hands to his temples and fell to the floor. "Help!" his wife wept. "Heart attack! Help!"

But Mendel and Isaac ran through the streets with the rabbi's new fur-lined caftan. After them noiselessly ran Ginzburg.

It was very late when Mendel bought the train ticket in the only booth open.

There was no time to stop for a sandwich so Isaac ate his peanuts and they hurried to the train in the vast deserted station.

"So in the morning," Mendel gasped as they ran, "there comes a man that he sells sandwiches and coffee. Eat but get change. When reaches California the train, will be waiting for you on the station Uncle Leo. If you don't recognize him he will recognize you. Tell him I send best regards."

But when they arrived at the gate to the platform it was shut, the light out.

"Too late," said the uniformed ticket collector, a bulky, bearded man with hairy nostrils and a fishy smell.

He pointed to the station clock. "Already past twelve."

"But I see standing there still the train," Mendel said, hopping in his grief.

"It just left—in one more minute."

"A minute is enough. Just open the gate."

"Too late I told you."

Mendel socked his bony chest with both hands. "With my whole heart I beg you this little favor."

"Favors you had enough already. For you the train is gone. You shoulda been dead already at midnight. I told you that yesterday. This is the best I can do."

"Ginzburg!" Mendel shrank from him.

"Who else?" The voice was metallic, eyes glittered, the expression amused.

"For myself," the old man begged, "I don't ask a thing. But what will happen to my boy?"

Ginzburg shrugged slightly. "What will happen happens. This isn't my responsibility. I got enough to think about without worrying about somebody on one cylinder."

"What then is your responsibility?"

"To create conditions. To make happen what happens. I ain't in the anthropomorphic business."

"Whichever business you in, where is your pity?"

"This ain't my commodity. The law is the law."

"Which law is this?"

"The cosmic, universal law, goddamn it, the one I got to follow myself."

"What kind of a law is it?" cried Mendel. "For God's sake, don't you understand what I went through in my life with this poor boy? Look at him. For thirty-nine years, since the day he was born, I wait for him to grow up, but he don't. Do you understand what this means in a father's heart? Why don't you let him go to his uncle?" His voice had risen and he was shouting.

Isaac mewled loudly.

"Better calm down or you'll hurt somebody's feelings," Ginzburg said, with a wink toward Isaac.

"All my life," Mendel cried, his body trembling, "what did I have? I was poor. I suffered from my health. When I worked I worked too hard. When I didn't work was worse. My wife died a young woman. But I didn't ask from anybody nothing. Now I ask a small favor. Be so kind, Mr. Ginzburg."

The ticket collector was picking his teeth with a matchstick.

"You ain't the only one, my friend, some got it worse than you. That's how it goes."

"You dog you." Mendel lunged at Ginzburg's throat and began to choke. "You bastard, don't you understand what it means human?"

They struggled nose to nose. Ginzburg, though his astonished eyes bulged, began to laugh. "You pipsqueak nothing. I'll freeze you to pieces."

His eyes lit in rage, and Mendel felt an unbearable cold like an icy dagger invading his body, all of his parts shriveling.

Now I die without helping Isaac.

A crowd gathered. Isaac yelped in fright.

Clinging to Ginzburg in his last agony, Mendel saw reflected in the ticket collector's eyes the depth of his terror. Ginzburg, staring at himself in Mendel's eyes, saw mirrored in them the extent of his own awful wrath. He beheld a shimmering, starry, blinding light that produced darkness.

Ginzburg looked astounded. "Who, me?"

His grip on the squirming old man loosened, and Mendel, his heart barely beating, slumped to the ground.

"Go," Ginzburg muttered, "take him to the train."

"Let pass," he commanded a guard.

The crowd parted. Isaac helped his father up and they tottered down the steps to the platform where the train waited, lit and ready to go.

Mendel found Isaac a coach seat and hastily embraced him. "Help Uncle Leo, Isaakl. Also remember your father and mother."

"Be nice to him," he said to the conductor. "Show him where everything is."

He waited on the platform until the train began slowly to move. Isaac sat at the edge of his seat, his face strained in the direction of his journey. When the train was gone, Mendel ascended the stairs to see what had become of Ginzburg.

JEAN STAFFORD

In the Zoo

Keening harshly in his senility, the blind polar bear slowly and ceaselessly shakes his head in the stark heat of the July and mountain noon. His open eyes are blue. No one stops to look at him; an old farmer, in passing, sums up the old bear's situation by observing, with a ruthless chuckle, that he is a "back number." Patient and despairing, he sits on his yellowed haunches on the central rock of his pool, his huge toy paws wearing short boots of mud.

The grizzlies to the right of him, a conventional family of father and mother and two spring cubs, alternately play the clown and sleep. There is a blustery, scoundrelly, half-likable bravado in the manner of the black bear on the polar's left; his name, according to the legend on his cage, is Clancy, and he is a rough-and-tumble, brawling blowhard, thundering continually as he paces back and forth, or pauses to face his audience of children and mothers and release from his great, gray-tongued mouth a perfectly Vesuvian roar. If he were to be reincarnated in human form, he would be a man of action, possibly a football coach, probably a politician. One expects to see his black hat hanging from a branch of one of his trees; at any moment he will light a cigar.

The polar bear's next-door neighbors are not the only ones who offer so sharp and sad a contrast to him. Across a reach of scrappy grass and litter is the convocation of conceited monkeys, burrowing into each other's necks and chests for fleas, picking their noses with their long, black, finicky fingers, swinging by their gifted tails on the flying trapeze, screaming bloody murder. Even when they mourn—one would think the male orangutan was on the very brink of suicide—they are comedians; they only fake depression, for they are firmly secure in their rambunctious tribalism and in their appalling insight and contempt. Their flibbertigibbet gamboling is a sham, and, stealthily and shiftily, they are really watching the pitiful polar bear ("Back number," they quote the farmer. "That's *his* number all right," they snigger), and the windy black bear ("Life of the party. Gasbag. Low I.Q.," they note scornfully on his dossier), and the stupid, bourgeois grizzlies ("It's feed the face and hit the sack for them," the monkeys say). And they are watching my sister and me, two middle-aged women, as we sit on a bench between the exhibits, eating popcorn, growing thirsty. We are thoughtful.

A chance remark of Daisy's a few minutes before has turned us to memory and meditation. "I don't know why," she said, "but that poor blind bear reminds me of Mr. Murphy." The name "Mr. Murphy" at once returned us both to childhood, and we were floated far and fast, our later lives diminished. So now we eat our popcorn in silence with the ritualistic appetite of childhood, which has little to do with hunger; it is not so much food as a sacrament, and in tribute to our sisterliness and our friendliness I break the silence to say that this is the best popcorn I have ever eaten in my life. The extravagance of my statement instantly makes me feel self-indulgent, and for some time I uneasily avoid looking at the blind bear. My sister does not agree or disagree; she simply says that popcorn is the only food she has ever really liked. For a long time, then, we eat without a word, but I know, because I know her well and know her similarity to me, that Daisy is thinking what I am thinking; both of us are mournfully remembering Mr. Murphy, who, at one time in our lives, was our only friend.

This zoo is in Denver, a city that means nothing to my sister and me except as a place to take or meet trains. Daisy lives two hundred miles farther west, and it is her custom, when my every-other-year visit with her is over, to come across the mountains to see me off on my eastbound train. We know almost no one here, and because our stays are short, we have never bothered to learn the town in more than the most desultory way. We know the Burlington uptown office and the respectable hotels, a restaurant or two, the Union Station, and, beginning today, the zoo in the city park.

But since the moment that Daisy named Mr. Murphy by name our situation in Denver has been only corporeal; our minds and our hearts are in Adams, fifty miles north, and we are seeing, under the white sun at its pitiless meridian, the streets of that ugly town, its parks and trees and bridges, the bandstand in its dreary park, the roads that lead away from it, west to the mountains and east to the plains, its mongrel and multitudinous churches, its high school shaped like a loaf of bread, the campus of its college, an oasis of which we had no experience except to walk through it now and then, eyeing the woodbine on the impressive buildings. These things are engraved forever on our minds with a legibility so insistent that you have only to say the name of the town aloud to us to rip the rinds from our nerves and leave us exposed in terror and humiliation.

We have supposed in later years that Adams was not so bad as all that, and we know that we magnified its ugliness because we looked upon it as the extension of the possessive, unloving, scornful, complacent foster mother, Mrs. Placer, to whom, at the death of our parents within a month of each other, we were sent like Dickensian grotesqueries—cowardly, weak-stomached, given to tears, backward in school. Daisy was ten and I was eight when, unaccompanied, we made the long trip from Marblehead to our benefactress, whom we had never seen and, indeed, never heard of until the pastor of our church came to tell us of the arrangement our father had made on his deathbed, seconded by our mother on hers. This man, whose name and face I have forgotten and whose parting speeches to us I have not forgiven, tried to dry our tears with talk of Indians and of buffaloes; he spoke, however, at much greater length, and in preaching cadences, of the Christian goodness of Mrs. Placer. She was, he said, childless and fond of children, and for many years she had been a widow, after the lingering demise of her tubercular husband, for whose sake she had moved to the Rocky Mountains. For his support and costly medical care, she had run a boarding house, and after his death, since he had left her nothing, she was obliged to continue running it. She had been a girlhood friend of our paternal grandmother, and our father, in the absence of responsible relatives, had made her the beneficiary of his life insurance on the condition that she lodge and rear us. The pastor, with a frankness remarkable considering that he was talking to children, explained to us that our father had left little more than a drop in the bucket for our care, and he enjoined us to give Mrs. Placer, in return for her hospitality and sacrifice, courteous help and eternal thanks. "Sacrifice" was a word we were never allowed to forget.

And thus it was, in grief for our parents, that we came cringing to the dry Western town and to the house where Mrs. Placer lived, a house in which the square, uncushioned furniture was cruel and the pictures on the walls were either dour or dire and the lodgers, who lived in the upper floors among shadowy wardrobes and chiffoniers, had come through the years to resemble their landlady in appearance as well as in deportment.

After their ugly-colored evening meal, Gran—as she bade us call her—and her paying guests would sit, rangy and aquiline, rocking on the front porch on spring and summer and autumn nights, tasting their delicious grievances: those slights delivered by ungrateful sons and daughters, those impudences committed by trolley-car conductors and uppity salesgirls in the ready-to-wear, all those slurs and calculated elbow-jostlings that were their daily crucifixion and their staff of life. We little girls, washing the dishes in the cavernous kitchen, listened to their even, martyred voices, fixed like leeches to their solitary subject and their solitary creed—that life was essentially a matter of being done in, let down, and swindled.

At regular intervals, Mrs. Placer, chairwoman of the victims, would say, "Of course, I don't care; I just have to laugh," and then would tell a shocking tale of an intricate piece of skulduggery perpetrated against her by someone she did not even know. Sometimes, with her avid, partial jury sitting there on the porch behind the bitter hopvines in the heady mountain air, the cases she tried involved Daisy and me, and, listening, we travailed, hugging each other, whispering, "I wish she wouldn't! Oh, how did she find out?" How *did* she? Certainly we never told her when we were snubbed or chosen last on teams, never admitted to a teacher's scolding or to the hoots of laughter that greeted us when we bit on silly, unfair jokes. But she knew. She knew about the slumber parties we were not invited to, the beefsteak fries at which we were pointedly left out; she knew that the singing teacher had said in so many words that I could not carry a tune in a basket and that the sewing superintendent had said that Daisy's fingers were all thumbs. With our teeth chattering in the cold of our isolation, we would hear her protestant, litigious voice defending our right to be orphans, paupers, wholly dependent on her—except for the really ridiculous pittance from our father's life insurance—when it was all she could do to make ends meet. She did not care, but she had to laugh that people in general were so small-minded that they looked down on fatherless, motherless waifs like us and, by association, looked down on her. It seemed funny to her that people gave her no credit for taking on these sickly youngsters who were not even kin but only the grandchildren of a friend.

If a child with braces on her teeth came to play with us, she was, according to Gran, slyly lording it over us because our teeth were crooked but there was no money to have them straightened. And what could be the meaning of our being asked to come for supper at the doctor's house? Were the doctor and his la-di-da New York wife and those pert girls with their solid-gold barrettes and their Shetland pony going to shame her poor darlings? Or shame their poor Gran by making them sorry to come home to the plain but honest life that was all she could provide for them?

There was no stratum of society not reeking with the effluvium of fraud and pettifoggery. And the school system was almost the worst of all: if we could not understand fractions, was that not our teacher's fault? And therefore what right had she to give us F? It was as plain as a pikestaff to Gran that the teacher was only covering up her own inability to teach. It was unlikely, too—highly unlikely—that it was by accident that time and time again the free medical clinic was closed for the day just as our names were about to be called out, so that nothing was done about our bad tonsils, which meant that we were repeatedly sick in the winter, with Gran fetching and carrying for us, climbing those stairs a jillion times a day with her game leg and her heart that was none too strong.

Steeped in these mists of accusation and hidden plots and double meanings, Daisy and I grew up like worms. I think no one could have withstood the atmosphere in that house where everyone trod on eggs that a little bird had told them were bad. They spied on one another, whispered behind doors, conjectured, drew parallels beginning "With all due respect . . ." or "It is a matter of indifference to *me* but . . ." The vigilantes patrolled our town by day, and by night returned to lay their goodies at their priestess's feet and wait for her oracular interpretation of the innards of the butcher, the baker, the candlestick maker, the soda jerk's girl, and the barber's unnatural deaf white cat.

Consequently, Daisy and I also became suspicious. But it was suspicion of ourselves that made us mope and weep and grimace with self-judgment. Why were we not happy when Gran had sacrificed herself to the bone for us? Why did we not cut dead the paper boy who had called her a filthy name? Why did we persist in our willful friendliness with the grocer who had tried, unsuccessfully, to overcharge her on a case of pork and beans?

Our friendships were nervous and surreptitious; we sneaked and lied, and as our hungers sharpened, our debasement deepened; we were pitied; we were shifty-eyed, always on the lookout for Mrs. Placer or one of her tattletale lodgers; we were hypocrites.

Nevertheless, one thin filament of instinct survived, and Daisy and I in time found asylum in a small menagerie down by the railroad tracks. It belonged to a gentle alcoholic ne'er-do-well, who did nothing all day long but drink bathtub gin in rickeys and play solitaire and smile to himself and talk to his animals. He had a little, stunted red vixen and a deodorized skunk, a parrot from Tahiti that spoke Parisian French, a woe-begone coyote, and two capuchin monkeys, so serious and humanized, so small and sad and sweet, and so religious-looking with their tonsured heads that it was impossible not to think their gibberish was really an ordered language with a grammar that some day some philologist would understand.

Gran knew about our visits to Mr. Murphy and she did not object, for it gave her keen pleasure to excoriate him when we came home. His vice was not a matter of guesswork; it was an established fact that he was half-seas over from dawn till midnight. "With the black Irish," said Gran, "the taste for drink is taken in with the mother's milk and is never mastered. Oh, I know all about those promises to join the temperance movement and not to touch another drop. The way to hell is paved with good intentions."

We were still little girls when we discovered Mr. Murphy, before the shattering disease of adolescence was to make our bones and brains ache even more painfully than before, and we loved him and we hoped to marry him when we grew up. We loved him, and we loved his monkeys to exactly the same degree and in exactly the same way; they were husbands and fathers and brothers, these three little, ugly, dark, secret men who minded their own business and let us mind ours. If we stuck our fingers through the bars of the cage, the monkeys would sometimes take them in their tight, tiny hands and look into our faces with a tentative, somehow absent-minded sorrow, as if they terribly regretted that they could not place us but were glad to see us all the same. Mr. Murphy, playing a solitaire game of cards called "once in a blue moon" on a kitchen table in his back yard beside the pens, would occasionally look up and blink his beautiful blue eyes and say, "You're peaches to make over my wee friends. I love you for it." There was nothing demanding in his voice, and nothing sticky; on his lips the word "love" was jocose and forthright, it had no strings attached. We would sit on either side of him and watch him regiment his ranks of cards and stop to drink as deeply as if he were dying of thirst and wave to his animals and say to them, "Yes, lads, you're dandies."

Because Mr. Murphy was as reserved with us as the capuchins were, as courteously noncommittal, we were surprised one spring day when he told us that he had a present for us, which he hoped Mrs. Placer would let us keep; it was a puppy, for whom the owner had asked him to find a home—half collie and half Labrador retriever, blue-blooded on both sides.

"You might tell Mrs. Placer—" he said, smiling at the name, for Gran was famous in the town. "You might tell Mrs. Placer," said Mr. Murphy, "that this lad will make a fine watchdog. She'll never have to fear for her spoons again. Or her honor." The last he said to himself, not laughing but tucking his chin into his collar; lines sprang to the corners of his eyes. He would not let us see the dog, whom we could hear yipping and squealing inside his shanty, for he said that our disappointment would weigh on his conscience if we lost our hearts to the fellow and then could not have him for our own.

That evening at supper, we told Gran about Mr. Murphy's present. A dog? In the first place, why a dog? Was it possible that the news had reached Mr. Murphy's ears that Gran had just this very day finished planting her spring garden, the very thing that a rampageous dog would have in his mind to destroy? What sex was it? A male! Females, she had heard, were more trustworthy; males roved and came home smelling of skunk; such a consideration as this, of course, would not have crossed Mr. Murphy's fuddled mind. Was this young male dog housebroken? We had not asked? That was the limit!

Gran appealed to her followers, too raptly fascinated by Mr. Murphy's machinations to eat their Harvard beets. "Am I being farfetched or does it strike you as decidedly queer that Mr. Murphy is trying to fob off on my little girls a young cur that has not been trained?" she asked them. "If it were housebroken, he would have said so, so I feel it is safe to assume that it is not. Perhaps cannot *be* housebroken. I've heard of such cases."

The fantasy spun on, richly and rapidly, with all the skilled helping hands at work at once. The dog was tangibly in the room with us, shedding his hair, scratching his fleas, shaking rain off himself to splatter the walls, dragging some dreadful carcass across the floor, chewing up slippers, knocking over chairs with his tail, gobbling the chops from the platter, barking, biting, fathering, fighting, smelling to high heaven of carrion, staining the rug with his muddy feet, scratching the floor with his claws. He developed rabies; he bit a child, two children! Three! Everyone in town! And Gran and her poor darlings went to jail for harboring this murderous, odoriferous, drunk, Roman Catholic dog.

And yet, astoundingly enough, she came around to agreeing to let us have the dog. It was, as Mr. Murphy had predicted, the word "watchdog" that deflected the course of the trial. The moment Daisy uttered it, Gran halted, marshaling her reverse march; while she rallied and tacked and reconnoitered, she sent us to the kitchen for the dessert. And by the time this course was under way, the uses of a dog, the enormous potentialities for investigation and law enforcement in a dog trained by Mrs. Placer, were being minutely and passionately scrutinized by the eight upright bloodhounds sitting at the table wolfing their brown Betty as if it were fresh-killed rabbit. The dog now sat at attention beside his mistress, fiercely alert, ears cocked, nose aquiver, the protector of widows, of orphans, of lonely people who had no homes. He made short shrift of burglars, homicidal maniacs, Peeping Toms, gypsies, bogus missionaries, Fuller Brush men with a risqué spiel. He went to the store and brought back groceries, retrieved the evening paper from the awkward place the boy had meanly thrown it, rescued cripples from burning houses, saved children from drowning, heeled at command, begged, lay down, stood up, sat, jumped through a hoop, ratted.

Both times—when he was a ruffian of the blackest delinquency and then a pillar of society—he was full-grown in his prefiguration, and when Laddy appeared on the following day, small, unsteady, and whimpering lonesomely, Gran and her lodgers were taken aback; his infant, clumsy paws embarrassed them, his melting eyes were unapropos. But it could never be said of Mrs. Placer, as Mrs. Placer her own self said, that she was a woman who went back on her word, and her darlings were going to have their dog, softheaded and feckless as he might be. All the first night, in his carton in the kitchen, he wailed for his mother, and in the morning, it was true, he had made a shambles of the room—fouled the floor, and pulled off the tablecloth together with a ketchup bottle, so that thick gore lay everywhere. At breakfast, the lodgers confessed they had had a most amusing night, for it had actually been funny the way the dog had been determined not to let anyone get a wink of sleep. After that first night, Laddy slept in our room, receiving from us, all through our delighted, sleepless nights, pats and embraces and kisses and whispers. He was our baby, our best friend, the smartest, prettiest, nicest dog in the entire wide world. Our soft and rapid blandishments excited him to yelp at us in pleased bewilderment, and then we would playfully grasp his muzzle, so that he would snarl, deep in his throat like an adult dog, and shake his head violently, and, when we freed him, nip us smartly with great good will.

He was an intelligent and genial dog and we trained him quickly. He steered clear of Gran's radishes and lettuce after she had several times given him a brisk comeuppance with a strap across the rump, and he soon left off chewing shoes and the laundry on the line, and he outgrew his babyish whining. He grew like a weed; he lost his spherical softness, and his coat, which had been sooty fluff, came in stiff and rusty black; his nose grew aristocratically long, and his clever, pointed ears stood at attention. He was all bronzy, lustrous black except for an Elizabethan ruff of white and a tip of white at the end of his perky tail. No one could deny that he was exceptionally handsome and that he had, as well, great personal charm and style. He escorted Daisy and me to school in the morning, laughing interiorly out of the enormous pleasure of his life as he gracefully cantered ahead of us, distracted occasionally by his private interest in smells or unfamiliar beings in the grass but, on the whole, engrossed in his role of chaperon. He made friends easily with other dogs, and sometimes he went for a long hunting weekend into the mountains with a huge and bossy old red hound named Mess, who had been on the county most of his life and had made a good thing of it, particularly at the fire station.

It was after one of these three-day excursions into the high country that Gran took Laddy in hand. He had come back spent and filthy, his coat a mass of cockleburs and ticks, his eyes bloodshot, loud *râles* in his chest; for half a day he lay motionless before the front door like someone in a hangover, his groaning eyes explicitly saying "Oh, for God's sake, leave me be" when we offered him food or bowls of water. Gran was disapproving, then affronted, and finally furious. Not, of course, with Laddy, since all inmates of her house enjoyed immunity, but with Mess, whose caddish character, together with that of his nominal masters, the firemen, she examined closely under a strong light, with an air of detachment, with her not caring but her having, all the same, to laugh. A lodger who occupied the back west room had something to say about the fire chief and his nocturnal visits to a certain house occupied by a certain group of young women, too near the same age to be sisters and too old to be the daughters of the woman who claimed to be their mother. What a story! The exophthalmic librarian—she lived in one of the front rooms—had some interesting insinuations to make about the deputy marshal, who had borrowed, significantly, she thought, a book on hypnotism. She also knew—she was, of course, in a most useful position in the town, and from her authoritative pen in the middle of the library her mammiform and azure eyes and her eager ears missed nothing—that the fire chief's wife was not as scrupulous as she might be when she was keeping score on bridge night at the Sorosis.

There was little at the moment that Mrs. Placer and her disciples could do to save the souls of the Fire Department and their families, and therefore save the town from holocaust (a very timid boarder—a Mr. Beaver, a newcomer who was not to linger long—had sniffed throughout this recitative as if he were smelling burning flesh), but at least the unwholesome bond between Mess and Laddy could and would be severed once and for all. Gran looked across the porch at Laddy, who lay stretched at full length in the darkest corner, shuddering and baying abortively in his throat as he chased jack rabbits in his dreams, and she said, "A dog can have morals like a human." With this declaration Laddy's randy, manly holidays were finished. It may have been telepathy that woke him; he lifted his heavy head from his paws, laboriously got up, hesitated for a moment, and then padded languidly across the porch to Gran. He stood docilely beside her chair, head down, tail drooping as if to say, "O.K., Mrs. Placer, show me how and I'll walk the straight and narrow."

The very next day, Gran changed Laddy's name to Caesar, as being more dignified, and a joke was made at the supper table that he had come, seen, and conquered Mrs. Placer's heart—for within her circle, where the magnanimity she lavished upon her orphans was daily demonstrated, Mrs. Placer's heart was highly thought of. On that day also, although we did not know it yet, Laddy ceased to be our dog. Before many weeks passed, indeed, he ceased to be anyone we had ever known. A week or so after he became Caesar, he took up residence in her room, sleeping alongside her bed. She broke him of the habit of taking us to school (temptation to low living was rife along those streets; there was a chow—well, never mind) by the simple expedient of chaining him to a tree as soon as she got up in the morning. This discipline, together with the stamina-building cuffs she gave his sensitive ears from time to time, gradually but certainly remade his character. From a sanguine, affectionate, easygoing Gael (with the fits of melancholy that alternated with the larkiness), he turned into an overbearing, military, efficient, loud-voiced Teuton. His bark, once wide of range, narrowed to one dark, glottal tone.

Soon the paper boy flatly refused to serve our house after Caesar efficiently removed the bicycle clip from his pants leg; the skin was not broken, or even bruised, but it was a matter of principle with the boy. The milkman approached the back door in a seizure of shakes like St. Vitus's dance. The metermen, the coal men, and the garbage collector crossed themselves if they were Catholics and, if they were not, tried whistling in the dark. "Good boy, good Caesar," they caroled, and, unctuously lying, they said they knew his bark was worse than his bite, knowing full well that it was not, considering the very nasty nip, requiring stitches, he had given a representative of the Olson Rug Company, who had had the folly to pat him on the head. Caesar did not molest the lodgers, but he disdained them and he did not brook being personally addressed by anyone except Gran. One night, he wandered into the dining room, appearing to be in search of something he had mislaid, and, for some reason that no one was ever able to divine, suddenly stood stock-still and gave the easily upset Mr. Beaver a long and penetrating look. Mr. Beaver, trembling from head to toe, stammered, "Why—er, hello there, Caesar, old boy, old boy," and Caesar charged. For a moment, it was touch and go, but Gran saved Mr. Beaver, only to lose him an hour later when he departed, bag and baggage, for the Y.M.C.A. This rout and the consequent loss of revenue would more than likely have meant Caesar's downfall and his deportation to the pound if it had not been that a newly widowed druggist, very irascible and very much Gran's style, had applied for a room in her house a week or so before, and now he moved in delightedly, as if he were coming home.

Finally, the police demanded that Caesar be muzzled and they warned that if he committed any major crime again—they cited the case of the Olson man—he would be shot on sight. Mrs. Placer, although she had no respect for the law, knowing as much as she did about its agents, obeyed. She obeyed, that is, in part; she put the muzzle on Caesar for a few hours a day, usually early in the morning when the traffic was light and before the deliveries had started, but the rest of the time his powerful jaws and dazzling white saber teeth were free and snapping. There was between these two such preternatural rapport, such an impressive conjugation of suspicion, that he, sensing the approach of a policeman, could convey instantly to her the immediate necessity of clapping his nose cage on. And the policeman, sent out on the complaint of a terrorized neighbor, would be greeted by this law-abiding pair at the door.

Daisy and I wished we were dead. We were divided between hating Caesar and loving Laddy, and we could not give up the hope that something, some day, would change him back into the loving animal he had been before he was appointed vice-president of the Placerites. Now at the meetings after supper on the porch he took an active part, standing rigidly at Gran's side except when she sent him on an errand. He carried out these assignments not with the air of a servant but with that of an accomplice. "Get me the paper, Caesar," she would say to him, and he, dismayingly intelligent and a shade smart-alecky, would open the screen door by himself and in a minute come back with the *Bulletin,* from which Mrs. Placer would then read an item, like the Gospel of the day, and then read between the lines of it, scandalized.

In the deepening of our woe and our bereavement and humiliation, we mutely appealed to Mr. Murphy. We did not speak outright to him, for Mr. Murphy lived in a state of indirection, and often when he used the pronoun "I," he seemed to be speaking of someone standing a little to the left of him, but we went to see him and his animals each day during the sad summer, taking what comfort we could from the cozy, quiet indolence of his back yard, where small black eyes encountered ours politely and everyone was half asleep. When Mr. Murphy inquired about Laddy in his bland, inattentive way, looking for a stratagem whereby to shift the queen of hearts into position by the king, we would say, "Oh, he's fine," or "Laddy is a nifty dog." And Mr. Murphy, reverently slaking the thirst that was his talent and his concubine, would murmur, "I'm glad."

We wanted to tell him, we wanted his help, or at least his sympathy, but how could we cloud his sunny world? It was awful to see Mr. Murphy ruffled. Up in the calm clouds as he generally was, he could occasionally be brought to earth with a thud, as we had seen and heard one day. Not far from his house, there lived a bad, troublemaking boy of twelve, who was forever hanging over the fence trying to teach the parrot obscene words. He got nowhere, for she spoke no English and she would flabbergast him with her cold eye and sneer, "*Tant pis.*" One day, this boorish fellow went too far; he suddenly shot his head over the fence like a jack-in-the-box and aimed a water pistol at the skunk's face. Mr. Murphy leaped to his feet in a scarlet rage; he picked up a stone and threw it accurately, hitting the boy square in the back, so hard that he fell right down in a mud puddle and lay there kicking and squalling and, as it turned out, quite badly hurt. "If you ever come back here again, I'll kill you!" roared Mr. Murphy. I think he meant it, for I have seldom seen an anger so resolute, so brilliant, and so voluble. "How dared he!" he cried, scrambling into Mallow's cage to hug and pet and soothe her. "He must be absolutely mad! He must be the Devil!" He did not go back to his game after that but paced the yard, swearing a blue streak and only pausing to croon to his animals, now as frightened by him as they had been by the intruder, and to drink straight from the bottle, not bothering with fixings. We were fascinated by this unfamiliar side of Mr. Murphy, but we did not want to see it ever again, for his face had grown so dangerously purple and the veins of his forehead seemed ready to burst and his eyes looked scorched. He was the closest thing to a maniac we had ever seen. So we did not tell him about Laddy; what he did not know would not hurt him, although it was hurting us, throbbing in us like a great, bleating wound.

But eventually Mr. Murphy heard about our dog's conversion, one night at the pool hall, which he visited from time to time when he was seized with a rare but compelling garrulity, and the next afternoon when he asked us how Laddy was and we replied that he was fine, he tranquilly told us, as he deliberated whether to move the jack of clubs now or to bide his time, that we were sweet girls but we were lying in our teeth. He did not seem at all angry but only interested, and all the while he questioned us, he went on about his business with the gin and the hearts and spades and diamonds and clubs. It rarely happened that he won the particular game he was playing, but that day he did, and when he saw all the cards laid out in their ideal pattern, he leaned back, looking disappointed, and he said, "I'm damned." He then scooped up the cards, in a gesture unusually quick and tidy for him, stacked them together, and bound them with a rubber band. Then he began to tell us what he thought of Gran. He grew as loud and apoplectic as he had been that other time, and though he kept repeating that he knew *we* were innocent and he put not a shred of the blame on us, we were afraid he might suddenly change his mind, and, speechless, we cowered against the monkeys' cage. In dread, the monkeys clutched the fingers we offered to them and made soft, protesting noises, as if to say, "Oh, stop it, Murphy! Our nerves!"

As quickly as it had started, the tantrum ended. Mr. Murphy paled to his normal complexion and said calmly that the only practical thing was to go and have it out with Mrs. Placer. "At once," he added, although he said he bitterly feared that it was too late and there would be no exorcising the fiend from Laddy's misused spirit. And because he had given the dog to us and not to her, he required that we go along with him, stick up for our rights, stand on our own mettle, get up our Irish, and give the old bitch something to put in her pipe and smoke.

Oh, it was hot that day! We walked in a kind of delirium through the simmer, where only the grasshoppers had the energy to move, and I remember wondering if ether smelled like the gin on Mr. Murphy's breath. Daisy and I, in one way or another, were going to have our gizzards cut out along with our hearts and our souls and our pride, and I wished I were as drunk as Mr. Murphy, who swam effortlessly through the heat, his lips parted comfortably, his eyes half closed. When we turned in to the path at Gran's house, my blood began to scald my veins. It was so futile and so dangerous and so absurd. Here we were on a high moral mission, two draggletailed, gumptionless little girls and a toper whom no one could take seriously, partly because he was little more than a gurgling bottle of booze and partly because of the clothes he wore. He was a sight, as he always was when he was out of his own yard. There, somehow, in the carefree disorder, his clothes did not look especially strange, but on the streets of the town, in the barbershop or the post office or on Gran's path, they were fantastic. He wore a pair of hound's-tooth pants, old but maintaining a vehement pattern, and with them he wore a collarless blue flannelette shirt. His hat was the silliest of all, because it was a derby three sizes too big. And as if Shannon, too, was a part of his funny-paper costume, the elder capuchin rode on his shoulder, tightly embracing his thin red neck.

Gran and Caesar were standing side by side behind the screen door, looking as if they had been expecting us all along. For a moment, Gran and Mr. Murphy faced each other across the length of weedy brick between the gate and the front porch, and no one spoke. Gran took no notice at all of Daisy and me. She adjusted her eyeglasses, using both hands, and then looked down at Caesar and matter-of-factly asked, "Do you want out?"

Caesar flung himself full-length upon the screen and it sprang open like a jaw. I ran to meet him and head him off, and Daisy threw a library book at his head, but he was on Mr. Murphy in one split second and had his monkey off his shoulder and had broken Shannon's neck in two shakes. He would have gone on nuzzling and mauling and growling over the corpse for hours if Gran had not marched out of the house and down the path and slapped him lightly on the flank and said, in a voice that could not have deceived an idiot, "Why, Caesar, you scamp! You've hurt Mr. Murphy's monkey! Aren't you ashamed!"

Hurt the monkey! In one final, apologetic shudder, the life was extinguished from the little fellow. Bloody and covered with slather, Shannon lay with his arms suppliantly stretched over his head, his leather fingers curled into loose, helpless fists. His hind legs and his tail lay limp and helter-skelter on the path. And Mr. Murphy, all of a sudden reeling drunk, burst into the kind of tears that Daisy and I knew well—the kind that time alone could stop. We stood aghast in the dark-red sunset, killed by our horror and our grief for Shannon and our unforgivable disgrace. We stood upright in a dead faint, and an eon passed before Mr. Murphy picked up Shannon's body and wove away, sobbing, "I don't believe it! I don't *believe* it!"

The very next day, again at morbid, heavy sunset, Caesar died in violent convulsions, knocking down two tall hollyhocks in his throes. Long after his heart had stopped, his right hind leg continued to jerk in aimless reflex. Madly methodical, Mr. Murphy had poisoned some meat for him, had thoroughly envenomed a whole pound of hamburger, and early in the morning, before sunup, when he must have been near collapse with his hangover, he had stolen up to Mrs. Placer's house and put it by the kitchen door. He was so stealthly that Caesar never stirred in his fool's paradise there on the floor by Gran. We knew these to be the facts, for Mr. Murphy made no bones about them. Afterward, he had gone home and said a solemn Requiem for Shannon in so loud a voice that someone sent for the police, and they took him away in the Black Maria to sober him up on strong green tea. By the time he was in the lockup and had confessed what he had done, it was far too late, for Caesar had already gulped down the meat. He suffered an undreamed-of agony in Gran's flower garden, and Daisy and I, unable to bear the sight of it, hiked up to the red rocks and shook there, wretchedly ripping to shreds the sand lilies that grew in the cracks. Flight was the only thing we could think of, but where could we go? We stared west at the mountains and quailed at the look of the stern white glacier; we wildly scanned the prairies for escape. "If only we were something besides kids! Besides girls!" mourned Daisy. I could not speak at all; I huddled in a niche of the rocks and cried.

No one in town, except, of course, her lodgers, had the slightest sympathy for Gran. The townsfolk allowed that Mr. Murphy was a drunk and was fighting Irish, but he had a heart and this was something that could never be said of Mrs. Placer. The neighbor who had called the police when he was chanting the *Dies Irae* before breakfast in that deafening monotone had said, "The poor guy is having some kind of a spell, so don't be rough on him, hear?" Mr. Murphy became, in fact, a kind of hero; some people, stretching a point, said he was a saint for the way that every day and twice on Sunday he sang a memorial Mass over Shannon's grave, now marked with a chipped, cheap plaster figure of Saint Francis. He withdrew from the world more and more, seldom venturing into the streets at all, except when he went to the bootlegger to get a new bottle to snuggle into. All summer, all fall, we saw him as we passed by his yard, sitting at his dilapidated table, enfeebled with gin, graying, withering, turning his head ever and ever more slowly as he maneuvered the protocol of the kings and the queens and the knaves. Daisy and I could never stop to visit him again.

It went on like this, year after year. Daisy and I lived in a mesh of lies and evasions, baffled and mean, like rats in a maze. When we were old enough for beaux, we connived like sluts to see them, but we would never admit to their existence until Gran caught us out by some trick. Like this one, for example: Once, at the end of a long interrogation, she said to me, "I'm more relieved than I can tell you that you *don't* have anything to do with Jimmy Gilmore, because I happen to know that he is after only one thing in a girl," and then, off guard in the loving memory of sitting in the movies the night before with Jimmy, not even holding hands, I defended him and defeated myself, and Gran, smiling with success, said, "I *thought* you knew him. It's a pretty safe rule of thumb that where there's smoke there's fire." That finished Jimmy and me, for afterward I was nervous with him and I confounded and alarmed and finally bored him by trying to convince him, although the subject had not come up, that I did not doubt his good intentions.

Daisy and I would come home from school, or, later, from our jobs, with a small triumph or an interesting piece of news, and if we forgot ourselves and, in our exuberance, told Gran, we were hustled into court at once for cross-examination. Once, I remember, while I was still in high school, I told her about getting a part in a play. How very nice for me, she said, if that kind of make-believe seemed to me worth while. But what was my role? An old woman! A widow woman believed to be a witch? She did not care a red cent, but she did have to laugh in view of the fact that Miss Eccles, in charge of dramatics, had almost run her down in her car. And I would forgive her, would I not, if she did not come to see the play, and would not think her eccentric for not wanting to see herself ridiculed in public?

My pleasure strangled, I crawled, joy-killed, to our third-floor room. The room was small and its monstrous furniture was too big and the rag rugs were repulsive, but it was bright. We would not hang a blind at the window, and on this day I stood there staring into the mountains that burned with the sun. I feared the mountains, but at times like this their massiveness consoled me; they, at least, could not be gossiped about.

Why did we stay until we were grown? Daisy and I ask ourselves this question as we sit here on the bench in the municipal zoo, reminded of Mr. Murphy by the polar bear, reminded by the monkeys not of Shannon but of Mrs. Placer's insatiable gossips at their post-prandial feast.

"But how could we have left?" says Daisy, wringing her buttery hands. "It was the depression. We had no money. We had nowhere to go."

"All the same, we could have gone," I say, resentful still of the waste of all those years. "We could have come here and got jobs as waitresses. Or prostitutes, for that matter."

"I wouldn't have wanted to be a prostitute," says Daisy.

We agree that under the circumstances it would have been impossible for us to run away. The physical act would have been simple, for the city was not far and we could have stolen the bus fare or hitched a ride. Later, when we began to work as salesgirls in Kress's, it would have been no trick at all to vanish one Saturday afternoon with our week's pay, without so much as going home to say goodbye. But it had been infinitely harder than that, for Gran, as we now see, held us trapped by our sense of guilt. We were vitiated, and we had no choice but to wait, flaccidly, for her to die.

You may be sure we did not unlearn those years as soon as we put her out of sight in the cemetery and sold her house for a song to the first boob who would buy it. Nor did we forget when we left the town for another one, where we had jobs at a dude camp—the town where Daisy now lives with a happy husband and two happy sons. The succubus did not relent for years, and I can still remember, in the beginning of our days at the Lazy S3, overhearing an edgy millionaire say to his wife, naming my name, "That girl gives me the cold shivers. One would think she had just seen a murder." Well, I had. For years, whenever I woke in the night in fear or pain or loneliness, I would increase my suffering by the memory of Shannon, and my tears were as bitter as poor Mr. Murphy's.

We have never been back to Adams. But we see that house plainly, with the hopvines straggling over the porch. The windows are hung with the cheapest grade of marquisette, dipped into coffee to impart to it an unwilling color, neither white nor tan but individual and spitefully unattractive. We see the wicker rockers and the swing, and through the screen door we dimly make out the slightly veering corridor, along one wall of which stands a glass-doored bookcase; when we were children, it had contained not books but stale old cardboard boxes filled with such things as W.C.T.U. tracts and anti-cigarette literature and newspaper clippings relating to sexual sin in the Christianized islands of the Pacific.

Even if we were able to close our minds' eyes to the past, Mr. Murphy would still be before us in the apotheosis of the polar bear. My pain becomes intolerable, and I am relieved when Daisy rescues us. "We've got to go," she says in a sudden panic. "I've got asthma coming on." We rush to the nearest exit of the city park and hail a cab, and, once inside it, Daisy gives herself an injection of adrenalin and then leans back. We are heartbroken and infuriated, and we cannot speak.

Two hours later, beside my train, we clutch each other as if we were drowning. We ought to go out to the nearest policeman and say, "We are not responsible women. You will have to take care of us because we cannot take care of ourselves." But gradually the storm begins to lull.

"You're sure you've got your ticket?" says Daisy. "You'll surely be able to get a roomette once you're on."

"I don't know about that," I say. "If there are any V.I.P.s on board, I won't have a chance. 'Spinsters and Orphans Last' is the motto of this line."

Daisy smiles. "I didn't care," she says, "but I had to laugh when I saw that woman nab the redcap you had signaled to. I had a good notion to give her a piece of my mind."

"It will be a miracle if I ever see my bags again," I say, mounting the steps of the train. "Do you suppose that blackguardly porter knows about the twenty-dollar gold piece in my little suitcase?"

"Anything's possible!" cries Daisy, and begins to laugh. She is so pretty, standing there in her bright-red linen suit and her black velvet hat. A solitary ray of sunshine comes through a broken pane in the domed vault of the train shed and lies on her shoulder like a silver arrow.

"So long, Daisy!" I call as the train begins to move.

She walks quickly along beside the train. "Watch out for pickpockets!" she calls.

"You, too!" My voice is thin and lost in the increasing noise of the speeding train wheels. "Goodbye, old dear!"

I go at once to the club car and I appropriate the writing table, to the vexation of a harried priest, who snatches up the telegraph pad and gives me a sharp look. I write Daisy approximately the same letter I always write her under this particular set of circumstances, the burden of which is that nothing for either of us can ever be as bad as the past before Gran mercifully died. In a postscript I add: "There is a Roman Catholic priest (that is to say, he is *dressed* like one) sitting behind me although all the chairs on the opposite side of the car are empty. I can only conclude that he is looking over my shoulder, and while I do not want to cause you any alarm, I think you would be advised to be on the lookout for any appearance of miraculous medals, scapulars, papist booklets, etc., in the shops of your town. It really makes me laugh to see the way he is pretending that all he wants is for me to finish this letter so that he can have the table."

I sign my name and address the envelope, and I give up my place to the priest, who smiles nicely at me, and then I move across the car to watch the fields as they slip by. They are alfalfa fields, but you can bet your bottom dollar that they are chockablock with marijuana.

I begin to laugh. The fit is silent but it is devastating; it surges and rattles in my rib cage, and I turn my face to the window to avoid the narrow gaze of the Filipino bar boy. I must think of something sad to stop this unholy giggle, and I think of the polar bear. But even his bleak tragedy does not sober me. Wildly I fling open the newspaper I have brought and I pretend to be reading something screamingly funny. The words I see are in a Hollywood gossip column: "How a well-known starlet can get a divorce in Nevada without her crooner husband's consent, nobody knows. It won't be worth a plugged nickel here."

SHIRLEY JACKSON

The Lottery

The morning of June 27th was clear and sunny, with the fresh warmth of a full-summer day; the flowers were blossoming profusely and the grass was richly green. The people of the village began to gather in the square, between the post office and the bank, around ten o'clock; in some towns there were so many people that the lottery took two days and had to be started on June 26th, but in this village, where there were only about three hundred people, the whole lottery took less than two hours, so it could begin at ten o'clock in the morning and still be through in time to allow the villagers to get home for noon dinner.

The children assembled first, of course. School was recently over for the summer, and the feeling of liberty sat uneasily on most of them; they tended to gather together quietly for a while before they broke into boisterous play, and their talk was still of the classroom and the teacher, of books and reprimands. Bobby Martin had already stuffed his pockets full of stones, and the other boys soon followed his example, selecting the smoothest and roundest stones; Bobby and Harry Jones and Dickie Delacroix—the villagers pronounced this name "Dellacroy"—eventually made a great pile of stones in one corner of the square and guarded it against the raids of the other boys. The girls stood aside, talking among themselves, looking over their shoulders at the boys, and the very small children rolled in the dust or clung to the hands of their older brothers or sisters.

Soon the men began to gather, surveying their own children, speaking of planting and rain, tractors and taxes. They stood together, away from the pile of stones in the corner, and their jokes were quiet and they smiled rather than laughed. The women, wearing faded house dresses and sweaters, came shortly after their menfolk. They greeted one another and exchanged bits of gossip as they went to join their husbands. Soon the women, standing by their husbands, began to call to their children, and the children came reluctantly, having to be called four or five times. Bobby Martin ducked under his mother's grasping hand and ran, laughing, back to the pile of stones. His father spoke up sharply, and Bobby came quickly and took his place between his father and his oldest brother.

The lottery was conducted—as were the square dances, the teen-age club, the Halloween program—by Mr. Summers, who had time and energy to devote to civic activities. He was a round-faced, jovial man and he ran the coal business, and people were sorry for him, because he had no children and his wife was a scold. When he arrived in the square, carrying the black wooden box, there was a murmur of conversation among the villagers, and he waved and called, "Little late today, folks." The postmaster, Mr. Graves, followed him, carrying a three-legged stool, and the stool was put in the center of the square and Mr. Summers set the black box down on it. The villagers kept their distance, leaving a space between themselves and the stool, and when Mr. Summers said, "Some of you fellows want to give me a hand?" there was a hesitation before two men, Mr. Martin and his oldest son, Baxter, came forward to hold the box steady on the stool while Mr. Summers stirred up the papers inside it.

The original paraphernalia for the lottery had been lost long ago, and the black box now resting on the stool had been put into use even before Old Man Warner, the oldest man in town, was born. Mr. Summers spoke frequently to the villagers about making a new box, but no one liked to upset even as much tradition as was represented by the black box. There was a story that the present box had been made with some pieces of the box that had preceded it, the one that had been constructed when the first people settled down to make a village here. Every year, after the lottery, Mr. Summers began talking again about a new box, but every year the subject was allowed to fade off without anything's being done. The black box grew shabbier each year; by now it was no longer completely black but splintered badly along one side to show the original wood color, and in some places faded or stained.

Mr. Martin and his oldest son, Baxter, held the black box securely on the stool until Mr. Summers had stirred the papers thoroughly with his hand. Because so much of the ritual had been forgotten or discarded, Mr. Summers had been successful in having slips of paper substituted for the chips of wood that had been used for generations. Chips of wood, Mr. Summers had argued, had been all very well when the village was tiny, but now that the population was more than three hundred and likely to keep on growing, it was necessary to use something that would fit more easily into the black box. The night before the lottery, Mr. Summers and Mr. Graves made up the slips of paper and put them in the box, and it was then taken to the safe of Mr. Summers's coal company and locked up until Mr. Summers was ready to take it to the square next morning. The rest of the year, the box was put away, sometimes one place, sometimes another; it had spent one year in Mr. Graves's barn and another year underfoot in the post office, and sometimes it was set on a shelf in the Martin grocery and left there.

There was a great deal of fussing to be done before Mr. Summers declared the lottery open. There were the lists to make up—of heads of families, heads of households in each family, members of each household in each family. There was the proper swearing-in of Mr. Summers by the postmaster, as the official of the lottery; at one time, some people remembered, there had been a recital of some sort, performed by the official of the lottery, a perfunctory, tuneless chant that had been rattled off duly each year; some people believed that the official of the lottery used to stand just so when he said or sang it, others believed that he was supposed to walk among the people, but years and years ago this part of the ritual had been allowed to lapse. There had been, also, a ritual salute, which the official of the lottery had had to use in addressing each person who came up to draw from the box, but this also had changed with time, until now it was felt necessary only for the official to speak to each person approaching. Mr. Summers was very good at all this; in his clean white shirt and blue jeans, with one hand resting carelessly on the black box, he seemed very proper and important as he talked interminably to Mr. Graves and the Martins.

Just as Mr. Summers finally left off talking and turned to the assembled villagers, Mrs. Hutchinson came hurriedly along the path to the square, her sweater thrown over her shoulders, and slid into place in the back of the crowd. "Clean forgot what day it was," she said to Mrs. Delacroix, who stood next to her, and they both laughed softly. "Thought my old man was out back stacking wood," Mrs. Hutchinson went on, "and then I looked out the window and the kids was gone, and then I remembered it was the twenty-seventh and came a-running." She dried her hands on her apron, and Mrs. Delacroix said, "You're in time, though. They're still talking away up there."

Mrs. Hutchinson craned her neck to see through the crowd and found her husband and children standing near the front. She tapped Mrs. Delacroix on the arm as a farewell and began to make her way through the crowd. The people separated good-humoredly to let her through; two or three people said, in voices just loud enough to be heard across the crowd, "Here comes your Missus, Hutchinson," and "Bill, she made it after all." Mrs. Hutchinson reached her husband, and Mr. Summers, who had been waiting, said cheerfully, "Thought we were going to have to get on without you, Tessie." Mrs. Hutchinson said, grinning,

"Wouldn't have me leave m'dishes in the sink, now, would you, Joe?" and soft laughter ran through the crowd as the people stirred back into position after Mrs. Hutchinson's arrival.

"Well, now," Mr. Summers said soberly, "guess we better get started, get this over with, so's we can go back to work. Anybody ain't here?"

"Dunbar," several people said. "Dunbar, Dunbar."

Mr. Summers consulted his list. "Clyde Dunbar," he said. "That's right. He's broke his leg, hasn't he? Who's drawing for him?"

"Me, I guess," a woman said, and Mr. Summers turned to look at her. "Wife draws for her husband," Mr. Summers said. "Don't you have a grown boy to do it for you, Janey?" Although Mr. Summers and everyone else in the village knew the answer perfectly well, it was the business of the official of the lottery to ask such questions formally. Mr. Summers waited with an expression of polite interest while Mrs. Dunbar answered.

"Horace's not but sixteen yet," Mrs. Dunbar said regretfully. "Guess I gotta fill in for the old man this year."

"Right," Mr. Summers said. He made a note on the list he was holding. Then he asked, "Watson boy drawing this year?"

A tall boy in the crowd raised his hand. "Here," he said. "I'm drawing for m'mother and me." He blinked his eyes nervously and ducked his head as several voices in the crowd said things like "Good fellow, Jack," and "Glad to see your mother's got a man to do it."

"Well," Mr. Summers said, "guess that's everyone. Old Man Warner make it?"

"Here," a voice said, and Mr. Summers nodded.

A sudden hush fell on the crowd as Mr. Summers cleared his throat and looked at the list. "All ready?" he called. "Now, I'll read the names—heads of families first—and the men come up and take a paper out of the box. Keep the paper folded in your hand without looking at it until everyone has had a turn. Everything clear?"

The people had done it so many times that they only half listened to the directions; most of them were quiet, wetting their lips, not looking around. Then Mr. Summers raised one hand high and said, "Adams." A man disengaged himself from the crowd and came forward. "Hi, Steve," Mr. Summers said, and Mr. Adams said, "Hi, Joe." They grinned at one another humorlessly and nervously. Then Mr. Adams reached into the black box and took out a folded paper. He held it firmly by one corner as he turned and went hastily back to his place in the crowd, where he stood a little apart from his family, not looking down at his hand.

"Allen," Mr. Summers said. "Anderson. . . . Bentham."

"Seems like there's no time at all between lotteries any more," Mrs. Delacroix said to Mrs. Graves in the back row. "Seems like we got through with the last one only last week."

"Time sure goes fast," Mrs. Graves said.

"Clark. . . . Delacroix."

"There goes my old man," Mrs. Delacroix said. She held her breath while her husband went forward.

"Dunbar," Mr. Summers said, and Mrs. Dunbar went steadily to the box while one of the women said, "Go on, Janey," and another said, "There she goes."

"We're next," Mrs. Graves said. She watched while Mr. Graves came around from the side of the box, greeted Mr. Summers gravely, and selected a slip of paper from the box. By now, all through the crowd there were men holding the small folded papers in their large hands, turning them over and over nervously. Mrs. Dunbar and her two sons stood together, Mrs. Dunbar holding the slip of paper.

"Harburt. . . . Hutchinson."

"Get up there, Bill," Mrs. Hutchinson said, and the people near her laughed.

"Jones."

"They do say," Mr. Adams said to Old Man Warner, who stood next to him, "that over in the north village they're talking of giving up the lottery."

Old Man Warner snorted. "Pack of crazy fools," he said. "Listening to the young folks, nothing's good enough for *them.* Next thing you know, they'll be wanting to go back to living in caves, nobody work any more, live *that* way for a while. Used to be a saying about 'Lottery in June, corn be heavy soon.' First thing you know, we'd all be eating stewed chickweed and acorns. There's *always* been a lottery," he added petulantly. "Bad enough to see young Joe Summers up there joking with everybody."

"Some places have already quit lotteries," Mrs. Adams said.

"Nothing but trouble in *that,*" Old Man Warner said stoutly. "Pack of young fools."

"Martin." And Bobby Martin watched his father go forward. "Overdyke. . . . Percy."

"I wish they'd hurry," Mrs. Dunbar said to her older son. "I wish they'd hurry."

"They're almost through," her son said.

"You get ready to run tell Dad," Mrs. Dunbar said.

Mr. Summers called his own name and then stepped forward precisely and selected a slip from the box. Then he called, "Warner."

"Seventy-seventh year I been in the lottery," Old Man Warner said as he went through the crowd. "Seventy-seventh time."

"Watson." The tall boy came awkwardly through the crowd. Someone said, "Don't be nervous, Jack," and Mr. Summers said, "Take your time, son."

"Zanini."

After that, there was a long pause, a breathless pause, until Mr. Summers, holding his slip of paper in the air, said, "All right, fellows." For a minute, no one moved, and then all the slips of paper were opened. Suddenly, all the women began to speak at once, saying, "Who is it?," "Who's got it?," "Is it the Dunbars?," "Is it the Watsons?" Then the voices began to say, "It's Hutchinson. It's Bill," "Bill Hutchinson's got it."

"Go tell your father," Mrs. Dunbar said to her older son.

People began to look around to see the Hutchinsons. Bill Hutchinson was standing quiet, staring down at the paper in his hand. Suddenly, Tessie Hutchinson shouted to Mr. Summers, "You didn't give him time enough to take any paper he wanted. I saw you. It wasn't fair!"

"Be a good sport, Tessie," Mrs. Delacroix called, and Mrs. Graves said, "All of us took the same chance."

"Shut up, Tessie," Bill Hutchinson said.

"Well, everyone," Mr. Summers said, "that was done pretty fast, and now we've got to be hurrying a little more to get done in time." He consulted his next list. "Bill," he said, "you draw for the Hutchinson family. You got any other households in the Hutchinsons?"

"There's Don and Eva," Mrs. Hutchinson yelled. "Make *them* take their chance!"

"Daughters draw with their husbands' families, Tessie," Mr. Summers said gently. "You know that as well as anyone else."

"It wasn't *fair,*" Tessie said.

"I guess not, Joe," Bill Hutchinson said regretfully. "My daughter draws with her husband's family, that's only fair. And I've got no other family except the kids."

"Then, as far as drawing for families is concerned, it's you," Mr. Summers said in explanation, "and as far as drawing for households is concerned, that's you, too. Right?"

"Right," Bill Hutchinson said.

"How many kids, Bill?" Mr. Summers asked formally.

"Three," Bill Hutchinson said. "There's Bill, Jr., and Nancy, and little Dave. And Tessie and me."

"All right, then," Mr. Summers said. "Harry, you got their tickets back?"

Mr. Graves nodded and held up the slips of paper. "Put them in the box, then," Mr. Summers directed. "Take Bill's and put it in."

"I think we ought to start over," Mrs. Hutchinson said, as quietly as she could. "I tell you it wasn't *fair.* You didn't give him time enough to choose. *Every*body saw that."

Mr. Graves had selected the five slips and put them in the box, and he dropped all the papers but those onto the ground, where the breeze caught them and lifted them off.

"Listen, everybody," Mrs. Hutchinson was saying to the people around her.

"Ready, Bill?" Mr. Summers asked, and Bill Hutchinson, with one quick glance around at his wife and children, nodded.

"Remember," Mr. Summers said, "take the slips and keep them folded until each person has taken one. Harry, you help little Dave." Mr. Graves took the hand of the little boy, who came willingly with him up to the box. "Take a paper out of the box, Davy," Mr. Summers said. Davy put his hand into the box and laughed. "Take just *one* paper," Mr. Summers said. "Harry, you hold it for him." Mr. Graves took the child's hand and removed the folded paper from the tight fist and held it while little Dave stood next to him and looked up at him wonderingly.

"Nancy next," Mr. Summers said. Nancy was twelve, and her school friends breathed heavily as she went forward, switching her skirt, and took a slip daintily from the box. "Bill, Jr.," Mr. Summers said, and Billy, his face red and his feet overlarge, nearly knocked the box over as he got a paper out. "Tessie," Mr. Summers said. She hesitated for a minute, looking around defiantly, and then set her lips and went up to the box. She snatched a paper out and held it behind her.

"Bill," Mr. Summers said, and Bill Hutchinson reached into the box and felt around, bringing his hand out at last with the slip of paper in it.

The crowd was quiet. A girl whispered, "I hope it's not Nancy," and the sound of the whisper reached the edges of the crowd.

"It's not the way it used to be," Old Man Warner said clearly. "People ain't the way they used to be."

"All right," Mr. Summers said. "Open the papers. Harry, you open little Dave's."

Mr. Graves opened the slip of paper and there was a general sigh through the crowd as he held it up and everyone could see that it was blank. Nancy and Bill, Jr., opened theirs at the same time, and both beamed and laughed, turning around to the crowd and holding their slips of paper above their heads.

"Tessie," Mr. Summers said. There was a pause, and then Mr. Summers looked at Bill Hutchinson, and Bill unfolded his paper and showed it. It was blank.

"It's Tessie," Mr. Summers said, and his voice was hushed. "Show us her paper, Bill."

Bill Hutchinson went over to his wife and forced the slip of paper out of her hand. It had a black spot on it, the black spot Mr. Summers had made the night before with the heavy pencil in the coal-company office. Bill Hutchinson held it up, and there was a stir in the crowd.

"All right, folks," Mr. Summers said. "Let's finish quickly."

Although the villagers had forgotten the ritual and lost the original black box, they still remembered to use stones. The pile of stones the boys had made earlier was ready; there were stones on the ground with the blowing scraps of paper that had come out of the box. Mrs. Delacroix selected a stone so large she had to pick it up with both hands and turned to Mrs. Dunbar. "Come on," she said. "Hurry up."

Mrs. Dunbar had small stones in both hands, and she said, gasping for breath, "I can't run at all. You'll have to go ahead and I'll catch up with you."

The children had stones already, and someone gave little Davy Hutchinson a few pebbles.

Tessie Hutchinson was in the center of a cleared space by now, and she held her hands out desperately as the villagers moved in on her. "It isn't fair," she said. A stone hit her on the side of the head.

Old Man Warner was saying, "Come on, come on, everyone." Steve Adams was in the front of the crowd of villagers, with Mrs. Graves beside him.

"It isn't fair, it isn't right," Mrs. Hutchinson screamed, and then they were upon her.

J. F. POWERS

The Valiant Woman

They had come to the dessert in a dinner that was a shambles. "Well, John," Father Nulty said, turning away from Mrs. Stoner and to Father Firman, long gone silent at his own table. "You've got the bishop coming for confirmations next week."

"Yes," Mrs. Stoner cut in, "and for dinner. And if he don't eat any more than he did last year——"

Father Firman, in a rare moment, faced it. "Mrs. Stoner, the bishop is not well. You know that."

"And after I fixed that fine dinner and all." Mrs. Stoner pouted in Father Nulty's direction.

"I wouldn't feel bad about it, Mrs. Stoner," Father Nulty said. "He never eats much anywhere."

"It's funny. And that new Mrs. Allers said he ate just fine when he was there," Mrs. Stoner argued, and then spit out, "but she's a damned liar!"

Father Nulty, unsettled but trying not to show it, said, "Who's Mrs. Allers?"

"She's at Holy Cross," Mrs. Stoner said.

"She's the housekeeper," Father Firman added, thinking Mrs. Stoner made it sound as though Mrs. Allers were the pastor there.

"I swear I don't know what to do about the dinner this year," Mrs. Stoner said.

Father Firman moaned. "Just do as you've always done, Mrs. Stoner."

"Huh! And have it all to throw out! Is that any way to do?"

"Is there any dessert?" Father Firman asked coldly.

Mrs. Stoner leaped up from the table and bolted into the kitchen, mumbling. She came back with a birthday cake. She plunged it in the center of the table. She found a big wooden match in her apron pocket and thrust it at Father Firman.

"I don't like this bishop," she said. "I never did. And the way he went and cut poor Ellen Kennedy out of Father Doolin's will!"

She went back into the kitchen.

"Didn't they talk a lot of filth about Doolin and the housekeeper?" Father Nulty asked.

"I should think they did," Father Firman said. "All because he took her to the movies on Sunday night. After he died and the bishop cut her out of the will, though I hear he gives her a pension privately, they talked about the bishop."

"I don't like this bishop at all," Mrs. Stoner said, appearing with a cake knife. "Bishop Doran—there was the man!"

"We know," Father Firman said. "All man and all priest."

"He did know real estate," Father Nulty said.

Father Firman struck the match.

"Not on the chair!" Mrs. Stoner cried, too late.

Father Firman set the candle burning—it was suspiciously large and yellow, like a blessed one, but he could not be sure. They watched the fluttering flame.

"I'm forgetting the lights!" Mrs. Stoner said, and got up to turn them off. She went into the kitchen again.

The priests had a moment of silence in the candlelight.

"Happy birthday, John," Father Nulty said softly. "Is it fifty-nine you are?"

"As if you didn't know, Frank," Father Firman said, "and you the same but one."

Father Nulty smiled, the old gold of his incisors shining in the flickering light, his collar whiter in the dark, and raised his glass of water, which would have been wine or better in the bygone days, and toasted Father Firman.

"Many of 'em, John."

"Blow it out," Mrs. Stoner said, returning to the room. She waited by the light switch for Father Firman to blow out the candle.

Mrs. Stoner, who ate no desserts, began to clear the dishes into the kitchen, and the priests, finishing their cake and coffee in a hurry, went to sit in the study.

Father Nulty offered a cigar.

"John?"

"My ulcers, Frank."

"Ah, well, you're better off." Father Nulty lit the cigar and crossed his long black legs. "Fish Frawley has got him a Filipino, John. Did you hear?"

Father Firman leaned forward, interested. "He got rid of the woman he had?"

"He did. It seems she snooped."

"Snooped, eh?"

"She did. And gossiped. Fish introduced two town boys to her, said, 'Would you think these boys were my nephews?' That's all, and the next week the paper had it that his two nephews were visiting him from Erie. After that, he let her believe he was going East to see his parents, though both are dead. The paper carried the story. Fish returned and made a sermon out of it. Then he got the Filipino."

Father Firman squirmed with pleasure in his chair. "That's like Fish, Frank. He can do that." He stared at the tips of his fingers bleakly. "You could never get a Filipino to come to a place like this."

"Probably not," Father Nulty said. "Fish is pretty close to Minneapolis. Ah, say, do you remember the trick he played on us all in Marmion Hall?"

"That I'll not forget!" Father Firman's eyes remembered. "Getting up New Year's morning and finding the toilet seats all painted!"

"Happy Circumcision! Hah!" Father Nulty had a coughing fit.

When he had got himself together again, a mosquito came and sat on his wrist. He watched it a moment before bringing his heavy hand down. He raised his hand slowly, viewed the dead mosquito, and sent it spinning with a plunk of his middle finger.

"Only the female bites," he said.

"I didn't know that," Father Firman said.

"Ah, yes . . ."

Mrs. Stoner entered the study and sat down with some sewing—Father Firman's black socks.

She smiled pleasantly at Father Nulty. "And what do you think of the atom bomb, Father?"

"Not much," Father Nulty said.

Mrs. Stoner had stopped smiling. Father Firman yawned.

Mrs. Stoner served up another: "Did you read about this communist convert, Father?"

"He's been in the Church before," Father Nulty said, "and so it's not a conversion, Mrs. Stoner."

"No? Well, I already got him down on my list of Monsignor's converts."

"It's better than a conversion, Mrs. Stoner, for there is more rejoicing in heaven over the return of . . . uh, he that was lost, Mrs. Stoner, is found."

"And that congresswoman, Father?"

"Yes. A convert—she."

"And Henry Ford's grandson, Father. I got him down."

"Yes, to be sure."

Father Firman yawned, this time audibly, and held his jaw.

"But he's one only by marriage, Father," Mrs. Stoner said. "I always say you got to watch those kind."

"Indeed you do, but a convert nonetheless, Mrs. Stoner. Remember, Cardinal Newman himself was one."

Mrs. Stoner was unimpressed. "I see where Henry Ford's making steering wheels out of soybeans, Father."

"I didn't see that."

"I read it in the *Reader's Digest* or some place."

"Yes, well . . ." Father Nulty rose and held his hand out to Father Firman. "John," he said. "It's been good."

"I heard Hirohito's next," Mrs. Stoner said, returning to converts.

"Let's wait and see, Mrs. Stoner," Father Nulty said.

The priests walked to the door.

"You know where I live, John."

"Yes. Come again, Frank. Good night."

Father Firman watched Father Nulty go down the walk to his car at the curb. He hooked the screen door and turned off the porch light. He hesitated at the foot of the stairs, suddenly moved to go to bed. But he went back into the study.

"Phew!" Mrs. Stoner said. "I thought he'd never go. Here it is after eight o'clock."

Father Firman sat down in his rocking chair. "I don't see him often," he said.

"I give up!" Mrs. Stoner exclaimed, flinging the holey socks upon the horsehair sofa. "I'd swear you had a nail in your shoe."

"I told you I looked."

"Well, you ought to look again. And cut your toenails, why don't you? Haven't I got enough to do?"

Father Firman scratched in his coat pocket for a pill, found one, swallowed it. He let his head sink back against the chair and closed his eyes. He could hear her moving about the room, making the preparations; and how he knew them—the fumbling in the drawer for a pencil with a point, the rip of the page from his daily calendar, and finally the leg of the card table sliding up against his leg.

He opened his eyes. She yanked the floor lamp alongside the table, setting the bead fringe tinkling on the shade, and pulled up her chair on the other side. She sat down and smiled at him for the first time that day. Now she was happy.

She swept up the cards and began to shuffle with the abandoned virtuosity of an old river-boat gambler, standing them on end, fanning them out, whirling them through her fingers, dancing them halfway up her arms, cracking the whip over them. At last they lay before him tamed into a neat deck.

"Cut?"

"Go ahead," he said. She liked to go first.

She gave him her faint, avenging smile and drew a card, cast it aside for another which he thought must be an ace from the way she clutched it face down.

She was getting all the cards, as usual, and would have been invincible if she had possessed his restraint and if her cunning had been of a higher order. He knew a few things about leading and lying back that she would never learn. Her strategy was attack, forever attack, with one baffling departure: she might sacrifice certain tricks as expendable if only she could have the last ones, the heartbreaking ones, if she could slap them down one after another, shatteringly.

She played for blood, no bones about it, but for her there was no other way; it was her nature, as it was the lion's, and for this reason he found her ferocity pardonable, more a defect of the flesh, venial, while his own trouble was all in the will, mortal. He did not sweat and pray over each card as she must, but he did keep an eye out for reneging and demanded a cut now and then just to aggravate her, and he was always secretly hoping for aces.

With one card left in her hand, the telltale trick coming next, she delayed playing it, showing him first the smile, the preview of defeat. She laid it on the table—so! She held one more trump than he had reasoned possible. Had she palmed it from somewhere? No, she would not go that far; that would not be fair, was worse than reneging, which so easily and often happened accidentally, and she believed in being fair. Besides he had been watching her.

God smote the vines with hail, the sycamore trees with frost, and offered up the flocks to the lightning—but Mrs. Stoner! What a cross Father Firman had from God in Mrs. Stoner! There were other housekeepers as bad, no doubt, walking the rectories of the world, yes, but . . . yes. He could name one and maybe two priests who were worse off. One, maybe two. Cronin. His scraggly blonde of sixty—take her, with her everlasting banging on the grand piano, the gift of the pastor; her proud talk about the goiter operation at the Mayo Brothers', also a gift; her honking the parish Buick at passing strange priests because they were all in the game together. She was worse. She was something to keep the home fires burning. Yes sir. And Cronin said she was not a bad person really, but what was he? He was quite a freak himself.

For that matter, could anyone say that Mrs. Stoner was a bad person? No. He could not say it himself, and he was no freak. She had her points,

Mrs. Stoner. She was clean. And though she cooked poorly, could not play the organ, would not take up the collection in an emergency, and went to card parties, and told all—even so, she was clean. She washed everything. Sometimes her underwear hung down beneath her dress like a paratrooper's pants, but it and everything she touched was clean. She washed constantly. She was clean.

She had her other points, to be sure—her faults, you might say. She snooped—no mistake about it—but it was not snooping for snooping's sake; she had a reason. She did other things, always with a reason. She overcharged on rosaries and prayer books, but that was for the sake of the poor. She censored the pamphlet rack, but that was to prevent scandal. She pried into the baptismal and matrimonial records, but there was no other way if Father was out, and in this way she had once uncovered a bastard and flushed him out of the rectory, but that was the perverted decency of the times. She held her nose over bad marriages in the presence of the victims, but that was her sorrow and came from having her husband buried in a mine. And he had caught her telling a bewildered young couple that there was only one good reason for their wanting to enter into a mixed marriage—the child had to have a name, and that—that was what?

She hid his books, kept him from smoking, picked his friends (usually the pastors of her colleagues), bawled out people for calling after dark, had no humor, except at cards, and then it was grim, very grim, and she sat hatchet-faced every morning at Mass. But she went to Mass, which was all that kept the church from being empty some mornings. She did annoying things all day long. She said annoying things into the night. She said she had given him the best years of her life. Had she? Perhaps—for the miner had her only a year. It was too bad, sinfully bad, when he thought of it like that. But all talk of best years and life was nonsense. He had to consider the heart of the matter, the essence. The essence was that housekeepers were hard to get, harder to get than ushers, than willing workers, than organists, than secretaries—yes, harder to get than assistants or vocations.

And she was a *saver*—saved money, saved electricity, saved string, bags, sugar, saved—him. That's what she did. That's what she said she did, and she was right, in a way. In a way, she was usually right. In fact, she was always right—in a way. And you could never get a Filipino to come way out here and live. Not a young one anyway, and he had never seen an old one. Not a Filipino. They liked to dress up and live.

Should he let it drop about Fish having one, just to throw a scare into her, let her know he was doing some thinking? No. It would be a perfect cue for the one about a man needing a woman to look after him. He was not up to that again, not tonight.

Now she was doing what she liked most of all. She was making a grand slam, playing it out card for card, though it was in the bag, prolonging what would have been cut short out of mercy in gentle company. Father Firman knew the agony of losing.

She slashed down the last card, a miserable deuce trump, and did in the hapless king of hearts he had been saving.

"Skunked you!"

She was awful in victory. Here was the bitter end of their long day together, the final murderous hour in which all they wanted to say—all he wouldn't and all she couldn't—came out in the cards. Whoever won at honeymoon won the day, slept on the other's scalp, and God alone had to help the loser.

"We've been at it long enough, Mrs. Stoner," he said, seeing her assembling the cards for another round.

"Had enough, huh!"

Father Firman grumbled something.

"No?"

"Yes."

She pulled the table away and left it against the wall for the next time. She went out of the study carrying the socks, content and clucking. He closed his eyes after her and began to get under way in the rocking chair, the nightly trip to nowhere. He could hear her brewing a cup of tea in the kitchen and conversing with the cat. She made her way up the stairs, carrying the tea, followed by the cat, purring.

He waited, rocking out to sea, until she would be sure to be through in the bathroom. Then he got up and locked the front door (she looked after the back door) and loosened his collar going upstairs.

In the bathroom he mixed a glass of antiseptic, always afraid of pyorrhea, and gargled to ward off pharyngitis.

When he turned on the light in his room, the moths and beetles began to batter against the screens, the lighter insects humming. . . .

Yes, and she had the guest room. How did she come to get that? Why wasn't she in the back room, in her proper place? He knew, if he cared to remember. The screen in the back room—it let in mosquitoes, and if it didn't do that she'd love to sleep back there, Father, looking out at the steeple and the blessed cross on top, Father, if it just weren't for the screen, Father. Very well, Mrs. Stoner, I'll get it fixed or fix it myself. Oh, could you now, Father? I could, Mrs. Stoner, and I will. In the meantime you take the guest room. Yes, Father, and thank you, Father, the house ringing with amenities then. Years ago, all that. She was a pie-faced girl then, not really a girl perhaps, but not too old to marry again. But she never had. In fact, he could not remember that she had even tried for a husband since coming to the rectory, but, of course, he could be wrong, not knowing how they went about it. God! God save us! Had she got her wires crossed and mistaken him all these years for *that? That!* Him! Suffering God! No. That was going too far. That was getting morbid. No. He must not think of that again, ever. No.

But just the same she had got the guest room and she had it yet. Well, did it matter? Nobody ever came to see him any more, nobody to stay overnight anyway, nobody to stay very long . . . not any more. He knew how they laughed at him. He had heard Frank humming all right—before he saw how serious and sad the situation was and took pity—humming, "Wedding Bells Are Breaking Up That Old Gang of Mine." But then they'd always laughed at him for something—for not being an athlete, for wearing glasses, for having kidney trouble . . . and mail coming addressed to Rev. and Mrs. Stoner.

Removing his shirt, he bent over the table to read the volume left open from last night. He read, translating easily, "Eisdem licet cum illis . . . Clerics are allowed to reside only with women about whom there can be no suspicion, either because of a natural bond (as mother, sister, aunt) or of advanced age, combined in both cases with good repute."

Last night he had read it, and many nights before, each time as though this time to find what was missing, to find what obviously was not in the paragraph, his problem considered, a way out. She was not mother, not sister, not aunt, and *advanced age* was a relative term (why, she was younger than he was) and so, eureka, she did not meet the letter of the law—but, alas, how she fulfilled the spirit! And besides it would be a slimy way of handling it after all her years of service. He could not afford to pension her off, either.

He slammed the book shut. He slapped himself fiercely on the back, missing the wily mosquito, and whirled to find it. He took a magazine and folded it into a swatter. Then he saw it—oh, the preternatural cunning of it!—poised in the beard of St. Joseph on the bookcase. He could not hit it there. He teased it away, wanting it to light on the wall, but it knew his thoughts and flew high away. He swung wildly, hoping to stun it, missed, swung back, catching St. Joseph across the neck. The statue fell to the floor and broke.

Mrs. Stoner was panting in the hall outside his door.

"What is it?"

"Mosquitoes!"

"What is it, Father? Are you hurt?"

"Mosquitoes—damn it! And only the female bites!"

Mrs. Stoner, after a moment, said, "Shame on you, Father. She needs the blood for her eggs."

He dropped the magazine and lunged at the mosquito with his bare hand.

She went back to her room, saying, "Pshaw, I thought it was burglars murdering you in your bed."

He lunged again.

GRACE PALEY

A Subject of Childhood

At home one Saturday and every Saturday, Richard drew eight-by-eleven portraits of stick men waving their arms. Tonto held a plastic horse in his hand and named it Tonto because its eyes were painted blue as his had been. I revised the hem of last year's dress in order to be up to the minute, chic, and *au courant* in the midst of spring. Strangers would murmur, "Look at her, isn't she wonderful? Who's her couturier?"

Clifford scrubbed under the shower, singing a Russian folk song. He rose in a treble of cold water to high C, followed by the scourging of the flesh. At last after four hots and three colds, he was strong and happy and he entered the living room, a steaming emanation. His face was round and rosy. He was noticeably hairless on the head. What prevented rain and shower water from running foolishly down his face? Heavy dark down-sloping brows. Beneath these his eyes were round and dark, amazed. This Clifford, my close friend, was guileless. He would not hurt a fly and he was a vegetarian.

As always, he was glad to see us. He had wrapped a large sun-bathing towel around his damp body. "Behold the man!" he shouted, and let the towel fall. He stood for a moment, gleaming and pleasant. Richard and Tonto glanced at him. "Cover yourself, for God's sakes, Clifford," I said.

"Take it easy, Faith," he called to the ear of reason. "the world is changing." Actually propriety did not embarrass him. It did not serve him. He peeked from behind the rubber plant where his pants, under and over, were heaped. When he reappeared, snapped and buttoned, he said, "Wake up, wake up. What's everyone slouching around for?" He poked Richard in the tummy. "A little muscle tone there, boy. Wake up."

Richard said, "I want to draw, Clifford."

"You can draw any time. I'm not always here. Draw tomorrow, Rich. Come on—fight me, boy. Fight. Come on . . . let's go, get me. You better get started, Richy, 'cause I'm gonna really punch you one. Here I come, ready or not!"

"Here *I* come," said Tonto, dropping his horse, and he whacked Clifford hard across the kidneys.

"Who did that?" asked Clifford. "What boy did that?"

"Me, me," said Tonto, jumping up and down. "Did I hurt you bad?"

"Killed me, yes sir, yes you did, and now I'm going to get *you.*" He whirled. "I'm going to tickle you, that's what." He raised Tonto high above his head, a disposable item, then pitched him into the air-foam belly of the couch.

Richard tiptoed with the Teddy bear to a gentle rise, the sofa cushion, from which he crowned Clifford three times.

"Oh, I'm getting killed," cried Clifford. "They're all after me. They're very rough." Richard kicked him in the shin. "That's it," said Clifford. "Get it out! Get it all out! Boys! Out! Out!"

Tonto spit right into his eye. He wiped his cheek. He feinted and dodged the Teddy bear that was coming down again on his bowed head. Tonto leaped onto his back and got hold of his ears. "Ouch," said Clifford.

Richard found a tube of rubber cement in the bookcase and squirted it at Clifford's hairy chest.

"I'm wild," said Richard. "I am, I'm wild."

"So am I," said Tonto. "I'm the wildest boy in the whole park." He tugged at Clifford's ears. "I'll ride you away. I'm an elephant boy."

"He's a lazy camel," screamed Richard. "Bubbles, I want you to work."

"Pretend I'm the djinn," said Tonto in a high wail. "Giddap, Clifford."

"Me, me, me," said Richard, sinking to the floor. "It's me. I'm a poison snake," he said, slithering to Clifford's foot. "I'm a poison snake," he said, resting his chin on Clifford's instep. "I'm a terrible poison snake," he swore. Then he raised his head like the adder he is, and after a prolonged hiss, with all his new front teeth, he bit poor Clifford above the bone, in his Achilles' heel, which is his weak left ankle.

"Oh no, oh no . . ." Clifford moaned, then folded neatly at all joints.

"Mommy, Mommy, Mommy," cried Richard, for Clifford fell, twelve stone, on him.

"Oh, it's me," screamed Tonto, an elephant boy thrown by his horse, headlong into a trap of table legs.

And he was the one I reached first. I hugged him to my lap. "Mommy," he sobbed, "my head hurts me. I wish I could get inside you." Richard lay, a crushed snake in the middle of the floor, without breath, without tears, angry.

Well, what of Clifford? He had hoisted his sorrowful self into an armchair and lay there lisping on a bloody tongue which he himself had bitten, "Faith, Faith, the accumulator, the accumulator!"

Bruised and tear-stricken, the children agreed to go to bed. They forgot to say it was too early to nap. They forgot to ask for their bears. They lay side by side and clutched each other's thumb. Here was the love that myth or legend has imposed on brothers.

I re-entered the living room where Clifford sat, a cone like an astrologer's hat on his skin-punctured place. Just exactly there, universal energies converged. The stationary sun, the breathless air in which the planets swing were empowered now to make him well, to act, in their remarkable art, like aspirin.

"We've got to have a serious talk," he said. "I really can't take those kids. I mean, Faith, you know yourself I've tried and tried. But you've done something to them, corrupted their instincts in some way or other. Here we were, having an absolutely marvelous time, rolling around making all kinds of free noise, and look what happened—like every other time, someone got hurt. I mean I'm really hurt. We should have all been relaxed. Easy. It should have been all easy. Our bodies should have been so easy. No one should've been hurt, Faith."

"Do you mean it's my fault you all got hurt?"

"No doubt about it, Faith, you've done a rotten job."

"Rotten job?" I said.

"Lousy," he said.

I gave him one more chance. "Lousy?" I asked.

"Oh my god! Stinking!" he said.

Therefore, the following—a compendium of motivations and griefs, life to date:

Truthfully, Mondays through Fridays—because of success at work—my ego is hot; I am a star; whoever can be warmed by me, I may oblige. The flat scale stones of abuse that fly into that speedy atmosphere are utterly consumed. Untouched, I glow my little thermodynamic way.

On Saturday mornings in my own home, however, I face the sociological law called the Obtrusion of Incontrovertibles. For I have raised these kids, with one hand typing behind my back to earn a living. I have raised them all alone without a father to identify themselves with in the bathroom like all the other little boys in the playground. Laugh. I was forced by inclement management into a yellow-dog contract with Bohemia, such as it survives. I have stuck by it despite the encroachments of kind relatives who offer ski pants, piano lessons, tickets to the rodeo. Meanwhile I have serviced Richard and Tonto, taught them to keep clean and hold an open heart on the subjects of childhood. We have in fact risen mightily from toilets in the hall and scavenging in great cardboard boxes at the Salvation Army for underwear and socks. It has been my perversity to do this alone, except for the one year their father was living in Chicago with Claudia Lowenstill and she was horrified that he only sent bicycles on the fifth birthday. A whole year of gas and electricity, rent and phone payments followed. One day she caught him in the swiveling light of truth, a grand figure who took a strong stand on a barrel of soapsuds and went down clean. He is now on the gold coast of another continent, enchanted by the survival of clandestine civilizations. Courts of kitchen drama cannot touch him.

All the same, I gave Clifford one more opportunity to renege and be my friend. I said, "Stinking? I raised them lousy?"

This time he didn't bother to answer because he had become busy gathering his clothes from different parts of the room.

Air was filtering out of my two collapsing lungs. Water rose, bubbling to enter, and I would have died of instantaneous pneumonia—something I never have heard of—if my hand had not got hold of a glass ash tray and, entirely apart from my personal decision, flung it.

Clifford was on his hands and knees looking for the socks he'd left under the armchair on Friday. His back was to me; his head convenient to the trajectory. And he would have passed away a blithering idiot had I not been blind with tears and only torn off what is anyway a vestigial ear lobe.

Still, Clifford is a gentle person, a consortment of sweet dispositions. The sight of all the blood paralyzed him. He hulked, shuddering; he waited on his knees to be signaled once more by Death, the Sheriff from the Styx.

"You don't say things like that to a woman," I whispered. "You damn stupid jackass. You just don't say anything like that to a woman. Wash yourself, moron, you're bleeding to death."

I left him alone to tie a tourniquet around his windpipe or doctor himself according to present-day plans for administering first aid in the Great Globular and Coming War.

I tiptoed into the bedroom to look at the children. They were asleep. I covered them and kissed Tonto, my baby, and "Richard, what a big boy you are," I said. I kissed him too. I sat on the floor, rubbing my cheek on Richard's rubbly fleece blanket until their sweet breathing in deep sleep quieted me.

A couple of hours later Richard and Tonto woke up picking their noses, sneezing, grumpy, then glad. They admired the ticktacktoes of Band-Aid I had created to honor their wounds. Richard ate soup and Tonto ate ham. They didn't inquire about Clifford, since he had a key which had always opened the door in or out.

That key lay at rest in the earth of my rubber plant. I felt discontinued. There was no one I wanted to offer it to.

"Still hungry, boys?" I asked. "No, sir," said Tonto. "I'm full up to here," leveling at the eyes.

"I'll tell you what," I came through with a stunning notion. "Go on down and play."

"Don't shove, miss," said Richard.

I looked out the front window. Four flights below, armed to the teeth, Lester Stukopf waited for the enemy. Carelessly I gave Richard this classified information. "Is he all alone?" asked Richard.

"He is," I said.

"O.K., O.K." Richard gazed sadly at me. "Only, Faith, remember, I'm going down because I feel like it. Not because you told me."

"Well, naturally," I said.

"Not me," said Tonto.

"Oh, don't be silly, you go too, Tonto. It's so nice and sunny. Take your new guns that Daddy sent you. Go on, Tonto."

"No, sir, I hate Richard and I hate Lester. I hate those guns. They're baby guns. He thinks I'm a baby. You better send him a picture."

"Oh, Tonto——"

"He thinks I suck my thumb. He thinks I wet my bed. That's why he sends me baby guns."

"No, no, honey. You're no baby. Everybody knows you're a big boy."

"He is not," said Richard. "And he does so suck his thumb and he does so wet his bed."

"Richard," I said, "Richard, if you don't have anything good to say, shut your rotten mouth. That doesn't help Tonto, to keep reminding him."

"Goodbye," said Richard, refusing to discuss, but very high and first-born. Sometimes he is nasty, but he is never lazy. He returned in forty-five seconds from the first floor to shout, "As long as he doesn't wet my bed, what do I care?"

Tonto did not hear him. He was brushing his teeth, which he sometimes does vigorously seven times a day, hoping they will loosen. I think they are loosening.

I served myself hot coffee in the living room. I organized comfort in the armchair, poured the coffee black into a white mug that said MAMA, tapped cigarette ash into a ceramic hand-hollowed by Richard. I looked into the square bright window of daylight to ask myself the sapping question: What is man that woman lies down to adore him?

At the very question mark Tonto came softly, sneaky in socks, to say, "I have to holler something to Richard, Mother."

"Don't lean out that window, Tonto. Please, it makes me nervous."

"I have to tell him something."

"No."

"Oh yes," he said. "It's awful important, Faith. I really *have* to."

How could I permit it? If he should fall, everyone would think I had neglected them, drinking beer in the kitchen or putting eye cream on at the vanity table behind closed doors. Besides, I would be bereaved forever. My grandmother mourned all her days for some kid who'd died of earache at the age of five. All the other children, in their own municipal-pension and federal-welfare years, gathered to complain at her deathside when she was ninety-one and heard her murmur, "Oh, oh, Anita, breathe a little, try to breathe, my little baby."

With tears in my eyes I said, "O.K., Tonto, I'll hold onto you. You can tell Richard anything you have to."

He leaned out onto the air. I held fast to one thick little knee. "Richie," he howled. "Richie, hey, Richie!" Richard looked up, probably shielding his eyes, searching for the voice. "Richie, hey, listen, I'm playing with your new birthday-present army fort and all them men."

Then he banged the window shut as though he knew nothing about the nature of glass and tore into the bathroom to brush his teeth once more in triumphant ritual. Singing through toothpaste and gargle, "I bet he's mad," and in lower key, "He deserves it, he stinks."

"So do you," I shouted furiously. While I sighed for my grandmother's loss, he had raised up his big mouth against his brother. "You really stink!"

"Now listen to me. I want you to get out of here. Go on down and play. I need ten minutes all alone. Anthony, I might kill you if you stay up here."

He reappeared, smelling like peppermint sticks at Christmas. He stood on one foot, looked up into my high eyes, and said, "O.K., Faith. Kill me."

I had to sit immediately then, so he could believe I was his size and stop picking on me.

"Please," I said gently, "go out with your brother. I have to think, Tonto."

"I don't wanna. I don't have to go anyplace I don't wanna," he said. "I want to stay right here with you."

"Oh, please, Tonto, I have to clean the house. You won't be able to do a thing or start a good game or anything."

"I don't care," he said. "I want to stay here with you. I want to stay right next to you."

"O.K., Tonto. O.K. I'll tell you what, go to your room for a couple of minutes, honey, go ahead."

"No," he said, climbing onto my lap. "I want to be a baby and stay right next to you every minute."

"Oh, Tonto," I said, "please, Tonto." I tried to pry him loose, but he put his arm around my neck and curled up right there in my lap, thumb in mouth, to be my baby.

"Oh, Tonto," I said, despairing of one solitary minute. "Why can't you go play with Richard? You'll have fun."

"No," he said, "I don't care if Richard goes away, or Clifford. They can go do whatever they wanna do. I don't even care. I'm never gonna go away. I'm gonna stay right next to you forever, Faith."

"Oh, Tonto," I said. He took his thumb out of his mouth and placed his open hand, its fingers stretching wide, across my breast. "I love you, Mama," he said.

"Love," I said. "Oh love, Anthony, I know."

I held him so and rocked him. I cradled him. I closed my eyes and leaned on his dark head. But the sun in its course emerged from among the water towers of downtown office buildings and suddenly shone white and bright on me. Then through the short fat fingers of my son, interred forever, like a black and white barred king in Alcatraz, my heart lit up in stripes.

WILLIAM H. GASS

In the Heart of the Heart of the Country

A PLACE

So I have sailed the seas and come . . .

to B . . .

a small town fastened to a field in Indiana. Twice there have been twelve hundred people here to answer to the census. The town is outstandingly neat and shady, and always puts its best side to the highway. On one lawn there's even a wood or plastic iron deer.

You can reach us by crossing a creek. In the spring the lawns are green, the forsythia is singing, and even the railroad that guts the town has straight bright rails which hum when the train is coming, and the train itself has a welcome horning sound.

Down the back streets the asphalt crumbles into gravel. There's Westbrook's, with the geraniums, Horsefall's, Mott's. The sidewalk shatters. Gravel dust rises like breath behind the wagons. And I am in retirement from love.

WEATHER

In the Midwest, around the lower Lakes, the sky in the winter is heavy and close, and it is a rare day, a day to remark on, when the sky lifts and allows the heart up. I am keeping count, and as I write this page, it is eleven days since I have seen the sun.

MY HOUSE

There's a row of headless maples behind my house, cut to free the passage of electric wires. High stumps, ten feet tall, remain, and I climb these like a boy to watch the country sail away from me. They are ordinary fields, a little more uneven than they should be, since in the spring they puddle. The topsoil's thin, but only moderately stony. Corn is grown one year, soybeans another. At dusk starlings darken the single tree—a larch—which stands in the middle. When the sky moves, fields move under it. I feel, on my perch, that I've lost my years. It's as though I were living at last in my eyes, as I have always dreamed of doing, and I think then I know why I've come here: to see, and so to go out against new things—oh god how easily—like air in a breeze. It's true there are moments—foolish moments, ecstasy on a tree stump—when I'm all but gone, scattered I like to think like seed, for I'm the sort now in the fool's position of having love left over which I'd like to lose; what good is it now to me, candy ungiven after Halloween?

A PERSON

There are vacant lots on either side of Billy Holsclaw's house. As the weather improves, they fill with hollyhocks. From spring through fall, Billy collects coal and wood and puts the lumps and pieces in piles near his door, for keeping warm is his one work. I see him most often on mild days sitting on his doorsill in the sun. I notice he's squinting a little, which is perhaps the reason he doesn't cackle as I pass. His house is the size of a single garage, and very old. It shed its paint with its youth, and its boards are a warped and weathered gray. So is Billy. He wears a short lumpy faded black coat when it's cold, otherwise he always goes about in the same loose, grease-spotted shirt and trousers. I suspect his galluses were yellow once, when they were new.

WIRES

These wires offend me. Three trees were maimed on their account, and now these wires deface the sky. They cross like a fence in front of me, enclosing the crows with the clouds. I can't reach in, but like a stick, I throw my feelings over. What is it that offends me? I am on my stump, I've built a platform there and the wires prevent my going out. The cut trees, the black wires, all the beyond birds therefore anger me. When I've wormed through a fence to reach a meadow, do I ever feel the same about the field?

THE CHURCH

The church has a steeple like the hat of a witch, and five birds, all doves, perch in its gutters.

MY HOUSE

Leaves move in the windows. I cannot tell you yet how beautiful it is, what it means. But they do move. They move in the glass.

POLITICS

. . . for all those not in love.

I've heard Batista described as a Mason. A farmer who'd seen him in Miami made this claim. He's as nice a fellow as you'd ever want to meet. Of Castro, of course, no one speaks.

For all those not in love there's law: to rule . . . to regulate . . . to rectify. I cannot write the poetry of such proposals, the poetry of politics, though sometimes—often—always now—I am in that uneasy peace of equal powers which makes a State; then I communicate by passing papers, proclamations, orders, through my bowels. Yet I was not a State with you, nor were we both together any Indiana. A squad of Pershing Rifles at the moment, I make myself Right Face! Legislation packs the screw of my intestines. Well, king of the classroom's king of the hill. You used to waddle when you walked because my sperm between your legs was draining to a towel. Teacher, poet, folded lover—like the politician, like those drunkards, ill, or those who faucet-off while pissing heartily to preach upon the force and fullness of that stream, or pause from vomiting to praise the purity and passion of their puke—I chant, I beg, I orate, I command, I sing—

> Come back to Indiana—not too late!
>   (Or will you be a ranger to the end?)
> Good-bye . . . Good-bye . . . oh, I shall always wait
>   You, Larry, traveler—
>   stranger,
>   son,
>   —my friend—

my little girl, my poem by heart, my self, my childhood.

But I've heard Batista described as a Mason. That dries up my pity, melts my hate. Back from the garage where I have overheard it, I slap the mended fender of my car to laugh, and listen to the metal stinging tartly in my hand.

PEOPLE

Their hair in curlers and their heads wrapped in loud scarves, young mothers, fattish in trousers, lounge about in the speedwash, smoking cigarettes, eating candy, drinking pop, thumbing magazines, and screaming at their children above the whir and rumble of the machines.

At the bank a young man freshly pressed is letting himself in with a key. Along the street, delicately teetering, many grandfathers move in a dream. During the murderous heat of summer, they perch on window ledges, their feet dangling just inside the narrow shelf of shade the store has made, staring steadily into the street. Where their consciousness has gone I can't say. It's not in the eyes. Perhaps it's diffuse, all temperature and skin, like an infant's, though more mild. Near the corner there are several large overalled men employed in standing. A truck turns to be weighed on the scales at the Feed and Grain. Images drift on the drugstore window. The wind has blown the smell of cattle into town. Our eyes have been driven in like the eyes of the old men. And there's no one to have mercy on us.

VITAL DATA

There are two restaurants here and a tearoom. two bars. one bank, three barbers, one with a green shade with which he blinds his window. two groceries. a dealer in Fords. one drug, one hardware, and one appliance store. several that sell feed, grain, and farm equipment. an antique shop. a poolroom. a laundromat. three doctors. a dentist. a plumber. a vet. a funeral home in elegant repair the color of a buttercup. numerous beauty parlors which open and shut like night-blooming plants. a tiny dime and department store of no width but several floors. a hutch, homemade, where you can order, after lying down or squirming in, furniture that's been fashioned from bent lengths of stainless tubing, glowing plastic, metallic thread, and clear shellac. an American Legion Post and a root beer stand. little agencies for this and that: cosmetics, brushes, insurance, greeting cards and garden produce—anything—sample shoes—which do their business out of hats and satchels, over coffee cups and dissolving sugar. a factory for making paper sacks and pasteboard boxes that's lodged in an old brick building bearing the legend OPERA HOUSE, still faintly golden, on its roof. a library given by Carnegie. a post office. a school. a railroad station. fire station. lumberyard. telephone company. welding shop. garage . . . and spotted through the town from one end to the other in a line along the highway, gas stations to the number five.

EDUCATION

In 1833, Colin Goodykoontz, an itinerant preacher with a name from a fairytale, summed up the situation in one Indiana town this way:

> Ignorance and her squalid brood. A universal dearth of intellect. Total abstinence from literature is very generally practiced. . . . There is not a scholar in grammar or geography, or a *teacher capable* of *instructing* in them, to my knowledge. . . . Others are supplied a few months of the year with the most antiquated & unreasonable forms of teaching reading, writing & cyphering. . . . Need I stop to remind you of the host of loathsome reptiles such a stagnant pool is fitted to breed! Croaking jealousy; bloated bigotry; coiling suspicion; wormish blindness; crocodile malice!

Things have changed since then, but in none of the respects mentioned.

BUSINESS

One side section of street is blocked off with sawhorses. Hard, thin, bitter men in blue jeans, cowboy boots and hats, untruck a dinky carnival. The merchants are promoting themselves. There will be free rides, raucous music, parades and coneys, pop, popcorn, candy, cones, awards and drawings, with all you can endure of pinch, push, bawl, shove, shout, scream, shriek, and bellow. Children pedal past on decorated bicycles, their wheels a blur of color, streaming crinkled paper and excited dogs. A little later there's a pet show for a prize—dogs, cats, birds, sheep, ponies, goats—none of which wins. The whirlabouts whirl about. The Ferris wheel climbs dizzily into the sky as far as a tall man on tiptoe might be persuaded to reach, and the irritated operators measure the height and weight of every child with sour eyes to see if they are safe for the machines. An electrical megaphone repeatedly trumpets the names of the generous sponsors. The following day they do not allow the refuse to remain long in the street.

MY HOUSE, THIS PLACE AND BODY

I have met with some mischance, wings withering, as Plato says obscurely, and across the breadth of Ohio, like heaven on a table, I've fallen as far as the poet, to the sixth sort of body, this house in B, in Indiana, with its blue and gray bewitching windows, holy magical insides. Great thick evergreens protect its entry. And I live *in.*

Lost in the corn rows, I remember feeling just another stalk, and thus this country takes me over in the way I occupy myself when I am well . . . completely—to the edge of both my house and body. No one notices, when they walk by, that I am brimming in the doorways. My house, this place and body, I've come in mourning to be born in. To anybody else it's pretty silly: love. Why should I feel a loss? How am I bereft? She was never mine; she was a fiction, always a golden tomgirl, barefoot, with an adolescent's slouch and a boy's taste for sports and fishing, a figure out of Twain, or worse, in Riley. Age cannot be kind.

There's little hand-in-hand here . . . not in B. No one touches except in rage. Occasionally girls will twine their arms about each other and lurch along, school out, toward home and play. I dreamed my lips would drift down your back like a skiff on a river. I'd follow a vein with the point of my finger, hold your bare feet in my naked hands.

THE SAME PERSON

Billy Holsclaw lives alone—how alone it is impossible to fathom. In the post office he talks greedily to me about the weather. His head bobs on a wild flood of words, and I take this violence to be a measure of his eagerness for speech. He badly needs a shave, coal dust has layered his face, he spits when he speaks, and his fingers pick at his tatters. He wobbles out in the wind when I leave him, a paper sack mashed in the fold of his arm, the leaves blowing past him, and our encounter drives me sadly home to poetry—where there's no answer. Billy closes his door and carries coal or wood to his fire and closes his eyes, and there's simply no way of knowing how lonely and empty he is or whether he's as vacant and barren and loveless as the rest of us are—here in the heart of the country.

WEATHER

For we're always out of luck here. That's just how it is—for instance in the winter. The sides of the buildings, the roofs, the limbs of the trees are gray. Streets, sidewalks, faces, feelings—they are gray. Speech is gray, and the grass where it shows. Every flank and front, each top is gray. Everything is gray: hair, eyes, window glass, the hawkers' bills and touters' posters, lips, teeth, poles and metal signs—they're gray, quite gray. Cars are gray. Boots, shoes, suits, hats, gloves are gray. Horses, sheep, and cows, cats killed in the road, squirrels in the same way, sparrows, doves, and pigeons, all are gray, everything is gray, and everyone is out of luck who lives here.

A similar haze turns the summer sky milky, and the air muffles your head and shoulders like a sweater you've got caught in. In the summer light, too, the sky darkens a moment when you open your eyes. The heat is pure distraction. Steeped in our fluids, miserable in the folds of our bodies, we can scarcely think of anything but our sticky parts. Hot cyclonic winds and storms of dust crisscross the country. In many places, given an indifferent push, the wind will still coast for miles, gathering resource and edge as it goes, cunning and force. According to the season, paper, leaves, field litter, seeds, snow, fill up the fences. Sometimes I think the land is flat because the winds have leveled it, they blow so constantly. In any case, a gale can grow in a field of corn that's as hot as a draft from hell, and to receive it is one of the most dismaying experiences of this life, though the smart of the same wind in winter is more humiliating, and in that sense even worse. But in the spring it rains as well, and the trees fill with ice.

PLACE

Many small Midwestern towns are nothing more than rural slums, and this community could easily become one. Principally during the first decade of the century, though there were many earlier instances, well-to-do farmers moved to town and built fine homes to contain them in their retirement. Others desired a more social life, and so lived in, driving to their fields like storekeepers to their businesses. These houses are now dying like the bereaved who inhabit them; they are slowly losing their senses—deafness, blindness, forgetfulness, mumbling, an insecure gait, an uncontrollable trembling has overcome them. Some kind of Northern Snopes will occupy them next: large-familied, Catholic, Democratic, scrambling, vigorous, poor; and since the parents will work in larger, nearby towns, the children will be loosed upon themselves and upon the hapless neighbors much as the fabulous Khan loosed his legendary horde. These Snopes will undertake makeshift repairs with materials that other people have thrown away; paint halfway round their house, then quit; almost certainly maintain an ugly loud cantankerous dog and underfeed a pair of cats to keep the rodents down. They will collect piles of possibly useful junk in the back yard, park their cars in the front, live largely leaning over engines, give not a hoot for the land, the old community, the hallowed ways, the established clans. Weakening widow ladies have already begun to hire large rude youths from families such as these to rake and mow and tidy the grounds they will inherit.

PEOPLE

In the cinders at the station boys sit smoking steadily in darkened cars, their arms bent out the windows, white shirts glowing behind the glass. Nine o'clock is the best time. They sit in a line facing the highway—two or three or four of them—idling their engines. As you walk by a machine may growl at you or a pair of headlights flare up briefly. In a moment one will pull out, spinning cinders behind it, to stalk impatiently up and down the dark streets or roar half a mile into the country before returning to its place in line and pulling up.

MY HOUSE, MY CAT, MY COMPANY

I must organize myself. I must, as they say, pull myself together, dump this cat from my lap, stir—yes, resolve, move, do. But do what? My will is like the rosy dustlike light in this room: soft, diffuse, and gently comforting. It lets me do . . . anything . . . nothing. My ears hear what they happen to; I eat what's put before me; my eyes see what blunders into them; my thoughts are not thoughts, they are dreams. I'm empty or I'm full . . . depending; and I cannot choose. I sink my claws in Tick's fur and scratch the bones of his back until his rear rises amorously. Mr. Tick, I murmur, I must organize myself. I must pull myself together. And Mr. Tick rolls over on his belly, all ooze.

I spill Mr. Tick when I've rubbed his stomach. Shoo. He steps away slowly, his long tail rhyming with his paws. How beautifully he moves, I think; how beautifully, like you, he commands his loving, how beautifully he accepts. So I rise and wander from room to room, up and down, gazing through most of my forty-one windows. How well this house receives its loving too. Let out like Mr. Tick, my eyes sink in the shrubbery. I am not here; I've passed the glass, passed second-story spaces, flown by branches, brilliant berries, to the ground, grass high in seed and leafage every season; and it is the same as when I passed above you in my aged, ardent body; it's, in short, a kind of love; and I am learning to restore myself, my house, my body, by paying court to gardens, cats, and running water, and with neighbors keeping company.

Mrs. Desmond is my right-hand friend; she's eighty-five. A thin white mist of hair, fine and tangled, manifests the climate of her mind. She is habitually suspicious, fretful, nervous. Burglars break in at noon. Children trespass. Even now they are shaking the pear tree, stealing rhubarb, denting lawn. Flies caught in the screens and numbed by frost awake in the heat to buzz and scrape the metal cloth and frighten her, though she is deaf to me, and consequently cannot hear them. Boards creak, the wind whistles across the chimney mouth, drafts cruise like fish through the hollow rooms. It is herself she hears, her own flesh failing, for only death will preserve her from those daily chores she climbs like stairs, and all that anxious waiting. Is it now, she wonders. No? Then: is it now?

We do not converse. She visits me to talk. My task to murmur. She talks about her grandsons, her daughter who lives in Delphi, her sister or her husband—both gone—obscure friends—dead—obscurer aunts and uncles—lost—ancient neighbors, members of her church or of her clubs—passed or passing on; and in this way she brings the ends of her life together with a terrifying rush: she is a girl, a wife, a mother, widow, all at once. All at once—appalling—but I believe it; I wince in expectation of the clap. Her talk's a fence—a shade drawn, window fastened, door that's locked—for no one dies taking tea in a kitchen; and as her years compress and begin to jumble, I really believe in the brevity of life; I sweat in my wonder; death is the dog down the street, the angry gander, bedroom spider, goblin who's come to get her; and it occurs to me that in my listening posture I'm the boy who suffered the winds of my grandfather with an exactly similar politeness, that I am, right now, all my ages, out in elbows, as angular as badly stacked cards. Thus was I, when I loved you, every man I could be, youth and child—far from enough—and you, so strangely ambiguous a being, met me, heart for spade, play after play, the whole run of our suits.

Mr. Tick, you do me honor. You not only lie in my lap, but you remain alive there, coiled like a fetus. Through your deep nap, I feel you hum. You are, and are not, a machine. You are alive, alive exactly, and it means nothing to you—much to me. You are a cat—you cannot understand—you are a cat so easily. Your nature is not something you must rise to. You, not I, live in: in house, in skin, in shrubbery. Yes. I think I shall hat my head with a steeple; turn church; devour people. Mr. Tick, though, has a tail he can twitch, he need not fly his Fancy. Claws, not metrical schema, poetry his paws; while smoothing . . . smoothing . . . smoothing roughly, his tongue laps its neatness. O Mr. Tick, I know you; you are an electrical penis. Go on now, shoo. Mrs. Desmond doesn't like you. She thinks you will tangle yourself in her legs and she will fall. You murder her birds, she knows, and walk upon her roof with death in your jaws. I must gather myself together for a bound. What age is it I'm at right now, I wonder. The heart, don't they always say, keeps the true time. Mrs. Desmond is knocking. Faintly, you'd think, but she pounds. She's brought me a cucumber. I believe she believes I'm a woman. Come in, Mrs. Desmond, thank you, be my company, it looks lovely, and have tea. I'll slice it, crisp, with cream, for luncheon, each slice as thin as me.

POLITICS

O all ye isolate and separate powers, Sing! Sing, and sing in such a way that from a distance it will seem a harmony, a Strindberg play, a friendship ring . . . so happy—happy, happy, happy—as here we go hand in handling, up and down. Our union was a singing, though we were silent in the songs we sang like single notes are silent in a symphony. In no sense sober, we barbershopped together and never heard the discords in our music or saw ourselves as dirty, cheap, or silly. Yet cats have worn out better shoes than those thrown through our love songs at us. Hush. Be patient—prudent—politic. Still, Cleveland killed you, Mr. Crane. Were you not politic enough and fond of being beaten? Like a piece of sewage, the city shat you from its stern three hundred miles from history—beyond the loving reach of sailors. Well, I'm not a poet who puts Paris to his temple in his youth to blow himself from Idaho, or—fancy that—Missouri. My god, I said, this is my country, but must my country go so far as Terre Haute or Whiting, go so far as Gary?

When the Russians first announced the launching of their satellite, many people naturally refused to believe them. Later others were outraged that they had sent a dog around the earth. I wouldn't want to take that mutt from out that metal flying thing if he's still living when he lands, our own dog catcher said; anybody knows you shut a dog up by himself to toss around the first thing he'll be setting on to do you let him out is bite somebody.

This Midwest. A dissonance of parts and people, we are a consonance of Towns. Like a man grown fat in everything but heart, we overlabor; our outlook never really urban, never rural either, we enlarge and linger at the same time, as Alice both changed and remained in her story. You are blond. I put my hand upon your belly; feel it tremble from my trembling. We always drive large cars in my section of the country. How could you be a comfort to me now?

MORE VITAL DATA

The town is exactly fifty houses, trailers, stores, and miscellaneous buildings long, but in places no streets deep. It takes on width as you drive south, always adding to the east. Most of the dwellings are fairly spacious farm houses in the customary white, with wide wraparound porches and tall narrow windows, though there are many of the grander kind—fretted, scalloped, turreted, and decorated with clapboards set at angles or on end, with stained-glass windows at the stair landings and lots of wrought iron full of fancy curls—and a few of these look like castles in their rarer brick. Old stables serve as garages now, and the lots are large to contain them and the vegetable and flower gardens which, ultimately, widows plant and weed and then entirely disappear in. The shade is ample, the grass is good, the sky a glorious fall violet; the apple trees are heavy and red, the roads are calm and empty; corn has sifted from the chains of tractored wagons to speckle the streets with gold and with the russet fragments of the cob, and a man would be a fool who wanted, blessed with this, to live anywhere else in the world.

EDUCATION

Buses like great orange animals move through the early light to school. There the children will be taught to read and warned against Communism. By Miss Janet Jakes. That's not her name. Her name is Helen something—Scott or James. A teacher twenty years. She's now worn fine and smooth, and has a face, Wilfred says, like a mail-order ax. Her voice is hoarse, and she has a cough. For she screams abuse. The children stare, their faces blank. This is the thirteenth week. They are used to it. You will all, she shouts, you will all draw pictures of me. No. She is a Mrs.—someone's missus. And in silence they set to work while Miss Jakes jabs hairpins in her hair. Wilfred says an ax, but she has those rimless tinted glasses, graying hair, an almost dimpled chin. I must concentrate. I must stop making up things. I must give myself to life; let it mold me: that's what they say in *Wisdom's Monthly Digest* every day. Enough, enough—you've been at it long enough; and the children rise formally a row at a time to present their work to her desk. No, she wears rims; it's her chin that's dimpleless. Well, it will take more than a tablespoon of features to sweeten that face. So she grimly shuffles their sheets, examines her reflection crayoned on them. I would not dare . . . allow a child . . . to put a line around me. Though now and then she smiles like a nick in the blade, in the end these drawings depress her. I could not bear it—how can she ask?—that anyone . . . draw me. Her anger's lit. That's why she does it: flame. There go her eyes; the pink in her glasses brightens, dims. She is a pumpkin, and her rage is breathing like the candle in. No, she shouts, no—the cartoon trembling—no, John Mauck, John Stewart Mauck, this will not do. The picture flutters from her fingers. You've made me too muscular.

I work on my poetry. I remember my friends, associates, my students, by their names. Their names are Maypop, Dormouse, Upsydaisy. Their names are Gladiolus, Callow Bladder, Prince and Princess Oleo, Hieronymus, Cardinal Mummum, Mr. Fitchew, The Silken Howdah, Spot. Sometimes you're Tom Sawyer, Huckleberry Finn; it is perpetually summer; your buttocks are my pillow; we are adrift on a raft; your back is our river. Sometimes you are Major Barbara, sometimes a goddess who kills men in battle, sometimes you are soft like a shower of water; you are bread in my mouth.

I do not work on my poetry. I forget my friends, associates, my students, and their names: Gramophone, Blowgun, Pickle, Serenade . . . Marge the Barge, Arena, Uberhaupt . . . Doctor Dildoe, The Fog Machine. For I am now in B, in Indiana: out of job and out of patience, out of love and time and money, out of bread and out of body, in a temper, Mrs. Desmond, out of tea. So shut your fist up, bitch, you bag of death; go bang another door; go die, my dearie. Die, life-deaf old lady. Spill your breath. Fall over like a frozen board. Gray hair grows from the nose of your mind. You are a skull already—*memento mori*—the foreskin retracts from your teeth. Will your plastic gums last longer than your bones, and color their grinning? And is your twot still hazel-hairy, or are you bald as a ditch? . . . bitch . . . . . . bitch . . . . bitch. I wanted to be famous, but you bring me age—my emptiness. Was it *that* which I thought would balloon me above the rest? Love? where are you? . . . love me. I want to rise so high, I said, that when I shit I won't miss anybody.

BUSINESS

For most people, business is poor. Nearby cities have siphoned off all but a neighborhood trade. Except for feed and grain and farm supplies, you stand a chance to sell only what one runs out to buy. Chevrolet has quit, and Frigidaire. A locker plant has left its afterimage. The lumberyard has been, so far, six months about its going. Gas stations change hands clumsily, a restaurant becomes available, a grocery closes. One day they came and knocked the cornices from the watch repair and pasted campaign posters on the windows. Torn across, by now, by boys, they urge you still to vote for half an orange beblazoned man who as a whole one failed two years ago to win at his election. Everywhere, in this manner, the past speaks, and it mostly speaks of failure. The empty stores, the old signs and dusty fixtures, the debris in alleys, the flaking paint and rusty gutters, the heavy locks and sagging boards: they say the same disagreeable things. What do the sightless windows see, I wonder, when the sun throws a passerby against them? Here a stair unfolds toward the street—dark, rickety, and treacherous—and I always feel, as I pass it, that if I just went carefully up and turned the corner at the landing, I would find myself out of the world. But I've never had the courage.

THAT SAME PERSON

The weeds catch up with Billy. In pursuit of the hollyhocks, they rise in coarse clumps all around the front of his house. Billy has to stamp down a circle by his door like a dog or cat does turning round to nest up, they're so thick. What particularly troubles me is that winter will find the weeds still standing stiff and tindery to take the sparks which Billy's little mortarless chimney spouts. It's true that fires are fun here. The town whistle, which otherwise only blows for noon (and there's no noon on Sunday), signals the direction of the fire by the length and number of its blasts, the volunteer firemen rush past in their cars and trucks, houses empty their owners along the street every time like an illustration in a children's book. There are many bikes, too, and barking dogs, and sometimes—halleluiah—the fire's right here in town—a vacant lot of weeds and stubble flaming up. But I'd rather it weren't Billy or Billy's lot or house. Quite selfishly I want him to remain the way he is—counting his sticks and logs, sitting on his sill in the soft early sun—though I'm not sure what his presence means to me . . . or to anyone. Nevertheless, I keep wondering whether, given time, I might not someday find a figure in our language which would serve him faithfully, and furnish his poverty and loneliness richly out.

WIRES

Where sparrows sit like fists. Doves fly the steeple. In mist the wires change perspective, rise and twist. If they led to you, I would know what they were. Thoughts passing often, like the starlings who flock these fields at evening to sleep in the trees beyond, would form a family of paths like this; they'd foot down the natural height of air to just about a bird's perch. But they do not lead to you.

Of whose beauty it was sung
She shall make the old man young.

They fasten me.

If I walked straight on, in my present mood, I would reach the

Wabash. It's not a mood in which I'd choose to conjure you. Similes dangle like baubles from me. This time of year the river is slow and shallow, the clay banks crack in the sun, weeds surprise the sandbars. The air is moist and I am sweating. It's impossible to rhyme in this dust. Everything—sky, the cornfield, stump, wild daisies, my old clothes and pressless feelings—seem fabricated for installment purchase. Yes. Christ. I am suffering a summer Christmas; and I cannot walk under the wires. The sparrows scatter like handfuls of gravel. Really, wires are voices in thin strips. They are words wound in cables. Bars of connection.

WEATHER

I would rather it were the weather that was to blame for what I am and what my friends and neighbors are—we who live here in the heart of the country. Better the weather, the wind, the pale dying snow . . . the snow—why not the snow? There's never much really, not around the lower Lakes anyway, not enough to boast about, not enough to be useful. My father tells how the snow in the Dakotas would sweep to the roofs of the barns in the old days, and he and his friends could sled on the crust that would form because the snow was so fiercely driven. In Bemidji trees have been known to explode. That would be something—if the trees in Davenport or Francisville or Carbondale or Niles were to go blam some winter—blam! blam! blam! all the way down the gray, cindery, snow-sick streets.

A cold fall rain is blackening the trees or the air is like lilac and full of parachuting seeds. Who cares to live in any season but his own? Still I suspect the secret's in this snow, the secret of our sickness, if we could only diagnose it, for we are all dying like the elms in Urbana. This snow—like our skin it covers the country. Later dust will do it. Right now—snow. Mud presently. But it is snow without any laughter in it, a pale gray pudding thinly spread on stiff toast, and if that seems a strange description, it's accurate all the same. Of course soot blackens everything, but apart from that, we are never sufficiently cold here. The flakes as they come, alive and burning, we cannot retain, for if our temperatures fall, they rise promptly again, just as, in the summer, they bob about in the same feckless way. Suppose though . . . suppose they were to rise some August, climb and rise, and then hang in the hundreds like a hawk through December, what a desert we could make of ourselves—from Chicago to Cairo, from Hammond to Columbus—what beautiful Death Valleys.

PLACE

I would rather it were the weather. It drives us in upon ourselves—an unlucky fate. Of course there is enough to stir our wonder anywhere; there's enough to love, anywhere, if one is strong enough, if one is diligent enough, if one is perceptive, patient, kind enough—whatever it takes; and surely it's better to live in the country, to live on a prairie by a drawing of rivers, in Iowa or Illinois or Indiana, say, than in any city, in any stinking fog of human beings, in any blooming orchard of machines. It ought to be. The cities are swollen and poisonous with people. It ought to be better. Man has never been a fit environment for man—for rats, maybe, rats do nicely, or for dogs or cats and the household beetle.

And how long the street is, nowadays. These endless walls are fallen to keep back the tides of earth. Brick could be beautiful but we have covered it gradually with gray industrial vomits. Age does not make concrete genial, and asphalt is always—like America—twenty-one, until it breaks up in crumbs like stale cake. The brick, the asphalt, the concrete, the dancing signs and garish posters, the feed and excrement of the automobile, the litter of its inhabitants: they compose, they decorate, they line our streets, and there is nowhere, nowadays, our streets can't reach.

A man in the city has no natural thing by which to measure himself. His parks are potted plants. Nothing can live and remain free where he resides but the pigeon, starling, sparrow, spider, cockroach, mouse, moth, fly and weed, and he laments the existence of even these and makes his plans to poison them. The zoo? There *is* the zoo. Through its bars the city man stares at the great cats and dully sucks his ice. Living, alas, among men and their marvels, the city man supposes that his happiness depends on establishing, somehow, a special kind of harmonious accord with others. The novelists of the city, of slums and crowds, they call it love—and break their pens.

Wordsworth feared the accumulation of men in cities. He foresaw their "degrading thirst after outrageous stimulation," and some of their hunger for love. Living in a city, among so many, dwelling in the heat and tumult of incessant movement, a man's affairs are touch and go—that's all. It's not surprising that the novelists of the slums, the cities, and the crowds, should find that sex is but a scratch to ease a tickle, that we're most human when we're sitting on the john, and that the justest image of our life is in full passage through the plumbing.

That man, immur'd in cities, still retains
His inborn inextinguishable thirst
Of rural scenes, compensating his loss
By supplemental shifts, the best he may.

Come into the country, then. The air nimbly and sweetly recommends itself unto our gentle senses. Here, growling tractors tear the earth. Dust roils up behind them. Drivers sit jouncing under bright umbrellas. They wear refrigerated hats and steer by looking at the tracks they've cut behind them, their transistors blaring. Close to the land, are they? good companions to the soil? Tell me: do they live in harmony with the alternating seasons?

It's a lie of old poetry. The modern husbandman uses chemicals from cylinders and sacks, spike-ball-and-claw machines, metal sheds, and cost accounting. Nature in the old sense does not matter. It does not exist. Our farmer's only mystical attachment is to parity. And if he does not realize that cows and corn are simply different kinds of chemical engine, he cannot expect to make a go of it.

It isn't necessary to suppose our cows have feelings; our neighbor hasn't as many as he used to have either; but think of it this way a moment, you can correct for the human imputations later: how would it feel to nurse those strange tentacled calves with their rubber, glass, and metal lips, their stainless eyes?

PEOPLE

Aunt Pet's still able to drive her car—a high square Ford—even though she walks with difficulty and a stout stick. She has a watery gaze, a smooth plump face despite her age, and jet black hair in a bun. She has the slowest smile of anyone I ever saw, but she hates dogs, and not very long ago cracked the back of one she cornered in her garden. To prove her vigor she will tell you this, her smile breaking gently while she raises the knob of her stick to the level of your eyes.

HOUSE, MY BREATH AND WINDOW

My window is a grave, and all that lies within it's dead. No snow is falling. There's no haze. It is not still, not silent. Its images are not an animal that waits, for movement is no demonstration. I have seen the sea slack, life bubble through a body without a trace, its spheres impervious as soda's. Downwound, the whore at wagtag clicks and clacks. Leaves wiggle. Grass sways. A bird chirps, pecks the ground. An auto wheel in penning circles keeps its rigid spokes. These images are stones; they are memorials. Beneath this sea lies sea: god rest it . . . rest the world beyond my window, me in front of my reflection, above this page, my shade. Death is not so still, so silent, since silence implies a falling quiet, stillness a stopping, containing, holding in; for death is time in a clock, like Mr. Tick, electric . . . like wind through a windup poet. And my blear floats out to visible against the glass, befog its country and bespill myself. The mist lifts slowly from the fields in the morning. No one now would say: the Earth throws back its covers; it is rising from sleep. Why is the feeling foolish? The image is too Greek. I used to gaze at you so wantonly your body blushed. Imagine: wonder: that my eyes could cause such flowering. Ah, my friend, your face is pale, the weather cloudy; a street has been felled through your chin, bare trees do nothing, houses take root in their rectangles, a steeple stands up in your head. You speak of loving; then give me a kiss. The pane is cold. On icy mornings the fog rises to greet me (as you always did); the barns and other buildings, rather than ghostly, seem all the more substantial for looming, as if they grew in themselves while I watched (as you always did). Oh my approach, I suppose, was like breath in a rubber monkey. Nevertheless, on the road along the Wabash in the morning, though the trees are sometimes obscured by fog, their reflection floats serenely on the river, reasoning the banks, the sycamores in French rows. Magically, the world tips. I'm led to think that only those who grow down live (which will scarcely win me twenty-five from *Wisdom's Monthly Digest),* but I find I write that only those who live down grow; and what I write, I hold, whatever I really know. My every word's inverted, or reversed—or I am. I held you, too, that way. You were so utterly provisional, subject to my change. I could inflate your bosom with a kiss, disperse your skin with gentleness, enter your vagina from within, and make my love emerge like a fresh sex. The pane is cold. Honesty is cold, my inside lover. The sun looks, through the mist, like a plum on the tree of heaven, or a bruise on the slope of your belly. Which? The grass crawls with frost. We meet on this window, the world and I, inelegantly, swimmers of the glass; and swung wrong way round to one another, the world seems in. The world—how grand, how monumental, grave and deadly, that word is: the world, my house and poetry. All poets have their inside lovers. Wee penis does not belong to me, or any of this foggery. It is *his* property which he's thrust through what's womanly of me to set down this. These wooden houses in their squares, gray streets and fallen sidewalks, standing trees, your name I've written sentimentally across my breath into the whitening air, pale birds: they exist in me now because of him. I gazed with what intensity . . . A bush in the excitement of its roses could not have bloomed so beautifully as you did then. It was a look I'd like to give this page. For that is poetry: to bring within about, to change.

POLITICS

Sports, politics, and religion are the three passions of the badly educated. They are the Midwest's open sores. Ugly to see, a source of constant discontent, they sap the body's strength. Appalling quantities of money, time, and energy are wasted on them. The rural mind is narrow, passionate, and reckless on these matters. Greed, however shortsighted and direct, will not alone account for it. I have known men, for instance, who for years have voted squarely against their interests. Nor have I ever noticed that their surly Christian views prevented them from urging forward the smithereening, say, of Russia, China, Cuba, or Korea. And they tend to back their country like they back their local team: they have a fanatical desire to win; yelling is their forte; and if things go badly, they are inclined to sack the coach. All in all, then, Birch is a good name. It stands for the bigot's stick, the wild-child-tamer's cane.

Forgetfulness—is that their object?

Oh, I was new, I thought. A fresh start: new cunt, new climate, and new country—there you were, and I was pioneer and had no history. That language hurts me, too, my dear. You'll never hear it.

FINAL VITAL DATA

The Modern Homemakers' Demonstration Club. The Prairie Home Demonstration Club. The Night-outers' Home Demonstration Club. The IOOF, FFF, VFW, WCTU, WSCS, 4-H, 40 and 8, Psi Iota Chi, and PTA. The Boy and Girl Scouts, Rainbows, Masons, Indians and Rebekah Lodge. Also the Past Noble Grand Club of the Rebekah Lodge. As well as the Moose and the Ladies of the Moose. The Elks, the Eagles, the Jaynettes and the Eastern Star. The Women's Literary Club, the Hobby Club, the Art Club, the Sunshine Society, the Dorcas Society, the Pythian Sisters, the Pilgrim Youth Fellowship, the American Legion, the American Legion Auxiliary, the American Legion Junior Auxiliary, the Gardez Club, the Bridge for Fun Club, the What-can-you-do? Club, the Get Together Club, the Coterie Club, the Worthwhile Club, the Let's Help Our Town Club, the No Name Club, the Forget-me-not Club, the Merry-go-round Club . . .

EDUCATION

Has a quarter disappeared from Paula Frosty's pocket book? Imagine the landscape of that face: no crayon could engender it; soft wax is wrong; thin wire in trifling snips might do the trick. Paula Frosty and Christopher Roger accuse the pale and splotchy Cheryl Pipes. But Miss Jakes, I *saw* her. Miss Jakes is so extremely vexed she snaps her pencil. What else is missing? I appoint you a detective, John: search her desk. Gum, candy, paper, pencils, marble, round eraser—whose? A thief. I can't watch her all the time, I'm here to teach. Poor pale fossetted Cheryl, it's determined, can't return the money because she took it home and spent it. Cindy, Janice, John, and Pete—you four who sit around her—you will be detectives this whole term to watch her. A thief. In all my time. Miss Jakes turns, unfists, and turns again. I'll handle you, she cries. To think. A thief. In all my years. Then she writes on the blackboard the name of Cheryl Pipes and beneath that the figure twenty-five with a large sign for cents. Now Cheryl, she says, this won't be taken off until you bring that money out of home, out of home straight up to here, Miss Jakes says, tapping her desk.

Which is three days.

ANOTHER PERSON

I was raking leaves when Uncle Halley introduced himself to me. He said his name came from the comet, and that his mother had borne him prematurely in her fright of it. I thought of Hobbes, whom fear of the Spanish Armada had hurried into birth, and so I believed Uncle Halley to honor the philosopher, though Uncle Halley is a liar, and neither the one hundred twenty-nine nor the fifty-three he ought to be. That fall the leaves had burned themselves out on the trees, the leaf lobes had curled, and now they flocked noisily down the street and were broken in the wires of my rake. Uncle Halley was himself (like Mrs. Desmond and history generally) both deaf and implacable, and he shooed me down his basement stairs to a room set aside there for stacks of newspapers reaching to the ceiling, boxes of leaflets and letters and programs, racks of photo albums, scrapbooks, bundles of rolled-up posters and maps, flags and pennants and slanting piles of dusty magazines devoted mostly to motoring and the Christian ethic. I saw a bird cage, a tray of butterflies, a bugle, a stiff straw boater, and all kinds of tassels tied to a coat tree. He still possessed and had on display the steering lever from his first car, a linen duster, driving gloves and goggles, photographs along the wall of himself, his friends, and his various machines, a shell from the first war, a record of "Ramona" nailed through its hole to a post, walking sticks and fanciful umbrellas, shoes of all sorts (his baby shoes, their counters broken, were held in sorrow beneath my nose—they had not been bronzed, but he might have them done someday before he died, he said), countless boxes of medals, pins, beads, trinkets, toys, and keys (I scarcely saw—they flowed like jewels from his palms), pictures of downtown when it was only a path by the railroad station, a brightly colored globe of the world with a dent in Poland, antique guns, belt buckles, buttons, souvenir plates and cups and saucers (I can't remember all of it—I won't), but I recall how shamefully, how rudely, how abruptly, I fled, a good story in my mouth but death in my nostrils; and how afterward I busily, righteously, burned my leaves as if I were purging the world of its years. I still wonder if this town—its life, and mine now—isn't really a record like the one of "Ramona" that I used to crank around on my grandmother's mahogany Victrola through lonely rainy days as a kid.

THE FIRST PERSON

Billy's like the coal he's found: spilled, mislaid, discarded. The sky's no comfort. His house and his body are dying together. His windows are boarded. And now he's reduced to his hands. I suspect he has glaucoma. At any rate he can scarcely see, and weeds his yard of rubble on his hands and knees. Perhaps he's a surgeon cleansing a wound or an ardent and tactile lover. I watch, I must say, apprehensively. Like mine-war detectors, his hands graze in circles ahead of him. Your nipples were the color of your eyes. Pebble. Snarl of paper. Length of twine. He leans down closely, picks up something silvery, holds it near his nose. Foil? cap? coin? He has within him—what, I wonder? Does he know more now because he fingers everything and has to sniff to see? It would be romantic cruelty to think so. He bends the down on your arms like a breeze. You wrote me: something is strange when we don't understand. I write in return: I think when I loved you I fell to my death.

Billy, I could read to you from Beddoes; he's your man perhaps; he held with dying, freed his blood of its arteries; and he said that there were many wretched love-ill fools like me lying alongside the last bone of their former selves, as full of spirit and speech, nonetheless, as Mrs. Desmond, Uncle Halley and the Ferris wheel, Aunt Pet, Miss Jakes, Ramona or the megaphone; yet I reverse him finally, Billy, on no evidence but braggadocio, and I declare that though my inner organs were devoured long ago, the worm which swallowed down my parts still throbs and glows like a crystal palace.

Yes, you were younger. I was Uncle Halley, the museum man and infrequent meteor. Here is my first piece of ass. They weren't so flat in those days, had more round, more juice. And over here's the sperm I've spilled, nicely jarred and clearly labeled. Look at this tape like lengths of intestine where I've stored my spew, the endless worm of words I've written, a hundred million emissions or more: oh I was quite a man right from the start; even when unconscious in my cradle, from crotch to cranium, I was erectile tissue; though mostly, after the manner approved by Plato, I had intercourse by eye. Never mind, old Holsclaw, you are blind. We pull down darkness when we go to bed; put out like Oedipus the actually offending organ, and train our touch to lies. All cats are gray, says Mr. Tick; so under cover of glaucoma you are sack gray too, and cannot be distinguished from a stallion.

I must pull myself together, get a grip, just as they say, but I feel spilled, bewildered, quite mislaid. I did not restore my house to its youth, but to its age. Hunting, you hitch through the hollyhocks. I'm inclined to say you aren't half the cripple I am, for there is nothing left of me but mouth. However, I resist the impulse. It is another lie of poetry. My organs are all there, though it's there where I fail—at the roots of my experience. Poet of the spiritual, Rilke, weren't you? yet that's what you said. Poetry, like love, is—in and out—a physical caress. I can't tolerate any more of my sophistries about spirit, mind, and breath. Body equals being, and if your weight goes down, you are the less.

HOUSEHOLD APPLES

I knew nothing about apples. Why should I? My country came in my childhood, and I dreamed of sitting among the blooms like the bees. I failed to spray the pear tree too. I doubled up under them at first, admiring the sturdy low branches I should have pruned, and later I acclaimed the blossoms. Shortly after the fruit formed there were falls—not many—apples the size of goodish stones which made me wobble on my ankles when I walked about the yard. Sometimes a piece crushed by a heel would cling on the shoe to track the house. I gathered a few and heaved them over the wires. A slingshot would have been splendid. Hard, an unattractive green, the worms had them. Before long I realized the worms had them all. Even as the apples reddened, lit their tree, they were being swallowed. The birds preferred the pears, which were small—sugar pears I think they're called—with thick skins of graying green that ripen on toward violet. So the fruit fell, and once I made some applesauce by quartering and paring hundreds; but mostly I did nothing, left them, until suddenly, overnight it seemed, in that ugly late September heat we often have in Indiana, my problem was upon me.

My childhood came in the country. I remember, now, the flies on our snowy luncheon table. As we cleared away they would settle, fastidiously scrub themselves and stroll to the crumbs to feed where I would kill them in crowds with a swatter. It was quite a game to catch them taking off. I struck heavily since I didn't mind a few stains; they'd wash. The swatter was a square of screen bound down in red cloth. It drove no air ahead of it to give them warning. They might have thought they'd flown headlong into a summered window. The faint pink dot where they had died did not rub out as I'd supposed, and after years of use our luncheon linen would faintly, pinkly, speckle.

The country became my childhood. Flies braided themselves on the flypaper in my grandmother's house. I can smell the bakery and the grocery and the stables and the dairy in that small Dakota town I knew as a kid; knew as I dreamed I'd know your body, as I've known nothing, before or since; knew as the flies knew, in the honest, unchaste sense: the burned house, hose-wet, which drew a mist of insects like the blue smoke of its smolder, and gangs of boys, moist-lipped, destructive as its burning. Flies have always impressed me; they are so persistently alive. Now they were coating the ground beneath my trees. Some were ordinary flies; there were the large blue-green ones; there were swarms of fruit flies too, and the red-spotted scavenger beetle; there were a few wasps, several sorts of bees and butterflies—checkers, sulphurs, monarchs, commas, question marks—and delicate dragonflies . . . but principally houseflies and horseflies and bottleflies, flies and more flies in clusters around the rotting fruit. They loved the pears. Inside, they fed. If you picked up a pear, they flew, and the pear became skin and stem. They were everywhere the fruit was: in the tree still—apples like a hive for them—or where the fruit littered the ground, squashing itself as you stepped . . . there was no help for it. The flies droned, feasting on the sweet juice. No one could go near the trees; I could not climb; so I determined at last to labor like Hercules. There were fruit baskets in the barn. Collecting them and kneeling under the branches, I began to gather remains. Deep in the strong rich smell of the fruit, I began to hum myself. The fruit caved in at the touch. Glistening red apples, my lifting disclosed, had families of beetles, flies, and bugs, devouring their rotten undersides. There were streams of flies; there were lakes and cataracts and rivers of flies, seas and oceans. The hum was heavier, higher, than the hum of the bees when they came to the blooms in the spring, though the bees were there, among the flies, ignoring me—ignoring everyone. As my work went on and juice covered my hands and arms, they would form a sleeve, black and moving, like knotty wool. No caress could have been more indifferently complete. Still I rose fearfully, ramming my head in the branches, apples bumping against me before falling, bursting with bugs. I'd snap my hand sharply but the flies would cling to the sweet. I could toss a whole cluster into a basket from several feet. As the pear or apple lit, they would explosively rise, like monads for a moment, windowless, certainly, with respect to one another, sugar their harmony. I had to admit, though, despite my distaste, that my arm had never been more alive, oftener or more gently kissed. Those hundreds of feet were light. In washing them off, I pretended the hose was a pump. What have I missed? Childhood is a lie of poetry.

THE CHURCH

Friday night. Girls in dark skirts and white blouses sit in ranks and scream in concert. They carry funnels loosely stuffed with orange and black paper which they shake wildly, and small megaphones through which, as drilled, they direct and magnify their shouting. Their leaders, barely pubescent girls, prance and shake and whirl their skirts above their bloomers. The young men, leaping, extend their arms and race through puddles of amber light, their bodies glistening. In a lull, though it rarely occurs, you can hear the squeak of tennis shoes against the floor. Then the yelling begins again, and then continues; fathers, mothers, neighbors joining in to form a single pulsing ululation—a cry of the whole community—for in this gymnasium each body becomes the bodies beside it, pressed as they are together, thigh to thigh, and the same shudder runs through all of them, and runs toward the same release. Only the ball moves serenely through this dazzling din. Obedient to law it scarcely speaks but caroms quietly and lives at peace.

BUSINESS

It is the week of Christmas and the stores, to accommodate the rush they hope for, are remaining open in the evening. You can see snow falling in the cones of the street lamps. The roads are filling—undisturbed. Strings of red and green lights droop over the principal highway, and the water tower wears a star. The windows of the stores have been bedizened. Shamelessly they beckon. But I am alone, leaning against a pole—no . . . there is no one in sight. They're all at home, perhaps by their instruments, tuning in on their evenings, and like Ramona, tirelessly playing and replaying themselves. There's a speaker perched in the tower, and through the boughs of falling snow and over the vacant streets, it drapes the twisted and metallic strains of a tune that can barely be distinguished—yes, I believe it's one of the jolly ones, it's "Joy to the World." There's no one to hear the music but myself, and though I'm listening, I'm no longer certain. Perhaps the record's playing something else.

FLANNERY O'CONNOR

Revelation

The doctor's waiting room, which was very small, was almost full when the Turpins entered and Mrs. Turpin, who was very large, made it look even smaller by her presence. She stood looming at the head of the magazine table set in the center of it, a living demonstration that the room was inadequate and ridiculous. Her little bright black eyes took in all the patients as she sized up the seating situation. There was one vacant chair and a place on the sofa occupied by a blond child in a dirty blue romper who should have been told to move over and make room for the lady. He was five or six, but Mrs. Turpin saw at once that no one was going to tell him to move over. He was slumped down in the seat, his arms idle at his sides and his eyes idle in his head; his nose ran unchecked.

Mrs. Turpin put a firm hand on Claud's shoulder and said in a voice that included anyone who wanted to listen, "Claud, you sit in that chair there," and gave him a push down into the vacant one. Claud was florid and bald and sturdy, somewhat shorter than Mrs. Turpin, but he sat down as if he were accustomed to doing what she told him to.

Mrs. Turpin remained standing. The only man in the room besides Claud was a lean stringy old fellow with a rusty hand spread out on each knee, whose eyes were closed as if he were asleep or dead or pretending to be so as not to get up and offer her his seat. Her gaze settled agreeably on a well-dressed gray-haired lady whose eyes met hers and whose expression said: if that child belonged to me, he would have some manners and move over—there's plenty of room there for you and him too.

Claud looked up with a sigh and made as if to rise.

"Sit down," Mrs. Turpin said. "You know you're not supposed to stand on that leg. He has an ulcer on his leg," she explained.

Claud lifted his foot onto the magazine table and rolled his trouser leg up to reveal a purple swelling on a plump marble-white calf.

"My!" the pleasant lady said. "How did you do that?"

"A cow kicked him," Mrs. Turpin said.

"Goodness!" said the lady.

Claud rolled his trouser leg down.

"Maybe the little boy would move over," the lady suggested, but the child did not stir.

"Somebody will be leaving in a minute," Mrs. Turpin said. She could not understand why a doctor—with as much money as they made charging five dollars a day to just stick their head in the hospital door and look at you—couldn't afford a decent-sized waiting room. This one was hardly bigger than a garage. The table was cluttered with limp-looking magazines and at one end of it there was a big green glass ash tray full of cigarette butts and cotton wads with little blood spots on them. If she had had anything to do with the running of the place, that would have been emptied every so often. There were no chairs against the wall at the head of the room. It had a rectangular-shaped panel in it that permitted a view of the office where the nurse came and went and the secretary listened to the radio. A plastic fern in a gold pot sat in the opening and trailed its fronds down almost to the floor. The radio was softly playing gospel music.

Just then the inner door opened and a nurse with the highest stack of yellow hair Mrs. Turpin had ever seen put her face in the crack and called for the next patient. The woman sitting beside Claud grasped the two arms of her chair and hoisted herself up; she pulled her dress free from her legs and lumbered through the door where the nurse had disappeared.

Mrs. Turpin eased into the vacant chair, which held her tight as a corset. "I wish I could reduce," she said, and rolled her eyes and gave a comic sigh.

"Oh, *you* aren't fat," the stylish lady said.

"Ooooo I am too," Mrs. Turpin said. "Claud he eats all he wants to and never weighs over one hundred and seventy-five pounds, but me I just look at something good to eat and I gain some weight," and her stomach and shoulders shook with laughter. "You can eat all you want to, can't you, Claud?" she asked, turning to him.

Claud only grinned.

"Well, as long as you have such a good disposition," the stylish lady said, "I don't think it makes a bit of difference what size you are.

You just can't beat a good disposition."

Next to her was a fat girl of eighteen or nineteen, scowling into a thick blue book which Mrs. Turpin saw was entitled *Human Development.* The girl raised her head and directed her scowl at Mrs. Turpin as if she did not like her looks. She appeared annoyed that anyone should speak while she tried to read. The poor girl's face was blue with acne and Mrs. Turpin thought how pitiful it was to have a face like that at that age. She gave the girl a friendly smile but the girl only scowled the harder. Mrs. Turpin herself was fat but she had always had good skin, and, though she was forty-seven years old, there was not a wrinkle in her face except around her eyes from laughing too much.

Next to the ugly girl was the child, still in exactly the same position, and next to him was a thin leathery old woman in a cotton print dress. She and Claud had three sacks of chicken feed in their pump house that was in the same print. She had seen from the first that the child belonged with the old woman. She could tell by the way they sat—kind of vacant and white-trashy, as if they would sit there until Doomsday if nobody called and told them to get up. And at right angles but next to the well-dressed pleasant lady was a lank-faced woman who was certainly the child's mother. She had on a yellow sweat shirt and wine-colored slacks, both gritty-looking, and the rims of her lips were stained with snuff. Her dirty yellow hair was tied behind with a little piece of red paper ribbon. Worse than niggers any day, Mrs. Turpin thought.

The gospel hymn playing was, "When I looked up and He looked down," and Mrs. Turpin, who knew it, supplied the last line mentally, "And wona these days I know I'll we-eara crown."

Without appearing to, Mrs. Turpin always noticed people's feet. The well-dressed lady had on red and gray suede shoes to match her dress. Mrs. Turpin had on her good black patent leather pumps. The ugly girl had on Girl Scout shoes and heavy socks. The old woman had on tennis shoes and the white-trashy mother had on what appeared to be bedroom slippers, black straw with gold braid threaded through them—exactly what you would have expected her to have on.

Sometimes at night when she couldn't go to sleep, Mrs. Turpin would occupy herself with the question of who she would have chosen to be if she couldn't have been herself. If Jesus had said to her before he made her, "There's only two places available for you. You can either be a nigger or white-trash," what would she have said? "Please, Jesus, please," she would have said, "just let me wait until there's another place available," and he would have said, "No, you have to go right now and I have only those two places so make up your mind." She would have wiggled and squirmed and begged and pleaded but it would have been no use and finally she would have said, "All right, make me a nigger then—but that don't mean a trashy one." And he would have made her a neat clean respectable Negro woman, herself but black.

Next to the child's mother was a red-headed youngish woman, reading one of the magazines and working a piece of chewing gum, hell for leather, as Claud would say. Mrs. Turpin could not see the woman's feet. She was not white-trash, just common. Sometimes Mrs. Turpin occupied herself at night naming the classes of people. On the bottom of the heap were most colored people, not the kind she would have been if she had been one, but most of them; then next to them—not above, just away from—were the white-trash; then above them were the home-owners, and above them the home-and-land owners, to which she and Claud belonged. Above she and Claud were people with a lot of money and much bigger houses and much more land. But here the complexity of it would begin to bear in on her, for some of the people with a lot money were common and ought to be below she and Claud and some of the people who had good blood had lost their money and had to rent and then there were colored people who owned their homes and land as well. There was a colored dentist in town who had two red Lincolns and a swimming pool and a farm with registered white-face cattle on it. Usually by the time she had fallen asleep all the classes of people were moiling and roiling around in her head, and she would dream they were all crammed in together in a box car, being ridden off to be put in a gas oven.

"That's a beautiful clock," she said and nodded to her right. It was a big wall clock, the face encased in a brass sunburst.

"Yes, it's very pretty," the stylish lady said agreeably. "And right on the dot too," she added, glancing at her watch.

The ugly girl beside her cast an eye upward at the clock, smirked, then looked directly at Mrs. Turpin and smirked again. Then she returned her eyes to her book. She was obviously the lady's daughter because, although they didn't look anything alike as to disposition, they both had the same shape of face and the same blue eyes. On the lady they sparkled pleasantly but in the girl's seared face they appeared alternately to smolder and to blaze.

What if Jesus had said, "All right, you can be white-trash or a nigger or ugly"!

Mrs. Turpin felt an awful pity for the girl, though she thought it was one thing to be ugly and another to act ugly.

The woman with the snuff-stained lips turned around in her chair and looked up at the clock. Then she turned back and appeared to look a little to the side of Mrs. Turpin. There was a cast in one of her eyes.

"You want to know wher you can get you one of themther clocks?" she asked in a loud voice.

"No, I already have a nice clock," Mrs. Turpin said. Once somebody like her got a leg in the conversation, she would be all over it.

"You can get you one with green stamps," the woman said. "That's most likely wher he got hisn. Save you up enough, you can get you most anythang. I got me some joo'ry."

Ought to have got you a wash rag and some soap, Mrs. Turpin thought.

"I get contour sheets with mine," the pleasant lady said.

The daughter slammed her book shut. She looked straight in front of her, directly through Mrs. Turpin and on through the yellow curtain and the plate glass window which made the wall behind her. The girl's eyes seemed lit all of a sudden with a peculiar light, an unnatural light like night road signs give. Mrs. Turpin turned her head to see if there was anything going on outside that she should see, but she could not see anything. Figures passing cast only a pale shadow through the curtain. There was no reason the girl should single her out for her ugly looks.

"Miss Finley," the nurse said, cracking the door. The gum-chewing woman got up and passed in front of her and Claud and went into the office. She had on red high-heeled shoes.

Directly across the table, the ugly girl's eyes were fixed on Mrs. Turpin as if she had some very special reason for disliking her.

"This is wonderful weather, isn't it?" the girl's mother said.

"It's good weather for cotton if you can get the niggers to pick it," Mrs. Turpin said, "but niggers don't want to pick cotton any more. You can't get the white folks to pick it and now you can't get the niggers—because they got to be right up there with the white folks."

"They gonna *try* anyways," the white-trash woman said, leaning forward.

"Do you have one of the cotton-picking machines?" the pleasant lady asked.

"No," Mrs. Turpin said, "they leave half the cotton in the field. We don't have much cotton anyway. If you want to make it farming now, you have to have a little of everything. We got a couple of acres of cotton and a few hogs and chickens and just enough white-face that Claud can look after them himself."

"One thing I don't want," the white-trash woman said, wiping her mouth with the back of her hand. "Hogs. Nasty stinking things, a-gruntin and a-rootin all over the place."

Mrs. Turpin gave her the merest edge of her attention. "Our hogs are not dirty and they don't stink," she said. "They're cleaner than some children I've seen. Their feet never touch the ground. We have a pig-parlor—that's where you raise them on concrete," she explained to the pleasant lady, "and Claud scoots them down with the hose every afternoon and washes off the floor." Cleaner by far than that child right there, she thought. Poor nasty little thing. He had not moved except to put the thumb of his dirty hand into his mouth.

The woman turned her face away from Mrs. Turpin. "I know I wouldn't scoot down no hog with no hose," she said to the wall.

You wouldn't have no hog to scoot down, Mrs. Turpin said to herself.

"A-gruntin and a-rootin and a-groanin," the woman muttered.

"We got a little of everything," Mrs. Turpin said to the pleasant lady. "It's no use in having more than you can handle yourself with help like it is. We found enough niggers to pick our cotton this year but Claud he has to go after them and take them home again in the evening. They can't walk that half a mile. No they can't. I tell you," she said and laughed merrily, "I sure am tired of buttering up niggers, but you got to love em if you want em to work for you. When they come in the morning, I run out and I say, 'Hi yawl this morning?' and when Claud drives them off to the field I just wave to beat the band and they just wave back." And she waved her hand rapidly to illustrate.

"Like you read out of the same book," the lady said, showing she understood perfectly.

"Child, yes," Mrs. Turpin said. "And when they come in from the field, I run out with a bucket of icewater. That's the way it's going to be from now on," she said. "You may as well face it."

"One thang I know," the white-trash woman said. "Two thangs I ain't going to do: love no niggers or scoot down no hog with no hose." And she let out a bark of contempt.

The look that Mrs. Turpin and the pleasant lady exchanged indicated they both understood that you had to *have* certain things before you could *know* certain things. But every time Mrs. Turpin exchanged a look with the lady, she was aware that the ugly girl's peculiar eyes were still on her, and she had trouble bringing her attention back to the conversation.

"When you got something," she said, "you got to look after it." And when you ain't got a thing but breath and britches, she added to herself, you can afford to come to town every morning and just sit on the Court House coping and spit.

A grotesque revolving shadow passed across the curtain behind her and was thrown palely on the opposite wall. Then a bicycle clattered down against the outside of the building. The door opened and a colored boy glided in with a tray from the drugstore. It had two large red and white paper cups on it with tops on them. He was a tall, very black boy in discolored white pants and a green nylon shirt. He was chewing gum slowly, as if to music. He set the tray down in the office opening next to the fern and stuck his head through to look for the secretary. She was not in there. He rested his arms on the ledge and waited, his narrow bottom stuck out, swaying to the left and right. He raised a hand over his head and scratched the base of his skull.

"You see that button there, boy?" Mrs. Turpin said. "You can punch that and she'll come. She's probably in the back somewhere."

"Is thas right?" the boy said agreeably, as if he had never seen the button before. He leaned to the right and put his finger on it. "She sometime out," he said and twisted around to face his audience, his elbows behind him on the counter. The nurse appeared and he twisted back again. She handed him a dollar and he rooted in his pocket and made the change and counted it out to her. She gave him fifteen cents for a tip and he went out with the empty tray. The heavy door swung to slowly and closed at length with the sound of suction. For a moment no one spoke.

"They ought to send all them niggers back to Africa," the white-trash woman said. "That's wher they come from in the first place."

"Oh, I couldn't do without my good colored friends," the pleasant lady said.

"There's a heap of things worse than a nigger," Mrs. Turpin agreed. "It's all kinds of them just like it's all kinds of us."

"Yes, and it takes all kinds to make the world go round," the lady said in her musical voice.

As she said it, the raw-complexioned girl snapped her teeth together. Her lower lip turned downwards and inside out, revealing the pale pink inside of her mouth. After a second it rolled back up. It was the ugliest face Mrs. Turpin had ever seen anyone make and for a moment she was certain that the girl had made it at her. She was looking at her as if she had known and disliked her all her life—all of Mrs. Turpin's life, it seemed too, not just all the girl's life. Why, girl, I don't even know you, Mrs. Turpin said silently.

She forced her attention back to the discussion. "It wouldn't be practical to send them back to Africa," she said. "They wouldn't want to go. They got it too good here."

"Wouldn't be what they wanted—if I had anythang to do with it," the woman said.

"It wouldn't be a way in the world you could get all the niggers back over there," Mrs. Turpin said. "They'd be hiding out and lying down and turning sick on you and wailing and hollering and raring and pitching. It wouldn't be a way in the world to get them over there."

"They got over here," the trashy woman said. "Get back like they got over."

"It wasn't so many of them then," Mrs. Turpin explained.

The woman looked at Mrs. Turpin as if here was an idiot indeed but Mrs. Turpin was not bothered by the look, considering where it came from.

"Nooo," she said, "they're going to stay here where they can go to New York and marry white folks and improve their color. That's what they all want to do, every one of them, improve their color."

"You know what comes of that, don't you?" Claud asked.

"No, Claud, what?" Mrs. Turpin said.

Claud's eyes twinkled. "White-faced niggers," he said with never a smile.

Everybody in the office laughed except the white-trash and the ugly girl. The girl gripped the book in her lap with white fingers. The trashy woman looked around her from face to face as if she thought they were all idiots. The old woman in the feed sack dress continued to gaze expressionless across the floor at the high-top shoes of the man opposite her, the one who had been pretending to be asleep when the Turpins came in. He was laughing heartily, his hands still spread out on his knees. The child had fallen to the side and was lying now almost face down in the old woman's lap.

While they recovered from their laughter, the nasal chorus on the radio kept the room from silence.

"You go to blank blank
And I'll go to mine
But we'll all blank along
To-geth-ther,
And all along the blank
We'll hep eachother out
Smile-ling in any kind of
Weath-ther!"

Mrs. Turpin didn't catch every word but she caught enough to agree with the spirit of the song and it turned her thoughts sober. To help anybody out that needed it was her philosophy of life. She never spared herself when she found somebody in need, whether they were white or black, trash or decent. And of all she had to be thankful for, she was most thankful that this was so. If Jesus had said, "You can be high society and have all the money you want and be thin and svelte-like, but you can't be a good woman with it," she would have had to say, "Well don't make me that then. Make me a good woman and it don't matter what else, how fat or how ugly or how poor!" Her heart rose. He had not made her a nigger or white-trash or ugly! He had made her herself and given her a little of everything. Jesus, thank you! she said. Thank you thank you thank you! Whenever she counted her blessings she felt as buoyant as if she weighed one hundred and twenty-five pounds instead of one hundred and eighty.

"What's wrong with your little boy?" the pleasant lady asked the white-trashy woman.

"He has a ulcer," the woman said proudly. "He ain't give me a minute's peace since he was born. Him and her are just alike," she said, nodding at the old woman, who was running her leathery fingers through the child's pale hair. "Look like I can't get nothing down them two but Co' Cola and candy."

That's all you try to get down em, Mrs. Turpin said to herself. Too lazy to light the fire. There was nothing you could tell her about people like them that she didn't know already. And it was not just that they didn't have anything. Because if you gave them everything, in two weeks it would all be broken or filthy or they would have chopped it up for lightwood. She knew all this from her own experience. Help them you must, but help them you couldn't.

All at once the ugly girl turned her lips inside out again. Her eyes fixed like two drills on Mrs. Turpin. This time there was no mistaking that there was something urgent behind them.

Girl, Mrs. Turpin exclaimed silently, I haven't done a thing to you! The girl might be confusing her with somebody else. There was no need to sit by and let herself be intimidated. "You must be in college," she said boldly, looking directly at the girl. "I see you reading a book there."

The girl continued to stare and pointedly did not answer.

Her mother blushed at this rudeness. "The lady asked you a question, Mary Grace," she said under her breath.

"I have ears," Mary Grace said.

The poor mother blushed again. "Mary Grace goes to Wellesley College," she explained. She twisted one of the buttons on her dress. "In Massachusetts," she added with a grimace. "And in the summer she just keeps right on studying. Just reads all the time, a real book worm. She's done real well at Wellesley; she's taking English and Math and History and Psychology and Social Studies," she rattled on, "and I think it's too much. I think she ought to get out and have fun."

The girl looked as if she would like to hurl them all through the plate glass window.

"Way up north," Mrs. Turpin murmured and thought, well, it hasn't done much for her manners.

"I'd almost rather to have him sick," the white-trash woman said, wrenching the attention back to herself. "He's so mean when he ain't. Look like some children just take natural to meanness. It's some gets bad when they get sick but he was the opposite. Took sick and turned good. He don't give me no trouble now. It's me waitin to see the doctor," she said.

If I was going to send anybody back to Africa, Mrs. Turpin thought, it would be your kind, woman. "Yes, indeed," she said aloud, but looking up at the ceiling, "it's a heap of things worse than a nigger." And dirtier than a hog, she added to herself.

"I think people with bad dispositions are more to be pitied than anyone on earth," the pleasant lady said in a voice that was decidedly thin.

"I thank the Lord he has blessed me with a good one," Mrs. Turpin said. "The day has never dawned that I couldn't find something to laugh at."

"Not since she married me anyways," Claud said with a comical straight face.

Everybody laughed except the girl and the white-trash.

Mrs. Turpin's stomach shook. "He's such a caution," she said, "that I can't help but laugh at him."

The girl made a loud ugly noise through her teeth.

Her mother's mouth grew thin and tight. "I think the worst thing in the world," she said, "is an ungrateful person. To have everything and not appreciate it. I know a girl," she said, "who has parents who would give her anything, a little brother who loves her dearly, who is getting a good education, who wears the best clothes, but who can never say a kind word to anyone, who never smiles, who just criticizes and complains all day long."

"Is she too old to paddle?" Claud asked.

The girl's face was almost purple.

"Yes," the lady said, "I'm afraid there's nothing to do but leave her to her folly. Some day she'll wake up and it'll be too late."

"It never hurt anyone to smile," Mrs. Turpin said. "It just makes you feel better all over."

"Of course," the lady said sadly, "but there are just some people you can't tell anything to. They can't take criticism."

"If it's one thing I am," Mrs. Turpin said with feeling, "it's grateful. When I think who all I could have been besides myself and what all I got, a little of everything, and a good disposition besides, I just feel like shouting, 'Thank you, Jesus, for making everything the way it is!' It could have been different!" For one thing, somebody else could have got Claud. At the thought of this, she was flooded with gratitude and a terrible pang of joy ran through her. "Oh thank you, Jesus, Jesus, thank you!" she cried aloud.

The book struck her directly over her left eye. It struck almost at the same instant that she realized the girl was about to hurl it. Before she could utter a sound, the raw face came crashing across the table toward her, howling. The girl's fingers sank like clamps into the soft flesh of her neck. She heard the mother cry out and Claud shout, "Whoa!" There was an instant when she was certain that she was about to be in an earthquake.

All at once her vision narrowed and she saw everything as if it were happening in a small room far away, or as if she were looking at it through the wrong end of a telescope. Claud's face crumpled and fell out of sight. The nurse ran in, then out, then in again. Then the gangling figure of the doctor rushed out of the inner door. Magazines flew this way and that as the table turned over. The girl fell with a thud and Mrs. Turpin's vision suddenly reversed itself and she saw everything large instead of small. The eyes of the white-trashy woman were staring hugely at the floor. There the girl, held down on one side by the nurse and on the other by her mother, was wrenching and turning in their grasp. The doctor was kneeling astride her, trying to hold her arm down. He managed after a second to sink a long needle into it.

Mrs. Turpin felt entirely hollow except for her heart which swung from side to side as if it were agitated in a great empty drum of flesh.

"Somebody that's not busy call for the ambulance," the doctor said in the off-hand voice young doctors adopt for terrible occasions.

Mrs. Turpin could not have moved a finger. The old man who had been sitting next to her skipped nimbly into the office and made the call, for the secretary still seemed to be gone.

"Claud!" Mrs. Turpin called.

He was not in his chair. She knew she must jump up and find him but she felt like some one trying to catch a train in a dream, when everything moves in slow motion and the faster you try to run the slower you go.

"Here I am," a suffocated voice, very unlike Claud's, said.

He was doubled up in the corner on the floor, pale as paper, holding his leg. She wanted to get up and go to him but she could not move. Instead, her gaze was drawn slowly downward to the churning face on the floor, which she could see over the doctor's shoulder.

The girl's eyes stopped rolling and focused on her. They seemed a much lighter blue than before, as if a door that had been tightly closed behind them was now open to admit light and air.

Mrs. Turpin's head cleared and her power of motion returned. She leaned forward until she was looking directly into the fierce brilliant eyes. There was no doubt in her mind that the girl did know her, knew her in some intense and personal way, beyond time and place and condition. "What you got to say to me?" she asked hoarsely and held her breath, waiting, as for a revelation.

The girl raised her head. Her gaze locked with Mrs. Turpin's. "Go back to hell where you came from, you old wart hog," she whispered. Her voice was low but clear. Her eyes burned for a moment as if she saw with pleasure that her message had struck its target.

Mrs. Turpin sank back in her chair.

After a moment the girl's eyes closed and she turned her head wearily to the side.

The doctor rose and handed the nurse the empty syringe. He leaned over and put both hands for a moment on the mother's shoulders, which were shaking. She was sitting on the floor, her lips pressed together, holding Mary Grace's hand in her lap. The girl's fingers were gripped like a baby's around her thumb. "Go on to the hospital," he said. "I'll call and make the arrangements."

"Now let's see that neck," he said in a jovial voice to Mrs. Turpin. He began to inspect her neck with his first two fingers. Two little moon-shaped lines like pink fish bones were indented over her windpipe. There was the beginning of an angry red swelling above her eye. His fingers passed over this also.

"Lea' me be," she said thickly and shook him off. "See about Claud. She kicked him."

"I'll see about him in a minute," he said and felt her pulse. He was a thin gray-haired man, given to pleasantries. "Go home and have yourself a vacation the rest of the day," he said and patted her on the shoulder.

Quit your pattin me, Mrs. Turpin growled to herself.

"And put an ice pack over that eye," he said. Then he went and squatted down beside Claud and looked at his leg. After a moment he pulled him up and Claud limped after him into the office.

Until the ambulance came, the only sounds in the room were the tremulous moans of the girl's mother, who continued to sit on the floor. The white-trash woman did not take her eyes off the girl. Mrs. Turpin looked straight ahead at nothing. Presently the ambulance drew up, a long dark shadow, behind the curtain. The attendants came in and set the stretcher down beside the girl and lifted her expertly onto it and carried her out. The nurse helped the mother gather up her things. The shadow of the ambulance moved silently away and the nurse came back in the office.

"That ther girl is going to be a lunatic, ain't she?" the white-trash woman asked the nurse, but the nurse kept on to the back and never answered her.

"Yes, she's going to be a lunatic," the white-trash woman said to the rest of them.

"Po' critter," the old woman murmured. The child's face was still in her lap. His eyes looked idly out over her knees. He had not moved during the disturbance except to draw one leg up under him.

"I thank Gawd," the white-trash woman said fervently, "I ain't a lunatic."

Claud came limping out and the Turpins went home.

As their pick-up truck turned into their own dirt road and made the crest of the hill, Mrs. Turpin gripped the window ledge and looked out suspiciously. The land sloped gracefully down through a field dotted with lavender weeds and at the start of the rise their small yellow frame house, with its little flower beds spread out around it like a fancy apron, sat primly in its accustomed place between two giant hickory trees. She would not have been startled to see a burnt wound between two blackened chimneys.

Neither of them felt like eating so they put on their house clothes and lowered the shade in the bedroom and lay down, Claud with his leg on a pillow and herself with a damp washcloth over her eye. The instant she was flat on her back, the image of a razor-backed hog with warts on its face and horns coming out behind its ears snorted into her head. She moaned, a low quiet moan.

"I am not," she said tearfully, "a wart hog. From hell." But the denial had no force. The girl's eyes and her words, even the tone of her voice, low but clear, directed only to her, brooked no repudiation. She had been singled out for the message, though there was trash in the room to whom it might justly have been applied. The full force of this fact struck her only now. There was a woman there who was neglecting her own child but she had been overlooked. The message had been given to Ruby Turpin, a respectable, hard-working, church-going woman. The tears dried. Her eyes began to burn instead with wrath.

She rose on her elbow and the washcloth fell into her hand. Claud was lying on his back, snoring. She wanted to tell him what the girl had said. At the same time, she did not wish to put the image of herself as a wart hog from hell into his mind.

"Hey, Claud," she muttered and pushed his shoulder.

Claud opened one pale baby blue eye.

She looked into it warily. He did not think about anything. He just went his way.

"Wha, whasit?" he said and closed the eye again.

"Nothing," she said. "Does your leg pain you?"

"Hurts like hell," Claud said.

"It'll quit terreckly," she said and lay back down. In a moment Claud was snoring again. For the rest of the afternoon they lay there. Claud slept. She scowled at the ceiling. Occasionally she raised her fist and made a small stabbing motion over her chest as if she was defending her innocence to invisible guests who were like the comforters of Job, reasonable-seeming but wrong.

About five-thirty Claud stirred. "Got to go after those niggers," he sighed, not moving.

She was looking straight up as if there were unintelligible handwriting on the ceiling. The protuberance over her eye had turned a greenish-blue. "Listen here," she said.

"What?"

"Kiss me."

Claud leaned over and kissed her loudly on the mouth. He pinched her side and their hands interlocked. Her expression of ferocious concentration did not change. Claud got up, groaning and growling, and limped off. She continued to study the ceiling.

She did not get up until she heard the pick-up truck coming back with the Negroes. Then she rose and thrust her feet in her brown oxfords, which she did not bother to lace, and stumped out onto the back porch and got her red plastic bucket. She emptied a tray of ice cubes into it and filled it half full of water and went out into the back yard. Every afternoon after Claud brought the hands in, one of the boys helped him put out hay and the rest waited in the back of the truck until he was ready to take them home. The truck was parked in the shade under one of the hickory trees.

"Hi yawl this evening?" Mrs. Turpin asked grimly, appearing with the bucket and the dipper. There were three women and a boy in the truck.

"Us doin nicely," the oldest woman said. "Hi you doin?" and her gaze stuck immediately on the dark lump on Mrs. Turpin's forehead. "You done fell down, ain't you?" she asked in a solicitous voice. The old woman was dark and almost toothless. She had on an old felt hat of Claud's set back on her head. The other two women were younger and lighter and they both had new bright green sunhats. One of them had hers on her head; the other had taken hers off and the boy was grinning beneath it.

Mrs. Turpin set the bucket down on the floor of the truck. "Yawl hep yourselves," she said. She looked around to make sure Claud had gone. "No, I didn't fall down," she said, folding her arms. "It was something worse than that."

"Ain't nothing bad happen to you!" the old woman said. She said it as if they all knew that Mrs. Turpin was protected in some special way by Divine Providence. "You just had you a little fall."

"We were in town at the doctor's office for where the cow kicked Mr. Turpin," Mrs. Turpin said in a flat tone that indicated they could leave off their foolishness. "And there was this girl there. A big fat girl with her face all broke out. I could look at that girl and tell she was peculiar but I couldn't tell how. And me and her mama was just talking and going along and all of a sudden WHAM! She throws this big book she was reading at me and . . ."

"Naw!" the old woman cried out.

"And then she jumps over the table and commences to choke me."

"Naw!" they all exclaimed, "naw!"

"Hi come she do that?" the old woman asked. "What ail her?"

Mrs. Turpin only glared in front of her.

"Somethin ail her," the old woman said.

"They carried her off in an ambulance," Mrs. Turpin continued, "but before she went she was rolling on the floor and they were trying to hold her down to give her a shot and she said something to me." She paused. "You know what she said to me?"

"What she say?" they asked.

"She said," Mrs. Turpin began, and stopped, her face very dark and heavy. The sun was getting whiter and whiter, blanching the sky overhead so that the leaves of the hickory tree were black in the face of it. She could not bring forth the words. "Something real ugly," she muttered.

"She sho shouldn't said nothin ugly to you," the old woman said. "You so sweet. You the sweetest lady I know."

"She pretty too," the one with the hat on said.

"And stout," the other one said. "I never knowed no sweeter white lady."

"That's the truth befo' Jesus," the old woman said. "Amen! You des as sweet and pretty as you can be."

Mrs. Turpin knew exactly how much Negro flattery was worth and it added to her rage. "She said," she began again and finished this time with a fierce rush of breath, "that I was an old wart hog from hell."

There was an astounded silence.

"Where she at?" the youngest woman cried in a piercing voice.

"Lemme see her. I'll kill her!"

"I'll kill her with you!" the other one cried.

"She b'long in the sylum," the old woman said emphatically. "You the sweetest white lady I know."

"She pretty too," the other two said. "Stout as she can be and sweet. Jesus satisfied with her!"

"Deed he is," the old woman declared.

Idiots! Mrs. Turpin growled to herself. You could never say anything intelligent to a nigger. You could talk at them but not with them. "Yawl ain't drunk your water," she said shortly. "Leave the bucket in the truck when you're finished with it. I got more to do than just stand around and pass the time of day," and she moved off and into the house.

She stood for a moment in the middle of the kitchen. The dark protuberance over her eye looked like a miniature tornado cloud which might any moment sweep across the horizon of her brow. Her lower lip protruded dangerously. She squared her massive shoulders. Then she marched into the front of the house and out the side door and started down the road to the pig parlor. She had the look of a woman going single-handed, weaponless, into battle.

The sun was a deep yellow now like a harvest moon and was riding westward very fast over the far tree line as if it meant to reach the hogs before she did. The road was rutted and she kicked several good-sized stones out of her path as she strode along. The pig parlor was on a little knoll at the end of a lane that ran off from the side of the barn. It was a square of concrete as large as a small room, with a board fence about four feet high around it. The concrete floor sloped slightly so that the hog wash could drain off into a trench where it was carried to the field for fertilizer. Claud was standing on the outside, on the edge of the concrete, hanging onto the top board, hosing down the floor inside. The hose was connected to the faucet of a water trough nearby.

Mrs. Turpin climbed up beside him and glowered down at the hogs inside. There were seven long-snouted bristly shoats in it—tan with liver-colored spots—and an old sow a few weeks off from farrowing. She was lying on her side grunting. The shoats were running about shaking themselves like idiot children, their little slit pig eyes searching the floor for anything left. She had read that pigs were the most intelligent animal. She doubted it. They were supposed to be smarter than dogs. There had even been a pig astronaut. He had performed his assignment perfectly but died of a heart attack afterwards because they left him in his electric suit, sitting upright throughout his examination when naturally a hog should be on all fours.

A-gruntin and a-rootin and a-groanin.

"Gimme that hose," she said, yanking it away from Claud. "Go on and carry them niggers home and then get off that leg."

"You look like you might have swallowed a mad dog," Claud observed, but he got down and limped off. He paid no attention to her humors.

Until he was out of earshot, Mrs. Turpin stood on the side of the pen, holding the hose and pointing the stream of water at the hind quarters of any shoat that looked as if it might try to lie down. When he had had time to get over the hill, she turned her head slightly and her wrathful eyes scanned the path. He was nowhere in sight. She turned back again and seemed to gather herself up. Her shoulders rose and she drew in her breath.

"What do you send me a message like that for?" she said in a low fierce voice, barely above a whisper but with the force of a shout in its concentrated fury. "How am I a hog and me both? How am I saved and from hell too?" Her free fist was knotted and with the other she gripped the hose, blindly pointing the stream of water in and out of the eye of the old sow whose outraged squeal she did not hear.

The pig parlor commanded a view of the back pasture where their twenty beef cows were gathered around the hay-bales Claud and the boy had put out. The freshly cut pasture sloped down to the highway. Across it was their cotton field and beyond that a dark green dusty wood which they owned as well. The sun was behind the wood, very red, looking over the paling of trees like a farmer inspecting his own hogs.

"Why me?" she rumbled. "It's no trash around here, black or white, that I haven't given to. And break my back to the bone every day working. And do for the church."

She appeared to be the right size woman to command the arena before her. "How am I a hog?" she demanded. "Exactly how am I like them?" and she jabbed the stream of water at the shoats. "There was plenty of trash there. It didn't have to be me.

"If you like trash better, go get yourself some trash then," she railed. "You could have made me trash. Or a nigger. If trash is what you wanted why didn't you make me trash?" She shook her fist with the hose in it and a watery snake appeared momentarily in the air. "I could quit working and take it easy and be filthy," she growled. "Lounge about the sidewalks all day drinking root beer. Dip snuff and spit in every puddle and have it all over my face. I could be nasty.

"Or you could have made me a nigger. It's too late for me to be a nigger," she said with deep sarcasm, "but I could act like one. Lay down in the middle of the road and stop traffic. Roll on the ground."

In the deepening light everything was taking on a mysterious hue.

The pasture was growing a peculiar glassy green and the streak of highway had turned lavender. She braced herself for a final assault and this time her voice rolled out over the pasture. "Go on," she yelled, "call me a hog! Call me a hog again. From hell. Call me a wart hog from hell. Put that bottom rail on top. There'll still be a top and bottom!"

A garbled echo returned to her.

A final surge of fury shook her and she roared, "Who do you think you are?"

The color of everything, field and crimson sky, burned for a moment with a transparent intensity. The question carried over the pasture and across the highway and the cotton field and returned to her clearly like an answer from beyond the wood.

She opened her mouth but no sound came out of it.

A tiny truck, Claud's, appeared on the highway, heading rapidly out of sight. Its gears scraped thinly. It looked like a child's toy. At any moment a bigger truck might smash into it and scatter Claud's and the niggers' brains all over the road.

Mrs. Turpin stood there, her gaze fixed on the highway, all her muscles rigid, until in five or six minutes the truck reappeared, returning. She waited until it had had time to turn into their own road. Then like a monumental statue coming to life, she bent her head slowly and gazed, as if through the very heart of mystery, down into the pig parlor at the hogs. They had settled all in one corner around the old sow who was grunting softly. A red glow suffused them. They appeared to pant with a secret life.

Until the sun slipped finally behind the tree line, Mrs. Turpin remained there with her gaze bent to them as if she were absorbing some abysmal life-giving knowledge. At last she lifted her head. There was only a purple streak in the sky, cutting through a field of crimson and leading, like an extension of the highway, into the descending dusk. She raised her hands from the side of the pen in a gesture hieratic and profound. A visionary light settled in her eyes. She saw the streak as a vast swinging bridge extending upward from the earth through a field of living fire. Upon it a vast horde of souls were rumbling toward heaven. There were whole companies of white-trash, clean for the first time in their lives, and bands of black niggers in white robes, and battalions of freaks and lunatics shouting and clapping and leaping like frogs. And bringing up the end of the procession was a tribe of people whom she recognized at once as those who, like herself and Claud, had always had a little of everything and the God-given wit to use it right. She leaned forward to observe them closer. They were marching behind the others with great dignity, accountable as they had always been for good order and common sense and respectable behavior. They alone were on key. Yet she could see by their shocked and altered faces that even their virtues were being burned away. She lowered her hands and gripped the rail of the hog pen, her eyes small but fixed unblinkingly on what lay ahead. In a moment the vision faded but she remained where she was, immobile.

At length she got down and turned off the faucet and made her slow way on the darkening path to the house. In the woods around her the invisible cricket choruses had struck up, but what she heard were the voices of the souls climbing upward into the starry field and shouting hallelujah.

CYNTHIA OZICK

Levitation

A pair of novelists, husband and wife, gave a party. The husband was also an editor; he made his living at it. But really he was a novelist. His manner was powerless; he did not seem like an editor at all. He had a nice plain pale face, likable. His name was Feingold.

For love, and also because he had always known he did not want a Jewish wife, he married a minister's daughter. Lucy too had hoped to marry out of her tradition. (These words were hers. "Out of my tradition," she said. The idea fevered him.) At the age of twelve she felt herself to belong to the people of the Bible. ("A Hebrew," she said. His heart lurched, joy rocked him.) One night from the pulpit her father read a Psalm; all at once she saw how the Psalmist meant *her;* then and there she became an Ancient Hebrew.

She had huge, intent, sliding eyes, disconcertingly luminous, and copper hair, and a grave and timid way of saying honest things.

They were shy people, and rarely gave parties.

Each had published one novel. Hers was about domestic life; he wrote about Jews.

All the roil about the State of the Novel had passed them by. In the evening after the children had been put to bed, while the portable dishwasher rattled out its smell of burning motor oil, they sat down, she at her desk, he at his, and began to write. They wrote not without puzzlements and travail; nevertheless as naturally as birds. They were devoted to accuracy, psychological realism, and earnest truthfulness; also to virtue, and even to wit. Neither one was troubled by what had happened to the novel: all those declarations about the end of Character and Story. They were serene. Sometimes, closing up their notebooks for the night, it seemed to them that they were literary friends and lovers, like George Eliot and George Henry Lewes.

In bed they would revel in quantity and murmur distrustingly of theory. "Seven pages so far this week." "Nine-and-a-half, but I had to throw out four. A wrong tack." "Because you're doing first person. First person strangles. You can't get out of their skin." And so on. The one principle they agreed on was the importance of never writing about writers. Your protagonist always has to be someone *real,* with real work-in-the-world—a bureaucrat, a banker, an architect (ah, they envied Conrad his shipmasters!)—otherwise you fall into solipsism, narcissism, tedium, lack of appeal-to-the-common-reader; who knew what other perils.

This difficulty—seizing on a concrete subject—was mainly Lucy's. Feingold's novel—the one he was writing now—was about Menachem ben Zerach, survivor of a massacre of Jews in the town of Estella in Spain in 1328. From morning to midnight he hid under a pile of corpses, until a "compassionate knight" (this was the language of the history Feingold relied on) plucked him out and took him home to tend his wounds. Menachem was then twenty; his father and mother and four younger brothers had been cut down in the terror. Six thousand Jews died in a single day in March. Feingold wrote well about how the mild winds carried the salty fragrance of fresh blood, together with the ashes of Jewish houses, into the faces of the marauders. It was nevertheless a triumphant story: at the end Menachem ben Zerach becomes a renowned scholar.

"If you're going to tell about how after he gets to be a scholar he just sits there and *writes,*" Lucy protested, "then you're doing the Forbidden Thing." But Feingold said he meant to concentrate on the massacre, and especially on the life of the "compassionate knight." What had brought him to this compassion? What sort of education? What did he read? Feingold would invent a journal for the compassionate knight, and quote from it. Into this journal the compassionate knight would direct all his gifts, passions, and private opinions.

"Solipsism," Lucy said. "Your compassionate knight is only another writer. Narcissism. Tedium."

They talked often about the Forbidden Thing. After a while they began to call it the Forbidden City, because not only were they (but Lucy especially) tempted to write—solipsistically, narcissistically, tediously, and without common appeal—about writers, but, more narrowly yet, about writers in New York.

"The compassionate knight," Lucy said, "lived on the Upper West Side of Estella. He lived on the Riverside Drive, the West End Avenue, of Estella. He lived in Estella on Central Park West."

The Feingolds lived on Central Park West.

In her novel—the published one, not the one she was writing now—Lucy had described, in the first person, where they lived:

> By now I have seen quite a few of those West Side apartments. They have mysterious layouts. Rooms with doors that go nowhere—turn the knob, open: a wall. Someone is snoring behind it, in another apartment. They have made two and three or even four and five flats out of these palaces. The toilet bowls have antique cracks that shimmer with moisture like old green rivers. Fluted columns and fireplaces. Artur Rubinstein once paid rent here. On a gilt piano he raced a sonata by Beethoven. The sounds went spinning like mercury. Breathings all lettered now. Editors. Critics. Books, old, old books, heavy as centuries. Shelves built into the cold fireplace; Freud on the grate, Marx on the hearth, Melville, Hawthorne, Emerson. Oh God, the weight, the weight.

Lucy felt herself to be a stylist; Feingold did not. He believed in putting one sentence after another. In his publishing house he had no influence. He was nervous about his decisions. He rejected most manuscripts because he was afraid of mistakes; every mistake lost money. It was a small house panting after profits; Feingold told Lucy that the only books his firm respected belonged to the accountants. Now and then he tried to smuggle in a novel after his own taste, and then he would be brutal to the writer. He knocked the paragraphs about until they were as sparse as his own. "God knows what you would do to mine," Lucy said; "bald man, bald prose." The horizon of Feingold's head shone. She never showed him her work. But they understood they were lucky in each other. They pitied every writer who was not married to a writer. Lucy said: "At least we have the same premises."

Volumes of Jewish history ran up and down their walls; they belonged to Feingold. Lucy read only one book—it was *Emma*—over and over again. Feingold did not have a "philosophical" mind. What he liked was event. Lucy liked to speculate and ruminate. She was slightly more intelligent than Feingold. To strangers he seemed very mild. Lucy, when silent, was a tall copper statue.

They were both devoted to omniscience, but they were not acute enough to see what they meant by it. They thought of themselves as children with a puppet theater: they could make anything at all happen, speak all the lines, with gloved hands bring all the characters to shudders or leaps. They fancied themselves in love with what they called "imagination." It was not true. What they were addicted to was counterfeit pity, and this was because they were absorbed by power, and were powerless.

They lived on pity, and therefore on gossip: who had been childless for ten years, who had lost three successive jobs, who was in danger of being fired, which agent's prestige had fallen, who could not get his second novel published, who was *persona non grata* at this or that magazine, who was drinking seriously, who was a likely suicide, who was dreaming of divorce, who was secretly or flamboyantly sleeping with whom, who was being snubbed, who counted or did not count; and toward everyone in the least way victimized they appeared to feel the most immoderate tenderness. They were, besides, extremely "psychological": kind listeners, helpful, lifting hot palms they would gladly put to anyone's anguished temples. They were attracted to bitter lives.

About their own lives they had a joke: they were "secondary-level" people. Feingold had a secondary-level job with a secondary-level house. Lucy's own publisher was secondary-level; even the address was Second Avenue. The reviews of their books had been written by secondary-level reviewers. All their friends were secondary-level: not the presidents or partners of the respected firms, but copy editors and production assistants; not the glittering eagles of the intellectual organs, but the wearisome hacks of small Jewish journals; not the fiercely cold-hearted literary critics, but those wan and chattering daily reviewers of film. If they knew a playwright, he was off-off-Broadway in ambition and had not yet been produced. If they knew a painter, he lived in a loft and had exhibited only once, against the wire fence in the outdoor show at Washington Square in the spring. And this struck them as mean and unfair; they liked their friends, but other people—why not they?—were drawn into the deeper caverns of New York, among the lions.

New York! They risked their necks if they ventured out to Broadway for a loaf of bread after dark; muggers hid behind the seesaws in the playgrounds, junkies with knives hung upside down in the jungle gym. Every apartment a lit fortress; you admired the lamps and the locks, the triple locks on the caged-in windows, the double locks and the police rods on the doors, the lamps with timers set to make burglars think you were always at home. Footsteps in the corridor, the elevator's midnight grind; caution's muffled gasps. Their parents lived in Cleveland and St. Paul, and hardly ever dared to visit. All of this: grit and unsuitability (they might have owned a snowy lawn somewhere else); and no one said their names, no one had any curiosity about them, no one ever asked whether they were working on anything new. After half a year their books were remaindered for eighty-nine cents each. Anonymous mediocrities. They could not call themselves forgotten because they had never been noticed.

Lucy had a diagnosis: they were, both of them, sunk in a ghetto. Feingold persisted in his morbid investigations into Inquisitional autos-da-fé in this and that Iberian marketplace. She herself had supposed the inner life of a housebound woman—she cited *Emma*—to contain as much comedy as the cosmos. Jews and women! They were both beside the point. It was necessary to put aside pity; to look to the center; to abandon selflessness; to study power.

They drew up a list of luminaries. They invited Irving Howe, Susan Sontag, Alfred Kazin, and Leslie Fiedler. They invited Norman Podhoretz and Elizabeth Hardwick. They invited Philip Roth and Joyce Carol Oates and Norman Mailer and William Styron and Donald Barthelme and Jerzy Kosinski and Truman Capote. None of these came; all of them had unlisted numbers, or else machines that answered the telephone, or else were in Prague or Paris or out of town. Nevertheless the apartment filled up. It was a Saturday night in a chill November. Taxis whirled on patches of sleet. On the inside of the apartment door a mound of rainboots grew taller and taller. Two closets were packed tight with raincoats and fur coats; a heap of coats smelling of skunk and lamb fell tangled off a bed.

The party washed and turned like a sluggish tub; it lapped at all the walls of all the rooms. Lucy wore a long skirt, violet-colored, Feingold a lemon shirt and no tie. He looked paler than ever. The apartment had a wide center hall, itself the breadth of a room; the dining room opened off it to the left, the living room to the right. The three party-rooms shone like a triptych: it was as if you could fold them up and enclose everyone into darkness. The guests were free-standing figures in the niches of a cathedral; or else dressed-up cardboard dolls, with their drinks, and their costumes all meticulously hung with sashes and draped collars and little capes, the women's hair variously bound, the men's sprouting and spilling: fashion stalked, Feingold moped. He took in how it all flashed, manhattans and martinis, earrings and shoe-tips—he marveled, but knew it was a falsehood, even a figment. The great world was somewhere else. The conversation could fool you: how these people talked! From the conversation itself—grains of it, carried off, swallowed by new eddyings, swirl devouring swirl, every moment a permutation in the tableau of those freestanding figures or dolls, all of them afloat in a tub—from this or that hint or syllable you could imagine the whole universe in the process of ultimate comprehension. Human nature, the stars, history—the voices drummed and strummed. Lucy swam by blank-eyed, pushing a platter of mottled cheeses. Feingold seized her: "It's a waste!" She gazed back. He said, "No one's here!" Mournfully she rocked a stump of cheese; then he lost her.

He went into the living room: it was mainly empty, a few lumps on the sofa. The lumps wore business suits. The dining room was better. Something in formation: something around the big table: coffee cups shimmering to the brim, cake cut onto plates (the mock-Victorian rosebud plates from Boots's drug store in London: the year before their first boy was born Lucy and Feingold saw the Brontës' moors; Coleridge's house in Highgate; Lamb House, Rye, where Edith Wharton had tea with Henry James; Bloomsbury; the Cambridge stairs Forster had lived at the top of)—it seemed about to become a regular visit, with points of view, opinions; a discussion. The voices began to stumble; Feingold liked that, it was nearly human. But then, serving round the forks and paper napkins, he noticed the awful vivacity of their falsetto phrases: actors, theater chatter, who was directing whom, what was opening where; he hated actors. Shrill puppets. Brainless. A double row of faces around the table; gurgles of fools.

The center hall—swept clean. No one there but Lucy, lingering.

"Theater in the dining room," he said. "Junk."

"Film. I heard film."

"Film too," he conceded. "Junk. It's mobbed in there."

"Because they've got the cake. They've got all the food. The living room's got nothing."

"My God," he said, like a man choking, "do you realize *no one came?*"

The living room had—had once had—potato chips. The chips were gone, the carrot sticks eaten, of the celery sticks nothing left but threads. One olive in a dish; Feingold chopped it in two with vicious teeth. The business suits had disappeared. "It's awfully early," Lucy said; "a lot of people had to leave." "It's a cocktail party, that's what happens," Feingold said. "It isn't *exactly* a cocktail party," Lucy said. They sat down on the carpet in front of the fireless grate. "Is that a real fireplace?" someone inquired. "We never light it," Lucy said. "Do you light those candlesticks ever?" "They belonged to Jimmy's grandmother," Lucy said, "we never light them."

She crossed no-man's-land to the dining room. They were serious in there now. The subject was Chaplin's gestures.

In the living room Feingold despaired; no one asked him, he began to tell about the compassionate knight. A problem of ego, he said: compassion being superconsciousness of one's own pride. Not that he believed this; he only thought it provocative to say something original, even if a little muddled. But no one responded. Feingold looked up. "Can't you light that fire?" said a man. "All right," Feingold said. He rolled a paper log made of last Sunday's *Times* and laid a match on it. A flame as clear as a streetlight whitened the faces of the sofa-sitters. He recognized a friend of his from the Seminary—he had what Lucy called "theological" friends—and then and there, really very suddenly, Feingold wanted to talk about God. Or, if not God, then certain historical atrocities, abominations: to wit, the crime of the French nobleman Draconet, a proud Crusader, who in the spring of the year 1247 arrested all the Jews of the province of Vienne, castrated the men, and tore off the breasts of the women; some he did not mutilate, and only cut in two. It interested Feingold that Magna Carta and the Jewish badge of shame were issued in the same year, and that less than a century afterward all the Jews were driven out of England, even families who had been settled there seven or eight generations. He had a soft spot for Pope Clement IV, who absolved the Jews from responsibility for the Black Death. "The plague takes the Jews themselves," the Pope said. Feingold knew innumerable stories about forced conversions, he felt at home with these thoughts, comfortable, the chairs seemed dense with family. He wondered whether it would be appropriate—at a cocktail party, after all!—to inquire after the status of the Seminary friend's agnosticism: was it merely that God had stepped out of history, left the room for a moment, so to speak, without a pass, or was there no Creator to begin with, nothing had been created, the world was a chimera, a solipsist's delusion?

Lucy was uneasy with the friend from the Seminary; he was the one who had administered her conversion, and every encounter was like a new stage in a perpetual examination. She was glad there was no Jewish catechism. Was she a backslider? Anyhow she felt tested. Sometimes she spoke of Jesus to the children. She looked around—her great eyes wheeled—and saw that everyone in the living room was a Jew.

There were Jews in the dining room too, but the unruffled, devil-may-care kind: the humorists, the painters, film reviewers who went off to studio showings of *Screw on Screen* on the eve of the Day of Atonement. Mostly there were Gentiles in the dining room. Nearly the whole cake was gone. She took the last piece, cubed it on a paper plate, and carried it back to the living room. She blamed Feingold, he was having one of his spasms of fanaticism. Everyone normal, everyone with sense—the humanists and humorists, for instance—would want to keep away. What was he now, after all, but one of those boring autodidacts who spew out everything they read? He was doing it for spite, because no one had come. There he was, telling about the blood-libel. Little Hugh of Lincoln. How in London, in 1279, Jews were torn to pieces by horses, on a charge of having crucified a Christian child. How in 1285, in Munich, a mob burned down a synagogue on the same pretext. At Eastertime in Mainz two years earlier. Three centuries of beatified child martyrs, some of them figments, all called "Little Saints." The Holy Niño of LaGuardia. Feingold was crazed by these tales, he drank them like a vampire. Lucy stuck a square of chocolate cake in his mouth to shut him up. Feingold was waiting for a voice. The friend from the Seminary, pragmatic, licked off his bit of cake hungrily. It was a cake sent from home, packed by his wife in a plastic bag, to make sure there was something to eat. It was a guaranteed no-lard cake. They were all ravenous. The fire crumpled out in big paper cinders.

The friend from the Seminary had brought a friend. Lucy examined him: she knew how to give catechisms of her own, she was not a novelist for nothing. She catechized and catalogued: a refugee. Fingers like long wax candles, snuffed at the nails. Black sockets: was he blind? It was hard to tell where the eyes were under that ledge of skull. Skull for a head, but such a cushioned mouth, such lips, such orderly expressive teeth. Such a bone in such a dry wrist. A nose like a saint's. The face of Jesus. He whispered. Everyone leaned over to hear. He was Feingold's voice: the voice Feingold was waiting for.

"Come to modern times," the voice urged. "Come to yesterday." Lucy was right: she could tell a refugee in an instant, even before she heard any accent. They all reminded her of her father. She put away this insight (the resemblance of Presbyterian ministers to Hitler refugees) to talk over with Feingold later: it was nicely analytical, it had enough mystery to satisfy. "Yesterday," the refugee said, "the eyes of God were shut." And Lucy saw him shut his hidden eyes in their tunnels. "Shut," he said, "like iron doors"—a voice of such nobility that Lucy thought immediately of that eerie passage in Genesis where the voice of the Lord God walks in the Garden in the cool of the day and calls to Adam, "Where are you?"

They all listened with a terrible intensity. Again Lucy looked around. It pained her how intense Jews could be, though she too was intense. But she was intense because her brain was roiling with ardor, she wooed mind-pictures, she was a novelist. *They* were intense all the time; she supposed the grocers among them were as intense as any novelist; was it because they had been Chosen, was it because they pitied themselves every breathing moment?

Pity and shock stood in all their faces.

The refugee was telling a story. "I witnessed it," he said, "I am the witness." Horror; sadism; corpses. As if—Lucy took the image from the elusive wind that was his voice in its whisper—as if hundreds and hundreds of Crucifixions were all happening at once. She visualized a hillside with multitudes of crosses, and bodies dropping down from big bloody nails. Every Jew was Jesus. That was the only way Lucy could get hold of it: otherwise it was only a movie. She had seen all the movies, the truth was she could feel nothing. That same bulldozer shoveling those same sticks of skeletons, that same little boy in a cap with twisted mouth and his hands in the air—if there had been a camera at the Crucifixion Christianity would collapse, no one would ever feel anything about it. Cruelty came out of the imagination, and had to be witnessed by the imagination.

All the same, she listened. What he told was exactly like the movies. A gray scene, a scrubby hill, a ravine. Germans in helmets, with shining tar-black belts, wearing gloves. A ragged bundle of Jews at the lip of the ravine—an old grandmother, a child or two, a couple in their forties. All the faces stained with grayness, the stubble on the ground stained gray, the clothes on them limp as shrouds but immobile, as if they were already under the dirt, shut off from breezes, as if they were already stone. The refugee's whisper carved them like sculptures—there they stood, a shadowy stone asterisk of Jews, you could see their nostrils, open as skulls, the stony round ears of the children, the grandmother's awful twig of a neck, the father and mother grasping the children but strangers to each other, not a touch between them, the grandmother cast out, claiming no one and not claimed, all prayerless stone gums. There they stood. For a long while the refugee's voice pinched them and held them, so that you had to look. His voice made Lucy look and look. He pierced the figures through with his whisper. Then he let the shots come. The figures never teetered, never shook: the stoniness broke all at once and they fell cleanly, like sacks, into the ravine. Immediately they were in a heap, with random limbs all tangled together. The refugee's voice like a camera brought a German boot to the edge of the ravine. The boot kicked sand. It kicked and kicked, the sand poured over the family of sacks.

Then Lucy saw the fingers of the listeners—all their fingers were stretched out.

The room began to lift. It ascended. It rose like an ark on waters. Lucy said inside her mind, "This chamber of Jews." It seemed to her that the room was levitating on the little grains of the refugee's whisper. She felt herself alone at the bottom, below the floorboards, while the room floated upward, carrying Jews. Why did it not take her too? Only Jesus could take her. They were being kidnapped, these Jews, by a messenger from the land of the dead. The man had a power. Already he was in the shadow of another tale: she promised herself she would not listen, only Jesus could make her listen. The room was ascending. Above her head it grew smaller and smaller, more and more remote, it fled deeper and deeper into upwardness.

She craned after it. Wouldn't it bump into the apartment upstairs? It was like watching the underside of an elevator, all dirty and hairy, with dust-roots wagging. The black floor moved higher and higher. It was getting free of her, into loftiness, lifting Jews.

The glory of their martyrdom.

Under the rising eave Lucy had an illumination: she saw herself with the children in a little city park. A Sunday afternoon early in May. Feingold has stayed home to nap, and Lucy and the children find seats on a bench and wait for the unusual music to begin. The room is still levitating, but inside Lucy's illumination the boys are chasing birds. They run away from Lucy, they return, they leave. They surround a pigeon. They do not touch the pigeon; Lucy has forbidden it. She has read that city pigeons carry meningitis. A little boy in Red Bank, New Jersey, contracted sleeping sickness from touching a pigeon; after six years, he is still asleep. In his sleep he has grown from a child to an adolescent; puberty has come on him in his sleep, his testicles have dropped down, a benign blond beard glints mildly on his cheeks. His parents weep and weep. He is still asleep. No instruments or players are visible. A woman steps out onto a platform. She is an anthropologist from the Smithsonian Institution in Washington, D.C. She explains that there will be no "entertainment" in the usual sense; there will be no "entertainers." The players will not be artists; they will be "real peasants." They have been brought over from Messina, from Calabria. They are shepherds, goatherds. They will sing and dance and play just as they do when they come down from the hills to while away the evenings in the taverns. They will play the instruments that scare away the wolves from the flock. They will sing the songs that celebrate the Madonna of Love. A dozen men file onto the platform. They have heavy faces that do not smile. They have heavy dark skins, cratered and leathery. They have ears and noses that look like dried twisted clay. They have gold teeth. They have no teeth. Some are young; most are in their middle years. One is very old; he wears bells on his fingers. One has an instrument like a butter churn: he shoves a stick in and out of a hole in a wooden tub held under his arm, and a rattling screech spurts out of it. One blows on two slender pipes simultaneously. One has a long strap, which he rubs. One has a frame of bicycle bells; a descendant of the bells the priests used to beat in the temple of Minerva.

The anthropologist is still explaining everything. She explains the "male" instrument: three wooden knockers; the innermost one lunges up and down between the other two. The songs, she explains, are mainly erotic. The dances are suggestive.

The unusual music commences. The park has filled with Italians—greenhorns from Sicily, settled New Yorkers from Naples. An ancient people. They clap. The old man with the bells on his fingers points his dusty shoe-toes and slowly follows a circle of his own. His eyes are in trance, he squats, he ascends. The anthropologist explains that up-and-down dancing can also be found in parts of Africa. The singers wail like Arabs; the anthropologist notes that the Arab conquest covered the southernmost portion of the Italian boot for two hundred years. The whole chorus of peasants sings in a dialect of archaic Greek; the language has survived in the old songs, the anthropologist explains. The crowd is laughing and stamping. They click their fingers and sway. Lucy's boys are bored. They watch the man with the finger-bells; they watch the wooden male pump up and down. Everyone is clapping, stamping, clicking, swaying, thumping. The wailing goes on and on, faster and faster. The singers are dancers, the dancers are singers, they turn and turn, they are smiling the drugged smiles of dervishes. At home they grow flowers. They follow the sheep into the deep grass. They drink wine in the taverns at night. Calabria and Sicily in New York, sans wives, in sweat-blotched shirts and wrinkled dusty pants, gasping before strangers who have never smelled the sweetness of their village grasses!

Now the anthropologist from the Smithsonian has vanished out of Lucy's illumination. A pair of dancers seize each other. Leg winds over leg, belly into belly, each man hopping on a single free leg. Intertwined, they squat and rise, squat and rise. Old Hellenic syllables fly from them. They send out high elastic cries. They celebrate the Madonna, giver of fertility and fecundity. Lucy is glorified. She is exalted. She comprehends. Not that the musicians are peasants, not that their faces and feet and necks and wrists are blown grass and red earth. An enlightenment comes on her: she sees what is eternal: before the Madonna there was Venus; before Venus, Aphrodite; before Aphrodite, Astarte. The womb of the goddess is garden, lamb, and babe. She is the river and the waterfall. She causes grave men of business—goatherds are men of business—to cavort and to flash their gold teeth. She induces them to blow, beat, rub, shake and scrape objects so that music will drop out of them.

Inside Lucy's illumination the dancers are seething. They are writhing. For the sake of the goddess, for the sake of the womb of the goddess, they are turning into serpents. When they grow still they are earth. They are from always to always. Nature is their pulse. Lucy sees: she understands: the gods are God. How terrible to have given up Jesus, a man like these, made of earth like these, with a pulse like these, God entering nature to become god! Jesus, no more miraculous than an ordinary goatherd; is a goatherd miracle? Is a leaf? A nut, a pit, a core, a seed, a stone? Everything is miracle! Lucy sees how she has abandoned nature, how she has lost true religion on account of the God of the Jews. The boys are on their bellies on the ground, digging it up with sticks. They dig and dig: little holes with mounds beside them. They fill them with peach pits, cherry pits, cantaloupe rinds. The Sicilians and Neapolitans pick up their baskets and purses and shopping bags and leave. The benches smell of eaten fruit, running juices, insect-mobbed. The stage is clean.

The living room has escaped altogether. It is very high and extremely small, no wider than the moon on Lucy's thumbnail. It is still sailing upward, and the voices of those on board are so faint that Lucy almost loses them. But she knows which word it is they mainly use. How long can they go on about it? How long? A morbid cud-chewing. Death and death and death. The word is less a human word than an animal's cry; a crow's. Caw caw. It belongs to storms, floods, avalanches. Acts of God. "Holocaust," someone caws dimly from above; she knows it must be Feingold. He always says this word over and over and over. History is bad for him: how little it makes him seem! Lucy decides it is possible to become jaded by atrocity. She is bored by the shootings and the gas and the camps, she is not ashamed to admit this. They are as tiresome as prayer. Repetition diminishes conviction; she is thinking of her father leading the same hymns week after week. If you said the same prayer over and over again, wouldn't your brain turn out to be no better than a prayer wheel?

In the dining room all the springs were running down. It was stale in there, a failed party. They were drinking beer or Coke or whiskey-and-water and playing with the cake crumbs on the tablecloth. There was still some cheese left on a plate, and half a bowl of salted peanuts. "The impact of Romantic Individualism," one of the humanists objected. "At the Frick?" "I never saw that." "They certainly are deliberate, you have to say that for them." Lucy, leaning abandoned against the door, tried to tune in. The relief of hearing atheists. A jacket designer who worked in Feingold's art department came in carrying a coat. Feingold had invited her because she was newly divorced; she was afraid to live alone. She was afraid of being ambushed in her basement while doing laundry. "Where's Jimmy?" the jacket designer asked. "In the other room." "Say goodbye for me, will you?" "Goodbye," Lucy said. The humanists—Lucy saw how they were all compassionate knights—stood up. A puddle from an overturned saucer was leaking onto the floor. "Oh, I'll get that," Lucy told the knights, "don't think another thought about it."

Overhead Feingold and the refugee are riding the living room. Their words are specks. All the Jews are in the air.

URSULA K. LE GUIN

The Ones Who Walk Away from Omelas

(Variations on a theme by William James)

With a clamor of bells that set the swallows soaring, the Festival of Summer came to the city Omelas, bright-towered by the sea. The rigging of the boats in harbor sparkled with flags. In the streets between houses with red roofs and painted walls, between old moss-grown gardens and under avenues of trees, past great parks and public buildings, processions moved. Some were decorous: old people in long stiff robes of mauve and grey, grave master workmen, quiet, merry women carrying their babies and chatting as they walked. In other streets the music beat faster, a shimmering of gong and tambourine, and the people went dancing, the procession was a dance. Children dodged in and out, their high calls rising like the swallows' crossing flights over the music and the singing. All the processions wound towards the north side of the city, where on the great water-meadow called the Green Fields boys and girls, naked in the bright air, with mud-stained feet and ankles and long, lithe arms, exercised their restive horses before the race. The horses wore no gear at all but a halter without bit. Their manes were braided with streamers of silver, gold, and green. They flared their nostrils and pranced and boasted to one another; they were vastly excited, the horse being the only animal who has adopted our ceremonies as his own. Far off to the north and west the mountains stood up half encircling Omelas on her bay. The air of morning was so clear that the snow still crowning the Eighteen Peaks burned with white-gold fire across the miles of sunlit air, under the dark blue of the sky. There was just enough wind to make the banners that marked the racecourse snap and flutter now and then. In the silence of the broad green meadows one could hear the music winding through the city streets, farther and nearer and ever approaching, a cheerful faint sweetness of the air that from time to time trembled and gathered together and broke out into the great joyous clanging of the bells.

Joyous! How is one to tell about joy? How describe the citizens of Omelas?

They were not simple folk, you see, though they were happy. But we do not say the words of cheer much any more. All smiles have become archaic. Given a description such as this one tends to make certain assumptions. Given a description such as this one tends to look next for the King, mounted on a splendid stallion and surrounded by his noble knights, or perhaps in a golden litter borne by great-muscled slaves. But there was no king. They did not use swords, or keep slaves. They were not barbarians. I do not know the rules and laws of their society, but I suspect that they were singularly few. As they did without monarchy and slavery, so they also got on without the stock exchange, the advertisement, the secret police, and the bomb. Yet I repeat that these were not simple folk, not dulcet shepherds, noble savages, bland utopians. They were not less complex than us. The trouble is that we have a bad habit, encouraged by pedants and sophisticates, of considering happiness as something rather stupid. Only pain is intellectual, only evil interesting. This is the treason of the artist: a refusal to admit the banality of evil and the terrible boredom of pain. If you can't lick 'em, join 'em. If it hurts, repeat it. But to praise despair is to condemn delight, to embrace violence is to lose hold of everything else. We have almost lost hold, we can no longer describe a happy man, nor make any celebration of joy. How can I tell you about the people of Omelas? They were not naïve and happy children—though their children were, in fact, happy. They were mature, intelligent, passionate adults whose lives were not wretched. O miracle! but I wish I could describe it better. I wish I could convince you. Omelas sounds in my words like a city in a fairy tale, long ago and far away, once upon a time. Perhaps it would be best if you imagined it as your own fancy bids, assuming it will rise to the occasion, for certainly I cannot suit you all. For instance, how about technology? I think that there would be no cars or helicopters in and above the streets; this follows from the fact that the people of Omelas are happy people. Happiness is based on a just discrimination of what is necessary, what is neither necessary nor destructive, and what is destructive. In the middle category, however—that of the unnecessary but undestructive, that of comfort, luxury, exuberance, etc.—they could perfectly well have central heating, subway trains, washing machines, and all kinds of marvelous devices not yet invented here, floating light-sources, fuelless power, a cure for the common cold. Or they could have none of that: it doesn't matter. As you like it. I incline to think that people from towns up and down the coast have been coming in to Omelas during the last days before the Festival on very fast little trains and double-decked trams, and that the train station of Omelas is actually the handsomest building in town, though plainer than the magnificent Farmers' Market. But even granted trains, I fear that Omelas so far strikes some of you as goody-goody. Smiles, bells, parades, horses, bleh. If so, please add an orgy. If an orgy would help, don't hesitate. Let us not, however, have temples from which issue beautiful nude priests and priestesses already half in ecstasy and ready to copulate with any man or woman, lover or stranger, who desires union with the deep godhead of the blood, although that was my first idea. But really it would be better not to have any temples in Omelas—at least, not manned temples. Religion yes, clergy no. Surely the beautiful nudes can just wander about, offering themselves like divine soufflés to the hunger of the needy and the rapture of the flesh. Let them join the processions. Let tambourines be struck above the copulations, and the glory of desire be proclaimed upon the gongs, and (a not unimportant point) let the offspring of these delightful rituals be beloved and looked after by all. One thing I know there is none of in Omelas is guilt. But what else should there be? I thought at first there were no drugs, but that is puritanical. For those who like it, the faint insistent sweetness of *drooz* may perfume the ways of the city, *drooz* which first brings a great lightness and brilliance to the mind and limbs, and then after some hours a dreamy languor, and wonderful visions at last of the very arcana and inmost secrets of the Universe, as well as exciting the pleasure of sex beyond all belief; and it is not habit-forming. For more modest tastes I think there ought to be beer. What else, what else belongs in the joyous city? The sense of victory, surely, the celebration of courage. But as we did without clergy, let us do without soldiers. The joy built upon successful slaughter is not the right kind of joy; it will not do; it is fearful and it is trivial. A boundless and generous contentment, a magnanimous triumph felt not against some outer enemy but in communion with the finest and fairest in the souls of all men everywhere and the splendor of the world's summer: this is what swells the hearts of the people of Omelas, and the victory they celebrate is that of life. I really don't think many of them need to take *drooz.*

Most of the processions have reached the Green Fields by now. A marvelous smell of cooking goes forth from the red and blue tents of the provisioners. The faces of small children are amiably sticky; in the benign grey beard of a man a couple of crumbs of rich pastry are entangled. The youths and girls have mounted their horses and are beginning to group around the starting line of the course. An old woman, small, fat, and laughing, is passing out flowers from a basket, and tall young men wear her flowers in their shining hair. A child of nine or ten sits at the edge of the crowd, alone, playing on a wooden flute. People pause to listen, and they smile, but they do not speak to him, for he never ceases playing and never sees them, his dark eyes wholly rapt in the sweet, thin magic of the tune.

He finishes, and slowly lowers his hands holding the wooden flute.

As if that little private silence were the signal, all at once a trumpet sounds from the pavilion near the starting line: imperious, melancholy, piercing. The horses rear on their slender legs, and some of them neigh in answer. Sober-faced, the young riders stroke the horses' necks and soothe them, whispering, "Quiet, quiet, there my beauty, my hope. . . ." They begin to form in rank along the starting line. The crowds along the racecourse are like a field of grass and flowers in the wind. The Festival of Summer has begun.

Do you believe? Do you accept the festival, the city, the joy? No? Then let me describe one more thing.

In a basement under one of the beautiful public buildings of Omelas, or perhaps in the cellar of one of its spacious private homes, there is a room. It has one locked door, and no window. A little light seeps in dustily between cracks in the boards, secondhand from a cobwebbed window somewhere across the cellar. In one corner of the little room a couple of mops, with stiff, clotted, foul-smelling heads, stand near a rusty bucket. The floor is dirt, a little damp to the touch, as cellar dirt usually is. The room is about three paces long and two wide: a mere broom closet or disused tool room. In the room a child is sitting. It could be a boy or a girl. It looks about six, but actually is nearly ten. It is feeble-minded. Perhaps it was born defective, or perhaps it has become imbecile through fear, malnutrition, and neglect. It picks its nose and occasionally fumbles vaguely with its toes or genitals, as it sits hunched in the corner farthest from the bucket and the two mops. It is afraid of the mops. It finds them horrible. It shuts its eyes, but it knows the mops are still standing there; and the door is locked; and nobody will come. The door is always locked; and nobody ever comes, except that sometimes—the child has no understanding of time or interval—sometimes the door rattles terribly and opens, and a person, or several people, are there. One of them may come in and kick the child to make it stand up. The others never come close, but peer in at it with frightened, disgusted eyes. The food bowl and the water jug are hastily filled, the door is locked, the eyes disappear. The people at the door never say anything, but the child, who has not always lived in the tool room, and can remember sunlight and its mother's voice, sometimes speaks. "I will be good," it says. "Please let me out. I will be good!" They never answer. The child used to scream for help at night, and cry a good deal, but now it only makes a kind of whining, "eh-haa, eh-haa," and it speaks less and less often. It is so thin there are no calves to its legs; its belly protrudes; it lives on a half-bowl of corn meal and grease a day. It is naked. Its buttocks and thighs are a mass of festered sores, as it sits in its own excrement continually.

They all know it is there, all the people of Omelas. Some of them have come to see it, others are content merely to know it is there. They all know that it has to be there. Some of them understand why, and some do not, but they all understand that their happiness, the beauty of their city, the tenderness of their friendships, the health of their children, the wisdom of their scholars, the skill of their makers, even the abundance of their harvest and the kindly weathers of their skies, depend wholly on this child's abominable misery.

This is usually explained to children when they are between eight and twelve, whenever they seem capable of understanding; and most of those who come to see the child are young people, though often enough an adult comes, or comes back, to see the child. No matter how well the matter has been explained to them, these young spectators are always shocked and sickened at the sight. They feel disgust, which they had thought themselves superior to. They feel anger, outrage, impotence, despite all the explanations. They would like to do something for the child. But there is nothing they can do. If the child were brought up into the sunlight out of the vile place, if it were cleaned and fed and comforted, that would be a good thing, indeed; but if it were done, in that day and hour all the prosperity and beauty and delight of Omelas would wither and be destroyed. Those are the terms. To exchange all the goodness and grace of every life in Omelas for that single, small improvement: to throw away the happiness of thousands for the chance of the happiness of one: that would be to let guilt within the walls indeed.

The terms are strict and absolute; there may not even be a kind word spoken to the child.

Often the young people go home in tears, or in a tearless rage, when they have seen the child and faced this terrible paradox. They may brood over it for weeks or years. But as time goes on they begin to realize that even if the child could be released, it would not get much good of its freedom: a little vague pleasure of warmth and food, no doubt, but little more. It is too degraded and imbecile to know any real joy. It has been afraid too long ever to be free of fear. Its habits are too uncouth for it to respond to humane treatment. Indeed, after so long it would probably be wretched without walls about it to protect it, and darkness for its eyes, and its own excrement to sit in. Their tears at the bitter injustice dry when they begin to perceive the terrible justice of reality, and to accept it. Yet it is their tears and anger, the trying of their generosity and the acceptance of their helplessness, which are perhaps the true source of the splendor of their lives. Theirs is no vapid, irresponsible happiness. They know that they, like the child, are not free. They know compassion. It is the existence of the child, and their knowledge of its existence, that makes possible the nobility of their architecture, the poignancy of their music, the profundity of their science. It is because of the child that they are so gentle with children. They know that if the wretched one were not there snivelling in the dark, the other one, the flute-player, could make no joyful music as the young riders line up in their beauty for the race in the sunlight of the first morning of summer.

Now do you believe in them? Are they not more credible? But there is one more thing to tell, and this is quite incredible.

At times one of the adolescent girls or boys who go to see the child does not go home to weep or rage, does not, in fact, go home at all. Sometimes also a man or woman much older falls silent for a day or two, and then leaves home. These people go out into the street, and walk down the street alone. They keep walking, and walk straight out of the city of Omelas, through the beautiful gates. They keep walking across the farmlands of Omelas. Each one goes alone, youth or girl, man or woman. Night falls; the traveler must pass down village streets, between the houses with yellow-lit windows, and on out into the darkness of the fields. Each alone, they go west or north, towards the mountains. They go on. They leave Omelas, they walk ahead into the darkness, and they do not come back. The place they go towards is a place even less imaginable to most of us than the city of happiness. I cannot describe it at all. It is possible that it does not exist. But they seem to know where they are going, the ones who walk away from Omelas.

STANLEY ELKIN

A Poetics for Bullies

I'm Push the bully, and what I hate are new kids and sissies, dumb kids and smart, rich kids, poor kids, kids who wear glasses, talk funny, show off, patrol boys and wise guys and kids who pass pencils and water the plants—and cripples, *especially* cripples. I love nobody loved.

One time I was pushing this red-haired kid (I'm a pusher, no hitter, no belter; an aggressor of marginal violence, I hate *real* force) and his mother stuck her head out the window and shouted something I've never forgotten. "*Push,*" she yelled. "*You, Push.* You pick on him because you wish you had his red hair!" It's true; I *did* wish I had his red hair. I wish I were tall, or fat, or thin. I wish I had different eyes, different hands, a mother in the supermarket. I wish I were a man, a small boy, a girl in the choir. I'm a coveter, a Boston Blackie of the heart, casing the world. Endlessly I covet and case. (Do you know what makes me cry? The Declaration of Independence. "All men are created equal." That's beautiful.)

If you're a bully like me, you use your head. Toughness isn't enough. You beat them up, they report you. Then where are you? I'm not even particularly strong. (I used to be strong. I used to do exercise, work out, but strength implicates you, and often isn't an advantage anyway—read the judo ads. Besides, your big bullies aren't bullies at all—they're *athletes.* With them, beating guys up is a sport.) But what I lose in size and strength I make up in courage. I'm very brave. That's a lie about bullies being cowards underneath. If you're a coward, get out of the business.

I'm best at torment.

A kid has a toy bow, toy arrows. "Let Push look," I tell him.

He's suspicious, he knows me. "Go way, Push," he says, this mama-warned Push doubter.

"Come on," I say, "come on."

"No, Push. I can't. My mother said I can't."

I raise my arms, I spread them. I'm a bird—slow, powerful, easy, free.

I move my head offering profile like something beaked. I'm the Thunderbird. "In the school where I go I have a teacher who teaches me magic," I say. "Arnold Salamancy, give Push your arrows. Give him one, he gives back two. Push is the God of the Neighborhood."

"Go way, Push," the kid says, uncertain.

"Right," Push says, himself again. "Right. I'll disappear. First the fingers." My fingers ball to fists. "My forearms next." They jackknife into my upper arms. "The arms." Quick as bird-blink they snap behind my back, fit between the shoulder blades like a small knapsack. (I am double-jointed, protean.) "My head," I say.

"No, Push," the kid says, terrified. I shudder and everything comes back, falls into place from the stem of self like a shaken puppet.

"The arrow, the arrow. Two where was one." He hands me an arrow.

"*Trouble, trouble, double rubble!*" I snap it and give back the pieces.

Well, sure. There *is* no magic. If there were I would learn it. I would find out the words, the slow turns and strange passes, drain the bloods and get the herbs, do the fires like a vestal. I would look for the main chants. *Then* I'd change things. *Push* would!

But there's only casuistical trick. Sleight-of-mouth, the bully's poetics.

You know the formulas:

"Did you ever see a match burn twice?" you ask. Strike. Extinguish. Jab his flesh with the hot stub.

"Play 'Gestapo'?"

"How do you play?"

"What's your name?"

"It's Morton."

I slap him. "You're lying."

"Adam and Eve and Pinch Me Hard went down to the lake for a swim. Adam and Eve fell in. Who was left?"

"Pinch Me Hard."

I do.

Physical puns, conundrums. Push the punisher, the conundrummer!

But there has to be more than tricks in a bag of tricks.

I don't know what it is. Sometimes I think *I'm* the only new kid. In a room, the school, the playground, the neighborhood, I get the feeling I've just moved in, no one knows me. You know what I like? To stand in crowds. To wait with them at the airport to meet a plane. Someone asks what time it is. I'm the first to answer. Or at the ball park when the vendor comes. He passes the hot dog down the long row. I want *my* hands on it, too. On the dollar going up, the change coming down.

I am ingenious, I am patient.

A kid is going downtown on the elevated train. He's got his little suit on, his shoes are shined, he wears a cap. This is a kid going to the travel bureaus, the foreign tourist offices to get brochures, maps, pictures of the mountains for a unit at his school—a kid looking for extra credit. I follow him. He comes out of the Italian Tourist Information Center. His arms are full. I move from my place at the window. I follow for two blocks and bump into him as he steps from a curb. It's a *collision*—The pamphlets fall from his arms. Pretending confusion, I walk on his paper Florence. I grind my heel in his Riviera. I climb Vesuvius and sack his Rome and dance on the Isle of Capri.

The Industrial Museum is a good place to find children. I cut somebody's five- or six-year-old kid brother out of the herd of eleven- and twelve-year-olds he's come with. *"Quick,"* I say. I pull him along the corridors, up the stairs, through the halls, down to a mezzanine landing. Breathless, I pause for a minute. "I've got some gum. Do you want a stick?" He nods; I stick him. I rush him into an auditorium and abandon him. He'll be lost for hours.

I sidle up to a kid at the movies. "You smacked my brother," I tell him. "After the show—I'll be outside."

I break up games. I hold the ball above my head. "You want it? Take it."

I go into barber shops. There's a kid waiting. "I'm next," I tell him, "understand?"

One day Eugene Kraft rang my bell. Eugene is afraid of me, so he helps me. He's fifteen and there's something wrong with his saliva glands and he drools. His chin is always chapped. I tell him he has to drink a lot because he loses so much water.

"Push? Push," he says. He's wiping his chin with his tissues. "Push, there's this kid—"

"Better get a glass of water, Eugene."

"No, Push, no fooling, there's this new kid—he just moved in. You've got to see this kid."

"Eugene, get some water, please. You're drying up. I've never seen you so bad. There are deserts in you, Eugene."

"All right, Push, but then you've got to see—"

"Swallow, Eugene. You better swallow."

He gulps hard.

"Push, this is a kid and a half. Wait, you'll see."

"I'm very concerned about you, Eugene. You're dying of thirst, Eugene. Come into the kitchen with me."

I push him through the door. He's very excited. I've never seen him so excited. He talks at me over his shoulder, his mouth flooding, his teeth like the little stone pebbles at the bottom of a fishbowl. "He's got this sport coat, with a patch over the heart. Like a king, Push. No kidding."

"Be careful of the carpet, Eugene."

I turn on the taps in the sink. I mix in hot water. "Use your tissues, Eugene. Wipe your chin."

He wipes himself and puts the Kleenex in his pocket. All of Eugene's pockets bulge. He looks, with his bulging pockets, like a clumsy smuggler.

"Wipe, Eugene. Swallow, you're drowning."

"He's got this funny accent—you could die." Excited, he tamps at his mouth like a diner, a tubercular.

"Drink some water, Eugene."

"No, Push. I'm not thirsty—really."

"Don't be foolish, kid. That's because your mouth's so wet. Inside where it counts you're drying up. It stands to reason. Drink some water."

"He has this crazy haircut."

"Drink," I command. I shake him. *"Drink!"*

"Push, I've got no glass. Give me a glass at least."

"I can't do that, Eugene. You've got a terrible sickness. How could I let you use our drinking glasses? Lean under the tap and open your mouth."

He knows he'll have to do it, that I won't listen to him until he does. He bends into the sink.

"Push, it's hot," he complains. The water splashes into his nose, it gets on his glasses and for a moment his eyes are magnified, enormous. He pulls away and scrapes his forehead on the faucet.

"Eugene, you touched it. Watch out, please. You're too close to the tap. Lean your head deeper into the sink."

"It's *hot,* Push."

"Warm water evaporates better. With your affliction you've got to evaporate fluids before they get into your glands."

He feeds again from the tap.

"Do you think that's enough?" I ask after a while.

"I do, Push, I really do," he says. He is breathless.

"Eugene," I say seriously, "I think you'd better get yourself a canteen."

"A canteen, Push?"

"That's right. Then you'll always have water when you need it. Get one of those Boy Scout models. The two-quart kind with a canvas strap."

"But you hate the Boy Scouts, Push."

"They make very good canteens, Eugene. *And wear it!* I never want to see you without it. Buy it today."

"All right, Push."

"Promise!"

"All right, Push."

"Say it out."

He made the formal promise that I like to hear.

"Well, then," I said, "let's go see this new kid of yours."

He took me to the schoolyard. "Wait," he said, "you'll see." He skipped ahead.

"Eugene," I said, calling him back. "Let's understand something. No matter what this new kid is like, nothing changes as far as you and I are concerned."

"Aw, Push," he said.

"Nothing, Eugene. I mean it. You don't get out from under me."

"Sure, Push, I know that."

There were some kids in the far corner of the yard, sitting on the ground, leaning up against the wire fence. Bats and gloves and balls lay scattered around them. (It was where they told dirty jokes. Sometimes I'd come by during the little kids' recess and tell them all about what their daddies do to their mommies.)

"There. See? Do you see him?" Eugene, despite himself, seemed hoarse.

"Be quiet," I said, checking him, freezing as a hunter might. I stared.

He was a *prince,* I tell you.

He was tall, tall, even sitting down. His long legs comfortable in expensive wool, the trousers of a boy who had been on ships, jets; who owned a horse, perhaps; who knew Latin—what *didn't* he know?—somebody made up, like a kid in a play with a beautiful mother and a handsome father; who took his breakfast from a sideboard, and picked, even at fourteen and fifteen and sixteen, his mail from a silver plate. He would have hobbies—stamps, stars, things lovely dead. He wore a sport coat, brown as wood, thick as heavy bark. The buttons were leather buds. His shoes seemed carved from horses' saddles, gunstocks. His clothes had once grown in nature. *What it must feel like inside those clothes,* I thought.

I looked at his face, his clear skin, and guessed at the bones, white as bleached wood. His eyes had skies in them. His yellow hair swirled on his head like a crayoned sun.

"Look, look at him," Eugene said. "The sissy. Get him, Push."

He was talking to them and I moved closer to hear his voice. It was clear, beautiful, but faintly foreign—like herb-seasoned meat.

When he saw me he paused, smiling. He waved. The others didn't look at me.

"Hello there," he called. "Come over if you'd like. I've been telling the boys about tigers."

"Tigers," I said.

"Give him the 'match burn twice,' Push," Eugene whispered.

"Tigers, is it?" I said. "What do you know about tigers?" My voice was high.

"The 'match burn twice,' Push."

"Not so much as a Master *Tugjah.* I was telling the boys. In India there are men of high caste—*Tugjahs,* they're called. I was apprenticed to one once in the Southern Plains and might perhaps have earned my mastership, but the Red Chinese attacked the northern frontier and . . . well, let's just say I had to leave. At any rate, these *Tugjahs* are as intimate with the tiger as you are with dogs. I don't mean they keep them as pets. The relationship goes deeper. Your dog is a service animal, as is your elephant."

"Did you ever see a match burn twice?" I asked suddenly.

"Why no, can you do that? Is it a special match you use?"

"No," Eugene said, "it's an ordinary match. He uses an ordinary match."

"Can you do it with one of mine, do you think?"

He took a matchbook from his pocket and handed it to me. The cover was exactly the material of his jacket, and in the center was a patch with a coat-of-arms identical to the one he wore over his heart.

I held the matchbook for a moment and then gave it back to him. "I don't feel like it," I said.

"Then some other time, perhaps," he said.

Eugene whispered to me. "His accent, Push, his funny *accent.*"

"Some other time, perhaps," I said. I am a good mimic. I can duplicate a particular kid's lisp, his stutter, a thickness in his throat. There were two or three here whom I had brought close to tears by holding up my mirror to their voices. I can parody their limps, their waddles, their girlish runs, their clumsy jumps. I can throw as they throw, catch as they catch. I looked around. "Some other time, perhaps," I said again. No one would look at me.

"I'm *so* sorry," the new one said, "we don't know each other's names. You are?"

"I'm so sorry," I said. "You are?"

He seemed puzzled. Then he looked sad, disappointed. No one said anything.

"It don't sound the same," Eugene whispered.

It was true. I sounded nothing like him. I could imitate only defects, only flaws.

A kid giggled.

"Shh," the prince said. He put one finger to his lips.

"Look at that," Eugene said under his breath. "He's a sissy."

He had begun to talk to them again. I squatted, a few feet away. I ran gravel through my loose fists, one bowl in an hourglass feeding another.

He spoke of jungles, of deserts. He told of ancient trade routes traveled by strange beasts. He described lost cities and a lake deeper than the deepest level of the sea. There was a story about a boy who had been captured by bandits. A woman in the story—it wasn't clear whether she was the boy's mother—had been tortured. His eyes clouded for a moment when he came to this part and he had to pause before continuing. Then he told how the boy escaped—it was cleverly done—and found help, mountain tribesmen riding elephants. The elephants charged the cave in which the mo—the *woman*—was still a prisoner. It might have collapsed and killed her, but one old bull rushed in and, shielding her with his body, took the weight of the crashing rocks. Your elephant is a service animal.

I let a piece of gravel rest on my thumb and flicked it in a high arc above his head. Some of the others who had seen me stared, but the boy kept on talking. Gradually I reduced the range, allowing the chunks of gravel to come closer to his head.

"You see?" Eugene said quietly. "He's afraid. He pretends not to notice."

The arcs continued to diminish. The gravel went faster, straighter. No one was listening to him now, but he kept talking.

"—of magic," he said, "what occidentals call 'a witch doctor.' There are spices that induce these effects. The *Bogdovii* was actually able to stimulate the growth of rocks with the powder. The Dutch traders were ready to go to war for the formula. Well, you can see what it could mean for the Low Countries. Without accessible quarries they've never been able to construct a permanent system of dikes. But with the *Bogdovii's* powder"—he reached out and casually caught the speeding chip as if it had been a ping-pong ball—"they could turn a grain of sand into a pebble, use the pebbles to grow stones, the stones to grow rocks. This little piece of gravel, for example, could be changed into a mountain." He dipped his thumb into his palm as I had and balanced the gravel on his nail. He flicked it; it rose from his nail like a missile and climbed an impossible arc. It disappeared. "The *Bogdovii* never revealed how it was done."

I stood up. Eugene tried to follow me.

"Listen," he said, "you'll get him."

"Swallow," I told him. "Swallow, you pig!"

I have lived my life in pursuit of the vulnerable: Push the chink seeker, wheeler dealer in the flawed cement of the personality, a collapse maker. But what isn't vulnerable, *who* isn't? There is that which is unspeakable, so I speak it, that which is unthinkable, which I think. Me and the devil, we do God's dirty work, after all.

I went home after I left him. I turned once at the gate, and the boys were around him still. The useless Eugene had moved closer. *He* made room for him against the fence.

I ran into Frank the fat boy. He made a move to cross the street, but I had seen him and he went through a clumsy retractive motion. I could tell he thought I would get him for that, but I moved by, indifferent to a grossness in which I had once delighted. As I passed he seemed puzzled, a little hurt, a little—this was astonishing—guilty. *Sure* guilty. Why *not* guilty? The forgiven tire of their exemption. Nothing could ever be forgiven, and I forgave nothing. I held them to the mark. Who else cared about the fatties, about the dummies and slobs and clowns, about the gimps and squares and oafs and fools, the kids with a mouthful of mush, all those shut-ins of the mind and heart, all those losers? Frank the fat boy knew, and passed me shyly. His wide, fat body, stiffened, forced jokishly martial when he saw me, had already become flaccid as he moved by, had already made one more forgiven surrender. Who cared?

The streets were full of failure. Let them. Let them be. There was a paragon, a paragon loose. What could he be doing here, why had he come, what did he want? It was impossible that this hero from India and everywhere had made his home here; that he lived, as Frank the fat boy did, as Eugene did, as *I* did, in an apartment; that he shared our lives.

In the afternoon I looked for Eugene. He was in the park, in a tree. There was a book in his lap. He leaned against the thick trunk.

"Eugene," I called up to him.

"Push, they're closed. It's Sunday, Push. The stores are closed. I looked for the canteen. The stores are closed."

"Where is he?"

"Who, Push? What do you want, Push?"

"*Him.* Your pal. The prince. Where? Tell me, Eugene, or I'll shake you out of that tree. I'll burn you down. I swear it. Where is he?"

"No, Push. I was wrong about that guy. He's nice. He's really nice. Push, he told me about a doctor who could help me. Leave him alone, Push."

"Where, Eugene? *Where?* I count to three."

Eugene shrugged and came down the tree.

I found the name Eugene gave me—funny, foreign—over the bell in the outer hall. The buzzer sounded and I pushed open the door. I stood inside and looked up the carpeted stairs, the angled banisters.

"What is it?" She sounded old, worried.

"The new kid," I called, "the new kid."

"It's for you," I heard her say.

"Yes?" His voice, the one I couldn't mimic. I mounted the first stair. I leaned back against the wall and looked up through the high, boxy banister poles. It was like standing inside a pipe organ.

"Yes?"

From where I stood at the bottom of the stairs I could see only a boot. He was wearing boots.

"Yes? What is it, please?"

"*You,*" I roared. "Glass of fashion, mold of form, it's me! It's Push the bully!"

I heard his soft, rapid footsteps coming down the stairs—a springy, spongy urgency. He jingled, the bastard. He had coins—I could see them: rough, golden, imperfectly round; raised, massively gowned goddesses, their heads fingered smooth, their arms gone—and keys to strange boxes, thick doors. I saw his boots. I backed away.

"I brought you down," I said.

"Be quiet, please. There's a woman who's ill. A boy who must study. There's a man with bad bones. An old man needs sleep."

"He'll get it," I said.

"We'll go outside," he said.

"No. Do you live here? What do you do? Will you be in our school? Were you telling the truth?"

"Shh. Please. You're very excited."

"Tell me your name," I said. It could be my campaign, I thought. His *name.* Scratched in new sidewalk, chalked onto walls, written on papers dropped in the street. To leave it behind like so many clues, to give him a fame, to take it away, to slash and cross out, to erase and to smear—my kid's witchcraft. "Tell me your name."

"It's John," he said softly.

"What?"

"It's John."

"John what? Come on now. I'm Push the bully."

"John Williams," he said.

"John Williams? John Williams? Only that? Only John Williams?"

He smiled.

"Who's that on the bell? The name on the box?"

"She needs me," he said.

"Cut it out."

"I help her," he said.

"You stop that."

"There's a man that's in pain. A woman who's old. A husband that's worried. A wife that despairs."

"You're the bully," I said. "Your John Williams is a service animal," I yelled in the hall.

He turned and began to climb the stairs. His calves bloomed in their leather sheathing.

"Lover," I whispered to him.

He turned to me at the landing. He shook his head sadly.

"We'll see," I said.

"We'll see what we'll see," he said.

That night I painted his name on the side of the gymnasium in enormous letters. In the morning it was still there, but it wasn't what I meant. There was nothing incantatory in the huge letters, no scream, no curse. I had never traveled with a gang, there had been no togetherness in my tearing, but this thing on the wall seemed the act of vandals, the low production of ruffians. When you looked at it you were surprised they had gotten the spelling right.

Astonishingly, it was allowed to remain. And each day there was something more celebrational in the giant name, something of increased hospitality, lavish welcome. John Williams might have been a football hero, or someone back from the kidnapers. Finally I had to take it off myself.

Something had changed.

Eugene was not wearing his canteen. Boys didn't break off their conversations when I came up to them. One afternoon a girl winked at me. (Push has never picked on girls. *Their* submissiveness is part of their nature. They are ornamental. Don't get me wrong, please. There is a way in which they function as part of the landscape, like flowers at a funeral. They have a strange cheerfulness. They are the organizers of pep rallies and dances. They put out the Year Book. They are *born* Gray Ladies. I can't bully them.)

John Williams was in the school, but except for brief glimpses in the hall I never saw him. Teachers would repeat the things he had said in their other classes. They read from his papers. In the gym the coach described plays he had made, set shots he had taken. Everyone talked about him, and girls made a reference to him a sort of love signal. If it was suggested that he had smiled at one of them, the girl referred to would blush or, what was worse, look aloofly mysterious. (*Then* I could have punished her, *then* I could.) Gradually his name began to appear on all their notebooks, in the margins of their texts. (It annoyed me to remember what *I* had done on the wall.) The big canvas books, with their careful, elaborate J's and W's, took on the appearance of ancient, illuminated fables. It was the unconscious embroidery of love, hope's bright doodle. Even the administration was aware of him. In Assembly the principal announced that John Williams had broken all existing records in the school's charity drives. She had never seen good citizenship like his before, she said.

It's one thing to live with a bully, another to live with a hero.

Everyone's hatred I understand, no one's love; everyone's grievance, no one's content.

I saw Mimmer. Mimmer should have graduated years ago. I saw Mimmer the dummy.

"Mimmer," I said, "you're in his class."

"He's very smart."

"Yes, but is it fair? You work harder. I've seen you study. You spend hours. Nothing comes. He was born knowing. You could have used just a little of what he's got so much of. It's not fair."

"He's very clever. It's wonderful," Mimmer says.

Slud is crippled. He wears a shoe with a built-up heel to balance himself.

"Ah, Slud," I say, "I've seen him run."

"He has beaten the horses in the park. It's very beautiful," Slud says.

"He's handsome, isn't he, Clob?" Clob looks contagious, radioactive. He has severe acne. He is ugly *under* his acne.

"He gets the girls," Clob says.

He gets *everything,* I think. But I'm alone in my envy, awash in my lust. It's as if I were a prophet to the deaf. Schnooks, schnooks, I want to scream, dopes and settlers. What good does his smile do you, of what use is his good heart?

The other day I did something stupid. I went to the cafeteria and shoved a boy out of the way and took his place in line. It was foolish, but their fear is almost all gone and I felt I had to show the flag. The boy only grinned and let me pass. Then someone called my name. It was *him.* I turned to face him. "Push," he said, "you forgot your silver." He handed it to a girl in front of him and she gave it to the boy in front of her and it came to me down the long line.

I plot, I scheme. Snares, I think; tricks and traps. I remember the old days when there were ways to snap fingers, crush toes, ways to pull noses, twist heads and punch arms—the old-timey Flinch Law I used to impose, the gone bully magic of deceit. But nothing works against him, I think. How does he know so much? He is bully-prepared, that one, not to be trusted.

It is worse and worse.

In the cafeteria he eats with Frank. "You don't want those potatoes," he tells him. "Not the ice cream, Frank. One sandwich, remember. You lost three pounds last week." The fat boy smiles his fat love at him. John Williams puts his arm around him. He seems to squeeze him thin.

He's helping Mimmer to study. He goes over his lessons and teaches him tricks, short cuts. "I want you up there with me on the Honor Roll, Mimmer."

I see him with Slud the cripple. They go to the gym. I watch from the balcony. "Let's develop those arms, my friend." They work out with weights. Slud's muscles grow, they bloom from his bones.

I lean over the rail. I shout down, "He can bend iron bars. Can he peddle a bike? Can he walk on rough ground? Can he climb up a hill? Can he wait on a line? Can he dance with a girl? Can he go up a ladder or jump from a chair?"

Beneath me the rapt Slud sits on a bench and raises a weight. He holds it at arm's length, level with his chest. He moves it high, higher. It rises above his shoulders, his throat, his head. He bends back his neck to see what he's done. If the weight should fall now it would crush his throat. I stare down into his smile.

I see Eugene in the halls. I stop him. "Eugene, what's he done for you?" I ask. He smiles—he never did this—and I see his mouth's flood. "High tide," I say with satisfaction.

Williams has introduced Clob to a girl. They have double-dated.

A week ago John Williams came to my house to see me! I wouldn't let him in.

"Please open the door, Push. I'd like to chat with you. Will you open the door? Push? I think we ought to talk. I think I can help you to be happier."

I was furious. I didn't know what to say to him. "I don't want to be happier. Go way." It was what little kids used to say to me.

"*Please* let me help you."

"*Please* let me—" I begin to echo. "Please let me alone."

"We ought to be friends, Push."

"No deals." I am choking, I am close to tears. What can I do? *What?* I want to kill him.

I double-lock the door and retreat to my room. He is still out there.

I have tried to live my life so that I could keep always the lamb from my door.

He has gone too far this time; and I think sadly, I will have to fight him, I will have to fight him. Push pushed. I think sadly of the pain. Push pushed. I will have to fight him. Not to preserve honor but its opposite. Each time I see him I will have to fight him. And then I think—*of course!* And *I* smile. He has done *me* a favor. I know it at once. If he fights me he fails. He fails if he fights me. *Push pushed pushes!* It's physics! Natural law! I know he'll beat me, but I won't prepare, I won't train, I won't use the tricks I know. It's strength against strength, and my strength is as the strength of ten because my jaw is glass! *He doesn't know everything, not everything he doesn't.* And I think, I could go out now, he's still there, I could hit him in the hall, but I think, No, I want them to see, I want *them* to see!

The next day I am very excited. I look for Williams. He's not in the halls. I miss him in the cafeteria. Afterward I look for him in the schoolyard where I first saw him. (He has them organized now. He teaches them games of Tibet, games of Japan; he gets them to play lost sports of the dead.) He does not disappoint me. He is there in the yard, a circle around him, a ring of the loyal.

I join the ring. I shove in between two kids I have known. They try to change places; they murmur and fret.

Williams sees me and waves. His smile could grow flowers. "Boys," he says, "boys, make room for Push. Join hands, boys." They welcome me to the circle. One takes my hand, then another. I give to each calmly.

I wait. *He doesn't know everything.*

"Boys," he begins, "today we're going to learn a game that the knights of the lords and kings of old France used to play in another century. Now you may not realize it, boys, because today when we think of a knight we think, too, of his fine charger, but the fact is that a horse was a rare animal—not a domestic European animal at all, but Asian. In western Europe, for example, there was no such thing as a work horse until the eighth century. Your horse was just too expensive to be put to heavy labor in the fields. (This explains, incidentally, the prevalence of famine in western Europe, whereas famine is unrecorded in Asia until the ninth century, when Euro-Asian horse trading was at its height.) It wasn't only expensive to purchase a horse, it was expensive to keep one. A cheap fodder wasn't developed in Europe until the tenth century. Then, of course, when you consider the terrific risks that the warrior horse of a knight naturally had to run, you begin to appreciate how expensive it would have been for the lord—unless he was extremely rich—to provide all his knights with horses. He'd want to make pretty certain that the knights who got them knew how to handle a horse. (Only your knights errant—an elite, crack corps—ever had horses. We don't realize that most knights were *home* knights; *chevalier chez* they were called.)

"This game, then, was devised to let the lord, or king, see which of his knights had the skill and strength in his hands to control a horse. Without moving your feet, you must try to jerk the one next to you off balance. Each man has two opponents, so it's very difficult. If a man falls, or if his knee touches the ground, he's out. The circle is diminished but must close up again immediately. Now, once for practice only—"

"Just a minute," I interrupt.

"Yes, Push?"

I leave the circle and walk forward and hit him as hard as I can in the face.

He stumbles backward. The boys groan. He recovers. He rubs his jaw and smiles. I think he is going to let me hit him again. I am prepared for this. He knows what I'm up to and will use his passivity. Either way I win, but I am determined he shall hit me. I am ready to kick him, but as my foot comes up he grabs my ankle and turns it forcefully. I spin in the air. He lets go and I fall heavily on my back. I am surprised at how easy it was, but am content if they understand. I get up and am walking away, but there is an arm on my shoulder. He pulls me around roughly. He hits me.

"*Sic semper tyrannus,*" he exults.

"Where's your other cheek?" I ask, falling backward.

"One cheek for tyrants," he shouts. He pounces on me and raises his fist and I cringe. His anger is terrific. I do not want to be hit again.

"You see? You see?" I scream at the kids, but I have lost the train of my former reasoning. I have in no way beaten him. I can't remember now what I had intended.

He lowers his fist and gets off my chest and they cheer. "Hurrah," they yell. "Hurrah, hurrah." The word seems funny to me.

He offers his hand when I try to rise. It is so difficult to know what to do. Oh God, it is so difficult to know which gesture is the right one. I don't even know this. He knows everything, and I don't even know this. I am a fool on the ground, one hand behind me pushing up, the other not yet extended but itching in the palm where the need is. It is better to give than receive, surely. It is best not to need at all.

Appalled, guessing what I miss, I rise alone.

"Friends?" he asks. He offers to shake.

"Take it, Push." It's Eugene's voice.

"Go ahead, Push." Slud limps forward.

"Push, hatred's so ugly," Clob says, his face shining.

"You'll feel better, Push," Frank, thinner, taller, urges softly.

"Push, don't be foolish," Mimmer says.

I shake my head. I may be wrong. I am probably wrong. All I know at last is what feels good. "Nothing doing," I growl. "No deals." I begin to talk, to spray my hatred at them. They are not an easy target even now. "Only your knights errant—your crack corps—ever have horses. Slud may dance and Clob may kiss but they'll never be good at it. *Push is no service animal.* No. *No.* Can you hear that, Williams? There isn't any magic, but your no is still stronger than your yes, and distrust is where I put my faith." I turn to the boys. "What have you settled for? Only your knights errant ever have horses. *What have you settled for?* Will Mimmer do sums in his head? How do you like your lousy hunger, thin boy? Slud, you can break me but you can't catch me. And Clob will never shave without pain, and ugly, let me tell you, is *still* in the eye of the beholder!"

John Williams mourns for me. He grieves his gamy grief. No one has everything—not even John Williams. He doesn't have *me.* He'll never have me, I think. If my life were only to deny him that, it would almost be enough. I could do his voice now if I wanted. His corruption began when he lost me. "You," I shout, rubbing it in, *"indulger,* dispense me no dispensations. Push the bully hates your heart!"

"Shut him up, somebody," Eugene cries. His saliva spills from his mouth when he speaks.

"Swallow! *Pig, swallow!*"

He rushes toward me.

Suddenly I raise my arms and he stops. I feel a power in me. I am Push, Push the bully, God of the Neighborhood, its incarnation of envy and jealousy and need. I vie, strive, emulate, compete, a contender in every event there is. I didn't make myself. I probably can't save myself, but maybe that's the only need I don't have. I taste my lack and that's how I win—by having nothing to lose. It's not good enough! I want and I want and I will die wanting, but first I will have something. This time I will have something. I say it aloud. "This time I will have something." I step toward them. The power makes me dizzy. It is enormous. They feel it. They back away. They crouch in the shadow of my outstretched wings. It isn't deceit this time but the real magic at last, the genuine thing: the cabala of my hate, of my irreconcilableness.

Logic is nothing. Desire is stronger.

I move toward Eugene. *"I will have something,"* I roar.

"Stand back," he shrieks, "I'll spit in your eye."

"I will have something. I will have terror. I will have drought. I bring the dearth. Famine's contagious. Also is thirst. Privation, privation,

barrenness, void. I dry up your glands, I poison your well."

He is choking, gasping, chewing furiously. He opens his mouth. It is dry. His throat is parched. There is sand on his tongue.

They moan. They are terrified, but they move up to see. We are thrown together. Slud, Frank, Clob, Mimmer, the others, John Williams, myself. I will not be reconciled, or halve my hate. *It's* what I have, all I can keep. My bully's sour solace. It's enough, I'll make do.

I can't stand them near me. I move against them. I shove them away. I force them off. I press them, thrust them aside. *I push through.*

DONALD BARTHELME

Robert Kennedy Saved from Drowning

K. AT HIS DESK

He is neither abrupt with nor excessively kind to associates. Or he is both abrupt and kind.

The telephone is, for him, a whip, a lash, but also a conduit for soothing words, a sink into which he can hurl gallons of syrup if it comes to that.

He reads quickly, scratching brief comments ("Yes," "No") in corners of the paper. He slouches in the leather chair, looking about him with a slightly irritated air for new visitors, new difficulties. He spends his time sending and receiving messengers.

"I spend my time sending and receiving messengers," he says. "Some of these messages are important. Others are not."

DESCRIBED BY SECRETARIES

A: "Quite frankly I think he forgets a lot of things. But the things he forgets are those which are inessential. I even think he might forget deliberately, to leave his mind free. He has the ability to get rid of unimportant details. And he does."

B: "Once when I was sick, I hadn't heard from him, and I thought he had forgotten me. You know usually your boss will send flowers or something like that. I was in the hospital, and I was mighty blue. I was in a room with another girl, and *her* boss hadn't sent her anything either. Then suddenly the door opened and there he was with the biggest bunch of yellow tulips I'd ever seen in my life. And the other girl's boss was with him, and he had tulips too. They were standing there with all those tulips, smiling."

BEHIND THE BAR

At a crowded party, he wanders behind the bar to make himself a Scotch and water. His hand is on the bottle of Scotch, his glass is waiting. The bartender, a small man in a beige uniform with gilt buttons, politely asks K. to return to the other side, the guests' side, of the bar. "You let one behind here, they all be behind here," the bartender says.

K. READING THE NEWSPAPER

His reactions are impossible to catalogue. Often he will find a note that amuses him endlessly, some anecdote involving, say, a fireman who has propelled his apparatus at record-breaking speed to the wrong address. These small stories are clipped, carried about in a pocket, to be produced at appropriate moments for the pleasure of friends. Other manifestations please him less. An account of an earthquake in Chile, with its thousands of dead and homeless, may depress him for weeks. He memorizes the terrible statistics, quoting them everywhere and saying, with a grave look: "We must do something." Important actions often follow, sometimes within a matter of hours. (On the other hand, these two kinds of responses may be, on a given day, inexplicably reversed.)

The more trivial aspects of the daily itemization are skipped. While reading, he maintains a rapid drumming of his fingertips on the desktop. He receives twelve newspapers, but of these, only four are regarded as serious.

ATTITUDE TOWARD HIS WORK

"Sometimes I can't seem to do anything. The work is there, piled up, it seems to me an insurmountable obstacle, really out of reach. I sit and look at it, wondering where to begin, how to take hold of it. Perhaps I pick up a piece of paper, try to read it but my mind is elsewhere, I am thinking of something else, I can't seem to get the gist of it, it seems meaningless, devoid of interest, not having to do with human affairs, drained of life. Then, in an hour, or even a moment, everything changes suddenly: I realize I only have to *do* it, hurl myself into the midst of it, proceed mechanically, the first thing and then the second thing, that it is simply a matter of moving from one step to the next, plowing through it. I become interested, I become excited, I work very fast, things fall into place, I am exhilarated, amazed that these things could ever have seemed dead to me."

SLEEPING ON THE STONES OF UNKNOWN TOWNS (RIMBAUD)

K. is walking, with that familiar slight dip of the shoulders, through the streets of a small city in France or Germany. The shop signs are in a language which alters when inspected closely, MÖBEL becoming MEUBLES for example, and the citizens mutter to themselves with dark virtuosity a mixture of languages. K. is very interested, looks closely at everything, at the shops, the goods displayed, the clothing of the people, the tempo of street life, the citizens themselves, wondering about them. What are their water needs?

"In the West, wisdom is mostly gained at lunch. At lunch, people tell you things."

The nervous eyes of the waiters.

The tall bald cook, white apron, white T-shirt, grinning through an opening in the wall.

"Why is that cook looking at me?"

"The transportation problems of our cities and their rapidly expanding suburbs are the most urgent and neglected transportation problems confronting the country. In these heavily populated and industrialized areas, people are dependent on a system of transportation that is at once complex and inadequate. Obsolete facilities and growing demands have created seemingly insoluble difficulties and present methods of dealing with these difficulties offer little prospect of relief."

K. PENETRATED WITH SADNESS

He hears something playing on someone else's radio, in another part of the building.

The music is wretchedly sad; now he can (barely) hear it, now it fades into the wall.

He turns on his own radio. There it is, on his own radio, the same music. The sound fills the room.

KARSH OF OTTAWA

"We sent a man to Karsh of Ottawa and told him that we admired his work very much. Especially, I don't know, the Churchill thing and, you know, the Hemingway thing, and all that. And we told him we wanted to set up a sitting for K. sometime in June, if that would be convenient for him, and he said yes, that was okay, June was okay, and where did we want to have it shot, there or in New York or where. Well, that was a problem because we didn't know exactly what K.'s schedule would be for June, it was up in the air, so we tentatively said New York around the fifteenth. And he said, that was okay, he could do that. And he wanted to know how much time he could have, and we said, well, how much time do you need? And he said he didn't know, it varied from sitter to sitter. He said some people were very restless and that made it difficult to get just the right shot. He said there was one shot in each sitting that was, you know, the key shot, the right one. He said he'd have to see, when the time came."

DRESS

He is neatly dressed in a manner that does not call attention to itself. The suits are soberly cut and in dark colors. He must at all times present an aspect of freshness difficult to sustain because of frequent movements from place to place under conditions which are not always the most favorable. Thus he changes clothes frequently, especially shirts. In the course of a day he changes his shirt many times. There are always extra shirts about, in boxes.

"Which of you has the shirts?"

A FRIEND COMMENTS: K.'S ALONENESS

"The thing you have to realize about K. is that essentially he's absolutely alone in the world. There's this terrible loneliness which prevents people from getting too close to him. Maybe it comes from something in his childhood, I don't know. But he's very hard to get to know, and a lot of people who think they know him rather well don't really know him at all. He says something or does something that surprises you, and you realize that all along you really didn't know him at all.

"He has surprising facets. I remember once we were out in a small boat. K. of course was the captain. Some rough weather came up and we began to head back in. I began worrying about picking up a landing and I said to him that I didn't think the anchor would hold, with the wind and all. He just looked at me. Then he said: 'Of course it will hold. That's what it's for.' "

K. ON CROWDS

"There are exhausted crowds and vivacious crowds.

"Sometimes, standing there, I can sense whether a particular crowd is one thing or the other. Sometimes the mood of the crowd is disguised, sometimes you only find out after a quarter of an hour what sort of crowd a particular crowd is.

"And you can't speak to them in the same way. The variations have to be taken into account. You have to say something to them that is meaningful to them *in that mood.*"

GALLERY-GOING

K. enters a large gallery on Fifty-seventh Street, in the Fuller Building. His entourage includes several ladies and gentlemen. Works by a geometricist are on show. K. looks at the immense, rather theoretical paintings.

"Well, at least we know he has a ruler."

The group dissolves in laughter. People repeat the remark to one another, laughing.

The artist, who has been standing behind a dealer, regards K. with hatred.

K. PUZZLED BY HIS CHILDREN

The children are crying. There are several children, one about four, a boy, then another boy, slightly older, and a little girl, very beautiful, wearing blue jeans, crying. There are various objects on the grass, an electric train, a picture book, a red ball, a plastic bucket, a plastic shovel.

K. frowns at the children whose distress issues from no source immediately available to the eye, which seems indeed uncaused, vacant, a general anguish. K. turns to the mother of these children who is standing nearby wearing hip-huggers which appear to be made of linked marshmallows studded with diamonds but then I am a notoriously poor observer.

"Play with them," he says.

This mother of ten quietly suggests that K. himself "play with them."

K. picks up the picture book and begins to read to the children. But the book has a German text. It has been left behind, perhaps, by some foreign visitor. Nevertheless K. perseveres.

"A ist der Affe, er isst mit der Pfote." ("A is the Ape, he eats with his Paw.")

The crying of the children continues.

A DREAM

Orange trees.

Overhead, a steady stream of strange aircraft which resemble kitchen implements, bread boards, cookie sheets, colanders.

The shiny aluminum instruments are on their way to complete the bombings of Sidi-Madani.

A farm in the hills.

MATTERS (FROM AN ADMINISTRATIVE ASSISTANT)

"A lot of matters that had been pending came to a head right about that time, moved to the front burner, things we absolutely had to take care of. And we couldn't find K. Nobody knew where he was. We had looked everywhere. He had just withdrawn, made himself unavailable. There was this one matter that was probably more pressing than all the rest put together. Really crucial. We were all standing around wondering what to do. We were getting pretty nervous because this thing was really . . . Then K. walked in and disposed of it with a quick phone call. A quick phone call!"

CHILDHOOD OF K. AS RECALLED BY A FORMER TEACHER

"He was a very alert boy, very bright, good at his studies, very thorough, very conscientious. But that's not unusual; that describes a good number of the boys who pass through here. It's not unusual, that is, to find these qualities which are after all the qualities that we look for and encourage in them. What *was* unusual about K. was his compassion, something very rare for a boy of that age—even if they have it, they're usually very careful not to display it for fear of seeming soft, girlish. I remember, though, that in K. this particular attribute was very marked. I would almost say that it was his strongest characteristic."

SPEAKING TO NO ONE BUT WAITERS, HE—

"The dandelion salad with bacon, I think."

"The *rysstafel.*"

"The poached duck."

"The black bean purée."

"The cod fritters."

K. EXPLAINS A TECHNIQUE

"It's an expedient in terms of how not to destroy a situation which has been a long time gestating, or, again, how to break it up if it appears that the situation has changed, during the gestation period, into one whose implications are not quite what they were at the beginning. What I mean is that in this business things are constantly altering (usually for the worse) and usually you want to give the impression that you're not watching this particular situation particularly closely, that you're paying no special attention to it, until you're ready to make your move. That is, it's best to be sudden, if you can manage it. Of course you can't do that all the time. Sometimes you're just completely wiped out, cleaned out, totaled, and then the only thing to do is shrug and forget about it."

K. ON HIS OWN ROLE

"Sometimes it seems to me that it doesn't matter what I do, that it is enough to exist, to sit somewhere, in a garden for example, watching whatever is to be seen there, the small events. At other times, I'm aware that other people, possibly a great number of other people, could be affected by what I do or fail to do, that I have a responsibility, as we all have, to make the best possible use of whatever talents I've been given, for the common good. It is not enough to sit in that garden, however restful or pleasurable it might be. The world is full of unsolved problems, situations that demand careful, reasoned and intelligent action. In Latin America, for example."

AS ENTREPRENEUR

The original cost estimates for burying the North Sea pipeline have been exceeded by a considerable margin. Everyone wonders what he will say about this contretemps which does not fail to have its dangers for those responsible for the costly miscalculations, which are viewed in many minds as inexcusable.

He says only: "Exceptionally difficult rock conditions."

WITH YOUNG PEOPLE

K., walking the streets of unknown towns, finds himself among young people. Young people line these streets, narrow and curving, which are theirs, dedicated to them. They are everywhere, resting on the embankments, their guitars, small radios, long hair. They sit on the sidewalks, back to back, heads turned to stare. They stand implacably on street corners, in doorways, or lean on their elbows in windows, or squat in small groups at that place where the sidewalk meets the walls of buildings. The streets are filled with these young people who say nothing, reveal only a limited interest, refuse to declare themselves. Street after street contains them, a great number, more displayed as one turns a corner, rank upon rank stretching into the distance, drawn from the arcades, the plazas, staring.

HE DISCUSSES THE FRENCH WRITER, POULET

"For Poulet, it is not enough to speak of *seizing the moment.* It is rather a question of, and I quote, 'recognizing in the instant which lives and dies, which surges out of nothingness and which ends in dream, an intensity and depth of significance which ordinarily attaches only to the whole of existence.'

"What Poulet is describing is neither an ethic nor a prescription but rather what he has discovered in the work of Marivaux. Poulet has taken up the Marivaudian canon and squeezed it with both hands to discover the essence of what may be called the Marivaudian being, what Poulet in fact calls the Marivaudian being.

"The Marivaudian being is, according to Poulet, a pastless futureless man, born anew at every instant. The instants are points which organize themselves into a line, but what is important is the instant, not the line. The Marivaudian being has in a sense no history. Nothing follows from what has gone before. He is constantly surprised. He cannot predict his own reaction to events. He is constantly being *overtaken* by events. A condition of breathlessness and dazzlement surrounds him. In consequence he exists in a certain freshness which seems, if I may say so, very desirable. This freshness Poulet, quoting Marivaux, describes very well."

K. SAVED FROM DROWNING

K. in the water. His flat black hat, his black cape, his sword are on the shore. He retains his mask. His hands beat the surface of the water which tears and rips about him. The white foam, the green depths. I throw a line, the coils leaping out over the surface of the water. He has missed it. No, it appears that he has it. His right hand (sword arm) grasps the line that I have thrown him. I am on the bank, the rope wound round my waist, braced against a rock. K. now has both hands on the line. I pull him out of the water. He stands now on the bank, gasping.

"Thank you."

ROBERT COOVER

The Babysitter

She arrives at 7:40, ten minutes late, but the children, Jimmy and Bitsy, are still eating supper, and their parents are not ready to go yet. From other rooms come the sounds of a baby screaming, water running, a television musical (no words: probably a dance number—patterns of gliding figures come to mind). Mrs. Tucker sweeps into the kitchen, fussing with her hair, and snatches a baby bottle full of milk out of a pan of warm water, rushes out again. "Harry!" she calls. "The babysitter's here already!"

That's My Desire? I'll Be Around? He smiles toothily, beckons faintly with his head, rubs his fast balding pate. Bewitched, maybe? Or, What's the Reason? He pulls on his shorts, gives his hips a slap. The baby goes silent in mid-scream. Isn't this the one who used their tub last time? Who's Sorry Now, that's it.

Jack is wandering around town, not knowing what to do. His girlfriend is babysitting at the Tuckers', and later, when she's got the kids in bed, maybe he'll drop over there. Sometimes he watches TV with her when she's babysitting, it's about the only chance he gets to make out a little since he doesn't own wheels, but they have to be careful because most people don't like their sitters to have boyfriends over. Just kissing her makes her nervous. She won't close her eyes because she has to be watching the door all the time. Married people really have it good, he thinks.

"Hi," the babysitter says to the children, and puts her books on top of the refrigerator. "What's for supper?" The little girl, Bitsy, only stares at her obliquely. She joins them at the end of the kitchen table. "I don't have to go to bed until nine," the boy announces flatly, and stuffs his mouth full of potato chips. The babysitter catches a glimpse of Mr. Tucker hurrying out of the bathroom in his underwear.

Her tummy. Under her arms. And her feet. Those are the best places. She'll spank him, she says sometimes. Let her.

That sweet odor that girls have. The softness of her blouse. He catches a glimpse of the gentle shadows amid her thighs, as she curls her legs up under her. He stares hard at her. He has a lot of meaning packed into that stare, but she's not even looking. She's popping her gum and watching television. She's sitting right there, inches away, soft, fragrant, and ready: but what's his next move? He notices his buddy Mark in the drugstore, playing the pinball machine, and joins him. "Hey, this mama's cold, Jack baby! She needs your touch!"

Mrs. Tucker appears at the kitchen doorway, holding a rolled-up diaper. "Now, don't just eat potato chips, Jimmy! See that he eats his hamburger, dear." She hurries away to the bathroom. The boy glares sullenly at the babysitter, silently daring her to carry out the order. "How about a little of that good hamburger now, Jimmy?" she says perfunctorily. He lets half of it drop to the floor. The baby is silent and a man is singing a love song on the TV. The children crunch chips.

He loves her. She loves him. They whirl airily, stirring a light breeze, through a magical landscape of rose and emerald and deep blue. Her light brown hair coils and wisps softly in the breeze, and the soft folds of her white gown tug at her body and then float away. He smiles in a pulsing crescendo of sincerity and song.

"You mean she's alone?" Mark asks. "Well, there's two or three kids," Jack says. He slides the coin in. There's a rumble of steel balls tumbling, lining up. He pushes a plunger with his thumb, and one ball pops up in place, hard and glittering with promise. His stare? to say he loves her. That he cares for her and would protect her, would shield her, if need be, with his own body. Grinning, he bends over the ball to take careful aim: he and Mark have studied this machine and have it figured out, but still it's not that easy to beat.

On the drive to the party, his mind is partly on the girl, partly on his own high-school days, long past. Sitting at the end of the kitchen table there with his children, she had seemed to be self-consciously arching her back, jutting her pert breasts, twitching her thighs: and for whom if not for him? So she'd seen him coming out of there, after all. He smiles. Yet what could he ever do about it? Those good times are gone, old man. He glances over at his wife, who, readjusting a garter, asks: "What do you think of our babysitter?"

He loves her. She loves him. And then the babies come. And dirty diapers and one goddamn meal after another. Dishes. Noise. Clutter. And fat. Not just tight, her girdle actually hurts. Somewhere recently she's read about women getting heart attacks or cancer or something from too-tight girdles. Dolly pulls the car door shut with a grunt, strangely irritated, not knowing why. Party mood. Why is her husband humming, "Who's Sorry Now?" Pulling out of the drive, she glances back at the lighted kitchen window. "What do you think of our babysitter?" she asks. While her husband stumbles all over himself trying to answer, she pulls a stocking tight, biting deeper with the garters.

"Stop it!" she laughs. Bitsy is pulling on her skirt and he is tickling her in the ribs. "Jimmy! Don't!" But she is laughing too much to stop him. He leaps on her, wrapping his legs around her waist, and they all fall to the carpet in front of the TV, where just now a man in a tuxedo and a little girl in a flouncy white dress are doing a tapdance together. The babysitter's blouse is pulling out of her skirt, showing a patch of bare tummy: the target. "I'll spank!"

Jack pushes the plunger, thrusting up a steel ball, and bends studiously over the machine. "You getting any off her?" Mark asks, and clears his throat, flicks ash from his cigarette. "Well, not exactly, not yet," Jack says, grinning awkwardly, but trying to suggest more than he admits to, and fires. He heaves his weight gently against the machine as the ball bounds off a rubber bumper. He can feel her warming up under his hands, the flippers suddenly coming alive, delicate rapid-fire patterns emerging in the flashing of the lights. 1000 WHEN LIT: *now!* "Got my hand on it, that's about all." Mark glances up from the machine, cigarette dangling from his lip. "Maybe you need some help," he suggests with a wry one-sided grin. "Like maybe together, man, we could do it."

She likes the big tub. She uses the Tuckers' bath salts, and loves to sink into the hot fragrant suds. She can stretch out, submerged, up to her chin. It gives her a good sleepy tingly feeling.

"What do you think of our babysitter?" Dolly asks, adjusting a garter. "Oh, I hardly noticed," he says. "Cute girl. She seems to get along fine with the kids. Why?" "I don't know." His wife tugs her skirt down, glances at a lighted window they are passing, adding: "I'm not sure I trust her completely, that's all. With the baby, I mean. She seems a little careless. And the other time, I'm almost sure she had a boyfriend over." He grins, claps one hand on his wife's broad gartered thigh. "What's wrong with that?" he asks. Still in anklets, too. Bare thighs, no girdles, nothing up there but a flimsy pair of panties and soft adolescent flesh. He's flooded with vague remembrances of football rallies and movie balconies.

How tiny and rubbery it is! she thinks, soaping between the boy's legs, giving him his bath. Just a funny jiggly little thing that looks like it shouldn't even be there at all. Is that what all the songs are about?

Jack watches Mark lunge and twist against the machine. Got her running now, racking them up. He's not too excited about the idea of Mark fooling around with his girlfriend, but Mark's a cooler operator than he is, and maybe, doing it together this once, he'd get over his own timidity. And if she didn't like it, there were other girls around. If Mark went too far, he could cut him off, too. He feels his shoulders tense: enough's enough, man . . . but sees the flesh, too. "Maybe I'll call her later," he says.

"Hey, Harry! Dolly! Glad you could make it!" "I hope we're not late." "No, no, you're one of the first, come on in! By golly, Dolly, you're looking younger every day! How do you do it? Give my wife your secret, will you?" He pats her on her girdled bottom behind Mr. Tucker's back, leads them in for drinks.

8:00. The babysitter runs water in the tub, combs her hair in front of the bathroom mirror. There's a western on television, so she lets Jimmy watch it while she gives Bitsy her bath. But Bitsy doesn't want a bath. She's angry and crying because she has to be first. The babysitter tells her if she'll take her bath quickly, she'll let her watch television while Jimmy takes his bath, but it does no good. The little girl fights to get out of the bathroom, and the babysitter has to squat with her back against the door and forcibly undress the child. There are better places to babysit. Both children mind badly, and then, sooner or later, the baby is sure to wake up for a diaper change and more bottle. The Tuckers do have a good color TV, though, and she hopes things will be settled down enough to catch the 8:30 program. She thrusts the child into the tub, but she's still screaming and thrashing around. "Stop it now, Bitsy, or you'll wake the baby!" "I have to go potty!" the child wails, switching tactics. The babysitter sighs, lifts the girl out of the tub and onto the toilet, getting her skirt and blouse all wet in the process. She glances at herself in the mirror. Before she knows it, the girl is off the seat and out of the bathroom. "Bitsy! Come back here!"

"Okay, that's enough!" Her skirt is ripped and she's flushed and crying. "Who says?" "I do, man!" The bastard goes for her, but he tackles him. They roll and tumble. Tables tip, lights topple, the TV crashes to the floor. He slams a hard right to the guy's gut, clips his chin with a rolling left.

"We hope it's a girl." That's hardly surprising, since they already have four boys. Dolly congratulates the woman like everybody else, but she doesn't envy her, not a bit. That's all she needs about now. She stares across the room at Harry, who is slapping backs and getting loud, as usual. He's spreading out through the middle, so why the hell does he have to complain about her all the time? "Dolly, you're looking younger every day!" was the nice greeting she got tonight. "What's your secret?" And Harry: "It's all those calories. She's getting back her baby fat." "Haw haw! Harry, have a heart!"

"Get her feet!" he hollers at Bitsy, his fingers in her ribs, running over her naked tummy, tangling in the underbrush of straps and strange clothing. "Get her shoes off!" He holds her pinned by pressing his head against her soft chest. "No! No, Jimmy! Bitsy, stop!" But though she kicks and twists and rolls around, she doesn't get up, she can't get up, she's laughing too hard, and the shoes come off, and he grabs a stockinged foot and scratches the sole ruthlessly, and she raises up her legs, trying to pitch him off, she's wild, boy, but he hangs on, and she's laughing, and on the screen there's a rattle of hooves, and he and Bitsy are rolling around and around on the floor in a crazy rodeo of long bucking legs.

He slips the coin in. There's a metallic fall and a sharp click as the dial tone begins. "I hope the Tuckers have gone," he says. "Don't worry, they're at your place," Mark says. "They're always the first ones to come and the last ones to go home. My old man's always bitching about them." Jack laughs nervously and dials the number. "Tell her we're coming over to protect her from getting raped," Mark suggests, and lights a cigarette. Jack grins, leaning casually against the door jamb of the phonebooth, chewing gum, one hand in his pocket. He's really pretty uneasy, though. He has the feeling he's somehow messing up a good thing.

Bitsy runs naked into the livingroom, keeping a hassock between herself and the babysitter. "Bitsy . . . !" the babysitter threatens. Artificial reds and greens and purples flicker over the child's wet body, as hooves clatter, guns crackle, and stagecoach wheels thunder over rutted terrain. "Get outa the way, Bitsy!" the boy complains. "I can't see!" Bitsy streaks past and the babysitter chases, cornering the girl in the back bedroom. Bitsy throws something that hits her softly in the face: a pair of men's undershorts. She grabs the girl scampering by, carries her struggling to the bathroom, and with a smart crack on her glistening bottom, pops her back into the tub. In spite, Bitsy peepees in the bathwater.

Mr. Tucker stirs a little water into his bourbon and kids with his host and another man, just arrived, about their golf games. They set up a match for the weekend, a threesome looking for a fourth. Holding his drink in his right hand, Mr. Tucker swings his left through the motion of a tee-shot. "You'll have to give me a stroke a hole," he says. "I'll give you a stroke!" says his host: "Bend over!" Laughing, the other man asks: "Where's your boy Mark tonight?" "I don't know," replies the host, gathering up a trayful of drinks. Then he adds in a low growl: "Out chasing tail probably." They chuckle loosely at that, then shrug in commiseration and return to the livingroom to join their women.

Shades pulled. Door locked. Watching the TV. Under a blanket maybe. Yes, that's right, under a blanket. Her eyes close when he kisses her. Her breasts, under both their hands, are soft and yielding.

A hard blow to the belly. The face. The dark beardy one staggers. The lean-jawed sheriff moves in, but gets a spurred boot in his face. The dark one hurls himself forward, drives his shoulder into the sheriff's hard midriff, her own tummy tightens, withstands, as the sheriff smashes the dark man's nose, slams him up against a wall, slugs him again! and again! The dark man grunts rhythmically, backs off, then plunges suicidally forward—her own knees draw up protectively—the sheriff staggers! caught low! but instead of following through, the other man steps back—a pistol! the dark one has a pistol! the sheriff draws! shoots from the hip! explosions! she clutches her hands between her thighs—no! the sheriff spins! wounded! the dark man hesitates, aims, her legs stiffen toward the set, the sheriff rolls desperately in the straw, fires: dead! the dark man is dead! groans, crumples, his pistol drooping in his collapsing hand, dropping, he drops. The sheriff, spent, nicked, watches weakly from the floor where he lies. Oh, to be whole! to be good and strong and right! to embrace and be embraced by harmony and wholeness! The sheriff, drawing himself painfully up on one elbow, rubs his bruised mouth with the back of his other hand.

"Well, we just sorta thought we'd drop over," he says, and winks broadly at Mark. "Who's we?" "Oh, me and Mark here." "Tell her, good thing like her, gotta pass it around," whispers Mark, dragging on his smoke, then flicking the butt over under the pinball machine. "What's that?" she asks. "Oh, Mark and I were just saying, like two's company, three's an orgy," Jack says, and winks again. She giggles. "Oh, Jack!" Behind her, he can hear shouts and gunfire. "Well, okay, for just a little while, if you'll both be good." Way to go, man.

Probably some damn kid over there right now. Wrestling around on the couch in front of his TV. Maybe he should drop back to the house. Just to check. None of that stuff, she was there to do a job! Park the car a couple doors down, slip in the front door before she knows it. He sees the disarray of clothing, the young thighs exposed to the flickering television light, hears his baby crying. "Hey, what's going on here! Get outa here, son, before I call the police!" Of course, they haven't really been doing anything. They probably don't even know how. He stares benignly down upon the girl, her skirt rumpled loosely around her thighs. Flushed, frightened, yet excited, she stares back at him. He smiles. His finger touches a knee, approaches the hem. Another couple arrives. Filling up here with people. He wouldn't be missed. Just slip out, stop back casually to pick up something or other he forgot, never mind what. He remembers that the other time they had this babysitter, she took a bath in their house. She had a date afterwards, and she'd just come from cheerleading practice or something. Aspirin maybe. Just drop quietly and casually into the bathroom to pick up some aspirin. "Oh, excuse me, dear! I only . . . !" She gazes back at him, astonished, yet strangely moved. Her soft wet breasts rise and fall in the water, and her tummy looks pale and ripply. He recalls that her pubic hairs, left in the tub, were brown. Light brown.

She's no more than stepped into the tub for a quick bath, when Jimmy announces from outside the door that he has to go to the bathroom. She sighs: just an excuse, she knows. "You'll have to wait." The little nuisance. "I can't wait." "Okay, then come ahead, but I'm taking a bath." She supposes that will stop him, but it doesn't. In he comes. She slides down into the suds until she's eye-level with the edge of the tub. He hesitates. "Go ahead, if you have to," she says, a little awkwardly, "but I'm not getting out." "Don't look," he says. She: "I will if I want to."

She's crying. Mark is rubbing his jaw where he's just slugged him. A lamp lies shattered. "Enough's enough, Mark! Now get outa here!" Her skirt is ripped to the waist, her bare hip bruised. Her panties lie on the floor like a broken balloon. Later, he'll wash her wounds, help her dress, he'll take care of her. Pity washes through him, giving him a sudden hard-on. Mark laughs at it, pointing. Jack crouches, waiting, ready for anything.

Laughing, they roll and tumble. Their little hands are all over her, digging and pinching. She struggles to her hands and knees, but Bitsy leaps astride her neck, bowing her head to the carpet. "Spank her, Jimmy!" His swats sting: is her skirt up? The phone rings. "The cavalry to the rescue!" she laughs, and throws them off to go answer.

Kissing Mark, her eyes closed, her hips nudge toward Jack. He stares at the TV screen, unsure of himself, one hand slipping cautiously under her skirt. Her hand touches his arm as though to resist, then brushes on by to rub his leg. This blanket they're under was a good idea. "Hi! This is Jack!"

Bitsy's out and the water's running. "Come on, Jimmy, your turn!" Last time, he told her he took his own baths, but she came in anyway. "I'm not gonna take a bath," he announces, eyes glued on the set. He readies for the struggle. "But I've already run your water. Come on, Jimmy, please!" He shakes his head. She can't make him, he's sure he's as strong as she is. She sighs. "Well, it's up to you. I'll use the water myself then," she says. He waits until he's pretty sure she's not going to change her mind, then sneaks in and peeks through the keyhole in the bathroom door: just in time to see her big bottom as she bends over to stir in the bubblebath. Then she disappears. Trying to see as far down as the keyhole will allow, he bumps his head on the knob. "Jimmy, is that you?" "I—I have to go to the bathroom!" he stammers.

Not actually in the tub, just getting in. One foot on the mat, the other in the water. Bent over slightly, buttocks flexed, teats swaying, holding on to the edge of the tub. "Oh, excuse me! I only wanted . . . !" He passes over her astonishment, the awkward excuses, moves quickly to the part where he reaches out to—"What on earth are you doing, Harry?" his wife asks, staring at his hand. His host, passing, laughs. "He's practicing his swing for Sunday, Dolly, but it's not going to do him a damn bit of good!" Mr. Tucker laughs, sweeps his right hand on through the air as though lifting a seven-iron shot onto the green. He makes a *dok!* sound with his tongue. "In there!"

"No, Jack, I don't think you'd better." "Well, we just called, we just, uh, thought we'd, you know, stop by for a minute, watch television for thirty minutes, or, or something." "Who's we?" "Well, Mark's here, I'm with him, and he said he'd like to, you know, like if it's all right, just—" "Well, it's *not* all right. The Tuckers said no." "Yeah, but if we only—" "And they seemed awfully suspicious about last time." "Why? We didn't—I mean, I just thought—" "No, Jack, and that's period." She hangs up. She returns to the TV, but the commercial is on. Anyway, she's missed most of the show. She decides maybe she'll take a quick bath. Jack might come by anyway, it'd make her mad, that'd be the end as far as he was concerned, but if he should, she doesn't want to be all sweaty. And besides, she likes the big tub the Tuckers have.

He is self-conscious and stands with his back to her, his little neck flushed. It takes him forever to get started, and when it finally does come, it's just a tiny trickle. "See, it was just an excuse," she scolds, but she's giggling inwardly at the boy's embarrassment. "You're just a nuisance, Jimmy." At the door, his hand on the knob, he hesitates, staring timidly down on his shoes. "Jimmy?" She peeks at him over the edge of the tub, trying to keep a straight face, as he sneaks a nervous glance back over his shoulder. "As long as you bothered me," she says, "you might as well soap my back."

"The aspirin . . ." They embrace. She huddles in his arms like a child. Lovingly, paternally, knowledgeably, he wraps her nakedness. How compact, how tight and small her body is! Kissing her ear, he stares down past her rump at the still clear water. "I'll join you," he whispers hoarsely.

She picks up the shorts Bitsy threw at her. Men's underwear. She holds them in front of her, looks at herself in the bedroom mirror. About twenty sizes too big for her, of course. She runs her hand inside the opening in front, pulls out her thumb. How funny it must feel!

"Well, man, I say we just go rape her," Mark says flatly, and swings his weight against the pinball machine. "Uff! Ahh! Get in there, you mother! Look at that! Hah! Man, I'm gonna turn this baby over!" Jack is embarrassed about the phone conversation. Mark just snorted in disgust when he hung up. He cracks down hard on his gum, angry that he's such a chicken. "Well, I'm game if you are," he says coldly.

8:30. "Okay, come on, Jimmy, it's time." He ignores her. The western gives way to a spy show. Bitsy, in pajamas, pads into the livingroom. "No, Bitsy, it's time to go to bed." "You said I could watch!" the girl whines, and starts to throw another tantrum. "But you were too slow and it's late. Jimmy, you get in that bathroom, and right now!" Jimmy stares sullenly at the set, unmoving. The babysitter tries to catch the opening scene of the television program so she can follow it later, since Jimmy gives himself his own baths. When the commercial interrupts, she turns off the sound, stands in front of the screen. "Okay, into the tub, Jimmy Tucker, or I'll take you in there and give you your bath myself!" "Just try it," he says, "and see what happens."

They stand outside, in the dark, crouched in the bushes, peeking in. She's on the floor, playing with the kids. Too early. They seem to be tickling her. She gets to her hands and knees, but the little girl leaps on her head, pressing her face to the floor. There's an obvious target, and the little boy proceeds to beat on it. "Hey, look at that kid go!" whispers Mark, laughing and snapping his fingers softly. Jack feels uneasy out here. Too many neighbors, too many cars going by, too many people in the world. That little boy in there is one up on him, though: he's never thought about tickling her as a starter.

His little hand, clutching the bar of soap, lathers shyly a narrow space between her shoulderblades. She is doubled forward against her knees, buried in rich suds, peeking at him over the edge of her shoulder. The soap slithers out of his grip and plunks into the water. "I . . . I dropped the soap," he whispers. She: "Find it."

"I dream of Jeannie with the light brown pubic hair!" "Harry! Stop that! You're drunk!" But they're laughing, they're all laughing, damn! he's feeling pretty goddamn good at that, and now he just knows he needs that aspirin. Watching her there, her thighs spread for him, on the couch, in the tub, hell, on the kitchen table for that matter, he tees off on Number Nine, and—*whap!*—swats his host's wife on the bottom. "Hole in one!" he shouts. "Harry!" Why can't his goddamn wife Dolly ever get happy-drunk instead of sour-drunk all the time? "Gonna be tough Sunday, old buddy!" "You're pretty tough right now, Harry," says his host.

The babysitter lunges forward, grabs the boy by the arms and hauls him off the couch, pulling two cushions with him, and drags him toward the bathroom. He lashes out, knocking over an endtable full of magazines and ashtrays. "You leave my brother alone!" Bitsy cries and grabs the sitter around the waist. Jimmy jumps on her and down they all go. On the silent screen, there's a fade-in to a dark passageway in an old apartment building in some foreign country. She kicks out and somebody falls between her legs. Somebody else is sitting on her face. "Jimmy! Stop that!" the babysitter laughs, her voice muffled.

She's watching television. All alone. It seems like a good time to go in. Just remember: really, no matter what she says, she wants it. They're standing in the bushes, trying to get up the nerve. "We'll tell her to be good," Mark whispers, "and if she's not good, we'll spank her." Jack giggles softly, but his knees are weak. She stands. They freeze. She looks right at them. "She can't see us," Mark whispers tensely. "Is she coming out?" "No," says Mark, "she's going into—that must be the bathroom!" Jack takes a deep breath, his heart pounding. "Hey, is there a window back there?" Mark asks.

The phone rings. She leaves the tub, wrapped in a towel. Bitsy gives a tug on the towel. "Hey, Jimmy, get the towel!" she squeals. "Now stop that, Bitsy!" the babysitter hisses, but too late: with one hand on the phone, the other isn't enough to hang on to the towel. Her sudden nakedness awes them and it takes them a moment to remember about tickling her. By then, she's in the towel again. "I hope you got a good look," she says angrily. She feels chilled and oddly a little frightened.

"Hello?" No answer. She glances at the window—is somebody out there? Something, she saw something, and a rustling—footsteps?

"Okay, I don't care, Jimmy, don't take a bath," she says irritably. Her blouse is pulled out and wrinkled, her hair is all mussed, and she feels sweaty. There's about a million things she'd rather be doing than babysitting with these two. Three: at least the baby's sleeping. She knocks on the overturned endtable for luck, rights it, replaces the magazines and ashtrays. The one thing that really makes her sick is a dirty diaper. "Just go on to bed." "I don't have to go to bed until nine," he reminds her. Really, she couldn't care less. She turns up the volume on the TV, settles down on the couch, poking her blouse back into her skirt, pushing her hair out of her eyes. Jimmy and Bitsy watch from the floor. Maybe, once they're in bed, she'll take a quick bath. She wishes Jack would come by. The man, no doubt the spy, is following a woman, but she doesn't know why. The woman passes another man. Something seems to happen, but it's not clear what. She's probably already missed too much. The phone rings.

Mark is kissing her. Jack is under the blanket, easing her panties down over her squirming hips. Her hand is in his pants, pulling it out, pulling it toward her, pulling it hard. She knew just where it was! Mark is stripping, too. God, it's really happening! he thinks with a kind of pious joy, and notices the open door. "Hey! What's going on here?"

He soaps her back, smooth and slippery under his hand. She is doubled over, against her knees, between his legs. Her light brown hair, reaching to her gleaming shoulders, is wet at the edges. The soap slips, falls between his legs. He fishes for it, finds it, slips it behind him. "Help me find it," he whispers in her ear. "Sure Harry," says his host, going around behind him. "What'd you lose?"

Soon be nine, time to pack the kids off to bed. She clears the table, dumps paper plates and leftover hamburgers into the garbage, puts glasses and silverware into the sink, and the mayonnaise, mustard, and ketchup in the refrigerator. Neither child has eaten much supper finally, mostly potato chips and ice cream, but it's really not her problem. She glances at the books on the refrigerator. Not much chance she'll get to them, she's already pretty worn out. Maybe she'd feel better if she had a quick bath. She runs water into the tub, tosses in bubblebath salts, undresses. Before pushing down her panties, she stares for a moment at the smooth silken panel across her tummy, fingers the place where the opening would be if there were one. Then she steps quickly out of them, feeling somehow ashamed, unhooks her brassiere. She weighs her breasts in the palms of her hands, watching herself in the bathroom mirror, where, in the open window behind her, she sees a face. She screams.

She screams: "Jimmy! Give me that!" "What's the matter?" asks Jack on the other end. "Jimmy! Give me my towel! Right now!" "Hello? Hey, are you still there?" "I'm sorry, Jack," she says, panting. "You caught me in the tub. I'm just wrapped in a towel and these silly kids grabbed it away!" "Gee, I wish I'd been there!" "Jack—!" "To protect you, I mean." "Oh, sure," she says, giggling. "Well, what do you think, can I come over and watch TV with you?" "Well, not right this minute," she says. He laughs lightly. He feels very cool. "Jack?" "Yeah?" "Jack, I . . . I think there's somebody outside the window!"

She carries him, fighting all the way, to the tub, Bitsy pummeling her in the back and kicking her ankles. She can't hang on to him and undress him at the same time. "I'll throw you in, clothes and all, Jimmy Tucker!" she gasps. "You better not!" he cries. She sits on the toilet seat, locks her legs around him, whips his shirt up over his head before he knows what's happening. The pants are easier. Like all little boys his age, he has almost no hips at all. He hangs on desperately to his underpants, but when she succeeds in snapping these down out of his grip, too, he gives up, starts to bawl, and beats her wildly in the face with his fists. She ducks her head, laughing hysterically, oddly entranced by the spectacle of that pale little thing down there, bobbing and bouncing rubberily about with the boy's helpless fury and anguish.

"Aspirin? Whaddaya want aspirin for, Harry? I'm sure they got aspirin here, if you—" "Did I say aspirin? I meant, uh, my glasses. And, you know, I thought, well, I'd sorta check to see if everything was okay at home." Why the hell is it his mouth feels like it's got about six sets of teeth packed in there, and a tongue the size of that liverwurst his host's wife is passing around? "Whaddaya want your glasses for, Harry? I don't understand you at all!" "Aw, well, honey, I was feeling kind of dizzy or something, and I thought—" "Dizzy is right. If you want to check on the kids, why don't you just call on the phone?"

They can tell she's naked and about to get into the tub, but the bathroom window is frosted glass, and they can't see anything clearly. "I got an idea," Mark whispers. "One of us goes and calls her on the phone, and the other watches when she comes out." "Okay, but who calls?" "Both of us, we'll do it twice. Or more."

Down forbidden alleys. Into secret passageways. Unlocking the world's terrible secrets. Sudden shocks: a trapdoor! a fall! or the stunning report of a rifle shot, the *whaaii-ii-iing!* of the bullet biting concrete by your ear! Careful! Then edge forward once more, avoiding the light, inch at a time, now a quick dash for an open doorway—*look out!* there's a knife! a struggle! no! the long blade glistens! jerks! thrusts! *stabbed!* No, no, it missed! The assailant's down, yes! the spy's on top, pinning him, a terrific thrashing about, the spy rips off the assailant's mask: *a woman!*

Fumbling behind her, she finds it, wraps her hand around it, tugs. "Oh!" she gasps, pulling her hand back quickly, her ears turning crimson. "I . . . I thought it was the soap!" He squeezes her close between his thighs, pulls her back toward him, one hand sliding down her tummy between her legs. I Dream of Jeannie—"I have to go to the bathroom!" says someone outside the door.

She's combing her hair in the bathroom when the phone rings. She hurries to answer it before it wakes the baby. "Hello, Tuckers." There's no answer. "Hello?" A soft click. Strange. She feels suddenly alone in the big house, and goes in to watch TV with the children.

"Stop it!" she screams. "Please, stop!" She's on her hands and knees, trying to get up, but they're too strong for her. Mark holds her head down. "Now, baby, we're gonna teach you how to be a nice girl," he says coldly, and nods at Jack. When she's doubled over like that, her skirt rides up her thighs to the leg bands of her panties. "C'mon, man, go! This baby's cold! She needs your touch!"

Parks the car a couple blocks away. Slips up to the house, glances in his window. Just like he's expected. Her blouse is off and the kid's shirt is unbuttoned. He watches, while slowly, clumsily, childishly, they fumble with each other's clothes. My God, it takes them forever. "Some party!" "You said it!" When they're more or less naked, he walks in. "Hey! What's going on here?" They go white as bleu cheese. Haw haw! "What's the little thing you got sticking out there, boy?" "Harry, behave yourself!" No, he doesn't let the kid get dressed, he sends him home bareassed. "Bareassed!" He drinks to that. "Promises, promises," says his host's wife. "I'll mail you your clothes, son!" He gazes down on the naked little girl on his couch. "Looks like you and me, we got a little secret to keep, honey," he says coolly. "Less you wanna go home the same way your boyfriend did!" He chuckles at his easy wit, leans down over her, and unbuckles his belt. "Might as well make it two secrets, right?" "What in God's name are you talking about, Harry?" He staggers out of there, drink in hand, and goes to look for his car.

"Hey! What's going on here?" They huddle half-naked under the blanket, caught utterly unawares. On television: the clickety-click of frightened running feet on foreign pavements. Jack is fumbling for his shorts, tangled somehow around his ankles. The blanket is snatched away. "On your feet there!" Mr. Tucker, Mrs. Tucker, Mark's mom and dad, the police, the neighbors, everybody comes crowding in. Hopelessly, he has a terrific erection. So hard it hurts. Everybody stares down at it.

Bitsy's sleeping on the floor. The babysitter is taking a bath. For more than an hour now, he's had to use the bathroom. He doesn't know how much longer he can wait. Finally, he goes to knock on the bathroom door. "I have to use the bathroom." "Well, come ahead, if you have to." "Not while you're in there." She sighs loudly. "Okay, okay, just a minute," she says, "but you're a real nuisance, Jimmy!" He's holding on, pinching it as tight as he can. *"Hurry!"* He holds his breath, squeezing shut his eyes. No. Too late. At last, she opens the door. "Jimmy!" "I *told* you to hurry!" he sobs. She drags him into the bathroom and pulls his pants down.

He arrives just in time to see her emerge from the bathroom, wrapped in a towel, to answer the phone. His two kids sneak up behind her and pull the towel away. She's trying to hang onto the phone and get the towel back at the same time. It's quite a picture. She's got a sweet ass. Standing there in the bushes, pawing himself with one hand, he lifts his glass with the other and toasts her sweet ass, which his son now swats. Haw haw, maybe that boy's gonna shape up, after all.

They're in the bushes, arguing about their next move, when she comes out of the bathroom, wrapped in a towel. They can hear the baby crying. Then it stops. They see her running, naked, back to the bathroom like she's scared or something. "I'm going in after her, man, whether you're with me or not!" Mark whispers, and he starts out of the bushes. But just then, a light comes sweeping up through the yard, as a car swings in the drive. They hit the dirt, hearts pounding. "Is it the cops?" "I don't know!" "Do you think they saw us?" "Sshh!" A man comes staggering up the walk from the drive, a drink in his hand, stumbles on in the kitchen door and then straight into the bathroom. "It's Mr. Tucker!" Mark whispers. A scream. "Let's get outa here, man!"

9:00. Having missed most of the spy show anyway and having little else to do, the babysitter has washed the dishes and cleaned the kitchen up a little. The books on the refrigerator remind her of her better intentions, but she decides that first she'll see what's next on TV. In the livingroom, she finds little Bitsy sound asleep on the floor. She lifts her gently, carries her into her bed, and tucks her in. "Okay, Jimmy, it's nine o'clock, I've let you stay up, now be a good boy." Sullenly, his sleepy eyes glued still to the set, the boy backs out of the room toward his bedroom. A drama comes on. She switches channels. A ballgame and a murder mystery. She switches back to the drama. It's a love story of some kind. A man married to an aging invalid wife, but in love with a younger girl. "Use the bathroom and brush your teeth before going to bed, Jimmy!" she calls, but as quickly regrets it, for she hears the baby stir in its crib.

Two of them are talking about mothers they've salted away in rest homes. Oh boy, that's just wonderful, this is one helluva party. She leaves them to use the john, takes advantage of the retreat to ease her girdle down awhile, get a few good deep breaths. She has this picture of her three kids carting her off to a rest home. In a wheelbarrow. That sure is something to look forward to, all right. When she pulls her girdle back up, she can't seem to squeeze into it. The host looks in. "Hey, Dolly, are you all right?" "Yeah, I just can't get into my damn girdle, that's all." "Here, let me help."

She pulls them on, over her own, standing in front of the bedroom mirror, holding her skirt bundled up around the waist. About twenty sizes too big for her, of course. She pulls them tight from behind, runs her hand inside the opening in front, pulls out her thumb. "And what a good boy am I!" She giggles: how funny it must feel! Then, in the mirror, she sees him: in the doorway behind her, sullenly watching. "Jimmy! You're supposed to be in bed!" "Those are my daddy's!" the boy says. "I'm gonna tell!"

"Jimmy!" She drags him into the bathroom and pulls his pants down. "Even your shoes are wet! Get them off!" She soaps up a warm washcloth she's had with her in the bathtub, scrubs him from the waist down with it. Bitsy stands in the doorway, staring. "Get out! Get out!" the boy screams at his sister. "Go back to bed, Bitsy. It's just an accident." "Get out!" The baby wakes and starts to howl.

The young lover feels sorry for her rival, the invalid wife; she believes the man has a duty toward the poor woman and insists she is willing to wait. But the man argues that he also has a duty toward himself: his life, too, is short, and he could not love his wife now even were she well. He embraces the young girl feverishly; she twists away in anguish. The door opens. They stand there grinning, looking devilish, but pretty silly at the same time. "Jack! I thought I told you not to come!" She's angry, but she's also glad in a way: she was beginning to feel a little too alone in the big house, with the children all sleeping. She should have taken that bath, after all. "We just came by to see if you were being a good girl," Jack says and blushes. The boys glance at each other nervously.

She's just sunk down into the tubful of warm fragrant suds, ready for a nice long soaking, when the phone rings. Wrapping a towel around her, she goes to answer: no one there. But now the baby's awake and bawling. She wonders if that's Jack bothering her all the time. If it is, brother, that's the end. Maybe it's the end anyway. She tries to calm the baby with the half-empty bottle, not wanting to change it until she's finished her bath. The bathroom's where the diapers go dirty, and they make it stink to high heaven. "Shush, shush!" she whispers, rocking the crib. The towel slips away, leaving an airy empty tingle up and down her backside. Even before she stoops for the towel, even before she turns around, she knows there's somebody behind her.

"We just came by to see if you were being a good girl," Jack says, grinning down at her. She's flushed and silent, her mouth half open. "Lean over," says Mark amiably. "We'll soap your back, as long as we're here." But she just huddles there, down in the suds, staring up at them with big eyes.

"Hey! What's going on here?" It's Mr. Tucker, stumbling through the door with a drink in his hand. She looks up from the TV. "What's the matter, Mr. Tucker?" "Oh, uh, I'm sorry, I got lost—no, I mean, I had to get some aspirin. Excuse me!" And he rushes past her into the bathroom, caroming off the livingroom door jamb on the way. The baby wakes.

"Okay, get off her, Mr. Tucker!" "Jack!" she cries, "what are *you* doing here?" He stares hard at them a moment: so that's where it goes. Then, as Mr. Tucker swings heavily off, he leans into the bastard with a hard right to the belly. Next thing he knows, though, he's got a face full of an old man's fist. He's not sure, as the lights go out, if that's his girlfriend screaming or the baby. . . .

Her host pushes down on her fat fanny and tugs with all his might on her girdle, while she bawls on his shoulder: "I don't *wanna* go to a rest home!" "Now, now, take it easy, Dolly, nobody's gonna make you—" "Ouch! Hey, you're hurting!" "You should buy a bigger girdle, Dolly." "You're telling me?" Some other guy pokes his head in. "What-samatter? Dolly fall in?" "No, she fell out. Give me a hand."

By the time she's chased Jack and Mark out of there, she's lost track of the program she's been watching on television. There's another woman in the story now for some reason. That guy lives a very complicated life. Impatiently, she switches channels. She hates ballgames, so she settles for the murder mystery. She switches just in time, too: there's a dead man sprawled out on the floor of what looks like an office or a study or something. A heavyset detective gazes up from his crouch over the body: "He's been strangled." Maybe she'll take that bath, after all.

She drags him into the bathroom and pulls his pants down. She soaps up a warm washcloth she's had in the tub with her, but just as she reaches between his legs, it starts to spurt, spraying her arms and hands. "Oh, Jimmy! I thought you were done!" she cries, pulling him toward the toilet and aiming it into the bowl. How moist and rubbery it is! And you can turn it every which way. How funny it must feel!

"Stop it!" she screams. "Please stop!" She's on her hands and knees and Jack is holding her head down. "Now we're gonna teach you how to be a nice girl," Mark says and lifts her skirt. "Well, I'll be damned!" "What's the matter?" asks Jack, his heart pounding. "Look at this big pair of men's underpants she's got on!" "Those are my daddy's!" says Jimmy, watching them from the doorway. "I'm gonna tell!"

People are shooting at each other in the murder mystery, but she's so mixed up, she doesn't know which ones are the good guys. She switches back to the love story. Something seems to have happened, because now the man is kissing his invalid wife tenderly. Maybe she's finally dying. The baby wakes, begins to scream. Let it. She turns up the volume on the TV.

Leaning down over her, unbuckling his belt. It's all happening just like he's known it would. Beautiful! The kid is gone, though his pants, poor lad, remain. "Looks like you and me, we got a secret to keep, child!" But he's cramped on the couch and everything is too slippery and small. "Lift your legs up, honey. Put them around my back." But instead, she screams. He rolls off, crashing to the floor. There they all come, through the front door. On television, somebody is saying: "Am I a burden to you, darling?" "Dolly! My God! Dolly, I can explain . . .!"

The game of the night is Get Dolly Tucker Back in Her Girdle Again. They've got her down on her belly in the livingroom and the whole damn crowd is working on her. Several of them are stretching the girdle, while others try to jam the fat inside. "I think we made a couple inches on this side! Roll her over!" Harry?

She's just stepped into the tub, when the phone rings, waking the baby. She sinks down in the suds, trying not to hear. But that baby doesn't cry, it screams. Angrily, she wraps a towel around herself, stamps peevishly into the baby's room, just letting the phone jangle. She tosses the baby down on its back, unpins its diapers hastily, and gets yellowish baby stool all over her hands. Her towel drops away. She turns to find Jimmy staring at her like a little idiot. She slaps him in the face with her dirty hand, while the baby screams, the phone rings, and nagging voices argue on the TV. There are better things she might be doing.

What's happening? Now there's a young guy in it. Is he after the young girl or the old invalid? To tell the truth, it looks like he's after the same man the women are. In disgust, she switches channels. "The strangler again," growls the fat detective, hands on hips, staring down at the body of a half-naked girl. She's considering either switching back to the love story or taking a quick bath, when a hand suddenly clutches her mouth.

"You're both chicken," she says, staring up at them. "But what if Mr. Tucker comes home?" Mark asks nervously.

How did he get here? He's standing pissing in his own goddamn bathroom, his wife is still back at the party, the three of them are, like good kids, sitting in there in the livingroom watching TV. One of them is his host's boy Mark. "It's a good murder mystery, Mr. Tucker," Mark said, when he came staggering in on them a minute ago. "Sit still!" he shouted, "I'm just home for a moment!" Then whump thump on into the bathroom. Long hike for a weewee, Mister. But something keeps bothering him. Then it hits him: the girl's panties, hanging like a broken balloon from the rabbit-ear antennae on the TV! He barges back in there, giving his shoulder a helluva crack on the livingroom door jamb on the way—but they're not hanging there any more. Maybe he's only imagined it. "Hey, Mr. Tucker," Mark says flatly. "Your fly's open."

The baby's dirty. Stinks to high heaven. She hurries back to the livingroom, hearing sirens and gunshots. The detective is crouched outside a house, peering in. Already, she's completely lost. The baby screams at the top of its lungs. She turns up the volume. But it's all confused. She hurries back in there, claps an angry hand to the baby's mouth. "Shut up!" she cries. She throws the baby down on its back, starts to unpin the diaper, as the baby tunes up again. The phone rings. She answers it, one eye on the TV. "*What?*" The baby cries so hard it starts to choke. Let it. "I said, hi, this is Jack!" Then it hits her: oh no! the diaper pin!

"The aspirin . . ." But she's already in the tub. Way down in the tub. Staring at him through the water. Her tummy looks pale and ripply. He hears sirens, people on the porch.

Jimmy gets up to go to the bathroom and gets his face slapped and smeared with baby poop. Then she hauls him off to the bathroom, yanks off his pajamas, and throws him into the tub. That's okay, but next she gets naked and acts like she's gonna get in the tub, too. The baby's screaming and the phone's ringing like crazy and in walks his dad. Saved! he thinks, but, no, his dad grabs him right back out of the tub and whales the dickens out of him, no questions asked, while she watches, then sends him—*whack!*—back to bed. So he's lying there, wet and dirty and naked and sore, and he still has to go to the bathroom, and outside his window he hears two older guys talking. "Listen, you know where to do it if we get her pinned?" "No! Don't you?"

"Yo ho heave ho! *Ugh!*" Dolly's on her back and they're working on the belly side. Somebody got the great idea of buttering her down first. Not to lose the ground they've gained, they've shot it inside with a basting syringe. But now suddenly there's this big tug-of-war under way between those who want to stuff her in and those who want to let her out. Something rips, but she feels better. The odor of hot butter makes her think of movie theaters and popcorn. "Hey, has anybody seen Harry?" she asks. "Where's Harry?"

Somebody's getting chased. She switches back to the love story, and now the man's back kissing the young lover again. What's going on? She gives it up, decides to take a quick bath. She's just stepping into the tub, one foot in, one foot out, when Mr. Tucker walks in. "Oh, excuse me! I only wanted some aspirin . . ." She grabs for a towel, but he yanks it away. "Now, that's not how it's supposed to happen, child," he scolds. "Please! Mr. Tucker . . .!" He embraces her savagely, his calloused old hands clutching roughly at her backside. "Mr. Tucker!" she cries, squirming. "Your wife called—!" He's pushing something between her legs, hurting her. She slips, they both slip—something cold and hard slams her in the back, cracks her skull, she seems to be sinking into a sea. . . .

They've got her over the hassock, skirt up and pants down. "Give her a little lesson there, Jack baby!" The television lights flicker and flash over her glossy flesh. 1000 WHEN LIT. Whack! Slap! Bumper to bumper! He leans into her, feeling her come alive.

The phone rings, waking the baby. "Jack, is that you? Now, you listen to me—!" "No, dear, this is Mrs. Tucker. Isn't the TV awfully loud?" "Oh, I'm sorry, Mrs. Tucker! I've been getting—" "I tried to call you before, but I couldn't hang on. To the phone, I mean. I'm sorry, dear." "Just a minute, Mrs. Tucker, the baby's—" "Honey, listen! Is Harry there? Is Mr. Tucker there, dear?"

"Stop it!" she screams and claps a hand over the baby's mouth. "Stop it! Stop it! *Stop it!*" Her other hand is full of baby stool and she's afraid she's going to be sick. The phone rings. "No!" she cries. She's hanging on to the baby, leaning woozily away, listening to the phone ring. "Okay, okay," she sighs, getting ahold of herself. But when she lets go of the baby, it isn't screaming any more. She shakes it. Oh no. . . .

"Hello?" No answer. Strange. She hangs up and, wrapped only in a towel, stares out the window at the cold face staring in—she screams!

She screams, scaring the hell out of him. He leaps out of the tub, glances up at the window she's gaping at just in time to see two faces duck away, then slips on the bathroom tiles, and crashes to his ass, whacking his head on the sink on the way down. She stares down at him, trembling, a towel over her narrow shoulders. "Mr. Tucker! Mr. Tucker, are you all right . . .?" Who's Sorry Now? Yessir, who's back is breaking with each . . . He stares up at the little tufted locus of all his woes, and passes out, dreaming of Jeannie . . .

The phone rings. "Dolly! It's for you!" "Hello?" "Hello, Mrs. Tucker?" "Yes, speaking." "Mrs. Tucker, this is the police calling . . ."

It's cramped and awkward and slippery, but he's pretty sure he got it in her, once anyway. When he gets the suds out of his eyes, he sees her staring up at them. Through the water. "Hey, Mark! Let her up!"

Down in the suds. Feeling sleepy. The phone rings, startling her. Wrapped in a towel, she goes to answer. "No, he's not here, Mrs. Tucker." Strange. Married people act pretty funny sometimes. The baby is awake and screaming. Dirty, a real mess. Oh boy, there's a lot of things she'd rather be doing than babysitting in this madhouse. She decides to wash the baby off in her own bathwater. She removes her towel, unplugs the tub, lowers the water level so the baby can sit. Glancing back over her shoulder, she sees Jimmy staring at her. "Go back to bed, Jimmy!" "I have to go to the bathroom." "Good grief, Jimmy! It looks like you already have!" The phone rings. She doesn't bother with the towel—what can Jimmy see he hasn't already seen?—and goes to answer. "No, Jack, and that's final." Sirens, on the TV, as the police move in. But wasn't that the channel with the love story? Ambulance maybe. Get this over with so she can at least catch the news. "Get those wet pajamas off, Jimmy, and I'll find clean ones. Maybe you better get in the tub, too." "I think something's wrong with the baby," he says. "It's down in the water and it's not swimming or anything."

She's staring up at them from the rug. They slap her. Nothing happens. "You just tilted her, man!" Mark says softly. "We gotta get outta here!" Two little kids are standing wide-eyed in the doorway. Mark looks hard at Jack. "No, Mark, they're just little kids . . .!" "We gotta, man, or we're dead."

"Dolly! My God! Dolly, I can explain!" She glowers down at them, her ripped girdle around her ankles. "What the four of you are doing in the bathtub with *my* babysitter?" she says sourly. "I can hardly wait!"

Police sirens wail, lights flash. "I heard the scream!" somebody shouts. "There were two boys!" "I saw a man!" "She was running with the baby!" "My God!" somebody screams, "they're *all* dead!" Crowds come running. Spotlights probe the bushes.

"Harry, where the hell you been?" his wife whines, glaring blearily up at him from the carpet. "I can explain," he says. "Hey, whatsamatter, Harry?" his host asks, smeared with butter for some goddamn reason. "You look like you just seen a ghost!" Where did he leave his drink? Everybody's laughing, everybody except Dolly, whose cheeks are streaked with tears. "Hey, Harry, you won't let them take me to a rest home, will you, Harry?"

10:00. The dishes done, children to bed, her books read, she watches the news on television. Sleepy. The man's voice is gentle, soothing. She dozes—awakes with a start: a babysitter? Did the announcer say something about a babysitter?

"Just want to catch the weather," the host says, switching on the TV. Most of the guests are leaving, but the Tuckers stay to watch the news. As it comes on, the announcer is saying something about a babysitter. The host switches channels. "They got a better weatherman on four," he explains. "Wait!" says Mrs. Tucker. "There was something about a babysitter . . .!" The host switches back. "Details have not yet been released by the police," the announcer says. "Harry, maybe we'd better go. . . ."

They stroll casually out of the drugstore, run into a buddy of theirs. "Hey! Did you hear about the babysitter?" the guy asks. Mark grunts, glances at Jack. "Got a smoke?" he asks the guy.

"I think I hear the baby screaming!" Mrs. Tucker cries, running across the lawn from the drive.

She wakes, startled, to find Mr. Tucker hovering over her. "I must have dozed off!" she exclaims. "Did you hear the news about the babysitter?" Mrs. Tucker asks. "Part of it," she says, rising. "Too bad, wasn't it?" Mr. Tucker is watching the report of the ball scores and golf tournaments. "I'll drive you home in just a minute, dear," he says. "Why, how nice!" Mrs. Tucker exclaims from the kitchen. "The dishes are all done!"

"What can I say, Dolly?" the host says with a sigh, twisting the buttered strands of her ripped girdle between his fingers. "Your children are murdered, your husband gone, a corpse in your bathtub, and your house is wrecked. I'm sorry. But what can I say?" On the TV, the news is over, and they're selling aspirin. "Hell, *I* don't know," she says. "Let's see what's on the late late movie."

JOHN UPDIKE

When Everyone Was Pregnant

I'm in securities, but I read a lot, on the train. Read yesterday that the Fifties were coming back. All through the Sixties writers kept knocking them: Eisenhower, Lester Lanin, skirts below the knee, ho-hum. Well, turns out Eisenhower was a great non-war President. Rock is dead. Skirts have dropped to the ankle. But *my* Fifties won't come back.

Kind years to me. Entered them poor and left them comfortable. Entered them chaste and left them a father. Of four and a miscarriage. Those the years when everyone was pregnant. Not only kind but beautiful years.

How they would float across the sand like billowed sails. My wife and the wives of our friends. Shakespeare, Titania to Oberon: "laughed to see the sails conceive, And grow big-bellied with the wanton wind." In their sun-paled plaid maternity bathing suits, the pregnant young women. Tugging behind them the toddlers already born. Dinghies. Moved to a town with a beach in '54: my first promotion, Nancy's second child.

Coming along the water's edge, heads higher than the line of the sea. The horizon blue, sparkling, severe. Proust and the "little band" at Balbec. Yet more fully in flower than those, bellies swollen stately. Faces and limbs freckled in every hollow, burnished on the ball of the shoulder, the tip of the nose. Sunburned nostril-wings, peeling. The light in their eyes stealing sparkle from the far hard edge of the sea. Where a few sails showed, leaning, curling.

They would come up to us, join us. Laughter, aluminum chairs, towels, infant sun hats, baby-food jars, thermoses chuckling in the straw hampers. Above me, edge of maternity skirt lifted by touch of wind, curl of pubic hair high inside thigh showed. Sickening sensation of love. Sand-warmed wind blowing cool out of the future.

They would settle with us, forming a ring. Their heads inward with gossip, their bare legs spokes of a wheel. On the rim, children with sandpails each digging by the feet of his own mother. The shades of sand darkening as they dug. The milk smell of sun lotion. The way our words drifted up and out: sandwich wrappers blowing.

Katharine, Sarah, Liz, Peggy, Angela, June. Notes of a scale, colors of a rainbow. Nancy the seventh. Now in the Seventies two have moved. To Denver, to Birmingham. Two are divorced. Two still among us with their husbands. But all are gone, receding. Can never be revisited, that time when everyone was pregnant guiltlessly.

Guiltlessness. Our fat Fifties cars, how we loved them, revved them: no thought of pollution. Exhaust smoke, cigarette smoke, factory smoke, all romantic. Romance of consumption at its height. Shopping for baby food in the gaudy trash of the supermarkets. Purchasing power: young, newly powerful, born to consume. To procreate greedily. A smug conviction that the world was doomed. Beyond the sparkling horizon, an absolute enemy. Above us, bombs whose flash would fill the scene like a cup to overflowing.

Old slides. June's husband had a Kodak with a flash attachment (nobody owned Japanese cameras then). How young we were. The men scrawny as boys. Laughable military haircuts: the pea-brain look. The women with bangs and lipsticked smiles. We look drunk. Sometimes we were.

Jobs, houses, spouses of our own. Permission to drink and change diapers and operate power mowers and stay up past midnight. At college Nancy had not been allowed to smoke upstairs, made herself do it in our home. Like a sexual practice personally distasteful but recommended by Van der Velde. Dreadful freedom. Phrase fashionable then.

Had we expected to starve in the Depression? Be bayonetted by Japs when they invaded California? Korea seemed the best bargain we could strike: extremities of superpowers tactfully clashing in distant cold mud. The world's skin of fear shivered but held. Then came Eisenhower and gave us a precarious peace and a sluggishly rising market and a (revokable) license to have fun, to make babies. Viewed the world through two lenses since discarded: fear and gratitude. Young people now are many things but they aren't afraid, and aren't grateful.

Those summer parties. Should remember them better. Sunlight in the gin, the sprig of mint wilting. The smell of grass freshly mowed coming in through the evening screens. Children wandering in and out with complaints their mothers brushed away like cigarette smoke. What were we saying? The words we spoke were nonsense except the breath we took to speak them was life—us alive, able.

Katharine's husband Jerry had only one eye, the other frosted by childhood accident. No one felt sorry for him, too healthy, hearty. Born salesman. Him saying across to Sarah Harris, her pregnant in a big-flowered dress, sitting dreaming in a plush wing chair, "Sarah, sitting there you look just like a voluptuous big piece of wallpaper!" I thought, *has only one eye, everything looks flat to him.* Sickening sensation of love.

Years later I said to Sarah "You voluptuous piece of wallpaper you" but she had forgotten and I had to explain.

Another night, my flat tire in the Connellys' newly gravelled driveway. Sharp bluestones. Two in the morning. Ed came up out of his cellar holding high a cruciform lug wrench chanting Veni Creator Spiritus. Shocked me. My own footsteps on the gravel, *unch, unch.* A monster coming closer. Most of us at least sent the kids to Sunday school.

Dancing. Hand squeezes. Moonlight songs, smoke getting in your eyes. All innocent enough. The bump, bump of pregnant bellies against me. Seeing each other's names in the Birth column of the local paper a private joke. Hospital visits, wifeless nights. The time our fourth was born, night after the first storm of winter. Gynecologist swung by for her in his car on the way to the hospital. Just starting up practice, handsome man in ski hat. On the stark white empty street below our window looked like a lover tossing pebbles. Her contractions coming every three minutes, her little suitcase, hurrying from room to room kissing the children in their sleep. Gynecologist waiting, his face turned upward in the moonlight, in the silence. A lover howling.

Nervous of the creaking wind I slept one or two of those nights with a golf club in the bed. I think a seven iron. Figured I could get it around on a burglar quicker than a wood.

The time Sarah was with me. Nancy off in the hospital with varicose veins. Diagnosis: no more babies. Our last baby cried. Sarah rose and mothered it. Child went silent, laughed, knew something was funny, maybe thought Sarah was Nancy making a face, pretending something. Same smell, woman smell, same safety. Mullioned moonlight on Sarah's bare shoulders, bent over crib. Baby gurgled and laughed. "Crazy kid you have here." Too much love. Too many babies, breathing all over the dark house like searchlights that might switch on.

Sarah's lovely wide shoulders, big hips, breasts shallow and firm. First time I saw them it tore at me, exclaimed she had breasts like a Greek statue. She laughed and told me I read too much. But it had been torn out of me.

The ritual of taking out Nancy's hairpins one by one before making love. Rain on the roof. Fifties a house decade, never ventured into the streets. Cuba, Sputnik, Tibet. Rain on the roof.

The brown line on her belly a woman brings back from the hospital, after being pregnant. Nobody had ever told me that line existed. Why hadn't they?

The babies got bigger. The parties got wilder. Time at the beach, after Cancer dance, hot summer, might have been 1960. We took off our clothes and swam. Scary tide, strong moon, could see the women had aged. Slack bellies, knees and faces full of shadow. Used their long gauzy dance dresses as towels, wrapped around them as sarongs. Over the ocean, riots. Assassinations, protests, a decade's overdue bills heaped like surf thunder on the sand bar. We were no longer young. Embarrassed. Groped for our underclothes and shoes. Yet the warm kiss of wind off of sand, even at night.

I make some notes on the train. My hand shakes. My town slides by, the other comfortable small towns, the pastures and glimpses of sea, a single horse galloping, a golf course with a dawn foursome frozen on the green, dew-white, and then the lesser cities, the little one-hotel disgruntled cities, black walls hurled like fists at our windows, broken factory windows, a rusted drawbridge halted forever at almost-down, a gravel yard with bluestones pyramided by size, a dump smoldering, trash gaudy with all the colors of jewels; then the metropolis, the tracks multiplying in lightning calculations, the hazed skyscrapers changing relationship to one another like the steeples in Proust, the tunnels of billboards, the station, vast and derelict; the final stop. This evening, the same thing backwards.

But never get bored with how the train slices straight. Lightly rocking. Through intersections of warning bells tingling, past playgrounds and back yards, warehouses built on a bias to fit the right-of-way. Like time. Cuts sleepwalking through everything.

Notes not come to anything. Lives not come to anything. Life a common stock that fluctuates in value. But you cannot sell, you must hold, hold till it dips to nothing. The big boys sell you out.

Edgar to blinded Gloucester: Ripeness is all. Have never exactly understood. Ripeness is all that is left? Or, deeper and more hopeful, ripeness is all that matters? Encloses all, answers all, justifies all. Ripeness is God.

Now: our babies drive cars, push pot, shave, menstruate, riot for peace, eat macrobiotic. Wonderful in many ways, but not ours, never ours, we see now. Now: we go to a party and see only enemies. Fifteen shared years have made us wary, survival-conscious. Sarah looks away. Spokes of the wheel are missing. Our babies accuse us.

Did the Fifties exist? Voluptuous wallpaper. Crazy kid. Sickening sensation of love. The train slides forward. The decades slide seaward, taking us along. I am still afraid. Still grateful.

RICHARD BRAUTIGAN

Revenge of the Lawn

My grandmother, in her own way, shines like a beacon down the stormy American past. She was a bootlegger in a little county up in the state of Washington. She was also a handsome woman, close to six feet tall who carried 190 pounds in the grand operatic manner of the early 1900s. And her specialty was bourbon, a little raw but a welcomed refreshment in those Volstead Act days.

She of course was no female Al Capone, but her bootlegging feats were the cornucopia of legend in her neck of the woods, as they say. She had the county in her pocket for years. The sheriff used to call her up every morning and give her the weather report and tell her how the chickens were laying.

I can imagine her talking to the sheriff: "Well, Sheriff, I hope your mother gets better soon. I had a cold and a bad sore throat last week myself. I've still got the sniffles. Tell her hello for me and to drop by the next time she's down this way. And if you want that case, you can pick it up or I can have it sent over as soon as Jack gets back with the car.

"No, I don't know if I'm going to the firemen's ball this year, but you know that my heart is with the firemen. If you don't see me there tonight, you tell the boys that. No, I'll try to get there, but I'm still not fully recovered from my cold. It kind of climbs on me in the evening."

My grandmother lived in a three-story house that was old even in those days. There was a pear tree in the front yard which was heavily eroded by rain from years of not having any lawn.

The picket fence that once enclosed the lawn was gone, too, and people just drove their cars right up to the porch. In the winter the front yard was a mud hole and in the summer it was hard as a rock.

Jack used to curse the front yard as if it were a living thing. He was the man who lived with my grandmother for thirty years. He was not my grandfather, but an Italian who came down the road one day selling lots in Florida.

He was selling a vision of eternal oranges and sunshine door to door in a land where people ate apples and it rained a lot.

Jack stopped at my grandmother's house to sell her a lot just a stone's throw from downtown Miami, and he was delivering her whiskey a week later. He stayed for thirty years and Florida went on without him.

Jack hated the front yard because he thought it was against him. There had been a beautiful lawn there when Jack came along, but he let it wander off into nothing. He refused to water it or take care of it in any way.

Now the ground was so hard that it gave his car flat tires in the summer. The yard was always finding a nail to put in one of his tires or the car was always sinking out of sight in the winter when the rains came on.

The lawn had belonged to my grandfather who lived out the end of his life in an insane asylum. It had been his pride and joy and was said to be the place where his powers came from.

My grandfather was a minor Washington mystic who in 1911 prophesied the exact date when World War I would start: June 28, 1914, but it had been too much for him. He never got to enjoy the fruit of his labor because they had to put him away in 1913 and he spent seventeen years in the state insane asylum believing he was a child and it was actually May 3, 1872.

He believed that he was six years old and it was a cloudy day about to rain and his mother was baking a chocolate cake. It stayed May 3, 1872 for my grandfather until he died in 1930. It took seventeen years for that chocolate cake to be baked.

There was a photograph of my grandfather. I look a great deal like him. The only difference being that I am over six feet tall and he was not quite five feet tall. He had a dark idea that being so short, so close to the earth and his lawn would help to prophesy the exact date when World War I would start.

It was a shame that the war started without him. If only he could have held back his childhood for another year, avoided that chocolate cake, all of his dreams would have come true.

There were always two large dents in my grandmother's house that had never been repaired and one of them came about this way: In the autumn the pears would get ripe on the tree in the front yard and the pears would fall on the ground and rot and bees would gather by the hundreds to swarm on them.

The bees somewhere along the line had picked up the habit of stinging Jack two or three times a year. They would sting him in the most ingenious ways.

Once a bee got in his wallet and he went down to the store to buy some food for dinner, not knowing the mischief that he carried in his pocket.

He took out his wallet to pay for the food.

"That will be 72 cents," the grocer said.

"AAAAAAAAAAAAAAAAAAAAAA!" Jack replied, looking down to see a bee busy stinging him on the little finger.

The first large dent in the house was brought about by still another bee landing on Jack's cigar as he was driving the car into the front yard that peary autumn the stock market crashed.

The bee ran down the cigar, Jack could only stare at it cross-eyed in terror, and stung him on the upper lip. His reaction to this was to drive the car immediately into the house.

That front yard had quite a history after Jack let the lawn go to hell. One day in 1932 Jack was off running an errand or delivering something for my grandmother. She wanted to dump the old mash and get a new batch going.

Because Jack was gone, she decided to do it herself. Grandmother put on a pair of railroad overalls that she used for working around the still and filled a wheelbarrow with mash and dumped it out in the front yard.

She had a flock of snow-white geese that roamed outside the house and nested in the garage that had not been used to park the car since the time Jack had come along selling futures in Florida.

Jack had some kind of idea that it was all wrong for a car to have a house. I think it was something that he had learned in the Old Country. The answer was in Italian because that was the only language Jack used when he talked about the garage. For everything else he used English, but it was only Italian for the garage.

After Grandmother had dumped the mash on the ground near the pear tree, she went back to the still down in the basement and the geese all gathered around the mash and started talking it over.

I guess they came to a mutually agreeable decision because they all started eating the mash. As they ate the mash their eyes got brighter and brighter and their voices, in appreciation of the mash, got louder and louder.

After a while one of the geese stuck his head in the mash and forgot to take it out. Another one of the geese cackled madly and tried to stand on one leg and give a W. C. Fields imitation of a stork. He maintained that position for about a minute before he fell on his tail feathers.

My grandmother found them all lying around the mash in the positions that they had fallen. They looked as if they had been machine-gunned. From the height of her operatic splendor she thought they were all dead.

She responded to this by plucking all their feathers and piling their bald bodies in the wheelbarrow and wheeling them down to the basement. She had to make five trips to accommodate them.

She stacked them like cordwood near the still and waited for Jack to return and dispose of them in a way that would provide a goose for dinner and a small profit by selling the rest of the flock in town. She went upstairs to take a nap after finishing with the still.

It was about an hour later that the geese woke up. They had devastating hangovers. They had all kind of gathered themselves uselessly to their feet when suddenly one of the geese noticed that he did not have any feathers. He informed the other geese of their condition, too. They were all in despair.

They paraded out of the basement in a forlorn and wobbly gang. They were all standing in a cluster near the pear tree when Jack drove into the front yard.

The memory of the time he had been stung on the mouth by that bee must have come back to his mind when he saw the defeathered geese standing there, because suddenly like a madman he tore out the cigar he had stuck in his mouth and threw it away from him as hard as he could. This caused his hand to travel through the windshield. A feat that cost him thirty-two stitches.

The geese stood by staring on like some helpless, primitive American advertisement for aspirin under the pear tree as Jack drove his car into the house for the second and last time in the Twentieth Century.

The first time I remember anything in life occurred in my grandmother's front yard. The year was either 1936 or 1937. I remember a man, probably Jack, cutting down the pear tree and soaking it with kerosene.

It looked strange, even for a first memory of life, to watch a man pour gallons and gallons of kerosene all over a tree lying stretched out thirty feet or so on the ground, and then to set fire to it while the fruit was still green on the branches.

ELLEN GILCHRIST

Victory Over Japan

When I was in the third grade I knew a boy who had to have fourteen shots in the stomach as the result of a squirrel bite. Every day at two o'clock they would come to get him. A hush would fall on the room. We would all look down at our desks while he left the room between Mr. Harmon and his mother. Mr. Harmon was the principal. That's how important Billy Monday's tragedy was.

Mr. Harmon came along in case Billy threw a fit. Every day we waited to see if he would throw a fit but he never did. He just put his books away and left the room with his head hanging down on his chest and Mr. Harmon and his mother guiding him along between them like a boat.

"Would you go with them like that?" I asked Letitia at recess. Letitia was my best friend. Usually we played girls chase the boys at recess or pushed each other on the swings or hung upside down on the monkey bars so Joe Franke and Bobby Saxacorn could see our underpants but Billy's shots had even taken the fun out of recess. Now we sat around on the fire escape and talked about rabies instead.

"Why don't they put him to sleep first?" Letitia said. "I'd make them put me to sleep."

"They can't," I said. "They can't put you to sleep unless they operate."

"My father could," she said. "He owns the hospital. He could put me to sleep." She was always saying things like that but I let her be my best friend anyway.

"They couldn't give them to me," I said. "I'd run away to Florida and be a beachcomber."

"Then you'd get rabies," Letitia said. "You'd be foaming at the mouth."

"I'd take a chance. You don't always get it." We moved closer together, caught up in the horror of it. I was thinking about the Livingstons' bulldog. I'd had some close calls with it lately.

"It was a pet," Letitia said. "His brother was keeping it for a pet."

It was noon recess. Billy Monday was sitting on a bench by the swings. Just sitting there. Not talking to anybody. Waiting for two o'clock, a small washed-out-looking boy that nobody paid any attention to until he got bit. He never talked to anybody. He could hardly even read. When Mrs. Jansma asked him to read his head would fall all the way over to the side of his neck. Then he would read a few sentences with her having to tell him half the words. No one would ever have picked him out to be the center of a rabies tragedy. He was more the type to fall in a well or get sucked down the drain at the swimming pool.

Fourteen days. Fourteen shots. It was spring when it happened and the schoolroom windows were open all day long and every afternoon after Billy left we had milk from little waxy cartons and Mrs. Jansma would read us chapters from a wonderful book about some children in England that had a bed that took them places at night. There we were, eating graham crackers and listening to stories while Billy was strapped to the table in Doctor Finley's office waiting for his shot.

"I can't stand to think about it," Letitia said. "It makes me so sick I could puke."

"I'm going over there and talk to him right now," I said. "I'm going to interview him for the paper." I had been the only one in the third grade to get anything in the Horace Mann paper. I got in with a story about how Mr. Harmon was shell-shocked in the First World War. I was on the lookout for another story that good.

I got up, smoothed down my skirt, walked over to the bench where Billy was sitting and held out a vial of cinnamon toothpicks. "You want one," I said. "Go ahead. She won't care." It was against the rules to bring cinnamon toothpicks to Horace Mann. They were afraid someone would swallow one.

"I don't think so," he said. "I don't need any."

"Go on," I said. "They're really good. They've been soaking all week."

"I don't want any," he said.

"You want me to push you on the swings?"

"I don't know," he said. "I don't think so."

"If it was my brother's squirrel, I'd kill it," I said. "I'd cut its head off."

"It got away," he said. "It's gone."

"What's it like when they give them to you?" I said. "Does it hurt very much?"

"I don't know," he said. "I don't look." His head was starting to slip down onto his chest. He was rolling up like a ball.

"I know how to hypnotize people," I said. "You want me to hypnotize you so you can't feel it?"

"I don't know," he said. He had pulled his legs up on the bench. Now his chin was so far down into his chest I could barely hear him talk. Part of me wanted to give him a shove and see if he would roll. I touched him on the shoulder instead. I could feel his little bones beneath his shirt. I could smell his washed-out rusty smell. His head went all the way down under his knees. Over his shoulder I saw Mrs. Jansma headed our way.

"Rhoda," she called out. "I need you to clean off the blackboards before we go back in. Will you be a sweet girl and do that for me?"

"I wasn't doing anything but talking to him," I said. She was beside us now and had gathered him into her wide sleeves. He was starting to cry, making little strangled noises like a goat.

"Well, my goodness, that was nice of you to try to cheer Billy up. Now go see about those blackboards for me, will you?"

I went on in and cleaned off the blackboards and beat the erasers together out the window, watching the chalk dust settle into the bricks. Down below I could see Mrs. Jansma still holding on to Billy. He was hanging on to her like a spider but it looked like he had quit crying.

That afternoon a lady from the PTA came to talk to us about the paper drive. "One more time," she was saying. "We've licked the Krauts. Now all we have left is the Japs. Who's going to help?" she shouted.

"I am," I shouted back. I was the first one on my feet.

"Who do you want for a partner?" she said.

"Billy Monday," I said, pointing at him. He looked up at me as though I had asked him to swim the English Channel, then his head slid down on the desk.

"All right," Mrs. Jansma said. "Rhoda Manning and Billy Monday. Team number one. To cover Washington and Sycamore from Calvin Boulevard to Conner Street. Who else?"

"Bobby and me," Joe Franke called out. He was wearing his coonskin cap, even though it was as hot as summer. How I loved him! "We want downtown," he shouted. "We want Dirkson Street to the river."

"Done," Mrs. Jansma said. JoEllen Scaggs was writing it all down on the blackboard. By the time Billy's mother and Mr. Harmon came to get him the paper drive was all arranged.

"See you tomorrow," I called out as Billy left the room. "Don't forget. Don't be late."

When I got home that afternoon I told my mother I had volunteered to let Billy be my partner. She was so proud of me she made me some cookies even though I was supposed to be on a diet. I took the cookies and a pillow and climbed up into my treehouse to read a book. I was getting to be more like my mother every day. My mother was a saint. She fed hoboes and played the organ at early communion even if she was sick and gave away her ration stamps to anyone that needed them. She had only had one pair of new shoes the whole war.

I was getting more like her every day. I was the only one in the third grade that would have picked Billy Monday to help with a paper drive. He probably couldn't even pick up a stack of papers. He probably couldn't even help pull the wagon.

I bet this is the happiest day of her life, I was thinking. I was lying in my treehouse watching her. She was sitting on the back steps putting liquid hose on her legs. She was waiting for the Episcopal minister to come by for a drink. He'd been coming by a lot since my daddy was overseas. That was just like my mother. To be best friends with a minister.

"She picked out a boy that's been sick to help her on the paper drive," I heard her tell him later. "I think it helped a lot to get her to lose weight. It was smart of you to see that was the problem."

"There isn't anything I wouldn't do for you, Ariane," he said. "You say the word and I'll be here to do it."

I got a few more cookies and went back up into the treehouse to finish my book. I could read all kinds of books. I could read Book-of-the-Month Club books. The one I was reading now was called *Cakes and Ale.* It wasn't coming along too well.

I settled down with my back against the tree, turning the pages, looking for the good parts. Inside the house my mother was bragging on me. Above my head a golden sun beat down out of a blue sky. All around the silver maple leaves moved in the breeze. I went back to my book. "She put her arms around my neck and pressed her lips against mine. I forgot my wrath. I only thought of her beauty and her enveloping kindness.

" 'You must take me as I am, you know,' she whispered.

" 'All right,' I said."

Saturday was not going to be a good day for a paper drive. The sky was gray and overcast. By the time we lined up on the Horace Mann playground with our wagons a light rain was falling.

"Our boys are fighting in rain and snow and whatever the heavens send," Mr. Harmon was saying. He was standing on the bleachers wearing an old baseball shirt and a cap. I had never seen him in anything but his gray suit. He looked more shell-shocked than ever in his cap.

"They're working over there. We're working over here. The Germans are defeated. Only the Japs left to go. There're canvas tarps from Gentilly's Hardware, so take one to cover your papers. All right now. One grade at a time. And remember, Mrs. Winchester's third grade is still ahead by seventy-eight pounds. So you're going to have to go some to beat that. Get to your stations now. Get ready, get set, go. Everybody working together . . ."

Billy and I started off. I was pulling the wagon, he was walking along beside me. I had meant to wait awhile before I started interviewing him but I started right in.

"Are you going to have to leave to go get it?" I said.

"Go get what?"

"You know. Your shot."

"I got it this morning. I already had it."

"Where do they put it in?"

"I don't know," he said. "I don't look."

"Well, you can feel it, can't you?" I said. "Like, do they stick it in your navel or what?"

"It's higher than that."

"How long does it take? To get it."

"I don't know," he said. "Till they get through."

"Well, at least you aren't going to get rabies. At least you won't be foaming at the mouth. I guess you're glad about that." I had stopped in front of a house and was looking up the path to the door. We had come to the end of Sycamore, where our territory began.

"Are you going to be the one to ask them?" he said.

"Sure," I said. "You want to come to the door with me?"

"I'll wait," he said. "I'll just wait."

We filled the wagon by the second block. We took that load back to the school and started out again. On the second trip we hit an attic with bundles of the *Kansas City Star* tied up with string. It took us all afternoon to haul that. Mrs. Jansma said she'd never seen anyone as lucky on a paper drive as Billy and I. Our whole class was having a good day. It looked like we might beat everybody, even the sixth grade.

"Let's go out one more time," Mrs. Jansma said. "One more trip before dark. Be sure and hit all the houses you missed."

Billy and I started back down Sycamore. It was growing dark. I untied my Brownie Scout sweater from around my waist and put it on and pulled the sleeves down over my wrists. "Let's try that brick house on the corner," I said. "They might be home by now." It was an old house set back on a high lawn. It looked like a house where old people lived. I had noticed old people were the ones who saved things. "Come on," I said. "You go to the door with me. I'm tired of doing it by myself."

He came along behind me and we walked up to the door and rang the bell. No one answered for a long time although I could hear footsteps and saw someone pass by a window. I rang the bell again.

A man came to the door. A thin man about my father's age.

"We're collecting papers for Horace Mann School," I said. "For the war effort."

"You got any papers we can have?" Billy said. It was the first time he had spoken to anyone but me all day. "For the war," he added.

"There're some things in the basement if you want to go down there and get them," the man said. He turned a light on in the hall and we followed him into a high-ceilinged foyer with a set of winding stairs going up to another floor. It smelled musty, like my grandmother's house in Clarksville. Billy was right beside me, sticking as close as a burr. We followed the man through the kitchen and down a flight of stairs to the basement.

"You can have whatever you find down here," he said. "There're papers and magazines in that corner. Take whatever you can carry."

There was a large stack of magazines. Magazines were the best thing you could find. They weighed three times as much as newspapers.

"Come on," I said to Billy. "Let's fill the wagon. This will put us over the top for sure." I picked up a bundle and started up the stairs. I went in and out several times carrying as many as I could at a time. On the third trip Billy met me at the foot of the stairs. "Rhoda," he said. "Come here. Come look at this."

He took me to an old table in a corner of the basement. It was a walnut table with grapes carved on the side and feet like lion's feet. He laid one of the magazines down on the table and opened it. It was a photograph of a naked little girl, a girl smaller than I was. He turned the page. Two naked boys were standing together with their legs twined. He kept turning the pages. It was all the same. Naked children on every page. I had never seen a naked boy. Much less a photograph of one. Billy looked up at me. He turned another page. Five naked little girls were grouped together around a fountain.

"Let's get out of here," I said. "Come on. I'm getting out of here."

I headed for the stairs with him right behind me. We didn't even close the basement door. We didn't even stop to say thank you.

The magazines we had collected were in bundles. About a block from the house we stopped on a corner, breathless from running. "Let's see if there're any more," I said. We tore open a bundle. The first magazine had pictures of naked grown people on every page.

"What are we going to do?" he said.

"We're going to throw them away," I answered, and started throwing them into the nandina bushes by the Hancock's vacant lot. We threw them into the nandina bushes and into the ditch that runs into Mills Creek. We threw the last ones into a culvert and then we took our wagon and got on out of there. At the corner of Sycamore and Wesley we went our separate ways.

"Well, at least you'll have something to think about tomorrow when you get your shot," I said.

"I guess so," he replied.

"Look here, Billy. I don't want you to tell anyone about those magazines. You understand?"

"I won't." His head was going down again.

"I mean it, Billy."

He raised his head and looked at me as if he had just remembered something he was thinking about. "I won't," he said. "Are you really going to write about me in the paper?"

"Of course I am. I said I was, didn't I? I'm going to do it tonight."

I walked on home. Past the corner where the Scout hikes met. Down the alley where I found the card shuffler and the Japanese fan. Past the yard where the violets grew. I was thinking about the boys with their legs twined. They looked like earthworms, all naked like that. They looked like something might fly down and eat them. It made me sick to think about it and I stopped by Mrs. Alford's and picked a few iris to take home to my mother.

Billy finished getting his shots. And I wrote the article and of course they put it on page one. BE ON THE LOOKOUT FOR MAD SQUIRREL, the headline read. By Rhoda Katherine Manning. Grade 3.

> We didn't even know it was mean, the person it bit said. That person is in the third grade at our school. His name is William Monday. On April

> 23 he had his last shot. Mrs. Jansma's class had a cake and gave him a pencil set. Billy Monday is all right now and things are back to normal.
>
> I think it should be against the law to keep dangerous pets or dogs where they can get out and get people. If you see a dog or squirrel acting funny go in the house and stay there.

I never did get around to telling my mother about those magazines. I kept meaning to but there never seemed to be anywhere to start. One day in August I tried to tell her. I had been to the swimming pool and I thought I saw the man from the brick house drive by in a car. I was pretty sure it was him. As he turned the corner he looked at me. *He looked right at my face.* I stood very still, my heart pounding inside my chest, my hands as cold and wet as a frog, the smell of swimming pool chlorine rising from my skin. What if he found out where I lived? What if he followed me home and killed me to keep me from telling on him? I was terrified. At any moment the car might return. He might grab me and put me in the car and take me off and kill me. I threw my bathing suit and towel down on the sidewalk and started running. I ran down Linden Street and turned into the alley behind Calvin Boulevard, running as fast as I could. I ran down the alley and into my yard and up my steps and into my house looking for my mother to tell her about it.

She was in the living room, with Father Kenniman and Mr. and Mrs. DuVal. They lived across the street and had a gold star in their window. Warrene, our cook, was there. And Connie Barksdale, our cousin who was visiting from the Delta. Her husband had been killed on Corregidor and she would come up and stay with my mother whenever she couldn't take it anymore. They were all in the living room gathered around the radio.

"Momma," I said. "I saw this man that gave me some magazines . . ."

"Be quite, Rhoda," she said. "We're listening to the news. Something's happened. We think maybe we've won the war." There were tears in her eyes. She gave me a little hug, then turned back to the radio. It was a wonderful radio with a magic eye that glowed in the dark. At night when we had blackouts Dudley and I would get into bed with my mother and we would listen to it together, the magic eye glowing in the dark like an emerald.

Now the radio was bringing important news to Seymour, Indiana. Strange, confused, hush-hush news that said we had a bomb bigger than any bomb ever made and we had already dropped it on Japan and half of Japan was sinking into the sea. Now the Japs had to surrender. Now they couldn't come to Indiana and stick bamboo up our fingernails. Now it would all be over and my father would come home.

The grown people kept on listening to the radio, getting up every now and then to get drinks or fix each other sandwiches. Dudley was sitting beside my mother in a white shirt acting like he was twenty years old. He always did that when company came. No one was paying any attention to me.

Finally I went upstairs and lay down on the bed to think things over. My father was coming home. I didn't know how to feel about that. He was always yelling at someone when he was home. He was always yelling at my mother to make me mind.

"What do you mean, you can't catch her," I could hear him yelling. "Hit her with a broom. Hit her with a table. Hit her with a chair. But, for God's sake, Ariane, don't let her talk to you that way."

Well, maybe it would take a while for him to get home. First they had to finish off Japan. First they had to sink the other half into the sea. I curled up in my soft old eiderdown comforter. I was feeling great. We had dropped the biggest bomb in the world on Japan and there were plenty more where that one came from.

I fell asleep in the hot sweaty silkiness of the comforter. I was dreaming I was at the wheel of an airplane carrying the bomb to Japan. Hit 'em, I was yelling. Hit 'em with a mountain. Hit 'em with a table. Hit 'em with a chair. Off we go into the wild blue yonder, climbing high into the sky. I dropped one on the brick house where the bad man lived, then took off for Japan. Down we dive, spouting a flame from under. Off with one hell of a roar. We live in flame. Buckle down in flame. For nothing can stop the Army Air Corps. Hit 'em with a table, I was yelling. Hit 'em with a broom. Hit 'em with a bomb. Hit 'em with a chair.

FRANK CONROY

Midair

A sunny, windy day on the lower East Side of New York. The year is 1942. Sean, aged six, is being more or less pulled along the sidewalk by his father, who has shown up from nowhere to take him home from school. Sean tries to keep the pace, although he does not remember the last time he has seen this big, exuberant man, nor is he altogether sure that he trusts him. Mary, on the other side, is nine. Her legs are longer, and she seems happy, skipping every now and then, shouting into the wind, calling him Daddy. Sean cannot hear what they're saying except in fragments—the wind tears at the words. His hand, wrist, and part of his forearm are enclosed in his father's fist. The big man strides along, red-faced, chin jutting forward proudly, his whole carriage suggesting the eagerness and confidence of a soldier marching forward to receive some important, hard-won medal.

He is not a soldier, as Sean's mother has recently explained. He is not in the Army (although a war is going on) but in something called a rest home, where people go in order to rest. He does not seem tired, Sean thinks.

"It'll be a different story now, by God," his father says as they turn the corner onto Seventh Street. "A completely different story." Energy seems to radiate from the man like an electrical charge. His body carries a pale-blue corona, and when he speaks his white teeth give off white lightning. "What a day!" He lets go of the children's hands and makes a sweeping gesture. "An absolute pip of a day. Look at that blue sky! The clouds! Seventh Street! Look how vivid the colors are!"

Sean cannot look. He is preoccupied with the unnatural force of his father's enthusiasm. It is as if all that has been pointed out is too far away to be seen. The boy's awareness is focussed on the small bubble of space immediately surrounding himself, his father, and his sister. Within that area he sees clearly—as if his life depended on it—and there is no part of him left over to see anything else.

They reach the tenement building and climb the stoop. His father hesitates at the door.

"The key," he says.

"Mother has it," Mary says.

"You haven't got it?" He rolls his head in exasperation.

"I'm sorry." Mary is afraid she has failed him. "I'm sorry, Daddy."

Sean is uneasy with her use of the word "Daddy." It sounds strange, since they never use it. It is not part of their domestic vocabulary. On those extremely rare occasions when Sean, Mary, and their mother ever mention the man, the word they have always used is "Father."

Mrs. Rosenblum, second floor rear, emerges from the house.

"Good morning," his father says, smiling, catching the door. "In you go, children."

Mrs. Rosenblum has never seen this big man before but recognizes, from his expensive clothes and confident manner, that he is a gentleman, and the father of the children. A quick glance at Mary, smiling as he touches her head, confirms everything.

"Nice," Mrs. Rosenblum says. "Very nice."

Inside, Sean's father takes the steps two at a time. The children follow up to the top floor—the fourth—and find him standing at the door to the apartment, trying the knob.

"No key here, either, I suppose."

"It's the same one," Mary says.

He gives the door a hard push, as if testing. Then he steps back, looks around, and notices the iron ladder leading up to the hatch and the roof.

"Aha! More than one way to skin a cat." He strides over to the ladder and begins to climb. "Follow me, buckos. Up the mainmast!"

"Daddy, what are you doing?" Mary cries.

"We'll use the fire escape." He pushes up the hatch and sunlight pours down. "Come on. It's fun!"

Sean can hear the wind whistling up there as his father climbs through. Mary hesitates an instant and then mounts the ladder. As she approaches the top, Sean follows her. He ascends into the sunshine and the wind.

The big man moves rapidly across the tarred roof to the rear of the building and the twin hoops of the fire-escape railing. He shouts back at the children, but his words are lost. He beckons, turns, and grabs the railings. His feet go over the edge and he begins to descend. Then he stops—his head and shoulders visible—and shouts again. Mary moves forward, the big man sinks out of sight, and Sean follows.

The boy steps to the edge and looks over. His father is ten feet below, on the fire-escape landing, red face upturned.

"Come on!" The white teeth flash. "The window's open."

The wind whips Mary's skirt around her knees as she goes over. She has to stop and push the hair out of her eyes. When she reaches the landing below, Sean grabs the hoops. Five floors down, a sheet of newspaper flutters across the cement at the bottom of the airshaft. It seems no bigger than a page from a book. He climbs down. Pigeons rise from the airshaft and scatter. On the landing, he sees his father, already inside, lifting Mary through the kitchen window. He follows quickly on his own.

The kitchen, although entirely familiar in every detail, seems slightly odd in its totality. The abruptness of the entry—without the usual preparation of the other rooms—tinges the scene with unreality. Sean follows his father and sister through the kitchen, into the hall, and to the doorway of his mother's room. His father does not enter but simply stops and looks.

"Have you been here before?" Sean asks.

"Of course he has, silly," Mary says rapidly.

His father turns. "Don't you remember?"

"I don't think so," Sean says.

As they pass the main door to the apartment, toward the front of the hall, his father pauses to slip on the chain lock.

For more than an hour they have been rearranging the books on the living-room shelves, putting them in alphabetical order by author. Sean's father stops every now and then, with some favorite book, to do a dramatic reading. The readings become more and more dramatic. He leans down to the children to emphasize the dialogue, shouting in different voices, gesticulating with his free arm in the air, making faces. But then, abruptly, his mood changes.

"The windows are filthy," he says angrily, striding back and forth from one to another, peering at the glass. The books are forgotten now as he goes to the kitchen. Mary quickly pushes them over to the foot of the bookcase. Sean helps. While doing this, they look very quickly, almost furtively, into each other's eyes. It takes a fraction of a second, but Sean understands. He is aware that his father's unexplained abandonment of an activity in which he had appeared to be so deeply involved has frightened Mary. His own feelings are complex—he is gratified that she is scared, since in his opinion she should have been scared all along, while at the same time his own fear, because of hers, escalates a notch.

"What's going to happen?" Sean asks quietly.

"Nothing. It's O.K." She pretends not to be afraid.

"Get Mother." The sound of water running in the kitchen.

Mary considers this. "It's O.K. She'll come home from work the way she always does."

"That's a long time. That's too long."

The big man returns with a bucket and some rags. His face seems even more flushed. "We'll do it ourselves. Wait till you see the difference." He moves to the central window, and they are drawn in his wake. Sean recognizes a shift in the atmosphere: before, with the books, there was at least a pretense of the three of them doing something together—a game they might all enjoy—but now his father's attention has narrowed and intensified onto the question of the windows. He seems barely aware of the children.

He washes the panes with rapid, sweeping movements. Then he opens the lower frame, bends through, turns, and sits on the sill to do the outside. Sean can see his father's face, concentrated, frowning, eyes searching the glass for streaks.

Sean begins to move backward.

"No," Mary says quickly. "We have to stay."

The boy stops beside the rocking chair where his mother sits after dinner.

The big man reënters, and steps back to regard the results of his work. "Much better. Much, much better." He moves on to the next window. "Fresh water, Mary. Take the bucket."

Mary obeys, and goes back to the kitchen.

The big man stares down at the street. Sean stays by the rocking chair.

"You don't remember," the big man says. "Well, that's all right. Time is different for children. In any case, the past is behind us now. What counts is the future." He gives a short, barking laugh. "Another cliché rediscovered! But that's the way it is. You have to penetrate the clichés, you have to live them out to find out how true they are. What a joke!"

Mary brings the bucket of water to his side. Suddenly he moves closer to the window. He has seen something on the street.

"God damn." He moves back rapidly. He turns and runs down the hall to the kitchen. Sean and Mary can see him closing and locking the rear windows. "Bastards!" he shouts.

Mary moves sideways to glance through the window to the street.

"What is it?" Sean asks.

"An ambulance." Her voice is beginning to quaver. "It must be that ambulance."

Now he comes back into the living room and paces. Then he rushes to the newly washed window, opens it, and tears the gauzy curtains from the rod and throws them aside. Sean can see Mary flinch as the curtains are torn. The big man moves from one window to the next, opening them and tearing away the curtains. Wind rushes through the room. Torn curtains rise from the floor and swirl about.

He gathers the children and sits down on the couch, his arms around their shoulders. Sean feels crushed and tries to adjust his position, but his father only tightens his grip. The big man is breathing fast, staring into the hall, at the door.

"Daddy," Mary says. "It hurts."

A slight release of pressure, but Sean is still held so tightly to the man's side he can barely move.

"Oh, the bastards," his father says. "The tricky bastards."

The buzzer sounds. Then, after a moment, a knock on the door. The big man's grip tightens.

Another knock. The sound of a key. Sean watches the door open a few inches until the chain pulls it short. He sees the glint of an eye.

"Mr. Kennedy? This is Dr. Silverman. Would you open the door, please?"

"Alone, are you, Doctor?" An almost lighthearted tone.

A moment's pause. "No. I have Bob and James here with me." A calm voice, reassuring to Sean. "Please let us in."

"The goon squad," his father says.

"Bob in particular is very concerned. And so am I."

"Bob is a Judas."

"Mr. Kennedy. Be reasonable. We've been through this before, after all."

"No, no." As if correcting a slow student. "This is different. I'm through with you people. I'm through with all of that. I've come home, I'm here with my children, and I'm going to stay."

A pause. "Yes. I can see the children."

"We've been having a fine time. We've been washing the windows, Doctor." An almost inaudible chuckle.

"Mr. Kennedy, I implore you to open the door. We simply must come in. We must discuss your plans."

"I'm not going to open the door. And neither are you. What we have here, Doctor, is a Mexican standoff. Do you get my meaning?"

"I'm very sorry to hear you say that." Another pause—longer this time. "Bob would like a word with you."

"Mr. Kennedy? This is Bob." A younger voice.

"I'm not coming back, Bob. Don't try any crap with me. I know why you're here."

"I'm worried about you. You're flying. You know that."

"Got the little white jacket, eh, Bob? The one with the funny sleeves?"

"Look, if you don't come back they'll assign me to Mr. Farnsworth. You wouldn't do that to me. Please."

"Cut the crap, Bob."

"Listen. I'm with you. You know that. I mean, how many times have we talked about your—"

A tremendous crash as the door is kicked in, the frame splintering where the chain has come away. Sean is aware that things are happening very fast now, and yet he can see it all with remarkable clarity. Wood chips drift lazily through the air. Three men rush through the door—two in white uniforms, one in ordinary clothes. He knows they are running toward the couch as fast as they can—their faces frozen masks of strain—but time itself seems to have slowed down.

Still clamped to his father's side, Sean feels himself rise up into the air. He sees his father's other hand make a grab for Mary, who is trying to escape. He gets hold of her hair, but she twists away with a yell. Sean feels betrayed that she has gotten away. She was the one calling him Daddy. The wind roars as the big man rushes to the window and climbs out on the sill.

"Stop where you are!" he shouts back at the men.

Sean cannot see, but he senses that the men have stopped. He can hear Mary crying, hear the wind, and hear the sound of his father's heart racing under the rough tweed of his jacket. He stares down at the street, at the cracks in the sidewalk. With the very limited motion available to his arms, he finds his father's belt and hangs on with both fists.

"You bastards," his father shouts. "What you don't realize is I can do anything. Anything!"

Something akin to sleepiness comes over Sean. As time passes he realizes—a message from a distant outpost—that he has soiled himself. Finally, they are pulled back in, with great speed and strength, and fall to the floor. His father screams as the men cover him.

In college, his father long dead, and all memory of his father's visit in 1942 completely buried, Sean looks for a wife. He is convinced that if he doesn't find someone before he graduates, he will have missed his chance for all time. The idea of living alone terrifies him, although he is not aware that it terrifies him. He lives as if he did not have a past, and so there is a great deal about himself of which he is not aware. He is entirely ignorant of his lack of awareness, and believes himself to be in full control of his existence. He zeroes in on a bright, rather guarded girl he meets in Humanities 301, and devotes himself to winning her hand. It is a long campaign, and the odds are against him—her family disapproves vehemently, for reasons that are never made clear, and she is more intelligent than Sean, and ambitious, in a way he is not, for power in some as yet unnamed career. She is older than he is. She is not afraid of living alone. Yet in the end his tenacity prevails. Graduate school provides no route for her ambition, she drifts for a bit, and finally capitulates over the telephone. Sean is exultant.

They are married by a judge in her parents' midtown brownstone. Sean is six feet two inches tall, weighs a hundred and thirty-three pounds, and appears, with his Irish, slightly acned face, to be all of seventeen. (He is actually twenty-two.) His wife is struck by the irony of the fact that more than half of the relatives watching the event are divorced. Sean is impressed by the activity outside the window during the ceremony. The New York Foundling Hospital is being torn down—the wrecker's ball exploding walls even as the absurdly short judge drones on. For both of them—in a moment of lucidity whose importance they are too young to recognize—the ceremony is anticlimactic, and faintly ridiculous.

Four years pass, and nothing happens. They both have a small monthly income from trust funds. She dabbles in an occasional project or temporary job but always retreats in mysterious frustration to the safety of their apartment. He writes a book, but it contains nothing, since he knows very little about people, or himself. He remains a boy; the marriage that was to launch him into maturity serves instead to extend his boyhood. Husband and wife, they remain children. They live together in good will, oddly sealed off from one another, and from the world. He dreams of people jumping out of windows, holding hands, in eerie accord. He has no idea what the dreams mean, or where they come from. She confesses that she has never believed in romantic love. They are both frightened of the outside, but they respond differently. She feels that what is out there is too dangerous to fool with. He feels that, however dangerous, it is only out there that strength can be found. In some vague, inchoate way, he knows he needs strength.

Privately, without telling him, she decides to have children. Philip is born. John is born. Sean is exultant.

A summer night in 1966. Sean drives down from Harlem, where he has gotten drunk in a jazz club. The bouncer, an old acquaintance, has sold him an ounce of marijuana. Sean carries it in a sealed envelope in his back pocket. He turns off the Henry Hudson Parkway at Ninety-sixth Street, slips along Riverside Drive for a couple of blocks, turns, and pulls up in front of Judy's house. It's a strange little building—five floors with a turret up the side, a dormer window on her top-floor apartment, bits of crenellation and decoration, like some miniature castle. A Rapunzel house.

He had met her on the sidelines during a soccer game. Kneeling on the grass, he had turned his head to follow the fullback's kick, and found himself looking instead at the slender, blue-jeaned thigh of the girl standing next to him. Perhaps it was the suddenness, the abrupt nearness of the splendid curve of her backside, the images sinking into him before he had time to protect himself. The lust he felt was so pure it seemed, for all its power, magically innocent, and he got to his feet and began talking to her. (She was eventually to disappear into medical school, but never, as it turned out, from his memory.)

He stares up at the dark window. Behind the window is a room, and in the room a bed, in which for a year he has been making love to Judy. She is gone now, away for a month, driving around France in a *deux-chevaux* Citroën leased by him as a gift. The room is dark and empty, and yet he has to go in. He does not question the urge. He simply gets out of the car and approaches the building. Once he is in motion, a kind of heat suffuses him. He experiences something like tunnel vision.

Inside, he scans the mailboxes. A few letters are visible behind the grille in hers. He opens the door with his key and runs up the stairs—turning at landings, climbing, turning, climbing, until he is there, at the top floor. It is midnight, and the building is silent. He slips the key into the lock, turns and pushes. The door will not open. He has forgotten the police lock, the iron bar she'd had installed before she left—with a separate locking mechanism. He doesn't have that key. He leans against the door for a moment, and the faint scent of the room inside reaches him. He is dizzy with the scent, and the door suddenly enrages him. The scent is inside, and he must get inside.

He pounds his shoulder against the glossy black wood in a steady rhythm, putting all his weight against it. The door shakes in its hinges, but he can feel the solidity of the iron bar in the center. There is not an iota of movement in the bar. He moves back in the hallway—halfway to the rear apartment—runs forward, raises his right leg, and kicks the central panel of the door. A terrific crash, but the door does not yield. He continues to run and kick, in a frenzy, until he starts falling down.

Out of breath, he sits on the stairs to the roof and looks at Judy's door. He cannot believe there is no way to get it open. The wood is cracked in several places. Finally, as his breathing slows, he gives up. The iron bar will never move.

Slowly, swirling like smoke, an idea emerges. He turns and looks up the stairs, into the darkness. After a moment he stands up, mounts the stairs, opens the hatch, and climbs out onto the roof. The air cools him—he is drenched with sweat. Purple sky. Stars. He crosses the flat part of the roof to the front of the building, where it suddenly drops off in a steep slope—a Rapunzel roof, tiled with overlapping slate. There is a masonry ridge, perhaps an inch high, at the bottom edge, fifteen feet down. He moves sideways until he comes to a place he estimates lies directly above the dormer window. He gets down on his belly and carefully slides his legs over onto the tiles, lowering more and more of himself onto the steep incline, testing to see if he can control his downward motion. Sufficient control seems possible, and, very slowly, he releases his grip on the roof and begins to slide. His face presses against the slate, and he can feel the sweat from his cheek on the slate. From somewhere off toward Amsterdam Avenue comes the sound of a siren.

He descends blindly and stops when his toes touch the ridge. Beyond the ridge, there is empty space and a clear drop to the sidewalk, but he is unafraid. He remains motionless for several moments, and his noisy brain falls still. He is no longer drunk. A profound calm prevails, a sense of peacefulness—as sweet, to him, as water to some traveller in the desert. Carefully, he slides down sideways until his entire body lies along the ridge. He raises his head and looks at the deserted street below—the pools of light under the street lamps, the tops of the parked cars, the square patterns of the cracks in the sidewalk—and there is a cleanness and orderliness to things. He becomes aware that there is a reality that lies behind the appearance of the world, a pure reality he has never sensed before, and the knowledge fills him with gratitude.

He moves his head farther out and looks for the dormer window. There it is. He had thought to hang on to the edge of the roof and swing himself down and into the window. In his mind, it had been a perfectly straightforward procedure. In his mind, he had known he could do anything—anything he was capable of imagining. But now, as he looks at the dormer window—too far away, full of tricky angles—he sees that the plan is impossible. He immediately discards the plan, as if he had been caught up in a story that ended abruptly. He no longer has any interest in getting into the apartment.

Moving slowly and carefully, as calm in his soul as the calmness in the great purple sky above him, he retreats. Using the friction of his arms and legs, of his damp palms and the sides of his shoes, he inches his way up the sloping roof. He reaches the top of the building.

Once inside, he closes the roof door behind him and descends rapidly. He passes the door to the apartment without a glance.

As his children are born, Sean begins to write a book about his past. At first he is ebullient, possessed by gaiety. He doesn't remember much—his childhood all jumbled, without chronology. There are only isolated scenes, places, sights and sounds, moods, in no apparent order. It seems a small thing to write down these floating memories, to play with them at a distance. It seems like fun.

His children, simply by coming into the world, have got him started. As the work gets difficult, the fact of his children sustains him in some roundabout fashion. His gaiety changes to a mood of taut attentiveness, as the past he had trivialized with his amnesia begins, with tantalizing slowness, to reveal itself. He knows hard work for the first time in his life, and he is grateful. Soon he finds himself in a kind of trance; after hours of writing he will look down at a page or two with a sense of awe, because the work is better than anything he could reasonably have expected of himself. He will live this way for four years. In his mind, his writing, his ability to write at all, is connected to his children.

He develops a habit of going into their room late at night. Blue light from the street lamp outside angles through the large windows to spill on the waxed wooden floor. Philip is three, sleeping on his side, his small hand holding a rubber frog. Sean crosses the room and looks at John, aged two. Behind delicate eyelids, his eyes move in a dream. Sean goes to a spot equidistant from both beds and sits down on the floor, his legs folded. He stares at the pale-blue bars of light on the floor and listens. He hears the children breathe. When they move, he hears them move. His mind clears. After half an hour he gets up, adjusts their blankets, and goes to bed.

At a small dinner party with his wife, in Manhattan, he becomes aware that the host and hostess are tense and abstracted. The hostess apologizes and explains that she should have cancelled the dinner. There had been a tragedy that afternoon. The young couple living directly above, on the eighth floor, had left a window open, and their baby girl had somehow pulled herself up and fallen through to her death.

"You're white as a ghost," his wife says as they leave the table. "Sean, you're trembling!"

They forgo coffee, with apologies, and go home immediately. Sean drives fast, parks by a hydrant, and runs up the stoop into the house.

"It's O.K., it's O.K.," his wife says.

He nods to the sitter in the living room and keeps on going, up the stairs, to the children's room. They are asleep, safe in their beds.

"We have to get guardrails," he says, going to the windows, locking them. "Bars—those things—whatever they are."

"Yes. We will," his wife whispers. "O.K."

"All the windows. Front and back."

"Yes, yes. Don't wake them, now."

That night he must sleep in their room.

Sean lies full length in the oversize bathtub, hot water to his chin. When he comes home from work (he writes in a small office a mile away), he almost always takes a bath. Philip and John push the door open and rush, stark naked, to the tub. They're about to be put to bed, but they've escaped. Sean doesn't move. Philip's head and shoulders are visible, while John, shorter, shows only his head. Their faces are solemn. Sean stares into their clear, intelligent eyes—so near—and waits, showing no expression, so as to draw the moment out. The sight of them is a profound refreshment.

"Do it, Daddy," Philip says.

"Do what?"

"The noise. When you wash your face."

Sean rises to a sitting position. He washes his face, and then rinses by bending forward and lifting cupped handfuls of water. He simultaneously blows and moans into the handfuls of water, making a satisfying noise. The boys smile. The drama of Daddy-in-the-bath fascinates them. They can't get enough of it.

Sean reaches out and lifts first one and then the other over the edge and into the tub. His hands encompass their small chests, and he can feel the life in them. The boys laugh and splash about, slippery as pink seals fresh from the womb. They hang on his neck and slide over his chest.

His wife comes in and pulls them up, into towels. They go off to bed. Later, in the kitchen, she says, "I wish you wouldn't do that."

"What?"

"In the bath like that."

He is nonplussed. "Good heavens. Why not?"

"It could scare them."

"But they love it!"

"It's icky."

"Icky," he repeats. He goes to the refrigerator for some ice. He can feel the anger starting, his face beginning to flush. He makes a drink and goes into the living room. The anger mounts as he hears the sounds of her working in the kitchen, making dinner. Abruptly, he puts down his drink, goes into the hall, down the stairs, and out the front door. He spends the evening in a bar frequented by writers and returns home drunk at three in the morning.

A few years later, Sean drives home from the office. He has worked late, missed dinner. He thinks about his boys, and begins to weep. He pulls off the expressway and parks in the darkness by the docks. It occurs to him that he is in bad trouble. The weeping has come out of nowhere, to overwhelm him, like some exotic physical reflex, and it could as well have happened on the street or in a restaurant. There is more pressure in him than he can control, or even gauge, his pretenses to the contrary notwithstanding. As he calms down, he allows himself to face the fact that his wife has begun to prepare for the end: a whisper of discreet activity—ice-skating with a male friend on weekends, veiled references to an unknown future, a certain coyness around the house. When he goes, he will have to leave the children. He starts the car, and the boys are in his mind; he feels the weight of their souls in his mind.

He unlocks the front door of the house, hangs his coat in the closet, and climbs the stairs. Silence. A fire burns in the fireplace in the empty living room. The kitchen and dining room are empty. He moves along the landing and starts up the second flight of stairs.

"Daddy." Philip is out of sight in his bedroom, but his voice is clear, his tone direct, as if they'd been talking together, as if they were in the middle of a conversation.

"I'm coming." Sean wonders why the house is so quiet. His wife must be up in the attic. John must be asleep.

"Why were you crying?" Philip asks.

Sean stops at the top of the stairs. His first thought is not how the boy knows but if the knowledge has scared him. He goes into the room, and there is Philip, wide awake, kneeling at the foot of his bed, an expectant look on his face.

"Hi." Sean can see the boy is not alarmed. Curious, focussed, but not scared.

"Why?" the boy asks. He is six years old.

"Grownups cry sometimes, you know. It's O.K."

The boy takes it in, still waiting.

"I'm not sure," Sean says. "It's complicated. Probably a lot of things. But it's O.K. I feel better now."

"That's good."

Sean senses the boy's relief. He sits down on the floor. "How did you know I was crying?" He has never felt as close to another human being as he does at this moment. His tone is deliberately casual.

The boy starts to answer, his intelligent face eager, animated. Sean watches the clearly marked stages: First, Philip draws a breath to begin speaking. He is confident. Second, he searches for language to frame what he knows, but, to his puzzlement, it isn't there. Third, he realizes he can't answer the question. He stares into the middle distance for several moments. Sean waits, but he has seen it all in the boy's face.

"I don't know," the boy says. "I just knew."

"I understand."

After a while the boy gives a sudden large yawn, and gets under the covers. Sean goes downstairs.

The time arrives when he must tell the boys he is going away. Philip is eight, and John almost seven. They go up into the attic playroom. Sean masks the storm in his heart and explains that no one in the family is at fault. He has no choice—he must leave, and not live in the house anymore. As he says this, the boys glance quickly at each other—almost furtively—and Sean feels a special sharp, mysterious pang.

Twelve years later, Sean stands on line at Gate 6 in Boston's Logan Airport, waiting to check in for Eastern's 7:45 A.M. flight to Philadelphia. He is gray-haired, a bit thick around the middle, wears reading glasses low on his nose, and walks, as he moves closer to the desk, with a slight limp, from a cartilage operation on his right knee. He wears a dark suit and a trenchcoat, and carries a soft canvas overnight bag hanging from his shoulder.

"Morning." The attendant is a black woman with whom he has checked in every Monday morning for the last two years. "It's nowhere near full," she says. "I'll upgrade you now." Sean commutes weekly between the two cities, and the airline has provided him with a special card. When first class is not full, he gets a first-class seat at no extra charge. She hands him his boarding pass, and he nods as he moves away.

He sits down and waits for the boarding call. Businessmen surround him, two military officers, three stewardesses, a student carrying a book bag from the university in Boston where Sean teaches. He doesn't recognize the student but watches him abstractedly. Philip and John are that age now. Sean recalls that when his boys entered college, in Washington and Chicago, he found himself easing up on his own students in Boston, softening his style despite himself.

The flight is called. He surrenders his ticket and moves down the enclosed walkway to the open door of the plane. The stewardess recognizes him and takes his coat. He settles down in seat 2-A and accepts a cup of coffee. The ritual is familiar and reassuring. Sean is at ease.

It had not always been thus. When he'd begun commuting, Sean was tense in the air. It had been difficult for him to look out the window without a flash of panic. In his fear, he was abnormally sensitive to the other passengers—controlling his anger at loud conversations, conscious of any intrusion, however minute, into the space allotted to him. Expansive people irritated him the most. He could not abide the way they threw their elbows about, or thoughtlessly stretched their legs, or clumsily bumped into his seat. He found himself hating the other passengers, cataloguing their faults like a miser counting money. But eventually, as he got used to flying, he began to recognize the oddness, the almost pathological oddness of his hatred, and it went away. Only on very rough flights did it recur.

Now he can gaze down through miles of empty space without fear. He wonders why, and concludes that both his former fear of heights and his present lack of fear are inexplicable. The stewardess brings breakfast, and his right knee cracks painfully as he adjusts his position.

The tenth summer of Sunday softball. The game Sean helped to organize had become a tradition in the town of Siasconset. Philip and John began as small boys and grew to young men playing the infield. Sean's second wife had taken pictures from the start, and the effect was that of time-lapse photography—a collapsed history in which the father grew older, the sons grew taller and stronger, and everyone else stayed more or less the same. Sean stood on the mound with a one-run lead, runner at first, and two outs. The batter was Gino, a power hitter. Sean threw an inside pitch and watched Gino's hips come around, watched the bat come around, and heard the snap of solid contact. The ball disappeared in speed toward third base. Sean turned to see John frozen in the air, impossibly high off the ground, feet together, toes pointed down, his legs and torso perfectly aligned in a smooth curve, a continuous brushstroke, his long arm pointing straight up at full extension, and there, nestled deep in the pocket of his glove, the white ball. Sean gave a shout of joy, dimly aware of pain in his knee, shouting all the way down as he fell, twisting, utterly happy, numb with pleasure.

The stewardess clears away his breakfast. Below, New York City slips past. He finds the old neighborhood, even the street, but he can't make out the house where his first wife still lives. They have retained good relations, and talk on the phone every month or so. His second, younger wife approves of the first, and vice versa. Sean is absurdly proud of this.

"Do you ever dream about me?" he had once asked her on the phone. "I mean, do I ever appear in your dreams?"

Slightly taken aback, she had laughed nervously. "No. What an odd question."

"I only ask because you crop up in mine. What is it—eleven years now, twelve? You still show up now and then."

The plane lands smoothly at the Philadelphia airport. Looping his bag over his shoulder, Sean is out the door, through the building, and into a cab.

"Downtown. The Drexler Building."

In his late forties, to his amazement, and through a process he never completely understood, the board of the Drexler Foundation had asked him to direct that part of their organization which gave money to the arts. It is work he enjoys.

He pays the driver and stares up at the Drexler Building—seventy stories of glass reflecting the clouds, the sky. Pushing through the big revolving door, he crosses the lobby, quickening his step as he sees the express elevator ready to leave. He jumps through just as the doors close behind him, pushes the button for the sixty-fifth floor, and turns.

For a split second he is disoriented. Philip, his older son, stands before him on the other side of the elevator, facing front. Sean's heart lurches, and then he sees that it is a young man of Philip's age, size, and general appearance, delivering a large envelope to Glidden & Glidden, on sixty-four. For a moment the two ideas overlap—the idea of Philip and the idea of the young man—and in that moment time seems to slow down. It is as if Sean had seen his son across a supernatural barrier—as if he, Sean, were a ghost haunting the elevator, able to see the real body of his son but unable to be seen by him. An almost unbearable sadness comes over him. As he emerges from this illusion, he knows full well that his son is hundreds of miles away at college, and yet he finds within himself a pressure of love for the young man so great it is all he can do to remain silent. The elevator ascends, and Sean regains control of himself. Now he can see the young man clearly—alert, a little edgy, clear blue eyes, a bit of acne.

"I hate elevators," the young man says, his eyes fixed on the lights above the door indicating the floors.

"I'm not crazy about them, but it beats walking."

The elevator approaches sixty-four, but then the lights go out, the emergency light comes on, and it stops between sixty-three and sixty-four. A slight bump downward. Sean grabs the rail involuntarily. Under the flat white light of the emergency bulb, the young man is pale, gaunt-looking.

"Oh my God," he says.

They fall a few feet more.

The young man presses himself into a corner. His eyes are wild.

Sean is utterly calm.

"Oh God oh God oh God." The young man's voice begins to rise.

"This has happened to me several times," Sean lies. "In Chicago. Once in Baltimore. The elevators have brakes, non-electrical, separate from all the other systems, which automatically engage if the elevator exceeds a certain speed." This, he thinks, is the truth. "Do you understand what I'm saying?"

The young man's mouth is open, as if to scream. He looks in all directions, finally at Sean.

"It can't fall. It can't. Do you understand?"

"Yes." The young man swallows hard.

"We're perfectly safe."

Sean watches the young man as several minutes go by. He remains silent, remembering his own panic in airplanes, his own need for privacy on those occasions, guessing that the boy feels likewise. After another minute, however, he can see the fear rising again in the young man's face. Sean shrugs off his bag and crosses the space between them.

"Listen," he says quietly, "it's going to be O.K."

The young man is breathing fast. He stares at Sean without seeing him. Sean reaches out and takes the young man's head in his hands.

"I want you to listen to me, now. We are quite safe. Focus on me, now. I know we are safe, and if you focus on me *you* will know we are safe." The young man sees him now. He moves his head slightly in Sean's hands.

"Hypnotism," he whispers.

"No, for Christ's sake, it isn't hypnotism," Sean says. "We're going to stay like this until the lights come on. We're going to stay like this until the door opens, or they come get us, or whatever." Sean can feel the young man begin to calm down. He holds the boy's head gently and stares into his eyes. "Good. That's good."

After a while the lights come on, the elevator rises, and the doors open. The boy jumps out. "Come on, come on!" he cries.

Sean smiles. "This is sixty-four. I'm going to sixty-five."

The young man moves forward, but the door closes. The elevator goes up one floor, and Sean gets out.

That night, as he lies in bed waiting for sleep, Sean goes over the entire incident in his mind. He laughs aloud, remembering the young man's expression when he realized Sean was going to stay in the elevator.

Then he remembers the day in 1942 when his father showed up unexpectedly, took him home from school, washed the windows, and carried him out on the windowsill. He remembers looking down at the cracks in the sidewalk. Here, in the darkness, he can see the cracks in the sidewalk from more than forty years ago. He feels no fear—only a sense of astonishment.

RAYMOND CARVER

What We Talk About When We Talk About Love

My friend Mel McGinnis was talking. Mel McGinnis is a cardiologist, and sometimes that gives him the right.

The four of us were sitting around his kitchen table drinking gin. Sunlight filled the kitchen from the big window behind the sink. There were Mel and me and his second wife, Teresa—Terri, we called her—and my wife, Laura. We lived in Albuquerque then. But we were all from somewhere else.

There was an ice bucket on the table. The gin and the tonic water kept going around, and we somehow got on the subject of love. Mel thought real love was nothing less than spiritual love. He said he'd spent five years in a seminary before quitting to go to medical school. He said he still looked back on those years in the seminary as the most important years in his life.

Terri said the man she lived with before she lived with Mel loved her so much he tried to kill her. Then Terri said, "He beat me up one night. He dragged me around the living room by my ankles. He kept saying, 'I love you, I love you, you bitch.' He went on dragging me around the living room. My head kept knocking on things." Terri looked around the table. "What do you do with love like that?"

She was a bone-thin woman with a pretty face, dark eyes, and brown hair that hung down her back. She liked necklaces made of turquoise, and long pendant earrings.

"My God, don't be silly. That's not love, and you know it," Mel said. "I don't know what you'd call it, but I sure know you wouldn't call it love."

"Say what you want to, but I know it was," Terri said. "It may sound crazy to you, but it's true just the same. People are different, Mel. Sure, sometimes he may have acted crazy. Okay. But he loved me. In his own way maybe, but he loved me. There was love there, Mel. Don't say there wasn't."

Mel let out his breath. He held his glass and turned to Laura and me. "The man threatened to kill me," Mel said. He finished his drink and reached for the gin bottle. "Terri's a romantic. Terri's of the kick-me-so-I'll-know-you-love-me school. Terri, hon, don't look that way." Mel reached across the table and touched Terri's cheek with his fingers. He grinned at her.

"Now he wants to make up," Terri said.

"Make up what?" Mel said. "What is there to make up? I know what I know. That's all."

"How'd we get started on this subject, anyway?" Terri said. She raised her glass and drank from it. "Mel always has love on his mind," she said. "Don't you, honey?" She smiled, and I thought that was the last of it.

"I just wouldn't call Ed's behavior love. That's all I'm saying, honey," Mel said. "What about you guys?" Mel said to Laura and me. "Does that sound like love to you?"

"I'm the wrong person to ask," I said. "I didn't even know the man. I've only heard his name mentioned in passing. I wouldn't know. You'd have to know the particulars. But I think what you're saying is that love is an absolute."

Mel said, "The kind of love I'm talking about is. The kind of love I'm talking about, you don't try to kill people."

Laura said, "I don't know anything about Ed, or anything about the situation. But who can judge anyone else's situation?"

I touched the back of Laura's hand. She gave me a quick smile. I picked up Laura's hand. It was warm, the nails polished, perfectly manicured. I encircled the broad wrist with my fingers, and I held her.

"When I left, he drank rat poison," Terri said. She clasped her arms with her hands. "They took him to the hospital in Santa Fe. That's where we lived then, about ten miles out. They saved his life. But his gums went crazy from it. I mean they pulled away from his teeth. After that, his teeth stood out like fangs. My God," Terri said. She waited a minute, then let go of her arms and picked up her glass.

"What people won't do!" Laura said.

"He's out of the action now," Mel said. "He's dead."

Mel handed me the saucer of limes. I took a section, squeezed it over my drink, and stirred the ice cubes with my finger.

"It gets worse," Terri said. "He shot himself in the mouth. But he bungled that too. Poor Ed," she said. Terri shook her head.

"Poor Ed nothing," Mel said. "He was dangerous."

Mel was forty-five years old. He was tall and rangy with curly soft hair. His face and arms were brown from the tennis he played. When he was sober, his gestures, all his movements, were precise, very careful.

"He did love me though, Mel. Grant me that," Terri said. "That's all I'm asking. He didn't love me the way you love me. I'm not saying that. But he loved me. You can grant me that, can't you?"

"What do you mean, he bungled it?" I said.

Laura leaned forward with her glass. She put her elbows on the table and held her glass in both hands. She glanced from Mel to Terri and waited with a look of bewilderment on her open face, as if amazed that such things happened to people you were friendly with.

"How'd he bungle it when he killed himself?" I said.

"I'll tell you what happened," Mel said. "He took this twenty-two pistol he'd bought to threaten Terri and me with. Oh, I'm serious, the man was always threatening. You should have seen the way we lived in those days. Like fugitives. I even bought a gun myself. Can you believe it? A guy like me? But I did. I bought one for self-defense and carried it in the glove compartment. Sometimes I'd have to leave the apartment in the middle of the night. To go to the hospital, you know? Terri and I weren't married then, and my first wife had the house and kids, the dog, everything, and Terri and I were living in this apartment here. Sometimes, as I say, I'd get a call in the middle of the night and have to go in to the hospital at two or three in the morning. It'd be dark out there in the parking lot, and I'd break into a sweat before I could even get to my car. I never knew if he was going to come up out of the shrubbery or from behind a car and start shooting. I mean, the man was crazy. He was capable of wiring a bomb, anything. He used to call my service at all hours and say he needed to talk to the doctor, and when I'd return the call, he'd say, 'Son of a bitch, your days are numbered.' Little things like that. It was scary, I'm telling you."

"I still feel sorry for him," Terri said.

"It sounds like a nightmare," Laura said. "But what exactly happened after he shot himself?"

Laura is a legal secretary. We'd met in a professional capacity. Before we knew it, it was a courtship. She's thirty-five, three years younger than I am. In addition to being in love, we like each other and enjoy one another's company. She's easy to be with.

"What happened?" Laura said.

Mel said, "He shot himself in the mouth in his room. Someone heard the shot and told the manager. They came in with a passkey, saw what had happened, and called an ambulance. I happened to be there when they brought him in, alive but past recall. The man lived for three days. His head swelled up to twice the size of a normal head. I'd never seen anything like it, and I hope I never do again. Terri wanted to go in and sit with him when she found out about it. We had a fight over it. I didn't think she should see him like that. I didn't think she should see him, and I still don't."

"Who won the fight?" Laura said.

"I was in the room with him when he died," Terri said. "He never came up out of it. But I sat with him. He didn't have anyone else."

"He was dangerous," Mel said. "If you call that love, you can have it."

"It was love," Terri said. "Sure, it's abnormal in most people's eyes. But he was willing to die for it. He did die for it."

"I sure as hell wouldn't call it love," Mel said. "I mean, no one knows what he did it for. I've seen a lot of suicides, and I couldn't say anyone ever knew what they did it for."

Mel put his hands behind his neck and tilted his chair back. "I'm not interested in that kind of love," he said. "If that's love, you can have it."

Terri said, "We were afraid. Mel even made a will out and wrote to his brother in California who used to be a Green Beret. Mel told him who to look for if something happened to him."

Terri drank from her glass. She said, "But Mel's right—we lived like fugitives. We were afraid. Mel was, weren't you, honey? I even called the police at one point, but they were no help. They said they couldn't do anything until Ed actually did something. Isn't that a laugh?" Terri said.

She poured the last of the gin into her glass and waggled the bottle. Mel got up from the table and went to the cupboard. He took down another bottle.

"Well, Nick and I know what love is," Laura said. "For us, I mean," Laura said. She bumped my knee with her knee. "You're supposed to say something now," Laura said, and turned her smile on me.

For an answer, I took Laura's hand and raised it to my lips. I made a big production out of kissing her hand. Everyone was amused.

"We're lucky," I said.

"You guys," Terri said. "Stop that now. You're making me sick. You're still on the honeymoon, for God's sake. You're still gaga, for crying out loud. Just wait. How long have you been together now? How long has it been? A year? Longer than a year?"

"Going on a year and a half," Laura said, flushed and smiling.

"Oh, now," Terri said. "Wait awhile."

She held her drink and gazed at Laura.

"I'm only kidding," Terri said.

Mel opened the gin and went around the table with the bottle.

"Here, you guys," he said. "Let's have a toast. I want to propose a toast. A toast to love. To true love," Mel said.

We touched glasses.

"To love," we said.

Outside in the backyard, one of the dogs began to bark. The leaves of the aspen that leaned past the window ticked against the glass. The afternoon sun was like a presence in this room, the spacious light of ease and generosity. We could have been anywhere, somewhere enchanted. We raised our glasses again and grinned at each other like children who had agreed on something forbidden.

"I'll tell you what real love is," Mel said. "I mean, I'll give you a good example. And then you can draw your own conclusions." He poured more gin into his glass. He added an ice cube and a sliver of lime. We waited and sipped our drinks. Laura and I touched knees again. I put a hand on her warm thigh and left it there.

"What do any of us really know about love?" Mel said. "It seems to me we're just beginners at love. We say we love each other and we do, I don't doubt it. I love Terri and Terri loves me, and you guys love each other too. You know the kind of love I'm talking about now. Physical love, that impulse that drives you to someone special, as well as love of the other person's being, his or her essence, as it were. Carnal love and, well, call it sentimental love, the day-to-day caring about the other person. But sometimes I have a hard time accounting for the fact that I must have loved my first wife too. But I did, I know I did. So I suppose I am like Terri in that regard. Terri and Ed." He thought about it and then he went on. "There was a time when I thought I loved my first wife more than life itself. But now I hate her guts. I do. How do you explain that? What happened to that love? What happened to it, is what I'd like to know. I wish someone could tell me. Then there's Ed. Okay, we're back to Ed. He loves Terri so much he tries to kill her and he winds up killing himself." Mel stopped talking and swallowed from his glass. "You guys have been together eighteen months and you love each other. It shows all over you. You glow with it. But you both loved other people before you met each other. You've both been married before, just like us. And you probably loved other people before that too, even. Terri and I have been together five years, been married for four. And the terrible thing, the terrible thing is, but the good thing too, the saving grace, you might say, is that if something happened to one of us—excuse me for saying this—but if something happened to one of us tomorrow, I think the other one, the other person, would grieve for a while, you know, but then the surviving party would go out and love again, have someone else soon enough. All this, all of this love we're talking about, it would just be a memory. Maybe not even a memory. Am I wrong? Am I way off base? Because I want you to set me straight if you think I'm wrong. I want to know. I mean, I don't know anything, and I'm the first one to admit it."

"Mel, for God's sake," Terri said. She reached out and took hold of his wrist. "Are you getting drunk? Honey? Are you drunk?"

"Honey, I'm just talking," Mel said. "All right? I don't have to be drunk to say what I think. I mean, we're all just talking, right?" Mel said. He fixed his eyes on her.

"Sweetie, I'm not criticizing," Terri said.

She picked up her glass.

"I'm not on call today," Mel said. "Let me remind you of that. I am not on call," he said.

"Mel, we love you," Laura said.

Mel looked at Laura. He looked at her as if he could not place her, as if she was not the woman she was.

"Love you too, Laura," Mel said. "And you, Nick, love you too. You know something?" Mel said. "You guys are our pals," Mel said.

He picked up his glass.

Mel said, "I was going to tell you about something. I mean, I was going to prove a point. You see, this happened a few months ago, but it's still going on right now, and it ought to make us feel ashamed when we talk like we know what we're talking about when we talk about love."

"Come on now," Terri said. "Don't talk like you're drunk if you're not drunk."

"Just shut up for once in your life," Mel said very quietly. "Will you do me a favor and do that for a minute? So as I was saying, there's this old couple who had this car wreck out on the interstate. A kid hit them and they were all torn to shit and nobody was giving them much chance to pull through."

Terri looked at us and then back at Mel. She seemed anxious, or maybe that's too strong a word.

Mel was handing the bottle around the table.

"I was on call that night," Mel said. "It was May or maybe it was June. Terri and I had just sat down to dinner when the hospital called. There'd been this thing out on the interstate. Drunk kid, teenager, plowed his dad's pickup into this camper with this old couple in it. They were up in their mid-seventies, that couple. The kid—eighteen, nineteen, something—he was DOA. Taken the steering wheel through his sternum. The old couple, they were alive, you understand. I mean, just barely. But they had everything. Multiple fractures, internal injuries, hemorrhaging, contusions, lacerations, the works, and they each of them had themselves concussions. They were in a bad way, believe me. And, of course, their age was two strikes against them. I'd say she was worse off than he was. Ruptured spleen along with everything else. Both kneecaps broken. But they'd been wearing their seatbelts and, God knows, that's what saved them for the time being."

"Folks, this is an advertisement for the National Safety Council," Terri said. "This is your spokesman, Dr. Melvin R. McGinnis, talking." Terri laughed. "Mel," she said, "sometimes you're just too much. But I love you, hon," she said.

"Honey, I love you," Mel said.

He leaned across the table. Terri met him halfway. They kissed.

"Terri's right," Mel said as he settled himself again. "Get those seatbelts on. But seriously, they were in some shape, those oldsters. By the time I got down there, the kid was dead, as I said. He was off in a corner, laid out on a gurney. I took one look at the old couple and told the ER nurse to get me a neurologist and an orthopedic man and a couple of surgeons down there right away."

He drank from his glass. "I'll try to keep this short," he said. "So we took the two of them up to the OR and worked like fuck on them most of the night. They had these incredible reserves, those two. You see that once in a while. So we did everything that could be done, and toward morning we're giving them a fifty-fifty chance, maybe less than that for her. So here they are, still alive the next morning. So, okay, we move them into the ICU, which is where they both kept plugging away at it for two weeks, hitting it better and better on all the scopes. So we transfer them out to their own room."

Mel stopped talking. "Here," he said, "let's drink this cheapo gin the hell up. Then we're going to dinner, right? Terri and I know a new place. That's where we'll go, to this new place we know about. But we're not going until we finish up this cut-rate, lousy gin."

Terri said, "We haven't actually eaten there yet. But it looks good. From the outside, you know."

"I like food," Mel said. "If I had it to do all over again, I'd be a chef, you know? Right, Terri?" Mel said.

He laughed. He fingered the ice in his glass.

"Terri knows," he said. "Terri can tell you. But let me say this. If I could come back again in a different life, a different time and all, you know what? I'd like to come back as a knight. You were pretty safe wearing all that armor. It was all right being a knight until gunpowder and muskets and pistols came along."

"Mel would like to ride a horse and carry a lance," Terri said.

"Carry a woman's scarf with you everywhere," Laura said.

"Or just a woman," Mel said.

"Shame on you," Laura said.

Terri said, "Suppose you came back as a serf. The serfs didn't have it so good in those days," Terri said.

"The serfs never had it good," Mel said. "But I guess even the knights were vessels to someone. Isn't that the way it worked? But then everyone is always a vessel to someone. Isn't that right? Terri? But what I liked about knights, besides their ladies, was that they had that suit of armor, you know, and they couldn't get hurt very easy. No cars in those days, you know? No drunk teenagers to tear into your ass."

"Vassals," Terri said.

"What?" Mel said.

"Vassals," Terri said. "They were called vassals, not vessels."

"Vassals, vessels," Mel said, "what the fuck's the difference? You knew what I meant anyway. All right," Mel said. "So I'm not educated. I learned my stuff. I'm a heart surgeon, sure, but I'm just a mechanic. I go in and I fuck around and I fix things. Shit," Mel said.

"Modesty doesn't become you," Terri said.

"He's just a humble sawbones," I said. "But sometimes they suffocated in all that armor, Mel. They'd even have heart attacks if it got too hot and they were too tired and worn out. I read somewhere that they'd fall off their horses and not be able to get up because they were too tired to stand with all that armor on them. They got trampled by their own horses sometimes."

"That's terrible," Mel said. "That's a terrible thing, Nicky. I guess they'd just lay there and wait until somebody came along and made a shish kebab out of them."

"Some other vessel," Terri said.

"That's right," Mel said. "Some vassal would come along and spear the bastard in the name of love. Or whatever the fuck it was they fought over in those days."

"Same things we fight over these days," Terri said.

Laura said, "Nothing's changed."

The color was still high in Laura's cheeks. Her eyes were bright. She brought her glass to her lips.

Mel poured himself another drink. He looked at the label closely as if studying a long row of numbers. Then he slowly put the bottle down on the table and slowly reached for the tonic water.

"What about the old couple?" Laura said. "You didn't finish that story you started."

Laura was having a hard time lighting her cigarette. Her matches kept going out.

The sunshine inside the room was different now, changing, getting thinner. But the leaves outside the window were still shimmering, and I stared at the pattern they made on the panes and on the Formica counter. They weren't the same patterns, of course.

"What about the old couple?" I said.

"Older but wiser," Terri said.

Mel stared at her.

Terri said, "Go on with your story, hon. I was only kidding. Then what happened?"

"Terri, sometimes," Mel said.

"Please, Mel," Terri said. "Don't always be so serious, sweetie. Can't you take a joke?"

"Where's the joke?" Mel said.

He held his glass and gazed steadily at his wife.

"What happened?" Laura said.

Mel fastened his eyes on Laura. He said, "Laura, if I didn't have Terri and if I didn't love her so much, and if Nick wasn't my best friend, I'd fall in love with you. I'd carry you off, honey," he said.

"Tell your story," Terri said. "Then we'll go to that new place, okay?"

"Okay," Mel said. "Where was I?" he said. He stared at the table and then he began again.

"I dropped in to see each of them every day, sometimes twice a day if I was up doing other calls anyway. Casts and bandages, head to foot, the both of them. You know, you've seen it in the movies. That's just the way they looked, just like in the movies. Little eye-holes and nose-holes and mouth-holes. And she had to have her legs slung up on top of it. Well, the husband was very depressed for the longest while. Even after he found out that his wife was going to pull through, he was still very depressed. Not about the accident, though. I mean, the accident was one thing, but it wasn't everything. I'd get up to his mouth-hole, you know, and he'd say no, it wasn't the accident exactly but it was because he couldn't see her through his eye-holes. He said that was what was making him feel so bad. Can you imagine? I'm telling you, the man's heart was breaking because he couldn't turn his goddamn head and *see* his goddamn wife."

Mel looked around the table and shook his head at what he was going to say.

"I mean, it was killing the old fart just because he couldn't *look* at the fucking woman."

We all looked at Mel.

"Do you see what I'm saying?" he said.

Maybe we were a little drunk by then. I know it was hard keeping things in focus. The light was draining out of the room, going back through the window where it had come from. Yet nobody made a move to get up from the table to turn on the overhead light.

"Listen," Mel said. "Let's finish this fucking gin. There's about enough left here for one shooter all around. Then let's go eat. Let's go to the new place."

"He's depressed," Terri said. "Mel, why don't you take a pill?"

Mel shook his head. "I've taken everything there is."

"We all need a pill now and then," I said.

"Some people are born needing them," Terri said.

She was using her finger to rub at something on the table. Then she stopped rubbing.

"I think I want to call my kids," Mel said. "Is that all right with everybody? I'll call my kids," he said.

Terri said, "What if Marjorie answers the phone? You guys, you've heard us on the subject of Marjorie? Honey, you know you don't want to talk to Marjorie. It'll make you feel even worse."

"I don't want to talk to Marjorie," Mel said. "But I want to talk to my kids."

"There isn't a day goes by that Mel doesn't say he wishes she'd get married again. Or else die," Terri said. "For one thing," Terri said, "she's bankrupting us. Mel says it's just to spite him that she won't get married again. She has a boyfriend who lives with her and the kids, so Mel is supporting the boyfriend too."

"She's allergic to bees," Mel said. "If I'm not praying she'll get married again, I'm praying she'll get herself stung to death by a swarm of fucking bees."

"Shame on you," Laura said.

"Bzzzzzzz," Mel said, turning his fingers into bees and buzzing them at Terri's throat. Then he let his hands drop all the way to his sides.

"She's vicious," Mel said. "Sometimes I think I'll go up there dressed like a beekeeper. You know, that hat that's like a helmet with the plate that comes down over your face, the big gloves, and the padded coat? I'll knock on the door and let loose a hive of bees in the house. But first I'd make sure the kids were out, of course."

He crossed one leg over the other. It seemed to take him a lot of time to do it. Then he put both feet on the floor and leaned forward, elbows on the table, his chin cupped in his hands.

"Maybe I won't call the kids, after all. Maybe it isn't such a hot idea. Maybe we'll just go eat. How does that sound?"

"Sounds fine to me," I said. "Eat or not eat. Or keep drinking. I could head right on out into the sunset."

"What does that mean, honey?" Laura said.

"It just means what I said," I said. "It means I could just keep going. That's all it means."

"I could eat something myself," Laura said. "I don't think I've ever been so hungry in my life. Is there something to nibble on?"

"I'll put out some cheese and crackers," Terri said.

But Terri just sat there. She did not get up to get anything.

Mel turned his glass over. He spilled it out on the table.

"Gin's gone," Mel said.

Terri said, "Now what?"

I could hear my heart beating. I could hear everyone's heart. I could hear the human noise we sat there making, not one of us moving, not even when the room went dark.

JOYCE CAROL OATES

How I Contemplated the World from the Detroit House of Correction and Began My Life Over Again

Notes for an Essay for an English Class at Baldwin Country Day School; Poking Around in Debris; Disgust and Curiosity; a Revelation of the Meaning of Life; a Happy Ending . . .

I EVENTS

1. The girl (myself) is walking through Branden's, that excellent store. Suburb of a large famous city that is a symbol for large famous American cities. The event sneaks up on the girl, who believes she is herding it along with a small fixed smile, a girl of fifteen, innocently experienced. She dawdles in a certain style by a counter of costume jewelry. Rings, earrings, necklaces. Prices from $5 to $50, all within reach. All ugly. She eases over to the glove counter, where everything is ugly too. In her close-fitted coat with its black fur collar she contemplates the luxury of Branden's, which she has known for many years: its many mild pale lights, easy on the eye and the soul, its elaborate tinkly decorations, its women shoppers with their excellent shoes and coats and hairdos, all dawdling gracefully, in no hurry.

Who was ever in a hurry here?

2. The girl seated at home. A small library, paneled walls of oak. Someone is talking to me. An earnest, husky, female voice drives itself against my ears, nervous, frightened, groping around my heart, saying, "If you wanted gloves, why didn't you say so? Why didn't you ask for them?" That store, Branden's, is owned by Raymond Forrest who lives on Du Maurier Drive. We live on Sioux Drive. Raymond Forrest. A handsome man? An ugly man? A man of fifty or sixty, with gray hair, or a man of forty with earnest, courteous eyes, a good golf game; who is Raymond Forrest, this man who is my salvation? Father has been talking to him. Father is not his physician; Dr. Berg is his physician.

Father and Dr. Berg refer patients to each other. There is a connection. Mother plays bridge with . . . On Mondays and Wednesdays our maid Billie works at . . . The strings draw together in a cat's cradle, making a net to save you when you fall. . . .

3. *Harriet Arnold's.* A small shop, better than Branden's. Mother in her black coat, I in my close-fitted blue coat. Shopping. Now look at this, isn't this cute, do you want this, why don't you want this, try this on, take this with you to the fitting room, take this also, what's wrong with you, what can I do for you, why are you so strange . . . ? "I wanted to steal but not to buy," I don't tell her. The girl droops along in her coat and gloves and leather boots, her eyes scan the horizon, which is pastel pink and decorated like Branden's, tasteful walls and modern ceilings with graceful glimmering lights.

4. Weeks later, the girl at a bus stop. Two o'clock in the afternoon, a Tuesday; obviously she has walked out of school.

5. The girl stepping down from a bus. Afternoon, weather changing to colder. Detroit. Pavement and closed-up stores; grill-work over the windows of a pawnshop. What is a pawnshop, exactly?

II CHARACTERS

1. The girl stands five feet five inches tall. An ordinary height. Baldwin Country Day School draws them up to that height. She dreams along the corridors and presses her face against the Thermoplex glass. No frost or steam can ever form on that glass. A smudge of grease from her forehead . . . could she be boiled down to grease? She wears her hair loose and long and straight in suburban teen-age style, 1968. Eyes smudged with pencil, dark brown. Brown hair. Vague green eyes. A pretty girl? An ugly girl? She sings to herself under her breath, idling in the corridor, thinking of her many secrets (the thirty dollars she once took from the purse of a friend's mother, just for fun, the basement window she smashed in her own house just for fun) and thinking of her brother who is at Susquehanna Boys' Academy, an excellent preparatory school in Maine, remembering him unclearly . . . he has long manic hair and a squeaking voice and he looks like one of the popular teen-age singers of 1968, one of those in a group, *The Certain Forces, The Way Out, The Maniacs Responsible.* The girl in her turn looks like one of those fieldsful of girls who listen to the boys' singing, dreaming and mooning restlessly, breaking into high sullen laughter, innocently experienced.

2. The mother. A Midwestern woman of Detroit and suburbs. Belongs to the Detroit Athletic Club. Also the Detroit Golf Club. Also the Bloomfield Hills Country Club. The Village Women's Club at which lectures are given each winter on Genet and Sartre and James Baldwin, by the Director of the Adult Education Program at Wayne State University. . . . The Bloomfield Art Association. Also the Founders Society of the Detroit Institute of Arts. Also . . . Oh, she is in perpetual motion, this lady, hair like blown-up gold and finer than gold, hair and fingers and body of inestimable grace. Heavy weighs the gold on the back of her hairbrush and hand mirror. Heavy heavy the candlesticks in the dining room. Very heavy is the big car, a Lincoln, long and black, that on one cool autumn day split a squirrel's body in two unequal parts.

3. The father. Dr.   . He belongs to the same clubs as #2. A player of squash and golf; he has a golfer's umbrella of stripes. Candy stripes. In his mouth nothing turns to sugar, however; saliva works no miracles here. His doctoring is of the slightly sick. The sick are sent elsewhere (to Dr. Berg?), the deathly sick are sent back for more tests and their bills are sent to their homes, the unsick are sent to Dr. Coronet (Isabel, a lady), an excellent psychiatrist for unsick people who angrily believe they are sick and want to do something about it. If they demand a male psychiatrist, the unsick are sent by Dr.   (my father) to Dr. Lowenstein, a male psychiatrist, excellent and expensive, with a limited practice.

4. Clarita. She is twenty, twenty-five, she is thirty or more? Pretty, ugly, what? She is a woman lounging by the side of a road, in jeans and a sweater, hitchhiking, or she is slouched on a stool at a counter in some roadside diner. A hard line of jaw. Curious eyes. Amused eyes. Behind her eyes processions move, funeral pageants, cartoons. She says, "I never can figure out why girls like you bum around down here. What are you looking for anyway?" An odor of tobacco about her. Unwashed underclothes, or no underclothes, unwashed skin, gritty toes, hair long and falling into strands, not recently washed.

5. Simon. In this city the weather changes abruptly, so Simon's weather changes abruptly. He sleeps through the afternoon. He sleeps through the morning. Rising, he gropes around for something to get him going, for a cigarette or a pill to drive him out to the street, where the temperature is hovering around 35°. Why doesn't it drop? Why, why doesn't the cold clean air come down from Canada; will he have to go up into Canada to get it? will he have to leave the Country of his Birth

and sink into Canada's frosty fields . . . ? Will the F.B.I. (which he dreams about constantly) chase him over the Canadian border on foot, hounded out in a blizzard of broken glass and horns . . . ?

"Once I was Huckleberry Finn," Simon says, "but now I am Roderick Usher." Beset by frenzies and fears, this man who makes my spine go cold, he takes green pills, yellow pills, pills of white and capsules of dark blue and green . . . he takes other things I may not mention, for what if Simon seeks me out and climbs into my girl's bedroom here in Bloomfield Hills and strangles me, what then . . . ? (As I write this I begin to shiver. Why do I shiver? I am now sixteen and sixteen is not an age for shivering.) It comes from Simon, who is always cold.

III WORLD EVENTS

Nothing.

IV PEOPLE AND CIRCUMSTANCES CONTRIBUTING TO THIS DELINQUENCY

Nothing.

V SIOUX DRIVE

George, Clyde G. 240 Sioux. A manufacturer's representative; children, a dog, a wife. Georgian with the usual columns. You think of the White House, then of Thomas Jefferson, then your mind goes blank on the white pillars and you think of nothing. Norris, Ralph W. 246 Sioux. Public relations. Colonial. Bay window, brick, stone, concrete, wood, green shutters, sidewalk, lantern, grass, trees, blacktop drive, two children, one of them my classmate Esther (Esther Norris) at Baldwin. Wife, cars. Ramsey, Michael D. 250 Sioux. Colonial. Big living room, thirty by twenty-five, fireplaces in living room, library, recreation room, paneled walls wet bar five bathrooms five bedrooms two lavatories central air conditioning automatic sprinkler automatic garage door three children one wife two cars a breakfast room a patio a large fenced lot fourteen trees a front door with a brass knocker never knocked. Next is our house. Classic contemporary. Traditional modern. Attached garage, attached Florida room, attached patio, attached pool and cabana, attached roof. A front door mail slot through which pour *Time Magazine, Fortune, Life, Business Week,* the *Wall Street Journal,* the *New York Times,* the *New Yorker,* the *Saturday Review, M.D., Modern Medicine, Disease of the Month* . . . and also. . . . And in addition to all this, a quiet sealed letter from Baldwin saying: *Your daughter is not doing work compatible with her performance on the Stanford-Binet. . . .* And your son is not doing well, not well at all, very sad. Where is your son anyway? Once he stole trick-and-treat candy from some six-year-old kids, he himself being a robust ten. The beginning. Now your daughter steals. In the Village Pharmacy she made off with, yes she did, don't deny it, she made off with a copy of *Pageant Magazine* for no reason, she swiped a roll of Life Savers in a green wrapper and was in no need of saving her life or even in need of sucking candy; when she was no more than eight years old she stole, don't blush, she stole a package of Tums only because it was out on the counter and available, and the nice lady behind the counter (now dead) said nothing. . . . Sioux Drive. Maples, oaks, elms. Diseased elms cut down. Sioux Drive runs into Roosevelt Drive. Slow, turning lanes, not streets, all drives and lanes and ways and passes. A private police force. Quiet private police, in unmarked cars. Cruising on Saturday evenings with paternal smiles for the residents who are streaming in and out of houses, going to and from parties, a thousand parties, slightly staggering, the women in their furs alighting from automobiles bought of Ford and General Motors and Chrysler, very heavy automobiles. No foreign cars. Detroit. In 275 Sioux, down the block in that magnificent French-Normandy mansion, lives   himself, who has the C   account itself, imagine that! Look at where he lives and look at the enormous trees and chimneys, imagine his many fireplaces, imagine his wife and children, imagine his wife's hair, imagine her fingernails, imagine her bathtub of smooth clean glowing pink, imagine their embraces, his trouser pockets filled with odd coins and keys and dust and peanuts, imagine their ecstasy on Sioux Drive, imagine their income tax returns, imagine their little boy's pride in his experimental car, a scaled-down C   , as he roars around the neighborhood on the sidewalks frightening dogs and Negro maids, oh imagine all these things, imagine everything, let your mind roar out all over Sioux Drive and Du Maurier Drive and Roosevelt Drive and Ticonderoga Pass and Burning Bush Way and Lincolnshire Pass and Lois Lane.

When spring comes, its winds blow nothing to Sioux Drive, no odors of hollyhocks or forsythia, nothing Sioux Drive doesn't already possess, everything is planted and performing. The weather vanes, had they weather vanes, don't have to turn with the wind, don't have to contend with the weather. There is no weather.

VI DETROIT

There is always weather in Detroit. Detroit's temperature is always 32°. Fast-falling temperatures. Slow-rising temperatures. Wind from the north-northeast four to forty miles an hour, small-craft warnings, partly cloudy today and Wednesday changing to partly sunny through Thursday . . . small warnings of frost, soot warnings, traffic warnings, hazardous lake conditions for small craft and swimmers, restless Negro gangs, restless cloud formations, restless temperatures aching to fall out the very bottom of the thermometer or shoot up over the top and boil everything over in red mercury.

Detroit's temperature is 32°. Fast-falling temperatures. Slow-rising temperatures. Wind from the north-northeast four to forty miles an hour. . . .

VII EVENTS

1. The girl's heart is pounding. In her pocket is a pair of gloves! In a plastic bag! Airproof breathproof plastic bag, gloves selling for twenty-five dollars on Branden's counter! In her pocket! Shoplifted! . . . In her purse is a blue comb, not very clean. In her purse is a leather billfold (a birthday present from her grandmother in Philadelphia) with snapshots of the family in clean plastic windows, in the billfold are bills, she doesn't know how many bills. . . . In her purse is an ominous note from her friend Tykie *What's this about Joe H. and the kids hanging around at Louise's Sat. night? You heard anything?* . . . passed in French class. In her purse is a lot of dirty yellow Kleenex, her mother's heart would break to see such very dirty Kleenex, and at the bottom of her purse are brown hairpins and safety pins and a broken pencil and a ballpoint pen (blue) stolen from somewhere forgotten and a purse-size compact of Cover Girl Make-Up, Ivory Rose. . . . Her lipstick is Broken Heart, a corrupt pink; her fingers are trembling like crazy; her teeth are beginning to chatter; her insides are alive; her eyes glow in her head; she is saying to her mother's astonished face *I want to steal but not to buy.*

2. At Clarita's. Day or night? What room is this? A bed, a regular bed, and a mattress on the floor nearby. Wallpaper hanging in strips. Clarita says she tore it like that with her teeth. She was fighting a barbaric tribe that night, high from some pills; she was battling for her life with men wearing helmets of heavy iron and their faces no more than Christian crosses to breathe through, every one of those bastards looking like her

lover Simon, who seems to breathe with great difficulty through the slits of mouth and nostrils in his face. Clarita has never heard of Sioux Drive. Raymond Forrest cuts no ice with her, nor does the C account and its millions; Harvard Business School could be at the corner of Vernor and 12th Street for all she cares, and Vietnam might have sunk by now into the Dead Sea under its tons of debris, for all the amazement she could show . . . her face is overworked, overwrought, at the age of twenty (thirty?) it is already exhausted but fanciful and ready for a laugh. Clarita says mournfully to me *Honey somebody is going to turn you out let me give you warning.* In a movie shown on late television Clarita is not a mess like this but a nurse, with short neat hair and a dedicated look, in love with her doctor and her doctor's patients and their diseases, enamored of needles and sponges and rubbing alcohol. . . . Or no: she is a private secretary. Robert Cummings is her boss. She helps him with fantastic plots, the canned audience laughs, no, the audience doesn't laugh because nothing is funny, instead her boss is Robert Taylor and they are not boss and secretary but husband and wife, she is threatened by a young starlet, she is grim, handsome, wifely, a good companion for a good man. . . . She is Claudette Colbert. Her sister too is Claudette Colbert. They are twins, identical. Her husband Charles Boyer is a very rich handsome man and her sister, Claudette Colbert, is plotting her death in order to take her place as the rich man's wife, no one will know because they are *twins.* . . . All these marvelous lives Clarita might have lived, but she fell out the bottom at the age of thirteen. At the age when I was packing my overnight case for a slumber party at Toni Deshield's she was tearing filthy sheets off a bed and scratching up a rash on her arms. . . . Thirteen is uncommonly young for a white girl in Detroit, Miss Brock of the Detroit House of Correction said in a sad newspaper interview for the *Detroit News;* fifteen and sixteen are more likely. Eleven, twelve, thirteen are not surprising in colored . . . they are more precocious. What can we do? Taxes are rising and the tax base is falling. The temperature rises slowly but falls rapidly. Everything is falling out the bottom, Woodward Avenue is filthy, Livernois Avenue is filthy! Scraps of paper flutter in the air like pigeons, dirt flies up and hits you right in the eye, oh Detroit is breaking up into dangerous bits of newspaper and dirt, watch out. . . .

Clarita's apartment is over a restaurant. Simon her lover emerges from the cracks at dark. Mrs. Olesko, a neighbor of Clarita's, an aged white wisp of a woman, doesn't complain but sniffs with contentment at Clarita's noisy life and doesn't tell the cops, hating cops, when the cops arrive. I should give more fake names, more blanks, instead of telling all these secrets. I myself am a secret; I am a minor.

3. My father reads a paper at a medical convention in Los Angeles. There he is, on the edge of the North American continent, when the unmarked detective put his hand so gently on my arm in the aisle of Branden's and said, "Miss, would you like to step over here for a minute?"

And where was he when Clarita put her hand on my arm, that wintry dark sulphurous aching day in Detroit, in the company of closed-down barber shops, closed-down diners, closed-down movie houses, homes, windows, basements, faces . . . she put her hand on my arm and said, "Honey, are you looking for somebody down here?"

And was he home worrying about me, gone for two weeks solid, when they carried me off . . . ? It took three of them to get me in the police cruiser, so they said, and they put more than their hands on my arm.

4. I work on this lesson. My English teacher is Mr. Forest, who is from Michigan State. Not handsome, Mr. Forest, and his name is plain, unlike Raymond Forrest's, but he is sweet and rodentlike, he has conferred with the principal and my parents, and everything is fixed . . . treat her as if nothing has happened, a new start, begin again, only sixteen years old, what a shame, how did it happen?—nothing happened, nothing could have happened, a slight physiological modification known only to a gynecologist or to Dr. Coronet. I work on my lesson. I sit in my pink room. I look around the room with my sad pink eyes. I sigh, I dawdle, I pause, I eat up time, I am limp and happy to be home, I am sixteen years old suddenly, my head hangs heavy as a pumpkin on my shoulders, and my hair has just been cut by Mr. Faye at the Crystal Salon and is said to be very becoming.

(Simon too put his hand on my arm and said, "Honey, you have got to come with me," and in his six-by-six room we got to know each other. Would I go back to Simon again? Would I lie down with him in all that filth and craziness? Over and over again.

a Clarita is being betrayed as in front of a Cunningham Drug Store she is nervously eying a colored man who may or may not have money, or a nervous white boy of twenty with sideburns and an Appalachian look, who may or may not have a knife hidden in his jacket pocket, or a husky red-faced man of friendly countenance who may or may not be a member of the Vice Squad out for an early twilight walk.)

I work on my lesson for Mr. Forest. I have filled up eleven pages. Words pour out of me and won't stop. I want to tell everything . . . what was the song Simon was always humming, and who was Simon's friend in a very new trench coat with an old high school graduation ring on his finger . . . ? Simon's bearded friend? When I was down too low for him, Simon kicked me out and gave me to him for three days, I think, on Fourteenth Street in Detroit, an airy room of cold cruel drafts with newspapers on the floor. . . . Do I really remember that or am I piecing it together from what they told me? Did they tell the truth? Did they know much of the truth?

VIII CHARACTERS

1. Wednesdays after school, at four; Saturday mornings at ten. Mother drives me to Dr. Coronet. Ferns in the office, plastic or real, they look the same. Dr. Coronet is queenly, an elegant nicotine-stained lady who would have studied with Freud had circumstances not prevented it, a bit of a Catholic, ready to offer you some mystery if your teeth will ache too much without it. Highly recommended by Father! Forty dollars an hour, Father's forty dollars! Progress! Looking up! Looking better! That new haircut is so becoming, says Dr. Coronet herself, showing how normal she is for a woman with an I.Q. of 180 and many advanced degrees.

2. Mother. A lady in a brown suede coat. Boots of shiny black material, black gloves, a black fur hat. She would be humiliated could she know that of all the people in the world it is my exlover Simon who walks most like her . . . self-conscious and unreal, listening to distant music, a little bowlegged with craftiness. . . .

3. Father. Tying a necktie. In a hurry. On my first evening home he put his hand on my arm and said, "Honey, we're going to forget all about this."

4. Simon. Outside, a plane is crossing the sky, in here we're in a hurry. Morning. It must be morning. The girl is half out of her mind, whimpering and vague; Simon her dear friend is wretched this morning . . . he is wretched with morning itself . . . he forces her to give him an injection with that needle she knows is filthy, she has a dread of needles and surgical instruments and the odor of things that are to be sent into the blood, thinking somehow of her father. . . . This is a bad morning, Simon says that his mind is being twisted out of shape, and so he submits to the needle that he usually scorns and bites his lip with his yellowish teeth, his face going very pale. *Ah baby!* he says in his soft mocking voice, which with all women is a mockery of love, *do it like this—*

Slowly—And the girl, terrified, almost drops the precious needle but manages to turn it up to the light from the window . . . is it an extension of herself then? She can give him this gift then? *I wish you wouldn't do this to me,* she says, wise in her terror, because it seems to her that Simon's danger—in a few minutes he may be dead—is a way of pressing her against him that is more powerful than any other embrace. She has to work over his arm, the knotted corded veins of his arm, her forehead wet with perspiration as she pushes and releases the needle, staring at that mixture of liquid now stained with Simon's bright blood. . . . When the drug hits him she can feel it herself, she feels that magic that is more than any woman can give him, striking the back of his head and making his face stretch as if with the impact of a terrible sun. . . . She tries to embrace him but he pushes her aside and stumbles to his feet. *Jesus Christ,* he says. . . .

5. Princess, a Negro girl of eighteen. What is her charge? She is closed-mouthed about it, shrewd and silent, you know that no one had to wrestle her to the sidewalk to get her in here; she came with dignity. In the recreation room she sits reading *Nancy Drew and the Jewel Box Mystery,* which inspires in her face tiny wrinkles of alarm and interest: what a face! Light brown skin, heavy shaded eyes, heavy eyelashes, a serious sinister dark brow, graceful fingers, graceful wristbones, graceful legs, lips, tongue, a sugar-sweet voice, a leggy stride more masculine than Simon's and my mother's, decked out in a dirty white blouse and dirty white slacks; vaguely nautical is Princess' style. . . . At breakfast she is in charge of clearing the table and leans over me, saying, *Honey you sure you ate enough?*

6. The girl lies sleepless, wondering. Why here, why not there? Why Bloomfield Hills and not jail? Why jail and not her pink room? Why downtown Detroit and not Sioux Drive? What is the difference? Is Simon all the difference? The girl's head is a parade of wonders. She is nearly sixteen, her breath is marvelous with wonders, not long ago she was coloring with crayons and now she is smearing the landscape with paints that won't come off and won't come off her fingers either. She says to the matron *I am not talking about anything,* not because everyone has warned her not to talk but because, because she will not talk; because she won't say anything about Simon, who is her secret. And she says to the matron, *I won't go home,* up until that night in the lavatory when everything was changed. . . . "No, I won't go home I want to stay here," she says, listening to her own words with amazement, thinking that weeds might climb everywhere over that marvelous $180,000 house and

dinosaurs might return to muddy the beige carpeting, but never never will she reconcile four o'clock in the morning in Detroit with eight o'clock breakfasts in Bloomfield Hills. . . . oh, she aches still for Simon's hands and his caressing breath, though he gave her little pleasure, he took everything from her (five-dollar bills, ten-dollar bills, passed into her numb hands by men and taken out of her hands by Simon) until she herself was passed into the hands of other men, police, when Simon evidently got tired of her and her hysteria. . . . *No, I won't go home, I don't want to be bailed out.* The girl thinks as a *Stubborn and Wayward Child* (one of several charges lodged against her), and the matron understands her crazy white-rimmed eyes that are seeking out some new violence that will keep her in jail, should someone threaten to let her out. Such children try to strangle the matrons, the attendants, or one another . . . they want the locks locked forever, the doors nailed shut . . . and this girl is no different up until that night her mind is changed for her. . . .

IX THAT NIGHT

Princess and Dolly, a little white girl of maybe fifteen, hardy however as a sergeant and in the House of Correction for armed robbery, corner her in the lavatory at the farthest sink and the other girls look away and file out to bed, leaving her. God, how she is beaten up! Why is she beaten up? Why do they pound her, why such hatred? Princess vents all the hatred of a thousand silent Detroit winters on her body, this girl whose body belongs to me, fiercely she rides across the Midwestern plains on this girl's tender bruised body . . . revenge on the oppressed minorities of America! revenge on the slaughtered Indians! revenge on the female sex, on the male sex, revenge on Bloomfield Hills, revenge revenge. . . .

X DETROIT

In Detroit, weather weighs heavily upon everyone. The sky looms large. The horizon shimmers in smoke. Downtown the buildings are imprecise in the haze. Perpetual haze. Perpetual motion inside the haze. Across the choppy river is the city of Windsor, in Canada. Part of the continent has bunched up here and is bulging outward, at the tip of Detroit; a cold hard rain is forever falling on the expressways. . . . Shoppers shop grimly, their cars are not parked in safe places, their windshields may be smashed and graceful ebony hands may drag them out through their shatterproof smashed windshields, crying, *Revenge for the Indians!* Ah, they all fear leaving Hudson's and being dragged to the very tip of the city and thrown off the parking roof of Cobo Hall, that expensive tomb, into the river. . . .

XI CHARACTERS WE ARE FOREVER ENTWINED WITH

1. Simon drew me into his tender rotting arms and breathed gravity into me. Then I came to earth, weighed down. He said, *You are such a little girl,* and he weighed me down with his delight. In the palms of his hands were teeth marks from his previous life experiences. He was thirty-five, they said. Imagine Simon in this room, in my pink room: he is about six feet tall and stoops slightly, in a feline cautious way, always thinking, always on guard, with his scuffed light suede shoes and his clothes that are anyone's clothes, slightly rumpled ordinary clothes that ordinary men might wear to not-bad jobs. Simon has fair long hair, curly hair, spent languid curls that are like . . . exactly like the curls of wood shavings to the touch, I am trying to be exact . . . and he smells of unheated mornings and coffee and too many pills coating his tongue with a faint green-white scum. . . . Dear Simon, who would be panicked in this room and in this house (right now Billie is vacuuming next door in my parents' room; a vacuum cleaner's roar is a sign of all good things), Simon who is said to have come from a home not much different from this, years ago, fleeing all the carpeting and the polished banisters . . . Simon has a deathly face, only desperate people fall in love with it. His face is bony and cautious, the bones of his cheeks prominent as if with the rigidity of his ceaseless thinking, plotting, for he has to make money out of girls to whom money means nothing, they're so far gone they can hardly count it, and in a sense money means nothing to him either except as a way of keeping on with his life. *Each Day's Proud Struggle,* the title of a novel we could read at jail. . . . Each day he needs a certain amount of money. He devours it. It wasn't love he uncoiled in me with his hollowed-out eyes and his courteous smile, that remnant of a prosperous past, but a dark terror that needed to press itself flat against him, or against another man . . . but he was the first, he came over to me and took my arm, a claim. We struggled on the stairs and I said, *Let me loose, you're hurting my neck, my face,* it was such a surprise that my skin hurt where he rubbed it, and afterward we lay face to face and he breathed everything into me. In the end I think he turned me in.

2. Raymond Forrest. I just read this morning that Raymond Forrest's father, the chairman of the board at   , died of a heart attack on a plane bound for London. I would like to write Raymond Forrest a note

of sympathy. I would like to thank him for not pressing charges against me one hundred years ago, saving me, being so generous . . . well, men like Raymond Forrest are generous men, not like Simon. I would like to write him a letter telling of my love, or of some other emotion that is positive and healthy. Not like Simon and his poetry, which he scrawled down when he was high and never changed a word . . . but when I try to think of something to say, it is Simon's language that comes back to me, caught in my head like a bad song, it is always Simon's language:

> There is no reality only dreams
> Your neck may get snapped when you wake
> My love is drawn to some violent end
> She keeps wanting to get away
> My love is heading downward
> And I am heading upward
> She is going to crash on the sidewalk
> And I am going to dissolve into the clouds

XII EVENTS

1. Out of the hospital, bruised and saddened and converted, with Princess' grunts still tangled in my hair . . . and Father in his overcoat looking like a prince himself, come to carry me off. Up the expressway and out north to home. Jesus Christ, but the air is thinner and cleaner here. Monumental houses. Heartbreaking sidewalks, so clean.

2. Weeping in the living room. The ceiling is two stories high and two chandeliers hang from it. Weeping, weeping, though Billie the maid is *probably listening.* I will never leave home again. Never. Never leave home. Never leave this home again, never.

3. Sugar doughnuts for breakfast. The toaster is very shiny and my face is distorted in it. Is that my face?

4. The car is turning in the driveway. Father brings me home. Mother embraces me. Sunlight breaks in movieland patches on the roof of our traditional-contemporary home, which was designed for the famous automotive stylist whose identity, if I told you the name of the famous car he designed, you would all know, so I can't tell you because my teeth chatter at the thought of being sued . . . or having someone climb into my bedroom window with a rope to strangle me. . . . The car turns up the blacktop drive. The house opens to me like a doll's house, so lovely

in the sunlight, the big living room beckons to me with its walls falling away in a delirium of joy at my return, Billie the maid is *no doubt* listening from the kitchen as I burst into tears and the hysteria Simon got so sick of. Convulsed in Father's arms, I say I will never leave again, never, why did I leave, where did I go, what happened, my mind is gone wrong, my body is one big bruise, my backbone was sucked dry, it wasn't the men who hurt me and Simon never hurt me but only those girls . . . my God, how they hurt me . . . I will never leave home again. . . . The car is perpetually turning up the drive and I am perpetually breaking down in the living room and we are perpetually taking the right exit from the expressway (Lahser Road) and the wall of the rest room is perpetually banging against my head and perpetually are Simon's hands moving across my body and adding everything up and so too are Father's hands on my shaking bruised back, far from the surface of my skin on the surface of my good blue cashmere coat (dry-cleaned for my release). . . . I weep for all the money here, for God in gold and beige carpeting, for the beauty of chandeliers and the miracle of a clean polished gleaming toaster and faucets that run both hot and cold water, and I tell them, *I will never leave home, this is my home, I love everything here, I am in love with everything here. . . .*

I am home.

TONI CADE BAMBARA

Gorilla, My Love

That was the year Hunca Bubba changed his name. Not a change up, but a change back, since Jefferson Winston Vale was the name in the first place. Which was news to me cause he'd been my Hunca Bubba my whole lifetime, since I couldn't manage Uncle to save my life. So far as I was concerned it was a change completely to somethin soundin very geographical weatherlike to me, like somethin you'd find in a almanac. Or somethin you'd run across when you sittin in the navigator seat with a wet thumb on the map crinkly in your lap, watchin the roads and signs so when Granddaddy Vale say "Which way, Scout," you got sense enough to say take the next exit or take a left or whatever it is. Not that Scout's my name. Just the name Granddaddy call whoever sittin in the navigator seat. Which is usually me cause I don't feature sittin in the back with the pecans. Now, you figure pecans all right to be sittin with. If you thinks so, that's your business. But they dusty sometime and make you cough. And they got a way of slidin around and dippin down sudden, like maybe a rat in the buckets. So if you scary like me, you sleep with the lights on and blame it on Baby Jason and, so as not to waste good electric, you study the maps. And that's how come I'm in the navigator seat most times and get to be called Scout.

So Hunca Bubba in the back with the pecans and Baby Jason, and he in love. And we got to hear all this stuff about this woman he in love with and all. Which really ain't enough to keep the mind alive, though Baby Jason got no better sense than to give his undivided attention and keep grabbin at the photograph which is just a picture of some skinny woman in a countrified dress with her hand shot up to her face like she shame fore cameras. But there's a movie house in the background which I ax about. Cause I am a movie freak from way back, even though it do get me in trouble sometime.

Like when me and Big Brood and Baby Jason was on our own last Easter and couldn't go to the Dorset cause we'd seen all the Three Stooges they was. And the RKO Hamilton was closed readying up for the Easter Pageant that night. And the West End, the Regun and the Sunset was too far, less we had grownups with us which we didn't. So we walk up Amsterdam Avenue to the Washington and *Gorilla, My Love* playin, they say, which suit me just fine, though the "my love" part kinda drag Big Brood some. As for Baby Jason, shoot, like Granddaddy say, he'd follow me into the fiery furnace if I say come on. So we go in and get three bags of Havmore potato chips which not only are the best potato chips but the best bags for blowin up and bustin real loud so the matron come trottin down the aisle with her chunky self, flashin that flashlight dead in your eye so you can give her some lip, and if she answer back and you already finish seein the show anyway, why then you just turn the place out. Which I love to do, no lie. With Baby Jason kickin at the seat in front, egging me on, and Big Brood mumblin bout what fiercesome things we goin do. Which means me. Like when the big boys come up on us talkin bout Lemme a nickel. It's me that hide the money. Or when the bad boys in the park take Big Brood's Spaudeen way from him. It's me that jump on they back and fight awhile. And it's me that turns out the show if the matron get too salty.

So the movie come on and right away it's this churchy music and clearly not about no gorilla. Bout Jesus. And I am ready to kill, not cause I got anything gainst Jesus. Just that when you fixed to watch a gorilla picture you don't wanna get messed around with Sunday School stuff. So I am mad. Besides, we see this raggedy old brown film *King of Kings* every year and enough's enough. Grownups figure they can treat you just anyhow. Which burns me up. There I am, my feet up and my Havmore potato chips really salty and crispy and two jawbreakers in my lap and the money safe in my shoe from the big boys, and here comes this Jesus stuff. So we all go wild. Yellin, booin, stompin and carryin on. Really to wake the man in the booth up there who musta went to sleep and put on the wrong reels. But no, cause he holler down to shut up and then he turn the sound up so we really gotta holler like crazy to even hear ourselves good. And the matron ropes off the children section and flashes her light all over the place and we yell some more and some kids slip under the rope and run up and down the aisle just to show it take more than some dusty ole velvet rope to tie us down. And I'm flingin the kid in front of me's popcorn. And Baby Jason kickin seats. And it's really somethin. Then here come the big and bad matron, the one they let out in case of emergency. And she totin that flashlight like she gonna use it on somebody. This here the colored matron Brandy and her friends call Thunderbuns. She do not play. She do not smile. So we shut up and watch the simple ass picture.

Which is not so simple as it is stupid. Cause I realize that just about anybody in my family is better than this god they always talkin about. My daddy wouldn't stand for nobody treatin any of us that way. My mama specially. And I can just see it now, Big Brood up there on the cross talkin bout Forgive them Daddy cause they don't know what they doin. And my Mama say Get on down from there you big fool, whatcha think this is, playtime? And my Daddy yellin to Granddaddy to get him a ladder cause Big Brood actin the fool, his mother side of the family showin up. And my mama and her sister Daisy jumpin on them Romans beatin them with they pocketbooks. And Hunca Bubba tellin them folks on they knees they better get out the way and go get some help or they goin to get trampled on. And Granddaddy Vale sayin Leave the boy alone, if that's what he wants to do with his life we ain't got nothin to say about it. Then Aunt Daisy givin him a taste of that pocketbook, fussin bout what a damn fool old man Granddaddy is. Then everybody jumpin in his chest like the time Uncle Clayton went in the army and come back with only one leg and Granddaddy say somethin stupid about that's life. And by this time Big Brood off the cross and in the park playin handball or skully or somethin. And the family in the kitchen throwin dishes at each other, screamin bout if you hadn't done this I wouldn't had to do that. And me in the parlor trying to do my arithmetic yellin Shut it off.

Which is what I was yellin all by myself which make me a sittin target for Thunderbuns. But when I yell We want our money back, that gets everybody in chorus. And the movie windin up with this heavenly cloud music and the smart-ass up there in his hole in the wall turns up the sound again to drown us out. Then there comes Bugs Bunny which we already seen so we know we been had. No gorilla my nuthin. And Big Brood say Awwww sheeet, we goin to see the manager and get our money back. And I know from this we business. So I brush the potato chips out of my hair which is where Baby Jason like to put em, and I march myself up the aisle to deal with the manager who is a crook in the first place for lyin out there sayin *Gorilla, My Love* playin. And I never did like the man cause he oily and pasty at the same time like the bad guy in the serial, the one that got a hideout behind a push-button bookcase and play "Moonlight Sonata" with gloves on. I knock on the door and I am furious. And I am alone, too. Cause Big Brood suddenly got to go so bad even though my mama told us bout goin in them nasty bathrooms. And I hear him sigh like he disgusted when he get to the door and see only a little kid there. And now I'm really furious cause I get so tired grownups messin over kids just cause they little and can't take em to court. What is it, he say to me like I lost my mittens or wet on myself or am somebody's retarded child. When in reality I am the smartest kid P.S. 186 ever had in its whole lifetime and you can ax anybody. Even them teachers that don't like me cause I won't sing them Southern songs or back off when they tell me my questions are out of order. And cause my Mama come up there in a minute when them teachers start playin the dozens behind colored folks. She stalk in with her hat pulled down bad and that Persian lamb coat draped back over one hip on account of she got her fist planted there so she can talk that talk which gets us all hypnotized, and teacher be comin undone cause she know this could be her job and her behind cause Mama got pull with the Board and bad by her own self anyhow.

So I kick the door open wider and just walk right by him and sit down and tell the man about himself and that I want my money back and that goes for Baby Jason and Big Brood too. And he still trying to shuffle me out the door even though I'm sittin which shows him for the fool he is. Just like them teachers do fore they realize Mama like a stone on that spot and ain't backin up. So he ain't gettin up off the money. So I was forced to leave, takin the matches from under his ashtray, and set a fire under the candy stand, which closed the raggedy ole Washington down for a week. My Daddy had the suspect it was me cause Big Brood got a big mouth. But I explained right quick what the whole thing was about and I figured it was even-steven. Cause if you say Gorilla, My Love, you suppose to mean it. Just like when you say you goin to give me a party on my birthday, you gotta mean it. And if you say me and Baby Jason can go South pecan haulin with Granddaddy Vale, you better not be comin up with no stuff about the weather look uncertain or did you mop the bathroom or any other trickified business. I mean even gangsters in the movies say My word is my bond. So don't nobody get away with nothin far as I'm concerned. So Daddy put his belt back on. Cause that's the way I was raised. Like my Mama say in one of them situations when I won't back down, Okay Badbird, you right. Your point is well-taken. Not that Badbird my name, just what she say when she tired arguin and know I'm right. And Aunt Jo, who is the hardest head in the family and worse even than Aunt Daisy, she say, You absolutely right Miss Muffin, which also ain't my real name but the name she gave me one time when I got some medicine shot in my behind and wouldn't get up off her pillows for nothin. And even Granddaddy Vale—who got no memory to speak of, so sometime you can just plain lie to him, if you want to be like that—he say, Well if that's what I said, then that's it. But this name business was different they said. It wasn't like Hunca Bubba had gone back on his word or anything. Just that he was thinkin bout gettin married and was usin his real name now. Which ain't the way I saw it at all.

So there I am in the navigator seat. And I turn to him and just plain ole ax him. I mean I come right on out with it. No sense goin all around that barn the old folks talk about. And like my mama say, Hazel—which is my real name and what she remembers to call me when she bein serious—when you got somethin on your mind, speak up and let the chips fall where they may. And if anybody don't like it, tell em to come see your mama. And Daddy look up from the paper and say, You hear your mama good, Hazel. And tell em to come see me first. Like that. That's how I was raised.

So I turn clear round in the navigator seat and say, "Look here, Hunca Bubba or Jefferson Windsong Vale or whatever your name is, you gonna marry this girl?"

"Sure am," he say, all grins.

And I say, "Member that time you was baby-sittin me when we lived at four-o-nine and there was this big snow and Mama and Daddy got held up in the country so you had to stay for two days?"

And he say, "Sure do."

"Well. You remember how you told me I was the cutest thing that ever walked the earth?"

"Oh, you were real cute when you were little," he say, which is suppose to be funny. I am not laughin.

"Well. You remember what you said?"

And Granddaddy Vale squintin over the wheel and axin Which way, Scout. But Scout is busy and don't care if we all get lost for days.

"Watcha mean, Peaches?"

"My name is Hazel. And what I mean is you said you were going to marry *me* when I grew up. You were going to wait. That's what I mean, my dear Uncle Jefferson." And he don't say nuthin. Just look at me real strange like he never saw me before in life. Like he lost in some weird town in the middle of night and lookin for directions and there's no one to ask. Like it was me that messed up the maps and turned the road posts round. "Well, you said it, didn't you?" And Baby Jason lookin back and forth like we playin ping-pong. Only I ain't playin. I'm hurtin and I can hear that I am screamin. And Granddaddy Vale mumblin how we never gonna get to where we goin if I don't turn around and take my navigator job serious.

"Well, for cryin out loud, Hazel, you just a little girl. And I was just teasin."

" 'And I was just teasin,' " I say back just how he said it so he can hear what a terrible thing it is. Then I don't say nuthin. And he don't say nuthin. And Baby Jason don't say nuthin nohow. Then Granddaddy Vale speak up. "Look here, Precious, it was Hunca Bubba what told you them things. This here, Jefferson Winston Vale." And Hunca Bubba say, "That's right. That was somebody else. I'm a new somebody."

"You a lyin dawg," I say, when I meant to say treacherous dog, but just couldn't get hold of the word. It slipped away from me. And I'm cryin and crumplin down in the seat and just don't care. And Granddaddy say to hush and steps on the gas. And I'm losin my bearins and don't even know where to look on the map cause I can't see for cryin. And Baby Jason cryin too. Cause he is my blood brother and understands that we must stick together or be forever lost, what with grown-ups playin change-up and turnin you round every which way so bad. And don't even say they sorry.

ROBERT FLANAGAN

Teller's Ticket

The basic purpose of the ticket arrangement was to minimize if not completely eliminate difficulties, certainly not to cause more, and not by any stretch of the imagination to land Teller in such a hapless predicament that he wished he'd never conceived of the system.

He drove his white Rabbit at the legal limit in the expressway's slushy right lane, the gray wake of a tractor-trailer enveloping him as in a cloud. His windshield wipers slapped back and forth at a manic rate yet failed to clear his field of vision. The rear of the semi, intermittently visible, bore a yellow sticker with black block lettering: MY LIGHTS ARE ON FOR SAFETY. Teller's lights were on high. He wore his shoulder harness and seat belt. He felt utterly unsafe.

Teller believed on principle in conducting one's life in an orderly manner. Had his life worked out according to plan—he'd had his heart set on being elected a U.S. senator—he would have applied his idea of order to the affairs of the nation. He had failed to win election, however, to either city council or the local school board. Adjusting downward his career aims, he now labored as a lobbyist for Hartford Health Insurance. The statehouse was his beat. Bills affecting health care plans bore his anonymous stamp, and tens of thousands of heartland citizens were unknowingly in his debt for their extended coverage. Teller took satisfaction in pulling strings behind the scenes.

Nina, his wife, was a coronary care nurse. The Tellers' common interest was health. They jogged, dieted, and did slimnastics together. They drank only in moderation. Neither smoked. Had they chosen to have children, their offspring never would have become those lank and languid social excesses one saw smoking grass in city parks or lining up at public clinics for the legalized manna of methadone.

Not that Teller and Nina had no problems. Any two people living together for any length of time, whether husband and wife, parent and child, sibling and sibling, or POSSLQ's (persons of the opposite sex sharing living quarters, as per U.S. census category), had problems.

Teller, as he did in influencing bills and amendments, applied his considerable talents for meticulous analysis and reasoned compromise to his marital difficulties.

So how in the world had he gotten himself into this idiotic imbroglio—that's what he'd like to know.

Once a week he played poker, his minor vice. His doctor, Art Easterday, hosted the games at his comfortably cluttered bachelor's quarters. There was usually another doctor or two in attendance, besides Bill Modell, a pipe-sucking ad exec addicted to high stakes bluffing, and a CPA named Veering who was Teller's only match in estimating the odds of a given hand. Teller, although he infrequently won big, rarely ended up a loser. He folded early on weak cards, stood pat on a fair draw, seldom bluffed, and when blessed with a winning hand sucked in bets with artful raises.

Last night he had suffered a three-hour run of bad cards before being dealt, at midnight, four kings in a round of draw. He discarded a deuce, and drew an ace of spades. He bumped a raise and a bifocaled gynecologist folded. Easterday, an excessive mound of chips before his expansive paunch, met and raised Teller. Veering closed his eyes for a moment, consulting his internal calculator, before tossing in his hand. Modell called. Teller raised. Easterday raised again, giving Teller pause. Easterday too had drawn a single card, which probably meant he was drawing to a straight or a flush (the doctor's weakness was for filling inside straights) or was also holding four of a kind. Even so, Easterday couldn't do better than queens. Moving to raise, Teller noted with dismay that his run of bad luck had left him bereft of chips. It was the biggest pot of the entire night.

"You out?" Modell prompted, chomping at the bit to sweeten the pot. It appeared that the only reason he played was to prove how much he could afford to lose.

Teller produced his wallet. He had filled up his Rabbit's tank and had gotten his hair trimmed; two crinkled ones were all he had left. His checkbook was at home. Easterday displayed on his boneless face the mild smile that never failed to infuriate Teller. He fished out his one remaining monthly ticket, tapped its stiff edge on the table a moment, considering. Then, promising himself that he'd make up to Nina for his indiscretion with a gala evening out on his winnings, he placed the ticket atop the loaded pot.

Had he felt in his bones at that moment that he teetered on the brink of a deadly precipice? Now, he could not be certain. Then, he knew only that the pot was his.

Easterday picked up the ticket, read it, raised his eyebrows, and laid it back down. "I don't think you want to do this."

"Hey, what's going on here?" Modell was aiming the ticket at Teller's head.

The ticket was Teller's prize: *This entitles the bearer to one sex act of his choice.* Nina's signature slanted across the lower part of the card.

"I assume you can read," Teller said to Modell, then to the banker: "That ought to be worth at least fifty."

"I'd say a hundred at the very least," Easterday replied.

"A hundred it is," Teller snapped, a generous grin covering his pique at being topped by the doctor. "After all, it's your money." He resolutely appeared calm as the others looked first at the ticket and then at him with what he took to be a new regard.

Modell complained, "I thought this was table stakes."

"Pot limit," Teller reminded him.

Easterday leaned forward as he did in professional consultation. "I believe you are making a serious mistake."

"The question is, are you a gambler or not?" Teller let that sink in, then fixed Modell with a penetrating stare. "Too rich for your blood, big boy?"

"What the hell!" Modell flipped in ten blue chips.

"You're being foolish," Easterday said.

"Hey, it's my money," Modell whined.

"I was speaking to Byron."

If Teller had considered backing down and treating the incident as his little joke, Easterday's patronizing tone stiffened his resolution. Why did doctors think the world was obligated to defer to them? A man too old for his years, who obviously needed to be put on a strict diet, Easterday was forever giving Teller advice: slow down, develop a hobby, take your poor wife on vacation. When Teller countered that he knew how to manage his affairs, the doctor would only smile. Easterday seemed determined not to treat Teller as an equal. Had Teller risen to the Senate, he'd have sponsored a socialized medicine bill to put Easterday and his ilk in their place. "Does that mean you fold?" Teller asked.

Easterday blue-chipped the pot.

"Showdown!" Modell trumpeted, slapping down his pathetic full house. Easterday held a straight flush, hearts, queen high. Teller splayed his losing kings. He sensed the others' close attention. "Win some, lose some," he said. Rising from his chair, he donned his parka and went out to his Rabbit, the heart in his chest as frantic as a snared bird.

Now, his hands clutched the steering wheel like a lifeline. His nerves sang with the stored tension of a sleepless night and a distracted day at work. How to tell Nina what he had done? For after his noon confrontation with Easterday it was apparent that an explanation of sorts would be necessary. It wasn't only that he'd lost the ticket, but that he had dared show it to anyone. Nina would leave him, or kill him. She had always been the less rational partner in their marriage.

Although, to give her her due, she had come to admit the practicality of the ticket arrangement. The Tellers' bone of contention was sex, as it appeared to be with the majority of married couples, and he'd seen no reason that the problem could not be dealt with in a rational manner. Not given to hot-tubbing, standing on his head while chanting a mantra, nor self-hypnotizing his system into proper biorhythms, Teller sought release from tension in sex. Since he was on principle monogamous, Nina necessarily provided any release beyond that which he might handle himself. Teller's sexual needs were daily, Nina's weekly. Such disparity might drive some couples into divorce court to sunder their union and fragment their estate. None of that avoidable messiness for Teller. A booklet of detachable, redeemable love coupons spotted in a novelty shop prompted his plan. In consultation with his wife, he composed a series of fifteen monthly tickets on the reverse side of his business cards, fourteen tickets specifying particular sexual acts and a special one giving him free choice. Nina was issued three counter-claims to allow for occasional indisposition. Despite his wife's initial discomfiture, Teller felt reasonably assured that his system was both equitable and viable. Having read Kinsey, Masters and Johnson, *The Joy of Sex, More Joy,* Nancy Friday and Gay Talese, he was quite cognizant of the fact that the sexual revolution had rendered obsolete traditional strictures and customs. There was a whole lot of coupling going on, and Teller saw no reason that a loyal spouse need miss out on the action, not when he was capable of plotting a course of corrective action.

Of course Nina felt somewhat differently about it. Her lovemaking, although more regular since the system's inception, was marked by a sense of distance. Teller fully expected, however, that it would take time for her to adjust to such a frank and open approach to matters she'd been taught to regard as dark, dangerous secrets. Nina had been raised in the Roman Catholic religion, that primitive cult designed to scar one deeply enough in childhood that the remainder of one's life would be devoted to rituals in hope of a miraculous cure. Teller's parents were Christian Scientists. Although he practiced no religion, Teller did not inveigh against others' beliefs. While it was true that when traveling he relieved his motel room of the Gideon Bible, disposing of it in the nearest trash can, it had nothing to do with religion. He resisted on principle the invasion of one's privacy.

Which was precisely the reason he resented Easterday so. The good doctor was invading the Tellers' privacy now by pressing his claim just as surely as if he were inserting a rubber-gloved finger into Teller's rectum, which he did every six months. As he also did to Nina.

Could it be that having taken Pap smears, palpated her breasts, rapped her dimpled knees with his rubber-headed hammer, peered down her throat, lit up her ear canals and pupils, and listened to her heart beat, that Easterday secretly lusted for Nina?

In a moment of giddy paranoia Teller imagined the fat physician as having run the poker game for years waiting as patiently as a bullfrog for the butterfly of opportunity that last night had provided. Not so paranoid perhaps. Hadn't Teller off-handedly mentioned his ticket system during his recent physical? Hadn't Easterday displayed definite interest, his eyebrows lifting, and a light coming on in his eyes which Teller saw now as one not of surprise but rather of excitement? Not paranoia at all. The proof, if indeed Teller needed any, had come that noon when he'd tried to buy back his ticket. "I'm afraid that's not possible," Easterday had said. Teller had expected him to hand it over with a chuckle, to treat the affair as a joke between friends, a pardonable bit of gaucherie which Teller would pay for with rueful smiles and patient endurance of the doctor's waggish jibes. Teller doubled, then tripled, his offer. "What's lost is lost," was Easterday's reply.

"What kind of man are you anyway?" Teller had shrieked.

"The question is"—a slow grin suffused Easterday's pallid face,—"are you a gambler or not?"

Teller had slammed the door in leaving, nearly bowling over the young office nurse whom the fat quack no doubt spreadeagled on his desk after hours. Easterday probably had possessed dozens of women, no doubt illicitly diddling scores of his patients. What did he care if he shattered marriages, ruined people's lives, made it impossible for a man ever again to look his wife straight in the eye?

Nina's tan Rabbit was in the drive. Teller whipped in behind her. He entered their paid-for split-level as anxiously as a firefighter a blazing tenement.

"Any calls?" he called, his usual greeting sounding ominous to him. What did Easterday say? What did you say? What can I say to make it okay?

"Nothing," Nina called from the bathroom. She always popped into the tub directly on arriving home; it was hard work nursing hearts back to health.

Teller made a cup of Sanka and sagged into his armchair. Slowly, now that he was home and enclosed by known walls, some sense of safety returned.

Of course there existed not the slightest possibility that Nina would honor Easterday's ill-gotten claim. Medical ethics, marriage vows, and moral concerns gave her the perfect right to turn him away empty-handed. Moreover, strictly on a technical level, she had left one monthly counter-claim. The Tellers would scout about for a new doctor and that would be the end of the affair. Teller could explain to his wife that he'd had too much to drink that night, implying perhaps that his host may have spiked his drink. The fact that he rarely drank would only serve as further reason for his unaccountably erratic behavior.

Why was he thinking defensively? The situation called for action. Teller would sit his wife down and frankly explain to her that he had cause for concern. It appeared that one of his tickets had turned up missing. To make no bones about it, he'd lost it. They needed to be prepared for the unlikely event that someone might find it and, misunderstanding the nature of the Tellers' intimate agreement, attempt to redeem it.

Easterday had witnesses, though. Still, Teller found it difficult to believe the doctor would have the gall to call on them. And if he did? Why then he was lying and the others were lying too. At bottom, who was Nina going to believe—a bunch of drunken gambling braggarts, or her own husband?

Secure in his wife's trust, Teller felt his heart expand in magnanimity. To clear the air he would propose they drop the ticket system altogether. "I know you're not nuts about it, kid, so what say we forget it?" Well, not *kid.* He'd broach the subject as soon as she completed her bath, then take her out to dinner, someplace swank, and afterwards they might go dancing if she liked, or to a movie, or shopping, whatever. Actually though, he might better wait until they came home, buoyant with fun and champagne-giggly, before mentioning the ticket's loss in an offhand manner, a comical happenstance to amuse the two of them in years to come as they looked back from the snug comfort of maturity at their feckless youth.

The telephone rang. Teller froze.

"Would you get that?" Nina called.

Teller plucked up the receiver and replaced it on its cradle. "Wrong number," he shouted. He waited beside the phone. Pouncing, he strangled the first ring before it fully sounded, then left the phone off the hook.

He ran upstairs for his checkbook, changed his shirt and tie, and rapped on the bathroom door. "Shake a leg, sweetheart. I'm treating you to dinner."

Nina opened the door. Her small body encased in a nubby white towel, a turban of white hiding her hazel hair, she looked heartbreakingly innocent. Teller's glasses misted with steam. He saw her as a fetching waif he'd seduced only to sell into white slavery. Never could he tell her what he'd done, no matter how much champagne they'd had.

She smiled up at him. "What's the occasion?"

Assaulted by an image of Easterday as a giant pulsating larval creature bearing down on Nina, Teller blurted "You look lovely!"

"Why, thank you."

Urgent signals of disconnection sounded. "I'll get it!" Teller bounded downstairs to suffocate the phone with couch cushions.

Only one course of action lay open to him. Easterday's lust could not be so great that he was willing to die for it.

When they returned home from dinner and a movie, Nina dressed for bed. Teller sat staring at premium redemption forms at his study desk.

"Aren't you coming?" She was wearing her plum, empire-style nightgown, his favorite, and his heart stuttered as his eyes took them in, her gold hoop earrings and slave bracelet.

"Some business." Feeling her soft breasts against the back of his head, he resisted an urge to rise.

An hour later he tiptoed to the open door of their bedroom. She was sleeping. He eased downstairs to the phone. On the sixth ring, the toad's voice croaked "Hello?"

A handkerchief over the mouthpiece, Teller rasped "Better listen and listen good, fat man. You're in a jam, understand. You're in way over your head."

"Byron, whom do you think you are fooling?"

"I ain't saying who hired me. But I'm warning you, Sawbones, I get a contract, I get it done. I don't mess and I don't miss. You get on my list . . ."

The doctor clicked off. Teller wiped perspiration from his face with the handkerchief, then carefully replaced the weapon in its holder.

Addressing the mystery voice as Byron was more than a shot in the dark, of course, but Easterday could not be one hundred percent certain who the caller was. He had to be suffering some apprehension, if not terror.

Teller would confront Easterday first thing in the morning. Lay it on the line. "Five hundred cash. It's an offer you can't refuse."

The telephone rang. Teller seized the receiver, holding it six inches from his ear and watching it from the corner of an eye, the cord snaking about his wrist.

"Did you lose something?" The doctor's voice was saturated with the oil of self-satisfaction.

Teller's hand sagged to the cradle. How could a sensitive, sensible human being do this to a fellow creature? Easterday was often a joyous dinner guest at Teller's laden table. He'd sung the praises of Nina's cooking, of Nina's decorating, of Nina's nursing. How could he treat her like a common whore?

Teller's body trembled. He was furious, he thought; outraged. He didn't have to stand for such abuse. He knew people in power, he had connections on the state medical board, he was skilled in legal ins and outs. A supposedly reputable physician making late night crank calls to his patients! He'd have Easterday's license revoked. He'd haul the fat man into court on harassment charges. Tack on alienation of affections too. Any attorney worth his salt . . .

Teller hugged himself. He was terrified.

The next three days were hell for Teller. He calculated his moves about the house always to be nearer than Nina to the phone. He ate little and became the victim of aspirin-immune headaches. Sleeping fitfully, listening for the telephone or doorbell or a car turning into their drive, he felt acid bubbling in his stomach. When Nina touched him in bed, he turned his back to her, pleading fatigue.

Each day he left his office early to be home when Nina arrived. "Anything interesting happen today? Anything new?"

"Is there something wrong?" she asked.

"Work," he explained.

He knew he was beaten. The lost ticket had become a San Andreas fault underlying the seven year construction of their marriage. The claim presented would shift the earth, bringing who knew what all down about their ears.

And might the earth move for Nina with Easterday? As it had for Maria in *For Whom the Bell Tolls?* As it did less and less frequently for Nina with Teller?

Why had he done such a crazy thing? He'd known deep down that it was more than a joke. Yet in spite of his trembling hands, he'd gambled the ticket like a man on easy terms with deviance and danger. In fact, he saw now, placing the ticket on the gaming table was every bit as dangerous as if he'd plunked down a loaded revolver. It provoked unavoidable consequences. But surely he hadn't thought so at the time. At the time he'd thought of nothing but securing the loaded pot. His bet was a sure thing, damn it! No one needed to take the ticket seriously.

It was only there for show. Until Easterday's fluke of luck ruined everything.

Yet hadn't Teller at times sensed that the tickets, while apparently no more than convenient possessions, were charged with a possibly destructive power? Like money or cars or firearms?

If he'd suffered such doubts, they were easily dismissed by the flush feelings of sufficiency and control he had felt as his well-being. Ticketed Teller was a man to behold, there was confidence in his stride and steel in his eye; no-ticket Teller was a bum on his uppers, scrounging gutters for stogie stubs.

The truth was inescapable. He was a fool.

But Easterday! He was worse than a fool. An unprincipled opportunist, he would press his advantage although it caused crisis and anguish for people who had thought of him as healer and friend. What could the hypocritical physician, brain in his groin, hope to comprehend of the Tellers' complex human union? Teller and Nina shared so many memories, understood one another's codewords and looks, made allowances for moods and quirks, counterbalanced particular weaknesses with particular strengths. Teller needed Nina. She was like a best friend to him. Struck by the possibility of losing her, Teller saw that she *was* his best friend. The doctor, of course, saw her as another usable body. Why hadn't Teller recognized this weakness earlier?

The next day he left work at noon, legitimately claiming a migraine, and lunched on Excedrin and Tums. He knew he had to tell her, and the sooner the better. He went shopping. At Fredericks of Hollywood he bought Nina a black silk affair split to the hip on either side. Minutes later he returned it. At Sears he got the fuzzy green sleepsack he knew she'd prefer. He ran from the shopping mall to his parked car, sleet needling his cheeks.

Home, he rooted about in Nina's things. He found the pack of redeemed tickets bound by a rubber band and tucked in a drawer beneath his wife's white panties. Building a fire on the hearth, he tossed the tickets into the blaze. When they were reduced to ash, he wrapped the sleepsack in gold foil and stuck a green silk bow on the package, then sat in his armchair, allowing himself a snifter of sherry for courage. Three-thirty came and went. He phoned the hospital and found that Nina had left there at three.

The calendar magnet-stuck to the refrigerator gave him the reason: 3:30, Doctor. So the meeting had been arranged. Easterday must have gotten to her at work. There was nothing for Teller to do but take his lumps.

He was working on a second snifter—consolation now—when he jerked to attention. A knot popped in the grate. *His* lumps? Nina was the one being lumped with those personless, glossy bodies laid bare in centerfolds, stylish latrines for men's ease.

He sped off in his Rabbit. The sleet turned to snow on his windshield.

Nina sat in the waiting room reading *Family Circle.* Her face registered alarm when she saw him. "What are you doing here?"

The office nurse slid back a glass slat. "Mrs. Teller, the doctor will see you now."

"That's what he thinks!" Teller threw open the door and barged down the hall. Behind him he heard Nina call his name.

"Aha!" Easterday cried. "The high-roller! Or is this the pimp? Or the hit man?"

"Let's have it, Fatso."

"Have what?"

"My ticket!" Teller roared.

The door opened and Nina looked in. "Your what?"

Easterday exploded with an enormous laugh. "Your ticker is fine!" He grasped Teller by the arm, there was great strength in his oleaginous hand, and placed him in a plastic chair. "This husband of yours!" he said to Nina. "At poker the other night I told him he had a weak heart. I'm afraid he misunderstood me. Nina, dear, would you mind waiting a few more minutes?" He winked. "Man talk." He edged her into the hall and closed the door.

"I'm not leaving here without it," Teller cried, springing to his feet. "If you lay a hand on her, it'll be over my dead body."

"So what is your offer now?"

"Whatever you want."

"Anything?"

"Name it."

Easterday creased his massive rump on the edge of his costly desk. "Surely you wouldn't go so far as to offer to take your wife's place?"

"What?"

"To redeem the ticket, you would take her place?"

Dizzied, Teller slumped into the chair.

"Well, Byron?"

He saw the doctor's smile as a sign of degenerate delight. The consulting room became a sultan's chamber. He detected in the air a hint of jasmine: Easterday's cologne? A confirmed bachelor—what a farce! The truth was only too clear to Teller now. He slammed a door in his mind against a rush of disgusting images. An act done out of love was above disgust. He would do it out of love for Nina. Whatever the doctor desired could be no worse than what Teller had demanded she do for him. "Anything," he managed to say.

"As a gambling man, you understand, it does interest me to know whether or not you are bluffing."

Teller met and held the doctor's gelid stare. "You want to find out, you've got to call."

Easterday sighed, a flatulent elephant. "Your ticket was thrown away right after our game."

"What?"

"It has gone the way of all trash."

"Why didn't you tell me?"

"Did you ask?"

"I offered . . ."

"You actually believed I could bring myself to mention a thing like that? To Nina, of all people?"

"Then why didn't you just give it back to me?"

"And have you use it?"

A flare went off in the dark of Teller's skull. When jogging had given him knee pains, he'd joked about having prosthetic joints put in that would work better than the original equipment. "The body is a machine made by the hand of God," Easterday had replied, "infinitely better than any machine of human invention." A quotation from Descartes, he'd said; but the sentiment, Teller realized now, had come straight from Easterday's heart. The doctor's eye was aimed beyond organ and tissue, cell and chromosome, molecule, plasma, helical DNA. A mechanic of the corpus, Easterday aspired to Romance.

Teller spoke in open amazement. "You're in love with her."

"The question is," the doctor, dropping his eyes, seemed a shy fat boy of fifty, "are you?"

"She's my wife."

Easterday made a smacking sound with his lips.

"Am I in love with Nina?" Teller rose from his perch. "I am."

"You are—truly?"

"Heart and soul," he declared.

"Ah, a closet Quixote." The doctor's voice, barely audible, sounded no mockery. His slow smile seemed Buddha-like. "There's hope for you after all."

Teller captured one of Easterday's soft paws in his hands and warmly squeezed it. "Thank you." His heart went out to his physician. "You're a good man."

Easterday slid free. "Please."

Embarrassed by his overflow of emotion, Teller faced the door. After a moment, pink-cheeked, he turned back. Easterday's look stopped his hand on its way to his wallet. "No," Teller said, "I won't insult you."

"Good." The doctor had assumed his swivel seat, the desk a barrier of pale oak emphasizing his authority. "Your wife is here for her regular physical. I'm afraid I've kept her waiting too long already."

For twenty-eight minutes Teller endured the auger of doubt. He leaped to his feet as Nina reentered the waiting room. "You're all right?"

"Yes," she said. "Are you?"

"Of course."

"Why were you so upset? Is there really something wrong with your heart?"

"Only a misunderstanding."

They stepped from the office into a swirl of white flakes. When Nina offered her hand, he accepted it as a token of the gift of herself.

MAX APPLE

BRIDGING

At the Astrodome, Nolan Ryan is shaving the corners. He's going through the Giants in order. The radio announcer is not even mentioning that by the sixth the Giants haven't had a hit. The K's mount on the scoreboard. Tonight Nolan passes the Big Train and is now the all-time strikeout king. He's almost as old as I am and he still throws nothing but smoke. His fastball is an aspirin; batters tear their tendons lunging for his curve. Jessica and I have season tickets, but tonight she's home listening and I'm in the basement of St. Anne's Church watching Kay Randall's fingertips. Kay is holding her hands out from her chest, her fingertips on each other. Her fingers move a little as she talks and I can hear her nails click when they meet. That's how close I'm sitting.

Kay is talking about "bridging"; that's what her arched fingers represent.

"Bridging," she says, "is the way Brownies become Girl Scouts. It's a slow steady process. It's not easy, but we allow a whole year for bridging."

Eleven girls in brown shirts with red bandannas at their neck are imitating Kay as she talks. They hold their stumpy chewed fingertips out and bridge them. So do I.

I brought the paste tonight and the stick-on gold stars and the thread for sewing buttonholes.

"I feel a little awkward," Kay Randall said on the phone, "asking a man to do these errands . . . but that's my problem, not yours. Just bring the supplies and try to be at the church meeting room a few minutes before seven."

I arrive a half hour early.

"You're off your rocker," Jessica says. She begs me to drop her at the Astrodome on my way to the Girl Scout meeting. "After the game, I'll meet you at the main souvenir stand on the first level. They stay open an hour after the game. I'll be all right. There are cops and ushers every five yards."

She can't believe that I am missing this game to perform my functions as an assistant Girl Scout leader. Our Girl Scout battle has been going on for two months.

"Girl Scouts is stupid," Jessica says. "Who wants to sell cookies and sew buttons and walk around wearing stupid old badges?"

When she agreed to go to the first meeting, I was so happy I volunteered to become an assistant leader. After the meeting, Jessica went directly to the car the way she does after school, after a birthday party, after a ball game, after anything. A straight line to the car. No jabbering with girlfriends, no smiles, no dallying, just right to the car. She slides into the back seat, belts in, and braces herself for destruction. It has already happened once.

I swoop past five thousand years of stereotypes and accept my assistant leader's packet and credentials.

"I'm sure there have been other men in the movement," Kay says, "we just haven't had any in our district. It will be good for the girls."

Not for my Jessica. She won't bridge, she won't budge.

"I know why you're doing this," she says. "You think that because I don't have a mother, Kay Randall and the Girl Scouts will help me. That's crazy. And I know that Sharon is supposed to be like a mother too. Why don't you just leave me alone."

Sharon is Jessica's therapist. Jessica sees her twice a week. Sharon and I have a meeting once a month.

"We have a lot of shy girls," Kay Randall tells me. "Scouting brings them out. Believe me, it's hard to stay shy when you're nine years old and you're sharing a tent with six other girls. You have to count on each other, you have to communicate."

I imagine Jessica zipping up in her sleeping bag, mumbling good night to anyone who first says it to her, then closing her eyes and hating me for sending her out among the happy.

"She likes all sports, especially baseball," I tell my leader.

"There's room for baseball in scouting," Kay says. "Once a year the whole district goes to a game. They mention us on the big scoreboard."

"Jessica and I go to all the home games. We're real fans."

Kay smiles.

"That's why I want her in Girl Scouts. You know, I want her to go to things with her girlfriends instead of always hanging around with me at ball games."

"I understand," Kay says. "It's part of bridging."

With Sharon the term is "separation anxiety." That's the fastball, "bridging" is the curve. Amid all their magic words I feel as if Jessica and I are standing at home plate blindfolded.

While I await Kay and the members of Troop 111, District 6, I eye St. Anne in her grotto and St. Gregory and St. Thomas. Their hands are folded as if they started out bridging, ended up praying.

In October the principal sent Jessica home from school because Mrs. Simmons caught her in spelling class listening to the World Series through an earphone.

"It's against the school policy," Mrs. Simmons said. "Jessica understands school policy. We confiscate radios and send the child home."

"I'm glad," Jessica said. "It was a cheap-o radio. Now I can watch the TV with you."

They sent her home in the middle of the sixth game. I let her stay home for the seventh too.

The Brewers are her favorite American League team. She likes Rollie Fingers, and especially Robin Yount.

"Does Yount go in the hole better than Harvey Kuenn used to?"

"You bet," I tell her. "Kuenn was never a great fielder but he could hit three hundred with his eyes closed."

Kuenn is the Brewers' manager. He has an artificial leg and can barely make it up the dugout steps, but when I was Jessica's age and the Tigers were my team, Kuenn used to stand at the plate, tap the corners with his bat, spit some tobacco juice, and knock liners up the alley.

She took the Brewers' loss hard.

"If Fingers wasn't hurt they would have squashed the Cards, wouldn't they?"

I agreed.

"But I'm glad for Andujar."

We had Andujar's autograph. Once we met him at a McDonald's. He was a relief pitcher then, an erratic right-hander. In St. Louis he improved. I was happy to get his name on a napkin. Jessica shook his hand.

One night after I read her a story, she said, "Daddy, if we were rich could we go to the away games too? I mean, if you didn't have to be at work every day."

"Probably we could," I said, "but wouldn't it get boring? We'd have to stay at hotels and eat in restaurants. Even the players get sick of it."

"Are you kidding?" she said. "I'd never get sick of it."

"Jessica has fantasies of being with you forever, following baseball or whatever," Sharon says. "All she's trying to do is please you. Since she lost her mother she feels that you and she are alone in the world. She doesn't want to let anyone or anything else into that unit, the two of you. She's afraid of any more losses. And, of course, her greatest worry is about losing you."

"You know," I tell Sharon, "that's pretty much how I feel too."

"Of course it is," she says. "I'm glad to hear you say it."

Sharon is glad to hear me say almost anything. When I complain that her $100-a-week fee would buy a lot of peanut butter sandwiches, she says she is "glad to hear me expressing my anger."

"Sharon's not fooling me," Jessica says. "I know that she thinks drawing those pictures is supposed to make me feel better or something. You're just wasting your money. There's nothing wrong with me."

"It's a long, difficult, expensive process," Sharon says. "You and Jessica have lost a lot. Jessica is going to have to learn to trust the world again. It would help if you could do it too."

So I decide to trust Girl Scouts. First Girl Scouts, then the world. I make my stand at the meeting of Kay Randall's fingertips. While Nolan Ryan breaks Walter Johnson's strikeout record and pitches a two-hit shutout, I pass out paste and thread to nine-year-olds who are sticking and sewing their lives together in ways Jessica and I can't.

II

Scouting is not altogether new to me. I was a Cub Scout. I owned a blue beanie and I remember very well my den mother, Mrs. Clark. A den mother made perfect sense to me then and still does. Maybe that's why I don't feel uncomfortable being a Girl Scout assistant leader.

We had no den father. Mr. Clark was only a photograph on the living room wall, the tiny living room where we held our monthly meetings. Mr. Clark was killed in the Korean War. His son John was in the troop.

John was stocky but Mrs. Clark was huge. She couldn't sit on a regular chair, only on a couch or a stool without sides. She was the cashier in the convenience store beneath their apartment. The story we heard was that Walt, the old man who owned the store, felt sorry for her and gave her the job. He was her landlord too. She sat on a swivel stool and rang up the purchases.

We met at the store and watched while she locked the door; then we followed her up the steep staircase to her three-room apartment. She carried two wet glass bottles of milk. Her body took up the entire width of the staircase. She passed the banisters the way semi trucks pass each other on a narrow highway.

We were ten years old, a time when everything is funny, especially fat people. But I don't remember anyone ever laughing about Mrs. Clark. She had great dignity and character. So did John. I didn't know what to call it then, but I knew John was someone you could always trust.

She passed out milk and cookies, then John collected the cups and washed them. They didn't even have a television set. The only decoration in the room that barely held all of us was Mr. Clark's picture on the wall. We saw him in his uniform and we knew he died in Korea defending his country. We were little boys in blue beanies drinking milk in the apartment of a hero. Through that aura I came to scouting. I wanted Kay Randall to have all of Mrs. Clark's dignity.

When she took a deep breath and then bridged, Kay Randall had noticeable armpits. Her wide shoulders slithered into a tiny rib cage. Her armpits were like bridges. She said "bridging" like a mantra, holding her hands before her for about thirty seconds at the start of each meeting.

"A promise is a promise," I told Jessica. "I signed up to be a leader, and I'm going to do it with you or without you."

"But you didn't even ask me if I liked it. You just signed up without talking it over."

"That's true; that's why I'm not going to force you to go along. It was my choice."

"What can you like about it? I hate Melissa Randall. She always has a cold."

"Her mother is a good leader."

"How do you know?"

"She's my boss. I've got to like her, don't I?" I hugged Jessica. "C'mon, honey, give it a chance. What do you have to lose?"

"If you make me go I'll do it, but if I have a choice I won't."

Every other Tuesday, Karen, the fifteen-year-old Greek girl who lives on the corner, babysits Jessica while I go to the Scout meetings. We talk about field trips and how to earn merit badges. The girls giggle when Kay pins a promptness badge on me, my first.

Jessica thinks it's hilarious. She tells me to wear it to work.

Sometimes when I watch Jessica brush her hair and tie her ponytail and make up her lunch kit I start to think that maybe I should just relax and stop the therapy and the scouting and all my not-so-subtle attempts to get her to invite friends over. I start to think that, in spite of everything, she's a good student and she's got a sense of humor. She's barely nine years old. She'll grow up like everyone else does. John Clark did it without a father; she'll do it without a mother. I start to wonder if Jessica seems to the girls in her class the way John Clark seemed to me: dignified, serious, almost an adult even while we were playing. I admired him. Maybe the girls in her class admire her. But John had that hero on the wall, his father in a uniform, dead for reasons John and all the rest of us understood.

My Jessica had to explain a neurologic disease she couldn't even pronounce. "I hate it when people ask me about Mom," she says. "I just tell them she fell off the Empire State Building."

III

Before our first field trip I go to Kay's house for a planning session. We're going to collect wildflowers in East Texas. It's a one-day trip. I arranged to rent the school bus.

I told Jessica that she could go on the trip even though she wasn't a troop member, but she refused.

We sit on colonial furniture in Kay's den. She brings in coffee and we go over the supply list. Another troop is joining ours so there will be twenty-two girls, three women, and me, a busload among the bluebonnets.

"We have to be sure the girls understand that the bluebonnets they pick are on private land and that we have permission to pick them. Otherwise they might pick them along the roadside, which is against the law."

I imagine all twenty-two of them behind bars for picking bluebonnets and Jessica laughing while I scramble for bail money.

I keep noticing Kay's hands. I notice them as she pours coffee, as she checks off the items on the list, as she gestures. I keep expecting her to bridge. She has large, solid, confident hands. When she finishes bridging I sometimes feel like clapping the way people do after the national anthem.

"I admire you," she tells me. "I admire you for going ahead with

Scouts even though your daughter rejects it. She'll get a lot out of it indirectly from you."

Kay Randall is thirty-three, divorced, and has a Bluebird too. Her older daughter is one of the stubby-fingered girls, Melissa. Jessica is right; Melissa always has a cold.

Kay teaches fifth grade and has been divorced for three years. I am the first assistant she's ever had.

"My husband, Bill, never helped with Scouts," Kay says. "He was pretty much turned off to everything except his business and drinking. When we separated I can't honestly say I missed him; he'd never been there. I don't think the girls miss him either. He only sees them about once a month. He has girlfriends, and his business is doing very well. I guess he has what he wants."

"And you?"

She uses one of those wonderful hands to move the hair away from her eyes, a gesture that makes her seem very young.

"I guess I do too. I've got the girls and my job. I'm lonesome, though. It's not exactly what I wanted."

We both think about what might have been as we sit beside her glass coffeepot with our lists of sachet supplies. If she was Barbra Streisand and I Robert Redford and the music started playing in the background to give us a clue and there was a long close-up of our lips, we might just fade into middle age together. But Melissa called for Mom because her mosquito bite was bleeding where she scratched it. And I had an angry daughter waiting for me. And all Kay and I had in common was Girl Scouts. We were both smart enough to know it. When Kay looked at me before going to put alcohol on the mosquito bite, our mutual sadness dripped from us like the last drops of coffee through the grinds.

"You really missed something tonight," Jessica tells me. "The Astros did a double steal. I've never seen one before. In the fourth they sent Thon and Moreno together, and Moreno stole home."

She knows batting averages and won-lost percentages too, just like the older boys, only they go out to play. Jessica stays in and waits for me.

During the field trip, while the girls pick flowers to dry and then manufacture into sachets, I think about Jessica at home, probably beside the radio. Juana, our once-a-week cleaning lady, agreed to work on Saturday so she could stay with Jessica while I took the all-day field trip.

It was no small event. In the eight months since Vicki died I had not gone away for an entire day.

I made waffles in the waffle iron for her before I left, but she hardly ate.

"If you want anything, just ask Juana."

"Juana doesn't speak English."

"She understands, that's enough."

"Maybe for you it's enough."

"Honey, I told you, you can come; there's plenty of room on the bus. It's not too late for you to change your mind."

"It's not too late for you either. There's going to be plenty of other leaders there. You don't have to go. You're just doing this to be mean to me."

I'm ready for this. I spent an hour with Sharon steeling myself. "Before she can leave you," Sharon said, "you'll have to show her that you can leave. Nothing's going to happen to her. And don't let her be sick that day either."

Jessica is too smart to pull the "I don't feel good" routine. Instead she becomes more silent, more unhappy looking than usual. She stays in her pajamas while I wash the dishes and get ready to leave.

I didn't notice the sadness as it was coming upon Jessica. It must have happened gradually in the years of Vicki's decline, the years in which I paid so little attention to my daughter. There were times when Jessica seemed to recognize the truth more than I did.

As my Scouts picked their wildflowers, I remembered the last outing I had planned for us. It was going to be a Fourth of July picnic with some friends in Austin. I stopped at the bank and got $200 in cash for the long weekend. But when I came home Vicki was too sick to move and the air conditioner had broken. I called our friends to cancel the picnic; then I took Jessica to the mall with me to buy a fan. I bought the biggest one they had, a 58-inch oscillating model that sounded like a hurricane. It could cool 10,000 square feet, but it wasn't enough.

Vicki was home sitting blankly in front of the TV set. The fan could move eight tons of air an hour, but I wanted it to save my wife. I wanted a fan that would blow the whole earth out of its orbit.

I had $50 left. I gave it to Jessica and told her to buy anything she wanted.

"Whenever you're sad, Daddy, you want to buy me things." She put the money back in my pocket. "It won't help." She was seven years old, holding my hand tightly in the appliance department at J. C. Penney's.

I watched Melissa sniffle even more among the wildflowers, and I pointed out the names of various flowers to Carol and JoAnne and Sue and Linda and Rebecca, who were by now used to me and treated me pretty much as they treated Kay. I noticed that the Girl Scout flower book had very accurate photographs that made it easy to identify the bluebonnets and buttercups and poppies. There were also several varieties of wild grasses.

We were only 70 miles from home on some land a wealthy rancher long ago donated to the Girl Scouts. The girls bending among the flowers seemed to have been quickly transformed by the colorful meadow. The gigglers and monotonous singers on the bus were now, like the bees, sucking strength from the beauty around them. Kay was in the midst of them and so, I realized, was I, not watching and keeping score and admiring from the distance but a participant, a player.

JoAnne and Carol sneaked up from behind me and dropped some dandelions down my back. I chased them; then I helped the other leaders pour the Kool-Aid and distribute the Baggies and the name tags for each girl's flowers.

My daughter is home listening to a ball game, I thought, and I'm out here having fun with nine-year-olds. It's upside down.

When I came home with dandelion fragments still on my back, Juana had cleaned the house and I could smell the taco sauce in the kitchen. Jessica was in her room. I suspected that she had spent the day listless and tearful, although I had asked her to invite a friend over.

"I had a lot of fun, honey, but I missed you."

She hugged me and cried against my shoulder. I felt like holding her the way I used to when she was an infant, the way I rocked her to sleep. But she was a big girl now and needed not sleep but wakefulness.

"I heard on the news that the Rockets signed Ralph Sampson," she sobbed, "and you hardly ever take me to any pro basketball games."

"But if they have a new center things will be different. With Sampson we'll be contenders. Sure I'll take you."

"Promise?"

"Promise." I promise to take you everywhere, my lovely child, and then to leave you. I'm learning to be a leader.

RICHARD FORD

Communist

My mother once had a boyfriend named Glen Baxter. This was in 1961. We—my mother and I—were living in the little house my father had left her up the Sun River, near Victory, Montana, west of Great Falls.

My mother was thirty-two at the time. I was sixteen. Glen Baxter was somewhere in the middle, between us, though I cannot be exact about it.

We were living then off the proceeds of my father's life insurance policies, with my mother doing some part-time waitressing work up in Great Falls and going to the bars in the evenings, which I know is where she met Glen Baxter. Sometimes he would come back with her and stay in her room at night, or she would call up from town and explain that she was staying with him in his little place on Lewis Street by the GN yards. She gave me his number every time, but I never called it. I think she probably thought that what she was doing was terrible, but simply couldn't help herself. I thought it was all right, though. Regular life it seemed, and still does. She was young, and I knew that even then.

Glen Baxter was a Communist and liked hunting, which he talked about a lot. Pheasants. Ducks. Deer. He killed all of them, he said. He had been to Vietnam as far back as then, and when he was in our house he often talked about shooting the animals over there—monkeys and beautiful parrots—using military guns just for sport. We did not know what Vietnam was then, and Glen, when he talked about that, referred to it only as "the Far East." I think now he must've been in the CIA and been disillusioned by something he saw or found out about and been thrown out, but that kind of thing did not matter to us. He was a tall, dark-eyed man with short black hair, and was usually in a good humor. He had gone halfway through college in Peoria, Illinois, he said, where he grew up. But when he was around our life he worked wheat farms as a ditcher, and stayed out of work winters and in the bars drinking with women like my mother, who had work and some money. It is not an uncommon life to lead in Montana.

What I want to explain happened in November. We had not been seeing Glen Baxter for some time. Two months had gone by. My mother knew other men, but she came home most days from work and stayed inside watching television in her bedroom and drinking beers. I asked about Glen once, and she said only that she didn't know where he was, and I assumed they had had a fight and that he was gone off on a flyer back to Illinois or Massachusetts, where he said he had relatives. I'll admit that I liked him. He had something on his mind always. He was a labor man as well as a Communist, and liked to say that the country was poisoned by the rich, and strong men would need to bring it to life again, and I liked that because my father had been a labor man, which was why we had a house to live in and money coming through. It was also true that I'd had a few boxing bouts by then—just with town boys and one with an Indian from Choteau—

and there were some girlfriends I knew from that. I did not like my mother being around the house so much at night, and I wished Glen Baxter would come back, or that another man would come along and entertain her somewhere else.

At two o'clock on a Saturday, Glen drove up into our yard in a car. He had had a big brown Harley-Davidson that he rode most of the year, in his black-and-red irrigators and a baseball cap turned backwards. But this time he had a car, a blue Nash Ambassador. My mother and I went out on the porch when he stopped inside the olive trees my father had planted as a shelter belt, and my mother had a look on her face of not much pleasure. It was starting to be cold in earnest by then. Snow was down already onto the Fairfield Bench, though on this day a chinook was blowing, and it could as easily have been spring, though the sky above the Divide was turning over in silver and blue clouds of winter.

"We haven't seen you in a long time, I guess," my mother said coldly.

"My little retarded sister died," Glen said, standing at the door of his old car. He was wearing his orange VFW jacket and canvas shoes we called wino shoes, something I had never seen him wear before. He seemed to be in a good humor. "We buried her in Florida near the home."

"That's a good place," my mother said in a voice that meant she was a wronged party in something.

"I want to take this boy hunting today, Aileen," Glen said. "There're snow geese down now. But we have to go right away, or they'll be gone to Idaho by tomorrow."

"He doesn't care to go," my mother said.

"Yes I do," I said, and looked at her.

My mother frowned at me. "Why do you?"

"Why does he need a reason?" Glen Baxter said and grinned.

"I want him to have one, that's why." She looked at me oddly. "I think Glen's drunk, Les."

"No, I'm not drinking," Glen said, which was hardly ever true. He looked at both of us, and my mother bit down on the side of her lower lip and stared at me in a way to make you think she thought something was being put over on her and she didn't like you for it. She was very pretty, though when she was mad her features were sharpened and less pretty by a long way. "All right, then I don't care," she said to no one in particular. "Hunt, kill, maim. Your father did that too." She turned to go back inside.

"Why don't you come with us, Aileen?" Glen was smiling still, pleased.

"To do what?" my mother said. She stopped and pulled a package of cigarettes out of her dress pocket and put one in her mouth.

"It's worth seeing."

"See dead animals?" my mother said.

"These geese are from Siberia, Aileen," Glen said. "They're not like a lot of geese. Maybe I'll buy us dinner later. What do you say?"

"Buy what with?" my mother said. To tell the truth, I didn't know why she was so mad at him. I would've thought she'd be glad to see him. But she just suddenly seemed to hate everything about him.

"I've got some money," Glen said. "Let me spend it on a pretty girl tonight."

"Find one of those and you're lucky," my mother said, turning away toward the front door.

"I already found one," Glen Baxter said. But the door slammed behind her, and he looked at me then with a look I think now was helplessness, though I could not see a way to change anything.

My mother sat in the backseat of Glen's Nash and looked out the window while we drove. My double gun was in the seat between us beside Glen's Belgian pump, which he kept loaded with five shells in case, he said, he saw something beside the road he wanted to shoot. I had hunted rabbits before, and had ground-sluiced pheasants and other birds, but I had never been on an actual hunt before, one where you drove out to some special place and did it formally. And I was excited. I had a feeling that something important was about to happen to me, and that this would be a day I would always remember.

My mother did not say anything for a long time, and neither did I. We drove up through Great Falls and out the other side toward Fort Benton, which was on the benchland where wheat was grown.

"Geese mate for life," my mother said, just out of the blue, as we were driving. "I hope you know that. They're special birds."

"I know that," Glen said in the front seat. "I have every respect for them."

"So where were you for three months?" she said. "I'm only curious."

"I was in the Big Hole for a while," Glen said, "and after that I went over to Douglas, Wyoming."

"What were you planning to do there?" my mother asked.

"I wanted to find a job, but it didn't work out."

"I'm going to college," she said suddenly, and this was something I had never heard about before. I turned to look at her, but she was staring out her window and wouldn't see me.

"I knew French once," Glen said. "*Rosé*'s pink. *Rouge*'s red." He glanced at me and smiled. "I think that's a wise idea, Aileen. When are you going to start?"

"I don't want Les to think he was raised by crazy people all his life," my mother said.

"Les ought to go himself," Glen said.

"After I go, he will."

"What do you say about that, Les?" Glen said, grinning.

"He says it's just fine," my mother said.

"It's just fine," I said.

Where Glen Baxter took us was out onto the high flat prairie that was disked for wheat and had high, high mountains out to the east, with lower heartbreak hills in between. It was, I remember, a day for blues in the sky, and down in the distance we could see the small town of Floweree, and the state highway running past it toward Fort Benton and the Hi-line. We drove out on top of the prairie on a muddy dirt road fenced on both sides, until we had gone about three miles, which is where Glen stopped.

"All right," he said, looking up in the rearview mirror at my mother. "You wouldn't think there was anything here, would you?"

"*We're* here," my mother said. "You brought us here."

"You'll be glad though," Glen said, and seemed confident to me. I had looked around myself but could not see anything. No water or trees, nothing that seemed like a good place to hunt anything. Just wasted land. "There's a big lake out there, Les," Glen said. "You can't see it now from here because it's low. But the geese are there. You'll see."

"It's like the moon out here, I recognize that," my mother said, "only it's worse." She was staring out at the flat wheatland as if she could actually see something in particular, and wanted to know more about it. "How'd you find this place?"

"I came once on the wheat push," Glen said.

"And I'm sure the owner told you just to come back and hunt anytime you like and bring anybody you wanted. Come one, come all. Is that it?"

"People shouldn't own land anyway," Glen said. "Anybody should be able to use it."

"Les, Glen's going to poach here," my mother said. "I just want you to know that, because that's a crime and the law will get you for it. If you're a man now, you're going to have to face the consequences."

"That's not true," Glen Baxter said, and looked gloomily out over the steering wheel down the muddy road toward the mountains. Though for myself I believed it was true, and didn't care. I didn't care about anything at that moment except seeing geese fly over me and shooting them down.

"Well, I'm certainly not going out there," my mother said. "I like towns better, and I already have enough trouble."

"That's okay," Glen said. "When the geese lift up you'll get to see them. That's all I wanted. Les and me'll go shoot them, won't we, Les?"

"Yes," I said, and I put my hand on my shotgun, which had been my father's and was heavy as rocks.

"Then we should go on," Glen said, "or we'll waste our light."

We got out of the car with our guns. Glen took off his canvas shoes and put on his pair of black irrigators out of the trunk. Then we crossed the barbed wire fence, and walked out into the high, tilled field toward nothing. I looked back at my mother when we were still not so far away, but I could only see the small, dark top of her head, low in the backseat of the Nash, staring out and thinking what I could not then begin to say.

On the walk toward the lake, Glen began talking to me. I had never been alone with him, and knew little about him except what my mother said—that he drank too much, or other times that he was the nicest man she had ever known in the world and that someday a woman would marry him, though she didn't think it would be her. Glen told me as we walked that he wished he had finished college, but that it was too late now, that his mind was too old. He said he had liked the Far East very much, and that people there knew how to treat each other, and that he would go back some day but couldn't go now. He said also that he would like to live in Russia for a while and mentioned the names of people who had gone there, names I didn't know. He said it would be hard at first, because it was so different, but that pretty soon anyone would learn to like it and wouldn't want to live anywhere else, and that Russians treated Americans who came to live there like kings. There were Communists everywhere now, he said. You didn't know them, but they were there. Montana had a large number, and he was in touch with all of them. He said that Communists were always in danger and that he had to protect himself all the time. And when he said that he pulled back his VFW jacket and showed me the butt of a pistol he had stuck under his shirt against his bare skin. "There are people who want to kill me right now," he said, "and I would kill a man myself if I thought I had to." And we kept walking. Though in a while he said, "I don't think I know much about you, Les. But I'd like to. What do you like to do?"

"I like to box," I said. "My father did it. It's a good thing to know."

"I suppose you have to protect yourself too," Glen said.

"I know how to," I said.

"Do you like to watch TV," Glen asked, and smiled.

"Not much."

"I love to," Glen said. "I could watch it instead of eating if I had one."

I looked out straight ahead over the green tops of sage that grew to the edge of the disked field, hoping to see the lake Glen said was there. There was an airishness and a sweet smell that I thought might be the place we were going, but I couldn't see it. "How will we hunt these geese?" I said.

"It won't be hard," Glen said. "Most hunting isn't even hunting. It's only shooting. And that's what this will be. In Illinois you would dig holes in the ground and hide and set out your decoys. Then the geese come to you, over and over again. But we don't have time for that here." He glanced at me. "You have to be sure the first time here."

"How do you know they're here now," I asked. And I looked toward the Highwood Mountains twenty miles away, half in snow and half dark blue at the bottom. I could see the little town of Floweree then, looking shabby and dimly lighted in the distance. A red bar sign shone. A car moved slowly away from the scattered buildings.

"They always come November first," Glen said.

"Are we going to poach them?"

"Does it make any difference to you," Glen asked.

"No, it doesn't."

"Well then, we aren't," he said.

We walked then for a while without talking. I looked back once to see the Nash far and small in the flat distance. I couldn't see my mother, and I thought that she must've turned on the radio and gone to sleep, which she always did, letting it play all night in her bedroom. Behind the car the sun was nearing the rounded mountains southwest of us, and I knew that when the sun was gone it would be cold. I wished my mother had decided to come along with us, and I thought for a moment of how little I really knew her at all.

Glen walked with me another quarter-mile, crossed another barbed wire fence where sage was growing, then went a hundred yards through wheatgrass and spurge until the ground went up and formed a kind of long hillock bunker built by a farmer against the wind. And I realized the lake was just beyond us. I could hear the sound of a car horn blowing and a dog barking all the way down in the town, then the wind seemed to move and all I could hear then and after then were geese. So many geese, from the sound of them, though I still could not see even one. I stood and listened to the high-pitched shouting sound, a sound I had never heard so close, a sound with size to it—though it was not loud. A sound that meant great numbers and that made your chest rise and your shoulders tighten with expectancy. It was a sound to make you feel separate from it and everything else, as if you were of no importance in the grand scheme of things.

"Do you hear them singing," Glen asked. He held his hand up to make me stand still. And we both listened. "How many do you think, Les, just hearing?"

"A hundred," I said. "More than a hundred."

"Five thousand," Glen said. "More than you can believe when you see them. Go see."

I put down my gun and on my hands and knees crawled up the earthwork through the wheatgrass and thistle, until I could see down to the lake and see the geese. And they were there, like a white bandage laid on the water, wide and long and continuous, a white expanse of snow geese, seventy yards from me, on the bank, but stretching far onto the lake, which was large itself—a half-mile across, with thick tules on the far side and wild plums farther and the blue mountain behind them.

"Do you see the big raft?" Glen said from below me, in a whisper.

"I see it," I said, still looking. It was such a thing to see, a view I had never seen and have not since.

"Are any on the land?" he said.

"Some are in the wheatgrass," I said, "but most are swimming."

"Good," Glen said. "They'll have to fly. But we can't wait for that now."

And I crawled backwards down the heel of land to where Glen was, and my gun. We were losing our light, and the air was purplish and cooling. I looked toward the car but couldn't see it, and I was no longer sure where it was below the lighted sky.

"Where do they fly to?" I said in a whisper, since I did not want anything to be ruined because of what I did or said. It was important to Glen to shoot the geese, and it was important to me.

"To the wheat," he said. "Or else they leave for good. I wish your mother had come, Les. Now she'll be sorry."

I could hear the geese quarreling and shouting on the lake surface. And I wondered if they knew we were here now. "She might be," I said with my heart pounding, but I didn't think she would be much.

It was a simple plan he had. I would stay behind the bunker, and he would crawl on his belly with his gun through the wheatgrass as near to the geese as he could. Then he would simply stand up and shoot all the ones he could close up, both in the air and on the ground. And when all the others flew up, with luck some would turn toward me as they came into the wind, and then I could shoot them and turn them back to him, and he would shoot them again. He could kill ten, he said, if he was lucky, and I might kill four. It didn't seem hard.

"Don't show them your face," Glen said. "Wait till you think you can touch them, then stand up and shoot. To hesitate is lost in this."

"All right," I said. "I'll try it."

"Shoot one in the head, and then shoot another one," Glen said. "It won't be hard." He patted me on the arm and smiled. Then he took off his VFW jacket and put it on the ground, climbed up the side of the bunker, cradling his shotgun in his arms, and slid on his belly into the dry stalks of yellow grass out of my sight.

Then, for the first time in that entire day, I was alone. And I didn't mind it. I sat squat down in the grass, loaded my double gun and took my other two shells out of my pocket to hold. I pushed the safety off and on to see that it was right. The wind rose a little, scuffed the grass and made me shiver. It was not the warm chinook now, but a wind out of the north, the one geese flew away from if they could.

Then I thought about my mother, in the car alone, and how much longer I would stay with her, and what it might mean to her for me to leave. And I wondered when Glen Baxter would die and if someone would kill him, or whether my mother would marry him and how I would feel about it. And though I didn't know why, it occurred to me that Glen Baxter and I would not be friends when all was said and done, since I didn't care if he ever married my mother or didn't.

Then I thought about boxing and what my father had taught me about it. To tighten your fists hard. To strike out straight from the shoulder and never punch backing up. How to cut a punch by snapping your fist inwards, how to carry your chin low, and to step toward a man when he is falling so you can hit him again. And most important, to keep your eyes open when you are hitting in the face and causing damage, because you need to see what you're doing to encourage yourself, and because it is when you close your eyes that you stop hitting and get hurt badly. "Fly all over your man, Les," my father said. "When you see your chance, fly on him and hit him till he falls." That, I thought, would always be my attitude in things.

And then I heard the geese again, their voices in unison, louder and shouting, as if the wind had changed again and put all new sounds in the cold air. And then a *boom.* And I knew Glen was in among them and had stood up to shoot. The noise of geese rose and grew worse, and my fingers burned where I held my gun too tight to the metal, and I put it down and opened my fist to make the burning stop so I could feel the trigger when the moment came. *Boom,* Glen shot again, and I heard him shuck a shell, and all the sounds out beyond the bunker seemed to be rising—the geese, the shots, the air itself going up. *Boom,* Glen shot another time, and I knew he was taking his careful time to make his shots good. And I held my gun and started to crawl up the bunker so as not to be surprised when the geese came over me and I could shoot.

From the top I saw Glen Baxter alone in the wheatgrass field, shooting at a white goose with black tips of wings that was on the ground not far from him, but trying to run and pull into the air. He shot it once more, and it fell over dead with its wings flapping.

Glen looked back at me and his face was distorted and strange. The air around him was full of white rising geese and he seemed to want them all. "Behind you, Les," he yelled at me and pointed. "They're all behind you now." I looked behind me, and there were geese in the air as far as I could see, more than I knew how many, moving so slowly, their wings wide out and working calmly and filling the air with noise, though their voices were not as loud or as shrill as I had thought they would be. And they were so close! Forty feet, some of them. The air around me vibrated and I could feel the wind from their wings and it seemed to me I could kill as many as the times I could shoot—a hundred or a thousand—and I raised my gun, put the muzzle on the head of a white goose, and fired. It shuddered in the air, its wide feet sank below its belly, its wings cradled out to hold back air, and it fell straight down and landed with an awful sound, a noise a human would make, a thick, soft, *hump* noise. I looked up again and shot another goose, could hear the pellets hit its chest, but it didn't fall or even break its pattern for flying. *Boom,* Glen shot again. And then again. "Hey," I heard him shout, "Hey, hey." And there were geese flying over me, flying in line after line. I broke my gun and reloaded, and thought to myself as I did: I need confidence here, I need to be sure with this. I pointed at another goose and shot it in the head, and it fell the way the first one had, wings out, its belly down, and with the same thick noise of hitting. Then I sat down in the grass on the bunker and let geese fly over me.

By now the whole raft was in the air, all of it moving in a slow swirl above me and the lake and everywhere, finding the wind and heading out south in long wavering lines that caught the last sun and turned to silver as they gained a distance. It was a thing to see, I will tell you now. Five thousand white geese all in the air around you, making a noise like you have never heard before. And I thought to myself then: this is something I will never see again. I will never forget this. And I was right.

Glen Baxter shot twice more. Once he missed, but with the other he hit a goose flying away from him, and knocked it half falling and flying into the empty lake not far from shore, where it began to swim as though it was fine and make its noise.

Glen stood in the stubby grass, looking out at the goose, his gun lowered. "I didn't need to shoot that one, did I, Les?"

"I don't know," I said, sitting on the little knoll of land, looking at the goose swimming in the water.

"I don't know why I shoot 'em. They're so beautiful." He looked at me.

"I don't know either," I said.

"Maybe there's nothing else to do with them." Glen stared at the goose again and shook his head. "Maybe this is exactly what they're put on earth for."

I did not know what to say because I did not know what he could mean by that, though what I felt was embarrassment at the great numbers of geese there were, and a dulled feeling like a hunger because the shooting had stopped and it was over for me now.

Glen began to pick up his geese, and I walked down to my two that had fallen close together and were dead. One had hit with such an impact that its stomach had split and some of its inward parts were knocked out. Though the other looked unhurt, its soft white belly turned up like a pillow, its head and jagged bill-teeth, its tiny black eyes looking as they would if they were alive.

"What's happened to the hunters out here?" I heard a voice speak. It was my mother, standing in her pink dress on the knoll above us, hugging her arms. She was smiling though she was cold. And I realized that I had lost all thought of her in the shooting. "Who did all this shooting? Is this your work, Les?"

"No," I said.

"Les is a hunter, though, Aileen," Glen said. "He takes his time." He was holding two white geese by their necks, one in each hand, and he was smiling. He and my mother seemed pleased.

"I see you didn't miss too many," my mother said and smiled. I could tell she admired Glen for his geese, and that she had done some thinking in the car alone. "It *was* wonderful, Glen," she said. "I've never seen anything like that. They were like snow."

"It's worth seeing once, isn't it?" Glen said. "I should've killed more, but I got excited."

My mother looked at me then. "Where's yours, Les?"

"Here," I said and pointed to my two geese on the ground beside me.

My mother nodded in a nice way, and I think she liked everything then and wanted the day to turn out right and for all of us to be happy. "Six, then. You've got six in all."

"One's still out there," I said, and motioned where the one goose was swimming in circles on the water.

"Okay," my mother said and put her hand over her eyes to look. "Where is it?"

Glen Baxter looked at me then with a strange smile, a smile that said he wished I had never mentioned anything about the other goose. And I wished I hadn't either. I looked up in the sky and could see the lines of geese by the thousands shining silver in the light, and I wished we could just leave and go home.

"That one's my mistake there," Glen Baxter said and grinned. "I shouldn't have shot that one, Aileen. I got too excited."

My mother looked out on the lake for a minute, then looked at Glen and back again. "Poor goose." She shook her head. "How will you get it, Glen?"

"I can't get that one now," Glen said.

My mother looked at him. "What do you mean?"

"I'm going to leave that one," Glen said.

"Well, no. You can't leave one," my mother said. "You shot it. You have to get it. Isn't that a rule?"

"No," Glen said.

And my mother looked from Glen to me. "Wade out and get it, Glen," she said in a sweet way, and my mother looked young then, like a young girl, in her flimsy short-sleeved waitress dress and her skinny, bare legs in the wheatgrass.

"No." Glen Baxter looked down at his gun and shook his head. And I didn't know why he wouldn't go, because it would've been easy. The lake was shallow. And you could tell that anyone could've walked out a long way before it got deep, and Glen had on his boots.

My mother looked at the white goose, which was not more than thirty yards from the shore, its head up, moving in slow circles, its wings settled and relaxed so you could see the black tips. "Wade out and get it, Glenny, won't you, please?" she said. "They're special things."

"You don't understand the world, Aileen," Glen said. "This can happen. It doesn't matter."

"But that's so cruel, Glen," she said, and a sweet smile came on her lips.

"Raise up your own arms, 'Leeny," Glen said. "I can't see any angel's wings, can you, Les?" He looked at me, but I looked away.

"Then you go on and get it, Les," my mother said. "You weren't raised by crazy people." I started to go, but Glen Baxter suddenly grabbed me by my shoulder and pulled me back hard, so hard his fingers made bruises in my skin that I saw later.

"Nobody's going," he said. "This is over with now."

And my mother gave Glen a cold look then. "You don't have a heart, Glen," she said. "There's nothing to love in you. You're just a son of a bitch, that's all."

And Glen Baxter nodded at my mother, then, as if he understood something he had not understood before, but something that he was willing to know. "Fine," he said, "that's fine." And he took his big pistol out from against his belly, the big blue revolver I had only seen part of before and that he said protected him, and he pointed it out at the goose on the water, his arm straight away from him, and shot and missed. And then he shot and missed again. The goose made its noise once. And then he hit it dead, because there was no splash. And then he shot it three times more until the gun was empty and the goose's head was down and it was floating toward the middle of the lake where it was empty and dark blue. "Now who has a heart?" Glen said. But my mother was not there when he turned around. She had already started back to the car and was almost lost from sight in the darkness. And Glen smiled at me then and his face had a wild look on it. "Okay, Les?" he said.

"Okay," I said.

"There're limits to everything, right?"

"I guess so," I said.

"Your mother's a beautiful woman, but she's not the only beautiful woman in Montana." And I did not say anything. And Glen Baxter suddenly said, "Here," and he held the pistol out at me. "Don't you want this? Don't you want to shoot me? Nobody thinks they'll die. But I'm ready for it right now." And I did not know what to do then. Though it is true that what I wanted to do was to hit him, hit him as hard in the face as I could, and see him on the ground bleeding and crying and pleading for me to stop. Only at that moment he looked scared to me, and I had never seen a grown man scared before—though I have seen one since—and I felt sorry for him, as though he was already a dead man. And I did not end up hitting him at all.

A light can go out in the heart. All of this happened years ago, but I still can feel now how sad and remote the world was to me. Glen Baxter, I think now, was not a bad man, only a man scared of something he'd never seen before—something soft in himself—his life going a way he didn't like. A woman with a son. Who could blame him there? I don't know what makes people do what they do, or call themselves what they call themselves, only that you have to live someone's life to be the expert.

My mother had tried to see the good side of things, tried to be hopeful in the situation she was handed, tried to look out for us both, and it hadn't worked. It was a strange time in her life then and after that, a time when she had to adjust to being an adult just when she was on the thin edge of things. Too much awareness too early in life was her problem, I think.

And what I felt was only that I had somehow been pushed out into the world, into the real life then, the one I hadn't lived yet. In a year I was gone to hard-rock mining and no-paycheck jobs and not to college. And I have thought more than once about my mother saying that I had not been raised by crazy people, and I don't know what that could mean or what difference it could make, unless it means that love is a reliable commodity, and even that is not always true, as I have found out.

Late on the night that all this took place I was in bed when I heard my mother say, "Come outside, Les. Come and hear this." And I went out onto the front porch barefoot and in my underwear, where it was warm like spring, and there was a spring mist in the air. I could see the lights of the Fairfield Coach in the distance, on its way up to Great Falls.

And I could hear geese, white birds in the sky, flying. They made their high-pitched sound like angry yells, and though I couldn't see them high up, it seemed to me they were everywhere. And my mother looked up and said, "Hear them?" I could smell her hair wet from the shower. "They leave with the moon," she said. "It's still half wild out here."

And I said, "I hear them," and I felt a chill come over my bare chest, and the hair stood up on my arms the way it does before a storm. And for a while we listened.

"When I first married your father, you know, we lived on a street called Bluebird Canyon, in California. And I thought that was the prettiest street and the prettiest name. I suppose no one brings you up like your first love. You don't mind if I say that, do you?" She looked at me hopefully.

"No," I said.

"We have to keep civilization alive somehow." And she pulled her little housecoat together because there was a cold vein in the air, a part of the cold that would be on us the next day. "I don't feel part of things tonight, I guess."

"It's all right," I said.

"Do you know where I'd like to go?"

"No," I said. And I suppose I knew she was angry then, angry with life, but did not want to show me that.

"To the Straits of Juan de Fuca. Wouldn't that be something? Would you like that?"

"I'd like it," I said. And my mother looked off for a minute, as if she could see the Straits of Juan de Fuca out against the line of mountains, see the lights of things alive and a whole new world.

"I know you liked him," she said after a moment. "You and I both suffer fools too well."

"I didn't like him too much," I said. "I didn't really care."

"He'll fall on his face. I'm sure of that," she said. And I didn't say anything because I didn't care about Glen Baxter anymore, and was happy not to talk about him. "Would you tell me something if I asked you? Would you tell me the truth?"

"Yes," I said.

And my mother did not look at me. "Just tell the truth," she said.

"All right," I said.

"Do you think I'm still very feminine? I'm thirty-two years old now. You don't know what that means. But do you think I am?"

And I stood at the edge of the porch, with the olive trees before me, looking straight up into the mist where I could not see geese but could still hear them flying, could almost feel the air move below their white wings. And I felt the way you feel when you are on a trestle all alone and the train is coming, and you know you have to decide. And I said, "Yes, I do." Because that was the truth. And I tried to think of something else then and did not hear what my mother said after that.

And how old was I then? Sixteen. Sixteen is young, but it can also be a grown man. I am forty-one years old now, and I think about that time without regret, though my mother and I never talked in that way again, and I have not heard her voice now in a long, long time.

ALICE WALKER

EVERYDAY USE

for your grandmama

I will wait for her in the yard that Maggie and I made so clean and wavy yesterday afternoon. A yard like this is more comfortable than most people know. It is not just a yard. It is like an extended living room.

When the hard clay is swept clean as a floor and the fine sand around the edges lined with tiny, irregular grooves, anyone can come and sit and look up into the elm tree and wait for the breezes that never come inside the house.

Maggie will be nervous until after her sister goes: she will stand hopelessly in corners, homely and ashamed of the burn scars down her arms and legs, eying her sister with a mixture of envy and awe. She thinks her sister has held life always in the palm of one hand, that "no" is a word the world never learned to say to her.

You've no doubt seen those TV shows where the child who has "made it" is confronted, as a surprise, by her own mother and father, tottering in weakly from backstage. (A pleasant surprise, of course: What would they do if parent and child came on the show only to curse out and insult each other?) On TV mother and child embrace and smile into each other's faces. Sometimes the mother and father weep, the child wraps them in her arms and leans across the table to tell how she would not have made it without their help. I have seen these programs.

Sometimes I dream a dream in which Dee and I are suddenly brought together on a TV program of this sort. Out of a dark and soft-seated limousine I am ushered into a bright room filled with many people. There I meet a smiling, gray, sporty man like Johnny Carson who shakes my hand and tells me what a fine girl I have. Then we are on the stage and Dee is embracing me with tears in her eyes. She pins on my dress a large orchid, even though she has told me once that she thinks orchids are tacky flowers.

In real life I am a large, big-boned woman with rough, man-working hands. In the winter I wear flannel nightgowns to bed and overalls during the day. I can kill and clean a hog as mercilessly as a man. My fat keeps me hot in zero weather. I can work outside all day, breaking ice to get water for washing; I can eat pork liver cooked over the open fire minutes after it comes steaming from the hog. One winter I knocked a bull calf straight in the brain between the eyes with a sledge hammer and had the meat hung up to chill before nightfall. But of course all this does not show on television. I am the way my daughter would want me to be: a hundred pounds lighter, my skin like an uncooked barley pancake. My hair glistens in the hot bright lights. Johnny Carson has much to do to keep up with my quick and witty tongue.

But that is a mistake. I know even before I wake up. Who ever knew a Johnson with a quick tongue? Who can even imagine me looking a strange white man in the eye? It seems to me I have talked to them always with one foot raised in flight, with my head turned in whichever way is farthest from them. Dee, though. She would always look anyone in the eye. Hesitation was no part of her nature.

"How do I look, Mama?" Maggie says, showing just enough of her thin body enveloped in pink skirt and red blouse for me to know she's there, almost hidden by the door.

"Come out into the yard," I say.

Have you ever seen a lame animal, perhaps a dog run over by some careless person rich enough to own a car, sidle up to someone who is ignorant enough to be kind to him? That is the way my Maggie walks. She has been like this, chin on chest, eyes on ground, feet in shuffle, ever since the fire that burned the other house to the ground.

Dee is lighter than Maggie, with nicer hair and a fuller figure. She's a woman now, though sometimes I forget. How long ago was it that the other house burned? Ten, twelve years? Sometimes I can still hear the flames and feel Maggie's arms sticking to me, her hair smoking and her dress falling off her in little black papery flakes. Her eyes seemed stretched open, blazed open by the flames reflected in them. And Dee. I see her standing off under the sweet gum tree she used to dig gum out of; a look of concentration on her face as she watched the last dingy gray board of the house fall in toward the red-hot brick chimney. Why don't you do a dance around the ashes? I'd wanted to ask her. She had hated the house that much.

I used to think she hated Maggie, too. But that was before we raised the money, the church and me, to send her to Augusta to school. She used to read to us without pity; forcing words, lies, other folks' habits, whole lives upon us two, sitting trapped and ignorant underneath her voice. She washed us in a river of make-believe, burned us with a lot of knowledge we didn't necessarily need to know. Pressed us to her with the serious way she read, to shove us away at just the moment, like dimwits, we seemed about to understand.

Dee wanted nice things. A yellow organdy dress to wear to her graduation from high school; black pumps to match a green suit she'd made from an old suit somebody gave me. She was determined to stare down any disaster in her efforts. Her eyelids would not flicker for minutes at a time. Often I fought off the temptation to shake her. At sixteen she had a style of her own: and knew what style was.

I never had an education myself. After second grade the school was closed down. Don't ask me why: in 1927 colored asked fewer questions than they do now. Sometimes Maggie reads to me. She stumbles along good-naturedly but can't see well. She knows she is not bright. Like good looks and money, quickness passed her by. She will marry John Thomas (who has mossy teeth in an earnest face) and then I'll be free to sit here and I guess just sing church songs to myself. Although I never was a good singer. Never could carry a tune. I was always better at a man's job. I used to love to milk till I was hooked in the side in '49. Cows are soothing and slow and don't bother you, unless you try to milk them the wrong way.

I have deliberately turned my back on the house. It is three rooms, just like the one that burned, except the roof is tin; they don't make shingle roofs any more. There are no real windows, just some holes cut in the sides, like the portholes in a ship, but not round and not square, with rawhide holding the shutters up on the outside. This house is in a pasture, too, like the other one. No doubt when Dee sees it she will want to tear it down. She wrote me once that no matter where we "choose" to live, she will manage to come see us. But she will never bring her friends. Maggie and I thought about this and Maggie asked me, "Mama, when did Dee ever *have* any friends?"

She had a few. Furtive boys in pink shirts hanging about on washday after school. Nervous girls who never laughed. Impressed with her they worshiped the well-turned phrase, the cute shape, the scalding humor that erupted like bubbles in lye. She read to them.

When she was courting Jimmy T she didn't have much time to pay to us, but turned all her faultfinding power on him. He *flew* to marry a cheap city girl from a family of ignorant flashy people. She hardly had time to recompose herself.

When she comes I will meet—but there they are!

Maggie attempts to make a dash for the house, in her shuffling way, but I stay her with my hand. "Come back here," I say. And she stops and tries to dig a well in the sand with her toe.

It is hard to see them clearly through the strong sun. But even the first glimpse of leg out of the car tells me it is Dee. Her feet were always neat-looking, as if God himself had shaped them with a certain style. From the other side of the car comes a short, stocky man. Hair is all over his head a foot long and hanging from his chin like a kinky mule tail. I hear Maggie suck in her breath. "Uhnnnh," is what it sounds like. Like when you see the wriggling end of a snake just in front of your foot on the road. "Uhnnnh."

Dee next. A dress down to the ground, in this hot weather. A dress so loud it hurts my eyes. There are yellows and oranges enough to throw back the light of the sun. I feel my whole face warming from the heat waves it throws out. Earrings gold, too, and hanging down to her shoulders. Bracelets dangling and making noises when she moves her arm up to shake the folds of the dress out of her armpits. The dress is loose and flows, and as she walks closer, I like it. I hear Maggie go "Uhnnnh" again. It is her sister's hair. It stands straight up like the wool on a sheep. It is black as night and around the edges are two long pigtails that rope about like small lizards disappearing behind her ears.

"Wa-su-zo-Tean-o!" she says, coming on in that gliding way the dress makes her move. The short stocky fellow with the hair to his navel is all grinning and he follows up with "Asalamalakim, my mother and sister!" He moves to hug Maggie but she falls back, right up against the back of my chair. I feel her trembling there and when I look up I see the perspiration falling off her chin.

"Don't get up," says Dee. Since I am stout it takes something of a push. You can see me trying to move a second or two before I make it. She turns, showing white heels through her sandals, and goes back to the car. Out she peeks next with a Polaroid. She stoops down quickly and lines up picture after picture of me sitting there in front of the house with Maggie cowering behind me. She never takes a shot without making sure the house is included. When a cow comes nibbling around the edge of the yard she snaps it and me and Maggie *and* the house. Then she puts the Polaroid in the back seat of the car, and comes up and kisses me on the forehead.

Meanwhile Asalamalakim is going through motions with Maggie's hand. Maggie's hand is as limp as a fish, and probably as cold, despite the sweat, and she keeps trying to pull it back. It looks like Asalamalakim wants to shake hands but wants to do it fancy. Or maybe he don't know how people shake hands. Anyhow, he soon gives up on Maggie.

"Well," I say. "Dee."

"No, Mama," she says. "Not 'Dee,' Wangero Leewanika Kemanjo!"

"What happened to 'Dee'?" I wanted to know.

"She's dead," Wangero said. "I couldn't bear it any longer, being named after the people who oppress me."

"You know as well as me you was named after your aunt Dicie," I said. Dicie is my sister. She named Dee. We called her "Big Dee" after Dee was born.

"But who was *she* named after?" asked Wangero.

"I guess after Grandma Dee," I said.

And who was she named after?" asked Wangero.

"Her mother," I said, and saw Wangero was getting tired. "That's about as far back as I can trace it," I said. Though, in fact, I probably could have carried it back beyond the Civil War through the branches.

"Well," said Asalamalakim, "there you are."

"Uhnnnh," I heard Maggie say.

"There I was not," I said, "before 'Dicie' cropped up in our family, so why should I try to trace it that far back?"

He just stood there grinning, looking down on me like somebody inspecting a Model A car. Every once in a while he and Wangero sent eye signals over my head.

"How do you pronounce this name?" I asked.

"You don't have to call me by it if you don't want to," said Wangero.

"Why shouldn't I?" I asked. "If that's what you want us to call you, we'll call you."

"I know it might sound awkward at first," said Wangero.

"I'll get used to it," I said. "Ream it out again."

Well, soon we got the name out of the way. Asalamalakim had a name twice as long and three times as hard. After I tripped over it two or three times he told me to just call him Hakim-a-barber. I wanted to ask him was he a barber, but I didn't really think he was, so I didn't ask.

"You must belong to those beef-cattle peoples down the road," I said. They said "Asalamalakim" when they met you, too, but they didn't shake hands. Always too busy: feeding the cattle, fixing the fences, putting up salt-lick shelters, throwing down hay. When the white folks poisoned some of the herd the men stayed up all night with rifles in their hands. I walked a mile and a half just to see the sight.

Hakim-a-barber said, "I accept some of their doctrines, but farming and raising cattle is not my style." (They didn't tell me, and I didn't ask, whether Wangero (Dee) had really gone and married him.)

We sat down to eat and right away he said he didn't eat collards and pork was unclean. Wangero, though, went on through the chitlins and corn bread, the greens and everything else. She talked a blue streak over the sweet potatoes. Everything delighted her. Even the fact that we still used the benches her daddy made for the table when we couldn't afford to buy chairs.

"Oh, Mama!" she cried. Then turned to Hakim-a-barber. "I never knew how lovely these benches are. You can feel the rump prints," she said, running her hands underneath her and along the bench. Then she gave a sigh and her hand closed over Grandma Dee's butter dish. "That's it!" she said. "I knew there was something I wanted to ask you if I could have." She jumped up from the table and went over in the corner where the churn stood, the milk in it clabber by now. She looked at the churn and looked at it.

"This churn top is what I need," she said. "Didn't Uncle Buddy whittle it out of a tree you all used to have?"

"Yes," I said.

"Uh huh," she said happily. "And I want the dasher, too."

"Uncle Buddy whittle that, too?" asked the barber.

Dee (Wangero) looked up at me.

"Aunt Dee's first husband whittled the dash," said Maggie so low you almost couldn't hear her. "His name was Henry, but they called him Stash."

"Maggie's brain is like an elephant's," Wangero said, laughing. "I can use the churn top as a centerpiece for the alcove table," she said, sliding a plate over the churn, "and I'll think of something artistic to do with the dasher."

When she finished wrapping the dasher the handle stuck out. I took it for a moment in my hands. You didn't even have to look close to see where hands pushing the dasher up and down to make butter had left a kind of sink in the wood. In fact, there were a lot of small sinks; you could see where thumbs and fingers had sunk into the wood. It was beautiful light yellow wood, from a tree that grew in the yard where Big Dee and Stash had lived.

After dinner Dee (Wangero) went to the trunk at the foot of my bed and started rifling through it. Maggie hung back in the kitchen over the dishpan. Out came Wangero with two quilts. They had been pieced by Grandma Dee and then Big Dee and me had hung them on the quilt frames on the front porch and quilted them. One was in the Lone Star pattern. The other was Walk Around the Mountain. In both of them were scraps of dresses Grandma Dee had worn fifty and more years ago. Bits and pieces of Grandpa Jarrell's Paisley shirts. And one teeny faded blue piece, about the size of a penny matchbox, that was from Great Grandpa Ezra's uniform that he wore in the Civil War.

"Mama," Wangero said sweet as a bird. "Can I have these old quilts?"

I heard something fall in the kitchen, and a minute later the kitchen door slammed.

"Why don't you take one or two of the others?" I asked. "These old things was just done by me and Big Dee from some tops your grandma pieced before she died."

"No," said Wangero. "I don't want those. They are stitched around the borders by machine."

"That'll make them last better," I said.

"That's not the point," said Wangero. "These are all pieces of dresses Grandma used to wear. She did all this stitching by hand. Imagine!" She held the quilts securely in her arms, stroking them.

"Some of the pieces, like those lavender ones, come from old clothes her mother handed down to her," I said, moving up to touch the quilts.

Dee (Wangero) moved back just enough so that I couldn't reach the quilts. They already belonged to her.

"Imagine!" she breathed again, clutching them closely to her bosom.

"The truth is," I said, "I promised to give them quilts to Maggie, for when she marries John Thomas."

She gasped like a bee had stung her.

"Maggie can't appreciate these quilts!" she said. "She'd probably be backward enough to put them to everyday use."

"I reckon she would," I said. "God knows I been saving 'em for long enough with nobody using 'em. I hope she will!" I didn't want to bring up how I had offered Dee (Wangero) a quilt when she went away to college. Then she had told me they were old-fashioned, out of style.

"But they're *priceless!*" she was saying now, furiously; for she has a temper. "Maggie would put them on the bed and in five years they'd be in rags. Less than that!"

"She can always make some more," I said. "Maggie knows how to quilt."

Dee (Wangero) looked at me with hatred. "You just will not understand. The point is these quilts, *these* quilts!"

"Well," I said, stumped. "What would *you* do with them?"

"Hang them," she said. As if that was the only thing you *could* do with quilts.

Maggie by now was standing in the door. I could almost hear the sound her feet made as they scraped over each other.

"She can have them, Mama," she said, like somebody used to never winning anything, or having anything reserved for her. "I can 'member Grandma Dee without the quilts."

I looked at her hard. She had filled her bottom lip with checkerberry snuff and it gave her face a kind of dopey, hangdog look. It was Grandma Dee and Big Dee who taught her how to quilt herself. She stood there with her scarred hands hidden in the folds of her skirt. She looked at her sister with something like fear but she wasn't mad at her. This was Maggie's portion. This was the way she knew God to work.

When I looked at her like that something hit me in the top of my head and ran down to the soles of my feet. Just like when I'm in church and the spirit of God touches me and I get happy and shout. I did something I never had done before: hugged Maggie to me, then dragged her on into the room, snatched the quilts out of Miss Wangero's hands and dumped them into Maggie's lap. Maggie just sat there on my bed with her mouth open.

"Take one or two of the others," I said to Dee.

But she turned without a word and went out to Hakim-a-barber.

"You just don't understand," she said, as Maggie and I came out to the car.

"What don't I understand?" I wanted to know.

"Your heritage," she said. And then she turned to Maggie, kissed her, and said, "You ought to try to make something of yourself, too, Maggie. It's really a new day for us. But from the way you and Mama still live you'd never know it."

She put on some sunglasses that hid everything above the tip of her nose and her chin.

Maggie smiled; maybe at the sunglasses. But a real smile, not scared. After we watched the car dust settle I asked Maggie to bring me a dip of snuff. And then the two of us sat there just enjoying, until it was time to go in the house and go to bed.

MARK HELPRIN

Letters from the *Samantha*

These letters were recovered in good condition from the vault of the sunken *Samantha,* an iron-hulled sailing ship of one thousand tons, built in Scotland in 1879 and wrecked during the First World War in the Persian Gulf off Basra.

20 August, 1909, 20° 14′ 18″ S,
43° 51′ 57″ E
Off Madagascar

Dear Sir:

Many years have passed since I joined the Green Star Line. You may note in your records and logs, if not, indeed, by memory, the complete absence of disciplinary action against me. During my command, the *Samantha* has been a trim ship on time. Though my subordinates sometimes complain, they are grateful, no doubt, for my firm rule and tidiness. It saves the ship in storms, keeps them healthy, and provides good training—even though they will be masters of steamships.

No other vessel of this line has been as punctual or well run. Even today we are a week ahead and our Madagascar wood will reach Alexandria early. Bound for London, the crew are happy, and though we sail the Mozambique Channel, they act as if we had just caught sight of Margate. There are no problems on this ship. But I must in conscience report an irregular incident for which I am ready to take full blame.

Half a day out of Androka, we came upon a sea so blue and casual that its waters seemed fit to drink. Though the wind was slight and we made poor time, we were elated by perfect climate and painter's colors, for off the starboard side Madagascar rose as green and tranquil as a well-watered palm, its mountains engraved by thrashing freshwater streams which beat down to the coast. A sweet upwelling breeze blew steadily from shore and confounded our square sails. Twenty minutes after noon, the lookout sighted a tornado on land. In the ship's glass I saw it, horrifying and enormous. Though at a great distance, its column appeared as thick as a massive tree on an islet in an atoll, and stretched at least 70 degrees upward from the horizon.

I have seen these pipes of windy fleece before. If there is sea nearby, they rush to it. So did this. When it became not red and black from soil and debris but silver and green from the water it drew, I began to tighten ship. Were the typhoon to have struck us directly, no preparation would have saved us. But what a shame to be swamped by high waves, or to be dismasted by beaten sea and wind. Hatches were battened as if for storm, minor sails furled, and the mainsail driven down half.

It moved back and forth over the sea in illegible patterning, as if tacking to changing winds. To our dismay, the distance narrowed. We were afraid, though every man on deck wanted to see it, to feel it, perhaps to ride its thick swirling waters a hundred times higher than our mast—higher than the peaks inland. I confess that I have wished to be completely taken up by such a thing, to be lifted into the clouds, arms and legs pinned in the stream. The attraction is much like that of phosphorescent seas, when glowing light and smooth swell are dangerously magnetic even for hardened masters of good ships. I have wanted to surrender to plum-colored seas, to know what one might find there naked and alone. But I have not, and will not.

Finally, we began to run rough water. The column was so high that we bent our heads to see its height, and the sound was greater than any engine, causing masts and spars to resonate like cords. Waves broke over the prow. Wind pushed us on, and the curl of the sea rushed to fill the depression of the waters. No more than half a mile off the starboard bow, the column veered to the west, crossing our path to head for Africa as rapidly as an express. Within minutes, we could not even see it.

As it crossed our bows, I veered in the direction from which it had come. It seemed to communicate a decisiveness of course, and here I took opportunity to evade. In doing so we came close to land. This was dangerous not only for the presence of reefs and shoals but because of the scattered debris. Trees as tall as masts and much thicker, roots sucked clean, lay in puzzlement upon the surface. Brush and vines were everywhere. The water was reddish brown from earth which had fallen from the cone. We were meticulously careful in piloting through this fresh salad, as a good ram against a solid limb would have been the end. Our cargo is hardwoods, and would have sunk us like granite. I myself straddled the sprit stays, pushing aside small logs with a boat hook and calling out trim to the wheel.

Nearly clear, we came upon a clump of tangled vegetation. I could not believe my eyes, for floating upon it was a large monkey, bolt upright and dignified. I sighted him first, though the lookout called soon after. On impulse, I set trim for the wavy mat and, as we smashed into it, offered the monkey an end of the boat hook. When he seized it I was almost pulled in, for his weight is nearly equal to mine. I observed that he had large teeth, which appeared both white and sharp. He came close, and then took to the lines until he sat high on the topgallant. As he passed, his foot cuffed my shoulder and I could smell him.

My ship is a clean ship. I regretted immediately my gesture with the hook. We do not need the mysterious defecations of such a creature, or the threat of him in the rigging at night. But we could not capture him to throw him back into the sea and, even had we collared him, might not have been able to get him overboard without danger to ourselves. We are now many miles off the coast. It is dark, and he sits high off the deck. The night watch is afraid and requests that I fell him with my rifle. They have seen his sharp teeth, which he displays with much screaming and gesticulating when they near him in the rigging. I think he is merely afraid, and I cannot bring myself to shoot him. I realize that no animals are allowed on board and have often had to enforce this rule when coming upon a parrot or cat hidden belowdecks where some captains do not go. But this creature we have today removed from the sea is like a man, and he has ridden the typhoon. Perhaps we will pass a headland and throw him overboard on a log. He must eventually descend for want of food. Then we will have our way. I will report further when the matter is resolved, and assure you that I regret this breach of regulations.

Yours & etc.,
Samson Low
Master, S/V Samantha

23 August, 1909, 10° 43′ 3″ S,
49° 5′ 27″ E
South of the Seychelles

Dear Sir:

We have passed the Channel and are heading north-northeast, hoping to ride the summer monsoon. It is shamefully hot, though the breeze is less humid than usual. Today two men dropped from the heat but they resumed work by evening. Because we are on a homeward tack, morale is at its best, or rather would be were it not for that damned ape in the rigging. He has not come down, and we have left behind his island and its last headland. He will have to have descended by the time we breach passage between Ras Asir and Jazirat Abd al-Kuri. The mate has suggested that there we throw him into the sea on a raft, which the carpenter has already set about building. He has embarked upon this with my permission, since there is little else for him to do. It has been almost an overly serene voyage and the typhoon caused no damage.

The raft he designed is very clever and has become a popular subject of discussion. It is about six feet by three feet, constructed of spare pine dunnage we were about to cast away when the typhoon was sighted. On each side is an outrigger for stability in the swell. In the center is a box, in which is a seat. Flanking this box are several smaller ones for fruit, biscuit, and a bucket of fresh water, in case the creature should drift a long time on the sea. This probably will not be so; the currents off Ras Asir drive for the beach, and we have noted that dunnage is quickly thrown upon the strand. Nevertheless, the crew have added their own touch—a standard distress flag flying from a ten-foot switch. They do not know, but I will order it replaced by a banner of another color, so that a hapless ship will not endanger itself to rescue a speechless monkey.

The crew have divided into two factions—those who wish to have the monkey shot, and those who would wait for him to descend and then put him in his boat. I am with the latter, since I would be the huntsman, and have already mentioned my lack of enthusiasm for this. A delegation of the first faction protested. They claimed that the second faction comprised those who stayed on deck, that the creature endangered balance in the rigging, and that he produced an uncanny effect in his screeching and bellicose silhouettes, which from below are humorous but which at close range, they said, are disconcerting and terrifying.

Since I had not seen him for longer than a moment and wanted to verify their complaint, I went up. Though sixty years of age, I did not use the bosun's chair, and detest those masters who do. It is pharaonic, and smacks of days in my father's youth when he saw with his own eyes gentlemen in sedan chairs carried about the city. The sight of twenty men laboring to hoist a ship's rotund captain is simply Egyptian, and I will not have it. Seventy feet off the deck, a giddy height to which I have not ascended in years, I came even with the ape. The ship was passing a boisterous sea and had at least a twenty-degree roll, which flung the two of us from side to side like pendula.

I am not a naturalist, nor have we on board a book of zoology, so the most I can do is to describe him. He is almost my height (nearly five feet ten inches) and appears to be sturdily built. Feet and hands are human in appearance except that they have a bulbous, skew, arthritic look common to monkeys. He is muscular and covered with fine reddish-brown hair. One can see the whiteness of his tendons when he stretches an arm or leg. I have mentioned the sharp, dazzling white teeth, set in rows like a trap, canine and pointed. His face is curiously delicate, and covered with orange hair leading to a snow-white crown of fur. My breath nearly failed when I looked into his eyes, for they are a bright, penetrating blue.

At first, he began to scream and swing as if he would come at me. If he had, I would have fared badly. The sailors fear him, for there is no man on board with half his strength, no man on the sea with a tenth his agility in the ropes, and if there is a man with the glacierlike pinnacled teeth, then he must be in a Scandinavian or Eastern European circus, for there they are fond of such things. To my surprise, he stopped his pantomime and, with a gentle and quizzical tilt of the head, looked me straight in the eyes. I had been sure that as a man I could answer his gaze as if from infallibility, and I calmly looked back. But he had me. His eyes unset me, so that I nearly shook. From that moment, he has not threatened or bared his teeth, but merely rests near the top of the foremast. The crew have attributed his conversion to my special power. This is flattering, though not entirely, as it assumes my ability to commune with an ape. Little do they suspect that it is I and not the monkey who have been converted, although to what I do not know. I am still thoroughly ashamed of my indiscretion and the trouble arising from it. We will get him and put him adrift off Ras Asir.

This evening, the cook grilled up some beef. I had him thoroughly vent the galley and use a great many herbs. The aroma was maddening. I sat in near-hypnotic ease in a canvas chair on the quarterdeck, a glass of wine in hand, as the heat fell to a cool breeze. We are all sunburnt and have been working hard, as the ape silently watches, to trim regularly and catch the best winds. We are almost in the full swift of the monsoon, and shortly will ride it in all its speed. It was wonderful to sit on deck and smell the herb-laden meat. The sea itself must have been jealous. I had several men ready with cargo net and pikes, certain that he would come down. We stared up at him as if he were the horizon, waiting. He smelled the food and agitated back and forth. Though he fretted, he did not descend. Even when we ate we saw him shunting to and fro on a yardarm. We left a dish for him away from us but he did not venture to seize it. If he had, we would have seized him.

From his impatience, I predict that tomorrow he will surrender to his stomach. Then we will catch him and this problem will be solved. I truly regret such an irregularity, though it would be worthwhile if he could only tell us how far he was lifted inside the silvered cone, and what it was like.

Yours & etc.,
SAMSON LOW

25 August, 1909, 2° 13′ 10″ N,
51° 15′ 17″ E
Off Mogadishu

DEAR SIR:

Today he came down. After the last correspondence, it occurred to me that he might be vegetarian, and that though he was hungry, the meat had put him off. Therefore, I searched my memory for the most aromatic vegetable dish I know. In your service as a fourth officer, I called at Jaffa port, in Palestine, in January of 1873. We went up to Sfat, a holy town high in the hills, full of Jews and Arabs, quiet and mystical. There were so many come into that freezing velvet dome of stars that all hostelries were full. I and several others paid a small sum for private lodging and board. At two in the morning, after we had returned from Mt. Jermak, the Arabs made a hot lively fire from bundles of dry cyprus twigs, and in a great square iron pan heated local oil and herbs, in which they fried thick sections of potato. I have never eaten so well. Perhaps it was our hunger, the cold, the silence, being high in the mountains at Sfat, where air is like ether and all souls change. Today I made the cook follow that old receipt.

We had been in the monsoon for several hours, and the air was littered with silver sparks—apparitions of heat from a glittering afternoon. Though the sun was low, iron decks could not be tread. In the rigging, he appeared nearly finished, limp and slouching, an arm hanging without energy, his back bent. We put potatoes in a dish on the forecastle. He descended slowly, finally touching deck lightly and ambling to the bows like a spider, all limbs brushing the planks. He ate his fill, and we threw the net over him. We had expected a ferocious struggle, but his posture and expression were so peaceful that I ordered the net removed. Sailors stood ready with pikes, but he stayed in place. Then I approached him and extended my hand as if to a child.

In imitation, he put out his arm, looking much less fearsome. Without a show of teeth, in his tired state, crouched on all fours to half our heights, he was no more frightening than a hound. I led him to the stern and back again while the crew cheered and laughed. Then the mate took him, and then the entire hierarchy of the ship, down to the cabin boys, who are smaller than he and seemed to interest him the most. By dark, he had strolled with every member of the crew and was miraculously tame. But I remembered his teeth, and had him chained to his little boat.

He was comfortable there, surrounded by fruit and water (which he ate and drank methodically) and sitting on a throne of sorts, with half a dozen courtiers eager to look in his eyes and hold his obliging wrist. Mine is not the only London post in which he will be mentioned. Those who can write are describing him with great zeal. I have seen some of these letters. He has been portrayed as a "mad baboon," a "man-eating gorilla of horrible colors, muscled but as bright as a bird," a "pygmy man set down on the sea by miracle and typhoon," and as all manner of Latin names, each different from the others and incorrectly spelled.

Depending on the bend of the monsoon and whether it continues to run strongly, we will pass Ras Asir in three days. I thought of casting him off early but was implored to wait for the Cape. I relented, and in doing so was made to understand why those in command must stay by rules. I am sure, however, that my authority is not truly diminished, and when the ape is gone I will again tighten discipline.

I have already had the distress flag replaced by a green banner. It flies over the creature on his throne. Though in splendor, he is in chains and in three days' time will be on the sea once more.

Yours & etc.,
SAMSON LOW

28 August, 1909, 12° 4′ 39″ N,
50° 1′ 2″ E
North of Ras Asir

DEAR SIR:

A most alarming incident has occurred. I must report, though it is among the worst episodes of my command. This morning, I arose, expecting to put the ape over the side as we rounded Ras Asir at about eleven. (The winds have been consistently excellent and a northward breeze veering off the monsoon has propelled us as steadily as an engine.) Going out on deck, I discovered that his boat was nowhere to be seen. At first, I thought that the mate had already disposed of him, and was disappointed that we were far from the coast. Then, to my shock, I saw him sitting unmanacled atop the main cargo hatch.

I screamed at the mate, demanding to know what had happened to the throne (as it had come to be called). He replied that it had gone overboard during the twelve-to-four watch. I stormed below and got that watch out in a hurry. Though sleepy-eyed, they were terrified. I told them that if the guilty one did not come forth I would put them all in irons. My temper was short and I could have struck them down. Two young sailors, as frightened as if they were surrendering themselves to die, admitted that they had thrown it over. They said they did not want to see the ape put to drift.

They are in irons until we make Suez. Their names are Mulcahy and Esper, and their pay is docked until they are freed. As we rounded the Cape, cutting close in (for the waters there are deep), we could see that though the creature would have been immediately cast up on shore, the shore itself was barren and inhospitable, and surely he would have died there. My Admiralty chart does not detail the inland topography of this area and shows only a yellow tongue marked "Africa" thrusting into the Gulf of Aden.

I can throw him overboard now or later. I do not want to do it. I brought him on board in the first place. There is nothing with which to fashion another raft. We have many tons of wood below, but not a cubic foot of it is lighter than water. The wind is good and we are making for the Bab al-Mandab, where we will pass late tomorrow afternoon—after that, the frustrating run up the Red Sea to the Canal.

The mate suggests that we sell him to the Egyptians. But I am reluctant to make port with this in mind, as it would be a victory for the two in chains and in the eyes of many others. And we are not animal traders. If he leaves us at sea the effects of his presence will be invalidated, we will touch land with discipline restored, and I will have the option of destroying these letters, though everything here has been entered in short form in the log. I have ordered him not to be fed, but they cast him scraps. I must get back my proper hold on the ship.

Yours & etc.,
SAMSON LOW

30 August, 1909, 15° 49′ 30″ N,
41° 5′ 32″ E
Red Sea off Massawa

Dear Sir:

I have been felled by an attack of headaches. Never before has this happened. There is pressure in my skull enough to burst it. I cannot keep my balance; my eyes roam and I am drunk with pain. For the weary tack up the Red Sea I have entrusted the mate with temporary command, retiring to my cabin with the excuse of heat prostration. I have been in the Red Sea time and again but have never felt apprehension that death would follow its heat. We have always managed. To the east, the mountains of the Hijaz are so dry and forbidding that I have seen sailors look away in fright.

The ape has begun to suffer from the heat. He is listless and ignored. His novelty has worn off (with the heat as it is) and no one pays him any attention. He will not go belowdecks but spends most of the day under the canvas sun shield, chewing slowly, though there is nothing in his mouth. It is hot there—the light so white and uncompromising it sears the eyes. I have freed his champions from irons and restored their pay. By this act I have won over the crew and caused the factions to disappear. No one thinks about the ape. But I dare not risk a recurrence of bad feeling and have decided to cast him into the sea. Where we found him, a strong seaward current would have carried him to the open ocean. Here, at least, he can make the shore, although it is the most barren coast on earth. But who would have thought he might survive the typhoon? He has been living beyond his time. To be picked up and whirled at incomprehensible speed, carried for miles above the earth where no man has ever been, and thrown into the sea is a death sentence. If he survived that, perhaps he can survive Arabian desert.

His expression is neither sad nor fierce. He looks like an old man, neutral to the world. In the last two days he has become the target of provocation and physical blows. I have ordered this stopped, but a sailor will sometimes throw a nail or a piece of wood at him. We shall soon be rid of him.

Yesterday we came alongside another British ship, the *Stonepool,* of the Dutch Express Line. On seeing the ape, they were envious. What is it, their captain asked, amazed at its coloring. I replied that he was a Madagascar ape we had fished from the sea, and I offered him to them, saying he was as tame as a dog. At first, they wanted him. The crew cried out for his acceptance, but the captain demurred, shaking his head and looking into my eyes as if he were laughing at me. "Damn!" I said, and went below without even a salute at parting.

My head aches. I must stop. At first light tomorrow, I will toss him back.

Yours & etc.,
SAMSON LOW

3 September, 1909
Suez

DEAR SIR:

The morning before last I went on deck at dawn. The ape was sitting on the main hatch, his eyes upon me from the moment I saw him. I walked over to him and extended my arm, which he would not take in his customary manner. I seized his wrist, which he withdrew. However, as he did this I laid hold of the other wrist, and pulled him off the hatch. He did not bare his teeth. He began to scream. Awakened by this, most of the crew stood in the companionways or on deck, silently observing.

He was hard to drag, but I towed him to the rail. When I took his other arm to hoist him over, he bared his teeth with a frightening shriek. Everyone was again terrified. The teeth must be six inches long.

He came at me with those teeth, and I could do nothing but throttle him. With my hands on his throat, his arms were free. He grasped my side. I felt the pads of his hands against my ribs. I had to tolerate that awful sensation to keep hold of his throat. No man aboard came close. He shrieked and moaned. His eyes reddened. My response was to tighten my hold, to end the horror. I gripped so hard that my own teeth were bared and I made sounds similar to his. He put his hands around my neck as if to strangle me back, but I had already taken the inside position and, despite his great strength, lessened the power of his grip merely by lifting my arms against his. Nevertheless he choked me. But I had a great head start. We held this position for long minutes, sweating, until his arms dropped and his body convulsed. In rage, I threw him by the neck into the sea, where he quickly sank.

Some of the crew have begun to talk about him as if he were about to be canonized. Others see him as evil. I assembled them as the coasts began to close on Suez and the top of the sea was white and still. I made my views clear, for in years of command and in a life on the sea I have learned much. I felt confident of what I told them.

He is not a symbol. He stands neither for innocence nor for evil. There is no parable and no lesson in his coming and going. I was neither right nor wrong in bringing him aboard (though it was indeed incorrect) or in what I later did. We must get on with the ship's business. He does not stand for a man or men. He stands for nothing. He was an ape, simian and lean, half sensible. He came on board, and now he is gone.

Yours & etc.,
SAMSON LOW

MARIANNE WIGGINS

HERSELF IN LOVE

Here's what women say, they say: "I loved him for his way with words, I loved the skin around his eyes." They sub-divide their men, they apportion to them grassy knolls on which to lollygag, they create swamp bogs (the things they cannot love) and bottomlands (the areas with margins for improvements). They make mental lists: his nails, his teeth, his nose hairs. They think of men not so much as objects of their love but as a project that comes wrapped at Christmas, disassembled. His gentleness with dishes. His "visions." His wretched socks. The way he tells a joke, the way he shifts the Datsun. The way he lifts his head from kisses on our breasts and gives us back a breath of our perfume. His naïveté in face of doom. His stomach muscles and the sweep of his long back.

A man is something which is nothing like the full sum of its parts—the way a snow crystal is not. A little dust, a little air, a little water at high altitude do not freeze the mind in wondrous contemplation of the universe until, in combination, catching on a random tuft of crimson scarf, a snowflake, fluidizing, breaks a woman's heart.

What women say, they say: "He hit me like a ton of bricks. He took my breath away. He unhinged me and I started shaking. He undid me. He has done me in." They turn tin ears on the music of the spheres and talk about his *skin* his *smile* his *tender failings.* No enigma equals the obscurity of how a woman tries to justify her love. Love is not a theft; or is it. Love is not a treason, is it. Love is not a perjury, or crime. It cannot kill, or can it. It will not test the morals of a race, or raze civilization. It won't annihilate the native vegetation. It may not even exist. As God might not. Why bother with it.

But women say, they say: "I can't go on without him. I think about him night and day. He turns me inside-out." They say, "He has *spaces* between his fingers. He has *fine hairs* along his shoulders. He has *toes.*" It's as though discovery of the other sex, the sense of parts apart, discloses brand new meaning on existence. "I never knew who *I* was *'til,*" they say, he kissed me or he touched me or he closed his eyes and laid his head down and said "thank you."

Herself had had that kind of bliss and "You can keep it" was her attitude. Herself had said "No more." No more love for her. No more staring pie-eyed at the farthest wall, no more starving, no more feasting, no more fast breaks from routine. The work at hand was far too arduous *a menos de amor.* The work at hand was Living:

In walked Killebrew.

Killebrew that bastard couldn't put two things together without causing one of them to break out in a rash. Herself was decent, ordered, sedulous, just. Killebrew was seepage. "Oh god, it's Killebrew," herself might say in much the same way as, "Oh god, the sink is leaking." Killebrew appeared from time to time like water on the floor inside a house. Unwanted news.

You'd think if love were going to strike there'd be a sign, some *frissonnement,* the birds gone suddenly, scaremongeringly, *mute.* But nothing outside the mere ordinary graced the day, a Thursday, garbage pick-up day, when Killebrew accumulated like a puddle on her side of the road.

"Hey, Killebrew," she acknowledged.

"How's herself?" he said.

"Not bad. How's yours?"

"The same. I've been ringing your credenza there for half an hour."

He pointed toward the door. *Credenza* in this case might signify her doorbell. Or it might not. With Killebrew one never knew.

"So what's up?" she asked, while surveying him: motely moldy workpants with perhaps no zipper in the fly; workboots; several tattered layers of several tattered shirts topped with a red hooded sweatshirt bunched and tied around his face so he resembled Rumpelstiltskin in a baby bunting.

"Use your phone," he said.

"Sure. Wander in, you'll find it." She started walking up the driveway toward the backyard garbage bin. He fell in beside her. "What are you up to this morning?" he asked. He seemed to have forgotten his request to use her phone. "You like my sweatshirt?" he asked. He pulled two little peaks of it out from his topography and read the chest logo out loud as though he'd just discovered it: " 'NOAA.' Know what that stands for?"

"Nope."

"Me neither," he admitted.

"National Organization of Another Annoyance?" she guessed.

"Yep, that's me."

"I guess you'll want a cup of coffee, too," she guessed again.

"Oh, no, just the check will do, thank you. . . ."

Inside her house he wandered through the downstairs 'til he found the phone. It was an old house and the phone had been installed in a small front room by some windows. When herself moved in she'd left the phone where she had found it. It seemed inordinately housewifely to have a phone moved to the kitchen. As though a caller might expect to find her there. Battering fried chicken.

"Fred?" she heard him say. "Is Fred there? Fred is *out?* Well when's he due? No. Fine. No problem. I'll call back."

Killebrew came back into the kitchen, took his sweatshirt off, and sat down on the blue stool by the stove. Then he stood up, took a coffee cup from her cabinet and poured himself a cup of coffee. "Murphy's out, the dumb mullah," he announced. "Lucky thing I didn't go up there on time." Then he sat down.

"You want milk?" she asked.

He shook his head.

She leaned against the dishwasher and stared at him and thought this would be as good a time as any to start baking the rum raisin cake for Christmas. "Mind if I go about my chores?" she said.

"No, go right ahead. You like my sweater?"

There had been a sweater underneath the sweatshirt.

"It's very nice," she said.

He made the same gesture he had made before, lifting out the fabric with his thumb and forefinger.

"Did you get it at the thrift shop?" she asked, conversationally.

"It's brand new!" he protested. "Cosmic knitted it, my birthday was last week."

" 'Cosmic?' "

"And she never knitted anything before."

"Well, it's very nice. It will keep you very warm." It looked like vacuum cleaner fuzz, she thought. "Who's 'Cosmic?' " And because she didn't really care, she read the recipe: " 'Put the raisins in a bowl and add the rum. Let stand overnight. Stir occasionally.' Now *that's* real comic writing. . . ."

"You don't know about The Cosmic and myself? Been going on about four months. Call her The Cosmic Korean. After my divorce I took the pledge, you know: no more white women."

He looked at her.

"Yeah, they say whole wheat's a whole lot better for you," she said, pointedly.

"Definitely. Or rye," he answered. She heard it "wry."

He got up, left the kitchen, made another phone call and came back.

"One third cup dark rum to one cup raisins seems like a lot of rum to me," she said. She measured out the rum and poured it on the raisins. She looked worried. Killebrew came over and peered inside the bowl. "Those babies will sop it up in no time," he maintained. He lifted the rum bottle by its neck and took a large swallow of it. He lit a cigarette. He walked into the pantry, stared at all her plates and came back into the kitchen with an ashtray. He sat down.

" 'Sift together' . . . Right, I did that. 'A quarter teaspoon salt,' it says: *'if desired'* . . ."

"Don't use it," he said, emphatically.

She looked at him. "No?"

"No salt."

"Sometimes salt, though, brings out sweetness. Heightens it. . . ."

He was staring at her. He stood up, walked to the sink, put his cigarette out with running water and lit another. He left the room to make another call. She heard him say, "Fred? Killebrew. I'm socked in here in town so I'll be running late. A little late. How late? It won't be *days,* all right?" She thought, This is ridiculous—I don't want to bake this *cake.* I want him to *leave.* He came back into the kitchen and she thought, Ten minutes more and then you're finished, Killebrew.

They talked about a movie they had both just seen. They talked about a book or two, while he poured himself another cup of coffee and smoked another cigarette. She set aside the dry ingredients, chopped the walnuts, watched the clock. " 'Freshly grated nutmeg,' " she read: "Give me a break." She crossed the kitchen to the spice cabinet. "That's the sort of instruction we ignore, right? Like 'Whip to strong peaks over ice—' " She turned to smile at him and he was leaning at the counter, bent a little, both hands on his heart.

"John, what the hell—?"

He stared at her.

"For godsake, are you all right?"

"No. What? I'm with you."

He began to pace.

"Are you having an attack?"

"What? No."

"Are you in pain?"

"Pain? No. Yes. I don't know. My heart was beating very fast."

"Are you having palpitations?"

"No."

"Sit down."

"No. Fine. I'm fine. It's going to pass."

"For godsake, it's the coffee. I put in these espresso beans, not everyone can—"

"Not the coffee."

"Plus two cigarettes."

"Not the cigarettes."

"And rum."

"Oh, lady, lots of rum."

"Anxiety attack. Or stress. You're late for that appointment . . ."

"No."

"Do you have to do something today that you don't want to do? That could be the cause of the anxiety."

"I don't have to do a single thing today that I don't want to do. In fact, I don't have to do a thing, if I don't want to."

"Well, then, Killebrew, it's cigarettes."

She turned back to the recipe and its freshly grated rinds of lemons.

"In fact," he said, "it is anxiety."

He came to stand quite near her, then moved away.

"It *is* anxiety. It's anxiety over not being able to know how to start to begin to say what I'm going to say."

She smiled at him, as an encouragement, and walked over to the refrigerator and took out two lemons. He stopped. She looked at him. "Do I have to be over there," she joked, pointing to where he stood, "for you to say it?"

"Yes, m'am."

She returned.

With the lemons.

He sat down at the table a foot or so from where she was working. The scene smelled of rum, the open jar of nutmeg, and, now as she was grating it, tart lemon. "I wanted to say, what I didn't know if I was going to be able to say was how really nice it is, it's really nice, to come around and sit and drink your coffee and just talk to you. . . ."

She looked up and smiled and tilted her head and said, "Why, thank you, Killebrew."

". . . And then the other thing, when I was sitting over there,"—he pointed to the blue stool by the stove; she grated—"I was sitting over there and I was thinking why am I sitting here when I really want to walk over there"—he pointed to where she was standing—"and just kiss your face."

For what seemed a long time she stared at the lemon in her left hand and its odd grater in the other. Then she laid the lemon and the grater down. It seemed to her that some response was necessary and it seemed to her that anything that she could say would be an insult to his sensibility and that the only thing that she could do with any rightness would be bend to him and give him a sweet kiss right on his cheek and when she did that he very gently turned her lips to his and they were kissing. Soon, somehow, they were standing, too, and kissing and the aroma of the lemon from her hands encompassed them. "I want you," he whispered. "I've always wanted to make love to you. I've always acted like a gentleman."

"We would make very tenderhearted love," she heard herself observe.

After a while he murmured, "Let's go upstairs." She held her breath and considered the idea. "Oh, no," he said. "Oh, no, don't frown." He placed his lips between her eyebrows where years had traced a worry line. "I'll leave, if that's what you think I should do," he suggested, but he didn't budge. She heard herself admit, "If we don't do it now, we'll never do it."

"Then let's do it."

She sighed. "Well, alright, John."

He started to lead her to the stairs. "You sound so enthusiastic about it. You'll see. This is a great idea."

"It's not a *great* idea, John," she said, climbing the stairs in front of him.

"You'll see. It's a good idea."

"It's not the best idea I've ever heard. . . ."

"Oh, no, you're right. Print this on the front page of the *Times* and people won't say *that's* the best idea I've ever heard, but you'll see. It's a good idea. . . ."

Better than most.

In a little while, he was getting dressed again. "Are you leaving?" she asked. It was a stupid question.

He sat down on the bed next to where she lay and tied his shoes. "I wasn't even thinking about this when I woke up this morning," he explained. "You weren't even on my mind—I guess you were. Yeah, I think you were. I think I thought about you late last night. I was writing a letter to this girl named Connie that I knew once in the third grade back in Buffalo and I was trying to explain my life and this letter just kept going on and going on and I thought, Jesus, who could I ever show this to and I thought of you. I wasn't even writing it to Connie, after a while. I don't know *who* I was writing it to. To whom." He took her hand. "Then, I swear to God, I just stopped by your house to use your phone and my heart started pounding. I've never had that happen. Once. One time before. And I thought, John, boy, you've got to say something to her, or you've got to get your coat on and get out the door."

"You weren't wearing a coat, John."

"It's allegorical." He kissed her. "See me out?"

"No."

"No?"

"I'm staying in bed." She pulled a pillow close to her. "I'm somewhere close to being in a dream state. . . ."

"Well, you're right there. That says it." He looked at her and said, "This whole thing's put me on 'Stun.' . . ."

Friday she didn't run into him in town; nor Saturday. On Sunday she ran into him on Main Street when she went to buy her Sunday papers. He was with a group of other men, dressed for heavy weather, autumn weather; scallopers. He looked guilty of contrition and a mite confused. "Hey, Killebrew," she acknowledged. "How's herself?" he asked. The other men were watching carefully to see if something dropped. "I'm well," she nodded. "And how's *your* health, John?" His eyes revealed a clear understanding of her frame of reference, and a tinge of panic that accompanies the proximity to an incendiary substance. She slipped her hand inside her coat and laid her palm across one breast so everyone could see and said, "No more heart palpitations?"

"No, m'am," he said, smiling, walking backwards. "Got that matter well in hand. I saw a specialist."

"Well, good. You must be real glad it didn't keep you on my back for long—"

She colored furiously.

She'd meant to say, *your* back.

Monday came and went and Tuesday morning around ten o'clock she was unloading from her car some kindling she had gathered when Killebrew pulled up. He sat staring at her from the cab of his truck until she walked over to him. "Hey, Killebrew," she said. She thought she ought to be real angry with him but instead she started noticing the skin around his eyes, the different colors intermingling in his beard. "This is for you," he said. He handed her a file folder with a few typed pages in it. "It's the letter I started writing to that girl I used to know in the third grade back in Buffalo. Connie. She and I and her kid brother and my brother Rick grew up together. Long time ago." He touched a piece of tree bark where it had caught in the loose weave on the cuff of her sweater. "You shouldn't stand out in the rain," he told her. She hadn't even noticed it was raining. She said, "Can I give you a cup of coffee?" He held up a chipped mug of coffee and said, "I have mine," but he got out of the truck anyway. They walked up the front porch steps and he said, "Is it after ten o'clock? I promised this old geezer on Hines Point I'd drop off my sander by ten o'clock. He's got the whole day planned around my sander. . . ."

They were in the kitchen and she had taken down a clean cup from the cabinet for herself and gone to the refrigerator for the quart of milk and instead of letting the refrigerator door close automatically, she slammed it. They stared at one another. "Can I kiss you?" she asked. That part of her that's always squaring edges, crossing out, correcting, justifying, thought "Can"? *Can* I kiss you? Almost imperceptibly he nodded, yes. In less than a minute they were starting up the stairs, Killebrew shedding his sweater as he went and four minutes later he was lacing up his boots on his way down.

She thought her clock had stopped.

"What are we calling this, 'The Phantom Strikes'?" she asked.

"I'm really sorry. No kidding. I wasn't going to come here. Swear to God. This geezer on Hines Point is such a nice old guy. . . ."

John was leaving, half undressed.

She, herself, was in her bare feet, t-shirt and her underwear. He had gotten up as if the house had been on fire and she had followed right along with him.

"If you can find some time to read my letter I'll appreciate it. It won't take you long to read. It won't take up too much of your time."

"John, nothing could take less time than this—"

He put his arms around her and held her securely and kissed her. "Thank you," he told her.

"For godsake, Killebrew, you don't say 'thank you' to a lover."

"Right. You're right there. I'll go home and look that up in Webster's and it'll say 'Not said to a lover.' . . ."

The letter started workmanlike enough: Dear Connie, comma. He'd moved away, he'd gotten married, he'd dodged the draft, he'd had a son. He'd lived in Arizona where his marriage fell apart. He'd worked his trade and made a living, moved around; then finally followed his estranged wife and their son back East to this small fishing village on the bay. That seemed to sum it up, he wrote, except that that suggested a black vacuum at the center of his life into which his past, his present and his future seemed to float. And maybe that was why he was sitting down to try to write these things. To try to find out where the emptiness came from. Why it existed. When it had begun. Most people didn't understand what he did for a living, he wrote. Or what it meant to him. He was a carpenter. A good one. Most people thought of that profession as being "in the trades." And it was true, sometimes to pay his way he had to take the nothing job, nail-banging job. But what he loved to do was finework. Beading a moulding with a nineteenth century Stanley #45 Jack plane. Working wood: wood working. "I've seen men sign the top tread of a gooseneck staircase before fastening it in place," he wrote. "I've seen descriptions of the weather of the day on the back of mouldings applied sixty-five years ago, as well as a sequential signing of men who have removed the same moulding. Five names in sixty-five years. Names of extinct millhouses, newspapers—a crew of mine wrote a fifty chapter novel describing the exploits of, the building of, a house on its framing, to be covered for years to come by wallboard. I personally have taken to putting Latin epigrams and the latest barometric pressure on the back or bottom of piecework as an encouragement to those anonymous artisans, for whom the work is always more important than their names. I admire the ability of those," the letter ended, "who could spend fifteen or twenty years building a cathedral. I guess I'm sorry that I'll never get that chance."

She thought, Love is a Revelation, like a religion, some religions; like Islam. She thought about the tile-cutters, the tile-layers, the mosaicists of mosques. She thought about cathedral spires and pagodas. She thought about the artist's handprint on the cavewall at Lascaux. She thought about what sets humans apart—their art, their fossilizing edifices, love, and their devotion to their sense of time. But time is bogus. Time does not exist in any universal way. It's not the thread that twines through heaven—like gravity, the condition time imposes is exact, but not eternal. The act of even thinking of eternity is a captive act of sitting in time's trap. Without time, what is there. Days of staring pie-eyed at the farthest wall. Minutes leaning on a rake. Hours lost in random conversation.

Nights on "Stun."

"It's after one."

"It isn't."

"Yes."

"It can't be."

"Right you are. You're right there. In Vladivostok, it's not one. But around here, vampires are thinking about lunch. . . ."

They had been talking for five hours—making love, and talking. The candles had burned down on her bedside tables and her bedroom seemed a berth inside a floating ship. They had talked about their families and their pasts. Or, *he* had talked and she had listened. It seemed a natural balance, effortless, the way he talked; she listened. His way with words. They'd been lovers ten days, not that she was counting. A week from now, a month, a year: what then. Maybe they would dish their manic clever selves off cliffs into black water.

Here's what women think, they think: Forever.

"Tell me about Connie," she said.

"Connie. *Consuelo,*" he breathed. He settled down against the pillow and wrapped her in his arms. "She and I and her kid brother and my brother Rick were trouble on a stick in the third grade. Wasn't anything that could hold still between us. We were thick as thieves. Called ourselves the Chicken Eaters. I was Chicken John. Rick was Chicken Rick. Joe was Chicken Joe. And Con was Chicken Con. Then one day we were running chicken drills down by the river. We were standing in this burned out rubble field by the Niagara and we all, together, got to feeling really weird. Chicken Con, she was a real tomboy and I never saw her do a single thing that anyone could classify as sissy, but she took hold of my hand. They were diverting the water from the American Fall so they could measure its erosion. Whole bunch of geodesic gnomes from the Army Corps of Engineers. Big program. And us kids were standing down there by the river and this wall of water starts coming through the plain, this enormous wall, water backed up all over itself and the *sound* it makes is just amazing, it must have been, well, I don't know because we were all just kids, it must have been three or four storeys high. And Chicken Con, she got this mean determined look on not to be too scared and she takes hold of my hand. Then, the next thing that you know, it's come and gone. It was all over in a minute. There was nothing we could do but stand right there and stare at it. The most amazing thing. So that's who Connie is."

She wanted to say, "I love you, John."

She lay against him, as if she were his shore and she wanted to say, "I love you, John," but something told her he would turn to her and tell her "thank you" so she lay there, watching him, for what may have passed as hours as he turned in sleep and rolled, inexorably, toward dreaming.

JAYNE ANNE PHILLIPS

Lechery

Though I have no money I must give myself what I need. Yes I know which lovers to call when the police have caught me peddling pictures, the store detectives twisting my wrists pull stockings out of my sleeves. And the butchers pummel the small of my back to dislodge their wrapped hocks; white bone and marbled tendon exposed as the paper tears and they push me against the wall. They curse me, I call my lovers. I'm nearly fifteen, my lovers get older and older. I know which ones will look at me delightedly, pay my bail, take me home to warm whiskey and bed. I might stay with them all day; I might run as the doors of their big cars swing open. Even as I run I can hear them behind me, laughing.

I go down by the schools with my pictures. The little boys smoke cigarettes, they're girlish as faggots, they try to act tough. Their Camels are wrinkled from pockets, a little chewed. I imagine them wet and stained pinkish at the tips, pink from their pouty lips. The boys have tight little chests, I see hard nipples in their T-shirts. Lines of smooth stomach, little penis tucked into jockey briefs. Already they're growing shaggy hair and quirky curves around their smiles. But no acne, I get them before they get pimples, I get them those first few times the eyes flutter and get strange. I show them what I do. Five or six surround me, jingling coins, tapping toes in tennis shoes. I know they've got some grade-school basketball coach, some ex-jock with a beer gut and a hard-on under his sweat pants in the locker room; that kills me. They come closer, I'm watching the ridged toes of their shoes. Now I do it with my eyes, I look up and pick the one I want. I tell him to collect the money and meet me at lunch in a park across the street, in a culvert, in a soft ditch, in a car parked under a bridge or somewhere shaded. Maybe I show them a few pills. One picture; blowsy redhead with a young blond girl, the girl a kneeling eunuch on white knees. The redhead has good legs, her muscles stand out tensed and she comes standing up. I tell them about it. Did you ever come standing up. I ask them, they shift their eyes at each other. I know they've been in blankets in dark bedrooms, see who can beat off first. Slapping sounds and a dry urge. But they don't understand their soft little cocks all stiff when they wake up in daylight, how the bed can float around.

So at noon I wait for them. I don't smoke, it's filthy. I suck a smooth pebble and wait. I've brushed my teeth in a gas station. I press my lips with my teeth and suck them, make them soft. Press dots of oil to my neck, my hands. Ambergris or musk between my breasts, down in the shadowed place where hair starts in a line at my groin. Maybe I brush my hair. I let them see me do it, open a compact and tongue my lips real slow. They only see the soft tip of my tongue, I pretend it's not for them.

Usually just one of them comes, the one I chose, with a friend waiting out of sight where he can see us. If they came alone I can tell by looking at them. Sometimes they are high on something, I don't mind. Maybe I have them in an abandoned car down in a back lot, blankets on the seat or no back seat but an old mattress. Back windows covered up with paper sacks and speckled mud, sun through dirty windows or brown paper makes the light all patterns.

He is nervous. Right away he holds out the money. Or he is a little mean, he punches at me with his childish fist. A fine blond boy with a sweet neck and thin collarbones arched out like wings, or someone freckled whose ashen hair falls loose. A dark boy, thick lashes and cropped wooled hair, rose lips full and swelling a little in the darkened car. I give him a little whiskey, I rifle through the pictures and pretend to arrange them. I take a drink too, joke with him. This is my favorite time; he leans back against the seat with something like sleep in his eyes. I stroke his hard thighs, his chest, I comfort him.

I put the pictures beside us, some of them are smaller than postcards. We put our faces close to see them. A blond girl, a black girl, they like to see the girls. One bending back droops her white hair while the other arches over, holds her at the waist, puts her mouth to a breast so small only the nipple stands up. In the picture her mouth moves in and out, anyone can tell. A black hand nearly touching pale pubic hair, a forefinger almost tender curls just so, moves toward a slit barely visible just below the pelvic bone. I don't like pictures of shaven girls, it scares them to see so much. It makes them disappear.

I do things they've never seen, I could let them touch but no. I arrange their hands and feet, keep them here forever. Sometimes they tell me stories, they keep talking of baseball games and vicious battles with their friends. Lips pouty and soft, eyes a hard glass glitter. They

In the foster homes they used to give me dolls and I played the church game. At first I waited till everyone left the house. Then it didn't matter who was around. I lined up all the dolls on the couch, I sat them one after the other. They were ugly, most of them had no clothes or backward arms. They were dolls from the trash, the Salvation Army at Christmas, junk-sale dolls. One of them was in a fire. The plastic hand was missing, melted into a bubbled fountain dribbling in nubs down the arm. We faced the front of the room. I made us sit for hours unmoving, listening to nothing at all and watching someone preach.

Uncle Wumpy gave me a doll. They call him that. Like his pocked face had rabbit ears and soft gray flesh. His face is pitted with tiny scars, his skin is flushed. We won at the carnival: cowboy hats, a rubber six-gun, a stuffed leopard with green diamond eyes for Kitty. We were on our way out between booths and machines, sawdust sticky with old candy and beer, to pick Kitty up at work. We passed the duckshoot. Wumpy was so drunk I had to help him with the gun and we drowned them all. Little yellow ducks with flipped up tail feathers and no eyeballs; they glided by hooked to a string. We hit them, knocked them back with a snap like something breaking. We hit twelve; the whole group popped up, started gliding by again as eyeless as before. So we kept shooting and shooting . . . The barker came out from behind the counter with his fat long-ashed cigar. He held it pinched in two fingers like something dirty he respected. Then he sucked on it and took the gun away. The crowd behind us mumbled. He thrust the doll into my arms. She was nearly three feet tall, pearl earrings, patent leather heels. Long white dress and a veil fastened with a clear plastic bird. I took the bird, I lit it with

Wumpy's lighter. Its neck melted down to a curve that held its flat head molded to its wings. I liked to keep the bird where no one saw it. Finally I buried it in a hole, I took it to a place I knew I'd forget.

How I found Wumpy. I was twelve, I lived with Minnie. She made me work in the luncheonette, swab Formica tables with a rag. Bend over to wipe the aluminum legs, clotted ketchup. By the grill her frozen french fries thawed out limp and fishy. She threw them in sooty fat; they fizzled and jumped and came out shining. Her old face squinched like a rat's, she was forty. Wore thick glasses and a red handkerchief on her head, like the gospel shows turned up loud. One hand was twisted. She had the arthritis, the rheumatism, the corns, the bunions on her knotted toes as she walked to the shower at home. Hunched in her long robe, she fixed her eyes on the bathroom door. Scuttled clinching herself at the waist and slammed the door.

After school I walked to the restaurant and helped her clear tables till seven. She cursed the miners under her breath. Slapped my butt if I was slow, moved her hard hand, its big twisted knuckles. Grabbed the curve of my ass and squeezed.

Wumpy came in every night for coffee. He cut brush for the State Road Commission. Watched Minnie and me. Kitty started coming in with him. Cellophane Baggie full of white crosses, cheap speed. She'd order a Pepsi, take a few pills, grind a few more to powder on the tabletop. She winked, gave me hair ribbons, said she'd like to take me to the movies. Wumpy told Minnie I needed some clothes, he and Kitty would take me to Pittsburgh to buy me some dresses. They gave her thirty dollars.

In the motel I stood in the bathroom and vomited. Sopors floated in the bowl, clumps of white undissolved powder in a clear mucus. I puked so easy, again and again, I almost laughed. Then they came in naked and took off my clothes. I couldn't stand up, they carried me to the bed. Wumpy got behind her and fucked her, she kept saying words but I couldn't keep my eyes open. She pulled me down She said Honey Honey. In the bottom of something dark I rocked and rocked. His big arms put me there until he lifted me. Lifted me held my hips in the air and I felt her mouth on my legs, I felt bigger and bigger. The ceiling spun around like the lights at Children's Center spun in the dark halls when I woke up at night. Then a tight muscular flash, I curled up and hugged myself.

I stood by the window and fingered the flimsy curtains. I watched them sleeping, I didn't leave. I watched Wumpy's broad back rising and falling.

Wumpy would never do it to me, he gave me pictures to sell. I wanted to give him the money, he laughed at me. He had little stars in the flesh of his hands. He took me to bars. We took a man to some motel, Wumpy said he always had to watch . . . stood by the bed while I choked and gagged a little, salt exploding in my throat—

The dream is here again and again, the dream is still here. Natalie made the dream. I slept with her when I was eight, six months we slept together. She whimpered at night, she wet the bed. Both of us wards of the state, they got money for us. Cold in the bedroom, she wrapping her skinny arms around my chest. Asking can she look at me. But I fall asleep, I won't take off my clothes in bed with her. I fall asleep and the same dream comes.

Natalie is standing in the sand. Behind her the ocean spills over, the waves have thick black edges. Natalie in her shredded slip, knobby knees, her pale blue eyes all watery. Natalie standing still as a dead thing spreads her legs and holds herself with her hand. Her fingers groping, her white face. She squeezes and pulls so hard she bleeds She calls for help She wants me. Faces all around us, big faces just teeth and lips to hold me down for Natalie. Natalie on top of me Natalie pressing down. Her watery eyes say nothing. She sighs with pleasure and her hot urine boils all around us.

I remember like this: Natalie watches me all the time. They're gone all day, we stay alone with the silent baby. Once there's no food but a box of salt. Bright blue box, the silver spout pops out. The girl with the umbrella dimples and swings her pony tails, flashes her white skin. I can eat it Natalie. I can eat it all. She looks out the window at the snow. I know she's scared. I sit down on the floor at her feet. The box is round like a tom-tom, I tip it up. Salt comes in my mouth so fast, fills me up but I can't quit pouring it . . . I start to strangle but Natalie won't look, she screams and screams. She kicks at me with her bare blue feet, the box flies across the room throwing fans of salt. When it gets dark, salt gleams on the floor with a strange cool light. Natalie stays in her chair without moving and I get to sleep alone.

I got lavish cards at Children's Center, I think a jokester sent them. To Daughter From Mother At Christmas, scrolls of stand-up gold and velvet poinsettias. I used to think about the janitors, those high school boys with smirky eyes and beer breath, licking the envelopes . . . somehow mailing them from Wichita or Tucson. The agency moved me from home to home. Holidays I stayed at the center, they did paper work to place me again. Every time there was a different pasty-faced boy with ragged nails, dragging a dun-colored mop. The cards came, they were never quite right. When I was ten, For Baby's First Christmas—a fold-out hobbyhorse, a mommy with blond hair and popped eyes. I was seven, the card said Debutante in raised silver script, showed a girl in mink and heels. After I started getting arrested the psychiatrist told them to hold my mail. They said I might go to an asylum.

Baby Girl Approximately 14 Months Abandoned December 1960, Diagnosed As Mute. But when I was three I made sounds like trucks and wasps, I screamed and sang. They think I'm crazy, this is what happens—

I like to lock the bathroom door late at night. Stand in front of the mirrors, hold a candle under my chin. Stare at my shadowed face and see the white shape of a skull. I lay down on the cold tile floor and do it to myself by the stalls. I do it, I lay on my stomach. Hold my breath, riding on the heels of my hands I'm blind; I feel the hush hush of water pipes through the floor. Ride up over a hump into the heat the jangling it holds me. When I open my eyes and roll over, the ceiling is very high it is the color of bone, lamplight through the barred windows. I make myself good I do it. Lay on the cold floor, its tiny geometric blocks. My skin goes white as porcelain, I'm big as the old sinks and toilets, the empty white tubs. White glass, marble, rock, old pipes bubbling air. When those white streaks flash in my vision I run here. I watch her. I know she is me. She runs from stall to stall flushing toilets, she does it again and again. Slushing water louder and louder, then high-pitched wail of the tanks filling. Crash and wail. I crouch on the floor and listen. I don't let anyone in.

I think Natalie is dead, she said she would die when she was twelve. But only then. In August under trees we sat heaving rocks. She buried her feet in sand and said she was a stone. I could pinch her till my nails rimmed with red; if she didn't cry out I had to do what she said. She wanted to play house again: I'm a house I'm a giant house. Crawl through my legs Its the door. And she heaved herself onto my back, cupped my chin in her hands. Pulled my head back to see her face above me. She stroked my throat, pointed her pink tongue in my ear and hissed. Shhhh. Hissing. Shhhhhh. Purring, breathing deep in her belly. She pretended her voice was a man. I love you. You're mine Eat your food. And I licked her hand all over, up and down between her fingers.

Once the man came after us. We were in the shed behind the house. Natalie liked that room with the tools and jugs, rusted rakes, wood in splintered piles and the squeaking rats. She took off her clothes, draped them on random nails to make an armless girl. A man's big black boots swallowed her ankles. She white and hairless, jingling the metal clasps. Natalie laughing and laughing. We held the blunt-nosed hammers, we threw them hard. Indented circles in the floor, piles of circles pressing down in the old wood like invisible coins. Natalie said we made money. More and more, on the wall, on the floor. Natalie at the windows crashing, glass in glittered piles on her shiny black rubber boots.

He opens the creaky door. What the hell are you doing. I hide by the workbench, back in the webs and spiders. The unbuckling, quick snaky swish of his belt against his pants. He catches her, throws her over the workbench. Natalie gets quiet, the big boots fall off her feet. Her feet almost have faces, dangling, alabaster, by my face; her thin white legs hanging down. Slaps of the belt and drawn-out breathing. You little bitch. He takes a penny and throws it to shadows in the dust. She knows She always knows She finds it. Handfuls of clattering coins. Natalie walks in her goose-pimpled skin, makes a pile of copper pennies by his shoes. He pushes her down on her knees, Natalie is laughing just a little. I see his back, his wide hips, the green work pants. Touch it, he says. Natalie says she can't, her hands are poison.

I'm pure, driven snow. I clean the house, make soup from a can. Wumpy drinks a beer. Squeezes cans till they buckle and fold, throws them in a corner. I want to touch him, squeeze him hard; he closes his eyes to make sounds in his scratchy voice. If I take off my shirt he hits me. Kitty hugs me, My Baby. She wants me to do what she wants. Wumpy does what she says. More and more, she wants what I want. We move around on the checkerboard floor.

Kitty is on probation. We give her lots of coffee and get her walking. Every Saturday the parole officer wants her to talk. Maybe she scores, comes back with smack in an envelope. Darker and darker, snow feathers down to wrap us up. Kitty nods out on the windowsill, curls up like a dormer mouse in her bulky red coat. She likes to lean out almost too far. Wumpy: I watch him through a lopsided hole in the bathroom door, he wants to be alone. Ties off, bulges a vein to hit. Hums and sighs. Pipes make watery yawns and wheezes, they come together in the tunneled walls. It's so quiet I hear the click of the neon sign before it changes and throws a splattered word across the floor. Rooms, it says, blue Rooms. When I see someone move, I'm afraid: If Natalie weren't dead she would find me.

MICHAEL MARTONE

Biograph

Iced air. How do they do it? We could've gone to the Marbro, but they don't have it there. I like the sign outside here, snow on top of all the letters. Everybody sitting outside on the street, looking over at the glowing white in the light. Light bouncing off the awnings. People dying in the heat. But you got a little money, and you are in where it's cool. They must take the heat right out of the air. But how do they know which is the hot part? In the loft, one time, placing bets, I saw the guy who runs the machine out in the middle of the street looking at something he held in his hand. The drays and the trucks working their way around him. Only the trolleys creeping up to him, the motorman yanking on the bell. I couldn't hear it because the windows were closed. The iced air. Everybody squinting at the man in the street holding his hand up staring at it, at something in it. Things moving slow in the heat. Boy, it's swell. I want to stay for the whole show. Let my shirt dry out, roll my socks back up.

Everybody's sitting in the dark. Up there in the ceiling they got the little lights that are supposed to be stars. Palm trees in pots up there on the sides of the stage. Ushers in monkey suits by the fire doors. It's like in Mooresville at the Friends with everybody sitting and waiting for somebody to get up and talk. I could stand up here and tell them a story. Mrs. Mint is the only one who knows, and she's worried about getting back to Romania, thanks to the house she ran in Gary.

She treats me square. No trouble when I stay with Patty. And Patty, still married to the cop, doesn't have a clue.

Thanks me every time she smiles because I'm the one who got her teeth fixed for her.

Smiling at me in the dark.

Jimmie, she says, *when you going to take off those sunglasses. You can't see the movie.* She likes a man who carries a gun, but she can't say why.

The girls down where Patty works all tell her I look like him. I just laugh, buy her a diamond, tell her I work for the Board of Trade.

There's a guy named Ralph Alsman's arrested all the time because he looks like him. The story's in the papers. How he keeps robbing banks.

There's nothing better to do. Rob a bank, go to a movie, buy a paper. It's all the same.

I read the paper all the time, and I start out thinking I don't know the man. Then I think that could be me.

You have to keep your mind busy or you go nuts. Think of Homer beating it by tying strings to flies he caught while he stood time on the mats in Pendleton. You go nuts without something to do. You buy a little time out of the heat.

I bet the girls wouldn't know what to do if I was him. Wouldn't want me to really be him. It only gives them something to talk about without no customers while Patty's putting on her hat and I'm leaning in the doorway waiting for her to blow.

I like Patty good enough, with her smile and all. She is nice and heavy leaning on my arm when we walk on the street. My hand will be in my pocket on the gun, and I'll tap her leg with it through the clothes. She'll smile. Our secret. *My husband,* she says, *only has the revolver they gave him.*

I like Patty. She'll do for now. But she's not Terry.

Sometimes, I think I see Terry in the Loop when I'm down there with a bag of corn feeding pigeons. Out of the house pretending I'm working. I'll be looking at the birds and her legs will walk by and I'll follow them up and something will go wrong.

I want to ask the doll where she got those legs from, but they just clip along through the crowd of strutting pigeons.

It's like that with a day to kill downtown. Her hand waving for a cab. And in the store windows, I see all the things I could buy that she would like. And all the other women, their hair thrown off their forehead just like hers, tilting their heads and thinking that the stuff they see will make them look like Terry. I can't go and get her. South Bend wasn't enough, and they've hidden her in some county jail. For harboring.

There has been a fire on a boat that had a party going on it. A little boy in a sailor hat is crying behind a glass window. It's beginning to fill with smoke in there, and you can't hear him cry. People are jumping off the ship. The railings are giving out, and people are falling into the water. There is a priest swimming with the boys. And then it is night, and the moon is shining, and the burning ship is shining on the water. Along the shore bodies are washing up, and people and police are looking through them.

So, you're out, Pete is saying as we drive south out of Lima. *They'll go up to the farm while we'll go down to Cincinnati.*

You're out, I say. I hadn't seen them since I got parole. I was in Lima by the time they broke Michigan City. Dumb. *I see you got my message,* I say.

We're laughing. There he was standing at the dayroom door. Too many pistols. Too many shots had been fired. Terry would be at the house.

Thanks.

Mac is reading off directions. Left here, right, right here. Something they learned from Baron Lamm's gang. In the dark. Clark is sucking on his fingers. He shot himself. *Kind of rusty,* he is saying, his finger in his mouth. The sheriff didn't look too good.

We told him, Pete said, *that we were Indiana state parole officers.* Mac laughs. *He didn't believe us.* They laugh. Nervous.

You're out. You're out, I say.

You should've not locked up the sheriff's wife, Mac says. *Right here.*

I tell you he'll be all right, Pete says.

It's going to be tough watching him die from across the room and behind bars, Mac says.

It's not that bad. He'll be okay.

He'd been square with me. The food is good.

There's just no going back, somebody says in the dark.

The sun is just getting into people's eyes. The light going all one color on the store windows. Mothers yanking the kids on trolleys to get them home in time to make supper. It takes longer for the men to get off and on the Toledo scales by the door. Harder to think. Almost time to go home. Not enough time to start something new. The tellers begin stacking the coins, and the hack's in the basement looking for work.

When we were together around a kitchen table planning a job, drinking beers but no hard stuff, and it would come that time of day, why, we'd all know it. And someone goes to the window and looks out, another stretches out on the davenport, reads the morning papers again. Not working.

After getting out of the pen we'd show up at the bank, 2:45 on the dot. The bank was closed. Closed from Roosevelt's holiday and never opened. We'd stand there, heavy in the vests and the guns. Looking through the bars and then looking real quick to see if anyone has seen us. Time thrown all off by something that happened years ago when we weren't in the world.

I hear in Mexico they go to sleep all the afternoon.

It's too hot for anything, even robbing the banks.

Then there are just two pair of hands. Blackie's throwing dice, shuffling cards, and counting poker chips. Jim's writing, turning pages in a book, and accepting a law degree. Then just Blackie's hands, his fingers tapping on a felt-covered table, waiting for the cards to be dealt. Then Blackie spreading the cards in his hand, looking them over and getting ready to bet.

Somewhere in the Wisconsin countryside and Pete saying, *That's it.* I'm feeling pretty good. We could be anywhere now. The fields all gleaned. Some shocks still standing. It's a big Buick, and the cold wind is blowing through it since we've taken out the windows.

We're going to take them to the hideout, says Mac, kidding.

Meaning the two citizens we have.

Can you cook? I am asking the lady without smiling.

She's wearing Pete's coat. The fellow's got on Pete's hat.

Pete's not even cold.

After a fashion, says the lady.

So we go along watching the phone wires. Down to two and then one. Birds all puffed up on them. Then no wires at all, just the fields and the white sky.

Pete runs them out into a turned field. Mac changes the plates. Pete turns them away, back to the wind. The three of them out in the big field. Pete ties their hands and then he comes back half the way, stops and goes back to get his hat and coat.

After Greencastle, we could kick back. It had been Homecoming weekend at the college, and the stores were making big deposits. Pete feeling grand. I say to him, *Why don't we move in with you two and share a place?* He says, *Sure,* without asking the girls. At the Clarendon, we carried the bags with the guns while the boy took the rest. Margaret set out right away to bake the new money. Crumbling the bills as we made fists, then smoothing them out. All the time we talked about what to do next. Not thinking about it at all. It takes time for new money to get old. But it all fell apart when Terry didn't do her bit. She sat and made up for hours though we weren't going anywhere. One day there was no breakfast on the table. What gives?

There's your girl friend, says Margaret.

Terry starts right up. *I can't cook.*

Well, you better start learning, I say.

Pete making a fist all the time and the green squeezing out through the fingers.

If they don't know me, they don't know how to say my name. The *g* is like in girl or gun. When they showed up from the *Star* and *News* at the farm and asked Dad what he thought about me and said the name, Dad just said, *I don't know him,* never heard of me. *But he's a junior,* they said.

That's not my name, Dad said. And he pronounced it for them.

That's all changed now, they said to him.

The old man just sat there right in front of them.

That's okay. Left all that behind. Even left that *g* behind.

Who told me that? Toms of the *Star* in Tucson while we waited for Indiana, Ohio, and Wisconsin to double-cross us. He came up to the bars during the sideshow, all those locals going by to look at us for a quarter. Pete steaming at Leach. Mac saying how great the weather was down there. Toms called me by my real name and told me the story. He asks me if that's how I wanted to be known, by the other name and all. Hell, it wouldn't do any good. It's out of our hands, just like everything else.

The police are leaving after doing nothing. They open the door, and there is a woman standing on the other side just about to knock. Shows she's surprised to see them, but she knows them all by name. She asks them if it is that time of month again. They nod and file out, the plainclothes first and then the uniforms. She stops one who is eating a sandwich as he goes by, takes out a hanky, and polishes his badge. All I had was a big bolt wrapped up in a neckerchief. I kept hitting him but only knocking off his straw hat. He'd pick it up and put it on again, and I'd knock it off. He was making that godawful sound, and I could hear the Masons come running. He didn't have no money. I didn't know a thing then. Just a kid. Same grocer gave me a talking to when I'd swiped some jawbreakers. He knew my dad. I ran, and someone chucked a bottle after me. They found me in the barn.

It was to have been all set. But the judge didn't care. I heard he died falling asleep across some railroad tracks, a knife in his pocket because I was coming to get him.

Since the operation, it's been like I had on thimbles. Patty wonders what's happened to my fingers. She's got them spread out in front of her eyes, tired of my fortune. She says, *Well, hell. How do you pick up something like a dime?*

I start thinking about all the things I've touched. Chairs and guns and the counter I hopped over in Daleville. The glasses. The sinks. The steering wheels. The money. It's like those things remember how I felt. But me, I forgot it as soon as I let go.

Touched Terry all over. Must have left a print on her everywhere. Some cop dusting her rear, blowing it off, saying, *We got the son of a bitch.* And they're all looking at her, looking for me. All the other women too. Shaking hands with men and having them look into their palms.

You think twice about punching a light switch.

Red rushing in saying that he killed a cop at the garage. Lost the Auburn, and they got his girl. He quieted down, started in telling us all over again what had happened and that the girl could be trusted. We looked at each other's faces, knowing that we didn't look like anybody else no more. Mac looked like a banker. Pete like some college kid, he's going without a hat and wearing that floppy collar. He walked into Racine and put a big Red Cross poster on the window without anybody taking a second look. And I'm looking like a sissy bookkeeper. Putting on weight.

We got the girls to dye our hair. Thought it was funny, us sitting with sheets around our necks. I said red and let my mustache grow. Terry sitting on my lap, drawing the eyebrows in. *Didn't like your face to begin with,* she's saying. Pete telling me later about the two toes he's got grown together. And Red holding up his hand, saying, *What am I going to do with these.* I never thought about them before, the fingers he left on the railroad track in the Soo.

They're going to fry you, boy.

I could hear Pete calling from the next cell. Leach was taking me back to Indiana. I fought them off awhile and they put cuffs on too hard for it. Some vacation. There was the cop from East Chicago who ran away. *He tried to stop me,* I tell them. Where is Wisconsin's Lightning Justice now? I could hear Pete screaming from his cell about going to Wisconsin and staying together and Mac calling from someplace else, *See you, John!*

I'll never see them again. I can't remember their faces. They went from Tucson to Ohio when Indiana waived the bust-out from Michigan City. They'll get it for getting me out of Lima.

The last thing is voices.

So long, John. Sioux Falls, Mason City. South Bend wasn't enough. I met their Mouth on the fair grounds to pass them the money. The parachutes dropping from the tower. *Tell them I'll get more.*

Indiana flew me to Crown Point. The pilot said that over there is Mexico.

Blackie has won the boat on a bet. They sit together on the deck with the lights of the city behind them. He asks her what she wants to name the boat. She talks about having a house and family. It's old-fashioned, *she says but that is what she wants. Then Blackie kisses her, and she stops talking about leaving the city, sailing away.*

We called her Mack Truck. She made breakfast Christmas morning. The fight I had with Terry was all left over from that race driver. I told her to go back to the reservation. *Take my car.* She's packing and crying.

Pete's girl said, *A girl's got a right to choose who she wants to be with.*

But it was like I didn't know Terry no more, and she stopped being pretty.

Christmas in Florida.

Even the joint had snow.

I told her to go where it was snowing, with the race driver. And she left after Red told her how to work the spark on the Ford. *I can buy another car!* I shouted at her.

It was so hot. I sat around in pieces of suits, and the girls giggled about thinking the tide was a flood. They had never seen an ocean in Indiana.

It got hotter the week after Christmas. The papers said we were still raising hell in Chicago. They blame everything on us. On New Year's Eve, people were shooting off firecrackers to see the light on the water. Pete's girl got out a tommy gun, and it rode right up when she shot it. I took it from her and fired it out over the waves, a long rip. But it wasn't any good firing at nothing. The tracers looked just so pitiful. Everybody else had girls and was heading for Tucson. I said I was going north and look for Terry. Red said he'd come along. We'd fence some bonds in Chicago.

If I make it to Mexico, I'll never see any of them again. Terry lost in the jails, Pete and Mac in Ohio. We can't pull off the magic trick again. We broke out of too many places. Even if I could walk in with this new face, there'd be no way to walk them out. The farmers they got to sit with them are taking shots at airplanes flying by. South Bend wasn't enough.

I'll never see Sally Rand at the Fair again. Have the woman I'm with tugging at my sleeve to get the hell out of there. But only half pulling, looking up at the stage too, at the feathers and the shiny pieces of paper. A thing like that. You can't stop watching the fans and balloons—because they are moving and changing and her face is floating, floating above whatever it is she's using to cover herself where she has to. The cops making such a big deal of it, standing off to the side, looking just like the rest of us looking up at the parts of her. Hiding like that. She didn't have to hide!

The alarm is ringing on the building. Red is jumpy, getting the money when a cop walks in. He thinks it's some kind of mistake. His blue overcoat is buttoned over his gun. *Just what I was looking for,* but it's trouble. There are more outside. They're lining up behind cars. *Grab somebody and go!* I yell to Red.

Someone says, *Can I get my coat?*

Out the door with the cop ahead of me and someone is calling the cop's name and the cop is running off down the street. I feel the bullet hit the vest. It knocks me back. I shoot at where the smoke is, and get hit twice more. I hear glass crashing and the alarm. I shoot some more at the smoke, see Red go down to the right, grab him, grab the money. My back is to the guns.

We get away in the car.

East Chicago still has Christmas stuff up.

Red took the bullet under his arm. My chest hurts. Red says from the backseat that being shot ain't nothing like being shot.

The ramps are crowded with people. He runs into Jim, and they shake hands, leaning forward and grabbing each other's arms with their other hands. Jim tells Blackie that he is running for DA and that Blackie's crowd better watch out. Blackie tells Jim that he's all for him and that Blackie's going straight. There is a roar from the crowd and Blackie says, Dempsey. *They talk about the fight and say that they will have to get together. There is another roar, and Blackie says,* Firpo.

Patty wants to hold hands in the dark. Puts my hand on her knee. She's got no stockings on. It's warm between her legs. We're both looking straight ahead. Watching the movie. I'm slumped down and my hat's on my lap. I'd say the man next to me is crowding me. His arm takes up the arm rest.

Her dress is nice. I think about what it's made of, stitch by stitch. What if the parts fell apart? In the shop I made double task, triple sometimes—yoking sleeves, setting collars with a Tomcat. The white thread in the blue work shirts. Thinking of pulling one thread and having the whole thing fall apart. It just feels good now, the cloth and what's underneath. She is moving.

The new DA is tired. Election night and all that. A woman breaks through the crowd and hops into the limousine after him. She says that Blackie sent her. They settle back in the seat and pull a blanket over their legs.

In Tucson, they took us one at a time, and me and Terry just getting back from looking for Indians. She stood there with her fingers crossed and her hands on top of her head. They cuffed me.

I do some shouting. *Hey, I tell you, I'm Sullivan! You got the wrong man!*

Some vacation, says Terry.

They had the prints on Pete and Mac by the time I made it to the station.

I don't know them. That's what I say. The place is lousy with reporters. The cops take me into a room where they start going through papers. They snatch my hand, turn over my wrist.

Well, what do we have here?

One bent down and undid a shoe.

The other foot, Charlie, says a guy.

They look at my heel a long time. I remember Pendleton and the foundry and pouring metal on it to get out of the heat. And then Charlie, he takes my face in his hands, and I say, *Hey.* He holds my head still while his thumbs feel through my mustache, pressing my lip on my teeth, my head down. *This is the guy,* he says.

They open the door and the reporters come in.

Guess who we got, they say.

Where's Indiana? I ask a farmer who's standing in his field. He points to the road crossing just ahead. Terry says, *You can't tell them apart. Illinois looks just the same. It'd be something if they were the colors on the map.*

I stop to change the plates and put the chains on. The roads are thawing and it'll just get worse as it gets warm. My dad won't know me now with these new clothes and hat. I want him to see Terry and the car. Hubert'll be there and the sisters. We'll hide in the barn if anybody comes. The hay will all be gone, and we can shoot baskets in the loft.

It wasn't warm enough for a picnic. But they filled the house with everyone bringing a covered dish and their own service.

I told them all about Crown Point. Once in the front room. Once in the kitchen. The kids on the porch. The men around back. Hubert took my picture with Terry. Then with me alone with the gun. Says he'll not have it developed till they catch me.

The people on the floor kicked the gas candle back and forth. Homer went in to get Red out of the vault. I'd been shot already. Green bent over where the gas shell hit him. We're all crying. I'm holding a girl when we go through the revolving door. It's my right shoulder so it's her I push against the glass.

She gives a little grunt.

Homer's behind me.

We've got people lined up all over. It's like a picket fence.

Red comes out and gets hit. It's coming from up above us and behind. We all get our guns going. The people got their hands up. Lester sets them out on the Buick. Two on the fenders like deer. They're on the back bumper, the running board, between us in the car. There must be twenty.

Slow! I yell.

Homer's reading off the directions when someone on the running board says, *Here, right here is where I live.* We stop and she gets off. Cars go by honking, thinking it's a shivaree. My arm hurts, all crowded in like that. Lester's leaning out the back with a rifle. We stop to let some more off, and he gets out to spread some tacks. I'm thinking that he's getting them under our car.

Some law you got! he's yelling at the locals.

The new DA and Blackie's girl are sitting at a table in a nightclub. A woman is on the stage, singing. After the song, everyone pounds on the tables with little wooden hammers. Then we see Blackie asleep in a room. He wakes up, and magazines fall to the floor. The phone rings, and he answers it. A woman, in bed, is on the other end of the line. She asks him to guess who she saw that night at the nightclub. Blackie hangs up and looks at the magazines.

Tellers always telling you to use the next window. Not believing you unless you have a mask. Walking in the door and wasting a whole clip above their heads. Less chance of shooting maybe, but you never know when somebody will get a wise idea, think they're in a movie.

That boy in South Bend, looking at his hand where the bullet went through.

The sheriff in Lima saying, *I'm going to have to leave you, Mother.*

The bullet that killed him on the floor next to him.

Margaret so surprised when the gun went off on the beach in Florida.

All the things we didn't do too. And did.

They'd draw my face all wrong. I don't smoke. Finding out later, after Pete and Mac got shipped to Ohio, that Leach told the papers to give me all the play.

Didn't matter to Pete.

Blackie closes the door, leaving the body inside. He catches up with his bodyguard, who is waiting by the elevator. It is New Year's Eve. The bodyguard is wearing a derby.

Cops are at the door, Terry says. And I'm a Lawrence something, something Lawrence. *Get dressed,* I tell her, fitting in a drum.

I am always waking up to these things. I can't remember my name.

I'd been leaving every morning, heading downtown to make it look like I had a job.

Terry's put her blouse on backwards. She's remembering what happened at Dr. Eye's.

Shots from the hall.

That'll be Homer coming over for breakfast.

Hurry up, I tell her, and spray the door.

Think about the cake the neighbor lady from across the hall brought over the first day, her husband with the pipe, saying he has a crystal set.

Down the back stairs, back out the back door.

Terry dents a fender backing out the car. I'm waiting, watching the door. The birds are noisy in the vines on the side of the building.

The DA is in his office trying on an overcoat. He tugs on the lapels. He bends forward, clutching the coat together to see where it falls on his legs. He checks to see if there is a label. He turns around in it and asks his assistant for his comments. He looks over his shoulder and down the back of a sleeve. It could be yours, *says the assistant.* Yes, *says the DA, standing there, thinking. He's in the middle of the room, bundled up. They bring him another coat, and the DA tries it on. The DA reaches into the pocket and finds a small wooden hammer.*

I heard they let her finish her drink. Then they took her out of the bar.

She'll be out before you know it, Homer was saying.

We were on the Lincoln Highway, heading to his folks. All the little towns had banks to rob. *They're taking away parts of me,* I'm saying to Homer, who's humming. We'd been stumbling through jobs. Losing guns and money. Not even planning anything anymore. Just going in shooting. Trusting the vests.

I'm lost, I say.

Men are pushing carts of big steamer trunks through the crowd. A band is playing somewhere. There's a ship whistle blowing. The DA looks at his watch and out over the people. Everyone is waving and shouting. There is a siren and the crowd gives way. An ambulance pulls up to the dock. Blackie gets out.

The shooting started when three guys left the bar to head home. The cops must have thought they were us. Lester opened up right away.

He sleeps with that gun.

I took off up the stairs with Homer and Red. We fired some out the windows, then covered each other to get out the back, down the bank to the lake. Walking on the far side, we could hear the shots over the water. Flashes every now and then.

They kept shooting at the house.

We tied up Red's head and caught our breath. Nobody even knew we were gone. They'd upped the reward that week.

The lake was very smooth, and we could see because of the moon and stars. They had all different sizes of guns shooting at the lodge.

The DA is running for governor. Blackie is at the racetrack. He looks through binoculars. He sees her in another part of the grandstand. He goes over and sits down. She says she's worried about Jim's chances to become governor. Someone is trying to ruin him, and he won't do anything about it. Blackie tells her not to worry, that he'll take care of it. He looks at her, tilts his head, says she mustn't tell Jim they talked.

Crossing the Mississippi on the spiral bridge below St. Paul. Pretty tricky since we're coming from the north. We pick up a tail. They start shooting. I knock out some glass and shoot back. Homer guns it. Red gets it. Never lucky, Red. His head already tied up from the night before at the lodge.

We shake them on a farm road and leave the car. I hold on to Red in the ditch while Homer goes to flag down a Ford. A family out for a drive, it looks like. Homer goes in the back with them. Red says he needs something to drink. The car could use gas. I stop at a place. The bottles are cold. My hands leave marks on the glass.

A lady opens the bottles for me. I go back to the car and give one to Red and try to give one to the kid in the back.

He's had his lunch already. I don't want him to have it, says the mother.

Down on one lip of the gravel pit, a locomotive is pushing some empty cars around. Piles of snow left over from the winter. It's been easy to dig in the loose gravel and sand. They're pumping water down below. Homer slides the body down through the bushes, and we put him in the hole. We're taking off all the clothes.

You weren't there, I say to Homer, pointing out the scar under Red's arm.

It's how he missed Tucson.

I tie up his clothes. Homer has the lye, but I want to do it. Feel kind of bad pouring it on his face. Turn his hands over and pour it on his fingers.

It smells real bad.

A hockey game is going on. Lots of people hollering. But there's a man in a men's room, two men. You can see them both in the mirrors. One of them says, You wanted to see me? *The other man pulls some paper towels from the rack. He turns to answer the question. It's Blackie. He has a gun wrapped up in the paper towels. When he shoots, you see the flashes coming from the towels.*

They told me later I swallowed my tongue. Last thing I can remember is the towel on my face. *Hotel Drake* in gold. And the smell of the ether.

I should've had a local. But I couldn't stand the thought of that, of looking at them when they did it. I wanted to wake up different.

I was always waking up the same.

The dimple was gone. But I could see where it had been. And the mole left a mark.

I was puffy and sore.

I saw a picture in a newspaper of a boy that turned out to be a picture of all the boys in a high-school class, one face on top of another. It didn't look like anything, and it had all the parts. I remembered that picture, looking at my face. Rob another bank and I'd have to get rid of this one too.

I wonder what I looked like with my face all blue. No way to forget it. That's me, all right.

Homer was thinking twice, cursing the tattoo. Finally went ahead and called it a goddamn mess. Lester sitting around drinking from a bottle of beer changes his mind a couple of times. Keeps what he has. Damn doctor was probably glad to let him.

Blackie sits and sketches all through his trial. The DA is examining a witness. Blackie's lawyer starts to get up to make an objection. Blackie stops him, says, Relax, you've been beaten by the best, *smiles at the DA, who is telling the jury that people like Blackie must be stopped.*

The cops are happy to show us the guns and vests. We act dumb. *What do you call this?* we are saying.

Oh, that. That's your submachine gun.

They have some .45s too.

We tell them we're from the East, doing a story on the crime wave. *Sports is my regular beat,* says Homer.

Yeah, well I've never been east, says one cop.

You should see the Fair in Chicago while you're in this neck of the woods, says the other one.

They talk it up. We listen.

I like hearing about myself. It's like being at your own funeral.

Being tourists got us in trouble in Tucson. Pete telling a cop he thought he was being followed, and the cop saying no. Tourists from the North. And I take pictures of cops directing traffic. *You look good in a uniform,* I tell them. The Sam Browne belts. The buttons picking up the light, turning white in the picture.

Pete used to say, *I wish you'd stop that. It's not smart.*

I'd say, *It's my hobby.*

We tell the cops in Warsaw we'll send them the story when we get done writing it.

The governor is in his car, racing to Sing Sing so he can see Blackie before he goes to the chair at midnight. Sirens getting closer, governor's car, motorcycles, everything speeding.

Guess who, I say to Margaret through her door. When she opens it, she knows me right away.

What happened to your face? You in an accident? I try to laugh. It's not her fault. I go on in. She's tough, but she misses Pete. I give her some money from Mason City and tell her about the tear gas and the bag of pennies. She says she doesn't think it would do any good. *You never know,* I say.

I've been down seeing my folks on the farm, I say.

She says that she reads about me all the time in the papers.

You know half of it ain't true.

It wasn't no good with nothing to plan.

She says she was at a dance when I broke out of Crown Point. She says she made sure a cop saw her that night. Says she makes sure a cop see her every night. She tells me she's thinking about going into vaudeville. People had been around to ask.

I could hear her sister in the next room taking a bath.

It didn't matter now that we had shields. They kept shooting, and the people with their hands up got hit first. The bags were too light. I was working the inside with two guys I didn't know. They were the only ones who would work with us now. Homer was outside with a rifle and Lester by the Hudson.

We walked out and everyone started to get hit. Homer in the head from a shotgun that took the pants leg off a local. I pulled him into the car.

He said we should wear something different when we did South Bend. *New faces. Sure.*

So we had on overalls over the vests. Always a clown. We wore straws too. Changed his luck. Pieces of straw mixed in with his hair in the hole in his head. Lester wanted to count the money again.

Blackie walks with the priest. The warden is there, the governor, two guards. Blackie says so long. Someone is playing a harmonica.

Mrs. Mint saying again over ice cream that Romania isn't a country, just what was left of a place after the war. Patty holds the cherry up for me.

I don't know anything about the world.

I'm seen everywhere.

Cops in England are searching the boats going to France. Every body that turns up is what's left of me.

I could call the Leach home, hear him stutter while he tries to keep me on the line. But it could be anybody with a gun. I'm worth too much now that the governors got together.

I'll check in with Henry Ford. Send a messenger to Detroit with a note. All the models I left on the edge of Chicago. Good little cars.

Mrs. Mint told me she's already turned the bed down back at Patty's place. But I want to stay and watch the cartoons.

The lights are going up and everybody's squinting coming out of the dark. I can see who's been next to me. And Patty crying. Mrs. Mint looking through her purse for a hanky for her. I can't keep my eyes open. Pete, Mac. I'll see their Mouth at Wrigley tomorrow, give him what I can spare from the trip.

Patty touching my hand. Then both of the women are squeezing by, heading for the aisle. The crowd is buzzing and I can smell the smoke from the lobby. It's cold in here. Just this once I'd like to open my eyes and have it be all different.

BIOGRAPHICAL NOTES

BY E. G. DUSTWORTHY, M.A.

CONRAD AIKEN (1889–1973), born in Georgia and raised in Massachusetts, was a poet, critic, and novelist as well as a writer of stories. He won the Pulitzer Prize for his *Selected Poems* of 1929 and was instrumental in refurbishing Emily Dickinson's reputation. His autobiography, *Ushant,* was published in 1952 and again in 1971, with the real names of the people involved supplied.

SHERWOOD ANDERSON (1876–1941) was a businessman first, a writer after. Born in Ohio, he lived in Chicago, New Orleans, and Paris. His reputation rests almost entirely upon a single book, *Winesburg, Ohio,* which did much to alter the way Americans wrote about the experience of small-town American life. He wrote several novels and collections of stories. "Death in the Woods" is one of his later, yet best works.

MAX APPLE (1941–   ) grew up in Grand Rapids; he teaches at Rice University in Houston. He has written two novels, *Zip* and *The Propheteers,* and two collections of stories: *The Oranging of America* and *Free Agents.*

TONI CADE BAMBARA (1939–   ) was born in New York City. She has been a social worker and a teacher of English. She is the author of two collections of stories, *Gorilla, My Love* and *The Sea Birds Are Still Alive,* and has edited a collection, *The Black Woman.*

DONALD BARTHELME (1931–   ) is a Texan living in New York City who has written three short novels: *Snow White, The Dead Father,* and *Paradise,* for which he was nominated for a Pulitzer Prize. He is better known for his short stories, collected under such titles as *Come Back, Dr. Caligari, Unspeakable Practices, Unnatural Acts, Sadness,* and *Guilty Pleasures.*

AMBROSE BIERCE (1842–1914?) was born in Ohio and known for the savage journalism he wrote for the Hearst press in San Francisco. He also wrote short stories about the Civil War (in which he had fought) and about horror and the supernatural. His supremely cynical book of aphorisms, *The Devil's Dictionary,* seems hardly dated today. In 1913 this bitter man disappeared into the Mexican Revolution, apparently seeking death.

Richard Brautigan (1935–1984) lived in San Francisco. He wrote short, comic, surrealistic novels and stories, among them the classic *Trout Fishing in America* and *The Hawkline Monster: A Gothic Western.*

George Washington Cable (1844–1925) was born in New Orleans, center of the Creole culture that he chronicled in such novels as *The Grandissimes* and story collections like *Old Creole Days.*

James M. Cain (1892–1977) was born and died in Maryland. Before writing fiction, he worked as a teacher, reporter, and newspaper columnist and was for nine months managing editor of *The New Yorker* magazine. He was for many years a scriptwriter in Hollywood. His most famous novels are *The Postman Always Rings Twice, Double Indemnity,* and *Mildred Pierce.*

Erskine Caldwell (1903–1987) was born in Georgia. He worked as a cotton picker, stagehand, professional football player, and screenwriter. The novels and stories for which he is best known, including *God's Little Acre* and *Tobacco Road,* were written in the early 1930s and, for their depictions of human squalor, became extremely controversial. His writings earned him decorations in Poland and France.

Raymond Carver (1938–1988) was born in Clatskanie, Oregon, and grew up among the Cascade Mountains in Washington. Carver's collections of stories include *Will You Please Be Quiet, Please?, What We Talk About When We Talk About Love,* and *Cathedral.* He was also a poet; his last collection of verse was *Where Water Comes Together with Other Water.*

Willa Cather (1873–1947) was born in Virginia and raised in Nebraska, scene of much of her best fiction. Her first collection of stories, *The Troll Garden,* appeared in 1905. Among her most highly regarded novels are *My Antonía* and *Death Comes for the Archbishop.*

John Cheever (1912–1982), writer of episodic novels and luminous short stories, was born in Massachusetts. In five novels and over a hundred stories, he observed the disappointments and fears of contemporary urban and suburban men and women, as well as their intimations of redemption. He gave voice to the inarticulate agonies that lie beneath the surface of ordinary lives. For *The Wapshot Chronicle* he received a National Book Award; his collected stories received the Pulitzer Prize.

Kate Chopin (1851–1904) was born and died in St. Louis, but spent much of her life in New Orleans and on a plantation in Natchitoches Parish, Louisiana. There she observed the life of the Creoles about whom she would later write in stories collected in two volumes, *Bayou Folk* and *A Night in Acadie.* Her second novel, *The Awakening,* has emerged as a classic among contemporary feminists, yet upon its publication in 1899 it was savagely attacked for its grim, if realistic, psychological portraits.

SAMUEL LANGHORNE CLEMENS (1835–1910) was born in Missouri. After brief service with the Confederacy, he became, under the trademark Mark Twain, a writer and lecturer, none more famous in his day. The author of *Tom Sawyer* and *Huckleberry Finn* was always a great teller of tales, if never a great writer of short stories.

FRANK CONROY (1936–) published his autobiography, *Stop-time,* at the age of thirty-one. The influence of that book was such that he has been reckoned an important writer even though nearly two decades passed before *Midair,* a slim collection of his stories, appeared. In 1981 he was appointed director of the Literature Program at the National Endowment for the Arts.

ROBERT COOVER (1932–), born in Iowa, won the William Faulkner Award for his first novel, *The Origin of the Brunists.* His second novel, *The Universal Baseball Association, J. Henry Waugh, Prop.,* is the best novel ever written about the national game. Coover's stories are collected in two volumes: *Pricksongs and Descants* and *A Night at the Movies.*

STEPHEN CRANE (1871–1900) was born in New Jersey. Publishers thought his first novel, *Maggie: A Girl of the Streets,* too realistic; it proved a failure when privately printed. Crane is best known for *The Red Badge of Courage,* a Civil War novel so realistic that readers find it difficult to believe Crane had never seen a war. "The Open Boat," his best-known story, is based on an incident from his own life. He died of tuberculosis in Germany.

STANLEY ELKIN (1930–) was born in New York City and teaches at Washington University, St. Louis. Among his novels are *Boswell, A Bad Man,* and *The Dick Gibson Show.* His stories have been collected in *Criers and Kibitzers, Kibitzers and Criers.*

WILLIAM FAULKNER (1897–1962) was born near Oxford, Mississippi, the town which, under the name "Jefferson," he often wrote about in his many novels and stories. An occasional poet and screenwriter, Faulkner made money from the sale of his stories, but it is upon his longer fiction, particularly the tortuous, difficult, and at times self-indulgent novels he wrote before World War II, that his reputation rests. *The Sound and the Fury, As I Lay Dying, Absalom, Absalom!,* and *Light in August* are his most admired works. All had nearly vanished when, in 1946, Malcolm Cowley's *The Portable Faulkner* revived Faulkner's reputation. He was awarded the Nobel Prize in 1950 and, finally, in 1954, a Pulitzer Prize for an inferior novel, *A Fable.*

F. SCOTT FITZGERALD (1896–1940), born in St. Paul, Minnesota, was the exemplar of the Lost Generation of writers in the 1920s. His stories of the Jazz Age commanded immense fees; they both defined and reported on a world that became a legend even before it had expired. Drink and worry over his mentally unstable wife, Zelda, wore him down, and he died of a heart attack. Besides his stories, Fitzgerald is known primarily for two of his five novels: *The Great Gatsby* and *Tender Is the Night.*

ROBERT FLANAGAN (1941–) was born in Toledo, Ohio, and now professes English at Ohio Wesleyan University. He is the author of a novel, *Maggot,* two books of poetry, and a collection of stories, *Naked to Naked Goes.* He has won awards in fiction from the National Endowment for the Arts and for the Humanities, and from the Ohio Arts Council.

RICHARD FORD (1944–) lives in Mississippi and in western Montana. Besides *Rock Springs,* a collection of short stories, he has published three novels: *A Piece of My Heart, The Ultimate Good Luck,* and *The Sportswriter.*

BENJAMIN FRANKLIN (1706–1790), journalist, inventor, and diplomat, was the eldest and certainly most colorful of this country's Founding Fathers. "The Speech of Polly Baker" was published in 1747.

MARY E. WILKINS FREEMAN (1852–1930) was born in Massachusetts; it is as a writer of New England manners that she is best known. She began her career as a poet and author of children's books; later she wrote novels and stories. *Pembroke* is considered her best novel; among her collections of stories are *A Humble Romance, A New England Nun,* and *The Wind in the Rose-bush.*

WILLIAM H. GASS (1924–) was born in Fargo, South Dakota, and raised in Warren, Ohio. His books include a novel, *Omensetter's Luck,* and a collection of stories, *In the Heart of the Heart of the Country,* as well as collections of critical essays which emphasize the philosophy of language and the theory of metaphor.

ELLEN GILCHRIST (1935–) grew up on a plantation in Mississippi, the state in which she still lives. She has published a novel, *The Annunciation,* and three collections of stories: *In the Land of Dreamy Dreams, Victory Over Japan* (which won the American Book Award for fiction), and *Drunk with Love.*

CHARLOTTE PERKINS STETSON [GILMAN] (1860–1935) was not yet married to her cousin George Houghton Gilman when she wrote her most famous story, though it is under his name that this most feminist of stories invariably appears. Victim of a mental breakdown after the birth of her daughter, she went on to write such feminist tracts as "Women and Economics," "Man-Made World," and a utopia, "Herland."

JOEL CHANDLER HARRIS (1848–1908), a journalist born in rural Georgia, was a white man who collected black folk literature. His "Uncle Remus" stories combine authority with humor; they also created a vogue for dialect stories which lasted into the 1920s.

BRET HARTE (1836–1902), that most Western of writers, was born in Albany, New York. He went to California at eighteen and in time became a journalist in San Francisco. His early stories about California mining life brought him immense fame and wealth, but he lost his skill and ended his life as a hack writer, imitating his earlier work.

Nathaniel Hawthorne (1804–1864) was born in Salem, Massachusetts; his ancestors had been prominent Puritans. He was, with E. A. Poe, an inventor of the modern short story. Those collected in *Twice-Told Tales* had, according to their author, "the pale tint of flowers that blossomed in too retired a shade." Other stories, often allegories of guilt and the revelation of secret sin, appeared in *Mosses from an Old Manse.* His novels include *The Scarlet Letter* and *The House of Seven Gables.*

Mark Helprin (1947–) was born in New York City; he sold his first story to *The New Yorker* while still an undergraduate at Harvard. He is the author of two long novels, *Refiner's Fire* and the grandiose *Winter's Tale.* A much more effective writer in the short story form, he has also published two collections of stories, *A Dove of the East* and *Ellis Island.*

Ernest Hemingway (1899–1961) was born in Illinois. He worked as a journalist in Kansas City and Toronto and as an ambulance driver in World War I. A member of the American expatriate group in Paris during the 1920s, he invented both a sensibility ideally suited to those disillusioned times and a style to convey it. His best books are his earliest: the novel *The Sun Also Rises* and the story collections *In Our Time, Men Without Women,* and *Winner Take Nothing.* In later years, Hemingway seemed to devote as much energy to his public image as he did to finishing books. He was awarded the Nobel Prize in 1954. Seven years later he shot himself.

O. Henry, pseudonym of William Sidney Porter (1862–1910), was born in North Carolina. Indicted for embezzlement in 1896, he fled to Honduras, but was jailed for three years when he returned to Austin, Texas, to visit his wife on her deathbed. In jail he began to write brief, sentimental stories with surprise endings, which have been endlessly reprinted.

Langston Hughes (1902–1967), born in Missouri, became one of the leading figures of the Harlem Renaissance. Known primarily as a poet, he also wrote novels, plays, and five volumes of satirical sketches featuring a single character, Jesse B. Semple, known as "Simple." The story included here appeared in *The Ways of White Folks.*

Zora Neale Hurston (c. 1901–1960) was born in Eatonville, Florida, an all-black community where her father was mayor. At Barnard College on a scholarship she studied anthropology; at about that time she researched the folklore of her hometown. Among her books are a collection of folklore, *Mules and Men* and a novel, *Their Eyes Were Watching God.* Toward the end of her life, her fiction was rejected by publishers; she worked for a while as a maid in Miami and died a pauper.

Washington Irving (1783–1859) was born in New York City and set about satirizing its society as soon as he began writing. He wrote serious history as well as the sketches and tales for which he is remembered; he also managed to write gracefully and with humor about both American and European themes. Toward the end of his life he was considered America's greatest author.

Shirley Jackson (1916–1965), born in California, lived in Vermont, teaching at Bennington College. She wrote several novels about disturbed young people and a novel that may be the best of contemporary ghost stories: *The Haunting of Hill House.* She also wrote two light memoirs about her happy family life, thus incurring the distrust of feminist critics.

Henry James (1843–1916), considered by many to be the greatest American writer of fiction, was born in New York City. He left America in 1875 and from the following year lived primarily in England, becoming a British citizen in 1915. Among his most important works are the novels *The Portrait of a Lady* and *The Ambassadors* and such novellas as *The Aspern Papers* and *The Turn of the Screw.*

Sarah Orne Jewett (1849–1909), one of the best of the 19th-century regional writers, was born in Maine and encouraged by W. D. Howells, editor of *The Atlantic Monthly.* "The White Heron" appeared in a collection of stories published in 1886. Ten years later, Jewett published her most famous book, *The Country of the Pointed Firs.*

Ring Lardner (1885–1933) was born Ringgold Wilmer Lardner in Niles, Michigan. A sports writer in Chicago, and later a newspaper columnist, he began writing fiction in 1914. His most famous books are *You Know Me Al, How to Write Short Stories,* and *The Love Nest.* During his last years, he was repeatedly hospitalized for tuberculosis.

Ursula K. Le Guin (1929–) is the daughter of an anthropologist and a folklorist; the influence of both is strong in her work. One of the most imaginative of feminist writers, she is the best living writer of fantasy and science ficton. She is best known for such novels as *The Left Hand of Darkness, The Dispossessed,* and *Always Coming Home.*

Jack London (1876–1916) was born in San Francisco and joined the gold rush in the Klondike in 1897. From this experience came his stories of a brutal life at the edge of survival. London was both a socialist and a devotee of Nietzsche, a curious mixture that did nothing to diminish his immense popularity and success. Among his best-known novels are *The Call of the Wild* and *White Fang.*

Anita Loos (1893–1981) wrote far too much, yet in 1925 she assured her place in American letters with *Gentlemen Prefer Blondes,* one of the funniest novels this country has produced. Its delightful narrator, Lorelei Lee, appears again—and in just as good form—in the story included here. At her best, Loos wrote funny lines to convey a distinctly unamused view of the world.

Bernard Malamud (1914–1986) was born in Brooklyn. Equally adept at novels and short stories, he won the National Book Award and the Pulitzer Prize for

The Fixer. He won another National Book Award for his first collection of stories, *The Magic Barrel.* For many years, until his death, he taught English at Bennington College.

MICHAEL MARTONE (1955–) was born in Fort Wayne, Indiana. He has taught at Iowa State University, published poetry and two collections of short stories: *Alive and Dead in Indiana* and *Safety Patrol.* He has twice earned the Pushcart Prize for an outstanding writer and has received a grant from the National Endowment for the Arts.

JOYCE CAROL OATES (1938–) was born in Lockport, New York. For many years she has published three or four books a year; no living American writer as prolific as she is equally talented. Though she has written some engaging fantasies and historical pastiches, her method has largely been realistic and her concern has been with the dark forces that press her characters into criminal or insane behavior. Her best novel, *Them,* received a Pulitzer Prize.

FLANNERY O'CONNOR (1925–1964) was raised in Milledgeville, Georgia, where she continued to live with her mother after her father died of an incurable blood disease. A Roman Catholic, O'Connor infused her novels and stories with a ferocious Christianity. The disease that killed her father struck her, too, crippling her before it killed her. O'Connor's novels are *Wise Blood* and *The Violent Bear It Away;* her stories appeared in two volumes: *A Good Man Is Hard To Find* and *Everything That Rises Must Converge.*

JOHN O'HARA (1905–1970), born in Pottsville, Pennsylvania, was the most prolific serious writer of his time. He wrote far too many novels and stories, and those that appeared after World War II seem now bloated and lacking in the satirical energy that informed his early work. His best novel was probably his first, *Appointment in Samara,* and his best stories—most of them very short—appeared in such collections as *The Doctor's Son, Pipe Night,* and *Hellbox.*

TILLIE OLSEN (1913–), born in Nebraska, came late to writing. She had first to raise her four daughters, which she did by working as a maid. Besides her collection of stories, *Tell Me a Riddle,* she has written a novel, *Yonnondio,* and a book of essays, *Silences.*

CYNTHIA OZICK (1928–) was born and educated in New York City and lives now in New Rochelle. Her books include three novels—*Trust, The Cannibal Galaxy,* and *The Messiah of Stockholm*—and three collections of stories: *The Pagan Rabbi, Bloodshed,* and *Levitation.*

GRACE PALEY (1922–) was born and lives in New York City. The wry feminism that informs her adroit stories, many of which are obviously about her own family, has made her an influential and important writer. She has published three books: *The Little Disturbances of Man, Enormous Changes at the Last Minute,* and *Later the Same Day.*

DOROTHY PARKER (1893–1967), born in New York City, was the quintessential New York wit, known as much for what she said as for what she wrote. Whether she was writing light verse or short stories, she affected a jaded cynicism, expressed through a lapidary style; only occasionally does a glint of genuine emotion show through. Most of what she wrote is now available in a single volume, Viking's *The Portable Dorothy Parker.*

JAYNE ANNE PHILLIPS (1952–) was born in West Virginia. Among her books are a novel, *Machine Dreams,* and four collections of stories, of which *Black Tickets* and *Fast Lanes* are the best known. She has been a teaching-writing fellow at the Iowa Writers' Workshop and is the recipient of the Sue Kaufman Prize from the American Academy of Arts and Letters and a National Endowment for the Arts Fellowship in Fiction.

EDGAR ALLAN POE (1809–1849), born in Boston, was a poet, literary journalist, and, with Nathaniel Hawthorne, an inventor of the modern short story. The author of such often-printed stories as "The Tell-Tale Heart," "The Premature Burial," and "The Purloined Letter" suffered from a Gothic imagination, a rococo prose style, and an addiction to liquor; the last killed him, the other two have kept him alive, particularly in books meant to be read by the young.

KATHERINE ANNE PORTER (1890–1980) was born Callie Russell Porter in Indian Creek, Texas. Her three marriages ended in divorce. Her only novel, *Ship of Fools,* was written late in life and fared indifferently with the critics, but her elegant, ironic stories and such novellas as *Noon Wine* and *Pale Horse, Pale Rider* have since their publication in the 1930s been acclaimed as classics.

J. F. POWERS (1917–) was born in Illinois. Most of what he has written concerns Roman Catholic priests in off-duty moments. He has published five books: three collections of stories—*Prince of Darkness, The Presence of Grace, Look How the Fish Live*—and two novels: *Morte D'Urban,* which won the National Book Award, and *Wheat That Springeth Green.*

IRWIN SHAW (1913–1984), born in Brooklyn, wrote plays as well as the novels and stories that made him famous. His best-known novels are perhaps *The Young Lions* and *Rich Man, Poor Man.* His stories have been collected in *Five Decades.*

ISAAC BASHEVIS SINGER (1904–) was born in the Russian-ruled part of Poland; he came to America in 1935. In New York he wrote—and still writes—articles, reviews, and stories for a Yiddish newspaper, *The Jewish Daily Forward.* He has written—always in Yiddish—numerous novels, memoirs, and collections of stories. In 1978 he received the Nobel Prize.

TESS SLESINGER (1905–1945) was born in New York City. At the age of thirty she moved to Hollywood to write movie scripts, including that for *The Good Earth* and, in collaboration with Frank Davis, *A Tree Grows in Brooklyn.* Her fiction includes a novel, *The Unpossessed,* and a story collection, *Time: The Present,* which was reprinted as *On Being Told That Her Second Husband Has Taken His First Lover.*

JEAN STAFFORD (1915–1979) was born in California and raised in Colorado. Her novels include *Boston Adventure* and *The Mountain Lion.* Her *Collected Stories* of 1969 received a Pulitzer Prize. Stafford also wrote a book of nonfiction, *A Mother in History,* which dealt with Lee Harvey Oswald's mother. She was married to Robert Lowell and to A. J. Liebling.

WILBUR DANIEL STEELE (1886–1970) was born in North Carolina; an ancestor had come to this country in 1632. Nobody today remembers his novels or plays, but his short stories, written mainly in the 1920s and 1930s, are remarkable for their narrative strength. Like many good writers, Steele recognized that he was unfit for any other employment; he knew, too, that his tales of plot and dramatic suspense made him "the last gasp of an epoch."

JAMES THURBER (1894–1961) was born in Ohio. Most of his distinctive fables, essays, stories, and drawings appeared in *The New Yorker.* About that magazine and its first editor Thurber wrote an engaging book, *The Years with Ross.* There are many collections of his work, among them *Men, Women and Dogs* and *The Thurber Carnival* may be the most indispensable. Thurber also wrote several children's books; at least one, *The Thirteen Clocks,* has become a classic.

JEAN TOOMER (1894–1967) was born in Washington, D.C., and is remembered for a short book called *Cane* which, through a kaleidoscope of poems and prose narratives, spoke with more artistry of the Afro-American experience than any book had done before. On its publication in 1923, Toomer was proclaimed a leader of the Harlem Renaissance, a celebrity he detested. Toomer insisted he was not a "Negro writer," nor even a black man. Later he became involved with the fashionable mysticism of G. I. Gurdjieff.

JOHN UPDIKE (1932–   ), arguably the best living American fiction writer, is a native of Pennsylvania who has lived most of his adult life in Massachusetts. Updike writes light verse and book reviews for *The New Yorker,* as well as the stories and novels that have made him famous. Of the latter, the most famous are probably the overly ambitious *Couples* and the "Rabbit" trilogy: *Rabbit, Run, Rabbit Redux,* and *Rabbit is Rich,* which won the Pulitzer Prize. Updike's short stories—in such collections as *Pigeon Feathers, The Music School,* and *Too Far To Go*—lack the excesses of prose and architecture to which the novels sometimes succumb.

ALICE WALKER (1944–   ) was born in Eatonton, Georgia, the daughter of sharecroppers. A feminist, she insisted—when it was not politic to do so—that sexism existed within the black community. One can see this in her works. She has published poems, essays, and stories. Her novels include *The Third Life of Grange Copeland, Meridian,* and *The Color Purple,* for which she won the Pulitzer Prize.

JEROME WEIDMAN (1913–   ) is a novelist and playwright whose writing reflects New York's Lower East Side, where he grew up. His best-known novels are probably his first, *I Can Get It for You Wholesale,* and *The Enemy Camp.* He collaborated with George Abbott on *Fiorello!,* which won the Pulitzer Prize.

EUDORA WELTY (1909–) was born in Jackson, Mississippi, where she has lived virtually all of her life. Her collections of stories include *A Curtain of Green, The Wide Net,* and *Collected Stories.* Among her novels are *The Ponder Heart, Delta Wedding,* and *Losing Battles.* Her most recent novel, *The Optimist's Daughter,* won the Pulitzer Prize, and her recent memoir, *One Writer's Beginnings,* has been highly praised.

EDITH WHARTON (1862–1937), one of the few patricians to reach the front rank of American letters, was born in New York City. Her marriage was unhappy but her books were many. She is best known for two novels—*The House of Mirth* and *The Age of Innocence,* which won the Pulitzer Prize—and for a novella, *Ethan Frome.* In 1930 she became the first woman to be awarded the gold medal of the National Institute of Arts and Letters.

MARIANNE WIGGINS (1947–) was born in Lancaster, Pennsylvania. Having lived in Europe and America, she now resides in London. A former stockbroker, she has published three novels, *Separate Checks, Went South,* and *Babe,* and a collection of stories, *Herself in Love.*

ACKNOWLEDGMENTS

CONRAD AIKEN: "Silent Snow, Secret Snow." Copyright 1932 and renewed 1960 by Conrad Aiken. Reprinted from *The Collected Stories of Conrad Aiken,* by permission of Schocken Books, published by Pantheon Books, a Division of Random House, Inc.

SHERWOOD ANDERSON: "Death in the Woods" from *Death in the Woods* by Sherwood Anderson. Reprinted by permission of Harold Ober Associates Incorporated. Copyright 1926 by The American Mercury, Inc. Copyright renewed 1953 by Eleanor Copenhaver Anderson.

MAX APPLE: "Bridging" from *Free Agents* by Max Apple. Copyright © 1984 by Max Apple. Reprinted by permission of Harper & Row, Publishers, Inc.

TONI CADE BAMBARA: "Gorilla, My Love." Copyright © 1971 by Toni Cade Bambara. Reprinted from *Gorilla, My Love* by Toni Cade Bambara, reprinted by permission of Random House, Inc.

DONALD BARTHELME: "Robert Kennedy Saved from Drowning." Copyright © 1968 by Donald Barthelme. Reprinted by permission of International Creative Management, Inc.

RICHARD BRAUTIGAN: "Revenge of the Lawn" from *Revenge of the Lawn.* Copyright © 1963, 1964, 1965, 1966, 1967, 1969, 1970, 1971 by Richard Brautigan. Reprinted by permission of Simon & Schuster, Inc.

JAMES M. CAIN: "The Baby in the Icebox" from *The Baby in the Icebox and Other Short Fiction* by James M. Cain, edited by Roy Hoopes. Copyright © 1981 by Alice M. Piper. Reprinted by permission of Henry Holt and Company, Inc.

ERSKINE CALDWELL: "Kneel to the Rising Sun" from *Stories of Life North and South* by Erskine Caldwell. Copyright © 1935 by Charles Scribner's Sons. Copyright © 1963 by Erskine Caldwell. Reprinted by permission of Dodd, Mead & Company, Inc.

RAYMOND CARVER: "What We Talk About When We Talk About Love." Copyright © 1981 by Raymond Carver. Reprinted from *What We Talk About*

When We Talk About Love by Raymond Carver, by permission of Alfred A. Knopf, Inc.

JOHN CHEEVER: "The Swimmer." Copyright © 1964 by John Cheever. Reprinted from *The Stories of John Cheever,* by permission of Alfred A. Knopf, Inc.

FRANK CONROY: "Midair" from *Midair* by Frank Conroy. Copyright © 1985 by Frank Conroy. Reprinted by permission of the publisher, E. P. Dutton/Seymour Lawrence, a division of NAL Penguin Inc.

ROBERT COOVER: "The Babysitter" from *Pricksongs and Descants* by Robert Coover. Copyright © 1969 by Robert Coover. Reprinted by permission of the publisher, E. P. Dutton, a division of New American Library.

STANLEY ELKIN: "A Poetics for Bullies" from *Criers and Kibitzers, Kibitzers and Criers.* Copyright © 1965, 1963, 1962, 1961, 1960, 1959 by Stanley Elkin. Reprinted by permission of Georges Borchardt, Inc. and the author.

WILLIAM FAULKNER: "Wash" from *Collected Stories of William Faulkner.* Copyright © 1934 and renewed 1962 by William Faulkner. Reprinted by permission of Random House, Inc.

F. SCOTT FITZGERALD: "The Bridal Party" from *The Stories of F. Scott Fitzgerald.* Copyright 1930 Curtis Publishing Company; copyright renewed © 1958 Curtis Publishing Company and Frances S. F. Lanahan. Reprinted with the permission of Charles Scribner's Sons, an imprint of Macmillan Publishing Company.

ROBERT FLANAGAN: "Teller's Ticket" from *Naked to Naked Goes.* Copyright © 1986. Reprinted by permission of the author and the author's agent, Liz Darhansoff.

RICHARD FORD: "Communist" reprinted from *Rock Springs* by Richard Ford. Copyright © 1987 by Richard Ford. Reprinted by permission of the Atlantic Monthly Press.

WILLIAM H. GASS: "In the Heart of the Heart of the Country" from *In the Heart of the Heart of the Country* by William Gass. Copyright © 1958, 1961, 1962, 1967, 1968 by William Gass. Reprinted by permission of David R. Godine, Publisher.

ELLEN GILCHRIST: "Victory Over Japan" from *Victory Over Japan: Short Stories* by Ellen Gilchrist. Copyright © 1984 by Ellen Gilchrist. By permission of Little, Brown and Company.

MARK HELPRIN: "Letters from the *Samantha*" from *Ellis Island & Other Stories* by Mark Helprin. Copyright © 1976 by Mark Helprin. Originally published in *The New Yorker.* Reprinted by permission of Delacorte Press/Seymour Lawrence.

ERNEST HEMINGWAY: "Hills Like White Elephants" from *The Short Stories of Ernest Hemingway.* Copyright 1927 Charles Scribner's Sons; copyright renewed 1955 Ernest Hemingway. Reprinted with the permission of Charles Scribner's Sons, an imprint of Macmillan Publishing Company.

LANGSTON HUGHES: "Slave on the Block" from *The Ways of White Folks* by Langston Hughes. Copyright 1934 and renewed 1962 by Langston Hughes. Reprinted by permission of Alfred A. Knopf, Inc.

ZORA NEALE HURSTON: "The Eatonville Anthology." Reprinted by permission of the Estate of Zora Neale Hurston.

SHIRLEY JACKSON: "The Lottery" from *The Lottery* by Shirley Jackson. Copyright © 1948, 1949 by Shirley Jackson. Copyright renewed © 1976, 1977 by Laurence Hyman, Barry Hyman, Mrs. Sarah Webster, and Mrs. Joanne Schnurer. "The Lottery" originally appeared in *The New Yorker.* Reprinted by permission of Farrar, Straus & Giroux, Inc.

RING LARDNER: "Champion" from *The Best Short Stories of Ring Lardner.* Copyright © 1957 by Charles Scribner's Sons; copyright renewed © 1985 Charles Scribner's Sons. Reprinted with the permission of Charles Scribner's Sons, an imprint of Macmillan Publishing Company.

URSULA K. LE GUIN: "The Ones Who Walk Away from Omelas." Copyright © 1973, 1975 by Ursula K. Le Guin; reprinted by permission of the author and the author's agent, Virginia Kidd.

ANITA LOOS: "Liquor Makes You Smart" reprinted from *Fate Keeps on Happening* by Anita Loos, edited by Ray Pierre Corsini. Copyright © 1984 by Anita Loos Trusts. Published by Dodd, Mead & Company, Inc. First appeared in *Cosmopolitan* magazine, © 1927. Reprinted by permission.

BERNARD MALAMUD: "Idiots First" from *Idiots First* by Bernard Malamud. Copyright © 1961, 1963 by Bernard Malamud. Reprinted by permission of Farrar, Straus & Giroux, Inc.

MICHAEL MARTONE: "Biograph" from *Alive and Dead in Indiana* by Michael Martone. Copyright © 1983 by Michael Martone. Reprinted by permission of the author.

JOYCE CAROL OATES: "How I Contemplated the World from the Detroit House of Correction and Began My Life Over Again" reprinted from *The Wheel of Love* by Joyce Carol Oates by permission of the publisher, Vanguard Press, Inc. Copyright © 1970, 1969, 1968, 1967, 1966, 1965, by Joyce Carol Oates.

FLANNERY O'CONNOR: "Revelation" from *The Complete Stories* by Flannery O'Connor. Copyright © 1964–1965 by the Estate of Mary Flannery O'Connor. Reprinted by permission of Farrar, Straus & Giroux, Inc.

JOHN O'HARA: "Over the River and Through the Wood." Copyright 1934 and renewed 1962 by John O'Hara. Reprinted from *Collected Stories of John O'-Hara,* Edited by Frank MacShane, by permission of Random House, Inc.

Tillie Olsen: "I Stand Here Ironing" from *Tell Me a Riddle* by Tillie Olsen. Copyright © 1956, 1961 by Tillie Olsen. Reprinted by arrangement with Dell Publishing/Seymour Lawrence. All rights reserved.

Cynthia Ozick: "Levitation" from *Levitations: Five Fictions* by Cynthia Ozick. Copyright © 1982 by Cynthia Ozick. Reprinted by permission of Alfred A. Knopf, Inc.

Grace Paley: "A Subject of Childhood" from *The Little Disturbances of Man* by Grace Paley. Copyright © 1988 by Grace Paley. Originally published in the United States by Doubleday & Company, Inc., copyright © 1959. Reprinted by permission of the author and Elaine Markson Literary Agency, Inc.

Dorothy Parker: "The Standard of Living" from *The Portable Dorothy Parker.* Copyright 1941 by Dorothy Parker, renewed © 1969 by Lillian Hellman. Originally published in *The New Yorker.* Reprinted by permission of Viking Penguin Inc.

Jayne Anne Phillips: "Lechery" excerpted from the book *Black Tickets* by Jayne Anne Phillips. Copyright © 1979 by Jayne Anne Phillips. Reprinted by permission of Delacorte Press/Seymour Lawrence.

Katherine Anne Porter: "Theft" from *Flowering Judas and Other Stories,* copyright 1935, 1963 by Katherine Anne Porter. Reprinted by permission of Harcourt Brace Jovanovich, Inc.

J. F. Powers: "The Valiant Woman" from *Prince of Darkness* by J. F. Powers. Copyright © 1947, 1975 by J. F. Powers. Reprinted by permission of the author.

Irwin Shaw: "The Eighty-Yard Run" from *Short Stories: Five Decades* by Irwin Shaw. © Estate of Irwin Shaw. Reprinted by permission.

Isaac Bashevis Singer: "Gimpel the Fool," *A Treasury of Yiddish Stories,* ed. Irving Howe and Eliezer Greenberg. Copyright 1953, 1954 by The Viking Press, Inc. All rights reserved. Reprinted by permission of Viking Penguin Inc.

Tess Slesinger: "White on Black" from *On Being Told That Her Second Husband Has Taken His First Lover and Other Stories* by Tess Slesinger. Copyright 1935 by Tess Slesinger and renewed 1963 by Frank Davis. Reprinted by permission of Times Books, a Division of Random House, Inc.

Jean Stafford: "In the Zoo" from *The Collected Stories of Jean Stafford.* Copyright © 1953, 1959 by Jean Stafford. Originally appeared in *The New Yorker.* Reprinted by permission of Farrar, Straus & Giroux, Inc.

Wilbur Daniel Steele: "The Man Who Saw Through Heaven." Copyright 1925, Copyright renewed 1952 by Wilbur Daniel Steele. Reprinted by permission of Harold Matson Company, Inc.

James Thurber: "The Unicorn in the Garden." Copyright © 1940 James Thurber. Copyright © 1968 Helen Thurber. From *Fables For Our Time,* published by Harper & Row.

JEAN TOOMER: "Becky" is reprinted from *Cane* by Jean Toomer, by permission of Liveright Publishing Corporation. Copyright 1923 by Boni & Liveright. Copyright renewed 1951 by Jean Toomer.

JOHN UPDIKE: "When Everyone Was Pregnant." Copyright © 1971 by John Updike. Reprinted from *Museums and Women and Other Stories* by John Updike, by permission of Alfred A. Knopf, Inc.

ALICE WALKER: "Everyday Use" from *In Love & Trouble* by Alice Walker, copyright © 1973 by Alice Walker. Reprinted by permission of Harcourt Brace Jovanovich, Inc.

JEROME WEIDMAN: "My Father Sits in the Dark" from *My Father Sits in the Dark and Other Stories* by Jerome Weidman. Copyright 1934 by Jerome Weidman. Copyright renewed © 1961 by Jerome Weidman. Reprinted by permission of Brandt & Brandt Literary Agents, Inc.

EUDORA WELTY: "Why I Live at the P.O." from *A Curtain of Green and Other Stories,* copyright 1941, 1969 by Eudora Welty. Reprinted by permission of Harcourt Brace Jovanovich, Inc.

MARIANNE WIGGINS: "Herself in Love" from *Herself in Love* by Marianne Wiggins. Copyright © 1987 by Marianne Wiggins. All rights reserved. Reprinted by permission of Viking Penguin Inc.

A NOTE ON THE EDITOR

PETER S. PRESCOTT is a senior writer and book critic at *Newsweek* magazine. He has also taught a seminar, "Writing with Style," at Columbia's Graduate School of Journalism, which will presently be metamorphosed into a book of the same name, to be published by Norton. He is a recent Guggenheim Fellow and, for pieces collected in his most recent book, *Never in Doubt,* the recipient of the George Polk Award for Criticism. Mr. Prescott's previous book, *The Child Savers: Juvenile Justice Observed,* won first prize in the Robert F. Kennedy Book Awards.

A director of both the Authors Guild and the Authors League Fund, and president of the Authors Guild Foundation, Mr. Prescott has lectured under the auspices of the U.S. State Department in Syria, Egypt, and Ireland. He was for nine years an editor at E. P. Dutton, book publishers, and has been at various times a columnist for *Look* magazine and a syndicated columnist at *Women's Wear Daily.*

His earlier books include: *A World of Our Own: Notes on Life and Learning in a Boys' Preparatory School; Soundings: Encounters with Contemporary Books;* and *A Darkening Green: Notes from the Silent Generation.* Mr. Prescott is now writing a biography of Alfred A. Knopf.